THE VISITORS

The setting of this novel is a country behind the Iron Curtain recognisably Poland. The heroine is the wife of a member of a British Mission who has been posted to one of the major provincial cities. She becomes involved not only with other professional visitors, chiefly diplomats and journalists, whose attitude is tempered, like her own, by the knowledge that for them there is always an exit, but also with their hosts, eager or reluctant as they may be. These are the destitute relics of the former aristocracy and the agents, open and secret, of the new ruling authority who, in whatever manner they entertain their guests, are bound to remain. The result is a situation that is charged with comedy, tragedy and ever-increasing danger for all concerned.

No synopsis can attempt to do justice to the variety and profusion of the characters, or the skill with which the many strands are woven into the spacious yet tensely unified story. In the person of Milly, the author has been consciously influenced by Madame Bovary, and has come within respectable distance of justifying her admission into the gallery of heroines containing Flaubert's Emma. But there are fully another dozen genuine, living people in this book, not least of them Milly's two children.

By the Same Author
THE FLYING FOX

Mary McMinnies

THE
VISITORS

THE REPRINT SOCIETY LONDON

First published 1958

This edition published by The Reprint Society, Ltd.,
by arrangement with Wm. Collins, Sons & Co. Ltd.
1960

To John

Contents

PART ONE

Au fond de son âme, cependant, elle attendait
un événement.   Comme les matelots en
détresse, elle promenait sur la solitude de sa
vie des yeux désespérés, cherchant au loin
quelque voile blanche dans les brumes de
l'horizon.   Elle ne savait pas quel serait ce
hasard, le vent qui le pousserait jusqu'à elle,
vers quel rivage il la mènerait, s'il était
chaloupe ou vaisseau à trois ponts, chargé
d'angoisses ou plein de félicités jusqu'aux
sabords.   Mais, chaque matin, à son réveil,
elle l'espérait pour la journée, et elle écoutait
tous les bruits, se levait en sursaut, s'étonnait
qu'il ne vînt pas, puis, au coucher du soleil,
toujours plus triste, désirait être au lendemain.

FLAUBERT: *Madame Bovary*

Chapter One

"I'M SORRY," said Milly in her brisk way, "about the bag, Mr. Wragg."
She bit her lip, wanting to laugh. Not her fault—his, for having that
absurd name. She did not know him well enough to laugh, did not,
in fact, know him at all, although disliking him already on account
of his chawed finger nails and Midlands accent.

Wragg was standing with his back to her, his hands in his pockets,
gazing moodily out of the window at the long red banners flapping in
the wind. On the wall of the building opposite the compelling features
of Big Brother, blown up many times lifesize, shuddered as the wind
bellied out the canvas. Down below in the street a squad of workers
was marching past, men and bosomy girls in overalls brandishing new
spades, followed by a couple of tanks and a substantial wedge of
soldiery; beyond, the glitter of more spades, then more tanks, more
soldiers, and so on, all the way up the long broad street. The squad
swung past in step to the music which blared from all the loudspeakers
all over the city. The torrent of noise seemed to isolate them both,
him and her, high up in the hotel room. There would be no escaping
the radio anywhere in the city that day; it was a day of national
importance and the marching and the music had been going on since
dawn.

It was a day of some importance for Wragg, too, and he was reflecting
upon how badly it was turning out. He moved away from the window
and frowned at Milly, reciprocating her dislike and for roughly the
same reasons, namely, her finger nails and her voice. They had met
for the first time ten minutes ago.

"It's just an understood thing," he explained coldly. "Anyone
going to Grusnov from here takes down the bag—and the NAAFI."

"Why the NAAFI?"

"Why?" The question seemed to surprise him. "You wouldn't
get very far without it, that's why. So I think we'd better wait," he
added, and turned his back on her again.

"Well," she replied sweetly, crossing her slim feet and inspecting
them with an air of satisfaction, "we can't. Larry says not." Larry
Purdoe was her husband, and her tone was intended as a reminder
that he was also Wragg's new chief, a tone she had had occasion to
employ often enough in the past with other subordinates in other

11

countries to be assured of its effect. She got no change out of Wragg, however, who merely shrugged his shoulders, mumbling: " The Simpsons always waited." The name seemed to halt in the air between them—lame enough as an argument, God knew, he thought, cursing himself.

" We're not the Simpsons," said Milly tartly. She had stepped into too many strange shoes not to know how to deal with *that*. She got up.

" Larry'll be back in a minute. Have a drink or something, won't you? " There was a brand new cocktail shaker on the window-sill and a couple of bottles on the table. She nodded, vaguely indicating some sort of mating between them.

" No, thanks," he muttered, suddenly becoming conscious, under her amused glance, that not only did his sleeves seem mysteriously to have shrunk but also his hands, which were red and bony, to have swollen up; the sight of them bothered him and he stuck them back in his pockets, and just to show how carefree and confident he was he began to whistle, but soundlessly, through his teeth. He could have done with a drink but he didn't recognise either of the bottles on the table and as for fooling around with a cocktail shaker, that would be asking for trouble. Still, she was only trying to be kind, very likely. He looked up with the definite intention of smiling at her, but she had beaten him to it, and something about her smile put him off his stroke. Addressing a point some way above her head he said casually: " No, I'll just wait, thanks."

Horrid common young man, thought Milly. Chapel and high tea and youth hostels. I know that type. In fact she did not know it, but on the other hand she was not far wrong.

" Well, I must go and say good night to the children. You'll be all right? "

" Oh yes, thanks," he said hastily—too hastily. It sounded like relief. After she had gone he opened the window and coiling his long lanky shape on the sill, leaning his head back, brooded over the last half-hour, sick with shame at his own shortcomings. He took his hands out of his pockets and spread them in front of him. Now, perversely, they were back to their normal size. Normal, that's what they were— he clenched them—only, perhaps, stronger than most. They struck him as good strong capable hands. He practised a smile but his face felt stiff, rubbed his jaw, and tried again. There, that was it. Now all the jolly, friendly welcoming fatuities that were expected of him rolled smoothly off his tongue. In a minute or two, when they came back, the two of them, he would astonish them with his wit, his social charm, with little ironic asides that would reveal his far from superficial know- ledge of the set-up and the country. Surely it wasn't too late? Surely

12

strangers couldn't be so cruel as to judge a chap just like that—without giving him a second chance? He marched up and down the empty room, gesticulating, belatedly mouthing his pleasantries, persuading himself that it was not too late.

Milly walked down the corridor towards the sound of shrieks and splashing. She felt annoyed and, what was rare for her, worsted. She had made no visible impression on that young man—perhaps, even, had antagonised him. An impossible situation, as they would be seeing a great deal of him. Larry always managed to get on well with his staff—but then it was no effort to Larry. He was just naturally sunny and good-tempered. He seemed genuinely to like people, had time for everybody, no matter how boring or insignificant someone might be. Still, he was always pleased, and proud of her, too, when she made an effort to get on with the staff, so taking it all round, this unfortunate start must be remedied. She would set herself out to captivate Mr. Wragg on that long journey to-morrow. She would have him eating out of her hand in no time. It was not too late.

That problem as good as settled, smiling to herself she opened the bathroom door to come slap up against the tweed behind of Miss Raven who was energetically bent over the tub. Clarissa, pink-cheeked, wrapped in a towel on the lavatory seat, at sight of her mother squealed:

" Miss Raven won't let Dermot and me be bathed together ! " She relapsed into fits of derisive giggles.

" I should think not indeed." Miss Raven yanked Dermot's ears with a flannel, and straightened up. Her weatherbeaten face was flushed. " Had to clean the bath before we could even get in," she announced, as if scoring off Milly herself. " Did you say it was the best hotel? Well, I don't know, I must say. And Dermot was bitten during his rest. Look! " Proudly Dermot exhibited his scars. " A bare half-hour, it took, to get him into that state."

" Oh dear." Anxious to pacify her, Milly picked up a damp towel from the floor. " What a picnic we're going to have to-night. Perhaps we'd better look . . ."

" I have looked," snapped Miss Raven, hoisting Dermot out of the bath. " But you've got to know what you're looking for, haven't you? It's just not the sort of thing I *ever* expect to come across." She repeated, giving Milly a look, " *Ever*, Mrs. Purdoe."

" We must try and make the best of it, Miss Raven. It's only for one night, after all."

Miss Raven grunted, hustling the children into their pyjamas. " And what it'll be like in that Grusnov," she declared, without any pandering to heathen pronunciation, " I *don't* know." She laughed

13

ominously. "I've had a look at the map. Back of beyond, if you ask me."

Milly sighed, restraining herself from observing that Miss Raven had had ample opportunity to look at the map before leaving England. Miss Raven, engaged the week before in London, was going to be difficult. On top of Wragg, Miss Raven. Oh lord. Why did employees, inferiors, demand such perpetual cosseting—why did they act like *individuals*? One had to be sweet to them at whatever cost to oneself in order that things should run smoothly. She herself, she was convinced, was nothing like so exigent—on the contrary, she was most amiable and easy-going; after all, one was *paying* to have things made to run smoothly—and yet here one was, forever giving, giving—energy, patience, tact and sympathy, let alone money. This was the first time she had been able to have an English nurse for the children, a luxury she and Larry could ill afford even now, but an investment which had paid immediate and visible dividends in the form of the reactions of the Ambassadress that very morning. It would get about that Larry had private means—a rumour that never did any harm. All the same, she thought, shepherding the children down the corridor, Miss Raven stalking ahead, she would have greatly preferred, indeed had cherished, the dream of a cosy—but efficient—old thing, apple-cheeked and silvery-haired, who would be addressed as " Nanny " and who would just naturally reciprocate by addressing her employer as " madam "— but it had been all too plain from the outset that in respect of these requirements Miss Raven would neither submit herself to the one nor fulfil the other; however, she had the highest references. Just my luck, thought Milly gloomily, dumping the wet things on a chair. She watched Miss Raven, who had stripped back the beds and was staring suspiciously at the smooth white sheets. Why is it—when *I* get, at last, a mink coat, it has to be second-hand? When *I* engage a nurse —it has to be Miss Raven? The customary hiatus between the dream and reality. Other women seemed to acquire such possessions with no trouble at all, by miraculous sleights of hand—but not she, oh dear no.

" I want to whisper something." Clarissa nuzzled up against her.

" Go ahead." Obligingly she bent down, and Clarissa's lips tickled her ear. " Is it true we're going to have a picnic to-night? "

" You silly muggins—of course not. Now get into bed. You can't have picnics at night."

" But you *said* there would be . . ." wailed Clarissa.

" Darling, I never said anything of the sort . . . lie down, there's a good girl . . ." Milly bent over her son and kissed him. " Good night,

14

pet." She stood looking down at the hump in the neighbouring bed. "Good night, Clarissa." She paused. "Aren't you going to say good night?" Clarissa wriggled her behind in defiance.

"You've got a little black dog on your back," said her mother curtly. "Mind you get rid of him by morning. Good night, Miss Raven. Good night, my sweeties." She went out.

Clarissa sat up, accepted her mug of milk. "Mummy *did* say that about a picnic, didn't she, Miss Raven? In the bathroom?"

"Mmmmm . . ." said Miss Raven, who wasn't listening. She had caught sight of herself in the mirror.

"I *knew* she said it . . ." Clarissa pursued in triumph. "You can have picnics at night, can't you, Miss Raven?"

"I don't see why not," said Miss Raven rather absently. Then with reluctance abandoning her own reflection, "Good night," she said, and kissed Clarissa.

"Oooh . . . it's hot, your face," giggled Clarissa, submitting, however, to the kiss.

When Miss Raven had gone, Clarissa lay in the dark, thinking. This was the third time she had caught her mother out. The third time in— well, not long. Since Miss Raven came. She turned over on to her stomach, her favourite position for sleep. Then, cautiously, she put out first one hand, then the other, investigating her shoulder-blades. Smiling to herself, she buried her face in the pillow. It was all of a piece, to her way of thinking. There wasn't a trace of a little black dog on her back.

*   *   *

"Hallo, darling." Larry was mixing drinks, measuring from a toothglass. Wragg was still mooching about. Unreasonably, Milly suspected that if he hadn't already been on his feet as she entered he wouldn't have bothered to get up.

"Hallo," she said, and then, at once: "Where's the cocktail shaker?"

They stared at her.

"The shaker," she persisted. "The new one?"

"The *new* one?"

"Yes," she said impatiently. "I unpacked it just now. It was on the window-sill." She turned to Wragg. "You saw it there, didn't you?"

He mumbled something.

"It's not there now," said Larry.

"I can see that," she snapped, and darted over to the window. "But—where on earth . . . ?——" Suddenly she felt her nerves jangled,

15

a gust of anger swept over her. She spun round waspishly on Wragg, her plans for his captivation temporarily shelved: " You've been here all the time, haven't you? "

Nodding, speechless, he backed away from her. He had, as a matter of fact, availed himself of the adjoining bathroom during her absence, but it was already too late—he would gladly have died rather than admit to that now.

Larry laughed. " Must have blown out of the window. Never mind, sweetie—I never did believe in shakers. Try this." He sniffed his concoction. " Dynamite," he said happily.

" But, Larry, it *couldn't* have blown out—not with Mr. Wragg here." She tried to stem the rising hysteria in her voice. " It just couldn't *vanish*—not a great new cocktail shaker . . ."

" Darling, really . . ." Larry sighed. " Oh, well, all right." Wragg watched them as they searched the room.

" It's certainly very odd," said Larry at last. " It's gone."

" A mystery," Wragg put in helpfully.

" It's not just a *mystery* . . ." Milly snapped back at him. " It's more of a——" Larry saw that she was on the verge of tears. " More of an *omen* . . ."

" Rubbish, darling. Come on, drink this up, and don't be such a goose. It was only a little tin job."

" But it's so queer . . ." she sniffed, taking sips between sniffs as they stood watching her. Then, at sight of their grave faces her lips began to twitch and Larry knew the crisis was past. He chuckled and against her will she smiled, began to giggle and then they were both laughing, immoderately, uncontrollably, rolling about with laughter, although why, Wragg couldn't imagine. Utterly at sea, he stood there awkwardly, gazing down at them. All at once he hated them both. She had suspected him, he knew that. He thought they were very rude, laughing in this ridiculous way at some private joke of their own; there was nothing to laugh at, unless they were laughing at him.

It was true that she had suspected him, at once and instinctively; and although the mystery was never to be solved, so that months later when one would say to the other, " What do you suppose *did* happen to that shaker? " and both knew they would never be any the wiser, privately Milly still went on suspecting Wragg, and, as it happened, with good reason.

Because in fact Wragg knew very well what had become of the cocktail shaker, having not only been a witness to its fate, but indirectly the instrument of it. On his exit from the Purdoes' bathroom, the opening of the door had caused a gust of wind to sweep across the room when, to his horror, he had seen the " little tin job " somersault

16

merrily out of the window to be smashed to atoms in a bomb crater five stories below, and with it all his hopes of winning the friendship of the Purdoes, or even of retrieving their respect, had been shattered too. Before ever they had come back into the room Wragg was saddled with his load of guilt; once more he had started off on the wrong foot.

Chapter Two

" WRAGG'S GONE off to collect the bag," said Larry, " as we're so late starting."

Milly was sitting in the main hall of the hotel, surrounded by luggage, waiting for Miss Raven and the children to come down. Larry sat down next to her and lit a cigarette. They were late mainly on account of Miss Raven, whose experience was now enriched by her having encountered in and certainly on the flesh " something in her bed " during the night. Her story was—and Milly's head ached from the telling—that she had immediately woken the children, hunted through the bedclothes with a Flit spray, reberthed them, herself taken a Lysol bath—the hullabaloo apparently had gone on into the small hours—and then Miss Raven had overslept. " Never in all my born days," she kept repeating, two uproarious naked children leaping from one half-packed suit-case to the next, and Milly had steeled herself to listen to Miss Raven's reminiscences of her previous posts, when with the Gatleys in Bahrein, the Strutts in Seoul, the Watkins in Leopoldsville —all, Milly would have thought, posts calculated to make this one appear a bed of roses—all, however, according to Miss Raven, contrasting favourably with the present.

Larry glanced at his wife. " Where *is* the old crow? "

Milly stubbed out her cigarette savagely. " Flown home, for all I care. She doesn't seem to be madly efficient."

They sat on in silence. The main hall was large and dimly lighted; there was none of the cheerful bustle of the best hotel in a capital city. The illuminated showcases on the walls housed a collection of clumsy ceramics, bits of folk weave, ornamental glass; docketed, dingy, displayed in the manner of museum exhibits rather than to attract the tourist; logical enough, as there were no tourists. The smell of beer, boiled pork and cabbage swept in hot, unsavoury gusts from the bar and dining-room. They heard voices, laughter and singing, from the bar; the German trade delegation were starting the day off with a swing. A waiter was ambling about, collecting up ashtrays, or rather their contents. They watched him as he moved like a lazy old bee from flower to flower; he would hover over a table, carefully pick out the cigarette ends from a tray, drop a handful into his jacket pocket, take a casual swipe at the table with his napkin and, yawning, drift on to the next. The clerks behind the reception desk were whispering

18

together; the head porter looked up sharply each time somebody was batted through the swing doors.

" Look who've just come in," Larry murmured. Three men had entered; the first two, slung about with cameras, their profession printed on faces that were spongy-yellow with indigestion and insomnia, shuffled past into the bar. " That's Perry Game, did you see? *Daily Mail*. And Elmer Tripp."

" And who's that? " asked Milly, as the third man, who had stopped at the porter's desk, strode up the steps after the others. This was a very large man, dark, thick-lipped and obviously American. He glanced at the Purdoes as he passed and Milly imagined she caught a gleam of recognition in his eye. Larry turned and watched the three disappear into the bar.

" I don't know." He shook his head. " Seemed as if he knew us."

" Impossible," said Milly. " He was an American."

" Must be something going on. Game—and Tripp." Larry felt pleasurably excited. He loved capital cities—even this sort. Too few had come his way as yet. Then he thought of Grusnov, and that sobered him. Still—on his own. A responsible job, H.E. had said, briefing him, not half an hour ago. See what you can make of it. Call on us if you get stuck—and Larry had resolved he never would call on them if he could help it. One day—he considered his wife's profile— one day there would be a capital city, and then it would stay that way. This morning he had felt tremendously confident, energetic, keyed up; now, all of a sudden, a pinpoint of doubt pricked his swelling self-confidence. During the interview—had he or had he not sensed something?—he couldn't be sure—H.E. had been fiddling with a paperknife as he spoke, snapping it in and out, and Larry had missed one or two vital sentences wondering if the Old Man cleaned his nails with it in private—but still, he had sensed—what? No, perhaps nothing at all. He strove to recapture the tone of the interview, the half-and quarter-tones of that voice—weary, not especially hopeful, leaving open a world of room for doubt. If you're stuck—he took a deep breath. Stuck—unstuck. No—it was gone—that glimpse of a little red light. He must have imagined it. If it had been anything specific, surely that would have been said in so many words—not merely hinted at, if it had been hinted at all, and he was not even sure of that. He smoothed down his fears, varnished over that surface of his mind with a skin of self-confidence. Still, he would go carefully—that wouldn't be hard, it wasn't his nature to be rash. He would just watch his every step. And Milly—here she turned her head to smile at him and he smiled back—anyway, it wasn't her pigeon, was it? It was entirely his.

" Look at Wragg," she said. Wragg, engaged in the swing doors,

19

had become trapped by the hem of his coat. That was why she had smiled. They saw his pale desperate face swimming behind glass; he was tugging at his coat, even beginning in his frenzy to divest himself of it when an elderly porter, taking his time, hobbled over to release him. Then he arrived. The small mishap had flustered him.

" I've got it," he said, standing in front of Larry, breathing deeply. He ignored Milly.

" Oh? Oh, the bag. That's good. Well, we're all set then, just about."

" Good morning," said Milly.

Wragg drew out his handkerchief and wiped his hands and the back of his neck. He swallowed. " Good morning."

" Do sit down."

" Have a beer? "

" Oh no—no thanks." He stood there, shifting from one foot to another. " So we're off? "

At that moment, much to Milly's relief, as if on her cue Miss Raven appeared leading a child by either hand. She wore her usual tweed suit but her blouse was pinned at the neck by a Scottie brooch, and she had unbent so far as a touch of lipstick, which must surely be a good sign.

" We got stuck in the lift," she explained indignantly.

" Oh, poor Miss Raven. How awful. I'm so——"

" Stuck in the lift stuck in the lift," the children chorused in delight.

" The man didn't seem to know how to work it, Mrs. Purdoe."

" And Miss Raven called him a silly buzzer," said Dermot, loud and clear.

Miss Raven flushed. " I most certainly did not. I said he was a silly man," she added, unwisely.

" What's a *silly* buzzer, Daddy? " Clarissa leaned her cheek against her father's arm, naughtily eyeing Miss Raven's evident discomfiture.

Larry switched his glance from Miss Raven.

" A man who can't buzz," he said, giving prompt satisfaction.

" Can't buzz can't buzz stuck in the lift stuck in the——"

" Children, shut up," said Milly, at the end of her tether.

" It might have been very serious," said Miss Raven with dignity.

" But all's well that ends well, eh? " Larry was grinning at Miss Raven, a teasing impudent grin, and to Milly's surprise, Miss Raven's mouth curved into an unwilling little smile.

" Did you see Abe Schulman come in? " said Wragg. " With Elmer Tripp. I had a word with him outside. Schulman covers the Grusnov end for *Transatlantic*."

" Yes, we did. So he's one of us, eh? " One of the beleaguered

20

garrison, Larry was thinking. One of my responsibilities—no, American, so he's his own.

"Yes," said Wragg. "He's one of us." It did have an odd sound.

"A big dark man?" asked Milly. "American?"

"Yes," said Wragg, without turning her way. "That's him."

For some inexplicable reason, Milly forgot all her present irritations and her heart rose.

*   *   *

They all stood round the station wagon whilst the driver struggled with the luggage.

"It's going to be a ghastly squash," Milly said icily.

Larry walked round to the back.

"Good lord! Is that the bag?" Loosely swollen, the bag spread over the entire luggage space.

"It's always pretty hefty," said Wragg, on the defensive at once. "There are quite a few parcels for you, as a matter of fact. And I got the NAAFI too, of course."

"Couldn't that have come later?"

"I really don't know," he said stiffly. "I mean if you're prepared to go without tea, coffee, soap, and all the rest of it, I suppose it could." This sounded ruder than he had intended, and he flushed, stammered, "I mean, you can't do without it, you'll find."

"Yes, I see," said Larry amiably, although he had given Wragg a quick look. "I didn't think of all that. I'm sure you're quite right. Oh well, we'll manage somehow. You get in front, there's a good chap. We'll all squeeze in the back."

They drove out of the city, Larry asking questions to which Wragg, over his shoulder, replied:

"Yes, that's the Ghetto. Or was, rather." His resonant, not unpleasant voice boomed back at them. "Flamethrowers, yes . . . quick lime . . ." He reeled off statistics, in themselves so shocking that they had long since lost the power to shock. Miss Raven's gaze roamed suspiciously as if she were seeking to identify Marshall & Snelgrove's at least.

"What small shops," she commented at last.

"Rebuilding," said Wragg. "It was flat, you see. Flat as a pancake." He turned round as if to say more, his enthusiasm perhaps aroused, but he caught sight of Milly, yawning, fumbling with a powder puff, and stopped short.

They left the shattered skyline behind, and started on the road south. Often the driver had to swerve to avoid the long peasant carts, each with a sleepy horse between the shafts, rumbling along from nowhere to nowhere, the peasant and his wife huddled up together, dozing in front, reins slack; flocks of geese like scattered snowflakes drifted on either side of the road; now and again a row of cottages with a few dahlias blazing behind a wicker fence, a wrought-iron gate surmounted by a coat-of-arms, a lodge, a winding drive overgrown with willow-herb disappearing into a belt of pines, occasionally deer lolloping off into the trees, and then mile upon mile of land in stubble, no farm in sight, and then pine forests, then stubble and pasture and pines. It was flat country, but rolling, pleasant to the eye, and rich. The cows were fat, the geese, the pigs, the goats; the children plump and rosy, the women plain, sturdy, rather fierce-looking; logs of wood were stacked neatly against the cottage walls, the ripening apples weighed down the branches in the orchards, and there were rows of beehives under the apple-trees. Milly, squeezed into her corner, had had enough of first impressions, and reached into her bag for *Madame Bovary*. She had started to read it on the journey out, and had already discovered that there was almost no mood of hers that this novel did not fit.

"Very like England," Miss Raven observed with approval after a while. "All those woods."

"Not *woods*, Miss Raven," pleaded Clarissa. "Forests. Proper forests." She shivered with delight. "And wolves, Daddy?"

"Perhaps a wolf or two, eh, Wragg?"

"Wolves?" Wragg turned a startled face. The possibility seemed never to have occurred to him. Then he spoke rapidly to the driver in Slavonian. "Yes," he turned again, nodding gravely at Clarissa. "Sometimes. In a hard winter."

"Wheeee!" Her eyes shone. The deliberation with which he had treated her question had won her heart. More, she had obtained a straight answer. No one had contradicted the word forest, and there were wolves in it. One could scarcely hope for more in a single day.

Milly glanced up. She noted that Wragg's hair was sticky with brilliantine and could have done with a cut. He wore a silk scarf pulled up rather high and tight; probably had boils, or the remains of them, on the back of his neck. It occurred to her that you would have to be very sure of your loved one to risk travelling hundreds of miles in a closed car, with him sitting behind. Clarissa was singing under her breath, staring out of the window; she was over-excited, Milly could tell. Dermot was asleep, dribbling on to Miss Raven's tweedy lap; she, luckily, was leaning back with her eyes shut, sucking a mint humbug. Milly wondered what she was thinking about, and, with a more lively interest, whether at any time of her life Miss Raven had ever been pretty. No, she decided not. She had very fine straight

22

hair, in colour blonde to mouse—hopeless hair, was Milly's description of it: wisps escaped from under the correct felt hat—and blunt, rather stubby features, with full thick lips. Had her colouring been other than thoroughly Anglo-Saxon there would have been something negroid about her appearance; as it was, her face was ruddy, mottled, the blood-vessels broken under the rough dry skin, and her eyes were pale, a very pale blue. They were remarkable eyes, exactly the colour and with the clouded transparency of Lalique glass; glassy, too, in that they betrayed no expression whatsoever, the curious milky film preventing the light of Miss Raven's soul from filtering through.

Milly's critical gaze travelled down over Miss Raven's big-boned, wiry body. She had a thick, short neck, a red V of sunburn at the throat, and as if nature had played a final malicious prank on the poor thing, she was afflicted with that convex birdlike formation of the breast bone which Larry called the sign of the Iron Maiden—a challenge, according to him, that few men cared to accept. Milly grinned to herself, and nudged him with her foot, but he was engrossed in the map. She picked up her book once more.

Furry under the soft beams of the autumn sun, the pine forests swept down to the road and up to the sky. Now and again Wragg turned to peer over their heads through the rear window and on one occasion he muttered something to the driver, who nodded and accelerated. They were already travelling fairly fast. The next time Wragg looked round, Larry said:

" What's up? It's all right behind, isn't it? "

" His precious bag," Milly sniffed to herself.

" It's not that," said Wragg, his Adam's apple working overtime. " It—well, it just becomes automatic, you'll find. I was wondering when they'd catch up with us. They usually do about here."

" Oh, I see," said Larry, after he had thought this out. Presently he caught himself looking behind too, now and then. As they passed through the check-point outside the next small town a jeep swung out from a side road and thereafter maintained its pace within a quarter of a mile behind. It was a straight road now for quite a stretch, and the driver kept his foot hard down but the jeep was not to be shaken off.

" You see," said Wragg.

So this was it. It came to Larry with quite a shock—here he was with his wife and family, surrounded by forests, mile upon mile of lonely road ahead, he in charge—not only of them but of that small kingdom entrusted to him the other end, and almost at once this happened. They were being followed. As a situation, it was not unexhilarating. He looked at Wragg with a new appreciation: he certainly seemed to be taking it as a matter of course.

"Well," he said. "What do we do about it?"

Wragg turned and gave him a sort of grin. "Well, nothing, really." It might be possible, he thought, to get on with Purdoe after all; he seemed reasonable—at least he didn't flap. "We'll stop and eat at the next place if you like. That way we sometimes give him the slip."

"A very good idea," said Larry, and Wragg turned away to hide a blush. Even the most trivial word of approval caused him to blush, just as the merest hint of criticism would cause him to turn slightly pale, or alternatively white as a sheet.

They had to stop at a level crossing. The jeep halted coyly a hundred yards behind. For what seemed like ten minutes a train went by.

"Where's that train going?" asked Clarissa. Nobody answered. They were watching in the mirror the two young men in mackintoshes, high boots and green trilby hats who had got out of the jeep and were slouching off to the police point.

"Where's that train *going*?" she repeated.

"East," said Wragg.

"How do you know?"

"Because," he said patiently, "it's full of things."

"So it is," said Clarissa, satisfied with the obscure logic of this answer.

He means, thought Milly, that going West it would be empty. That's a good answer—impressive, even; now Clarissa and Larry and I shall remember this train. She, too, began to feel a flicker of excitement; the practical side of her mind appreciating the reality of the train, which was history in the making, and which summed up, made plain, all the things she had read countless times in newspapers but the significance of which she had never grasped until this moment. This was the way to learn. This was what it all boiled down to in the end; just as on occasion, in other countries, she had stood by when men took decisions—we had to strike camp because it was too misty to go farther—and it *was* too misty, you couldn't see a yard in front of your hand—so that she had suddenly had an inkling of what it must be like in battle—eyes, ears, influencing judgment, more to be relied on than a thousand instruments devised by man, and in any case after these instruments had failed. As a conception, it fascinated her; it had come to her so suddenly. "Then we sighted a ship," her father had said (but it was she, Milly, who had seen it first, by its smoke, naturally enough, but that was the fascinating part, just like that, searching the horizon with her eyes, she had seen it first), "and we set our course towards it." The memory of that occasion had always been of peculiar comfort to her, although she could never have told why. And so, now, similarly, as a great deal of what she had read and half-digested and

24

heard quoted and vaguely knew was going on between East and West suddenly became significant because intelligible, because this was evidence, proof of reality—the laden goods train snorting across their path from West to East—she felt happy and excited and alive, with an additional sense of security and comfort which she had not known she lacked.

Miss Raven, to whom this train was a train and a hindrance, nothing more, and whose attention had been caught by the sight of Larry's broad hands lying idle in his lap, lay back and closing her eyes once more, began painfully to rehash the silly buzzer remark.

In the next small town they stopped. The driver parked the car in a side street and Wragg led the way to the inn.

" This is where we usually . . ." he stooped, going under the archway into a courtyard, " I mean, the Simpsons used to . . ." His voice trailed off. In the presence of the Purdoes a strange paralysis seemed to affect him, robbing him of the ability to complete even the simplest remark. " That is . . ."

" Of course," said Larry, " I'm sure it'll do fine . . ."

The place was stuffy inside, thick with smoke and full of farmers in muddy high boots. At sight of Wragg the innkeeper pushed his way through the crowd and, hastily closing the door behind him, led the way down stone steps into what was clearly a private dining-room. They all sat down at a long refectory table covered with white paper. Wragg spoke at some length to the innkeeper, who then went away.

It was already late afternoon and the walls being oak-panelled, the room was rather dark. There were elaborate gilt lamp brackets on the walls, but the bulbs proved either to have fused or to be missing. The fast-vanishing light of day glimmered over the white surface of the table and the faces around it. The furnishings gave off a fusty smell of damp and moths. They waited for some time.

" Snappy service," remarked Larry, at last.

" I'm afraid that's usual," said Wragg. " Eastern Europe, you know," he added, and then, happening to glance at the wraith-like face of Milly, which was betraying unequivocally Western reactions to the delay : " I'll go and see what I can do," he muttered, and went out.

" Now we've lost *him*," she said.

" I'm hungry! " bleated Clarissa.

" So are we all," said her mother shortly. Presently Wragg returned, carrying a candle, followed by the innkeeper with glasses and a bottle and a light bulb. The bulb was fixed into a bracket set at a drunken angle on the wall and the light flickered between the ears and snouts of smallish beasts which, as they now saw, lined the walls. The room

25

was furnished in some splendour with a crimson plush couch, its under-belly stuffing trailing on the floor, oddments of tapestry, and a still life in an immense gilt frame which hung behind Larry's head, depicting a ham and a carp on a table, together with a duck, its throat cut and oozing blood, the whole tastefully garnished with oranges and onions. The children were entranced; in fact, everybody cheered up.

" Vodka, Miss Raven? "

" Is that what it is? " said Miss Raven, graciously holding out her glass.

They choked over the vodka, and Wragg looked fairly smug.

Eventually they were served with soup and lukewarm slabs of pork, potatoes and beetroot in sour cream.

" Too rich," said Miss Raven at once.

" Oh, but it's *lovely*, Miss Raven." Clarissa, despite her professed loathing for beetroot, busily set about making a goo of this vegetable with the mashed potato on her plate.

" I love fat," said Dermot, taking his cue from his sister.

" You don't, Dermot," said Milly. It had long been established that Dermot did not like fat. " You hate it."

" I *love* fat," he maintained. Shameless, his mouth stuffed with it, he lavished a warm and greasy smile on his mother.

" You'd better look out, Dermot," said Larry. " You're setting a precedent."

Dermot chewed steadily, considering his retort, gazing at the animals' heads and plainly gaining support from his exotic surroundings.

" *This* fat," he said at last with sophistication and point.

" Don't show off, Dermot," said Milly feebly.

It occurred to Wragg to wonder what it must be like to have children, not so much the process of procreation, parturition, and so on, as actually *having* them, ever-present, under one's feet. He himself, in his rare and fleeting brushes with the species, was accustomed to treat them with the utmost circumspection as undersized but none the less formidable adults. In fact, they appeared to him to be both sub- and superhuman. Brazen little hedonists with time on their hands, and irked, he supposed, by constant supervision, they seemed quite ruthless in exploiting their natural advantages, i.e. soundness of wind and limb, acuteness of eye and ear as yet unimpaired by depravities of habit, all of which made them more than a match for the old crocks with whom they came in daily conflict. Their sole disadvantage, so far as he could judge, lay in a lack of experience, which, far from being a handicap, allowed them the broadest possible latitude in their behaviour, exacerbated an already overweening self-assurance, and encouraged an irresponsibility in word and deed which they knew damn' well could always be covered by the blanket-excuse of youth. Now, as cautiously he took stock of first one young Purdoe then the other, he saw no grounds for any basic revision of these opinions.

"I'm going to live in a new house," Dermot had announced to no one in particular.

"You're not going to live in a house at all," said Miss Raven with a certain amount of suppressed enthusiasm.

"Not in a *house*?" His face puckered, as though he were rendered an orphan and homeless at her very words.

"Not in a *house*, darling," Milly comforted him. "You're going to live in a *hotel*."

"The Grand Hotel," said Miss Raven, a trifle self-consciously.

"The Grand Hotel," whispered Clarissa to herself. Then, smartly kicking her brother under the table to attract his attention, she began to gibber soundlessly, the words running into each other like a spell, granotelgranotelgranotel—until, Dermot obediently following suit, they were both gibbering like monkeys and no one could have guessed that Clarissa had instigated these antics the better to record those words, preserve the sound of that name—slow, solemn, portentous, out-stripping in fascination the forest, the wolves, even the train going "East"—"East" had been the keyword and here she glanced with affection at Mr. Wragg—The Grand Hotel. What a harvest of words to-day! She must garner them all, store them away for a rainy day, lock them up in her heart—and this, at the trifling cost of appearing temporarily deranged, she was achieving before their very eyes right there at the table.

"For God's sake," said Milly.

"The wind might change," said Miss Raven, "then where would you be?"

"I was wondering, Wragg . . ." Catching sight of his offspring, Larry broke off to say, with unaccustomed sharpness: "What's the matter with those children, Milly? Are they dotty, or what?"—and Milly and Miss Raven fairly jumped to action stations, but not before the children had already composed their faces, their separate objectives gained.

"So what are we in for, Wragg? What's it like?"

"Grusnov?" Wragg took out his handkerchief and blew his nose. "Well, it's very . . . er . . . very old."

"I meant the hotel, actually."

"Oh. Well, that's very . . . very——"

"Old too, I suppose?"

"Yes," Wragg smiled shyly. "It is rather, but quite comfortable, in a way. I mean, it's—it's rather up to you, really, what you make of

27

it." Milly shifted restlessly, and he looked nervous. " I mean, we all have our own—suites; like flats, you know. I suppose you'll have Number Nine. The Simpsons had that," he added.

" Well, I wonder if we shall," said Milly pleasantly.

Ignoring her, Wragg went on, " Schulman's in Number Twenty. I told you about him. Then we—Mrs. Wragg and I, I mean—have Forty-Five."

" Sound like house numbers."

" In a way they are." Wragg was frowning in the effort to explain. " We do keep ourselves pretty much to ourselves, you'll find. Have to—on top of each other like that." Milly saw his face suddenly stiffen with what she took to be anger, or disdain. Don't you fret, Mister Wragg, she thought, we'll respect your privacy. She began to dislike him in earnest, whilst he gazed at her, struck dumb with horror, hearing his own words reverberate back and forth as if rolled out by drums.

" Service any good? Food, and so on?"

" No, not really. I mean—there again, it's what you make it. We don't eat downstairs. You can't, really. We cook, of course . . . in the bathroom, actually."

" In the *bathroom*?" said Milly.

" Oh, yes." He looked surprised. " You'll see how—I mean, it's quite easy. Of course," he went on, turning to Larry, " you'll want to have a girl."

Larry, whose thoughts had been straying momentarily, stared at Wragg as if unable to believe his ears.

" Have a *girl*?" he repeated, and the expression on his face was such that Milly giggled. Wragg blushed to the eyebrows.

" A—a maid, I mean. You'll take on the Simpsons', I expect."

" I shouldn't think so," said Milly. She was against inheriting servants on principle, but it was not any sort of principle that prompted her to add, disagreeably: " I should think it most unlikely."

" She's a very good girl," Wragg mumbled. " She knows all the ropes."

" I dare say." She dismissed the subject by starting to make up her face, and it was Dermot, unexpectedly, who rallied the party.

" The Grand Hotel!" he announced in the firm voice of an impresario.

In a couple of hours they were there.

* * *

Grusnov, as Wragg had said, is very old. A walled city, dating from the times of Charlemagne, built for the most part of grey stone, it lies at the southernmost tip of Slavonia within sight of the Carpathians. It is a famous city, but it is by no means so easy to define what it is famous for—if there were a single simple symbol which could adequately represent it on one of those picture maps, as for instance, a herring for Grimsby, for Northampton a boot—but for Grusnov, what? No, instead, the more enthusiastically the conscientious chronicler chases after it, striving to snare it with words, put salt on its trailing tail of fame, the farther he is led, as he might have known was inevitable, into the maze of qualifying clauses, afterthoughts, Blicks hin and vor, which it would seem must surround any consideration of any aspect whatever of Slavonia; in the case in point, mercifully he loses his way and his quarry almost at the outset, running into the nebulous, messy, and thoroughly unsatisfactory word, culture.

Throughout the ages Grusnov has been the acknowledged centre of culture in Slavonia—so far so good, which is not, however, either as far or as good as one might have hoped; that is to say, bearing in view that a deeply-engrained cultural tradition is not perhaps what instantly springs to mind in connection with Slavonia, because not even the staunchest patriot could claim, or indeed would even wish to claim, that the Slavonians are primarily a culture-loving race. The pursuit of culture presupposes some leisure, and the Slavonians have had little enough of that. Geographically unlucky, placed between two great and greedy neighbours, but not, admittedly, on that account alone, it has been their unfortunate lot to have become embroiled, by no means always undeservedly, in every major European struggle since such struggles first began—a recreation which has accounted for rather more than half their time. Nevertheless, in the breathing-spaces between wars, artists, craftsmen and others did manage to put in a spot of work, and most of them seem to have preferred Grusnov not only as a place to do it in, but to be born in and die in, too: the tangible results, pretty things or simply large things, anyway, now all old things, being acquired by those who commissioned them, the noble families of Grusnov; the intangible, the fame, accruing to the city itself. In addition, it has an ancient university, which, if not of world renown, has been in the past second only to that of Vienna, in those parts; a magnificent castle, once the seat of kings, and several other lesser but respectable piles (all museums now), the atmospheres both scholarly and feudal having combined to give Grusnov the rather pompous reputation (although it must be added that there is no record of any spectacular substantiation of it) for being equally the stronghold of reactionary and the cradle of liberal and progressive thought. Times have changed. But Grusnov is still famous: in Western Europe (alas, by hearsay only) for its legacies of the past, its architecture, and its art treasures, some of which, evacuated to happier climes to escape the

29

perils of war, have been fostered so lovingly they have yet to be returned; and, in Slavonia, with a different kind of fame. In the eyes of the Government it is notorious: a city that is half-asleep, still wrapped in a cosy dream, in the grey fog of the Middle Ages which even on a clear day seems to cling about the rooftops; a city out on a limb, backward, *old*; a city that *wants watching*. So to grant Grusnov its due, its fame, let us say without qualification—and of course one is back to the start, but the conclusion contains all the foregoing—it is famous for being very old.

Perhaps because in distance it lies nearer to Vienna than to the Slavonian capital, perhaps because the Turks came within attacking distance of Grusnov and the Grusnovians shared the terrors, at least in prospect, of that invasion with the Viennese, there is something vaguely reminiscent of Vienna or rather, a flavour of the Austro-Hungarian Empire, in the atmosphere of Grusnov. Even in these days of the stakhanovite ideal, the city has an agreeably slothful and secretive air, which seems to hint at its having known not merely better days, but days so incomparably much better, a past so racy and conditions so luxurious, that it scorns to brag and is too lazy to do so anyway—an atmosphere which has a distinct appeal for the decadent Westerner. No mere revolution could dispel it overnight; it is the spirit of the city itself, and the city is too old to change.

The same influence is perceptible in the character of the inhabitants, the Grusnovians combining traits which are generally acknowledged to be part of the stock-in-trade of the Viennese with the more formidable selection boasted by their own race. More volatile, more easy-going than their compatriots in the north, with a reputation (relative) for charm, they are, notwithstanding, Slav—a full-time occupation, one would have thought. They have that fiery temperament which burns at a breath with ardour or anger, or, banked up, smoulders, sullenly; having, too, blind spots for dirt or time, they are slipshod, unpunctual; rash to the point of improvidence—and generous to that point; and, not least, having that weakness for gossip, the natural bent for conspiracy that would seem to be ineradicable characteristics of the race—small wonder that they have proved a sore trial to the Government. Like their city, of which they are proud, they do not take kindly to change.

As if the Grusnovians by themselves were not enough, there are the peasants—whose presence, in bulk, in any body of people, is a well-known corrective, having a stabilising if not downright constipating effect which encourages that body to withstand any sudden innovations of diet; and because it sits so solidly plump in the middle, in the stomach, in the bowels, permeating, too, all the vital organs, being

30

indeed essential to them, it stubbornly resists whatever purges, be their action never so violent, and is simply not to be budged.

The country surrounding Grusnov is rich and fertile. Before the war it belonged to the big estates of the Rapovskis, the Liehas, the Bielskis, now whomever the land belongs to is beside the point: it is farmed by the peasants. If the Government consisted of farmers . . . But it does not, and peasants have no need to be told when they are in a strong position—they exploit it. Several hundreds of miles removed from the eagle eye itself, they treat representative authority, when they meet it, with a sullen indifference and contrive so far as possible not to meet it. In between times they do pretty well as they please. Strict surveillance over those many outlying and prosperous farmsteads in the foothills of the mountains has proved an impossibility; and every farmer has an outhouse to which the visiting inspector is not invited, where sides of smoked pork hang from the ceiling and great cheeses squat in the gloom, where mead-honey ferments in a hip bath, and the corpse of a calf which has mysteriously met with an accident is dismembered into joints of choice and costly veal. The State shops are bare of delicacies, but in the Grusnov market all sorts of things are to be had—if you know where to look; much of the produce, by law due to the State, is rattled into market under cover of darkness, hidden beneath the mounds of turnips and cabbages in the long carts, and then sold hastily " under the counter," to friends. In Slavnik, the people live wretchedly; in Grusnov, the townspeople don't live too well, although at least they eat; but the kulaks in the Grusnov region fare like commissars, because they till the soil and the soil is rich. " You have but to scratch the Slavonian earth," said the invading Germans, " and it bears fruit. This country shall feed Europe." And for five years, under their occupation, in effect that is what Slavonia did.

Because Grusnov is a university town many of its inhabitants are of the intelligentsia; they still read foreign newspapers smuggled in as wrappings round parcels, and would still prefer to have their children taught French or English rather than political dogma. Dispossessed aristocrats who failed to make a getaway when the going was better have chosen to live there, too, conveniently far from the capital and near to the scenes of their childhood and their friends. The new class, so tiresomely conspicuous in the capital, of pushing boisterous young men and women who have grown up since the war and who are thoroughly impregnated by the Government doctrine, seem to stay there; at least in Grusnov, by constrast, they are scarcely to be seen. There are, it is true, quite a number of newcomers to Grusnov who could be included in that category—employees of government depart-

31

ments engaged on special work, but they do not behave noisily at all; rather the reverse.

The true Grusnovians, the dispossessed, the intelligentsia, the tradespeople, and the peasants, are devout Catholics, and the churches, again in contrast to Slavnik and other parts of Slavonia, are full to overflowing.

Lastly Grusnov has been lucky in that it has suffered none of the terrible devastation of war. The great grey buildings, intact, even whilst sheepishly wearing the banners with which they are decked, remain to frown defiance—a more discriminating defiance—still.

In Grusnov there are many churches; and at the hour, as in any other city, clocks strike, bells ring: high or low, late or early, each peal and chime eventually becomes familiar. But there, as in no other city, and always precisely on the hour, you will hear (if you listen carefully, because perhaps the wind will carry the first notes away) the bugler's call. It comes four times in all, to all four points of the compass. In the main square there is a watch tower, and at the top of this tower there is a chamber with apertures to north, south, east and west, and it is through these that the bugler blows his call; a call that has remained unchanged through the centuries, since the sounding of that alarm at sighting of the Tartar foe: each time the self-same warning notes, each time (as tradition decrees) the call cut short, on the verge of climax, on a breath. For it was at this point five hundred years ago that the Tartar's arrow pierced the bugler's throat. So, the call lopped off, its upward-swelling progress checked, the last note floats for a second on the air—all suspense, all promise, incomplete—and fades into silence, complete, the anti-climax of death. And this is the call that is to be heard every hour of every day and will continue to be heard so long as Grusnov remains a city.

At first it is disturbing to the newcomer, especially at night. Then he gets used to it. After a while he ceases to notice it at all.

An expression of astonishment came over the girl's face.

"Why—gnädige Frau, this is Number Nine. Naturally. This is the suite Mrs. Simpson had." She looked from one to the other, shy, puzzled, and then flitted out of the room.

"Hm," said Milly as the door closed. "Hear that? This is the suite the Simpsons had."

"Looks pretty good to me." Larry stretched comfortably. "Spot of Luxusleben just suits me fine. Anyway, it's probably the best they've got."

"I think it's a fast one."

Surprised, he turned to look at her. Her lips were set obstinately, in a way he knew.

"Whatever's got into you, darling? You fairly snapped that poor girl's head off."

"Well, I think she's a fast one too, come to that."

"Milly, for Pete's sake! Give her a chance. She shows willing enough, and at least you talk the same language. Honestly, sweetie, you're imagining things." He reached for her hand.

"Perhaps I am." She smiled as he lit two cigarettes and passed one to her. "What were the Simpsons like, I wonder?" she asked presently.

"Haven't a clue." Larry was walking round the room peering at the furniture. He pushed open the doors, and took a look at the adjoining room, then chuckled. "Know what it reminds me of? The Cavendish." It just needed, to complete the picture, old Rosa sitting in that high-backed chair, her blue eyes ablaze with curiosity and cognac. He could almost see her—hear her, too. "Didyagetyabeer, dear?" she'd ask, whether you'd been away five minutes or five years, and whatever the answer, nod affably.

"Reckon you could swing on those chandeliers, too. Good lord!" He bent down to examine one of the marble-topped commodes. "D'you know what, Milly? This stuff's *real*!" He stared round him. "It's *all* real! God! You could flog it for a fortune at home." He whacked a cushion on the daybed and a cloud of dust flew up. "See what I mean?" He grinned. "Just like the Cavendish."

She hadn't been listening.

"Why did they leave?" she said.

"Who? Oh, the Simpsons. I dunno. End of their time, I suppose. I didn't ask, and no one told me anything, up in Slavnik." He disappeared into the bathroom.

Milly lay thinking. So no one had told him anything. That in itself was odd, she reflected. In her experience, and in his too, you had scarcely set foot in a new post before you were inundated with conflicting reports on the subject of your predecessors. Once someone had left a post, he had left, and after that he and his were fair game for gossip, and the smaller the post the more scurrilous this was likely to be. So if Larry had heard nothing about the Simpsons in Slavnik, could that be, possibly, because he was not intended to hear anything? —and if so . . . her nose twitched. Sooner or later they would find out. There was a knock on the door in the far room.

" Come in," she called.

A man in a leather jerkin and peaked cap burst in, his arms laden with parcels. She recognised the driver of yesterday.

" Bag! " he called through the doorway, a broad grin on his face. It was apparently the only English word he knew. Placing his burden tenderly in an armchair he bowed, and still grinning, went out. She sprang out of bed.

" Darling! Look—what a lot of parcels. All for us—look! " Larry came out of the bathroom and stood in the doorway, shaving soap over his face.

" But what on earth . . . ? "

" Presents, I should think . . . for the children . . ." She was bending over the parcels, excitedly ripping off the string. " They're addressed to me, all of them . . . ooh, I wonder . . . ? "

Then he saw her face fall. She had torn off the outer wrappings, and scissors in hand, had paused. The parcels had been done up with great care in two separate layers of paper and string. They seemed to have been addressed twice over, too. She was picking them up one by one, staring in bewilderment at the inscription on the inner sheet of paper.

" Larry! But this one isn't for us at all! Nor *this*! Nor—Oh but *none* of them are," she wailed. " It's all a *mistake*."

" Who the hell are they for, then? " He wandered over to have a look.

" For a—yes, for a princess."

" A *princess*? " He looked at her kindly. " Now, Milly, just take it easy . . . it's been a strain, I know . . ."

" Don't be an ass," she said impatiently. " It's true. Look! Princess," she spelt out the name, " R A P O V S K A."

" Never heard of her," he said flatly. " No such name. Bet you it's not in the book."

" All those lovely parcels." She poked one fretfully.

" Well, don't muck them about, darling. They're not for us and that's that. I'll have to send them back to Slavnik. Some clot in Registry's made a balls-up. Bit odd, though, I must say." He frowned. It was as bad as having one's morning paper rumpled and read before

36

its appearance on the breakfast table. " Well, I've got to get a move on. Show my face at the office—Wragg'll have broken it to them that I'm here . . . Introductions—by Wragg. Indoctrination—by Wragg. Funny, it's just occurred to me. Wonder why he didn't ask for the job? "

" Perhaps he did." Milly sat back, looking up at him. " Didn't you think of that? "

" No," said Larry. " I didn't. I don't know . . ." he went on slowly, ". . . seems as if I don't know a thing, doesn't it? " He laughed, bent down and kissed her. " Your guess is as good as mine, darling, but don't start guessing too hard at this stage . . . we just don't know a thing."

When he had gone, she folded up the outer wrappings of the parcels; her name, she noticed, complete with initials, had been spelt correctly on each; she unravelled the string and twisted it into near little rolls. Really, it was very odd. Then she stacked the parcels in the bottom of the clothes press and locked it. She had been conscious of a mounting irritation ever since the moment of waking that morning and as she dropped the key of the cupboard into her bag she put her finger on the cause. She was uncomfortably aware that she had been at the receiving end of three successive fast ones since that time, and throughout had failed to acquit herself with her usual presence of mind, to deal with each as it deserved. Then she lay in a hot bath and gradually her sense of uneasiness melted away.

*   *   *

An additional suite of rooms had been necessary to accommodate the Purdoes and their entourage; thus a suite adjoining had been tacked on to the rooms originally occupied by the Simpsons, the whole now comprising Suite Nine.

The salon was the largest of the rooms; this led into the parents' bedroom, as has been described, which in turn led into the bathroom. There were two doors in the bathroom, the farther door having been the boundary of Suite Nine. Now unbolted, it led into the children's bedroom, which also had two doors, one leading into the main corridor and one into a small drawing-room which was to be the day nursery; a door off this room led into Miss Raven's bedroom, another door into what had originally been the bathroom of the annexed suite and which now, according to the practice of foreign residents in the Grand Hotel, was to serve as a kitchen. An electric plate had been rigged up on the bathroom table; food would be prepared on a wooden board laid across the bath, and the washing-up done in the hand-basin. On the far side of the kitchen was a small boxroom in which Gisela had erected

37

a camp bed. There was no communicating door between this box-room and the kitchen; both opened on to the main corridor.

The hotel, which had been converted from the town house of a nobleman, was not large, although the rooms were exceedingly spacious. It was built round a courtyard; thus the main corridor formed a square, and Suite Nine occupied one entire side of this square; beyond Gisela's room the corridor turned at right angles and somewhere round the corner was the Wraggs' apartment and farther on, the Americans'. All the rooms opened off one side of the corridor, that nearest the exterior walls of the hotel; on the other side, nearest the courtyard, was a blank wall with here and there a door leading down into the servants' regions, and into the courtyard. The first floor only was in use for guests; the only guests were foreigners and there were not many of these.

There was one other hotel in the town, with many more rooms, although not so luxurious, but if a foreigner chanced to go there first instead of to the Grand, he would invariably be told that all the rooms were occupied and be directed to the Grand, because the Grand was the foreigners' hotel. Thus matters were simplified for everybody concerned.

Milly put on her nicest tweeds, her thinnest stockings and a new hat and penetrated the labyrinth of rooms. Eventually she stumbled upon Miss Raven buttoning Dermot into gaiters.

" How's everything going, Miss Raven? All right? "

Miss Raven, who eschewed optimism on principle, and in particular the brand indulged in by employers, did not feel bound to make any such fatuous admission. All she said was: " I'm taking them out."

" Oh, I see." Milly stood hesitating, something in Miss Raven's tone making her uneasy. " Well, that's good," she said brightly, nervously.

Aware of having successfully lodged a shaft of disquietude into the breast of her employer, who would now enjoy her morning no more than she deserved to do, that is to say, no more than she herself would enjoy hers, Miss Raven cheered up. Consolidating her success, she went on: " It's the stove, I think, that's worrying them."

" Worrying them? "

" Oh yes. We've all got coughs this morning. Dries the air up so. You can't hardly breathe, can you? What with that and the dust as well."

" Nice and warm, though," pleaded Milly. " We'll be glad of it later."

" Later? " Miss Raven repeated, as if she could conceive of no time but the present, and that was bad enough.

38

"In—in the winter," stammered Milly, rashly laying herself open to the threat she dreaded most, and Miss Raven was not slow to seize the advantage.

"Oh, in the winter," she replied with a nicely calculated hint of vagueness to imply that the vicissitudes to be suffered by the Purdoes in that season might be no concern of hers.

Milly plunged through into the kitchen where she found Gisela standing on the edge of the bath, hammering hooks into shelves. As soon as she saw Milly she jumped down. She wore soft soles; all her movements were swift and noiseless, like a cat's.

"It pleases you, gnädige Frau, this way?" She gave Milly her rather touching smile. "I've tried to arrange it all as it was in Mrs. Simpson's time. Of course, then the Herrschaften only had the one bathroom and to cook and bath in one was difficult. Now we have space there should be no difficulty."

Milly decided to ignore the "we"; it annoyed her, nevertheless. She glanced at the shelves.

"It'll do for the moment. But why do we *have* to cook in the bathroom?"

"But—gnädigste—there's nowhere else!"

"There's a restaurant downstairs, isn't there?"

Gisela laughed, as if embarrassed. "It's a *public* restaurant," she said firmly, gently, as if to a child. "The Herrschaften will not eat there, of course."

"Oh? Won't we? I see . . ." But she did so. She decided to shelve the problem. She was at the mercy of everyone, it seemed. "Well, then, I'm going out to buy some food. Where's the market?"

"The *market*, gnädige Frau?" Gisela laughed. Her laugh was soft and low, exciting, like her voice. "You wish me to come with you, or to go for you? I always used to go for Mrs. Simpson."

"No, thank you," said Milly crossly. If there was any laughing to be done, especially in the kitchen, she was the one to do it. "I prefer to go by myself."

Gisela opened her eyes wide. "Alone—without knowing the language?" There was not a trace of impertinence in her voice nor in the smile which accompanied it, but Milly was convinced it lurked behind both.

"Yes," she replied smiling sweetly. "Without knowing the language. I shall speak in German, as I am speaking to you, or in French, and I dare say I shall get along very well. I am quite accustomed to markets, all over Europe, and I like to do my shopping for myself." No sooner had she finished this speech than she felt a fool. The girl was gazing at her in astonishment. Angry with herself, she became

39

flustered. " While I am out, please would you . . . well, lay clean paper on the shelves, with drawing-pins . . ."

" Already done, gnädige Frau." It was maddening, that meek voice. " Before ever your coffee was brought in, the shelves were already attended to."

Milly took a deep breath.

" Good," she said sharply, hating herself for not saying thank you. " Well, I expect you'll find lots of other little jobs . . ." she paused, glancing into the silver basket, which normally came in handy as a stop-gap, but the silver was already laid out, gleaming as never before. " Well . . ." she glanced up, almost, she could have sworn, in time to catch a smile on the girl's face, ". . . well, I'll bring the things for lunch. Good-bye."

Gisela sprang to open the door for her, and Milly went out into the main corridor. She felt quite rattled by the encounter. To make it worse, no sooner had she left the kitchen than she was convinced that she had been mistaken, indeed, had behaved quite unreasonably, not to say intolerably; the girl was simple and friendly and anxious to please—over-anxious, perhaps, but nothing more. I must be losing my grip, she thought. It's absurd to dislike her because she's *too* efficient. . . . She heard the chatter of the hotel chambermaids through the open doors along the passage. The girls curtsied, staring at her as she passed. A gnome-like creature, wearing felt slippers on his feet, was buffing up the parquet, bouncing rhythmically up and down, whistling. He stopped whistling as she went by. Happening to look back as she turned the corner, Milly saw that they were all still standing just as she had left them, watching her.

*　　　*　　　*

The porter behind the desk looked up as she came down the red-carpeted staircase. He was a stocky young man, swarthy, with oily black hair, his face pitted with smallpox scars. Somehow she knew that he was taking in every detail of her appearance as she approached. She handed him her key and he greeted her politely in French, allowing her, however, to push open the swing doors into the street for herself.

She walked through the park, which was laid out in the style of an English park. Dogs chased each other over the grass and drifts of leaves lay on the flower-beds and in the hollows under the chestnut trees. The trees were flaming gold, at the zenith of their autumnal beauty. An old man with a sack over his shoulder was collecting rubbish on the point of a stick. The benches were crowded with poorly dressed people, jostled close up against each other, most of them elderly, sitting with hands clasped, staring vacantly at the ground. She observed, because it was the sort of thing she did observe, that although she had every reason to be satisfied with her appearance, it excited no interest; not a single head turned to look at her as she passed. She felt piqued and then curiously ashamed, so that she hurried on faster. A much-travelled young woman, she was not ordinarily sensitive to the background of the stage on which in foreign cities her daily life was set; a monochrome background, grey as poverty, teeming with grey shadows. Here, however, in the twinkling of an eye, she herself seemed to have become the shadow, drifting by unremarked, apparently unremarkable, whilst these figures on the benches, silent, their shoulders bowed, in their ragged clothes and broken boots occupied with a strange dignity and an impression of permanence the centre of the stage. She hurried on and out of the park quite fast, towards the market.

*   *   *

Not long after, Miss Raven and her charges entered the park, and Miss Raven, seeing that it was quite a nice park, of the sort that she was used to, decided to take time off and said to her maid:

" I'll wear the Worth to-night."

The satin peignoir slid from her shoulders—she was standing on a white rug in front of an apple-log fire—and the girl's roughened fingers arrayed her slender body; smoothing on the gossamer stockings (half a tick, better sit down (Miss Raven, practically enough, hastily revised her dispositions) as her mistress reclined on a couch, Polly then held out the lingerie to warm in front of the fire.

" Not these, Polly—the orchid chiffon, I think." There was a hint of petulance in the voice and the girl hastened to the chest of drawers where the piles of French underwear lay in lavender-scented sachets. Why lavender? Well, verbena, then. Verbena to-day. When the white satin sheath had been slipped over the proud head, moulding the lovely body as though it had been poured into it, the young duchess gazed at her reflection in the mirror lit by silver sconces. She had never looked more exquisite.

" Oh, your Grace," breathed Polly—who was only a village girl— her eyes filling with tears.

" Hurry, child! " said the Duchess, time being short. Polly snatched up the brush and got to work on the thick bronze tresses, her deft fingers twisting the love curls at the nape in the way she had been taught by old Nanny (who lived in the turret, but I really can't go into all that now, thought Miss Raven). " Now the emeralds! " cried the Duchess, and Polly had scarcely clasped the jewels round the white throat before the Duke (attired in a silky sort of Paisley patterned dressing-gown) entered his wife's chamber. At the sight of her beauty

41

a strange look flashed over his saturnine—*saturnine*? repeated Miss Raven, momentarily at a loss; this was one of her favourite bits and she had never had any bother with it before. But " saturnine " wouldn't do—no, not for the Duke, anyway, not to-day. That face, that beloved old-timer, in the last few hours had somehow become transfigured, the savagery of the Mason profile softened, the famous snarl quite spoilt by the sunny smile of Mr. Purdoe. He's got to go on being Duke, she ruled severely, whichever he is, I can't change all that now. Ah-ha! She peered closer. A sensual curve did still betray the mouth. Her rebellious images under control, she was heartened, and fluency returned. He strode across the thick pile carpet, his body moving with animal grace. " You may go, Polly," he rasped kindly—*kindly*?—no, that wouldn't do; once more, hindered by artistic honesty, Miss Raven was forced to deviate from the script and the thought crossed her mind that it had lost a lot of the old kick—James had never caused her a mite of trouble—*said* then, kindly, and took the hairbrush from her hand. . . .

" I want to get out, Miss Raven." Dermot was drumming his feet on the step of the pram.

" Not yet," she murmured, pushing along faster.

" My lovely darling . . ." His lips caressed the hollow between . . .

" Look! " Clarissa uttered a scream fit to split the eardrums of a Sphinx. " Miss Raven, look! "

" Well, I'm looking," said Miss Raven.

" Over there . . . a *dachshund* . . . a darling little teeny-weeny . . ."

" What's a dachshund? " Her brother skilfully braked the passage of the pram with one gaitered foot.

" That is, you baby . . . oh, the sweetie sweet . . . it *is*, isn't it, Miss Raven? A dachshund? "

" Yes," replied Miss Raven, regretfully sheathing her wings and turning into wind preparatory to touching down.

*   *   *

Milly crossed over into the street leading to the market square. As she passed the corner, a swarm of women darted like angry wasps from a doorway; hovering in her path, brushing close, they almost seemed to settle upon her, their hands concealed beneath their aprons, hissing in her ear—" deedeeteedeedeetee." Alarmed, she walked on briskly, and they fell away, muttering. When she looked back, not one of them was to be seen.

A wind had got up. It swept the market square, tossing the skirts of the peasant women, tearing at the awnings, ruffling the shaggy bunches of dahlias in jampots on the flower stalls. The sunlight flickered over the heaps of corncobs, purple cabbages, shiny emerald peppers;

plaited baskets of bilberries, still misty with bloom; mounds of crab-apples, plums and pears. Rows of peasants squatted on their haunches, cheeses, butter and eggs spread on the ground before them; the poultry stalls were spread with plump corpses, geese, ducks, here and there a hare hanging muzzled with a tin mug; there were crayfish crawling in a bed of rushes, carp in a tank of mud, and everywhere, mushrooms. Garlands of dried mushrooms, like shrivelled bits of leather, swung in the wind. Gnarled and withered as their wares, the mushroom-sellers crouched over the mounds of fresh mushrooms, sorting them into heaps; handling them, not with casual familiarity, but almost with reverence, certainly with pride. Accustomed to the insipid cellar-grown type of fungus, Milly paused, fascinated.

There were all sorts. Some were improbable as mushrooms in a dream—grotesque, obscene, almost, and she was fairly sure, inedible; vast horny horrors, their stems covered with warts, soggy with rain; others ragged and shapeless, not like mushrooms at all, rather lopped-off elephants' ears, or old boots; heaps of pearly-white button mush-rooms, others like sugar biscuits, the upper layer set firm and white as icing, spongy beneath; a great pile of the sort that are the shape of *flutes de champagne*, mustard yellow, ribbed like parasols; and in the forefront a small heap of those most prized of all, which are found in a carpet of pine-needles, like scattered coins, flat and close, flush with the earth, but which when plucked seem to become mortal, oozing drops of scarlet juice like blood. She loitered up and down, peering, sniffing. They smelt fresh, of the morning; damp, of the forest; musty-sweet, of decay.

The peasants tittered and fingered her clothes as she fought her way through the crowd; when she bought butter she was mobbed by women offering her slices of butter to taste. Town-bred, she had always considered butter an absolute substance—but they waited anxiously as she rolled scraps of it on her tongue, and when she made her choice they screamed with delight. She bought a duck; then on her way back, calculating in terms of sterling, was appalled by the price. As she left the market, passing that corner of the street, the same grey shapes whirled around her—deedeeteedeedeetee—and then melted away.

The Grand Hotel was situated in the main shopping-street.

Dawdling along the row of shops, she discovered that the windows, which at a casual glance gave the impression of being well-stocked, were in reality almost empty, the displays padded out with bits of cardboard or consisting of an elaborately constructed " front " of a single product. Packets of detergent, skilfully erected in tiers, filled the entire window of a large grocery; inside the shop there was a queue. There was a queue outside the Bata shoe shop, a queue outside a

43

butcher's, the window empty except for a string of sausage; another outside a draper's, whose window was filled with hanks of coarse knitting-wool, all one colour, muddy brown. Sandwiched in between these shops, which were large and clean-looking and rather well-lit, there were one or two very small shops like little dark caves. These windows contained a jumble of stationery, apples and pears and chocolates; and inside, although it was dark, you could make out quite a crowd of customers, or friends of the proprietor, more likely, because they were not forming a queue but huddled round the counter, talking earnestly in whispers, or hanging about just inside the doorway, looking up and down the street.

It was very puzzling, she thought.

There were plenty of liquor shops. Brightly lit, with no queues outside, the windows were stacked with bottles which, without the well-known labels, the individuality of shape, the dusky charm of colour, lost much of their enchantment. These bottles were simply bottle-shaped, free of dust, the contents entirely masked by a uniform red label severely printed in black, whether denoting vinegar, vodka, or weedkiller seemed immaterial, yet the very innocence of presentation being somehow suggestive of evil, the corrupting anodyne; each guileless label the visiting-card of the guileful genie corked within. As for the bookshop window, the display was simply an author's success dream come true. Ousting unhealthy competition, copies of a single book in various poses, sideways, spine foremost, open, half-open, shut, in piles, more piles, higher piles, with and without jacket, even upside down, appropriated every inch of space. What a good book it must be, thought Milly in her simple way, staring; on the other hand, just as when one hears nothing but good of a stranger, the longer she looked the more she felt sure that she would dislike the book—did dislike it already, she decided, and walked on.

Just for fun, she went into the next draper's to buy a zip fastener, which she needed. They were quite friendly in the shop, in fact everybody crowded round. She explained what she wanted by showing them the zip fastener on her skirt. They were very attentive, patting her, and smiling, and so on, but it seemed they had no zip fasteners. Hooks and eyes, yes. Mammoth ones. No, nothing smaller. Buttons, yes, plain white bone. No, nothing else, neither smaller nor larger nor any other colour; no other buttons at all. She went out more puzzled than ever.

Then, just before she reached the hotel, she passed a different sort of shop. Lost in thought, she had gone by before she was struck by the incongruity of that window in contrast with the others, and frowning, she turned back. She stood in front of the window, her eyes screwed

44

up with astonishment. On the Ponte Lungho, or in Church Street, Kensington, or in the Faubourg St. Honoré, yes, one would expect to find a shop like this, but not here, surely. And yet ... she stared, spellbound, her eyes gradually disentangling one object from another; thickly coated with dust, stuffed in anyhow, with a carelessness which seemed to suggest not only that there was plenty more inside but that all hope of customers had long since been abandoned—a mother-of-pearl fan stuck into a teapot, an altar cloth, its silver and gold tarnished, the velvet rotting beneath the weight of heavy sand-coloured glass goblets set with jewels; a cupid on a candlestick, his chubby arm extended, draped with a necklace of garnets; a heap of inlaid snuff-boxes tossed together on a strip of brocade; a gold châtelaine, miniature ivory chessmen, a Florentine vase shrouded with lace, and a litter of sables nestling on the lid of a carved oak chest—the sight took her breath away. " Why," she whispered, fumbling for a word, as Larry had done earlier: " I do believe they're all *real!* "

She pushed open the door of the shop and a bell tinkled a long way off. Presently she heard slow footsteps descending the stairs and an old man with long white moustaches drifted out from behind a suit of armour. He glanced at her, nodded, and then stood chewing his moustaches, ignoring her, as if he hoped thereby to induce her to take herself off. He picked up something and began to rub it on his coat.

Milly was not so easily to be ignored. " Good morning," she said in French, advancing towards him. The old boy jumped; then he took off his spectacles and started blinking, between blinks giving her a sharp overall look, as if he had whipped out his antiquarian's glass and were appraising her—but this look, which appeared intermittently, might have been due merely to a trick of light.

" I am interested . . ." she began bravely, " in a . . . a . . . tea service . . ." Her voice died away in the gloom.

" Aaah . . ." He grunted sympathetically, as if, being broad-minded himself, he could tolerate the aberrations of his fellow-beings. He did, however, by making no move, even by blocking her way, seem to suggest that such interests might be pursued better elsewhere than in his shop.

" A tea service," she repeated, pointing to the one on the shelf behind him. " Could you tell me the price of that one, for instance? "

Reluctantly he shuffled across to the shelf and picking up one of the cups indicated, dusted it carefully with his pocket handkerchief and then replaced it without saying a word.

" The price? " she repeated.

He shrugged. " Ahhhh . . . the price . . . I would have to find that out . . . hard to say . . ."

" You mean you don't *know* the price? It's complete, isn't it? " she added suspiciously. Antique dealers, she knew, were up to all sorts of tricks.

" Ah, complete, yes . . ." he said sadly. " Very beautiful. Sèvres," he added casually, as if it were none of his business to extol, or explain the origin of, his wares. He shambled away down the aisle, dusting one or two objects with his handkerchief as he passed. Anxiously Milly pursued him. If this were a sales gambit, it was a successful one. She was suddenly determined to possess those cups. " I think I should like to buy it," she said loudly, catching up with him. " That tea service."

" Ah? " His eyebrows shot up so high they became tangled in his forelock.

" Je voudrais l'acheter," she said firmly, with her most winning smile, and yet something told her she was on the wrong tack. He looked at her, and she seemed to float into focus for an instant.

" Serait une belle possession," he agreed in his dreamy way, the use of the conditional form hinting not only at the existence of an insuperable obstacle to the fulfilment of her desire, but also at her own unsuitability as a candidate for ownership of such a treasure—in short, at the fantastic nature of her request.

" I will leave a deposit. I am living almost next door—at the Grand."

" The Grand? " He stopped chewing his moustaches. " Nice there, eh? Comfortable. The lady from there often came in to see me."

" Madame Simpson? " For the first time, and for the sake of the tea service, she exploited the name.

" Madame Simpson, c'est ça. Very nice lady . . . clever . . . good taste . . . liked pretty things . . ." Then, on an afterthought, he observed: " She, too, wanted that service."

" But I could leave a deposit, could I not? If you were to find out the price? . . . "

" Madame," he explained sadly, as if forced, out of honesty, to reveal the hidden flaw in the china. " There is no price . . . it is perfect, you see . . . I am sorry . . . a museum piece. . . . How would you transport it back to your country? It is forbidden, impossible . . . one does not wish for trouble. . . . I'll do my best to find you . . . some day soon . . . another one, pretty . . . not complete . . . sufficiently old . . . ." He was leading her to the door, soothing her as he might a child. . . . " Yes, come again . . . a pleasure . . . à bientôt. . . ." Blinking at the daylight, he shut the door behind her so smartly that the bell tinkled. She lingered, watched him trot down the aisle to the back of the shop —mopping his forehead with the handkerchief. Suddenly he was gone,

46

had dodged out of sight behind the armour, and the shop was as it had been, shadowy, silent, secret, stuffed with treasure trove, all of it, apparently, tantalisingly out of reach.

Back at the hotel, at the head of the stairs and turning the corner into the corridor, she saw Gisela slip out of the salon. In rather a furtive manner, it seemed to Milly, she flattened herself against the wall, closing the door behind her. In doing so she must have caught sight of her employer out of the corner of her eye because she looked up with a smile, without a trace of hesitation or surprise, as if she had expected Milly to come round the corner at precisely that moment, which could hardly have been the case. With her finger to her lips, her other hand still on the handle of the door, she waited until Milly came close.

" The housekeeper," she whispered; then, with a movement of her head, " in there."

" Look," Milly thrust the shopping-bag into her hands, " there's a duck——"

"Sssssh . . . gnädige Frau . . . the *housekeeper* . . . she is "—Gisela mouthed the words, rolling her eyes, accompanying the performance with becks and nods, and so on—"*sister* to the director of the hotel . . ." The role of conspirator, Milly recognised with almost a sense of relief, suited Gisela admirably; she fell into it not merely with ease, but as to the manner born. Anyway it was preferable to her previous one, Cinderella, Orphan of the Storm, or whatever it was meant to be, which was clearly a phoney. Stuffing the bag under her apron as if it contained contraband, Gisela belted off at the double down the corridor. Milly watched her, wondering a little; then opening the door, stepped briskly into the room.

A tall lean figure, dressed in black from head to foot, was fiddling with the drape of the curtains. She turned sharply at the click of the door handle, and seeing Milly, approached.

" I am the housekeeper, gnädige Frau. . . ."

" Oh, yes? "

" I hope you are comfortable? " She licked her lips, showing long yellow teeth. " You must tell me if anything is lacking. Everything is very clean, as you will see." She was ranging about the room, keys jangling. " We cleaned everything after Mrs. Simpson left—*everything* from top to bottom." From the emphasis one might suppose that Mrs. Simpson and family had been dirty in their habits.

" Quite comfortable . . . so far. Thank you."

" So far . . . yes . . ." she snickered. " You must please report immediately if anything is amiss. . . ." She looked Milly up and down, taking her measure.

"Do sit down," said Milly. "Have a glass of—well, of sherry or something? I usually do, about this time."

"Sherry?"

"It's a Spanish wine—very light. Cigarette?"

"Thank you, gnädige Frau." She watched Milly filling the glasses. "You are too kind, thank you . . . hmm . . . excellent . . ." She drained the glass at a gulp. "So long since I have tasted anything so good . . ." Milly refilled the glass. "In these difficult times . . ." murmured the housekeeper, interrupting herself briefly to dispatch the second glass. "Difficult times . . . yes, difficult . . ." Then, sitting bolt upright, she said suddenly: "You must not imagine that I am *really* a housekeeper, gnädige Frau."

"No?" said Milly, trying to be encouraging and merely feeling a fool. She poured more sherry.

"Ah *no.*" The housekeeper wagged her head mysteriously. "My brother and I—the manager, you know . . ." Milly nodded. "Yes, well, one must live . . . we were *placed* in the most unfortunate circumstances . . . coming of a very good family, as we do . . ." She brooded, fingering her glass, "My father had his estates . . . horses, peasants, everything, a fine gentleman, he was . . ." She reared her head and a wild look flashed from her eyes: "So fine . . . he would never . . ." she paused for dramatic effect and Milly wondered what on earth was coming next, ". . . he would *never* wear a shirt that had been laundered in the house. . . . No, his shirts had to be sent all the way to Vienna— in a special carriage, there and back—just for the ironing! . . . Think of that!"

Milly did think of it, and couldn't help reflecting that if such were the standards of the nobility, small wonder that a class so awkwardly exigent had not survived.

"Hmmm . . ." Absent-mindedly, the housekeeper took another cigarette. She seemed to have lost the thread. "You like the suite?" An odd look crept into her eyes. "Mrs. Simpson liked it," she went on; "Mrs. Simpson liked it very much . . ." Milly thought, she wants to talk, and experience told her to get up, which she did. At that moment there was a sort of scratching on the door; very slowly it opened, and the housekeeper sprang to her feet as a short fat old lady sidled in. Carefully closing the door behind her, her finger to her lips, her head on one side, the stranger listened at the keyhole for a second in the furtive manner which appeared to be a national characteristic of the Slavonians and which was rapidly getting on Milly's nerves, then strutted into the middle of the room. Shabbily dressed in woollies and button boots, carrying two large empty carpet bags, she stood there perfectly at ease, beaming graciously at Milly with hand outstretched.

48

" 'Ow d'yer do? " she said in a soft cooing voice, with a dazzling smile, and paused whilst the housekeeper withdrew from the room; then she continued: " 'Ow nice to meet yer . . ."

Milly took the hand held out to her, which was small, warm and chubby, the fingers armoured with rings. She had immediately identified the voice which had that peculiar enunciation, the slurred consonants, slovenly vowels, common to Cockney street urchins and certain polyglot beings who can—and frequently do—boast an entry in that famous studbook, the Almanach de Gotha. This was one of those well-preserved old things whose age it is impossible to guess; her cheeks pink and powdery and her white hair prettily arranged with a bang of fluffy curls in front. The smile, Milly noticed, did not extend to the eyes, which were round and innocent, in colour baby-blue; there was a twinkle in them, certainly, but they remained nevertheless quite frosty. Standing on tiptoe to reach Milly's ear, she whispered:

" I am the Princess Rapovska! " She nodded meaningly several times. " *Antoinette* Rapovska! " She looked sharply at Milly, and seemed gratified by her reactions to this statement, as though it were proper that one should be struck dumb at receiving such a visit. Then drawing her hand away she toddled over to the best chair, as if that were her accustomed place, and laid the bags down beside it and sat in it. " You 'ad a good journey? That's it, that's good. Ow! Sherry? Fine! " The princess tossed off her glass in the same uninhibited fashion as the housekeeper.

" Neow . . ." she went on, settling herself snugly and assuming a business-like tone, " you 'ave, 'aven't you, something for me? Yer know . . . parcels? "

" Yes. Of course . . . I mean, I'm so sorry . . . I . . ."

The princess, with a genial wave of her little hand, was pleased to accept the excuse. " Tha's awri' . . ." she said, holding out her sherry glass.

Milly refilled it, wondering how best to explain the crime she had committed. " I'm afraid . . . well, you see, there were all these parcels and we didn't understand . . . we thought they were for us . . so we . . . er . . . opened them."

" You *open* them? " exclaimed the princess, her eyes starting out of her head, her smile quite vanished.

" Well . . ." Milly floundered, " I mean, we didn't realise. Only the outer wrappers . . . then, of course, we saw right away they weren't for us . . . you see . . ." She smiled nervously.

" Ah-ah! . . ." The princess sank back into her chair, apparently mollified. " Tha's qui' righ' . . ." She nodded, approvingly. " Tha's jus' 'ow it's done . . ." Then some angle of the situation must have struck her as humorous, because she began to laugh. " You think they are for *you*—then you find they are for *us*! Ha-ha! . . . " She chuckled so merrily that out of politeness Milly joined in, although she was far from seeing the joke.

" Ow dear . . . but tha's jus' righ' . . . jus' the wye it's done . . ." she wiped her eyes, still chuckling, and whipped off her second glass of sherry. Then she continued more gravely, although her eyes still sparkled: " We poor Slavonians . . . gryteful, yer know, ever so gryteful for yer help . . . s'life an' death, yer know . . . the parcels . . . chère Madame Simpson . . . she 'ad yer nyme, tha's 'ow it 'appened . . . very obliging, Madame Simpson . . . 'elped us in the past, alwyes . . . ow, she was an angel, la Simpson . . . anywye," she went on briskly, angels being by their very nature neither here nor there, " now *you're* 'ere, yer see . . . an' we've all these friends, à Londres . . ." she rattled off a string of grand names, " an' so we tell 'em, send *this* wye . . . by you, yer see . . ." She sat back, flashing Milly another of her enchanting smiles. " S'quicker no trouble for nobody, eh ? " Then, casting a keen glance round the room, " You 'ave 'em 'ere ? My parcels ? "

Milly got up and lugged the parcels out of the cupboard. Once out on the carpet, they made a considerable pile. The princess stood over there, eyeing them shrewdly, prodding here and there. Then apparently satisfied that the overall bulk of the consignment tallied with some manifest of her own, she fetched the carpet bags and, kneeling beside the heap, began stuffing the parcels into the bags, wedging them down, now and then uttering little squeaks of delight. When they were all in, she raised herself on her short legs and hissed in Milly's ear: " Now I go out the back wye . . . the porter, yer know . . . 'e's . . . zzzz . . . ! "

" Oh," said Milly, " is he ? " She had no idea what was meant.

Stealing a last wistful glance at the sherry, the princess, clinging to her booty, made for the door. " Bye-bye," she whispered, adding graciously: " You can come an' 'ave coffee with me some time, you an' your 'usban'. Not to-dye "—hastily. " Sometime."

" Thank you. We should love to."

" Bien, alors. I will invite. An' tell your 'usban', more parcels arrive nex' week. A bientôt, alors, chère madame. Bye-bye." Off she went.

Weakened by these two encounters, Milly poured a glass of sherry for herself. Then, being methodical and in any case inclined to thrift, she seated herself at the bureau to write up her accounts. She was inclined, too, to the utmost neatness in her habits. That morning she had placed her account book in the right-hand top drawer. Now, on finding that it had been transferred to the lower drawer, she paused,

50

disconcerted. In her mind there was no margin for error or doubt. She was swept with a sudden cold wave of anger. But the princess had been under her eye all the time. She called Gisela.

"When I went to the market," she began pleasantly, watching the girl's startled face, "some women on the corner of the street rushed out at me. They said something like deedeeteedeedeetee—why did they do that? What does it mean?"

Gisela laughed, clearly relieved. "Because they think you are American. American D.D.T. is hard to get."

"I see. How is the duck getting on?"

"All right," said Gisela, "but it is rather an old duck. Only one stall sells them young . . . but naturally, the gnädige Frau could not have known that."

She was standing with one hand on the door in her racing start position, as if prepared to throw a belt about the world in no time at all, should her mistress so desire. Only an irritable or unreasonably suspicious employer might have sensed impertinence in that last remark, and even then she would have felt herself to be in the wrong. Milly, who chanced at that moment to be both irritable and suspicious, merely said:

"Never mind. I shall know next time. By the way," she added, "will you tell the housekeeper that I require keys for the drawers of the desk?" She met Gisela's eyes and smiled. "That's all. You may go now."

She made this request several times on subsequent occasions; the keys were lost, new keys were being made, the locksmith was ill—in any event, the keys were never forthcoming.

51

Chapter Four

SCOWLING FIERCELY, Olga Wragg levered the steak on to its raw side in the pan. Dripping sizzled and there was a smell of burning. Losing her head, she seized a wet fork and prodded the meat, an action which caused her to jump six inches into the air and clap her hand to her mouth; the fork clattered to the floor. She had received a mild to middling electric shock.

Anyone who cooked in the Grand Hotel bathrooms was subject to these shocks, the wiring of the hotel being haphazardly rigged and exceedingly faulty; sometimes, however, one suspected that it was the manager himself, an irascible old gnome who cultivated cacti in his bedroom, who, powerless to forbid the exploitation of wash-basin and power plug, from time to time emitted these malignant, if not lethal, currents of disapproval, just to show the foreigners he knew what they were at. Mrs. Wragg, who was slapdash in her methods, came in for more than her share of these shocks, which was unfair in view of the exemplary stoicism she displayed in her attitude towards them. Now she merely took another fork, a dry one, and went on manhandling the steak as before, her expression fiercer if anything, telling herself that having allowed her thoughts to wander she had none but herself to blame. She had evolved the theory that the only way of minimising the effect of contact with live current was by *thinking of it all the time*. Thus she would set out to cook a meal saying to herself, before ever approaching the electric plate—I am going to get a shock, I know it, so it won't be one. It annoyed her, nevertheless, that her mind should not have complete control over her body. She always jumped.

She slapped the plate on which lay the result of her efforts, a fair replica of Svidrigailov's " terrible-looking beefsteak," in front of her husband, spilling some of the gravy. There was a suppressed intensity, even violence, about all her movements which made for clumsiness.

" You may find the potatoes slightly burned," she said in her hoarse voice. " But it's all pure carbon. Quite harmless." She settled down to her own plate filled with cheese and raw shredded cabbage—she detested cooking and this was only one of her ways of showing it. They ate slowly, a journal propped in front of each. Wragg allowed a chuckle to escape him.

"What's the matter?" Mrs. Wragg asked suspiciously.

"Only the comp."

"Not up to the usual standard. Facetious treatment, I thought." Mrs. Wragg had once been commended in that very column, commended, however, in the preliminary paragraph, which, as everyone knows, is merely devoted to the egocentric maunderings of the competition setter; baulked of a share in the prize, she had never forgiven Tiny Tim—under which pseudonym the fellow lurked—and never more matched her wits with others at his behest.

"They sent the apple juice with the NAAFI," she said. "You need a laxative, Herbert. Better have some."

They sat sipping apple juice until Wragg took out his pencil. Once he became engaged with the crossword she knew she had lost him for the evening.

"Well, so what are they like, Herbert?"

"Who?"

His wife stared at him intently. She looked rather impressive. She had been experimenting with new make-up and her dark eyes, ringed about with pencil under glittering lids, dominated her face—no mean feat—let alone Wragg, which was easy by comparison.

"You know who I mean," she said quietly. She knew he was prevaricating and she was guessing why.

"Like?" He stirred restlessly. "Well, they're not *like* anything . . ."

She sighed.

"Knows his job?"

"Seems to. Knows what a half-tone block is."

"Well, that's a change. What's she——" she was going to say "like" but changed it. "What sort of woman is the wife?"

Wragg hesitated. What sort indeed? He had no idea. He could only think of chestnut hair gleaming whichever way you looked at it. Then he remembered the cocktail shaker episode, and blushed.

"Uppish," he said. "And spoilt. You wouldn't like her."

Mrs. Wragg looked faintly pleased.

"Good-looking?" she asked casually.

Wragg yawned and bit his pencil. "So-so." It was a shade overdone.

"I know that type," she snapped. "Superficial."

"Sure to be." Wragg glanced wistfully at the crossword.

"Still, I suppose we'll have to ask them to supper some time."

"I don't think we need," he said quickly, aware that engaging themselves with the Purdoes for supper would be simply throwing away the advantage of the home ground, ignoring the felicitous toss of the coin, a deliberate courting of disaster—opening up a whole avenue of possibilities for mistakes, of omission and commission—no, supper was unthinkable.

"You mean they ought to ask us first?"

He did not, but he let her think it. She began to clear away.

Wragg said: "I think I shall take a bath." After that, the crossword, in bed.

"If you're going to cut your toenails, spread the newspaper, Herbert, otherwise they get stuck in the cracks. The girl's complained."

"All right," said Wragg, sheepishly. It was the only answer he could make. If he had said, as tempted, that he had no intention of cutting his toenails, Olga merely had to look at him and score. It was true they needed cutting.

When he had gone into the bathroom she settled down in the armchair. She might put in a couple of hours' work before bed—it would depend on whether she was in the mood or not. She picked up her pencil and began chewing it, waiting for an idea.

She was writing a novel; that is to say, she had drafted the dedication and selected three of the four quotations to be incorporated as divisional headings; only the subject remained obstinately obscure. No need to worry about a plot; the plot would follow the subject, as night the day. She had for long entertained the idea of writing a novel, and of all the forms open to the creative writer that known as " fictionalised history " appealed to her most. In this field, to her way of thinking, one could scarcely go wrong; the facts, so long as one stuck to them—the names of characters, their appearances, idiosyncrasies, dates of birth, death, and even the circumstances in which they met their ends—providing a sturdy warp across which the novelist might weave her woof. Facts were facts, fiction—Olga's private synonym—a pack of lies; from a marriage of the two her novel was to be conceived.

That it would concern Napoleon, however obliquely, she was fairly sure. Her reading matter, permanently on show and a bore to dust, nevertheless an encouragement in itself, was assembled on the table beside her. An edition of *Chartreuse de Parme* in the original French, and also in minute and troublesome print, lay on top of the pile. Olga read French, but it seemed an exaggeration of effort to do so when alone with oneself, so now her pencil was skimming rapidly over the pages of an English translation of the same, but, to her distress, she discovered that her attention was but imperfectly held.

For one thing, she was uncomfortable. She was wearing a new black blouse, " a wisp of chiffon," and tight black velvet pants, " ideal for informal entertaining," both garments having arrived by the bag

54

the night before. Thus clothed, she was forced to sit bolt upright lest the blouse be creased, and lest the attendant strapless bra jab whalebone into her flesh; in which position the cut of the trousers contrived to catch her cruelly in the crutch. Her hair had been done in a new way, too, in a smooth sleek topknot; but now her head was itching and she badly wanted to scratch it (an eventuality for which her former style of hairdressing might have been designed) and that she was prevented from doing so merely aggravated a mounting sense of irritation, for which a scapegoat was at hand—or rather, at her feet under the table —in the shape of the weekly journal *Caprice*, and, more satisfactorily resolved into human shape, in that of one of its columnists, a certain Miss Annabel Andrews.

However, Olga was far from being a weak-minded woman, and her course once set she pursued it. Schooling herself to ignore mere physical discomfort, she reached for a cigarette and fitting it into a long amber holder—an accessory suggested by Miss Andrews—she was at once rewarded, consoled by a thought, no more than a flutter, an embryonic kick, connecting herself, black pants and amber holder, albeit tenuously, with George Sand (George Sand, the name flickered across her mind, that was all it amounted to) but as a link with literary endeavour it did the trick. Encouraged, with the intention of ploughing on, she wriggled her large limbs into an attitude that was at least bearable, in so doing disturbing with her foot the pile of magazines under the table, so that a headline was shuffled under her gaze. Painfully she read, upside down: " Three Musts for a Girl about Town " —by Lord Wother . . . but the nobleman's name was teasingly withheld beneath the pile. Olga, who could recognise the devil when she saw him, attacked Stendhal at a furious rate, but it was of no avail. Turning to the French and discovering the corresponding page uncut, she sighed . . . after all, one had to come up for air.

Lord Wotherspoon, as it turned out. Absorbed before she knew it, turning a page she was confronted by the familiar features, the critical eye, glossy hairdo, small, sharp " nosey " nose, of Annabel Andrews. Olga met that eye with respect, as always, but to-night she was aware of a totally new feeling in regard to Miss Andrews—sudden, violent dislike. For the past three months she had been that lady's most loyal acolyte, meekly submitted to her every counsel—and where had it got her? Ever since Molly Simpson, packing, had staggered down the corridor with an armful of magazines and said: " What am I going to do with all this trash? I can't throw them away."

" I'll get rid of them for you," Olga had said grimly. But instead she had sat down that very afternoon in front of the stove, and scornfully picking one up, had flicked through it—a serial, trash, it was true, but of academic interest as regards style, appeal—and thereafter never looked back.

Now, gazing about her in wonder, she appreciated for the first time the full effects of the influence of Miss Andrews, the transformation of the interior of Suite Number Forty-Five.

Gracious Living had set in. The knick-knacks which Herbert and she had collected in the course of their married life had been swept away and replaced by clever ceramics ordered from a London department store; the parquet was covered with folkweave mats; frilled nylon now bridged the gaps between the heavy plush curtains; posters, obtained from the London Passenger Transport Board, decorated the crimson damask walls. There was almost no corner of the suite that her fairy fingers, urged on by Miss Andrews, had left untouched. The day Wragg found, in the bathroom, a roll of paper tinted palest heliotrope, and the lavatory brush encased in a matching nylon bag, he had spoken:

" What *is* all this, Olga? What's going on? " He had waved at the sideboard. " Where's all the stuff we used to have? "

" We couldn't go on living with that sort of junk, Herbert."

" I don't see why not. We lived with it for years . . . I *liked* it."

" I'm sorry, Herbert." She had used that firm, quiet tone which almost always silenced him—but for good measure she had given him a look as well, one of her straight ones. " That's just the very worst reason you could produce. You liked it because you were used to it. We were due for a change. Personally, I'm rather pleased with the effect. It's very contemporary."

At that, for no reason that she could see, a shudder had passed over his face. Still, whether it was her voice, or the look, or what—something had silenced him. He had never said another word, let her have her own way, and in a remarkably short time the change-over to the contemporary had been accomplished.

Then Olga had started on herself. Professing to scorn fashion as a hindrance to the free expression of one's personality she had hitherto expressed hers in terms of gay dirndl skirts run up in no time, hand-woven tweeds, or rich furnishing fabrics tacked together and secured by jewelled pewter pins, but it had been made plain from the outset that that sort of thing wouldn't do at all for Miss Andrews. No one's appearance must be as contemporary as one's setting. And really it had been rather fun, experimenting with make-up, ordering new clothes —a late flowering, but an exotic one. The last three months, she could say, had been the happiest of her life—since the day when Molly Simpson left and she, Olga, had stepped straight into her shoes.

She had been astonished that the world, overnight, could have become such a pleasant place. The office staff, the porter at the desk downstairs, the maids, all of whom had snubbed her in Mrs. Simpson's day, now, aware of her position, had become respectful, even servile. Everyone knew, although it had not been confirmed, that Herbert would get Simpson's job—and indeed, Herbert had been the obvious choice.

So it had been all the worse when the blow had fallen—a week ago this very night, and how well she remembered it, Herbert coming it from the office and asking for cherry brandy. "Whatever for?" she had said, and he had surprised her by bursting out rudely: " Because I want a drink, that's what for." Then he had sat down at the table, just staring at his plate, and suddenly she had realised that something must have happened. She had fetched the cherry brandy and poured him out a glass and put it right in front of him, but he didn't seem to see it, he just went on staring at nothing. And she had stood there, waiting. " They're sending someone else," he had said at last. " No," she had said, and really she thought for a second he must be joking, although he never joked. " No."

" Yes," he had said, helping himself to beans or whatever it was. Vegetable stew, that was what it had been; a Thursday. " Yes, and I'm to go up to meet them."

" Married? "

" Oh yes." He was loading his fork, coating it with salt from the heap on his plate, one of those marital tricks which must often swing the balance towards murder. " With two children. And nanny," he had added, chewing stolidly.

And then she had started to create, well, yes, she had created, she would be the first to admit that. It was so grossly, monstrously unfair. She had continued all the time he was eating, while she cleared away and washed up, and then she had come back into the living-room and finding it empty had charged into the bedroom, and there he was, already in bed, turned over on his side, his back to her, and although even then she had been unable to stem the torrent of words, at last, the hump under the bedclothes remaining motionless, silent, her voice had died away.

So she had left him and gone into the other room and sat by the stove for a long time, thinking. In a few hours they would all know— the office staff, the porter, the maids, everybody. " He is a failure," she had murmured. " A failure. It all depends on me." So it was not to be in *that* way—the easy way, Molly Simpson's way. Of course not, not for *her*, Olga Wragg. But there must be a way, nevertheless. Having tasted the quality of Molly Simpson's very existence, she herself had developed a taste for what she imagined to be the fruits of power

—popularity and the centre of the stage, and it never once occurred to her that what she had recently and all too briefly enjoyed might merely be a legacy of Mrs. Simpson's own flamboyant personality. No, these were perquisites that went with the job; which resolved the problem in a nutshell. The job.

She had sat by the stove until one or two o'clock, brooding, thinking things out; and all through the past week she had been thinking and now, this evening, putting Stendhal to one side, she began to think things out all over again.

When Wragg came in from the bathroom, although she guessed that he had the paper with the crossword concealed in his dressing-gown pocket, she let him go by without a word. Careless of her seductive new clothes, huddled up in the arm-chair, she was pondering how best to employ her ingenuity that the future might be shaped in accordance with her own, and by now quite specific, blueprint.

58

Chapter Five

SOME DAYS LATER, when the second bag arrived, Larry said:

" Look, Milly, I'm damned if I'm just going to be a postbox. Half of this stuff is for that Rapovska woman. You'd better let her know this sort of thing isn't on."

" Darling, I don't even know her address."

" I bet Gisela does. Gisela! "

Gisela almost fell out of the bathroom door. How much English did she understand? None, so she said. Milly wondered. Even Larry, who professed to approve of Gisela, glanced at her sharply.

" Do you know where this Princess Rapovska lives? "

" Oh yes, sir," Gisela answered, in her soft breathless voice, her eyes sweeping the room. " For the parcels? " she said eagerly—too eagerly.

" Yes." Larry's cool grey eyes watched her face. " For the parcels."

" Of course . . ." Gisela gave him her winning smile. " I always used to take them for . . ."

" Oh, you did, did you? Well, perhaps you wouldn't mind obliging just once more? It'll be the last time." Milly seldom heard that chill note of authority in his voice, and never without admiring its instantaneous effect. Gisela glanced at him nervously, without a word swept the parcels into her apron and scuttled out of the room.

They were at lunch when she returned.

" A note, gnädige Frau," she whispered, stealthily laying it beside Milly's plate. " From the princess. Urgent, she said."

Milly spread the sheet of paper on the table, frowning. The message might have been in code, so cautiously was it phrased. Without date, heading, or signature, in capitals and in French it read:
WHAT WE SPOKE ABOUT WOULD BE AGREEABLE THIS EVENING NINE O'CLOCK. THE SERVANT KNOWS WHERE. DELIGHTED DEAR FRIENDS.
She passed it over to Larry.

He glanced at it. " What, no call signs? "

Milly giggled. " It means she's inviting us to coffee, darling, that's all."

" Oh, is that all? And what do we do back—inscribe her on the bag list? "

" Darling, don't be snooty. I think it would be rather fun. It's very *brave* of her, really. . . . Do let's go."

" Hm." He could be obstinate on occasion. " Something tells me she'll expect some kind of dash for this session."

" Oh, *Larry*! You've got it all wrong—she'd be awfully hurt. Wait till you meet her. She's a real old aristocrat."

" That's what I thought. They usually rate themselves pretty high, in my experience."

But curiosity and boredom prevailed. That evening Gisela escorted them through the back streets. A thin fog clung around the porticos. She sped on ahead of them, noiseless, swift; only the sound of their own footsteps rang out on the cobbles, echoing down the street. There was not a soul abroad apart from themselves—it was like wandering through a city of the dead. At last she stopped in front of a huge studded oak door: instead of using the brass knocker, she scratched with her fingernails until they heard shuffling footsteps on the other side of the door. " Viel Vergnügen! " she murmured, and melted away into the night. The door creaked slowly open. An old man in black bowed and stood aside for them to enter. When the door had shut behind them he turned to them, bowing again.

" Good evening," said Milly, holding out her hand. For all she knew he might be the prince.

Ignoring her hand, he said reprovingly: " Madame, je suis butler."

Milly bit her lip, following him up a flight of stairs. At the top there was a little antechamber, where he helped them off with their coats, and as he did so it struck Larry that the butler's eyes roamed over their innocent forms with a more than professional interest, as if his instructions had been to frisk them on arrival.

" Madame la princesse vient tout de suite." The butler disappeared into a room on the left, leaving the door open. Under the dim glow shed by a solitary bulb in a chandelier built to house a dozen such, Milly patted her hair in front of a mildewed gilt mirror.

Through the darkened doorway, a tremendous racket was going on in the room on the left. The background noise, the main blast, as it were, was identifiable as a cracked recording of Nelson Eddy singing " Rose Marie," played very loud and fast, simultaneously with a piano and voice rendering of " Tea for Two," executed in a staccato manner, the foot of the pianist pressing firmly on the loud pedal and the voice (a woman's) soaring with unusual range, verve and here and there with improvisation; an unequal contest out of which Nelson Eddy came but poorly. Above and below this mingling torrent there was some banging and crashing about, the slither of feet over parquet and shrill squeals of laughter.

The princess tottered into the doorway and stood blinking like a mole which has emerged from its burrow. She was dressed much in

60

the style of the occasion of Milly's first meeting with her, in all sorts of woollies with the addition of several brooches, and carpet slippers in place of boots. After a lapse of seconds—a pause calculated to inspire panic in any but the most confident of guests—as if, having with reluctance recognised them, she had decided to make the best of a bad job, shakily she advanced.

" Aaah ... chère amie ..." she patted Milly's arm ..." Charmante petite femme . . . this your 'usban'? Hmmm." She seemed to be appraising Larry's tailor rather than Larry himself. Apparently arriving at a favourable conclusion, she looked up at him and nodded in an offhand but friendly way. Larry smiled guardedly.

" So, come ..." She waved them inside, herself pausing to burrow amongst the pile of wraps they had discarded, mumbling to herself. " Go on, go," she urged testily, observing that they hung back. " Only a small soirée, fam'lee only."

She bustled them into a long dark hall with a raftered ceiling, which at first sight appeared to be a repository, or warehouse, the greater part being filled chock-a-block with solid pieces of furniture. At the far end of the room a log fire shed its light on several couples who were dancing resourcefully and with enthusiasm to the medley of music, weaving their way through the maze of sofas, cabinets, commodes, large upright cupboards, chairs and tables. The gramophone, an immense hooded monster, was set on one side of the fire; on the other side, in the shadows, a lady sat at a grand piano, bouncing up and down on the stool, her arms moving at a great rate. Some of the space was occupied by a billiard table covered with saucers containing onions and small fish and sweet biscuits; there was also a sort of tea urn, steaming, surrounded by dozens of cups and saucers. They dodged their way amongst the dancers to the fire, the princess at their heels.

" You like? " she said, gazing round her, and rubbing her little paws together, the rings sparkling in the firelight. " S'nice, isn't it? S'funny. They all like to come 'ere," she added, rather vaguely. Then, waving at the dancers, " This my fam'lee: Stas, Natalie, Mishka, Anni, Adas, Pierre . . ." Milly thought, as the butler handed her a cup of tea, how amusing, just like *War and Peace*.

" Rosa, Vassili . . . Louise . . ."

" *All* your family? "

" All, all related . . ." The princess shrugged, rather petulantly tapping the logs with her foot. The old butler was hanging about, waiting to catch her eye. When he did, Milly noticed that he shook his head, looking rather grim, and the princess sniffed. " You *like* tea? " she asked, suddenly turning to Larry. She seemed to be in a huff about something.

61

" Oh yes," he replied courteously. In fact he was dying for a drink.

In size and numbers the females of the Rapovski clan were in striking predominance over the males; Brünnhildes, Dianas, every man jack of them, they danced with a sort of belligerent enthusiasm, handling their partners rather roughly—with passion, certainly, but also with indifference. The latter, crouched beneath the shelving bosoms, suffering their faces to be swished by locks of black hair, wore identical fixed expressions of helpless resignation.

" That pore boy," the princess pointed out a young relative who was being waltzed past, " 'e 'as the teebee. 'Is father was the same—in six months, pff! " She made a telling little gesture, as if snuffing out a light. " Six months," she repeated in her uninhibited way as the wretched youth, dragged on by his partner, brushed the circle by the fire, "an' 'im," she went on, as another wilting specimen of the male line approached, " 'e's failed 'is examens but then 'e's a bit——" she had the delicacy to turn away to tap her forehead. " An' you see that one, over by the piano—quelle histoire—tragic . . . in love 'e is, à la folie, with the Stavrinska girl—'oo's married now, ça va sans dire, elle n'était pas tellement bête . . . but you see 'im, 'ow 'e is? . . .'ow pale, 'ow maigre . . . comme il souffre, pauvre garçon . . . 'e'll go like the rest, queek, yer know . . ."

The appearance of the young man did indeed bear out the likelihood of the fulfilment of this prognosis; catching the pitiless eye of the matriarch fixed upon him, he shuffled, looking more miserable than ever. The princess went on, smacking her rosy lips as if a pint or two of boy's blood were her favourite apéritif: " C'est toujours comme ça, ou la mélancolie, ou bien le galloping . . . they all go queek, queek, the men of our fam'lee . . ."

" But what a lot of lovely *girls*," said Milly politely. Indeed the young women, who were rollicking about like great awkward pieces of furniture come to life, seemed to fill the room.

" Ah, the *girls* . . ." She smiled rather complacently. " C'est bien autre chose."

Larry was frowning at the back view of the pianist.

" You know," he said, " I feel sure I've seen her before."

" 'Oo ? " The princess peered across. " Ooooh . . . *that* one . . ." She burst out laughing. " Sophie! " she yelled in the direction of the piano. " Viens tout de suite! Come meet our new British! "

The person at the piano immediately took her hands off the keys and stood up. As she did so, her arm caught against a sheaf of music, knocking it to the ground.

" Vous voyez? " said the princess, with a little grimace. " C'est notre Sophie—elle est toujours si maladroite! "

Larry had already crossed over to the piano and was helping to retrieve the scattered sheets. The princess sniggered, turning to Milly: " 'E's nice, your 'usban', to give himself the trouble."

" Who is she? " Amused, Milly connived at the evident amusement of her hostess. Whoever it was, she could see, was not very young and rather plain. Just Larry's luck, she thought.

The princess shrugged. " A relation," she said off-handedly. " Pas grand' chose. One 'as so many—and it's necessary to be agreeable to all. She speak English, 'er brother too—I think you like 'er brother. Where is 'e—ah, over there, look! " She pointed out yet another pale elegant young man, drifting in and out between the furniture, caught in the powerful embrace of a female whose cheek nuzzled his brow. ". . . Yer see, 'e 'as chic, eh? One sees it immediately . . . but 'is sister, la pauvre Sophie . . . du tout . . . du tout."

" There." Larry scrambled to his feet. " That's the lot." Puzzled, he stared at the woman who was re-arranging the music. She was quite tall, broadly built, dressed in an old-fashioned tweed suit, her brown hair done anyhow, in a bun of sorts. It was a bright brown, and rather curly, the type of hair which made you itch to see it done in a different way. Her hands, he noticed, were trembling. " I say—it's Miss Bielska, isn't it? "

She looked up, and a pair of warm brown eyes smiled shyly into his own. She had a very direct glance. She looked very healthy. She wore no make-up at all. At the sound of his voice all the lines in her face, and there were plenty, crinkled up with pleasure; although some more slowly than others, there wasn't one that didn't eventually crinkle up; a process that gave him pleasure to watch.

" Yes, Mr. Purdoe. Sophie Bielska." Her voice was shy, breathless, the voice of a girl, a little English girl.

" But—haven't I seen you before—in the office? "

" Oh, yes. I do translations—that is, sometimes I do—for you, and—for Mr. Schulman."

" Of course," he said slowly. " I remember. That's splendid. It is really. But isn't it rather difficult to arrange? "

" Well," she gave a doubtful little laugh—" perhaps not so easy."

" I think it's wonderful of you to come and help us out."

" Not at all," she said simply. " It gives me great joy."

" Sophie! " The princess hissed at her elbow, delivering some instructions in her own language which, to Larry's regret, caused Miss Bielska to vanish. Later he saw her collecting the used cups on a tray

63

which she carried away. "Excuse," the princess chuckled, taking his arm, "now you meet other people—my sister, Irène!"

"You dance?" murmured a gaunt, predatory-looking creature, purposefully bandaging a length of chiffon round her throat. "Come," and seized him bodily forthwith. He suffered himself to be led into the labyrinth, from which, enmeshed in her draperies, clasped against her bony chest, their knees clashing together like castanets, there was no immediate escape.

The butler, refilling the tea urn, whispered to his mistress. The princess suddenly shot round at Milly: "You *reelly* like tea?"

"Yes," said Milly, puzzled. "Thank you, I do." She was puzzled to see that her hostess and the butler once more exchanged a peculiarly significant glance; then the latter shuffled off, remaining, however, in earshot behind the urn.

"'E's our pore ol' Stefan," said the princess sentimentally. "Pore ol' man, been with us for years. Un très bon servant. Yer know, we try to send 'im awye in the bad days—but 'e's weeping—weeping—all the time . . . so we 'ave to keep 'im now . . ." The butler, who was listening hard, shot his mistress a look so black as to hint at another version of this touchingly feudal relationship. At that moment there was the sound of a hammering at the street door and he made off.

"Yer know 'oo that'll be?" exclaimed the princess. "*Your* friends"—in her excitement she pinched Milly quite hard—"the *Americans.*"

"*Our* friends?" Milly smiled, stepping out of reach. "We don't know any Americans."

"Yes, yes," the princess replied impatiently, "the journalist, Schulman, and"—she caught at the arm of a girl who was dancing past—"that other one 'oo is to come, Nina? the American Ambassador, eh?"

"Not the *Ambassador*, Granmamma"—at which a look of the most vivid disappointment came over the old lady's face—"Mr. Schwelling. But he's nice, too—high up in the American Embassy."

Comforted, the princess turned back to Milly.

"You 'ear what she sye? 'Igh up—'igh in the American Embassy. 'Igher than Schulman," she added practically, as the door opened and the butler announced: "Les messieurs américains."

Deserted, on the instant and completely, the British remained by the fireplace as the Rapovskis, in a body, surged to greet the new arrivals. Milly, who had caught sight of a tall figure with a shock of black hair in the fray at the doorway, turned to the fire and poked the logs absentmindedly with her toe. She put a hand to her cheeks.

"No."

Abe looked grave. "You oughta've done."

"Yes. I see that now."

"You couldn't know. What'll ya have? Scotch? Say when. I'll give you a tip." He patted the bottle. "This is your entrance fee. I mean, it's rationed and all that and it may be the only thing between you and insanity but now and again it's worth the sacrifice, just to come here. Specially when you've got some high-up from Slavnik on your hands—bring 'em here and they automatically file a glowing report. It impresses 'em, see? Look at old Smelling." Larry couldn't be sure he had heard aright. "Tickled pink. Thinks he's living in the past and the present—he'll dine off it for nights. None of the Embassy guys up in Slavnik ever see anything like this."

"Why not?"

"Too clamped down on, poor bastards. The Slavonians, I mean. They wouldn't dare invite you. Besides, up in Slavnik you're really watched. I had a whole gang of boys on me. Two on, two off, night and day. They always used the same pitch, a doorway one block along from where I lived. Goddammit, I used to get sorry for 'em—send 'em over a drink now and then. They didn't like that. Unprofessional, I guess. Anyway, it's different there. Here, they watch you, sure—but they do it gentlemanly. They choose someone you really *would* have a drink with—see what I mean?" Abe looked at him rather hard.

"I think so," said Larry slowly, looking round him with new eyes.

"Just so long as you do." Firmly corking the bottle, he went on: "I only got back just now, or I'd 've looked you up before. Tell you what, I'll drop old sugar puss soon as I can and we'll go back and have a drink. It's proles' night at the Grand—an education, you shouldn't miss it."

"I've got my wife here."

"Yeah." He grinned. "I saw. She can come too, there's no law against it. I'll give you the secret sign." He leaned over. "Say, do me a favour, will ya—keep an eye on the liquor. I don't want Antoinette snitching a coupla bottles round the back like she did last time. Help yourself, though."

"Thanks," said Larry and did as he was bid.

"You haven't met Abe Schulman?" Mr. Schwelling was saying to Milly. "Newspaper man. Top of his tree . . . an exceptionally fine person . . . in some ways," he added, catching a leer from Abe across the room. Mr. Schwelling frowned, but went on loyally: "Very sensitive boy, that . . ." His voice dropped. "Bears a scar, though."

"A scar?"

67

"A scar, Mrs. Purdoe—a deep and terrible wound. Abe was married to a lovely girl—a *very* lovely person—and then—one fine day—Tst!" He shook his head, stared into the fire.

"Oh dear," said Milly, after an appropriate pause. "What?"

"She passed away, Mrs. Purdoe. Terrible shock to that boy. Suddenly cut off—that young life. Terribly tragic thing." He took off his glasses and rubbed them briskly.

"How awful," said Milly weakly.

"Awful, you've said it . . . awful . . . hm . . . ah . . . hm . . ." Having elicited the desired reactions to his anecdote, he was not disposed, it seemed, to take further responsibility in the matter— already his eyes were wandering. Milly felt rather cross with him, leaving her saddled with some emotional baby.

"Hallo," said Abe Schulman at her elbow as Mr. Schwelling skipped off in pursuit of his prey, the gipsyish Natalie.

"Hallo."

"I saw you in the Imperial at Slavnik. Remember?"

"No, I—did you? I mean, I don't remember."

"You don't?" His eyes were black, shining with laughter, and she blushed furiously. "Hell, *I* put it in my diary. Do you care to crash around the Biedermeier, Mrs. Purdoe?"

"No, I—I don't think I will, thank you."

"We'll postpone it. What's Joe Schwelling been shooting his mouth off about to make you look at me like that?"

"Like what?"

"Like I wore a made-up tie or something."

"Oh, nothing."

"Nothing my foot. Whatever it was, don't you believe it. An old nanny-goat, that's what he is. Have some Scotch—here——" He held out his own glass. "Go on, it's not poison—at least it's British made."

She stood beside him, sipping, whilst he checked on her looks at his leisure. Aware that he would do so, some instinct had prompted her to turn her head so that her profile, her worst point, should strike him first. She could have given no reason for so doing; she was always careful to be photographed full face; full face, with a pussy-cat smile modelled on Vivien Leigh's, resulting, if the photographer knew his job, in a likeness which bore a startling resemblance to that famous beauty. In build and colouring, too, there was some resemblance, and Milly had always yearned to play Emma Hamilton or Scarlett, roles in which she was convinced she would acquit herself quite as well as Miss Leigh on-stage; off-stage she didn't do at all badly.

Abe thought: yes, it is not as good as I thought, not from this angle; the nose is small and sharp and turns up and there is the beginning of a line from nose to mouth, what must she be, all of thirty, I suppose, and the mouth is a little too thin for my liking and might become shrewish and the chin is too sharp and pointed, because at her age she should have the beginnings of a softness round the jaw, the line should be ever so faintly blurred, but it is not, it is too square, all her lines are too spare for comfort—except for her figure which is quite cute —and it will all harden into a face which could never lose me personally a wink of sleep unless—but at this moment she turned her head towards him, her wonderful great eyes smiling at him over the rim of the glass, and his thoughts whirled. She saw them whirl, just as she had reckoned on doing, whirl like specks of dust; giving them a chance to settle she waited, then looked again. Yes, that was better, that was how it was, usually; his thoughts had become resolved, she could see, into a single thought—thought, or purpose. Then she looked closer. All wasn't quite as it should be—wasn't there, this time, something rather unusual? Yes, it was true . . . there was something odd—on this occasion she couldn't be absolutely a hundred per cent certain what that single thought was—what *was* he thinking?

She was never to be quite certain of what Abe Schulman was thinking. Coming as he did from a country of beautiful women and long since conditioned to eyes as big as and even brighter than her own, the thought which had flashed into his mind was one she had never reckoned with. He thought: This baby's all clued-up. And from that moment this was the assumption upon which he based all his dealings with her. Mistakenly, because Abe, who was inclined to judge hastily in only this one respect, in judging women, was quite wrong about Milly.

Milly, who had none of that dazzling confidence which is the characteristic of American women, rather the humility which centuries of national statistics have bred in those of her race and sex, and who thankfully counted as blessings three love affairs and two proposals of marriage before meeting Larry, her fate; romantic and impulsive as well as hard-headed, was very far from being " all clued-up." She did have one or two clues, nevertheless, having worked during the war one afternoon a week in an American officers' club near Grosvenor Square, as a result of which it had become for her a matter both of principle and habit to deduct ten per cent off the charm, wit, assurance, and open enthusiasm regarding herself displayed by any American male. Now, after consideration, deciding that Abe Schulman displayed all these things including the last, she calmly made her customary deductions and in doing so, her mistake. Because as regards the last

—well, she couldn't have known it and there was no one by to tell her; for Schulman, deduct double.

" I hear you didn't know the password."

" Oh—you mean we didn't bring anything? Yes, I feel bad about that."

" Never mind—I dare say she'll forgive you. You'll have to play the import export game instead."

" You mean—parcels? " said Milly delicately.

" Uh-uh." He looked at her and laughed. " She's contacted you already, has she? No grass grows under those stout little boots. She tried that out on me too, but I wasn't having any—and good gracious, how smartly I was cut off her list—and for a *very* long time. We've made it up now, though, thanks to Haig an' Haig."

" I don't understand. Why didn't you? "

He seemed to be about to say something, but instead he took out a packet of cigarettes, opened it, transferred the cigarettes into a case, gave her one, took one himself, lit them and then said lamely: " I guess I just saw the red light. Our outfit's funny that way. You see, for one thing it's none of my business," he kicked the logs apart, and they watched the sparks fly, " and for another, if I shoot my mouth off to you, or to your husband, who's a good guy and I'm relieved to see him, I can tell you, it won't do any good. Neither of you'll believe what I say until you find it out for yourselves. Still—if you could just bear to hearken for just a minute to Uncle Abe—it might save you an awful lot of time and bother."

" Naturally," said Milly primly. " We're delighted to receive advice."

" Ah, phooey. No one is, ever. But listen all the same. Nothing's private in this place. Every move you make goes down in a little fat dossier—there's one for each of us, one for you, for me, for your husband—even the most trivial, nonsensical items—which, added up —don't look like that, Mrs. Purdoe, you know you have terrific eyes —added up, well, add up." He grinned. " But I don't want to alarm you."

" You don't alarm me," said Milly coolly, and to show she was cool took a swig from his glass. " We've heard all that before. Larry doesn't believe it. He says they're too incompetent." All this talk, she felt in a worldly way, was part of an enjoyably complicated flirtation.

" Incompetent? " He was weighing his words, she could see. Why, he was actually serious. " Sure they're incompetent, but not *in our way*, get it? They're competent and incompetent where you'd least expect. You can't rely—that's the trouble—you can't rely." It was

70

a trick of his, this denying of transitive verbs. He shook his great head, staring into the fire. " What was I saying? Who's Larry, anyway? Oh sure, Lawrence S. L. Purdoe, your husband. I looked it all up. Well, if the Slav mind's an open book to him after two weeks, he's wasted here. I've been here five years and it's still closed to me—but I know its cover awfully well."

" Five years! " She shuddered. " Doing what? "

" Watching my step," he said grimly.

" What could they do—to you? "

" Plenty. Give me twenty-four hours to leave, for one thing."

" Would that be so terrible? "

" Say, lady, I'm not a diplomat, you know. I'm just a lone, hard-working newspaper guy. The world's my oyster, but it's got to be the world, the whole world. If I got myself thrown out, I'd be on their black list for good. A third of Europe closed—and the dizziest third —and by now I've lasted quite a time, I'm a kinda specialist—closed to me? Ah, no . . . no, no. That just wouldn't combine. See what I mean? "

" Well, yes." Privately Milly made her own addition for sensationalism, deduction against veracity.

" Drink that up and I'll get you another."

" I don't want another."

" Say, you no drinker? You disappoint me, Mrs. Purdoe, just as I was thinking, at last the perfect woman. Whaddya say your husband's name was—Larry? Larry! " he bawled across the room. " Come over here! "

Larry stepped into the firelight. " Was that the secret sign? "

" Yep. That was it. Where's that stuffed shirt I brought along? Gosh, he looks happy as a king." Mr. Schwelling was sitting some distance off on a sofa next the princess, an album, tome or something, spread across their laps. " We can ditch him, I guess. They're in their element, combing through the Almanach de Gotha. C'marn, let's go."

*   *   *

They went into the Grand not by way of the main entrance, but through another door which led straight into the public restaurant, ballroom and bar; it was a part of the hotel which was strange to the Purdoes, the residential side being quite separate. Abe leading, they fought their way through to the bar; the tables in the restaurant were crowded, there was even a queue waiting for seats; the dance floor was packed, and the bar was full, too. The air was thick with smoke, and there was a smell of cheap scent, vodka fumes and the local brand of cigarettes. When they came up to the bar, however, people made way for them right and left, so that it was quite noticeable when they sat down on the stools at the bar, the gap all round, isolating the three of them. Even the buzz of conversation had died down.

Abe drew a bottle of Scotch from his pocket and put it on top of the bar.

" We can't drink that here, can we?"

" Oh, sure," he said easily, " we'd look funny without it. It's just one of the props . . . they expect it." Certainly the barman produced three clean glasses and soda without any fuss. Red and green spotlights were turned on in the ballroom. The tunes were unrecognisable, but mostly tangos. Whatever they were, it didn't seem to affect the style or the steps of the dancers, who jigged up and down, each couple clutched in a bear-like embrace; there was a good deal of barging and shrill laughter. Everyone seemed a little drunk. The faces of the women were plastered with make-up, uniform, swamping individuality; sticky raspberry lips, flaming cheeks, eye sockets which were dark hollows of shadow and mascara, and each head of hair identically crimped into unbecoming sausage curls; coarse white nylon blouses contributed to the effect of a uniform, also swinging ear-rings and thick platform shoes; nearly all the women had thick ankles, their figures were noticeably sloppy. Weight for weight, they were about equal with their partners; the latter, too, being short and stocky, their suits cut to one shape, with very square shoulders, in one of three colours. But the extraordinary thing was, to the eyes of the Westerner, that they all looked as if they were enjoying themselves, heartily even —which was more than you could say of the faces in the Berkeley Grill, thought Milly.

" You dance, madam?" A flushed young man in a peaked cap nudged her. She shook her head.

" English lady?" His eyes travelled to the bottle. " English whisky?"

" Yeah," said Abe. " Wanna shot?" He called for a fresh glass.

" Chin-chin," said the young man, knocking it back.

" Another?"

" Oh very fine, thanks." The young man suddenly glanced round him, which caused him to change his mind. " No," he said rather loudly, " I have vodka. You, too? All drink vodka?" He brought out a leather purse and spilled its contents on the bar. " Vodka— four!"

He insisted that Milly drink it in the Slavonian manner. They had three rounds, it seemed to her, in as many minutes. It was not a sociable way of drinking. After Larry's round, Abe ordered another.

72

The young man, by now scarlet in the face, was leaning heavily against the bar. He was really quite a nice young man and she felt rather sorry for him. Seizing his glass, he drained it and, for no apparent reason, hurled it on the floor. " Vodka," he smiled drunkenly, putting his arm round her shoulder. " Vodka . . ." Then he seemed to catch sight of somebody, an acquaintance, or an enemy, over her shoulder. His expression changed. Milly turned round. A small pale man at the end of the bar was watching them intently. " Vodka," the young man repeated, frowning. He seemed to be racking his brains for English words. " To—forget," he brought out with an effort, with a petulant movement of his hand sweeping all three glasses to the floor. " Vodka —forget . . . forget," he whispered, staring down at the wreckage. Then suddenly he leapt from his stool and disappeared through the door.

" Well, well," said Larry.

Abe leaned over. " Hi, Alby," he called to the pale man. " Have some Scotch? "

" Thank you." The man moved over and took the stool next to Milly. " Cheerio," he said. He drank slowly, and with every evidence of appreciation. " That young man, madam. I am afraid he annoyed you. He is just a student—a bit tipsy." He said to Larry, " You are from England, sir? "

" Yes," said Larry.

There was a silence. Seeing that Abe, who was just smiling to himself and pouring more whisky, wasn't going to help them out, Milly said in what Larry called her Camberley manner, " This is all *very* interesting—to us. Do they often have dances here? "

" Twice a week," the man replied.

" And the people—I mean—they're allowed to come—just whenever they like? "

" Of course." His eyebrows were raised in polite surprise.

" Just like in England? "

" I should say—just like."

" They all *look* quite happy," she said, puzzled. Larry wished he were near enough to give her a kick. Abe had winked at him.

" My dear lady, of course. They *are* quite happy."

" But—don't they—I mean, they must miss so much."

The stranger examined his nails with care, and then he asked gently:

" What, for instance? " His English was almost perfect.

It was difficult to say what. Surely it brooked of no argument— where Western standards did not obtain, they must be desired. That seemed to be self-evident. But on the other hand, for those who had

73

never had the privilege of knowing what those standards were—never, indeed, been permitted to know, nor permitted to have standards of any kind—then—but with her brain on fire with vodka, she was not going to go into all that—besides, it seemed vaguely disloyal.

" Well, what? " the man repeated, smiling faintly.

" Freedom," said Milly, frowning. " And things in the shops."

" La Liberté," Abe explained to no one in particular.

" But there is plenty in the shops," the man said calmly. " The shops are full. There is freedom, too. La Liberté," he added, after a pause. He finished his whisky, and turned to Abe. " Thank you for the drink. Good night, madam, sir." He bowed. " Good night, Mr. Schulman." He left the bar and they saw him cross the ballroom, weaving his way through the dancing couples, and take up a position at the far end, leaning against the wall, where he lit himself a cigarette.

" Mrs. Purdoe, you were terrific. What a gal."

" What have I done wrong? "

" On the contrary. You behaved wonderfully. Exactly as he expected you to behave."

" Now just who did you think he was, darling? " Larry said teasingly.

" I've no idea." Suddenly her hand flew to her throat. " Oh? Oh lord. You mean he was snooping? "

" Ah-ah, that's a harsh word, Mrs. P. Snooping?—Alby? Why, he's my closest friend! "

" You see, darling? " said Larry.

" Yes," she said. " Oh dear."

" So now you've met the works," said Abe. " Alby and the Rapovskis."

" And Sophie Bielska," said Larry.

" Darling, which one was that? Oh, yes—your great big governessy number in tweeds? Everything but the hockey stick, well "—she added, archly—" if not everything, something. You were talking to her long enough."

" Yes, she has something," said Larry, rather irritated.

Milly did the pussy-cat on them both in turn. " What did you say her name was? "

" She's a Miss Bielska."

" Hey, wait a minute," said Abe, " Countess, please. Not that she'd ever tell you. Also, just for the record "—he grinned at Milly—" she's my number one sweetiepie."

" I thought she was a poppet," said Larry. " What was she doing in that——"

" Rabble? You may well ask."

74

"I understood from the princess," said Milly sweetly, " that she was a sort of poor relation."

"Really? Uhuh. Well, she's certainly poor and I dare say she is a relation—almost all of them are related if you go back far enough —so I won't contradict. But she's also a very unusual person. She has a brother—I don't know if you saw him. He's a contemporary product if ever there was one—thinks the world owes him a living and because it doesn't pay up scrounges off his sister. Plenty like him. I don't care for him. His sister I happen to like very much. Nuts, of course." He laughed at the expression on Milly's face. She was regretting having encouraged the conversation along these lines; the governessy number was monopolising it.

"You'd find it hard to live up to her," Abe went on. "It's easy for me—but then, as she's rubbed in often enough, she only expects the worst from Americans. But *you*'d find it terribly hard."

"Hard to live up to her?" she asked crossly. "Why?" The boot, she felt, should surely be on the other foot.

"Well," he sighed, "it's this way. As I told you, she's screwy— like most of us. But with her, lunacy takes a peculiar form—you might call it, I'm afraid, acute Anglomania . . . yeah, I know . . ." he chuckled at sight of their faces, all at once frozen in the same wary disapproving expression, "Yeah . . . it is peculiar, I agree . . ."

"You mean—she *likes* us?" said Milly coldly.

"*Likes* you? No, my goodness, no. I mean she's *crazy* about you, the whole bunch of you, your climate, your Queen, your colonial policy, Shakespeare—Winston Churchill—the White Cliffs of Dover —your men's suitings, the elegance of your women, your spontaneous gaiety, friendliness to foreigners, even your cuisine—there's only one catch to it."

"What's that?" said Larry, grinning.

"She's never been to England in her life. Ah, well. No matter. Let her cherish her illusions. Howd'ya get on with Wragg?"

"*Wragg?*" they said, both together.

Abe looked from one to the other.

"You don't like him, huh?"

Larry said carefully, "I don't quite understand him. I think he's probably quite nice—but it's almost as though he had some grudge against me."

"You bet he has," Abe laughed. "The best grudge anyone can have. He wanted your job and he thinks you've gypped him out of it. Second time it's happened, too. First Simpson, then you. Wragg was here long before Simpson, you know."

"I didn't."

75

" No one tells you anything, eh? After Simpson—er—left, I guess Wragg thought it was all sewed up. Must've come as a bit of a shock——"

" Why didn't he get it? "

Abe looked deep into his glass. " Don't ask me. Sometimes they don't choose the old-timers—they know too much. And then Wragg might do worse than study those pamphlets on—what is it, how to win friends and influence people—he's not exactly the product of a charm school, is he? "

They laughed. Then Milly said boldly: " Why did Simpson leave?"

Accustomed to the company of men, she rarely bothered to prefix their names in conversation about them, the modified version of a trick she had picked up years ago in Rome from an elderly and highly successful English woman journalist, a lady who had presided over bachelor dinner-parties and also to some extent reigned over the cosmopolitan set, one of whose many mannerisms it had been to address all men, including her husband, by their surnames, *tout court*. It was a liberty willingly conceded her, partly because it didn't seem like a liberty, coming from her, more like an endearment, and if as sometimes happened she got the name right, more even like an accolade. As a gimmick it had struck Milly at once as being not only successful, but incredibly chic. Once away from the orbit of its originator she had purloined it for herself, but, like most copied " tricks," it had never quite come off; hence the modified version. She had overlooked the fact that a woman of sixty can get away with things which a woman of thirty cannot—although the converse was an axiom upon which she relied as naturally as she drew breath.

Schulman thought to himself, so she's a Little Pal, eh? Someone ought to put her over his knee and give her a good slapping. It was a type he detested. He had intended telling them quite a lot more, partly as a warning and partly because he felt sorry for Larry to whom he had taken an immediate liking. But he decided to be obstinate, and Larry never pressed him on the subject of the Simpsons again.

" He just left," Abbe answered smoothly.

" People are *very* mysterious about the Simpsons."

" Is that so? They were friends of mine." It was as if he had shut a door in her face.

" Tell you what," said Larry, " let's go upstairs. You take some whisky off us for a change."

In the salon Miss Raven was waiting up for them, sitting by the porcelain stove with her knitting. Her satin blouse was electric blue, a trying shade even to the most delicate of complexions; her face in contrast seemed abnormally red.

" Hallo, Miss Raven," said Larry kindly. " You shouldn't have stayed up." It occurred to him that she looked upset, and because he was habitually far more observant than Milly suspected, far more observant, that is, than she was herself, he noted that Miss Raven was quite breathless, although she was doing her best to conceal it, and that the hands holding the knitting were trembling; also, meticulous as he had thought her hitherto, the buttons of her blouse were done up wrong. He simply noted these details, indexed them as unimportant, but nevertheless filed them away in his mind. Then he went over to the table where the drinks were.

" Oh, *poor* Miss Raven," said Milly, exercising all her charm. " You really shouldn't have waited up. I *am* so sorry."

" I wasn't to know when you'd be in, was I ? " said Miss Raven in rather a martyred voice, dropping her knitting and clasping her troublesome hands on her knee. " I heard the dancing, you see."

" Yes, you should have been there. Such fun—well, no, rather awful, really. This is Mr. Schulman—the American journalist."

" *The* Mr. Schulman ? Abe Schulman ? "

" Well, anyway, Abe Schulman." He smiled at her.

" Oh, but I've read about you. In *Time* magazine, I think it was. Oh my goodness." Miss Raven squirmed with pleasure, and Milly thought, thank God for *Time* magazine.

" Something for you, Miss Raven ? A little nightcap, now ? "

" Ooooh—just a teeny one, Mr. Purdoe. Oooh, thanks." Her hands were still shaking, he saw.

" That's a very attractive colour you're wearing—most unusual."

Miss Raven bridled. " D'you like it, Mr. Purdoe ? A bit bright, perhaps—but once in a while . . . to cheer oneself up——"

She was interrupted by the violent slamming of a door in the bedroom, the bathroom door, it must have been. They heard a noise like a rushing wind, or even of a wild animal charging across the bedroom; there was a crash of a table overturned, and a sort of scrabbling at the double doors, when suddenly these were wrenched apart, screeching on their hinges, and a strange hooded monster—a man, although it was impossible to tell whether young or old—his overcoat was pulled right over his head—in a crouch position blundered across the room rather fast towards the far door and was out of it before they had come to their senses. Both Milly and Miss Raven screamed. The screams were not quite synchronised and afterwards Larry remembered that it was Milly who had screamed first.

" Friend of yours ? " Abe remarked.

Larry went to the door and peered out into the passage. " Not a sign." He shrugged. " Good God."

77

" Proles' night," said Abe calmly. " Anything can happen."

" But—how did he get in? You were in here all the time, weren't you, Miss Raven? " said Milly, ashamed that her first thought had been, not of the children, but of her mink coat.

" No," said Miss Raven. " Yes—that is——" and suddenly she dropped into a chair and burst into tears.

" Dear Miss Raven, don't be upset. He was just a drunk, I expect. I'll go and have a look at the children."

On her way through she called out: " Nothing's been touched," meaning the mink. Without thinking, she automatically unbolted the bathroom door into the children's room and went in. The bedside light was on, and she found Clarissa lying in bed staring at the ceiling. On seeing her mother she began to giggle.

Milly sat down on the edge of the bed. Now, all of a sudden, her knees were shaking under her and the sight of her giggling daughter did nothing to soothe her feelings.

" Well, what's the joke? " She spoke quite sharply.

" Oh, Mummy—a man." Clarissa leaned up on her elbow. " Such a *funny* man."

" Where? When? "

" Here." Clarissa pushed her hair away from her face. " Oh, hours ago, I think," she added vaguely.

" How did he get in? Which door did he come in by, darling? Try and think."

" Through there, of course." Clarissa pointed to the door leading into the passage. " He came in—then he went out." She dissolved into giggles once more. " He wanted—he wanted the toilet, he said."

" The lavatory," Milly corrected absently. " So he went through in there? " She pointed to the open bathroom door.

Clarissa sat bolt upright, looking rather shocked. " Oh, *no*, that's *your* bathroom. I told him to go the other way."

Milly summoned all her patience.

" Now, listen, Clarissa. He must have gone that way, darling, through Mummy's bathroom. Think what you're saying."

" But he *didn't* . . ." Clarissa stared at her mother, a wicked gleam in her eye. " You see, he couldn't've, could he? " She fell over on to her stomach, heaving with laughter. She considered that she had given her mother more than a fair chance . . . to say another word would be to spoil the game, and really, if grown-ups were so stupid . . . she mumbled under the bedclothes . . . " BECAUSE THE DOOR WAS LOCKED, YOU SILLY . . ."

Clarissa was engaged in playing her most fascinating, her latest game, which consisted of testing the wits of her maternal parent, or, if not too late, of sharpening them, by means of a series of traps, either by partially withholding intelligence which to her way of thinking should be self-evident, or now and then by deliberately embroidering, without actually falsifying the truth. Now, poking her face above the bedclothes, her eyes dancing at sight of her mother's bewilderment, she was prompted by pity to oblige with a last and wholly gratuitous clue. " Such a *funny* man," she whispered, and lying back on the pillows she began to pant. There was nothing equivocal in the performance of this exercise—Clarissa panted with all her might, great noisy rhythmic pants, in imitation of someone who has been running, or of a dog, or equally of what she had lately heard behind the bathroom door.

" Stop that," said Milly wearily. She got up, and with her hand on the light switch, gave her daughter a stern look. " Now just you go to sleep."

" I give up," she said as she came back into the salon. " I can't make head or tail of it. Children are quite hopeless."

Whereupon Miss Raven, to everybody's surprise, burst into peals of laughter.

Sleep did not come to Clarissa at once. She lay listening to the distant sounds of dance music, the rush of bath water next door, the scampering of feet up and down the passage; when Miss Raven tiptoed in to tuck the blanket round Dermot (who was already her favourite), Clarissa expertly feigned sleep and Miss Raven tiptoed out again. After that she lay awake for what seemed like hours, and to pass the time she recapitulated the moves of her game and the events which had led to its initial conception. She reviewed these with scrupulous justice to both parties, the dark encouraging in her a severity towards herself and a corresponding leniency towards her opponent which she would have scorned as weakness in the light of day. If it was a game, then she must not cheat. That is to say, she *could* cheat but only if notice of this irregularity were given, as in playing cards with her brother when one or the other would say: " Now this time we can cheat." She could not for obvious reasons indulge in this variation with her present opponent, her mother, because the essence of the game was secrecy. Therefore no cheating, for which she was rather thankful, for if it came to cheating there was small doubt who would win.

Before she slept Clarissa had recalled word for word the following events; events they were not, of course, by adult reckoning, but just as a yam falling from a tree may be an event to a man shipwrecked on a desert island, so is the destruction or confirmation of a conception, however trivial, in the eyes of a child.

The first: "We *are* living in the City of London, aren't we, Mummy?" Clarissa had thrown out casually one day.

Before replying Milly bit off a length of wool; she was darning socks, it being the end of their leave, and desperately counting the hours until the new nanny should arrive. Clarissa looked up anxiously.

"We *are* living——" she began but Milly cut her short.

"I heard you, darling—no, we're not. We're living in the City of Westminster."

"London isn't *two* cities," mumbled Clarissa, glancing out of the window, where the chimney-pots floated above the noon-day fog.

"Oh yes it is." Milly stuffed the socks into the basket with a sigh of relief. "The City of London and the City of Westminster."

"No, one, one, ONE!" she had cried, slamming her book on the table so that it fell on the floor.

"Darling, really. It's rather rude to contradict." Milly shrugged. "It's not very important, but it's two all the same. Now, how about a nice walk to blow the cobwebs away?"

But then, recently: "When we lived in London, Miss Raven," Clarissa began slyly, watching Miss Raven like a hawk.

"Yes?" said Miss Raven.

"We lived in Westminster."

"That's where I first met you."

"Yes, it is." Clarissa agreed, her voice soft. "London, wasn't it?"

"Of course." Miss Raven looked bewildered.

"The biggest city in the world?"

"Yes."

"One big city?"

"Of course."

An angelic smile spread over Clarissa's face.

Then, another time, that business about the sea.

"Are there *seven* seas, Mummy?"

"I don't know," said Milly, who had a headache. "I suppose so."

"Well, but then what's The Sea?"

"The Sea? There's no such thing as The Sea, really." Clarissa watched her anxiously. It was precisely on this point that she required support. "The sea's made up of the seven seas—or however many there are," she added hastily, this sort of thing being far from her strong point. "There's the Mediterranean, the Atlantic, the Pacific ... though those are Oceans ... I suppose they count ... then, let me see, the Adriatic—oh, darling, I expect there *are* seven. Ask your father."

"But it's all The Sea," insisted Clarissa, dropping her eyes to conceal her alarm.

80

" No, darling, don't you understand? " said her mother blithely, " they're all *different*, belonging to *different* countries."

" I don't believe it," wailed Clarissa and burst into tears.

She had bided her time, and then:

" What's the difference between an ocean and the sea, Miss Raven? "

" No difference, really," said Miss Raven, quite pat. " Only the name. They all join up."

" All *one* sea? "

" Yes, of course—except for the Dead Sea and the Caspian. Look at the map."

Clarissa, who was in bed, triumphantly dragged the atlas from beneath her pillow. " I've got it here," she said, smiling at Miss Raven. She's a funny one, thought Miss Raven.

" The Caspian," she muttered, poring over the map . . ." I've got it!—and the Dead . . . but they're not *seas*, Miss Raven. Just little lakes. You can't count *them*. This is The Sea! " She placed her hand flat on the satisfactory blue expanse and looked up, her eyes shining through her hair.

" I told you so," said Miss Raven placidly.

Out of kindness, Clarissa had decided not to reveal the results of her research to her mother, whose feelings might possibly have been wounded had she been confronted with the evidence of her fallibility. Besides, Clarissa was more than willing to make allowances for the odd lapse now and again. But from then on she treated with reservation the spars of wisdom which Milly occasionally threw overboard to drift her way; now, if the issue seemed important enough and if she had time, Clarissa usually checked up.

*   *   *

Some time during the night Miss Raven awoke with a start. She lay under the billowing feather coverlet, half-suffocated, her heart beating noisily in her chest. The door into the children's room was ajar and she could hear their quiet breathing; then, beneath her window, the noise which had awakened her started again, short sharp yelps, followed by a broken moaning which continued for several seconds, and she was still collecting courage to jump out of bed when it stopped. She glided to the window and pulling aside the heavy curtains—thick with dust, she noted—gazed out. There was nothing to be seen; the weaving tramlines glinting like snakes, the narrow street lay empty under the moon. On either side of the street the pavement was raised two or three feet, sheltered by stone archways which formed long galleries all the way down the street. These galleries were now tunnels of darkness. She strained her eyes to pierce the shadows, but in vain; she watched and waited, but nothing appeared. Suddenly the sound of a church-bell shattered the silence, striking the hour; then, one after another, from all the different churches round, the chimes rang out, echoed through the streets of the sleeping town, and died away; a second's silence—and then the bugler's call, sweet and clear, trembled in the air. There was no wind, and she heard it faint at first, then loud, then louder still, and then faint once more.

This scene, the town at night, the moonlit shadowy streets, and the bells, and now the thin queer notes of the bugle call, all seemed infinitely horrible to Miss Raven as though, like Rip Van Winkle, she had awoken to a century not her own. She would have no truck with any of it, and set about making her attitude quite clear. Tightening her dressing-gown cord about her thick waist, she tossed the feather quilt into a corner, unstrapped her own tartan rug and remade her bed in the austere style she preferred. Before getting into it, she hesitated; if she drew the curtains it would be stuffy and she would have a nightmare, very likely—but if she left them open she would be unable to sleep. She crossed over to the window and stood there in the pool of moonlight, looking out. Then she leaned right out, drinking in the air. It was a lovely night—crisp, with the smell of autumn. She watched a couple of cats emerge stealthily from the shadows of an archway, rub themselves up against a stone buttress, then off they streaked down the tramlines in the path of the moon. " So it was just a couple of cats," she murmured. She couldn't help feeling a bit disappointed. On a night like this a more romantic, or even a more sinister, explanation was due. " Still," she smiled tolerantly, " I suppose they have to have their bit of fun too."

The moonlight had already cast its spell upon Miss Raven and her mood, already softened, was beginning to suit the quality of the night. At any moment she would step off solid ground; once embarked, once she was happily afloat, nothing, nobody, must be allowed to spoil her trip. These excursions had become more frequent of late—although still made by choice—but certain routine preparations were involved. She fetched her tooth-glass and, unlocking her suitcase, crouched down behind the shelter of its lid, poured herself what she required, drank, poured more and then, rising swiftly, glass in hand, crossed over to the dressing-table. Seating herself in front of it, she switched on the lamp. Too bright, altogether too forthright: she swathed it with the nearest thing to hand, her peach-coloured lock-knit vest. Oblivious of everything but that which, already stirred by the currents of fancy, tugged impatiently at its moorings, she wasted no time on the reflection of the dowdy, middle-aged creature in the glass; instead, loosening the

82

belt of the dressing-gown, she shrugged her shoulders out of their covering, beneath which she wore a nylon nightgown which would have surprised Milly by its style and cut. Picking up her brush, Miss Raven hurriedly ruffled her coiffure, and then leaning her elbows on the dressing-table, she enfolded her rough cheeks between her hands. Closing her eyes, she stretched the skin at the corners outwards and upwards, tilting her head a little to one side, allowing her lips to curve into something that was not quite a smile, something quite special to the whole, until, all this being achieved, she could tell from experience and without the mirror that her face was playing its part. Yes, this was it. She could feel it now. Opening her eyes and deliberately disregarding such details as might impair whatever vision it was she had of herself, Miss Raven looked into the glass.

Presently she took another little nip from the suitcase and got into bed, where, cosy under the rugs, she lay musing happily until she fell asleep.

Chapter Six

ALREADY IT was October. That was how time passed. Between departure from the last place, arrival at the next, and for a week or two either side, miraculously it stood still—if you could always be doing that, coming and going, going and coming. But no sooner had you arrived than you began, because it had to be and you were experienced at it, to settle in. No sooner were you settled in and starting to find your feet, yet still making discoveries like where to buy the best sausage or the best spiced bread, still relishing the taste of the sausage and the bread and each day holding the promise of some novel experience before its close, then, before you knew where you were, the days would begin to assume a pattern to merge into each other, yesterday like to-day, to-day like to-morrow; and in front of your eyes, little by little, the excitement would be fading, the novelty becoming stale, until in no time at all you knew you would be passing through the intermediate stage, the seemingly endless one you cared for least, between coming and going. It would be like living in a dream; not uncomfortable, because only reality is that—your pulse-beat steady, you would be eating well, sleeping well; but certain times of day, the performing of certain actions, sherry at twelve, gin at six, brushing your teeth, pouring tea, seeming to come round with deadly regularity until you would feel something simply had to happen to jolt you out of it, the dream routine; even if it were to be no more than a gale, like the gale which had raged the night before and had swept not only a great many leaves off the trees but a leaf off the calendar, too, and now it was October.

At dawn the wind had dropped. At breakfast time the sky—as much as could be seen of it above the rooftops—was clear; it had been blown clear, drained of colour, until it was like a pigeon's egg, the palest grey-blue. In an hour or two, so gradually as to be scarcely perceptible, until quite suddenly, it seemed, the end of the street was invisible from the hotel, a mist had crept over the sky; a light vapour which at first had merely veiled the rooftops now hung in great billows there; streamers of mist floated down, twirled in between the buildings, caught on window-sills, fluttered under porticoes, sinking low, lower, until they settled in the street. At noon the sun was no more than a pale spot, like a primrose struggling into flower in a bank of mist, or fog, as it had become. On her way to the market, Milly had walked through the park. The leaves that had fallen during the night lay thick on the grass and the old man with the stick was standing in the middle of the lawn, leaning on his stick, gazing at the mess. She laughed to see him as he looked up at the trees, then down at the leaves. It was a Herculean task that faced him, and it was plain that he was not even going to begin to attempt it. There were still plenty more leaves to come down.

In the market some new stalls had been set up where peasant women were selling bunches of long white tapers. " Why? " she asked Gisela on her return. " What are they for? " " For All Saints' Eve," Gisela replied. " For the processions." " But that's not *yet*," she had objected. " Oh, but it's not far off," said Gisela indifferently.

Well, Gisela could afford to be indifferent, perhaps. To skip a whole month. A month here, a month there, what did it matter when you were twenty-three? But I'm thirty-three, thought Milly, pressed up against the window-pane, standing in the embrasure behind the curtains, staring out at the grey afternoon. It matters to me.

The street provided no spectacle. The trams went by, the people moved fast; most of them looked cold; the cobbles were all greasy with damp. The policeman whistled; a horse between the shafts of a cart slipped. She scratched with her fingernail on the pane, drawing a pattern in the film of dust encrusted on the glass. Her nail made a horrid squeak and she stopped. I'm bored, she thought. Bored, bored, bored. And time's passing. There was no one on whom to call, no one's call she might expect; no dressmaker, no hairdresser, with whom to while away the precious time. She had finished *Madame Bovary*. She was not going to read it again—not yet. She detested sewing. The children, as a form of distraction, had failed to come up to scratch. Dermot had a cold and Miss Raven was coddling him to her heart's content. Going into the day nursery a little while ago, Milly had found them there, Dermot and Miss Raven, on the floor in front of the stove playing draughts. She had at once offered to relieve Miss Raven but Dermot had said, kindly but firmly, " When I play with you, Mummy, I'm afraid I always win—and it's not nearly so much fun." So she had turned to Clarissa, who, taking advantage of Dermot's alleged indisposition, which meant no walk, was lying coiled up on the red plush sofa cracking hazel nuts between her teeth, in an ecstasy of enjoyment, the tears pouring down her face, having reached the chapter entitled " Dark Days " in Miss Alcott's famous story. Milly, who fancied herself at reading aloud, had said humbly: " Shall I read to you, Clarissa? " And Clarissa, for a brief second raising her eyes and favouring her immediate surroundings with her presence, had replied: " But I *am* reading, Mummy, and I really can't stop now."

85

So Milly had drifted back to her own quarters and for the last half-hour, possibly longer, there she had been standing, behind the curtains, ready to cry with boredom, staring down into the street.

Autumn. A grey afternoon. Between luncheon and tea—nearer tea. Time on one's hands and yet with each second that passed, less and less time; look at it that way and there was no time at all. At my back I always hear—that, certainly. And what was she doing about it? Just standing there, gazing out of a window. Like women all over the world, how often she had glimpsed them, behind lace curtains, leaning on balconies, crouched in the gloom screened by hideous plants—all over the world they were doing it now, and she one of them—gazing out of windows, wishing, waiting for something to happen. Whilst time passed.

Last year—but no, last year had been different. Last year was " before." Before what? Before three things had happened. They had happened in the summer, all at once in the way things do. First, her birthday. That had been bad enough. Thirty-three; the alliteration was like a couple of knells, a couple of hammer blows—as if one weren't enough, that's right, nail it fast. Then a day or two later she and Larry had gone to a party—nothing to do with her birthday; total strangers, actually, somewhere near Maidenhead. She had worn a new dress, white lace. She had been looking forward to the party, but what with the new dress, and her appearance after she had finished working on it, she became positively excited. " What a baby you are, Milly," Larry had said, driving there; but he was pleased, and she felt a baby, a heavenly, adorable, sweet-smelling bundle of lace and silk—and so on. But *then*, at the party; well, of course they were strangers, they knew nobody (she had told herself all this) and having lived abroad for so long, now and then in " bad stations," one had become perhaps a teeny bit spoilt; true, she *was* accustomed to making an entrance, and to a certain amount of attention afterwards. In fact, there had been no party for as long as she could remember when she had not been able to say to herself, half-way through and with honesty: " I am the prettiest girl in this room." But at *this* party—and it wasn't a very nice one, there was a lot of beer and some of the records were unfamiliar and people jigged about in rather a Palais de Danse way, she couldn't help feeling, and if *that* was the new dance they were all talking about she didn't want to learn it—things were different. For one thing, there were present two or three girls, one in particular, all rather *dim*, Milly thought, that is their faces seemed dim because they wore almost no make-up—whose behaviour she found extraordinarily irritating to watch. It was their manner towards the men, which was, well, not exactly *brazen*, but certainly challenging, your money or your life—highwaywomen, that's what they were; and the men, the silly dolts, couldn't even see through it, instead just lapped it up, crowded round to be robbed by these great dim creatures with their great—no, not dim, in all fairness, but anyway, great eyes. She had to admit that they seemed to have something, those girls (one, in particular), but she couldn't think what it was. I'm off form, she had thought; this dress —it doesn't suit me after all, and went away to a place where there was a mirror, and the only remedy for the evening and for her state of mind that had occurred to her had been to apply more lipstick and more mascara. When she had gone back into the room, Larry, she saw at once, was dancing with one of the girls—that particular one. She had danced herself once or twice, but had found the men all rather tiresome, not amusing even when drunk, either lugubrious or silly. In any event she didn't enjoy the evening one bit and on the way home she and Larry had had a row. Quite a bad row. But long after the row—during which all the familiar records were played, some sticking where they always stuck, although chipped, dented, still recognisable, here a new one, gingerly making its début, there a tried favourite one had thought smashed to smithereens turning up in a new version, all, of course, unforgettable, else why did they infallibly turn up, all eventually grinding through—no, long after, in the very act of comforting her, *not even in anger*, he had come out with it, the truly unforgivable remark: " Why shouldn't we," he had said, " step out of our age-group just once in a way? It does one good." For how many hours had she thought over that, not forgiving him for it? Then she had forgiven him because the posting had come through and there was suddenly a lot to do. A new passport for her, for one thing. The third thing, it turned out to be.

This time it'll *be* a passport, she was determined, her vanity having suffered—as whose has not?—some rude shocks in the past on this score. So she had a special photograph taken, no rush Oxford Street job, but a studio portrait in miniature, and very charming it turned out to be. Height: five feet four inches (giving herself an inch); colour of eyes, GREEN, she filled in boldly; distinguishing marks; mole under left ear; occupation? Well, they could *see* what sort of a person she was, couldn't they?—and she left that blank. So captivating was the description in combination with the photograph that had the official from the Passport Office called upon her to deliver the document in person, she would not have been at all surprised. But it arrived by post in the ordinary way, at the breakfast table. Glossy, slightly sticky, hairy, navy-blue; there it was. Without let or hindrance, her smile dazzled from the right-hand page; bags of personality, too, the scrawled signature was proof of that—five foot four, eyes green, a mole

—and then her heart stood still. Occupation: Housewife. Impossible —yet there it was, staring her in the face; in a cocky hand, block lettering, black ink: HOUSEWIFE. And she was doomed, was she, for the next five years to carry that smear round with her for all the world to see? Impossible.

" What on earth's the matter? " said Larry. She passed the thing over.

" But, darling, it's wonderful! This'll get us in and out of anywhere —iron or not, that curtain'll just fold up."

She couldn't speak. Her lips framed the word: " Housewife."

He took one look at her stricken face, then suddenly he burst out laughing. He roared with laughter. " But, my sweetheart—don't you understand? That's what you *are*! "

So it was on account of these three—well, *events*, she supposed you could call them—that she had begun to take stock; and the conclusions she had been forced to draw, remaining the same whichever way she reviewed the situation and in whatever mood, at whatever time of day, although the need for decisive action appeared perhaps slightly more urgent at three o'clock in the morning than at the corresponding time in the afternoon, were these: That she was thirty-three, that it was already autumn and would soon be winter, that time was passing, and nothing had happened yet.

*　　　*　　　*

She moved away from the window. The stove did make the room rather stuffy. As there was nothing else to do, she might as well have a nap. She made a nest of cushions and lay down on the sofa and was just dropping off when she heard a tapping, or scratching, on the door.

" Come in."

The princess Rapovska put her head round the door, her finger already to her lips. Seeing that Milly was alone, she came right in, closing the door behind her. Then, without a word, she trotted across the room towards the windows and dragged the curtains across. She raked the room with a glance, as if suspicious of some ambush having been prepared especially for her, and then, apparently satisfied, advanced towards the sofa.

" Ow! " she squeaked, clapping her little hands. " Pore madame Milly. I wake you up? What a shyme. 'Ow sorry I am." A totally unrepentant beam was spread over her face. Reluctantly Milly arose.

" Now what would you like, princess? Tea—or sherry, or something? "

" No, my dee-ur . . . no . . . nothing at all, but nothing. I come for one thing, yes, only one . . . you know wot? "

" No," said Milly, who had been wondering what. There was only one carpet bag to-day, it was true.

" To *give* you a little present! From my sister Irène and from me, with our kind regards . . . a little souvenir . . . to-dye we 'ave nyme-dye in our fam'lee, and I think—we all think—there is that pore Madame Milly, British, and the British 'ave not nyme-dyes, so . . . we myke one for 'er . . ." It sounded a flimsy enough excuse for present-giving, but the situation, obscured by giggles and coy looks on the part of the donor, had already resolved itself into a tiny package lying on Milly's lap. Bewildered, she opened it.

" Oh, but you shouldn't! . . . You really shouldn't, princess . . ." All the same, she couldn't resist examining, caressing the little box in her hand; a snuff-box, of tortoiseshell inlaid with silver.

" You like it? It's very owld . . ." said the princess solemnly. " It comes from my sister Irène's 'usban's fam'lee—'e's gone already, of course—not Rapovski . . . but a good noble family, quand même."

" But, dear princess, I can't really accept things like this . . . it's lovely, but . . . I—well, I scarcely know Princess Irène . . ."

" She's countess only," the princess corrected quickly. " But you like it? S'nice, eh? Tha's what I say to Irène—it's from both of us," she sank into her favourite chair, " to show 'ow we like you," she added ingenuously.

" Well, thank you. Thank you very much. I don't know what to say." Milly didn't know what to do, either, so she went over to the drinks table and poured two glasses of sherry.

Princess Rapovska, who was fumbling in her bag, accepted the glass absentmindedly and put it down on the table beside her. Fishing out a notebook from her bag, and a spectacle case, she placed a pair of spectacles on her nose and giving Milly a sharp look, like a hurdler who, the first lap completed, without slackening pace assesses his progress and that of his rival together with the obstacles ahead, she picked up the glass of sherry, drained it, and said briskly: " You enjoy our party? "

" Yes, indeed—it was——"

" Good, that's good." Clearly she was in a business-like mood with no time to dally. Her smile vanished; wriggling her plump little posterior into the chair, she heaved a great sigh and said: " I 'ave such bad news."

" Good heavens, what? "

She gazed at Milly sorrowfully over the rims of the spectacles. " You know my nephew, Paul? You don' remember? Tiens!—but

89

you saw 'im at the dancing. The doctor, 'e see 'im yesterday, and I fear . . . enfin, soon . . . very, very soon, I fear . . ." her voice dropped, " *e'll go, yer know*! "

" Oh dear," murmured Milly, at a loss to understand how the departure of yet another male Rapovski could be in any way her concern. They were always going—or on the point of going; there seemed to be no stopping them.

" *Unless*," the princess went on severely, as if reading her mind, " *unless* . . ." Grabbing her notebook, she began scuffling through it . . . " unless," she repeated, gaining time, " essential . . . wait, I 'ave it written down . . . essential, a medicine, a certain medicine . . . ah, 'ere!" She smiled triumphantly, then hastily readjusted her expression: " And the name, address in London, of the pharmacy, s'all written down very clear . . . 'ere! " She tore out the sheet and handed it over. " Now, you'll be so kind and order, yer know, from London, eh? That's good, eh? "

" Well, no . . . I mean, oh dear . . . I don't know what to say . . . I'm *terribly* sorry, princess, but I don't see how——" Larry? Goodness, she thought, he'd be wild.

" But it's very *easy*," said the princess loudly and firmly. " S'no trouble . . . not at all, s'all written down *'ere*. And the pore boy's at the door, yer know," she added quickly.

" At the——? Oh, I see, yes, but . . . surely it may cost quite a lot? "

" Oh, any amount! " The princess, like an irate penguin, waved her flippers. " Doesn't matter. Doesn't matter at all—when life's in danger, yer know." A little chuckle escaped her as if she were aware that there was no answer to this argument. " So you'll order queek, eh? I tell you, I think it's better ask for a big supply, as it's so awfool, 'is case . . . reelly desperate . . . yes, a big, big supply . . ." she repeated decisively. " And *immediately*, that's without saying." Suddenly there was a knock at the door and she leapt to her feet, clutching the notebook to her breast. " Oo's that? Don' answer . . . No! Ssssssh! . . . " But Abe Schulman came in.

" Hi," he said. " I just wondered if maybe there was a cup of tea going. Oh—hallo, Antoinette." He looked at the pair of them rather speculatively.

" Good evening Mr. Schulman," the princess replied, collecting herself and dignity too. " So, chère madame, we see you soon, eh? A pleasure, yes . . . very soon . . . and to yer 'usban' . . ." At the door she turned to survey them, Abe Schulman and Milly, her eyes snapping, greedily absorbing the setting for what she would be imagining, the sofa drawn up to the stove, the stove crackling through the grating, the brocade curtains shutting out the deepening twilight. " Bye-bye! " She smiled archly, waved, and then they heard her footsteps tittuping away down the corridor.

Abe had stretched himself full length on the sofa. He shifted his position, rootling beneath him with his hand for some object which was causing him discomfort. He pulled out the little snuff-box, raised his eyebrows when he saw what it was, then held it up to the light, examining it from all angles, opened and shut it, and without a word placed it on the table. He lay back, yawning.

Milly was leaning against the stove. The tiles through two layers of wool were just bearable to the touch.

" D'you really want tea? " Even to herself her voice sounded too casual.

" Nope. Changed my mind. Just give me a whisky and soda, my dear."

He waited until she stood with her back to him, pouring the drink, then he said in his lazy voice: " Now what was she after, I wonder— old Fairy Wishfulfilment? Pardon my curiosity, Milly. It's so easily aroused. Now what could it be? No—don't tell me, let me guess. Toothpaste, could it be? Or cocoa, or——" his hand moved to stroke the snuff-box but his eyes lingered on Milly's back view. She was taking a long time over pouring out that drink. " No," he went on, " no, I'd guess something a little more classy—a little more basic—essential, as dear old Antoinette would say." He saw her start and he smiled. " Yeah, something that represents life and death, say—yeah, that's it, I'd guess—penicillin, sulphanilamide, insulin "—the syllables, rather musical, floated in the air; a jet of soda had spurted over the edge of the glass on to the tray.

" As a matter of fact," she said calmly, bringing him his drink, " you're quite wrong. Princess Rapovska just came to call."

" My dear girl, then forgive me—thank you, thank you, fine—but you see, in my experience of Antoinette, long and fairly intimate as it's been, I may say, she *never* comes just to call." He added, idly. " Brought you this, did she? " He indicated the little box.

Without stopping to think, Milly snapped back at him:

" She did not. I—I bought it. Myself."

" Oh? Very pretty. You've got good taste." He lay down once more, balancing the glass on his chest. He appeared to have lost all interest in the discussion. She had flushed, and aware of it, fell on her knees in front of the stove and rattled the cinders with the poker.

" You're bored, aren't you? " he said unexpectedly, leaning up on his elbow to look at her. There was a sort of rough kindness in his voice which disarmed her completely.

91

" Yes, I am," she muttered. Then she turned round, sitting back on her heels. " *Horribly* bored."

" Oh dear me, that's the way it goes." He sighed, as if he sincerely commiserated with her lot. " What a heap of bother would be saved if—well, if they made this Operation Stag and we had none of you girls around."

" That's what you'd like! " she said resentfully.

" Oh, sure, I'm a man's man—didn't you know that? " He had never said a truer word but he said it with a smile which encouraged her to disbelieve him, which was in any case what she was inclined to do. He went on reflectively, casually almost, but she was not deceived: " I'd have thought a smart girl, like you—could've filled up her day all right. I mean, Milly, if you're short of literature, I've got plenty—or there's the language. Ever thought of tackling that? "

" The language? "

" Yeah—the language. Third most difficult in the world, so they say. There's a challenge for you. Strictly intellectual of course." He shook his head. " Never knew a woman yet who'd respond to that."

" Well, that's where you're wrong. *I* might, so there." She picked at some braiding round a cushion. " Yes, I might at that. *So* difficult, is it? "

" It has moods . . ."

" So have I," she interrupted flirtatiously.

" That's what makes it so difficult. And you'd have to have a teacher. Quite a problem."

She looked up in astonishment.

" But I should have thought there'd be masses of people only too keen . . ." A tried favourite, this, one of the assumptions that had always stood her in good stead when " fixing " her requirements— little men to do one's hair, to hand round at parties, little women round the corner, to run up this or that, run around with messages, walk dogs or children out, faithful little people, keen, all keen as mustard—she was disconcerted because Abe burst out laughing.

" You're terrific, Milly, you know that? " She did know it, but she kept quiet. " Who d'you think'd risk coming here just so you could get a smattering of Slavonian? Would anyone stick his neck out that far? I mean, would they? "

She was silent. " I see," she said at last. She scrambled up and took his glass.

" No, I won't, thanks. I gotta go." He got up too, and stood scratching his head. " Funny thing is, I've just thought of someone

92

who would . . ." He looked down at her doubtfully. " Stick her neck out, I mean. Honest now, you really want to learn? "

" Of course I do." After all, as he had said, it was a challenge—although, had she examined her motives more closely, she would have been bound to admit that the challenge lay in perfecting the arrangements rather than the language.

" Okay." He gave her an odd look, a searching one, taking her in from top to toe, and also her surroundings—the great gloomy room, even the snuffbox on the table. " I'll see if I can fix it." Then rather abruptly, he turned on his heel and went out.

She plumped up the cushions on which he had been lying, humming under her breath. " Of course," she said to herself, " it's just a *gambit*. Otherwise why should he bother? Yes, that's what it is—a gambit." Smiling, she peered into the glass, then she frowned; breathing on it, she rubbed it with her sleeve. There wasn't a mirror in Slavonia that didn't have this mildew—and they distorted too, quite dreadfully; now, for instance, her reflection was quite distorted. Old glass, she supposed vaguely, and left it at that.

The little box was such a pretty thing. She stroked it, holding it up to the light. The shell glowed like amber. She placed it on the mantelpiece. She was a woman, she murmured, looking at it, who loved to surround herself with beautiful things. Well, so she did . . . only she had never seriously considered this facet of her personality before. There wouldn't have been much point, would there? Still, it was by no means too late to begin—collecting. Little objects which took her fancy. Other women littered their houses with such things. Of course they did. One little snuff-box—oh dear, she whispered, now I should like *six*. She felt the virus of a new craze working in her blood. She had always been subject to these bouts of acquisitive passion; to be cured as soon as they were gratified, and if not gratified eventually they died away. Larry made a joke of it. " I want, I want," he would tease her. " You don't really *want* it, darling—what on earth would you do with it once you had it? " But that wasn't the point. In his masculine way, he often missed the point. The *wanting* and the *getting* of it was the thing. " Anyway," she picked up the box, " this is mine now." Still, better not let him see it, not yet. It would have to make its début rather shyly, gradually, like so many articles she was forced to buy on the sly. Not that he was mean, but well—one had to have so many new things so often; it was different for a man. Their things, suits and so on, actually *improved* with age.

Her eye fell on the slip of paper which Antoinette had left on the table. If the boy was *dying*—of course, that made it a different matter. Medicine—the very word had a kind of moral ring to it. If she ordered

93

the stuff, she would be saving a life, really. That was what it amounted to. Besides, the children were always needing things from the chemist and Larry never inquired into the details; so that was settled. She had fought down her scruples. Scruples? What nonsense. What scruples could she possibly have? She rather admired herself for taking the decision so boldly, as she folded up the paper and tucked it into her bag, next the snuff-box; then frowned, seeing them nestling together like that, as if there were some connection between them, which most definitely there was not. Still, lest any clandestine association arise from their proximity in that dark private place, her handbag, she took out the box and went into the bedroom where she found it separate accommodation in a drawer.

The same evening, as they were getting ready for bed, Milly was in her bath, prattling as her custom was through the open door.

"Abe says it's terribly hard—but he's going to find me a teacher. I'm longing to start. It's a good thing, isn't it? Then I can go round by myself more, and talk to people and all that." She got out of the bath, wrapped herself in the towel. "What do you think, darling? Is it a good thing, or isn't it?" she demanded, coming to the doorway. "I'm sure if——" She stopped short. Oh blast, she thought, damn and blast.

His back was turned to her and he was searching in the drawer of her night table. *Hers*—why, he had never gone to that drawer in all the time they had been there. Oh, God, I know what he wants, she thought, fool that I am, he wants that lighter stuff. Of course. He would. He just would. It had happened like this so often in the past, there was no reason to feel surprise; he had this extraordinary knack of stumbling upon whatever it was she might, just for the moment, wish to conceal from him; a knack with which she had never learned to reckon—because she was so trusting, she told herself, like a fool she trusted in his nature.

The truth was that it was Larry, not she, who was trusting by nature; without guile himself, he never suspected it in others unless and until he were confronted by proof. He did possess, however, this odd faculty that was almost a sixth sense, an equaliser as it were, which redressed any deficiency in worldly acumen, like a protective fairy leading him to the very spot where the evidence of his eyes would inevitably jog his brain to a conclusion, however reluctantly formed, upon which he would be forced to act; or at the least, take note. Milly had not only watched this phenomenon in motion time and time again in connection with herself, but she had heard tell of it from other sources, too. "At first you think he's easy," a Chief Clerk had confided in her, years ago. "And he *is* easy. But he's God knows hard to fool."

That had been intended as a compliment, of course—the Chief Clerk having been a Greek. She remembered this now, standing behind him, waiting, her heart in her mouth.

" I can't find the lighter fluid," he said at last. " I thought you'd put it here."

" Yes, I did." Her voice sounded unnaturally high and bright. " Perhaps Gisela moved it—it may be in the kitchen."

" This is pretty." He had the box in his hand, and was examining it under the light. " Real tortoiseshell. Where did you get it? "

" Get it? Oh, I just—just picked it up. That sort of thing's quite common round here—I mean, tortoiseshell—there's a lot of it about."

Larry looked about him, rather vaguely, as if he half-expected to locate the odd tortoise.

" I see," he said slowly. " Well, I've got some work to do. I'll be along later." He flicked a lock of hair off her forehead. " 'Night."

Chapter Seven

SOPHIE BIELSKA knelt on the floor and placed her right foot in its stout country shoe flat on a piece of cardboard. Scowling, she licked her pencil and drew round the outline. Tense with effort—she was by nature inaccurate—she whistled under her breath.

" Crikey! " She sat back, contemplating the result. " My fairy foot. More of a hoof, eh, Singe? " She passed the cardboard to her aunt, who was sitting on her bed carving up bits of felt with tailor's scissors; she was making dolls. " Darling, could you?—it won't take long. You see—just cut round a centimetre inside the line—that way they should fit. Last time they were a bit sloppy."

Obediently the old lady dropped the felt and began on the cardboard.

" And three layers, Singe, if you don't mind. I got two sheets."

Presently Sophie's aunt said in a whisper—both women spoke in whispers and in English: " You'll have to do the left one too, darling. It'll be different."

" Oh, will it? Drat. I never thought of that. At this rate I'm going to be late. Hurry, Singe, do. You are a slow coach."

" More haste less speed. These *won't* be sloppy." Her giggle was like the chirrup of a cricket. She was very old, Sophie's aunt, so old that it was impossible to guess her age. She had a wrinkled yellowish skin and her hair had receded from her forehead, leaving it smooth and shiny as a billiard ball. Her lower jaw protruded in a curious way; her obstinate little chin was egg-shaped. Sometimes, when deep in thought, she scratched it. Every feature of her face, whether singly or teamed up, was capable of conveying a variety of emotions, reactions, with a mobility that hinted at cynicism, even—to the sensitive— mockery; an impression reinforced by the heavy eyelids and the bright beady brown eyes beneath. Even the most unimaginative person would have perceived that her nickname was singularly apt. She had been known as Singe to family and friends as long as she or they could remember.

" Here's one, try it. It's all right? But what are you worrying about, Sophie? She won't inspect the soles of your feet, I should hope."

" But that's not the *point*, Singe. With these new soles I shall *feel* different. It's funny—shabby clothes don't matter—but *shoes*—ah, that's something else. Holes in your shoes—that really does something to you, *here*." She tapped her bosom. " Your courage melts away through the holes in your shoes. Now—yes, you are doing it beautifully, darling, but do please hurry up—now I shall be able to look her in the face."

" I wonder what she'll pay you," mused her aunt.

" Pay? " Sophie jumped to her feet. " I've no idea. What does it matter? You know I'd do it for nothing."

Singe smiled a little sadly at her niece. Poor Sophie—poor child. How old was she?—she must be nearly forty now. It was impossible to regard her as anything but the tomboy she had always been—a lovable, foolishly loving child.

" I know, Sophie." She sighed. " That's just it. You would do it for nothing."

Offended, Sophie hastily assumed her career-woman face. This expression, achieved by tightening the mouth, knitting the brows and narrowing the eyes, awe-inspiring as it was, would have been even more impressive had she ever succeeded in sustaining it for longer than a second and managed to conjure up a really scheming thought or two to match. Now, whilst her rather soft features were still fairly well knotted up, she made a stab at a commercial approach, saying loftily: " There is much devaluation, Singe—one must reckon with that. I read the papers, I know. Still," she walked about the room, her hands in her pockets, " it's true about money. To-day, for instance. We haven't any."

" Mischka comes this evening."

" So he does. Perhaps he'll have some. How many did he take last week? "

Their kinsman, Prince Michael Sopovski, paid weekly visits to several of his female relations in order to collect such merchandise as they manufactured in their homes—in Singe's case, dolls—which, in the course of the following week, he purveyed in the outlying villages. He covered a wide area on his bicycle and did a fairly good trade. The well-to-do peasants of the kulak class had money to burn, there being precious little to spend it on. The Prince was no longer young, in fact he was almost of an age with Singe, and the bicycling cost him a lot in effort; but only he knew how much more it cost him—and he regarded it as a weakness to be overcome—to approach and sell his wares in those villages whose names bore more than a chance resemblance to his own.

" Only six," said Singe, " last week. There was that tedious business of my hands, remember. But this week there will be eight."

It was hard on the hands, chopping the felt, stabbing it through with the thick needle, stuffing the shapes with sawdust—but no harder than roaming up hill and down dale in wind and rain with a heavy suitcase tied to the back of your bicycle; sleeping in haystacks and selling from door to door, always having to wear a smile, even when, as often happened, the kulak's wife shouted at you and turned you away, and sometimes those snappy farm dogs, she knew, although Mischka never spoke of these things. What changes they had seen, Mischka and she. Life was full of surprises. No end to the surprises and no end, it seemed, to life itself. How it went on and on. During the past year, since they had left the house in the country which she and Sophie had loved so much, a certain thought had often come to her—a wicked thought, and troublesome as it was wicked. She had confessed it to Father Joseph, who still came to see her regularly— a risk for him, poor man, but what a comfort—and he had rebuked her; in fact she had never seen him so stern. And afterwards she had said to herself, now that is destroyed for good, that thought, it will never come again. But it seemed one had less control over one's thoughts now that one was old—like a rat in a cupboard, you may kill it but you haven't destroyed the nest. There is a nest under the floor-boards you can't get at—so the next day another rat turns up in the cupboard, as sleek and black and evil as the first, indistinguishable, it might be the same one—so it is hopeless and you might as well face it that there will always be this thing in the cupboard, lurking. Oh, but she had such a *horror* of violence. Still, nowadays there was no choice, the violent way was the only way—you heard of it happening every day, to people you had known, quite close friends. What courage! Because although there were easy ways—and several that were not at all unpleasant, she knew that—it would mean going to the black market, and so many complications, even if one had the money, which one hadn't, that she herself wouldn't know where to begin. She thought, watching her niece at the window, digging a file into her nails, so long as I am still a comfort to Sophie, and after all I eat no more than a sparrow, and so long as I can get myself to that place in the passage and back and my hands are not too stiff to hold the scissors and not actually bleeding so as to mess up the felt which costs so much, it is really less trouble all round, just for the present, to continue living.

"Damn!" muttered Sophie. "What will she think I am—with the nails of a ploughboy. Ah, you should see hers—polished, like—like pink shells," she added unoriginally. "And her hair—how it shines! Like—well, like silk."

"Dark—or blonde?" Singe prompted timidly. She knew the answer but by now she also knew her cues.

"Dark. No, châtaine. And her face—so pale, you know, like a flower. And so dainty—that's what fascinated me above all . . . thin,

98

thin stockings . . . high heels, she's not very tall—although a perfect figure, of course."

"Of course," said Singe.

"You see, it came to me then, looking at her, Singe—and I must say I just fell in love with her at first sight—that we have *forgotten* so much—about the nice things. For instance, I had forgotten the smell of scent—and yet Mama always used scent, remember?—so I kept trying to get close to her to smell it. It made me dizzy—it was like a heavenly cloud. Then suddenly I got in an awful fright. You know how stupid I am. I thought—supposing Antoinette introduces me, I shall even have forgotten how to behave!"

"And did she?"

"What? Introduce me? Oh no, she never did, after all." She added vaguely, "I am so awfully busy, you see, what with the washing up . . ."

Singe, Maria-Theresa Luitpoldina Elzbieta Bielska, who had been born to the rank of countess, permitted herself for a fraction of a second to dwell upon the memory of a certain ball in Slavnik fifty years ago, before the débutante daughter of a self-made industrialist had become Princess Rapovska, indeed before the young lady had been considered anybody at all, and she chuckled to herself. In all the world there was only Mischka left, now, to share this joke.

"And her voice . . ." Sophie went on dreamily. "I could have cried with pleasure . . . a proper English voice. I kept edging up to her at the fireplace just to catch the sound of it. Of course, *he* has a nice voice, too."

"Who, Schulman?" her aunt inquired, teasing her.

"Schulman? Oh, Singe, don't be a donkey. Mr. Schulman has an *American* voice. No, Mr.—Mr. Purdoe." She brought out the name with a strange reluctance, as if it were already engraved on her heart. "*He* speaks clear and slow, so that you should understand. *She* speaks in the proper English way as if she didn't care two hoots whether we foreigners understood her or not."

"That's nice," said Singe, a shade tartly. "But surely it would inconvenience her if we did not?"

"No, darling," Sophie explained, "that's the real delightful English way, don't you see? After all, it's for *us* to understand *them*. Now I'm going to be late. I must wash my face! I must do my hair!"

She stamped up and down, working her feet into the new soles, and paused for a second in front of a square of glass on the wall. On a ledge beneath, laid out neatly, were a silver-backed brush with yellow bristles, a broken comb, a tube of Nivea cream, an ivory pen-tray used for hairpins and a tobacco tin filled with whitish face powder, also a piece of striped fur, a cat's paw, it looked like, with which to apply it. Absently, Sophie dabbed some on her nose, with an automatic grimace at her reflection.

It was a large room, with rather a low ceiling. The clean scrubbed floorboards were uncarpeted, here and there scarred with curious charred depressions, deep enough to make going difficult; Sophie, as she paced up and down, avoided them as one avoids holes in a familiar carpet. There was a sofa covered with a horse-blanket, a chest of drawers in one corner, the usual porcelain stove in another, and two beds, one on each side of the room. The bed on which Singe was sitting was enclosed by strange-looking canvas hangings; frayed at the edges, dirty-grey in colour, and even quite dirty, they formed a cubicle round the bed, by day one side being drawn back. Beside her bed was a large brass-bound leather trunk, beside Sophie's bed a wooden crate with the words TATE & LYLE stencilled on it; the sanctity of each was inviolable, containing, as each did, its owner's private possessions.

On the top of the chest of drawers there was a photograph in a silver frame of ladies and gentlemen in hunting costume gathered round a table set in the snow in a clearing in the forest. The snow had settled on the ladies' fur collars and seemed even to be falling on the feast spread before them; the ladies were laughing prettily beneath their fur hats, and the gentlemen, although their faces were somewhat obscured by luxuriant moustaches, seemed also to be in convivial mood; everyone held a glass outstretched. Huntsmen and servants stood in a group behind the host at the head of the table; in the foreground the carcases of three large boars lay propped up in the snow. Next to this photograph were some books; Hans Andersen, a Bible, a tattered paper edition of *The Tempest*, a bound copy of *Little Folks* and two novels by Angela Brazil. Flanking photograph and books, in positions of equal prominence, there was a plaster statue of Madonna and Child, and a tall square bottle, empty these ten years, which bore the label " The Lotion—Honey and Flowers " and beneath, the name of a famous barber in Jermyn Street, London, W. Above the chest of drawers was a shelf on which were piles of china, assorted pieces, the remains of a dozen different services united by a single feature, the crest stamped on each.

A kitchen table and three chairs completed the furniture of the room.

" Now I *am* in a hurry," muttered Sophie, lifting a drawer bodily out of the chest and throwing the contents on the floor. " A handkerchief, Singe, for pity's sake—oh, thanks—yes, and now I *must* wash . . ."

She picked up soap and towel, but becoming distracted, as she so easily did, started bundling the things back into the drawer.

"Sophie!" Singe sat up, her head cocked, listening. "Sophie!" she hissed. "Don't you hear? Hurry, before it's too late!"

Sophie turned her head, staring at the door. Both women listened, holding their breath as the heavy footsteps creaked along the passage, past their door, and through the kitchen. They heard a door shut, the grind of the key in the lock.

"Oh my God," said Sophie. Listlessly she threw the towel on the bed. "It's too late."

*   *   *

On the death of her father the previous winter, Sophie Bielska, together with her aunt and brother, removed from their country house, which was situated some distance away in the foothills of the Tartar mountains, to their town house in Grusnov—a statement which, whilst recording the event truthfully enough, unless modified and briefly explained might fall so far short of the truth as to be gravely misleading.

They had always considered the country house as "home" because they were country folk. Not smart, like the Rapovskis, who always wintered in Slavnik or abroad, the Bielskis were the sort of gentry whose interests and pleasures had to do with the land—a record harvest, their peasants' welfare, experiments with agricultural innovations, the breeding of bloodstock, hunting and shooting—and what else? Not much else. They used the town house very rarely, sometimes in winter, when there were balls, sometimes in summer for a change, never in the autumn or spring when the country was the only place to be.

Since the first year of the war they had been living in one wing of the huge country house, the wing formerly occupied by the servants. Sophie's father had passed away in the butler's pantry—a place in which he would never, in the ordinary course of events, have expected to draw breath in the whole of his life, let alone one so momentous as his last. The removal of the family to the town residence was not precisely voluntary; the death of old Count Bielski having reminded the preoccupied authorities not of his existence, of course, because by then he had managed to elude even their far-reaching grasp, but of that of his earthly possessions, by no means inconsiderable, which through some curious slip in the machinery of bureaucracy had hitherto been overlooked. In accordance with laws recently passed, the State, it seemed, was now the rightful heir to all such, and claimed them forthwith. Forthwith meant exactly that—or rather two hours' grace, during which time Sophie and her relations collected what they most

101

treasured, also some essential belongings, piled these and themselves into a borrowed peasant cart and drove off to Grusnov. They drove all night, arriving in the early hours of the morning.

The town house was pleasantly situated on the corner of a street overlooking the river and the public park. They soon discovered that in the years since they had seen it last changes had taken place. Sophie had, of course, brought her keys with her, but these, to her surprise, seemed to be unnecessary—the studded oak doors between the stone lions were already open, and even at that early hour all sorts of people were coming and going, in and out. Greatly puzzled, she left her brother and aunt to wait in the cart and went up the steps and inside. It was a four-story house and each story contained eight or ten rooms. Each of these rooms, she discovered, as she drifted along the corridors and up flights of stairs, apparently now housed an entire family. She paused outside the room that had been her own bedroom, on the third floor. As she was standing there a man came out and brushed past her, yelling something over his shoulders. She caught a glimpse of the room, washing strung up in rows, unmade camp beds and a woman with a red face. Then she said to herself in English, Sophie, pull yourself together, maybe there's still just a chance—and she went to the end of the passage where, round a corner and not very noticeable, there was a door that led to the attics, and to her relief it was still locked. She unlocked it and went up.

In the past the attics had been the maids' quarters, and they formed a self-contained flat. There were four rooms, two on one side overlooking the park and two on the other, separated by a passage and a kitchen with a small bathroom attached. There was a terrible stench, she noticed, directly she opened the door; the place was a pigsty—she heard later that Russian soldiers had bivouacked there during one winter—but it was unoccupied, which was the main thing, and so then she slipped downstairs and moved her family in.

Ten days went by before the new porter and his wife, who lived on the ground floor as befitted the most influential family in the block, discovered the unlocked door leading to the attics and reported the presence of the three reactionary undesirables to the police. In these ten days Sophie had cleaned up the two smaller rooms facing the park, also the kitchen and the bathroom, so that this part of the attic was now more or less habitable. She had scrubbed the floorboards which were pitted with the charred remains of fires, and caked with mud, spittle and food droppings; washed the walls of the infantile obscenities scrawled on them, although the cascading patterns of urine were impossible to remove; emptied the bath which had been half-full of sodden human excreta, and removed the heap of dried pellets of the same substance from the top of the porcelain stove. She had made a bonfire of family portraits which had been slashed and treated to the same acid spray as the walls; boarded up the broken window panes; and re-covered the sofa, which had been disembowelled by a bayonet or similar instrument, with a horse-blanket. When she had finished she arranged the few sticks of furniture and crockery they had brought with them and had scarcely heaved a sigh of relief when the police arrived.

By some miracle, perhaps because the police officers were Grus-novians, perhaps because desperation and weariness lent Sophie's soft voice a special charm and perhaps because there was plainly nowhere else for them to go, permission was granted for them to remain—on the understanding that this arrangement was on a temporary basis, a favour which might at any moment be withdrawn. They would be in a much stronger position, it was pointed out, not unkindly, if she and her brother could produce work-cards which would officially entitle them to rations and to a certain number of square feet of living space. There was work for the young man if he cared to take it—a clerk with languages could find employment—of course, there were certain formalities, also. . . . Dazed with relief, Sophie had scarcely listened. . . . " In any case, suitable tenants would be found without delay to occupy the remaining two rooms, with whom they would of course be required to share the kitchen and bathing facilities . . ." " Yes, of course . . ." she had agreed joyfully. " Thank you, thank you . . ." It had seemed too good to be true.

It was true all right. Within forty-eight hours their co-tenants had arrived; a youngish man, supervisor of a railway repair gang, with a wife and three children; not Grusnovians, but from a province in the north. The man was an ardent Party member, surly in his manner and openly suspicious. His wife, a brassy blonde employed in a State butcher's shop, appeared to have little or no control over her children, who were of school age, noisy, and dirty in their habits. From the point of view of the police the family were in every way " suitable " co-tenants—and doubtless had been carefully chosen. The domestic arrangements were far from ideal; sharing a kitchen was bad enough, but the greatest inconvenience, undoubtedly, arose from the sharing of the bathroom. This, as has been said, opened off the kitchen; it was also next door to Sophie's brother's bedroom, in other words, an excellent listening-post. The man and each member of his family spent far longer in the bathroom than was strictly necessary; at least there was never any audible evidence of ablutions being performed. It was for this reason that the Bielskis habitually conversed in English, and, when they remembered, in whispers.

The problem of accommodation settled, at least for the time being, the next immediate problem had been to find a means of earning enough to keep the three of them. Singe by reason of her age and infirmity was admitted even by the authorities to be incapable of work. Ludovic, Sophie's brother, was a couple of years younger than she, a young man of thirty-five or -six, who all his life had been accustomed to rely upon a weak chest to excuse him from strenuous and uncongenial physical effort. However, as the situation had really appeared to be desperate, that is, the small sums he required for cigarettes or the odd flutter at cards actually being denied him, he had, it was true, bestirred himself to the point of making one or two inquiries about a job. But it seemed that as he was totally untrained, and with no commercial assets other than fluency in English and French, the only work open to him was in a Government Office, where he would, of course, first be required to underwrite his loyalty. Except to himself, Ludovic admitted no loyalty of any kind, and, furthermore, he rightly guessed that this was one of the moral issues on which he could count on receiving his sister's support—" The last of the Bielskis to become one of ' them '?—no, never! " she would flash out at him—and as in any case the degrading proposition would have involved the grinding routine of office hours, the idea of which had always been repugnant to him, he had been content to sit back, nursing his chest and his high principles, and let his sister as she always did, find a way.

So, untrained like her brother, with nothing more to offer than he, namely fluency in English and French, but unlike her brother in that she had the stamina of a carthorse and the spirit of a tigress fighting for her young, she had set out to earn sufficient to support them all. It had been far from easy. The number of families who wished their children to receive instruction in the Western languages was decreasing month by month; still, there were a few, and she had some connections. Somehow, by suffering all manner of slights, by cadging for introductions to the new rich, by unashamedly cutting her fees lower than those of her competitors—and there were some—by dint of tramping over the town in all weathers, she had built up a sort of clientele. Then she had had her brainwave. Why not the British? They might need a translator. So she had approached the British office and Wragg, then in charge, had heard her out, rather aghast at her story; but it was Abe Schulman who shared the office, who had come to her rescue and immediately engaged her for three afternoons a week.

Poor Sophie—her English was impressively fluent but ungrammatical; she lived in constant terror lest her translations should be found wanting. Abe, who from the first day had chuckled over her basic English concoctions and prized them for their entertainment value, prized her for quite other reasons—her soothing presence, her ability to make coffee, and her rare, grave smile.

In one way and another she had succeeded, until now, in keeping their three heads above water. Only she knew how precarious their situation was. Sometimes her pupils kept her waiting for money. Quite often, without reasons given, without notice, they discontinued the lessons. And now Abe had found her this new pupil—and what a pupil! And now, just as she was about to set out, just when she wanted to make a good impression. . . . They were the footsteps of the railway gang supervisor which had creaked down the passage to the bathroom.

* * *

" So I shall smell, that's all. She will think I am a pig and a peasant, and it's better that she sees me in my true colours because that is what I have become. I don't care."

" Just put a dash of Cologne on your face, darling. It's wonderfully freshening."

" Cologne? " Sophie laughed shortly. " What a good idea. You have brilliant ideas, Singe."

Her aunt leaned forward. " Sophie," she whispered softly, " Ludo has Cologne. I happened to see it—in his box."

A look passed between them. Then Sophie marched across and knocked at the door of her brother's room.

" Ludo, it's me." She opened the door and went in.

Ludovic was lying on his bed, which was placed in similar position to that of his aunt; when the communicating door was open the two beds were opposite each other with the breadth of the rooms between. Supported by cushions, he was peacefully engaged with his knitting.

He was knitting a sock—he knitted all his own socks—of pure silk on rather fine needles. The source of the silk was a mystery to his aunt and sister alike, but he had quite a supply in different shades and never appeared to run short. He knitted exquisitely—for himself. It was strange, Sophie had remarked, how utterly his technical skill had deserted him, when after a certain amount of nagging, cajoling and coercion, he had been prevailed upon to attempt the manufacture of similar articles in coarser materials for more communally profitable ends. The experiment had proved a failure. The wool, which had been expensive, still lay, a tangled hank, in the chest of drawers. " You can take a horse to the water . . ." she had reflected, and Ludovic, having won his point, had commenced unmolested his umpteenth pair of silken hose.

" Ludo! "

" Well, Sophie, mon ange? " Ludovic smiled at his sister, laying

105

down his sock. He detested any invasion of his privacy, and in order to remind her of his idiosyncrasy, he sighed; then, taking up his nail file, with an appraising glance at his slender hands he applied himself to the maintenance of their rosy tips.

" Ludo, is *he* . . . ? " She jerked her head in the direction of the bathroom, door.

" Don't disturb him, darling," replied her brother in a lazy English drawl. " He mustn't be discouraged on any account. I do believe I heard him spit into the basin this time—and *not* into the bath. A smaller, altogether less satisfactory plop. Heaven for poor you, I thought—cleaning up. Comparatively speaking, of course. You know, Sophie, I've often wondered whether I ought to show him how the taps work. He may not *know* that from them *water flows*." He smoothed his hair thoughtfully. " I've a suspicion we're wronging him, my dear. Ignorance is not precisely a sin, after all."

Ludovic was wearing a silk dressing-gown that had belonged to their father. It reminded Sophie so much of her father that she could scarcely bring herself to look at him in it.

" Listen, Ludo—what I came for was—have you Cologne? I need some."

" Cologne? " he repeated to gain time, and raising his eyebrows for good measure. " *Cologne*, Sophie? " Here he happened to catch sight of his aunt's sharp little muzzle thrust forward, attentive to their conversation. She was as blind as a bat, he knew, but on the other hand she possessed certain other faculties, intuition, for instance, as yet singularly unimpaired by age. Ludovic maintained quite a respect for Singe.

" I have a drop," he admitted grudgingly.

" Well, hurry up, please. It's important. I want some now."

He bent over the bed and rummaged in his box; Sophie politely averting her eyes. Ludovic's box was labelled " DEL MONTE FRUITS— SLICED PEACHES."

" There you are." He sniffed appreciatively. " Don't chuck it about, Sophie. You know what you're like. It's got to last."

He watched her as she smeared it on her forehead, rubbing it in. What a great clumsy creature she was. More like a man than a woman, and more like a peasant than a Bielska.

" Anyway," he said, only faintly curious, but with the right to the information, in view of the Cologne, " where are you off to? "

" Oh, you'll never guess where! " Her eyes glowed, and suddenly she sat down on the bed, on his legs, as it happened, and he shifted them impatiently. She seemed so excited that she even caught his hand. He withdrew it at once—he disliked physical contact of any sort. He

106

noticed that specks of white powder were lodged amongst the hairs on her upper lip.

"You know where I'm going?" She clasped her hands. "To the British! Yes, to the Grand Hotel, to give lessons to Mrs. Purdoe. . . . Mr. Schulman has arranged it—wonderful, isn't it? What do you think of that?"

He lay back, staring at her. His eyes, she saw, had become quite bright and hard.

"What do I think? Of course, I think that you're out of your mind."

"But——"

"You're going *there*, to the Grand Hotel, regularly, I suppose, to give lessons? You're going to risk everything on account of that stupid Englishwoman?"

"Shut up!"

"No, I will not shut up. You know that anyone who goes in there is suspect, and to go there *regularly*——" As he spoke bubbles oozed out of the corners of his lips, a sign with him, of anger. Oh, he was really angry, you could see. "It's just like putting a noose round your neck. Round ours, too."

"I'm sorry," she said. "But I'm going all the same."

"Well, then you are mad." He shrugged. "Certifiable. Of course, at your age one expects that." He gave her a cold, insolent stare, but he was thinking hard. "Sophie," he changed his tone, forcing himself to take her hand, "don't do it, not for my sake, but for Singe."

Just then his aunt, as he might have known she would do, quite spoilt the effect by cackling across the two rooms: "Don't listen to him, Sophie. You do what you want."

"Oh, Ludo," Sophie turned to him in distress, her face quite white, "I *know* it's rash, but I think I must do it. I promised—if it were not the English—but you see, a promise is a promise. Please—won't you try to understand? Oh, dear, Ludo, *what* am I to do?"

The twin lights in his eyes shone cold and bright; they were pitiless, his eyes. In them, for the first time, she saw hatred—a real live hatred, for herself. Why, then, all these years she must have been blind—for how long had it existed, this hatred? Since heaven knows when—nourished by adversity, possibly, but conceived much earlier, way, way back. He hates me, she thought, he has always hated me. And what was he thinking? She had no idea.

Ludovic was thinking: look at her now. If my father could see her now. Sophie, the strong, Sophie the brave, Sophie who should have been the boy, who rides like a demon and shoots like a man, who, without turning a hair, can deliver a cow of a calf or a peasant

107

of a brat—and just look at her now. The old maid, the frump . . . she has no nerves, she's healthy and strong, always has been, and her duty lies clear before her, to care for us, for me and Singe. And now—to risk everything . . . even to seek his advice . . . when, from the very start—well, ever since his official abdication at their first boar-hunt, an occasion he still blushed to remember, he had taken trouble to make it quite clear that the boot was on the other foot. She might be the head of the family, but in that case, then—the head of the family she must be.

"It's quite simple," he said, "don't do it. Don't."

For one horrible second he thought that she might burst into tears. He had never yet seen her cry. But she was wavering. And then Singe, again. He could have throttled the old crow.

"Don't you listen to him, Sophie. You do what you want."

"You see, Ludo." She got up from the bed. "I'm afraid this time I must do what I want. It's *in* me," she touched her breast, gave him a funny little smile, "here. Never mind," she added dryly, "it'll mean a bit more money, too."

"Money," he murmured . . . "Hm . . ." Anger was a luxury really; one that in his position he couldn't afford; nobly, he denied himself of it. "D'you think, Sophie, you could . . . you see, I'm a bit short . . ."

"Oh, Ludo, to-day! Oh dear . . ."

"I've got a bit," croaked Singe. It was marvellous, he thought. You had to hand it to her. A kind of telepathy. She couldn't have heard. "I was keeping it for Sister Mary—but give it to him, Sophie." She grinned at her niece, whispered, "You did quite right, darling."

"Here," said Sophie, bringing him over the note. He tucked it under his pillow and, surprisingly, smiled. "Well, off you go," he said. "Have a nice time." Without returning the smile, she stumped out.

One or other of them, he reflected, examining the note with loving care, always had a bit of cash tucked away. Five hundred. That wouldn't get him far. Paul Rapovski, who had a garçonnière in the cellar of his grandmother's house and who was the acknowledged leader of the "smart set," had mentioned casually that there might be poker that afternoon. Ludovic had no idea of the stakes; the invitation had been so casual—perhaps they had banked on his not turning up. Still, with five hundred, he reckoned he could manage to muscle in. He had been muscling in all his life in default of invitations—he could do it again. He was handy with cards. Before he needed to begin dressing, how many hours to fill in?—three—four? All at once his expression became grave. He reached into his box for his clinical thermometer and put it under his tongue. His temperature was of absorbing interest to him—the taking of it one of his more

108

exacting hobbies which no startling development had as yet repaid. There was still hope, however, but not—he shook down the thermometer—it seemed, to-day. Oh, well.

A grey day. He liked a grey day. One could drowse it through. He took up his knitting once more, his head on one side, pursing his lips. He had been tempted to insert a touch of yellow at the ankle— no more than a row, or at most two. He had, as it chanced, some primrose silk which might have done very well. But this neat little monochrome rib was more distinguished, perhaps; the knitted silk crunched deliciously in the hand. Knitting—what a pleasure it was. Hypnotised by the gleaming needles, one could dream whole hours away. A soothing pastime. The last of the Bielskis applied himself to it.

Chapter Eight

" SHE'S NOT come yet, the Countess? " said Gisela. She was preparing mushrooms in the kitchen.

" No," said Milly shortly. " She's late."

" And for the first lesson, too." Gisela looked, and sounded, a little smug.

" Yes," said Milly. There was no doubt, it did make a very bad beginning. After all, in spite of what Abe had said, she was doing the poor woman a favour by engaging her at all.

" We haven't much sense of time in this country," Gisela went on philosophically, as if to excuse Sophie, but possibly also to irritate her mistress. " That's the way we are. Perhaps she may not come at all."

That had occurred to Milly, too. Then where would she be? A whole morning, a whole day, in fact—because Larry was away in Slavnik on a conference—alone with nothing to do. What, she wondered, would Mrs. Simpson have done, similarly placed? How had she filled her days? What sort of woman had she been? She would have given a lot to find out and the person who could undoubtedly have enlightened her was Gisela herself—but of course it was beneath one's dignity to ask. Still, the very thought of Mrs. Simpson was a challenge in itself, which prompted her to say, in her rather peremptory manner, just to show that she wasn't to be put upon, was mistress in her own kitchen, and so on: " You're quite sure, are you, Gisela, that those mushrooms are all quite—well, *safe*? "

Gisela laughed softly. It was a not unpleasing laugh, hers, but it never pleased Milly, who invariably caught a note of mockery in it, just as she fancied that in her smile there was always a trace of a sneer.

" Trust me, gnädige Frau. All are safe. Even this one—and look how ugly it is!—or that. I was brought up to know about mushrooms. I could never make a mistake." She went on chopping dill and onion, watching Milly out of the corner of her eye as she loitered round the kitchen, opening drawers, running her finger over surfaces, staring dubiously into the plughole of the hand-basin. There was no fault to be found, and Gisela, her head bent, smiled.

Milly sat down on the edge of the bath, watching the girl at work; she lit a cigarette. As she did so she noticed that Gisela glanced at it hungrily, and it crossed her mind to offer her one too—but that would

110

have been ridiculous, of course. Instead, she said kindly: " So you come from the country, do you? "

Gisela hesitated, then, with becoming shyness, launched into reminiscence. She was not such a fool as to stop work, however. She went on chopping. " Yes, from the country. We lived in the mountains." She waved the knife in the direction of the Tatars. " My father was a necromancer, gnädige Frau. A very unusual man, famous for miles around. You know what it means, necromancer? "

" Of course," said Milly impatiently. " Magic, and all that."

" Magic." Gisela nodded. " Spells and so on. He was clever with spells. A soothsayer, too, he was. The future, and the stars," she went on cosily, " and conversations with the dead; sometimes, that's to say —because he heard their voices, you know, but he would not always pass the messages—only when the fancy took him. Not even if they were ever so keen, the relations. Not even for money. He could be very stubborn, my father." She laughed dryly. " But that was not all. He cured people, too. It was for the cures that he became well known."

" Cured people? You mean—faith healing? " Against her will she was interested.

" Oh, no," said Gisela, full of scorn. " Dear me, no. He was very common-sense—almost like a real doctor. Better, according to him. No, he cured people with herbs and berries and teas made from roots and bark—all things he found in the forest. He knew about every plant that ever grew, I think—what would do this and what the other and how to undo, if necessary, what each had done. He knew how to prepare a certain tea so that a woman giving birth would feel no pain, and a different tea for a cough, or for colic, and worse things, even; oh, he made many, many cures. But the peasants, it's strange, they didn't like him the better for it, although they came to him from all around. When they were ill they were frightened, of course, and then they trusted him because he knew what to do—but afterwards? Oh, when they recovered . . . then it was a very different story! So he was only famous—not liked at all. No, they weren't a bit grateful, the peasants. If ever we came into the village—we lived in a hut in the forest, you see, quite apart—a large family, we were—they would often throw stones at us children." Her mouth tightened and for a second she looked quite grim. Then she went on, with indifference: " Of course it was the priest set them against us. My father was atheist, and, too, he would never let us eat meat, not a morsel. We lived on vegetables. That's why I eat so much meat now." She added slyly, " Perhaps the gnädige Frau has noticed? "

" No," said Milly, rather sharply. " I haven't." If Gisela intended

111

thereby to imply that she was mean, she was not. Although it had struck her, as it happened, that the girl had a voracious appetite.

" And what about your mother? " she said.

" My mother? " The question seemed to startle Gisela. A faint flush of colour came into her cheeks. " She's dead," she muttered and began re-chopping what had already been chopped.

" And your father—is he . . . ? "

Clearly she was happier on the topic of her paternal parent; fleetingly, Milly wondered why. With just a hint of an attitude, as if she knew from experience that the anecdote would prove a reliable tear-jerker, she said: " The Germans shot him, gnädige Frau. It was very sad. Only I and one brother escaped. We walked—I don't know how far . . ." Quick to sense the changing mood of her audience, she cut her story short: " Then I got a job—with a German officer's wife. A terrible woman."

" Good gracious! " said Milly, her attention caught once more.

" Yes, a terrible woman—but at least with her there was plenty to eat. I was very hungry by then, you see. My brother, too. For him, I used to smuggle food out of the kitchen at night. Because they were only Germans, after all . . ." She made as if to spit into the hand-basin —merely a token gesture, Milly was thankful to see.

Gisela had dropped the knife and picking up the mushrooms one by one, she examined them for grubs. If she found so much as a single grub, she threw the mushroom into a separate heap.

" You aren't going to waste all those, I should hope? "

" Oh, no, they won't be wasted, gnädigste. It is just that they are not fit to be eaten by the Herrschaften—but they are quite good enough for me. They will do very well for my supper to-night."

She is perfect, thought Milly. Larry is right. It is I who am impossible.

" I was there for nearly a year," Gisela went on in her singsong voice. " With that terrible woman. I suffered there. The woman was often alone when the officer had Dienst, you know. Then—I was made to— she made me——" she gulped, " *massage* her, yes, massage—oh, such things I had to do for her, you would not believe! " This reticence was far more telling than any description, however horrific. " A great fat woman—hard and fat as a rat. And if I did not obey—she would pinch, kick, slap, und so weiter . . . oh, the things I could—but one must forget, isn't it? It's the only way."

Milly's immediate reaction to this story was pity, and then a sense of guilt. Perhaps she herself was a " terrible woman "? certainly she had not been conspicuously kind to Gisela. She did wish, however, that there were not this suspicion of over-rehearsal, of calculated effect

112

in the telling of the tale. Rebuking herself, and resolving all sorts of amends, she said:

"You poor child." There was such mildness in her tone—because she never did things by halves, and if she were determined to be kind, kind she would be—that Gisela, after a little pause, looked up and smiled. It was a triumph of a smile, sad, humble, forbearing, withal wonderfully sunny—and yet it had the effect of dispelling all Milly's good resolutions so that they melted away like dew, of shrivelling her budding sympathy and of illuminating the motive behind her own attempt at kindliness, robbing her of any sense of virtue; the smile was too clever by half and it lingered a fraction too long. Suddenly she knew, without a shadow of doubt, that Gisela had read her mind like a book, had intended her to have just those reactions of pity and remorse—yes, and how very nearly she herself had been taken in. For a moment each held the other with her eyes. Staring at her, Milly thought—and it came to her with a shock—this is no peasant; she's as clever as I am. And pretty, too. Prettier than I am? Well, certainly younger. As to what Gisela was thinking, she could not even hazard a guess. Her eyes were blue as periwinkles, set wide apart, but opened too wide; her gaze was altogether too direct, too honest. She had wiped the smile off, that was something; all that was left of it was an ironical twist to the lips, which suited her better, much better. What *was* she thinking? For a moment, as their eyes met, they were two women taking stock of each other, no longer mistress and maid.

It was Gisela who disengaged first. She turned away, took up another onion and began peeling it. Milly got up from the edge of the bath, and unlocking the store cupboard started to re-arrange the tins on the shelf.

Presently:

"Gnädige Frau," the soft voice pleaded over her shoulder. "I—I have a request."

Milly turned round. The girl was standing just as one might have envisaged from the tone of her voice—cringing, like a thin stray dog which must beg, risking the blow it expects.

"Well?" She was exasperated and showed it.

"If it's not too much to ask—it's my shoes. I have not dared to clean them along with those of the Herrschaften. If I might, gnädigste, have just one tin of polish?"

"Of course." Mean, she told herself again, she was *not*. She took a couple of tins from the shelf. "Why didn't you ask me before?"

Gisela snatched the tins to her breast as if they were worth their weight in gold. "Oh, you are too good, gnädige Frau. Of course," she went on, thereby destroying a variety of created effects, "Mrs.

113

Simpson used to give me the same polish, often . . . but with you, I have not before had the courage to ask . . ."

" I don't see why," Milly replied curtly. Nevertheless, she recognised that a better humour was stealing over her. She was a model employer, approachable, generous, and just.

"The gnädige Frau is bored to-day." She took the saucepan of mushrooms off the stove, stirring in the chopped dill and sour cream. " And the Bielska not coming, too bad. And der Herr away, also. When ' die Nanny ' "—the title by which she referred to Miss Raven— " says that he is to be away, I thought then, the gnädige Frau, poor thing, how bored she will be to-day."

Now to be referred to as a " poor thing " has an irresistibly soothing effect upon the nerves of a person of strong character, and Milly was no exception to the rule, having long since reconciled herself to the inexplicable fact that she was rarely, if ever, no matter how piteously placed, regarded as an object of sympathy. Take to-day for instance: so she was—a poor thing. Gisela couldn't be more right. Enchanted to receive corroboration of this by no means novel conception of herself, and greatly softened by this token of the girl's perspicacity, she said wistfully:

" Yes, it's true, I am bored. I'd—well—if there were a cinema—or if I could go and have my hair done—anything, almost. But there's nothing. Nothing."

" The gnädige Frau misses the Western life . . . I know." Her voice had become velvety, insinuating. " There——" she tasted the mushrooms. " All done. Shall I suggest something? " Gaily she swept the pans off the stove. " Or not? " Her manner was coaxing, secretive, as if she were hinting a treat to a child. " To-day is the day of the market."

" The *market*? "

" Oh, not *that* market. This is a special market, only held once a week." She looked at her watch. A present from the open-handed Simpsons, Milly guessed. " I doubt that the Bielska will come to-day. It begins now, and it only stays open for an hour or two. Many Slavnik people attend just for the sight, the experience. There one may find "—she reeled off the items as if she were reciting a fairy story— " glass, porcelain, sometimes furs, even—those things, luxury things— and a lot of old rags too: what I go for, of course." Having thus casually listed the temptations, woven her spell, she took her account book from the shelf and sat down at the kitchen table; chewing her pencil, mumbling her additions, she allowed time for the magic to take effect.

Milly said at last: " You know where it is, this market? "

114

"Know? Oh yes, I always took"—she faltered, aware of the pitfall—"we often used to go," she finished demurely.

"Well, then, as I've nothing special to do . . . if the lunch really is ready . . . and I dare say it's something one *ought* to see . . ."

"Then let's go!" Springing up from her chair, Gisela slammed the account book back into the drawer and slammed the drawer shut.

* * *

They took the tram to the outskirts of the town, to the terminus, and then they walked until the cobbled street and the neat stone houses of the suburbs petered out together. The street became a muddy track leading over an area of flat waste land, the sort of no-man's land that is quite often to be seen outside large towns. On either side of the track there were scattered shacks inhabited by squatters; roughly built of wood, roofed with bits of corrugated iron or tarpaulin, these dwellings, although on hillocky ground, were surrounded by thick mud; planks of wood, bridging the mud, led from each down to the main track. One or two women at the doorways stared at Milly and Gisela as they passed, but sullenly, with indifference; they looked wretchedly poor.

"The ones who live there," Gisela remarked, "are very rough people. They came from Slavnik after the bombing. The Grusnov people don't like them. It was very bad, the bombing in Slavnik. There was no bombing here and so the Grusnovians don't understand how bad it was."

"How do they live? Is there work for them here?"

"They scratch a living," she replied grimly. "A bit here, a bit there—mostly in connection with the Kanetta, the market."

Milly darted a sideways glance at her companion, who, absorbed in her own thoughts, was staring straight ahead, and was struck by the beauty of that sharp profile. Stripped of its customary expression of humility, it was a face full of force and character, beautiful without being in the least prepossessing, and she was reminded of a young female wolf, gaunt, famished-looking, desperate, certainly cunning; Gisela even moved like a wolf, loping swiftly along. That's funny, thought Milly, I see her differently to-day—as if I'd never looked at her properly before. Possibly that was so; one avoids looking closely at those one instinctively dislikes. Her dislike for the girl was still as live as ever, but mingled now with another emotion which she failed to analyse, it being so alien to her own nature; once having looked at her, and in so doing having recognised some formidable quality in the other's personality—she felt her own self-confidence seeping away, to be replaced merely by a heightened sense of weariness; a poor substitute.

115

"This market," she began, wanting the girl to talk, "why is it so far out of the town?"

Without turning her head, Gisela said shortly: "Because it is—rather illegal."

"*Rather* illegal?" Milly smiled.

"Well, yes." She shrugged. "Not *very* illegal—only because of these stupid new laws." The distinction, over-subtle as it seemed, appeared to be quite clear to her. "Nowadays, if you have anything to sell you are supposed to take it to a State pawnshop—but there of course they charge ten per cent on the sale and they don't make any effort to sell your article quickly—or only if they know you; that is always the way in a State shop. Then again one is afraid to take valuable things to a State shop because there may be trouble." Her voice was drab as the picture of life that her words conjured up. "One is not supposed even to *possess* valuables now—all such things should have been handed in to the Government months ago. So—you want me to go on?"

"Yes," said Milly, "go on. It's all new to me."

"So whenever people need money quickly, an illness, or a funeral, or something, they prefer not to take their things to a State shop to sell, because perhaps the shop won't sell the goods anyway, or not for a long time, or perhaps even report them to the police as well—and where would be the point of that? You'd lose the goods and find yourself in prison too." She gave a dry little laugh. "So—they prefer to come here, to the Kanetta, where there is less risk and more likelihood of making a quick sale."

"But—I don't understand . . . surely here it's even more of a risk?"

"Oh, no—not so bad. You see, everybody comes here. They couldn't arrest all the thousands who come. In Slavnik, now, that would be a different matter. There is no such market in Slavnik," she added, and fell silent.

Rather uneasily Milly began pondering over all this information. She sensed that Gisela had presented her with the facts, leaving her to draw her own conclusions, and for some odd reason her brain was averse to performing that task. A certain word, or term, rather, which had been slipping elusively in and out between the facts whilst she considered them, now floated to the surface of her mind. It was an unattractive term, slimy, and she fished it out for scrutiny with distaste.

"So this market is—well, it's a *black* market, is it?"

She threw the expression in Gisela's direction, for her to pick up or not, as she pleased. But Gisela, apparently, was not squeamish at all.

"Yes," she said hardily, "it is that. A black market." She turned to Milly and grinned. "There has been a war, gnädige Frau. After a

116

war there is always the black market." She spoke in a manner so blasé, so utterly unemotional, that she seemed far older than her years. " If it had not been for the black market, well—I myself, for instance, would have starved." She jerked her head contemptuously towards the shacks. " I lived for a year in one of those. How? By running errands in the market—now and then picking something up cheap and selling it dear —making just enough so that my brother and I could eat. I dressed in rags. I took risks for those who preferred not to take risks . . . I learned—oh, such a lot—and you know, it was amusing. You wouldn't believe it, but I enjoyed it—until . . ." her voice, if anything, became more casual, hard with indifference, and she strode on faster than ever, ". . . until my brother died."

" Oh," said Milly, the cue for a spontaneous expression of sympathy as always catching her short. " Oh dear, how terrible."

" Yes, it was terrible. He caught cold. It was a bad winter and the roof leaked. We had not enough blankets. He had no overcoat. I had no overcoat, also, but I am very strong. There was no money for anything—for medicine or for a doctor—because you can't get a doctor to come out to this part of the town unless you pay very well, in advance. Still "—suddenly she looked fierce, but amused, too—" I found one, a doctor. But by then it was too late. My brother died very quickly, in two days. So after that—well, I . . ." she paused, " I realised something important." She fell silent, as if she had said more than she intended.

" Go on," said Milly. " What? "

Gisela, surprised by the note of interest in her voice, glanced at her shrewdly. " Something *very* important, gnädige frau. That I must look after myself." She smiled, seeing that Milly had expected some more sensational revelation. " Yes, just that. Well, the doctor was a kind man. I asked him to give me a reference and he lent me some money and so I made myself neat and presented myself at the Grand Hotel. I knew there was an English family staying there, and I pretended to the porter that I was a girl from a shop delivering something for the English lady. So he let me up stairs." Yes, thought Milly, that was how it would have been. She would probably get her own way with men, the doctor, the porter. . . . " And there I met—Mrs. Simpson."

" And she was—sympathetic? "

" An angel of goodness," Gisela answered readily—a shade too readily, perhaps; a nuance that was lost on Milly, however, who upon hearing this familiar description of her predecessor discovered that her own sympathy for the girl had scarcely arisen before it was already, mysteriously, beginning to wane.

The muddy track had come to an end. They had emerged on to a

117

wide open space, a patch of rough ground perhaps half a mile square, part of it used as a rubbish dump. In the far corner there was what looked from a distance like a gipsy encampment; caravans, covered carts, tents, and flimsy tarpaulin shelters. Nearer to, one saw that there were stalls set in rows, and the lanes between the stalls were thronged with people. A light drizzle was beginning to fall. If this was the famous market it was a desolate sight, and Milly felt bitterly disappointed. It was like an ant-heap, milling with activity, but the shapes who passed in a steady stream up and down the lanes between the stalls were grey and silent as ghosts; here and there in clusters, pressed together, furtively they handled the goods; money changed hands with scarcely a word being spoken.

In a wide circle round the stalls there were peasants squatting on the ground, each with his wares spread out in front of him; battered saucepans, rusty farm implements, sheepskin jackets, stained and filthy, the wool linings felted and yellow with age; patched farm boots and women's broken shoes—mass-produced Czech shoes which had not stood up to wear; second-hand clothes of all descriptions, long woollen underpants, overcoats with collars of mangy unidentifiable fur, even corsets. The smell that is inseparable from second-hand clothing was quite sickening. The only new articles were rabbit-skin coats and caps for children, in which there was a brisk trade.

" I don't see any china," said Milly crossly. What a wild-goose chase—and she was getting wet.

" It's farther on." Gisela, her face set hard like all the others, pushed her way through the crowd. Suddenly she stopped, whispered: " Sssssh! You see those two? " Quite near them, miraculously, a space had cleared in the lane of traffic around two young men in green hats and new mackintoshes who were chatting together, lighting cigarettes.

" Come." Gisela caught Milly's arm and they slipped down a side alley. She gave a little excited laugh. " Police," she said, and grimaced. " You see, gnädige Frau—there is the china, over there."

The stall was gaudy with pottery from Czechoslovakia, glossy figurines of ballet dancers, ladies in mauve crinolines or pink in the nude, Toby jugs, spaniels and roosters and spotted cats, all those ornaments which are treasured in humble houses throughout the world.

" But this is all junk! " Milly exclaimed, and turned to find Gisela watching her, her eyes dancing with amusement.

" Look underneath," she suggested softly.

The space beneath was crammed with dusty piles of china and glass; there was a heap of assorted silver implements, spoons, ladles, trowels, and so on, all very tarnished, in a tin basin. A couple of men in shabby overcoats were squatted down close to these objects, pouncing first on

118

one thing, then on another, their eyes darting here and there; occasionally one would put something aside on the grass, then they would both shake their heads, and muttering together, make rapid calculations on the back of an envelope.

" Dealers," said Gisela, in Milly's ear. " From Slavnik."

Milly's attention was elsewhere.

" D'you see that? " She pointed to a coffee-pot which lay on its side on the ground. She drew in her breath: " I think I'd like to have it," she said simply.

The coffee-pot was certainly a most pleasing shape, full-bellied yet slender, tapering at the neck, milky-white in colour, scrawled over with a pattern of roses in powder-blue. There was a tiny rosebud instead of a knob on the lid. Some subtle quality in the glaze of the china made one's fingers itch to touch it—but merely to touch was never enough for Milly—she must have it too.

" D'you suppose it's for sale? " She looked so anxious that Gisela smiled.

" Naturally. But it's Meissen, gnädige Frau. It'll be expensive. Still, I can ask."

It was expensive. " No, it's too much." Milly heaved a great sigh, her eyes lingering on it.

" You really want it? " whispered Gisela at her elbow. There was quite a teasing, merry look in her eyes—and how they shone! " You go on up a little way, see—wait for me behind that tent. I shan't be long." She vanished in the crowd.

Milly fought her way up to the tent and went round behind it, where she waited. She felt puzzled and somehow uneasy. No one, however, so much as looked at her. They were all too pre-occupied, and in too much of a hurry. Presently Gisela returned. She came up close, shielding the shopping bag with her coat.

" Look." She opened the bag. Inside was a paper parcel; she tore open a corner, and the immortal splendour of that blue on white gleamed through.

" But—my dear child! " Milly stared, aghast. " I told you—I simply can't afford . . ."

For answer, Gisela snapped the bag shut. Leaning against the framework of the tent, closing her eyes, she took a deep, deep breath. There was an extraordinary expression on her face—of triumph, no less. Then she muttered, in a tone and a manner that were both quite new, both urgent and intimate: " Give me a cigarette."

Milly, in a daze, produced her case and held it out.

" Here."

Gisela took one. " A light? "

119

Obediently she fumbled in her bag for her lighter. Snapping it open, she held the flame to the cigarette between the girl's lips. It was possibly in that second, with that action, that the relationship existing hitherto between them was severed, and another infinitely less resilient, incomparably more binding, forged. In any case, and each knew it, from then on they were no longer mistress and maid.

Gisela took a couple of deep gulps at the cigarette, then she tossed it away.

" You don't understand, eh? " She chuckled. " Shall I tell you how I did it? Two tins of Keevee, that's all."

" *You mean*——" Milly looked thunderstruck. Gisela patted her arm.

" Oh, but there's nothing wrong in *that*, gnädige Frau. Shoe polish is as rare as Meissen, that's all." She shrugged gaily. " And just think, to-morrow, when your man says: ' What a pretty coffee-pot! ' " The success of the transaction had put her in tremendous spirits, you could tell. " Come along now," she said briskly, rather as if she were in charge of a child. " Now we'd better get out quick." Then, back down the muddy lane, chattering on: " Mrs. Simpson," she began, as if the mention of that name were now permitted, that and a great deal else, " Mrs. Simpson obtained a whole service of the Meissen—nearly complete. This little article we've got to-day, although it's nice, bears the date. I looked. Hers was *without date*—just the mark, the crossed swords. That's much better. In fact, not to be compared."

" No," said Milly meekly, " I suppose not."

Back in the hotel she washed the coffee-pot in her own bathroom, dried it tenderly and put it on the mantelpiece where she could look at it. Then, after a while, for some reason she tired of looking at it. Its sheen was lustrous as ever, its shape as seductive, but curiously enough it seemed to have lost some of its original charm—in transit, perhaps. She put it away in the corner cupboard, where there was some other china, and pushed it right to the back. Then she poured herself a glass of sherry before lunch. After two or three glasses she felt much better. "There's nothing *wrong* in it," she kept saying to herself. "I gave something to Gisela and she made an exchange." People did that all over the world, made their living that way. People? What sort of people? Well—just people.

All during lunch, half-listening to Miss Raven, who said that a person had called and had seemed very upset—what sort of person? said Milly—oh, just a *person*, said Miss Raven, skilfully conveying her impression of whoever it was, but she'll call again, she said, this afternoon—Milly was thinking of her new possession, herself possessed at the thought of it, by a feeling of excitement, a sort of unholy joy. When

120

Gisela, demure as ever, handed round the plates, Milly was annoyed to find herself evading the girl's eye, and perceiving that an intolerable situation might rapidly develop, one that must be put a stop to, when lunch was over, determined to put a stop to it, she went straight into the kitchen and unlocked the store cupboard door.

" Here, Gisela," she said, taking out four tins of Kiwi and putting them on the kitchen table.

" Oh, thank you, gnädige Frau," said Gisela, with just the appropriate mixture of gratitude and surprise. Turning from the washing-up, with one of her swift movements she scooped the tins off the table top and dropped them into the pocket of her apron. Milly, humming a little tune to herself, locked the cupboard and then went off to lie down with a book, rather more cheerful now that the business was concluded and quite confidently supposing that she had settled up.

* * *

When Gisela had done the dishes and tidied up the kitchen, she went into her own room and washed her face and combed her hair, tying a ribbon round it, and then she put on some lipstick and rubbed a little rouge into her cheeks. The result was a startling difference in her appearance. The Waif of War, Orphan of the Storm no longer, eyeing herself in the glass she forswore both parts; now, made up, she certainly bore—as Mr. Simpson had once remarked—a distinct resemblance to Marlene. She ran down the front staircase into the hall; then sauntered up to the porter's desk.

" Good evening," she murmured.

" Good evening," the porter replied, without immediately looking up. Although apparently engaged in writing up his day-book, he had already glimpsed her approach out of the tail of his eye.

The porter, Kazimierz by name, was a young man who had spent some years as a prisoner-of-war in Silesia. He spoke five languages and he was ambitious. He had come quite far already (taking the start as the prison camp), due to having adhered, more or less steadfastly, to the principle of travelling light. More or less, because although he was a firm believer in that principle which many a great man has proved to be the key to success, the porter had a weakness; or rather, he had two —most men, great or otherwise, have more—and, like thorns in the flesh, and very ordinary common-or-garden thorns at that, he could not pluck them out: namely, vodka and women. In all other respects cool and calculating, as a cucumber and a Jew, prudent as a virgin and wily as a fox, under the influence of the one he would desire the other, and under the influence of both he would become garrulous, impulsive, and even rash. Although he recognised these failings and bitterly regretted them, on occasion he fell; that is, on regular occasions, just like other men. Small wonder that Gisela, who was his match and more, had long since decided that here was a man after her own heart. Their acquaintance was already of several months' standing, and it might be said that they knew each other quite well.

"I have a little present for you," she whispered. Sliding her hand out of her coat pocket and reaching across the desk, she dropped two tins of Kiwi, black, on to the ledge below.

In acknowledgment the porter, albeit rather reluctantly, looked up. He noted that Gisela had taken trouble with her appearance, and that her eyes were exceptionally bright. Experiencing a slight quickening of the pulse—he was a man, after all, he defended himself—he even smiled as he said: "They'll come in quite handy, Gisi. You had a nice outing this morning?"

"Yes, thank you," said Gisela, fluttering her eyelashes. "I took my lady to see the sights."

"Of course," said the porter, "it's the day of the Kanetta. Well, that's always interesting."

"Yes, it was of some interest. We found a little piece of china, nothing much, a coffee-pot, Meissen, quite pretty . . . which is now on the top shelf of the corner cupboard in the salon, right at the back . . . yes, only that, but next week, I dare say we shall be going again." She paused. "To-night," she added, her voice becoming husky, her eyes brooding—just a curl of cigarette smoke and there he would see, if he bothered to look, lucky man, Marlene—"after supper . . . I'll be free."

The porter inclined his head. Over her shoulder he had caught sight of the housekeeper, who had stepped out of her office into the hall.

"Same time, same place?" Gisela persisted, plugging away, pulling out all the throat-stops.

"Yes. But you'd better go back now, Gisi," he said, and Gisela went, just as the housekeeper approached. The porter had picked up his day-book and was studying the entries therein. "That girl," said the housekeeper, as she watched Gisela go upstairs. The porter was rather a favourite of hers.

"Yes," said the porter, frowning and dipping his pen in the ink. There was this entry to be made and he didn't wish to be disturbed. Someone else came through the swing doors and he looked up. He was on duty, after all.

"Oooooh . . ." sighed the housekeeper, all excited. Both pairs of eyes followed the progress of this new arrival up the stairs until she was out of sight.

" Know who that was? " The housekeeper leaned right over the desk. Her breath stank like mouldy cheese, but in the cause of his job he was prepared to suffer. " Countess Bielska," she said, licking her lips. " Bielska, Sophia," she added softly, lest there should be any mistake, and with a rattle of keys she took herself off.

After sucking his pen for quite a while, the porter, in his neat but crabbed script, made two fresh entries under the date of that day in his book.

* * *

Milly, who had fallen asleep on the sofa, was awakened by the knock at the door. She awoke with a start, her heart pounding. She had been dreaming. Rain lashed against the window-panes; the room had become quite dark. Still half-asleep, she crawled out of her nest of cushions and went to open the door, determined that if it were the princess she would send her packing.

It was not the princess.

The lights were dim in the corridor and she peered at the figure who stood there in the shadows.

" Mrs. Purdoe? "

She switched on the light. " Yes? " she said uncertainly.

The stranger was a woman, but in build more like a man, tall and broad, and rather peculiarly dressed, too, in a brown leather jerkin, of the type worn by bus drivers, and a brown beret set dead level, the headband pulled right down over her forehead. She stepped forward into the light.

" I am Sophie Bielska," she said in a breathless voice. Her lips twitched nervously, she was trying to smile, and a little smile came and went—she seemed painfully nervous, although her eyes which were brown and shining, full of an almost childlike candour, were fixed steadily on Milly's face.

" Oh yes, of course." Milly held out her hand. Seizing it, the odd creature sprang to attention in the manner of a French officer performing a military handshake, and some knuckles cracked.

" Do come in, won't you? " said Milly weakly, retrieving the crushed member and standing aside to allow her guest to enter—which she did, sweeping in and marching to the middle of the room where all at once she came to a halt. There she stood, shoulders back, head erect, eyes closed, snuffing the rather fetid air.

" I smell it! " she whispered, and took several deep shuddering breaths. " *I smell it*, Mrs. Purdoe! "

" Smell it? " said Milly, horrified. Timidly she approached. " Smell what? "

"The Red, White and Blue, Mrs. Purdoe!" she declared in ringing tones, her eyes still shut. "The Red, White and Blue!"

"Crumbs," murmured Milly, thoroughly alarmed.

On hearing this simple interjection, as if released from a trance the Bielska opened her eyes and giggled. It was an infectious school-girlish giggle and the face turned towards Milly was so radiant it might have been that of a young girl—or of a lunatic, she thought sourly.

"Ah!" She clasped Milly's hands between her own, which were big and capable and warm. "You must forgive me. You don't know how topping it is to come here. Yes, what joy." She was giggling with sheer happiness, it seemed. "I came this morning but I was late— I'm awfully sorry, it won't happen again."

"It doesn't matter a bit," said Milly graciously, disengaging her hands because she had a rooted dislike of a woman's touch. She had intended delivering some sort of lecture on the subject of unpunctuality —one must begin as one meant to go on—but now the ground was cut from under her feet.

"How perfectly understanding you are!" Sophie beamed at her hostess. "Generosity is your middle name, I should say. What a race!"

No suitable answer springing ready to her lips, Milly rang for tea. "Let me take your things," she said.

Sophie snatched off the beret and flung it on to a chair, along with her satchel; chuckling to herself, clearly in the grip of an uncontrollable excitement, she began stripping off the leather jerkin. Coming in with the tea-tray, Gisela shot her a single quick glance and then with the imperturbability of the perfect servant, after placing the tea-tray in front of her mistress, she moved nimbly about the room, emptying ash-trays, drawing the curtains and so forth. At her entrance, however, Milly had noticed that Sophie Bielska's manner had undergone a startling change. She sat down on the sofa, never taking her eyes off the maid all the time she was in the room. That radiant gaiety had vanished from her face; her expression had become wary, her eyes cool. So she's not mad, thought Milly. Not mad at all. She had been wondering.

"Milk?" she said. "Sugar?"

Gisela closed the door behind her and Sophie relaxed. That is, she let out a shrill squeal of excitement and Milly, pouring tea, slopped it over the tray.

"Look!" Entranced, she was gazing at the sugar bowl. "Oh, but look . . . *lump* sugar! Oh, it's too much, really it is. Who but the English would have *lump* sugar?"

124

" A whole lot of people have lump sugar," Milly said dryly. " It's nothing special. How many? "

" No, no, Mrs. Purdoe. It's an *English* delicacy, I'm sure . . . a true refinement and quite ripping, too. One lump, please."

" Cigarette? "

She wriggled with embarrassment. " I never have . . . but I could try."

" Well, try. No—not like that. Like this . . . ziehen, nicht blasen, you know." Accustomed to using German in her dealings with the maid, she uttered the words unthinkingly, and was startled by the violent reaction they produced.

" Swine . . .! " hissed Sophie. Vindictively she stubbed out the cigarette, mashing it in her passion as if it personified the foe. " Those swine! "

" Oh, but some are nice," said Milly soothingly. " Take another cigarette, do. It's a nice language, I think."

" Ah, but that's just *like* you English to be so generous. . . . You, with your cleverness, your *gift* for languages . . ."

" I wouldn't say that was a national trait," Milly murmured modestly. Then, determined to come to the point, " But I would like to learn yours."

" Bravo! *I* will teach you."

" D'you think you could manage it? Coming here, I mean. I know there are—well, difficulties . . ."

" Oh, *those* swine," Sophie agreed carelessly, puffing away.

" If it's a question of money . . ."

" My *dear* . . ." Ignoring the last remark, she went on, " What do I care about those devils? . . . Still, I think you should know . . ." Suddenly springing to her feet she prowled towards the door where she stood listening for a second, then flitted back to the sofa. For a large woman she moved with extraordinary grace. She bent over and whispered something that tickled into Milly's ear, then sat down again, nodding and looking very fierce. " Oh, yes," she said, " everybody knows that."

" Do—do they? " said Milly feebly. She felt completely at sea, and cast about desperately—the interview was not going according to plan. " I . . . er . . . hear the grammar's rather difficult," she said at last.

" The grammar? " Sophie, who had been lost in a trance momentarily, her thoughts running helter-skelter through a Slavonian maze of plot and counter-plot, shook herself. What *minds* they had, the English, really—they put one to shame, so purposeful they were, so direct. Her own mind was capable of immense concentration at times—now, for

125

instance, she had quite succeeded in forgetting how awful the day had been: coming here this morning and finding the bird flown, so that she had missed two other lessons, and Ludo so grumpy; and even yet she hadn't had time to stand in a queue to buy anything for supper, and how she would have liked just one of those biscuits instead of this cigarette; it would set her up, the biscuit, as there'd been no time for lunch, but if she kept her eyes away from the plate she forgot that, too, so she wasn't too bad at concentrating, was she? She had forgotten all those things while she had been thinking of the porter downstairs, whereas with equal intensity, just before, she had been thinking of Mrs. Purdoe's ear-rings, so chic, like nuggets of coal—yes, she *could* concentrate, but never, she reflected sadly, for very long. Now she saw that Mrs. Purdoe was looking at her rather oddly, and she took a deep breath.

" Oh—the *grammar*! The Slavonian grammar? " She laughed. " Certainly it's not like your perfect English grammar, so easy, smooth and regular. Mind you, I never actually learned English grammar myself because Miss Brownlow never bothered about grammar. She taught the *natural* way."

" Miss Brownlow? " said Milly, beginning to abandon hope.

" Yes, Miss Brownlow," repeated Sophie, in rather a strange voice. " Miss Brownlow." Suddenly she sprang up and leaning her elbow on the mantelpiece turned her head away, her cheek on her hand. Milly, who was becoming used to all this bounding about, catching sight in the glass of the expression on her face, which was one of acute distress, thought, what an extraordinary being, like a child, but a child would be more cunning; *her* feelings are all there, on the surface, but real none the less. . . . I do believe she's not *acting* at all. Still, I *was* having a nap, she thought, and what, I should like to know, has Miss Brownlow, whoever she is, got to do with me?

" It's like you to want to know," said Sophie softly, fingering the objects on the mantelpiece. " About Miss Brownlow, I mean. Your marvellous English gift for sympathy, of course. Miss Brownlow was my mother, Mrs. Purdoe." Instantly all sorts of hares started up in Milly's brain. " My mother, in a way," she went on, " I mean by that, she was everything to me. My own mother—she died when I was still quite a girl and there was always a distance, you know. In those days —there was *room* for that. I think that's good, I must say, a distance. Wherever I go now, giving lessons, there seems to be no *room*, and that's the main trouble—the children are brought up close, close to their parents—and of course they're idolised, the little beggars, because of the losses, you know, during the war—and at school they learn all sort of things, even to dislike their parents—certainly to criticise—to listen at

126

keyholes, all that. Well, that's not good. And the result? Our Slavonian children are not well-behaved as they used to be—no, they are shockingly—what was I saying?"

" Miss Brownlow," said Milly gently.

" Oh, yes. Well, I mean we didn't see our mother every day—we lived in a different wing of the house in the country and even here, in town, we lived on the third floor; still, most evenings, she would come up to say good night or, anyway, she would try to come. She was nice, you know, but severe—I was never pretty, and she would have liked a pretty daughter, and once I remember I stepped on the hem of her dress as she got out of the carriage—and how she scolded me! I was always clumsy, of course—a great fool. Then when she died—it was awful. Such a long procession and the peasants weeping and I wore a thick, thick veil—lucky in a way, because I couldn't weep . . ."

" But Miss Brownlow?" Milly prompted once more, as Sophie seemed to have fallen into one of her reveries. " Who was she?"

" Miss Brownlow?" She raised her face, astonished. " Oh, dash it! How badly I'm telling it! Of course, Miss Brownlow was there all the time, all through our lives as far back as I can remember—until— until the war. She was our English governess—an English ambassadress, my papa used to say. And just think, in all the years she was with us, she never learned a single word of Slavonian! She was a ripping good sort." She bit her lip. " That's slang, isn't it?"

" Yes," said Milly, who had smiled.

" She was very severe about slang. You may use it when you speak, she would say, but never when you write. And we never did. Not that we wrote much," she added. " But how one *enjoys* those words, ripping, awfully, jolly, tophole. Anyway . . . where was I? The war, yes. Well, it was all right for a year and more, then one day in June—a lovely evening, we had been haymaking and we were drinking tea on the steps in front of the house—the Germans came. Up the drive, quite suddenly, and simply ruining it, of course. My father was so vexed. They stayed a longish time—I forget how long, a month or two anyway, then one day . . . oh dear, I must get it in order, to tell you properly . . . I had a boxer, you see. As a matter of fact I had several, because we had a beautiful bitch who bred just like a—like a machine, but this one was my favourite. He had the intelligence of a Jew, I can tell you. Oh he was splendid, in every way. And I had called him—well, ' Emperor '— you know, in German." She would not say the German word. " Now this name happened to please the German officer very much, and some- times I would catch him sneaking a bone to the dog and calling him by name—but do you think that dog would touch one of those bones? Ha! But back to the day.

"So on this day I am speaking of, it was after second breakfast and rather late, I'm afraid, and Miss Brownlow, who disapproved of our Slavonian custom of two breakfasts, was already upstairs. I and my aunt and my father and my brother were all in the dining-room and the officer stayed with us whilst I made the dog do tricks. The officer was laughing, you know—each trick made him laugh more until I thought he would never stop. But it was necessary to keep him in a good humour, of course. Well, all this time one could hear the soldiers stamping overhead, all over the house. Then a soldier came in and said something to the officer and he got up and went to the door, and just as he was going out, just as we were breathing sighs of relief, he turned round and called to my dog to come—and, naturally, he wouldn't obey. So the officer said—he was smiling, by the way—' That's Slavonian discipline, is it?' Then, addressing me personally, he said, still smiling: ' Would he come if *you* told him to?' And I thought, I'll show you what our dogs are like, so I said softly to my dog, ' Go! '— and, naturally, he went."

"Well . . . then the door closed and we heard a commotion and when we tried the door we found it locked. After a bit we heard trucks going off down the drive and a few shots and we managed to break a window but by then everybody had gone. They had taken some things, pictures, ornaments, and so on—also Miss Brownlow. They had tried to take the dog, too, but he had resisted. He was such a very powerful brute, a chest like a barrel and great snarling lips—at heart just a sentimental old fool, no more harmful than a kitten—ah, but when he showed his teeth! Anyway, that was how we found him—with his teeth all bared, and still snarling. I dare say Miss Brownlow resisted, too, but it wasn't so easy for her, so they took her to Ravensbruck and now," Sophie smiled, " she has gone back to Durham where she came from and we correspond very often."

Milly thought, why, I can *see* all that, about the dog. How—how *terrible*. Ravensbruck? It had an unwholesome yet familiar ring. *Picture Post*, or something? Where was I—then? Larry at his OCTU —I was in Camberley—clothes rationing—goodness, I remember *that* —and Pearl Harbour, of course, though that wasn't so bad. All she could find to say was: " You do speak wonderful English."

" We were never permitted to speak a word of Slavonian as children, Mrs. Purdoe. And through Miss Brownlow we learned to *love* England; the Royal Family and the English aristocracy, their culture and their polished manners, and the English officers too—even the Tommies, although simple peasants, nature's gentlemen. . . ."

At this point Miss Raven walked in, for once clad, doubtless due to some unprecedented emergency, in the uniform of her calling, a starched white apron. Casting a swiftly appraising glance at the contents of the plates on the tea-tray, her suspicions allayed, she grunted and said: " I'll be needing that fresh cream from downstairs in future. The stuff you got from the NAAFI's no good."

" Oh," said Milly. Then, with a flash of maternal perception, " Has Dermot been sick? "

" He has."

" Oh, *poor* Miss Raven," began Milly but already Sophie had bounded across the room and clasped Miss Raven by the hand.

" An English *Nanny*! " she exclaimed in ecstasy; then stepping back, the better to admire the paragon from top to toe: " A *real English Nanny*! "

Scandalised, Miss Raven snatched her hand away and backed towards the door. In desperation resorting to the ignoblest means in order to repair the damage, Milly gabbled: " This is the Countess Bielska, Miss Raven . . . the *Countess* Bielska, Miss Raven . . ."

" Oh, yes? " said Miss Raven, meaning, oh yeah? She was groping for the door handle and clung to it when she found it: " Delighted, I'm sure . . . but, as I say, Dermot's been sick . . ." and she fled.

Sophie heaved a sigh as the door shut.

" Such *charm*," she crooned, " such devotion to duty . . . ah, what a *noble* race . . ."

" I think I'm going to have a drink," said Milly. " What about you? "

" Oh, yes," said Sophie, happily, her thoughts elsewhere.

" What would you like? "

" Oh—anything—anything at all, whatever you have." Chuckling, striding up and down, she kept bursting into little snatches of song. " Oh, thanks. What's this? " She sniffed eagerly at the glass handed to her.

" Gin. Most of it."

" *No!* " Sophie stared at it for a second as if it were some magic elixir. " *English gin!* Oh! " Tilting her head back, she drank. " Wonderful! Oh, what a taste. It's for the connoisseur, that taste— so refined . . ."

Milly had watched this performance with interest.

" You . . . er . . . you drink a fair amount of gin, do you? "

Sophie roared with laughter. " Never before in my life! But how superb it is—how I feel it now, strong, good, warm as fire in my tummy! " Noting the expression on the face of her hostess, she winked naughtily: ' Miss Brownlow considered the *other* word most shocking, you know . . . S . . . T . . . O . . . M . . ."

" Let me get you some more. Now," said Milly, returning with a fresh glass, " I'll show you how we drink it. Like this."

" I *see*, now I see! The *English* way. How sensible—how dignified —not like us, coarse brutes that we are." She practised sipping. " True—this way one gets the full flavour . . . now, Mrs. Purdoe! " Suddenly without warning, grabbing her satchel, she sat bolt upright. " We will have our first lesson! "

" Oh, do you think . . . ? "

" A short introductory lesson." She unstrapped the satchel, which was crammed with books, took them all out, scanned their titles one by one, muttering under her breath, and then stuffed them all back again. " Ready? " she snapped, the lines of her face combined in a pattern of severity.

" Yes," said Milly. Equipped with notebook and pencil she sat down meekly beside her teacher. Sophie, humming to herself, took the notebook from her and opening it on her lap, in heavy sprawling capitals headed the first page: LESSON ONE.

" Lesson One," she repeated, studying this title as if to gain inspiration from it. She took a sip of gin. " Hm. Lesson One."

" We could have it to-morrow instead," pleaded Milly.

" No, certainly not. C'est le premier pas qui coûte and it's no good putting it off. Lesson One." She deliberated for a while, then turning to Milly with an air of resolve, said: " In my opinion—in view of your intelligence, Mrs. Purdoe, your English brain, you see, I think it's better we approach this language the *natural* way . . ."

" Let's start by your calling me Milly, then. That's my name." Too late she realised her mistake. Sophie leapt to her feet, seizing Milly's hands in hers.

" *Milly!* Oh, Milly. You darling! What a name—what a dear elegant little cosy name it is—oh, what pleasure! Mine, then, as indeed you know, is Sophie. Now we must drink what those swine call a Bruderschaft—you know—here, with gin. Oh, Milly! " Ten minutes later the lesson recommenced.

" The natural way, you were saying."

" That's it. Now let me see. All we need is a sentence—a simple sentence—anything will do. Hm. It's dashed difficult to think of one, isn't it? Hm. For instance—last night . . ." she frowned.

" The thunder kept me awake," suggested her pupil flippantly. It had, too.

" Excellent! " Sophie clapped her hands. " Bravo! Now I'll write it, look . . ." Muttering to herself, what a sentence, just right, perfect, what brains, English brains, she traced a series of hieroglyphics generously spaced, ornamented with macabre dots and outlandish

130

squiggles, all over the first page of the notebook. " There! " she said triumphantly. " Now listen! " She read it over aloud two or three times, very fast. " That's your first Slavonian sentence! "

Stunned, Milly gazed at the furrowed page. Although she was relieved to see that the letters approximated recognisably to the Latin script, there seemed to be a marked preponderance of the more formidable consonants, s, t, z, w, y, r, and so on, arranged in bristling clumps with not a vowel in sight on either side for miles.

" Just read it again, would you? " she said nervously. Gaily Sophie obliged. " There! Learn—repeat—learn—that's the way, easy as winking."

" Yes. I see. But——" Milly stared at it unhappily—" I mean, you know best, Sophie, but do you really think this is a good sentence to kick off with? "

" *Good?* " she cried loyally, beaming at the originator, " it's *marvellous*! "

" Well, I'm not sure that—for instance, what's the present tense of —well, *what is*: ' I am being kept awake '? It does seem rather a tricky verb, perhaps. Oughtn't I to start with to be or to have, or something? "

" Darling . . . this is the *natural* way. Still," she shrugged, " to be and to have—certainly you'll need to know them—wait, I'll write them down." She snatched the notebook and made her indelible ravages on the second page. " There. That's that. As for the present tense you asked for—' I am being kept awake '—hmmm . . . well, it's rather unnecessary to go into all that now. Later, perhaps. You see, darling, *this* sentence—and what an excellent choice!—luckily, *very* luckily, in fact—is *not* in the present." She was fairly purring with the logic of her reasoning. " It was *last night* you were kept awake by the thunder —am I right? "

" Well, yes," admitted Milly. " That's true."

" Ha! You see. Now, I'll explain—because that was an intelligent question you asked and I *welcome* questions—ask whenever you're puzzled, darling, and then we'll just stop and put our thinking caps on, you know, and well—well, puzzle it out." Milly replenished the glasses.

" You see, I am getting into your way of it, the sipping. I must say it's lovely, this gin. You know, I felt rather blue when I came here this afternoon—it's not the gin, though, it's you, being so friendly and nice. Where were we? "

" I think—the present tense? "

" Ah, well, I advise you to forget it for the moment. Frankly, it's rather difficult. All the same I'll give you a hint as to where the

131

difficulty lies. Now. Oh dear, now we come into deep waters "—she took a strengthening sip or two—" in the *present*, in this crude language of ours, the verb changes according to whether you want to be kept awake all night—on occasion, you know, I suppose one *might* . . ." she said doubtfully, wrinkling her nose.

"Yes," said Milly. "I see. It all depends."

"Exactly. It all depends. On whether you are lying there prepared to grin and bear it, or whether you *anticipate* it'll go on *all* night and you feel a bit ratty, or—or whether you've just woken up fresh as a daisy and don't mind a bit being kept awake or—in other words, in the *present*—a dashed difficult tense, I repeat, for the beginner—you don't know how long it'll go on, do you? The thunder, I mean—so you don't know how you'll *feel*—until it stops. You see?"

"Ah," said Milly. "Moods?"

"My God, how *infernally* quick you are!" She tossed off the remains of her gin in delight. "What a pleasure to teach! Moods, that's it. Tst . . . the curse of the present, those moods! But *this*, in the *past*—thank God—is easy. You were kept awake last night. That's all we need to know, all being over and done with. Understand?"

"I *think* I do," said Milly cautiously.

"It's really awfully nice, the past," said Sophie happily. "Really splendid . . ." She broke off, a look of disquietude dawning as the past tense in all its awful splendour, its various facets twinkling, revolved before her eyes. "Oh well, never mind!" she added hastily, diving forward to seize Milly's hand. "I can see you'll be a topping pupil—ha! those English brains." She got up, collecting her satchel and other bits she had shed. "Shall I come to-morrow?"

"Oh, yes." Milly smiled. "Please—and I'll have the thunder sorted out, I promise."

When Sophie had gone she looked at the notebook and laughed. She felt more cheerful than she had felt for weeks and pouring herself a drink, sat down by the stove. "Last night . . . the thunder . . . kept me awake . . ." She was to remember the sentence all her life.

Later on that evening Abe Schulman dropped in; that is, he came in and dropped straight on to the sofa.

"Give me a Scotch, Milly," he said, rubbing his face hard all over, as men do when tired and women never.

"You're tired," she said, surprisingly for her. Because Larry never demanded sympathy or solicitude—and indeed would have been astonished had she proffered either—she was rather accustomed to take for granted a certain physiological status quo between the sexes, the balance heavily in favour of the female, the masculine metabolism being permanently set at fair the better to service the requirements of the other

132

more delicate frame, which after all, and there could scarcely be any argument about it, constituted a man's main duty in life.

"That's so. I am tired. Go get me that Scotch, there's a good girl."

While she was pouring it she said: "I had my lesson."

"Is that so? How d'ya make out?"

"Well, she's a perfect duck, isn't she? Oh, I'm quite a star pupil."

"Yeah, I somehow guessed you would be. Thanks. Discuss the dough?"

"The——? Oh, I see. Oh no, nor we did."

"No, really?" He grinned in a way she didn't care for. "Well, would you do me one favour, Milly? Go right ahead and discuss it next time. Gee, it's sordid, I know . . . but don't let it slip your mind. She's going to need it, that dough."

"Why?"

"Why? For Chrissake—because she's gotta eat, that's why. She and her whole family. And I've got bad news for her. They say she can't go on working for me. So she depends on you now and what she picks up elsewhere."

"Oh dear . . ."

"Oh dear," he mimicked nastily. "Whassamatter—you afraid of the responsibility, or something? It's terrible, I know—it'll cost you per week approximately, let's see now, a bottle of gin—export price," he added. "Gosh, that's ruinous."

"Don't be silly, Abe—why, of course, I shall be delighted."

"Good girl. I knew if I put it the right way I could rely on you. God, I've got a headache. Give me another drink."

"What's the matter?"

"Oh, I dunno. Everything. First this about Sophie—then—well, I guess I'm sickantired of this goddam country . . . seems they're tightening up all round. When'll Larry be in?"

"He's gone to Slavnik—I thought you knew." She smiled down at him, handing him his glass.

"No," he said, "I didn't know." To her amazement, he sounded genuinely disappointed. "That's why I came round," he went on, eyeing her rather oddly, "to have a chat with him—and some Scotch."

Now he was flirting, of course. She laughed.

"If there's anything I can do . . . ?"

"You?" he said, almost rudely. "No, my dear. This is serious." His glass was empty again and he got up and poured himself some more. When he came back she could see from his face that he was indeed quite serious. "They've arrested a friend of mine up there. Just had a signal now."

"But, Abe, how awful. What's he done?"

133

" Done? You don't have to *do* anything to get arrested—you just put those old-fashioned democratic notions right out of your mind. Hell, I liked him, though—he was a swell guy. Used to share a room with me in the hotel in Slavnik—way back in the bad old days after the war. Used to file my copy when I was too boozed up to—oh many and many a time. God, if only I could *do* something about it . . ."

She watched him as he leaned against the mantelpiece, his fingers running through his hair, his head in his hands. She thought, he wants Larry—not me. And she—what did she want? Above all she wanted to keep him with her, to have him stay talking to her, because—well, partly because she was bored but also because she was suddenly, and for no reason she could name, afraid. She simply did not want to be alone until midnight, until Larry got back, in this great silent room with its dark corners, with only the sound of the trams, and the church bells, and the rain on the window panes outside.

" But what could you do, Abe? "

" Oh, I dunno." He sighed, and began pacing up and down. " You just feel you have to do *something*—but there's never anything to be done. Trouble is, this character hasn't even an American passport."

" Why not? "

He stopped in his tracks and even took his cigarette out of his mouth to look at her.

" Because he isn't an American," he said.

" Oh." In that case, she couldn't help wondering why he was making such a fuss. The event, which otherwise might have merited headline status, she relegated immediately to a couple of lines on a back page. " What was he? " she asked politely.

" I dunno *what* he was. I doubt he had any sort of passport—I never asked him, Milly. But you get something like this every month or so—it goes in cycles. An arrest, a flap, all sorts of quite extraneous characters get involved, then the ones they've got the skids under, the ones they want to get rid of—well, they get rid of them and then it dies down. Hell, I'm sorry it's him—all the same, I'm mighty glad it's not me. And that's about all you can say. The standard obituary." His big mouth was pulled to one side in self-derision. Although apparently listening with sympathetic attention, Milly wasn't really listening at all. She was thinking, he can't go now, he mustn't . . . make him stay . . . oh, make him stay . . . But Abe, giving his scalp one final massage, shook himself like a dog and walked over to the door.

" Whaddya say to a picnic to-morrow—you and Larry and the kids? " he added, taking his time, teasing her, almost.

" In this weather? "

" Oh, it'll be fine to-morrow." He smiled at her as if he judged that the weather, too, were at his disposal.

" We'd have to take Miss Raven."

" That houri. Sure—the more the merrier. We'll go up river. I know a place—the kids can pick mushrooms. I gotta case of champagne. How about it? "

" Oh, yes! If Larry can get the day off."

" Sure he can get a day off. He'll need it after Slavnik." He was kicking at the tassels on the curtain of the door. " I sort of figure he'll come back pretty depressed "—he grinned—" so you be good to him to-night." He lounged out of the room and slammed the door behind him. She heard him whistling all the way down the passage. Really— her cheeks burned—what very *odd* things he said. And he had left her alone.

*   *   *

" Darling, how I've missed you."

" You shouldn't have stayed awake." Larry bent over the bed, his greatcoat falling over her like wings. His face felt hard and frosty.

" Did you miss me? "

" Of course I did." He was pulling off his things. " God, that was a bloody cold drive."

" Love me? "

" Mm." He was looking around for a coat hanger, blinking, dazed by the light.

" *Say* you love me."

Throwing his coat over a chair, he came and sat down on the bed.

" What is all this? "

" Just *say* it," she insisted, sitting up and shaking her hair over her shoulders.

" I love you. Satisfied? " He yawned. " I could do with a drink." She had put on a discreet bedtime make-up, he noticed, and all at once he did feel extraordinarily tired.

" You know, Larry—it's funny, I'm always asking *you*—and yet you never ask *me*."

" Silly pussycat. I don't have to ask. I know you do."

" That's what I *mean*," she wailed as he got up.

" I wonder if Gisela remembered the soda."

" Oh, darling, you want a drink? Of course you do. Wait, I'll get you one, I'll get it—wait." She ran into the next room, her frills floating behind her. Amused, a little puzzled, he watched her standing

135

barefoot on the cold parquet, carefully mixing his drink. His brain, trained to observation, deduction, to-night, he was thankful to note, owing to fatigue was content merely to perform the first function, and that perfunctorily. He picked up her dressing-gown and slippers.

" Here, you'll catch your death." He wrapped the dressing-gown round her shoulders. " Put these on at once."

" No, first try this." She was bent on outdoing him, it seemed.

" Sweetie. Wonderful."

" Was it an awful day? "

" Long—and damn' cold. That place gets you down."

" Abe said you'd say that."

" Abe? He's in, is he? That's good. I've got to see him now. There's a flap on up there—I couldn't get a thing done. Pure waste of time."

" He said someone had been arrested."

" Mm." He seemed scarcely to be listening. " I think I'll give him a ring now. You go to bed."

" *No!* " she said pettishly.

Larry picked up the telephone. She went into the bathroom and began to make up all over again—a vivid one this time.

Larry came to the bathroom door. " He's coming over."

" Yes, I'm just going to put on some clothes."

" Darling." He gave her a little smile. Funny, though—it struck her it was almost a grimace. " You go to bed, there's a good girl. Abe and I have to talk."

She flounced past him into the bedroom, sat down at the dressing-table, and jabbing her fingers into a jar of cold cream slathered it over her stormy face. He was watching her, she knew. After a moment, she stole a glance at him in the mirror and his expression, puzzled, anxious, smote her quite unexpectedly to the heart.

" I haven't had a very nice day either," she said in her smallest voice, and began snivelling. It wasn't hard; she was really near to tears.

" I know, my pet." He slid his hand round her warm soft neck. " I'll try and make it a nice one to-morrow."

She stopped snivelling at once.

" Abe wants us to go on a picnic to-morrow."

" Fine. Why not? "

" You mean we can go? " She picked up her hair brush, her eyes cast down. When he was gone she would give her hair one hundred and fifty strokes.

" You silly baby," he said, dropping a kiss on the top of her head. " Of course we can go. Good night."

136

She started to brush, counting under her breath; a propitiatory ritual in view of which to-morrow must surely come up to scratch.

Then, in bed, listening drowsily to the murmur of their voices in the next room, she hugged herself: " The thunder won't keep me awake to-night." And suddenly remembered. " Blast. Oh, well, I can send a note or something. Yes, I must remember to do that." But she didn't, of course. She quite forgot.

Chapter Nine

THAT LIFE was both real and earnest, and as much the one as the other, was not merely the way it seemed to Herbert Wragg, but the way he had always assumed it should be; a conception which, without modification or compromise, had been dinned into him from his earliest youth; moreover, as he had simultaneously been taught to shun the kind of experience which might have caused him to take a more lenient view, small wonder that it had yet to be disproved. Instead, once planted in his mind it had taken root, and deep roots at that, and had developed into the sturdy shape of a principle long before principles had any business there at all; an open mind was a luxury he had never been allowed to enjoy. At the age of thirty-six he found himself still clinging to it as a principle, partly—and he was not blind to it—out of habit, and partly for want of a better one; in short, he still clung to it, but rather as a drowning man clings to a spar, that is, with a desperation that was very far removed from the innocent fervour with which he had embraced it in youth.

There was no doubt that latterly he had been bothered by misgivings; even, one might say, that in his attitude a certain disaffection had set in. Why, for instance, if life were real and earnest, was it patently not so for everybody, and why, if it was intended to be so for him, if he had been singled out, as it would have been some consolation to believe, should it be *so* real and *so* earnest, that is, to such an appalling degree? Without ever arriving at a satisfactory explanation of either of these anomalies, lately he had taken to pondering them as and when they presented themselves to his mind—in between dreams.

As an " adolescent " (the term by which his parents had persisted in referring to him, it not being their custom to spare his blushes throughout the corresponding period) he had had his idle dreams, certainly, but on recognising them as such, he had smothered them with a promptitude and ruthlessness which had done him credit. Then the full life (politics and pacifism) had claimed him, during which time, ten years or so, he had not been troubled by them at all; he had thought them extinct. But his recent misgivings had coincided with a recurrence of the dreams, even fostered them, perhaps; or the other way about, he couldn't be sure now which had come first, they were so inextricably mixed. Yes, perhaps the other way about, because whereas the misgivings were still in their infancy, exploratory and

138

timorous, the dreams were hardy old-timers; nothing young about them. Tough, wiry, they weren't so easy to smother; they struggled, and one or two, one in particular, seemed to have as many lives as a cat. It kept rearing its by no means unattractive head; even slinking up on him unawares, purring, sidling around the back of his brain. If he didn't look out, it was on the way to becoming a pet.

In moments of despair, and poor Herbert had them along with everybody else, he was inclined to wonder whether after all he had not been defeated, worsted by his principle, because in these moments it rather appeared as if his life—at any rate one side of it, the more pleasurable side, when he was alone, in the bath, or walking to and from the office—far from being either real or earnest, was in a fair way to becoming the dreadful alternative—one long idle dream.

If this were so, and if he were to accept the conclusion to which it led, namely, that things were not what they seemed, his precious principle was no more than a hoax and he had been played a dirty trick somewhere along the line—that would mean, for one thing, a reassessment of the whole affair, and for another, that all his—well, sacrifices?—no, sacrifices were what one's parents made, he ought to know, he had been told often enough—all *his* efforts and *their* sacrifices had been in vain. With speculations like these he flagellated his soul.

His father, an ironmonger by trade, had started life with one rather small but handily-situated shop on the outskirts of Nottingham, and by the time his only son had reached the age of puberty (a term which, curiously enough, never achieved anything like the popularity of the more beastly-sounding "adolescence" in the enlightened conversation of the Wragg household) he had become the owner of a thriving business in the centre of the town. The family no longer lived "over the shop"; instead, they had moved to a nice residential quarter, to a villa, detached, three up four down and a gents, and Mrs. Wragg had a woman in twice a week to do the front. As to the formula for success, Wragg senior defined it with the rugged candour that was his characteristic, thus: " Drive a hard bargain but don't do the other fellow down; he's bound to find out." In other words honesty was the policy of Mr. Wragg, and an exceedingly profitable one it had proved.

Mr. Wragg was also a member of the Town Council, much admired for his forthrightness—cantankerousness, as it was unkindly termed by some—and appreciated by one and all (but never by all at once) for his " blockage " value; when it came to a vote, and Mr. Wragg's the casting one, all that was required was a whisper of the words "moral issue"—or—"conscience"—or—"matter of principle" for him to dig his heels in like a mule, and like a mule he was not thereafter to be budged. He was renowned, too, for his eloquence, and if ever a speaker failed the Rotarians reaped the benefit of that.

Both Mr. and Mrs. Wragg had early in life become converts of a free-thinking religious sect whose doctrines because ungilded, not to say unvarnished—being hewn from the sound, plain stuff of common sense—had proved of special appeal; in accepting which they had also acquired proficiency (although possibly both were naturally talented) in the craft of combination—a sort of spiritual carpentry whereby might be achieved, and so neatly as to make the joins barely perceptible, a dovetailing of the demands of both God and Mammon.

They managed to combine broadmindedness in respect of broad issues with intolerance in respect of petty ones in their domestic affairs; an attitude of charitable benevolence towards almost any geographically distant, sufficiently prolific and down-trodden bunch of strangers with a parsimonious severity towards their kith and kin; a naïveté, almost a childish simplicity as regards their expectations of the after-life with a healthy ambition to outstrip their next-door neighbours in the present one. Liberal in their public donations, frugal as to housekeeping and pocket-money, forbearing on Sundays, pernickety and fault-finding during the week, they were not as other mortals and they knew it; as certainly as they did not know that in being so they deprived themselves of many mortal pleasures too.

Herbert, their only child, of whom they had high hopes, was given no quarter. When he was not actually engaged in swotting for exams his free time was spent thus: on Sundays, Meetings for Worship (no Sunday papers); after Evening Meeting, useful hobbies (leather-work, his favourite, because of the rich smell and feel of the leather, although he would have blushed to confess it); on Thursdays, Discussion Groups in the front room, which he was permitted to attend in order to broaden his mind and hand round coffee; No More War Movement on Fridays, Sign the Pledge rallies every other Saturday, and on Mondays and Tuesdays, after prep, he would jaunt off on his bicycle distributing the King-Hall News Letter to outlying hamlets. So he was kept pretty busy. Sometimes, when his schoolfellows spoke of football matches, the cinema, the pantomime, he would listen in wonder, but without much envy; he was not as they, and therefore such frivolities were not for him.

His parents were loving in their way, just, according to their lights, and willing to make any and every sacrifice for his benefit. This word benefit—a favourite of theirs—was one he learned to dread, as being thoroughly tricky and open to a hundred interpretations, a word all too easily modified, planed down to suit; *real, lasting, eventual, ultimate*—which automatically ruled out a lot of simple things it now

140

and then occurred to him might be of immediate if merely temporary benefit. Furthermore, to encourage his development he was often allowed, in matters demanding those trivial decisions which are far more teasing and taxing than great ones, what they considered to be a free hand, partly to test him and partly to prove to themselves—as if proof were needed—what liberal, go-ahead parents they were. It would never have occurred to them that in foisting such decisions upon him they were asking too much. For instance: one occasion (he never forgot it) was when he was about thirteen years old, and a circus came to the town. Placards had been posted up everywhere and his school-fellows talked of nothing else. Herbert Wragg suddenly conceived a desire to go to that circus; that is to say, he wanted to go to it more than anything else in the world. By Sunday evening such was his state of excitement and desperation that after high tea he hinted as much to his mother. There was no immediate discernible reaction, this not being her way, but by Monday lunchtime a sixth sense told him that the project had been "put" to his father. He was kept on tenter-hooks until the middle of the week, by which time there was not a boy in the school except himself who had not been to the circus at least once. Then it so chanced that he caught sight of rival placards posted in the town, and his heart gave a jolt. A London company was coming down that very next week to perform *The Doctor's Dilemma*. Herbert, who had won more than one prize for Eng. Lit., that very night at tea was faced with his own dilemma. "The circus or the play," they said, "it is up to you." They watched him, his father gravely, his mother proudly, over lettuce and tinned salmon. A terrible test, but one that he passed with flying colours. He went to the play and loathed Shaw forever after.

Far from brilliant, he was hardworking and, shielded from the distractions which beset his fellows, forged ahead, eventually winning a scholarship to the school upon which his parents had set their heart; a co-educational establishment run on the progressive principles of the religious society to which they belonged. He liked being at school, even from the start. He was gratified to see the tears in his mother's eyes as she said good-bye to him. He enjoyed the journey into another county, obtaining a really solid satisfaction from counting the miles and months which stood between him and his parents. He revelled in his status as a boarder, and he found it a great relief to be one of a crowd. He liked his work, he quite liked one or two of the masters, he began to like football and he even liked the food—but he didn't like the girls. Lest there be the least suspicion of ambiguity on this point, let it be said at once that it was not so much that Herbert actually *dis*liked them—no, what he disliked was the distraction caused by their presence; it worried him.

There is no doubt that when the sexes are forced to congregate in large numbers during the years of adolescence, so coming into direct competition with each other in the classroom and at the dining-table, there does exist between them a curious basic antagonism—far more conspicuous and powerful than the little gusts of flirtatious hysteria which spring up alongside and as quickly die down. When placed side by side, feeding, or at their desks, they appear like creatures of two different species, and naturally hostile ones, at that; as different as whites from blacks, each sensitive to the other's distasteful and peculiar smell, due, in the case of the males, to simple unwashedness, and in that of the females to the neglect of more mysterious rites.

The girls also had certain natural advantages which they were not slow to exploit, possibly inspired by some subconscious desire to revenge their kind for centuries of subjection, and instinctively aware that now was the moment; they were never likely to have it so good again. However that may be, it is indisputable that the female of the species, Anglo-Saxon, in the process of budding into womanhood, develops both physically and mentally far more rapidly than the male. She is bigger and heavier and cleverer than her opposite number of corresponding age. The presence of the girls was generally acknowledged by the boys to be a distraction, but it was far more than that, inculcating as it did in all but the stoutest of hearts a sense of their masculine inferiority, and thus causing all manner of grave and interesting complexes from which few can ever have recovered.

As for Wragg, who was in any case unused to women, himself overgrown, weedy and further handicapped by a stutter, these great creatures with their plaits and their black-stockinged thighs and bulging shelves beneath gym-slips, their pert back-answers in class, their giggles and their sarcasm, inspired in him a mortal terror mixed with a very deep respect. What was more—as if superiority in size and wits were not enough—he early recognised them to be possessed, at least in the conditions obtaining—suffering as both sexes did the common yoke of masculine authority, of some incalculable additional advantage denied to their male school-fellows; it was a factor that in after life became even more apparent, and one he was never to underestimate. So far as women were concerned, Wragg threw in his hand almost at the outset. The dice were loaded all the other way.

Towards the end of his school career, when war was already judged to be inevitable, a publication called *Out of Bounds* was insinuated into the school. A rabid little journal, out for blood, its politics bright red, in flavour smacking of revolution not to say anarchy, it was calculated to appeal to anyone chafing under authority, and to encourage a sort of blind defiance to any and every rule of social behaviour. Wragg,

142

after slight persuasion and a flatteringly subversive correspondence with a real newspaper office in London, was appointed agent for the sale and distribution of this journal within the school. The responsibility caused him to blossom out in quite startling fashion, as an "intellectual" and a "character"; indeed, he became so absorbed in all three ventures that he neglected preparations for his final exams, sat them in a dreamy daze, a week later woke up to the fact that in all likelihood he had failed and, tortured with remorse, long before the results were out, he ran away from school and fled to his new friends in London.

These young gentlemen were by no means so keen to receive him in his present state, penniless and a fugitive, as he had been led to expect. Still, he was allowed to consider that in flouting authority he had struck a blow, however puny, for the cause, and they consented to employ his services, for which Wragg was humbly grateful. His father, finally tracking him down, was horrified to find young Herbert selling the *Daily Worker* outside Golders Green Tube Station. Mr. Wragg escorted his son, by now thoroughly chastened, back to Nottingham, where he was confined to his bedroom and forced to endure daily monologues from his father and wounded silence on the part of his mother until the examination results were announced. By some miracle, he had achieved a respectable pass. His enrolment at the London School of Economics coincided with the outbreak of war; and soon after, when his call-up papers arrived, he declared himself, to his parents' joy, a conscientious objector.

He was sent to work on a farm. However, proving himself to be not merely inept but of lethal menace with a bill-hook, apparently incapable of grasping the art of milking, the great swinging udders affecting him with a kind of neurosis which set his teeth a-chatter, willing but grossly inaccurate when it came to chucking muck, before long he was relieved of his duties on the land. It was a problem to know what to do with him; it seemed he fitted nowhere into the pattern of total war, not even the background. Then, through the influence of his father and the good offices of the religious society patronised by him, once the bombing had died down a job was arranged for Herbert with a refugee organisation in Russell Square. Here he found his spiritual home, and during the happy period which followed, met his fate. A two-fold fate; nothing could be simple for Herbert. He fell in love and he married Olga.

His love was a girl called Wendy who wore her blonde hair flowing to her shoulders and moved from the hips in a walking-on part at the Unity Theatre. Before meeting Wendy, Wragg had used to spend one evening a week at the Young Communists' League Headquarters, addressing envelopes, one with the No More War boys, and another

143

at Student Movement House; the other four evenings in his digs, making jottings for a pamphlet to be entitled " The Art of Living." Overnight, this routine was abandoned and his habits were transformed along with his thoughts, his dreams, his appetite and his appearance. Thereafter he spent most evenings in and around the Unity waiting for Wendy.

This placid scheme of things continued in the face of national disaster for quite some time. Wendy had many admirers but she was unexpectedly kind to Wragg, eventually allowing him, greatly to his own surprise, to kiss her in the black-out, leaning up against a lamp-post in Mecklenburgh Square. On this first occasion he was conscious of her rubbery lips and then of her cavernous mouth and of their teeth clashing together in no uncertain manner. It was a curious and not altogether pleasant sensation, saved by Wendy who achieved the slight adjustment necessary for perfect contact. On the second occasion the kissing went without a hitch. He also discovered that her breasts were large and rubbery, like her lips, rather malleable, an exquisite and novel delight. A week later he had still not recovered from the experience, remembering the smell of her hair, heathery, and of her breath, sardines and peppermint, like that of the nicest sort of cat. After that he thought very seriously about Wendy, and as a prelude to whatever he had in mind, he decided to invite her on a Ramble.

It was the custom on a Sunday morning for a score of young people of his acquaintance to assemble at a given rendezvous and then board a Green Line bus bound for the countryside. Once there, in a drove or splitting up into couples, they would tramp through muddy fields, stopping to eat sandwiches in a hedgerow, then tramp some more, finishing up with high tea at that particular café where the Ramble Leader obtained a cut rate. After tea there would be a singsong, quite rowdy, " Green Grow the Rushes " and " The Leather Bottèl " and so on, when those girls without men (there were never enough men to go round, and such as there were, mostly teeny) would launch into the descant, under cover of which their luckier sisters would grab for shy hands beneath the tables. Then the party would take the last bus home.

When Wragg, having described the delights of these excursions to Wendy, tentatively popped the question, she, to his surprise and joy, accepted without demur. Unwisely he allowed her a week's notice of the event. The next Sunday morning he waited at Hyde Park Corner, dressed, like the others, in shorts and stout boots, equipped with ruck-sack and alpenstock, his heart beating fast beneath his leatherette golfing jacket. Wendy was late, and when at last she appeared, her fair locks flying in the wind, wearing a red tam o' shanter and looking wonderfully pretty, she was accompanied by two strangers, a young man and

144

another person whom Wragg, speechless with distress, barely registered as female.

"Herbie!" Wendy danced up to him, laying a hand on his arm. "I'm not late, am I? It was Jumbo held us up. Jumbo, this is Herbie, like I told you." She distributed the warmth of her smile evenly between them. "And this is Olga," she went on—ah, base, perfidious Wendy. "A foursome's cosy, I always say."

All Wragg could say was, very sternly, "Here's your ticket, Wendy." Then he turned his back on them, pulling up the collar of his jacket. The cold wind whipped his bare shanks but he felt it in the pit of his stomach. Behind his back Wendy winked at the others as the Green Line bus trundled into sight.

In the bus she did sit next to him, however, because of the ticket, and after a bit, inclining her stubborn head to his, she whispered: "Like my friend? Guess what? He's in the R.A.F. Fighters." Then added tactlessly, "Don't tell the others—'cos they're just a lot of half-baked conchies, aren't they? So better not."

"No, better not," said Wragg, too deep in misery to be sensitive to insult. "You're pretty keen, I suppose?" he went on, lapsing into school slang.

"I'm nuts about him," she said simply. He sighed, and she squeezed his hand. Then in her kind way, wishing him to have the next best thing if he could not have her, she whispered cunningly: "What d'you think of Olga? Rather your type, I'd say." Unwillingly, Wragg swivelled his gaze across the bus and for the first time took account of the joker that Wendy had so deceitfully slipped into her hand to complete her cosy four.

Whoever she was, Wragg knew at once that this was no joker. Sensing his eyes upon her she turned her head and gave him that familiar look, the sort he always got and which he had deluded himself he need not suffer again—brooding, calculating, faintly contemptuous, pregnant with all kinds of meaning, mostly sinister. He looked away —Kilburn High Street and it had come on to rain. Of course he hadn't an earthly and he knew it, but out of sheer bravado he began humming to himself.

So Olga, then as now determined, jealous, radiating a malevolence towards the world at large, with then as now a sprinkling of black hairs on her upper lips, entered his life.

* * *

It was a long time before he made love to her. At first he accepted her as a convenience; he was lonely and she was an easy companion, that is, she would meet him faithfully at the places where he told her to meet him, wait hours at chilly bus-stops without complaining, sit in gallery queues, keeping his place, throughout paying scrupulously for herself, and her gloomy disposition suited Wragg's own; they neither of them talked much. It was not positively unpleasant to feel her hand on his arm, to have her nag him as to whether he had or had not eaten (they rarely ate together), remonstrate with him when he forgot his raincoat, inquire after his cold. Their association might have continued in this fashion indefinitely had not Wendy, one fine spring evening almost a year later, telephoned. He knew he was still in love with her the moment he heard her voice.

"Herbie, my pet!" she said. "Guess what? Congratulate me, I'm going to be married. Guess who? Yes, you met him. On Saturday —oh, I can't tell you—isn't it just—but what I rang up to say was, we're having a party. Oh, you *must*. Please."

So Wragg went, not to the wedding, but to the party, where there were men of a sort he had never met before in his life. "Whizzo!" —"Whacko!"—"Gone for a burton!"—they bawled, as the champagne corks dispersed in all directions, and Wendy looked so beautiful that he could only regard as a delusion of memory the occasions when he had kissed her. "Herbie!" she shrieked, putting her arms round his neck, her veil thrown back, cheeks flushed, a tiny speck of lipstick on her teeth. "Wish me luck! Where's his glass—give Herbie more pop!" He had lost her.

Afterwards he returned to Bloomsbury by tube, bought an evening paper in Southampton Row and allowed his feet to clump through the black-out in the direction of Olga's door. He rang the bell. She let him in and glancing at his face, never uttered a word.

Olga was to owe much to her behaviour that evening. On rare occasions a notoriously capricious Providence, perhaps from a bad conscience, attends to her ugly ducklings, taking them under her wing, indulging them even; not merely allowing the ill-favoured, the forlorn, a first and last chance, but also allowing them to appreciate it as such. On these occasions a plain woman may, by means of a trivial trick, the wearing of a certain shade, the cooking of a certain dish, a certain intuitive remark, or, more often, simply by keeping her mouth shut, win a disproportionately great reward. She may never again rise to such heights—but that once is usually enough. In this case Olga's inspiration took the form of silence, coupled with a freak of extravagance —a bottle of port.

Wragg lay back in an arm-chair, staring into the gas fire and still hearing Wendy's voice. The champagne at the wedding had made him feel rather queer, at the same time he felt like going on drinking. Olga, he realised vaguely, was struggling with some object in a corner, but he could not be bothered to turn his head. He heard a faint pop and then two tiny glasses filled with ruby liquid swam miraculously into view.

" What on earth? "

She knelt before him, all devotion, the light from the fire supporting her nobly, touching only those curves which served her best. " It's port . . ." she murmured. Her black eyes gleamed as she sat back on her haunches. " I thought you might feel like a drink." She even smiled. Then, wisely, she became silent; quite passive, when Wragg, mysteriously losing height after a couple of glasses, slid on to the hearthrug and began caressing her there. Later, on the divan, she tended to be fierce—but that again was all to the good; in spite of the port, he might otherwise never have made it. There was no faulting Olga that night.

* * *

Of course the affair was by no means concluded; it was by no means so simple as that. Wragg was a tricky fish to play, and although hooked he was not landed yet. Six months later, after much bickering, after some resourceful but sadly ineffectual dodging on his part countered by an easily-engineered but sufficiently horrific abortion on hers, after the delivery of countless coy ultimata, and this subterfuge finally worn threadbare, after its exposure; after tears, recriminations, sleepless nights spent thrashing it out—gas, a whiff of a threat of it, perpetually in the air and then, just clumsiness probably, a near do with a train door—after a whole war waged by different camps of friends, a parting that was intended to be final and a reunion that was not—for better or for worse, they married.

Chapter Ten

" THERE THEY GO," muttered Olga Wragg, behind the curtain. She breathed on the window pane, rubbing it with her sleeve. After a pause, during which her excitement mounted, she said: " It's the limit, Herbert."

Wragg waited, steeling himself to the inevitable, as had become his habit in defence of his sanity against the maddening trick of repetition which had become one of hers.

" I said, it's the limit, Herbert."

Now that it had come and gone he experienced the familiar faint spasm of relief—as though a tiny bubble had broken. No matter that it was merely the first to detach itself and that a string of others were to follow, bigger, brighter, bouncier—this one, at any rate, had been pricked.

" It is, isn't it? The limit? " Irked at receiving no audible response, Mrs. Wragg snatched the dainty nylon curtains aside and thrust her stormy face between.

" Yes," said Wragg, chasing honeygrains round his plate.

" Didn't even let you know, I suppose."

Strictly speaking, this was a statement, and as such required no answer; nevertheless, he hastened to respond lest she should presume upon his hardness of hearing and chalk up another.

" He sent a note, as a matter of fact."

" Oh, he did, did he? " She grunted, and then spun round, pressing her nose to the glass, fearful of missing some potential cause for grievance. " Office car," she intoned with satisfaction, " as well as Schulman's . . . and there's Vladek—well, I don't know"—although of course she did—" office driver—*and* office petrol, that goes without saying . . . Herbert! " Her head emerged, ludicrous amongst the frills. " You'll never let him get away with that! " She paused. " I said, you'll *never* . . ."

" No," mumbled Wragg, bogged down, chomping the splintery yet cloying breakfast food.

Appeased, she turned back to her post. " I can see you'll have to walk to the office to-day! "

" I always do." Wragg cut himself a piece of brown bread.

" Yes—but to-day you'll *have* to." Her ill-humour had passed.

" Purdoe," Wragg observed wistfully, " tells me they have toast for

148

breakfast. All one has to do is to buy a grill. They're quite cheap, he says."

"Toast?" She sprang out from behind the curtain. "Toast? What—and destroy all those vitamins? *Carbonise* them?" Her display of emotion would have done credit to a post-war journalist wallowing in the horrors of Auschwitz. "Yeast is a living thing, Herbert—it has special properties." She tossed her head. "I do actually know what I'm talking about," she added, with that vaguely allusive air of grandeur which usually sufficed to silence him. To-day, albeit defeated, he stuck to his guns.

"I just happen to like toast," he said doggedly.

What had come over him? She stared at him. Then, pensive, she returned to her vantage point. All right then, she would *buy* a grill, he should *have* his toast—but unreasonably she blamed this future complication of her morning routine on a certain figure now active in the scene below. Forgetting her annoyance, Olga gave herself up to pure enjoyment.

"*She's* going in Shulman's car," she reported over her shoulder. "Hm. That Nanny's got her hands full. . . . Well, what I mean to say is, if you can't manage your own two children, that's an admission of failure, I should say."

"But you *are* saying it," said Wragg, but not aloud—his inner man said it for him—" and you've said it before and God knows this won't be the last time, either," continued the I.M., who was rather a stout-hearted chap.

"Ridiculous!" exclaimed Olga, and such was his state of nerves that he jumped. "Quite ridiculous. You'd think they were going off to the North Pole." From this remark he interpreted, correctly, that Milly was in furs. "Three baskets. *And* a crate. Don't have to guess what's in there, do we?—not with Abe Schulman around. So you see," she turned to him with glee, " if they ring up from Slavnik, you'll just have to tell them you're all on your own. Holding the fort," she added, inadvertently seduced into the use of an abhorred cliché. "You'll have to tell them, Herbert, won't you? I'm sorry, you'll say—they're all out for the day."

His I.M. whispered mutinously, " If you have to tell them anything you certainly don't tell them that."

"Don't worry," said Wragg, reaching for his coat, " I'll tell them that."

"I might get that grill this morning," Olga said to herself, slapping the plates together in triumph as she cleared away. "Really, it's been worth it."

*   *   *

149

"All set?" Larry poked his head into the window of Abe's Citroën. "We'll follow you."

"So if you want to stop, you must stop too," said Milly.

"There'll be no stopping to-day, Milly. Don't you give way to her, Abe—this woman has a mania for stopping."

"I won't. We go there straight. Okay, we're off."

The Citroën nosed its way between the trams.

"Whats this stopping racket? I don't get it."

"Oh." It was a joke, she realised, that she shared with Larry. "I just like to stop if I see anything I fancy. Apples—eggs, maybe flowers. It makes Larry wild."

"It would make anyone wild. Why, for heaven's sake? You can buy them all in town."

"Mm, I know—but it's not the same thing. In the country—well, they're bound to be cheaper for one thing, and fresher, too. There they are, just *growing*—and somehow it hurts me to let them go by. One's meant to profit from nature," she added smugly.

"That's one way of putting it. Seems to me more like the eternal lure of a bargain. Anyway, what's nature got to do with it? Damn' all—as you'd know if you were a country girl. Someone's had to grow the flowers and feed the hens."

Milly was not accustomed to being taken up in this fashion. Sulking, she withdrew into her corner, and Abe laughed.

"You women, you're all alike. Acquisitive and greedy."

"That's just your personal opinion," Milly said sharply. She was annoyed. "Based on your experience, of course." She sniffed. "Which, I dare say, has been broad."

"Oh, sure, sure. Of broads, the broadest." He began to whistle and after a bit she looked round at him slyly. What a strange face he had—strangely attractive, although it was full of mistakes; the nose too large and fleshy, the lips too full and curly, the heavy black eyebrows unnecessarily emphasising the brow—which was impressive enough without that; the chin was obstinate, there was even the trace of a double chin. All the features were outsize and highly individual; each coolly asserting its independence, mischievously upsetting any tame notions as to harmony, team-spirit or design. This impression— as a whole, a restless and not especially happy one—you saw if you looked close was not created by mere accident of shape or size; each feature seemed to suggest a private history, as though each had matured separately, some jolted into maturity—the mouth, for instance —others naturally in their own time; the whole added up only when you looked at the lines. There were a lot of lines. Some of the lines were mistakes, too, and there was space for further mistakes and yet—

well, it was a comfortable face, that was how it struck her. It was like a not very new, even shabby, but familiar bed, with one or two of the springs gone but with plenty of bounce left in it; you could still bounce to the ceiling if you so pleased—although perhaps this one had been bounced on rather too much and showed it. Most of the lines were curves, adaptable, and springy, so that even the mistakes were oddly attractive, fitting in just where you would expect them to be—all except for one line. A rather small hard line at the corner of the mouth, at first glance it seemed to be a total outsider, a hanger-on, and yet even so it possibly had certain duties to perform—to remind the owner of the face of this and that, or to restrict the mouth from grinning too wide, occasionally to throttle down that great laugh, that sort of thing; because this little sneering line was practically all that the face possessed in the way of bodyguard. It never relaxed, whilst the others were in a constant state of flux. Yet once or twice already she had seen the face take shape, become a set piece set around that single hard line, and when that happened all the others became as taut as could be, merely the most economical lines of communication between certain points, no slack anywhere, no leeway for humour or mistakes; cut deep, to last. Then it became a face of exceptional power, as formidable as any she had ever come across, and not comfortable at all. She had seen it like that, and it gave her a definite thrill of pleasure to know that it could look like that; nevertheless, she preferred it as it was to-day.

And he was such a big man—that was nice. Two big men, she had to-day, the attentions of both devoted exclusively to herself; more, their very thoughts. At this moment—she hugged herself with glee— they are both thinking of me. To-day, on this picnic, everything centres round me. Everybody is thinking of me. The children are thinking of me, and so is Miss Raven—or if she isn't she ought to be. And so is Gisela thinking of me—it's an outing for her and a very pleasant one for which she has me to thank. And the driver—even he's probably thinking how best to please me, get round me, that is. So they are all mine—for to-day at least. Now I feel happy and it will be a day to remember—a happy day.

It had become her custom thus rapidly to weigh up the various factors, circumstances, attendant upon an expedition of this sort, and then, depending on the estimate arrived at—" To-day I shall (or shall not) be happy," she would say to herself. And although one might have supposed that this didactic and rather heavy-handed approach to something as evanescent as the glitter of a dragon-fly's wing, no more to be bullied than the wind, no more to be grasped than a rainbow, would have defeated its own ends, her will power was such that once

151

having decided that she was happy she was—and who is to say she was not? The converse also applied: thus a day in Milly's company might well progress from bad to worse, but it was unlikely to start off badly and end up well, or the reverse; her authority over herself was too strict for that. The fact of her having arrived at a favourable conclusion to-day was, as Larry would have appreciated, at the very least a good augury for the picnic.

She had adopted this curious procedure ever since the night of her thirtieth birthday, when, as she always did on every birthday, reviewing her life with an objectivity which would have done credit to a staff officer at a de-briefing, she had remarked that the total number of occasions which she could recall as " happy " ones were few and far between; yet many had existed, and so they must have slipped through her fingers unrecognised and unrecorded, and she had been cheated. Now she disliked above all things to be cheated—especially by something so intangible, transitory and yet, she was convinced, if she but kept her wits about her, biddable as happiness, so she made up her mind to put a stop to it, by disciplining herself, and it too, the slippery thing. Its appearances were altogether too casual—in future there must be none of this sneaking off before she had even had time to recognise it; the whole business must be on a more formal basis. In future *she* would stipulate those occasions, more, even *make* them, on which she expected happiness to turn up on parade, and see to it that it obeyed. That way, surely, there could be no cheating; that way, at least, she would have all that it seemed one could hope to have in the way of profit—the record of its presence on those occasions, whether a moment, an hour, or a day, now and for ever more.

It never occurred to her that she was cheated by nothing and nobody so much as by herself. There was no need, considering her circumstances, to make occasions for happiness; every day might have been a happy one. She enjoyed good health and looks, had a loving husband, charming children, sufficient money and an interesting and varied life —not one real care in the world, nor had she ever known one. Had she examined the matter more critically, instead of casting a hasty glance at it and then going straight ahead in her steamroller fashion, disciplining herself the better to snatch, she might have observed that the auguries which inclined her to decide on a happy day were as readily recognisable, indeed, being unvarying, as their malignant counterparts which caused her to decide the opposite. A happy day was a day which started off well and went according to plan, her plan, any deviations from which were due to charming little whims of her own with which everyone else fitted in. An unhappy day was likely to be when for some reason or another things shaped differently—you could tell from the start—

and she did not get her own way, and someone, or on memorably disastrous occasions, people—did not fit in.

But Milly would never have examined the matter in such an uncomfortable light and reduced it to proportions of such absurd simplicity, partly because her reasoning was apt to be exceedingly faulty—although she would have been the last to admit it—and partly from a sub-conscious desire to preserve her illusions intact; that is, from sheerly instinctive motives of self-protection. In other words, whilst admirable at assessing the contributory factors towards her fleeting spells of contentment or dissatisfaction she was innately incapable of linking these directly with the corresponding results, a flaw in her character which accounted for not a few of her many " blind spots." Genuinely puzzled by the frequency with which "unhappy" days came her way, sadly she observed—without dreaming of hingeing cause and effect—that as frequent were the occasions when she was surprised, grieved or disappointed at the behaviour of others, regrettably independent or awkward as it might be. Similarly, to-day for instance, whereas she could say with one breath, the thoughts of them all are centred on *me*, and with the next, *I* am happy, she was incapable of hinging the two with the simple word "therefore," because that would have formed an equation fundamentally unacceptable to her, one which could never have withstood even the most cursory examination because examination would have nullified the result. It would have made her unhappy, and happiness was what she still, naïvely enough, desired most from life.

* * *

As it was, the thoughts of the members of the picnic party at the moment pinpointed by Milly were not converging on any particular centre. Instead, as might have been expected, they were running haphazardly on various tracks and, in the case of each person, simultaneously on two levels: an upper and visible circuit; and that lower, but not necessarily subsidiary one which, plunging from view, pursues its devious course in and out those tunnels, grooves, blind alleys that honeycomb the mind, where the light of day and sanity never penetrates and whence the thoughts that enter emerge, if they emerge at all, as juggernauts, hurtling on to the upper circuit; but for each rare one of those a dozen more, going astray in the gloomy labyrinth, remain there, never to be thought of again.

They ran roughly as follows:

Abe was worrying about the champagne and concerned with avoiding the holes in the cobbles because it was likely to prove undrinkable if bounced up in the back, and he was also wondering whether there would be a telegram waiting for him on his return that evening,

153

and if so, what news it would contain, whether his friend who was being thrown out had in fact been thrown out or into prison, and whether he would, as he had once said he would in either eventuality, hang himself by the neck until he was dead.

In the other car, Larry was considering whether he had been justified in taking a day off, and speculating on what shape disaster, if it misconstrued his absence as a *carte blanche* invitation to materialise, would be likely to take, and whatever it was, whether Wragg could cope; and he was also consciously grateful for the fine weather and conscious, without any particular sense of gratitude, of Miss Raven's muscular thigh pressing into his own.

Miss Raven was thinking that she had forgotten Dermot's Thermos of milk which she had left on the kitchen table and was wondering whether, in view of his aversion to that beverage, she could rely on him as an accomplice in order that the omission should not be discovered by his mother. She was also cranking up the machine of fantasy, sluggish to-day, as always when the grit of reality, e.g. Larry's thigh next her own, sanded up the works. Still, she reckoned she had an hour, and she was already fixed up in a red chiffon gown cut low in the bosom, lying back in a rattan chair, the tropic moon like a gold coin sailing high in the black velvet sky pricked with stars. The drums were throbbing down in the native quarter and she was sipping her Martini, when all of a sudden Larry J. Mason dashed lithely up the steps.

" I don't want to alarm you, Lady Featherstone." He kissed her hand rather hurriedly. He had turned pale beneath his tan. " But the situation's pretty desperate. Getting worse every minute, as a matter of fact."

" Oh, God, so bad? " Her hand flew to her throat. " Would you care for a Martini? "

He gazed down at her, a strange yearning look on his handsome face. " Yes, I would," he said (well, he would, wouldn't he?) and then, patting the bulge beneath his impeccably cut dinner-jacket, " don't you worry—I'm not unprepared, and you won't be alone to-night."

Dermot was thinking, I've got to have freight, *proper* freight, not matches or marbles, and that coal was just right. One super run round and then she kicks up a fuss. Old fool. Typical, typical. (This was a phrase of his father's, greatly to his fancy. For good measure he tried it out again.) What does she think I am? Bullets would be best. Daddy's got bullets—but I don't know where, so I'd have to ask. He frowned, concentrating on his problem with cool objectivity, without harbouring any serious grudge against authority because of the satisfaction he was simultaneously deriving from the smooth chuggity-

154

chug rhythm of the rolling stock on the lower track. There was a lyric to fit, and it went like this:

> *Nobody knows, nobody knows*
> *What I've got in the little box under my bed.*

Indeed, he was right; nobody did know of the Vinolia Baby Soap carton under Dermot's bed, let alone what it contained. It had been there for over a week now, the little box which housed not merely an agreeably scandalous treasure trove, a portion of his own fæces, but the evidence, tangible, pungent, of his own cunning and splendid impregnability, his rebuke made manifest in respect of the indignities he daily suffered; in short, his answer to the adult world. A secret not to be shared with anyone, however—least of all with Clarissa. Here he glanced at his sister, who rolled her eyes at him lest he intrude on her own privacy.

Clarissa was thinking: Serve her right for forgetting the milk— I'm not sorry I put the Thermos under the chair—she could've looked under the chair, couldn't she? I mean, anyone else would. So when Mummy finds out—there *will* be a row, ha-ha. I don't *want* her to find out. I shan't do a thing. I'll just say, Dermot's thirsty, can he have a sip from my glass? It serves *her* right. That's twice she's allowed him to choose his biscuit first—greedy little pig, and then she lets him *go down to the second layer!* It's not fair. You're not supposed to start the second until the top's finished, everybody knows that. He's always wanting what I want, nowadays—copycat. And they all like him better than me. I wish I had someone to like—I'd like *anyone* who liked me best. At the same time Clarissa was listening to another voice, so soothing as to be the voice of sympathy itself, so faint as to impose on her no pressing obligation to acknowledge its origin: " If you go into the forest—if you can get away from the others, because they'll be picking mushrooms—and if you walk and walk until you lose your way and then walk some more until you're worn out, you'll have to sit down on the damp grass and if it's damp enough and you sit long enough you'll catch pneumonia—and then they'll be sorry. They'll start looking for you all over the place and when it gets dark perhaps wolves may come and get you. In any case, they'll be sorry. *Jolly* sorry."

Vladek, the driver, was thinking that this was more agreeable than waiting outside the office, that he would still get his pay plus, very likely, overtime as well. As a condition of employment by the British, Vladek had been subjected to the usual screening by the Embassy Visa Section, and he had emerged from it with his reputation as a rugged,

155

trustworthy, but bone-headed peasant with a gift for mechanics, unimpaired. No one had ever found fault with his driving nor with his maintenance of a vehicle, and although occasionally it had been suggested that he learn at least a few useful phrases of English to facilitate the execution of his duties, he had always met this suggestion with his famous cheerful grin and a negative shake of the head.

The fact was that Vladek preferred not to advertise his talents as a linguist; he spoke English very well, and indeed had been employed for this same job on that very account, but not by the British. He was in the unfortunate but by no means unique position of having to serve two masters. During the most unimpeachably documented period of his life, when, according to the file reposing in the archives of the British Embassy in Slavnik, he had been a young mechanic struggling to support an aged mother in a certain province of Lithuania, he had in fact been engaged very profitably in a totally different capacity several meridians west. In those days (which he remembered with a nostalgia flattering to his hosts) he had been a salesman, or traveller. Flitting up and down that stretch of coast which lies between Grimsby and Hull, paying particular attention to dockyards and to rumours of dissatisfaction amongst the labour, he was likely to have been found, albeit hovering shyly in the background, wherever trouble flared up. It was in such places and at such times that he himself had found the readiest market for his wares, and his present position, although ostensibly lowly, was actually promotion awarded him on the strength of those past laurels earned.

All of which goes to explain the thoughts now running through his head:

That is certainly champagne in the back of the American's car. How long since I've tasted champagne? Too long—I wonder, will they give me a glass or two? I should like that. Then I shall not be in a position to remember exactly all that is said—so much the better, I shall have to improvise—well, I've done that before now—but I won't make it hot, not if they give me champagne. It's a bother, though, improvising—perhaps I don't even need to do that—just say they gave me the drink and I got drunk. Awfully sorry—and grin! Yes, it would be safer like that—because of this girl, the maid. It's a nuisance, having this girl along too. What about her? That's just it, what? I haven't a clue. Maybe she's on a different net—maybe she isn't one at all. But it's likely she is, so better play safe—say nothing, drink champagne, take a holiday—and just say, *I got drunk*. That's it. Anyway, I'd prefer it that way—I like him, the American, and I like this new one, too. I don't care to drink their drink with *that* spoiling the taste— hell, they force one too much nowadays, there's no allowance for what

156

a man feels. Well, I'll wait and see how I feel after the champagne—if I get it.

But watch out for the girl, Vladek. I don't like this girl. What *is* her racket, I wonder? Ah-ha, what a lark! I never thought of that—it would be just like them, wouldn't it? No trust nowadays, no confidence. Perhaps I'm her bird—perhaps her racket is me?

All of a sudden his eyes switched from the road, which was straight, and swept over Gisela's face. She glanced at him vaguely, and he rolled back his lips in his most comradely grin, but Gisela, thereby confirming his worst suspicions, failed to respond to this approach.

Lost in meditation, she gazed stonily out of the window. Alone of them all Gisela confined her thoughts to a single track, and permitting no discursions drove them full steam ahead. Of them all, only her thoughts could truly be said to centre on Milly.

*   *   *

They were travelling south, in the opposite direction from Slavnik, towards the mountains. At the check point on the hill outside the town there was a halt whilst the numbers of the cars were taken. Then the barrier swung up.

" Now for the country," said Abe, and the country came singing up to greet them; a fairy-tale land of dashing streams and dark forest, dazzling flocks of geese on the grass verges by the roadside, here and there a lonely farmstead timbered with snow-eaves, the window-sills bright with geraniums. The soft damp air smelt of the pines but as the road climbed the air became fresh with a new smell that was sharper, more racy, even, than the smell of the pines, and on top of the pass there was a cold wind blowing and there ahead, fencing in the sky, like a glittering heap of bones raked across the horizon, a jumble of vertebræ, knuckles, teeth, shoulder-blades, smooth round skulls with black eyesockets, all ribbed over with snow and sunlight, were the Tatras.

Abe stole a look at Milly. Her lips were parted, moving. She was singing, he guessed. The wind fluttered the white fur in a ruff round her head.

" You're quite cute," he said, " in your way."

" In my *way*? " She was indignant at that.

" Oh, my heavens—you're not everyone's cup of tea. Not cosy enough, are you? "

" I wouldn't want to be—*cosy*! "

" You wouldn't want to scare people, would you? I bet you do, though—sometimes. Ah well, it's lucky . . ." He broke off and began to whistle.

" What's lucky? " she demanded.

" What? Oh, it's lucky it just so happens . . ." He grinned. " You don't scare *me*."

Her clear eyeballs jumped round at him. " Indeed, Mr. Schulman."

On the way down the pass they were ambushed by ragged urchins who sprang into the road, holding out baskets of mushrooms. Shouting and waving, they ran barefoot behind the cars, waving long after they were past, as they vanished into the distance. For quite a way the road was splashed on either side with patches of bright orange; rowans thick with berries.

" Be a hard winter," remarked Abe.

" How?—oh, the berries, you mean. Ah, but there's another way of telling, too," she went on chattily. " It's an old country saying. Apparently the field mice all know—when it's going to be—and then they make their holes facing south, or something . . ." Her voice trailed off. Was it south—or west, or what? She couldn't remember.

" You don't say? "

She sat back rather pleased with herself. She was fond of retailing, however inaccurately, such titbits of country lore as she had picked up, thereby revealing another, and, she considered, simpler side to her nature.

Presently Abe, who had been puzzling it out, said: " Can't see why they ever take a chance on it."

" Who? "

" Those *mice*." He fairly bit them in half. Milly made no reply. Frowning, she wondered whether she had been deceived in him. After a while he growled:

" Arptimistic little bastards."

Rather cross, she withdrew into her corner. She certainly had been wrong about him. He had completely missed the point.

Later on, he said pleasantly, breaking in on her thoughts: " That's a pretty nice husband you've got."

This was one of those standard American conversational gambits for which she had never yet discovered the correct reply. Was it an invitation to be openly disloyal? Or was a declaration of foolish devotion all that was required? Was one expected to make a frank appraisal of one's nearest and dearest? Or was one intended to feel merely a smug glow of satisfaction at the compliment to one's own taste, perspicacity and husband-sense—at having had the wit to select, from all the bargains available, this particular article which suited one so well? In that case—if a husband were to be regarded as a possession, like a dress, a hat, even a new novel or an Old Master—the cash once over the counter all rights, inclusive of design, etc., automatically reverting

158

to the owner, the purchaser—then she did know the correct, the transatlantic reply. " Thank you," she said.

" He's made a big hit with the staff, from all accounts."

" They just say that, I expect." She tried to keep the edge out of her voice. " Hoping it'll get back, you know."

Abe was silent for a moment. He liked the Slavonians and, sharing the conceit of all expatriates who adopted a certain country and a certain town in that country, prided himself on his own peculiar insight into the local character. He said, rather sharply: " You've no reason to say that."

" Well, it has—hasn't it? Got back, I mean."

Suddenly he laughed and reaching out his hand patted her knee. " Don't get sore now, Milly. Give 'em time—they don't know you yet."

She jerked away, furious that he had read her mind. She had listened for ten years to remarks like these, tributes to Larry, until she had reluctantly come to accept the inexplicable, namely, that of the two of them he was always the more immediately popular. " But he takes trouble," she would tell herself, full of resentment. " He likes to be liked." In the course of their rare quarrels, when hunting feverishly through her battered and depleted arsenal of blunted weapons, she invariably came across this trusty little tool, its business end still sharp, forged from the flinty stuff of truth.

Larry did like to be liked—but he was not, any more than any other person, liked on that account. Milly, as always, confused cause and effect. Larry instinctively radiated good will towards his fellow beings. He was sunny by nature, but the warmth he shed around him was not that of the sun, impersonal, falling on the backs of all created creatures alike, comforting some bones, picking others dry, then passing on— his was the antithesis, a personal warmth directed upon each individual he met and liked; moreover, directed with instinctive precision on that particular spot requiring its therapeutic properties most. It was one of his gifts—and small wonder that his wife, who distrusted and affected to despise those gifts with which she had not herself been endowed, had long since pounced on it, and when occasion demanded, turned it in the form of a weapon against him.

" I'm usually car sick," Clarissa informed Miss Raven, withdrawing her head from the window. Both children had been hanging their heads out of the windows like dogs.

Miss Raven, surfacing unwillingly, forced to grapple with the sudden change of atmospheric pressure, blinked foolishly at her charge.

" And Dermot is, *always*." Clarissa stifled a snigger.

159

Eardrums, eyeballs, adjusted with expert speed, Miss Raven had recovered.

" Always is what ? " she said sharply.

" Sick," said Clarissa with an angelic smile indicating her brother, and Miss Raven, making a grab at Dermot's flannel stern, hauled him in on to her lap.

Clarissa said to herself, viewing dispassionately his prostrate form: " He's sick all right." He was breathing noisily, yellow at the gills. " But not *so* sick." The spitting image of his father, her brother had, she reflected, a lot of their mother in him. You could rely on Dermot, just as you could rely on her—however propitious or forbidding the omens for the day, to pursue, undeterred, each his own course. At least you knew where you were with them. Once that course was set, and it was easy as pie to spot its direction, neither would ever be likely to confound you by deviating, by a change of mind, or the making of an exception. They never changed their minds nor made exceptions. She admired them both.

They turned off the main road and plunged down a cart track into the valley, for several miles following the course of the river, its waters churning ice-green beneath the great shaggy pines on the farther bank.

" This is the place," said Abe and stopped, and Vladek stopped too, and they all got out.

" I don't see any mushrooms," said Milly at once, as if she had expected a carpet of fungi to be laid out ready.

" You gotta go find them," said Abe, " in there." He jerked his head to where, on the other side of the road, the forest rose up steep, its outer edges fringed with yellow seedlings, darkness within.

" I don't want to go in there," said Dermot, who, having recovered to the extent of accepting a piece of chocolate, recognised too late that in so doing he had forfeited his claim to compassion. No amount of malingering would avail him now, and a firm stand must be made. " Wolves," he remarked hopefully, enlisting these beasts to his support.

" Nonsense, Dermot," said Miss Raven briskly, " it's not the time of year."

" He's funky," observed his sister. Dermot suffered the gibe in silence, sucking his chocolate, eyeing her stolidly. She bared her teeth at him and snarled.

" Don't make silly faces, Clarissa—and don't tease your brother. He's much younger than you," said Milly.

" He won't *always* be," she muttered, and dodging round behind her mother's back, she mouthed at him silently: " Funky-funk . . . Fraidy-cat . . . Cowardy-cee . . ." Dermot, in the public view, who knew when

160

he was on a good wicket, allowed his own mouth to droop, with an effective slackening and quivering of the lower lip.

" You'd like to come with me and pick mushrooms, wouldn't you, darling? " his mother suggested swiftly.

" Or stay here with Miss Raven, pet? " said that lady, and was rewarded by Dermot sliding his hand into hers.

" I'll count the ones you pick," he informed Milly kindly, the affair being concluded to his satisfaction.

Gisela spread rugs and Miss Raven plumped herself down in the middle and Gisela and Milly began to unpack the baskets. Miss Raven took out her knitting, a primrose yellow confection which seemed no nearer completion than on its first appearance, its shape being still undetermined, although its purpose was not. It was one of Miss Raven's most useful props.

" I don't want the children to get lost," she remarked, knitting placidly.

" Nor do I," said Milly with spirit. Then, seeing that Clarissa had wandered up the road and was nearly out of sight: " Clarissa, come back at once! Call that child, Larry! "

" Clarissa! Come back—and you can have some champagne! "

Clarissa wavered; then she came back. She had only been testing; but had she been allowed to reach the corner and disappear from view —an objective she had no particular wish to gain because the forest *was* frightening, close up—well, then, she would have known they did not care. As it was . . . she skipped back and thrust her nose into her father's glass. The bubbles tickled.

" Oh—but it's *sour*! "

" That's the way it should be."

" But I like things *sweet* . . ."

" You'll have to grow out of that," said Larry.

" It's lovely," said Miss Raven. " Nutty. That'll do, Clarissa."

Abe threw himself down on the rug, arranging his head in Miss Raven's lap.

" You don't mind, Miss Raven, do you? "

She had flushed scarlet. " Not at all, Mr. Schulman, if it makes you comfortable."

" I dunno that it does—now I come to think of it." He sat up. " Another illusion gone. All that about laps is hooey along with holding hands in the movie, sleeping with your arms——"

" Abe! " Milly burst out. Miss Raven, as was expected of her, assumed a mildly scandalised expression and concentrated on her knitting.

" Another glass, Miss Raven? "

" That's very kind, Mr. Purdoe. I wouldn't say no." Her cheeks and neck, he noticed, had become blotched with purple. Funny old thing, she likes a bit of a swig, he thought—and why ever not? "Abe, what about the driver?"

Vladek was polishing the windscreen with tremendous zest.

" Oh, sure." Lazily Abe held out his own glass. " Go ahead, give him a bottle to himself—there's plenty."

" The *driver*? " said Milly. " *Champagne?* " She laughed prettily, holding out her glass. " Thank you, darling, lovely. There's beer for him—I brought it specially. Personally, I would've thought he'd be only too *grateful* . . ."

" Would you really, now? " Abe chewed amiably on his cigarette. " That's very interesting. Now I wonder why you'd've thought that."

" He probably gets all the beer he wants, Milly, every day of his life."

" So much the better, then, if that's what he's used to." She smiled winningly. " After all, he's got to drive us back and there are the children to think of. So give him the beer, darling—it's in the basket."

" Hold on, Milly. Don't forget, it's Abe's champagne."

" And they're *my* children! " she snapped, a little too sharply.

" Aw, Larry, let it go . . ." Abe, who had been studying her, lay back with his arms behind his head. " Give the lady her own way, for Pete's sake."

Vladek, who had stopped polishing the windscreen, was discovered squatting in the grass on the far side of the car, smoking, with no particular expression on his face. When Larry presented him with the beer he jumped up and saluted, even mustering up a shadow of his famous grin.

" Well, he was grateful, wasn't he? " Milly demanded.

Larry shrugged. " Of course."

" What did I tell you? " Her expression grave, she was concentrating, impaling olives on sticks. " So you see—I was perfectly right."

Staring up at the trees, Abe began his tuneless whistle.

" Milly . . ." Larry shook his head. " Darling, you know . . . you are a . . ."

" A what? " Seeing that she could afford it, she gave him a nice smile.

" I don't know," said Larry helplessly, smiling back. " I can't think of a word."

Vladek, who was not smiling, but glumly chewing salami and washing it down with mouthfuls of flat beer, could without hesitation

162

have supplied a suitably descriptive word for Milly. Under his breath, he did. The long, cold hours stretched soberly ahead—well then, if he must be sober, how sober he would be.

*　　*　　*

"Who's going to find mushrooms, eh, Clarissa?" Abe squatted down beside her. "It's not so easy, you know. You've got to have specially sharp eyes and special fingers. Magic fingers." Clarissa stared at him. Then, as his expression remained perfectly grave, she spread out her two hands for his inspection.

He shook his head. "I can't tell that way. It's a question of magic, you see, and it's awful tricky stuff—mushrooms are just full of it. They're sensitive—they don't let themselves be picked by just anybody —they can creep right down under the pine needles, under the moss, if they don't like the looks of you, and that's why some people can't find them at all, not a single one. But there are just a few people—y'know, the ones with magic in their fingers—oh, they find beauties, any amount. Perhaps it'll turn out that way with you. And sometimes . . ."

"Magic!" said Milly scornfully. "Abe, I'm ashamed of you."

Clarissa gave her a quick look, and then nudged Abe. "Go on," she whispered, encouragingly, but he didn't seem in the least perturbed.

"Oh, I'm not *lying*, Milly, I assure you. You wait and see." He went on, smiling at Clarissa, "As I was saying, sometimes—it doesn't happen often, remember, and there's no telling who it may be—some smartie comes along who *seems* to be okay, y'know, special eyes, fingers, an' all, and he picks a whole heap of mushrooms and then—whaddya think?—magic, naturally—right there before his eyes, *those mushrooms turn to deadly poison!*"

"Deadly poison!" The children's eyes shone.

"Don't, Abe. You're scaring them out of their wits."

"I'm not frightened, Mummy. I should just like to see it happen, that's all."

"Me, too," breathed Dermot.

"Well, you won't. Mr. Schulman's only teasing."

He got to his feet. "So you don't believe in magic, Milly?" He grinned down at her. "Oh, my, you should. You miss a lot. But don't say you haven't been warned. C'marn, kids, let's go." Their enthusiasm reviving at the prospect of such supernatural hazards, obediently the children followed him into the forest.

"Gisela, go after them, will you? See they don't come to any harm."

Larry was stretched out beyond Miss Raven; he seemed to be asleep. Miss Raven was knitting. Milly lay down. It was warm out

163

of the wind, the sun stroking her face; lying there, somehow she couldn't rest; on the contrary, she felt her heart beating fast, pulses seemed to jump alive all over her body, in her ankles, her wrists, her throat. She stretched out her arms, flexing her fingertips like a cat its claws, pressing her shoulder blades flat against the earth. She tossed the rug away, just to be closer to the earth, to smell it. Beneath there were pine-needles, thick and slippery, silky against one's cheek. They smelt wonderful. She had a sudden ridiculous desire to kick off her shoes and curl her toes, arch her feet for the sheer pleasure of it. Electricity crackled through every fibre of her body. She forced herself to lie still, but it cost her a terrible effort; like the last few minutes in a Turkish bath or under a hair-drier, she almost had to count, but instead she listened to the noise of the river tumbling over the boulders, and the soughing of the wind in the pines, and the click of Miss Raven's knitting needles and the sound of her own heart beating. Suddenly she could bear it no longer and springing up, took to her heels and ran, crossed the road, leapt the ditch, and without a backward glance she too vanished into the forest.

Miss Raven, whose professional experience told her that Larry was merely feigning sleep, remarked: " Well, I never. Mrs. Purdoe sometimes moves quite like a young girl, doesn't she? "

Larry opened his eyes and lay staring at the treetops. Then he raised his head and looked around.

" She's gone off, too, has she? " He lay down again and yawned. " Thank God I haven't got magic fingers."

Miss Raven stopped knitting. " The sun's quite a treat, isn't it? But it's chilly. Mind you don't catch cold lying there like that, Mr. Purdoe."

He stirred, irritated. Lying there like what? As though he would have liked a nap, presumably. In that case, why the—unaccustomed to mothering, he had lost any taste for it he might ever have possessed. Contrary to popularly held, and expressed, feminine opinion, it is not invariably a safe bet to assume that all men are just little boys at heart. Some are not.

" Here." Miss Raven tucked a cushion under his head. " That's more comfy, isn't it? "

Larry, toying with the idea of letting out a sudden high-pitched yowl, resisted the temptation, and sat up. " Any more in that bottle, Miss Raven? "

Miss Raven rattled the bottle. " Only a drop. I'll get another, shall I? "

She eased the cork out of the new bottle rather deftly, he thought. " You know all the tricks of the trade, I see."

164

She blushed. " One learns these things," she said vaguely. " Cheerio, Mr. Purdoe."

" How green it all is," she mused, sipping. " And how damp. Oh, how it does remind me of Ireland." She heaved a sigh.

" Ireland?" His thoughts had been elsewhere, but when courtesy demanded he had a useful knack of picking up the last word spoken, disguising it with a thin coating of charm, and popping it back whence it had emerged. " Ireland, eh?"

" I was born in Ireland," Miss Raven admitted with an appropriate air of melancholy. Larry, seeing that her glass was empty, filled it up. It was not, however, the moment for an interruption and Miss Raven ignored it. " Yes," she went on, " that's where we had our country home. Within sight of the sea. A lovely old place—my sisters and I— I had three sisters, Mr. Purdoe, and such a happy childhood—until . . ." Her voice broke, and Larry turned his whole attention to his champagne. Miss Raven fortified herself too, and then continued, " Until . . . the crash came." She put down her glass and fixed him with a stern, sad look. ". . . Brought up to nothing but the best . . . quite suddenly . . . terrible losses . . . wildest dreams . . . ever to be in the position I'm in now . . ."

" Of course not," he stammered, ever so slightly hypnotised by those strange eyes. And *what* strange eyes—glassy, almost colourless, like the Adriatic under a white-hot sky. " No, no," he repeated, feeling excessively foolish, " of course not." Still, he reflected, her present position wasn't too bad, if it came to that—here she was, after all, sitting in the sun, relieved of her charges, drawing a jolly good screw, and sozzling champagne.

She went on rapidly in the same tense voice: " Who knows what life has in store? We were comfortably off, wealthy, even, when the . . ." She paused, as if at a loss, or as if she had caught sight of the flag marking the second time round. He went on for her: " When the . . . er . . . crash . . . came?"

Miss Raven nodded.

" Wasn't there—I mean, was there—well, was there really nothing left at all?" He cursed himself. It sounded crude, put like that.

Miss Raven tossed her head. " It's all in the hands of lawyers," she said, flashing him a bold yet meaningless smile—as bold as if she'd answered in terms of pounds, shillings, and pence, meaningless because she hadn't. Larry felt snubbed. Without warning she started off again, a jumble of disconnected phrases drifting his way, and much to his annoyance he was forced to rouse himself to keep track.

" Some day . . . photos . . . dear old place by the sea . . . stables . . . Hunt balls . . . known far and wide . . ."

165

He filled her glass again, and she seemed to buck up a bit, giggled, and said skittishly: " I'll tell you a secret, shall I? I was engaged, you know . . . once . . ." She gave him a quick look. " Perhaps you're surprised? "

He was, but he kept it to himself and she nodded, obviously pleased.

" To someone—but I simply daren't tell you who . . . he's very well known, you see . . . one of our most prominent . . . oh, I *wish* I could tell you, but I simply *can't* . . . but I took, I am sure, the wise decision . . . you see, I would not have harmed his career, not for the world . . . no, *don't* ask me his name, I beg of you . . ."

Larry gazed morosely at the river below. Nothing was farther from his mind than to press for details of Miss Raven's romance. Could he get up and go? Well, hardly. There was nowhere to go to, except the forest. My God, he thought, at this rate she'll drive me into the forest.

" Miss Raven——" he began.

" Ah, you're such a *wonderful* confidant, Mr. Purdoe. Life has taught me . . ." She paused, and he turned to look at her squarely, asking himself why to-day and for her his fount of sympathy should have run dry. Why was he not more touched? This situation, as Milly would have lost no time in pointing out, was right up his street.

" Cheer up, Miss Raven." Cautiously he patted her hand, and as it had occurred to him just too late that she might do, she caught it beneath her own. " You're amongst friends now. We're very fond of you, you know." Gently he extricated his hand. " Very . . . very *fond* . . ." he repeated uneasily, once more having glimpsed that certain fleeting look in her eyes. He decided it must be a trick of the light. " All of us," he added quickly, altering his tone with effect. She seemed to take warning at once.

" Thanks." She gave him a gallant little smile. " Thanks a million, as they say."

" That's the spirit, Miss Raven. Another drop? Now I'm going off to find those brats. You have a nap." He was extraordinarily thankful to be off. " Look, I'll cover you up, shall I? "

She lay down obediently and he brought a rug and tucked it round her. As he did so she murmured, as if to herself, her eyes shut: " Prince Charming."

" What was that? " He was picking up the glasses from the grass.

" Oh, nothing." Smiling, she snuggled under the rug. She knew he had heard, just as she had intended he should.

He ambled down to the river, faintly annoyed, or amused, or disgusted, he couldn't say which. All three, perhaps. Silly old trout. He certainly wouldn't breathe a word of it to Milly. Prince Charming, indeed. She'd think it was a tremendous joke, laugh her head off, say he had it coming to him. At that, she was probably right.

*   *   *

It was dark in the forest. When first she had plunged into the undergrowth she had been careless of her direction, laughing as she sprang over the fallen trunks and the boggy patches of bright green grass, trampling down the brambles which tore her stockings, bent simply on breasting this slope and the next until she was beneath the sheltering roof of trees. Once there the going was easier, and she paused to take breath, leaning against a tree. Not a single ray of sunlight penetrated the gloom, there was not a sound to be heard except her own breath coming in great gasps.

" Cooeeee . . ." she called, and a woodpigeon rattled off a few yards distant, a pine cone dropped to the ground, then silence. The brown-carpeted slopes stretched away on either hand like the vast shadowy halls of the underworld, peopled with black silent figures; as her eyes became used to the half-light, the tree trunks assumed individual shapes, personalities; they stood there watching, waiting. Out of the corner of her eye she caught a movement—turned her head swiftly—no, each stood silent, motionless; and yet—without turning her head her eyes moved—there! She spun round. Yes, surely? But she couldn't be sure, she couldn't watch every side at once; behind her now, for instance, they might be stealthily advancing. She leaned close up to the tree for protection, her back to it. A branch cracked above her head and every nerve in her body jumped. As though its snap had been the pistol shot to start her off, she was away like the wind up the slope; but now it seemed that her course was fixed, her direction set; zig-zagging through the trees, when forced to abandon her path in order to avoid this obstacle or that, she would double back, as if it were marked out. The slope became steep; she clambered up on hands and knees, grabbing at roots, selecting the green sinewy branches to hoist herself up, her feet slipping on the needles which lay in great drifts. Slipping, snatching at brambles, her hands torn and bleeding, she was sobbing for breath, but her legs and arms seemed to be moving of their own accord, and she felt herself driven on, knowing that she must reach the top and that she would reach it and when she did—a level glade on the far side of which a brook flowed between mossy banks—she flung herself down on the wet grass and lay there panting. Presently she began to laugh; she felt much better, and sat up.

It was dark in the glade, but not dark as it had been down below, where the pine-needles lay underfoot. Here copperbeech and maples were tangled with the pines and the green grass beneath reflected a

167

greenish light into the dome above. Still breathless, laughing to herself, she began pulling the twigs out of her hair. What a mess it was in!—sticky, covered with dust, matted with resin; when she shook her head a cloud of dust fell out and odds and ends of bark and stuff. "Crazy," she whispered, "that's what you are, crazy." But she didn't mind at all, not about her hair, nor even about her stockings which were quite spoilt. It had been too exciting for that. She still felt dreadfully excited, but she couldn't move another step.

Leaning back against a log, stretching her arms along it, the excitement flowing right down into her fingertips, she dug her nails into the bark; it was soft and rotten, covered with mould. Sniffing her fingers, all streaked with mould, mould under the nails, she thought she had never smelt anything so delicious. The smell of the mould was a compound of all the smells in the forest, of the earth and of the grass and of the trees, all quite pleasant smells but too fresh, too innocent, too vernal; no, there had to be just this rich sweet smell of corruption mixed in to give complete satisfaction, this hint of autumn and decay.

She was tugging up little handfuls of grass, singing under her breath, when her hand fell on an object in the grass, a round velvety shape. Rather absently she fondled it, when all at once, as if it were red hot, she snatched her hand away and jumped to her feet. She stared wildly about her, scarcely able to believe her eyes. Here, there, everywhere she was surrounded by mushrooms. Her heart started to beat fast, and she felt a pricking in her throat, that sure sign of collector's fever, a terrible lust, joy, too, and despair as well. Because she would never manage to pick them all. She tore off her scarf and her jacket, spreading them out flat. Whimpering under the stress of urgency, at the pity of it should she have to let so much as a single one go by, she fell on her knees and began picking.

It was a hopeless task. They grew thick, jostling each other in the grass, springing from the crevices of the very log against which she had been lying; they pushed up the carpet of pine-needles over the edge of the slope and all the way down the slope; wherever she looked there were mushrooms. They were of the type, too, that she particularly fancied, in form bisectional, the upper layer white and solid as coconut-ice, the under surface porous, honey-coloured. A different sort, the frilly yellow variety, cascaded down the banks of the brook. Chuckling to herself, she wasted no time on them; they were quite common—fetched almost nothing at the market.

When both scarf and jacket could hold no more, she sat back on her heels, gazing ruefully at the spread around her. It broke her heart to let them go and she heaved a great sigh. How quiet it was. The sound of a match being struck behind her made her whip round.

Abe Schulman was lounging against a tree, calmly drawing on his cigarette and watching her. He seemed to be amused. She scrambled to her feet.

" What are you up to? " she demanded furiously.

He took the cigarette out of his mouth and yawned. " Oh, I dunno, Milly . . . I was just watching . . . you, I mean. My, you were absorbed. Never even heard me crashing through the undergrowth." He chuckled.

How long had he been there? She stamped across towards him and for a second he thought she might be about to box his ears, and it occurred to Milly, too, that that was what she might do. But she stopped a couple of paces away and stood there, as angry as she had ever been in her life.

" Well, you've certainly struck a gold mine, my dear." He was laughing at her, she knew. " What a pity," he said softly, " you can't take 'em all." Suddenly, for no reason, she could have burst into tears. She wouldn't care, she thought, if she never saw another mushroom again.

" Here." He dived into his pocket. " I've got something for you." Curious, she took a step towards him.

" C'marn . . . it won't bite. Come an' take a look." He held out his closed hand. When she was near him he opened it; wrapped in a leaf there lay a score or so of wild strawberries.

" See, Milly? A delicacy—out of season. Worth more than all this." He indicated the floor of the forest. Unsmiling, puzzled, she reached out to take them, but as she did so he threw away his cigarette and with his other hand grasped her wrist and gently pulled her, unresisting, towards him; and as she still did not resist, after a second he kissed her, quite gently, on the mouth. Then he dropped her wrist and stood up, away from the tree. They stood there facing each other, he with the same little smile on his lips, she staring up at him, her eyes enormous in the twilight of the trees. At last she whispered: " Why did you do that? "

He said coolly, " I dunno. Just to see what it'd be like, I guess."

It was not the answer she had expected, obviously. Now, he thought, let's have it, that sizzling come-back.

Instead, in such a small voice, bewildered, like a child's: " You shouldn't 've done it," she said, and made a little gesture with her hand. Then he did look at her, peering forward to look at her as closely as she was looking at him, because suddenly it crossed his mind—but no, after all, it had been just a flicker, a movement, right at the back a door had opened and shut, maybe, but nothing came in or went out; nothing did cross his mind. He had her all weighed up. So he said:

169

" I shouldn't 've? I don't see why. It was such a very pure kiss, Mrs. Purdoe . . . considering . . ." He paused, just to tease her, not knowing that she waited as one waits for the next flash of lightning, the next drop of rain:

" Considering? " she said. She wasn't good at waiting.

He considered her, taking his time; then, in his lazy spaced-out drawl he said: " Oh, considering that I'm—well . . . that I'm just a very ordinary . . . sensual kind of a . . . *man*."

Unmoved until that moment—or so it seemed, because the kiss had not moved her, now suddenly at these words, closing her eyes, she felt all her strength desert her. As if he had cast a spell over her, when she tried to speak she could not; her limbs seemed to have become heavy as lead. She stood spellbound, trying to recapture the sound of his voice. Why? She had no idea why except that it was necessary to her —more, vital—to have him repeat those words again . . . because she was suffocating—no, drowning . . . in desire—for what? She had no idea for what, but it seemed that his voice, those words, contained the answer. She only knew that she ached with the sense of happiness at hand, a happiness so sweet, so near, that could she but stretch out her hand—and just as a drowning person instinctively clutches at his rescuer so, blindly, she put out her hand—but he was gone. Halfway down the slope she saw his coloured shirt moving between the trees.

Presently she picked up her jacket, shook the mushrooms out of it without so much as a glance at them, and put it on. Then she tied up the ends of the scarf with care, because she had to have something to show, and with the bundle in her hand, began the descent. She moved painfully, as if her bones were old and brittle, several times pausing for breath, supporting herself against the trunks of trees; the true culprits, heart and mind, already docile, now, perversely, it was her rebellious limbs that betrayed her. She was trembling from head to foot and her legs would barely carry her down. It was quite a while before she reached the edge of the forest.

* * *

" Good . . . no good . . . good . . . good . . . no good . . ." Gisela was squatting on the grass verge by the road, her face rapt, her expression stern as that of a high priestess; Abe, Larry, the two children and the driver sat in a circle round her, each with his offerings in front of him, humbly awaiting her judgment. The suspense was awful. Some she glanced at cursorily, then " Good," she would say with an approving nod, and the finder would smirk, he couldn't help it. Some she examined with the utmost care, prising open the gills,

170

sniffing, then, " Good "—and he wouldn't even smirk, it was such heady delight, that praise. Others she didn't even bother to examine. Picking them up with the tips of her fingers, she threw them straight over her shoulder in the direction of the river. Excitement mounted as the piles reduced.

" It's an education to me," said Larry. " I never knew there were so many kinds. Still, I doubt whether "—he touched one dubious-looking warty affair, not his, pronounced excellent—" whether we'd eat these at home."

" Don't fret," said Abe, " she knows what she's doing all right. The Slavonians are all a bit crazy when it comes to mushrooms—but that doesn't mean to say they're all potential suicides. Take a look at Vladek."

The driver's trophies, leathery monsters, had all passed muster. Grinning with pride, he was tenderly wrapping them in his coat.

" Now mine! " whispered Clarissa, pale with excitement.

Even Gisela had to smile at sight of the neat little heap of button mushrooms lying pearly white in the grass at her feet.

" All good. All very, very good." She turned to Larry. " Tell the little one, please. They are the best so far."

"Darling, Gisela says yours are the very best," said Larry generously, although worrying about his own. The enthusiasm was infectious. Clarissa bent her head to hide tears of sheer emotion.

" Magic fingers, Clarissa," said Abe, and she looked up, smiling shyly through her tears. " There's Mummy! " she shrieked. " Look! " They all looked at the bedraggled figure advancing towards them. " Oh, she's got the most—I *knew* she would! "

Milly came up, swinging her bundle in her hand. She stood there rather awkwardly, almost as if she were nervous, looking down at them. Larry thought: now I wonder what she's been up to? Struck by her expression and other things too, from habit, experience, he postponed his investigations and by not so much as the flicker of an eyelid did he betray his intuitive recognition of an event having taken place; an event that would be secret, her secret, and one which she would withhold, greedily keeping it to herself, or, if she so pleased, as sometimes happened, and as he always hoped might happen if he concealed from her the fact of his having divined its existence, share with him. Now all he said was: " Darling, where have you been? You *are* in a mess."

Abe, chewing a grass stalk, said: " Come on, Milly, let's see what you've got. My, after all that time they'd better be good."

Ignoring him, rather self-consciously she put down her bundle in the centre of the circle. They all clustered round.

171

"There," she said, shaking out the contents and smiling triumphantly at Larry.

From all about her there came a sharp hiss of indrawn breath. Her eyes flitted over the circle of faces; to her amazement, each, for an instant, seemed to be frozen into an identical expression of dismay. Really, they looked quite ludicrous. They were all staring—yes, in dismay—at what lay in the grass at her feet.

"I don't——" she began, and then glanced down and she, too, stared, unable to believe her eyes. Her spoils, which made a considerable pile, were already streaked with purple; livid patches, like bruises, on the smooth white caps seemed to be spreading under one's very eyes. They looked what they were, deadly.

"Magic!" whispered Dermot. Horrorstruck he gazed up at his mother. Then he poked one tentatively.

"Gib' Acht!" Quick as a flash Gisela had caught his arm, brushing him aside. Suddenly his sister burst into tears.

"Really, you two!" Larry, who had glanced at Milly, spoke sharply. "What a fuss about nothing. Pull yourself together, Clarissa. And Dermot, go and get a glass for your mother. Look lively, now. Abe, we'll crack another bottle, how about it?"

"Sure, I'll go get it." Abe went off to do so. They were all embarrassed by the sight of Milly's face.

"What a shame, darling," said Larry. "Never mind."

"It happens like that sometimes," said Gisela, who was busy trampling on Milly's mushrooms, grinding them underfoot. "With this kind there's no way of telling," she went on casually, "till you pick them."

"Hear that, Milly? You see, you couldn't 've known—there's no way of telling until you—until you pick them," he muttered, thinking, that's not a very happy way of putting it. He went off to get her champagne.

"Miss Raven—Miss Raven!" Clarissa whooped with glee, tossing aside the rug under which Miss Raven lay peacefully asleep. "Look—Miss Raven is *lying* on—get up, oh please get *up*, Miss Raven . . ." Roused at last, and indignant at the manner of it, Miss Raven sat up. Close to the earth, half-hidden in pine-needles, and crushed by the weight of her far from fragile form, the most delectable mushrooms of all lay bleeding.

"Well, I never!" she exclaimed, scrambling out of the way as the children swept down like locusts.

"Unter der Nanny are the finest," said Gisela, primly bestowing her accolade. In *that* case, thought Milly, and burst out laughing along with everybody else. Miss Raven, bridling as she accepted

172

champagne, looked as smug as if she had engendered the phenomena herself.

*   *   *

" Those very big ones of yours," murmured Gisela to the driver, " where did you find them? "

Vladek had thought her asleep. All the way home she had not uttered a word. The Herrschaften were asleep in the back. Now they were past the check-point, the lights of the town glinting ahead.

" I found them near the top of that steep slope," Vladek replied politely. " By the brook."

" Oh, so you went as far as that? "

" It wasn't so far," he said, leaving unspoken the retort, " no farther than you went yourself." He was not so generous, nor such a fool, that he felt called upon further to elaborate the point; that whereas she had seen only what she had doubtless hoped to see, he had seen that and her as well. All the same, it was a pity, he thought. Not about this girl; she could look after herself—anyway she wasn't his type. No, about the other, about *that*. So now—drop them at the hotel and then do his duty, he supposed. He sighed. He was an honest man at heart. He didn't much relish it, his duty; would vastly have preferred the champagne.

PART TWO

"Ere long, a bell tinkled and the curtain drew up. . . . Its second rising displayed a more elaborately prepared scene than the last. . . .

. . . The camels only were wanting."

CHARLOTTE BRONTE: *Jane Eyre*

Chapter One

THEY WERE to remember the day of the picnic as the last warm day of the year. A week later, overnight the weather changed and when they awoke next morning the frost had scrawled its crazy messages over the window-panes and the sky was sharp ice-blue. You could tell that the weather had changed from the way the horses' hooves rang out on the cobbles below, crisp and clear; the footsteps of the passers-by struck the pavement smartly; no one was dawdling about. The coffee smelt delicious; when Gisela drew the curtains, steam curled up from the spout in the sunlight, and a pale wash of sunlight streamed across the room. As soon as she put a match to the twigs in the stove, the red tongues of flame licked up the sunlight in a wide circle all round, until there was just the glow from the stove and one was thankful for it.

That morning another bag arrived. Larry, shivering in his dressing-gown, dragged it in from the salon where Vladek had left it and opened it in front of the stove. He tossed the parcels on to the bed one by one, delving down inside the sack.

" What's all this? Pharmaceutical goods . . . pharmaceutical . . . pharma . . . for heaven's sake, Milly! Are you starting up a shop? "

She struggled up in bed. " They're things for the children," she answered swiftly. " Miss Raven asked for them . . . cod liver oil, cough mixture, malted milk . . . I don't know, heaps of things."

" So I see."

" Well, you can't get that sort of thing in the NAAFI, so naturally I had to order."

" Poor little brutes. I've never seen so much dope."

" One has to be prepared," she said snappishly. " For any eventuality. After all, I'm the one that's responsible."

" All right, darling. Keep your hair on." He was opening his letters. " God, here's one from Schwelling. An invitation. Remember him? "

" No," said Milly.

" That old fuddy-duddy Abe brought to the Rapovskis. Wants us to dine—in Slavnik. Formal, it says. Wonder if he's asked Abe too? Probably. Like to go? "

Milly looked up from the letter she had read three times over in order to avoid opening the parcels in front of him.

" It might be fun. Hm. Formal . . .? " Her thoughts scampered ahead.

Larry grinned. " Make up your mind, darling. You can only wear one at a time." She picked up a roll from the tray and aimed it at his head. He dodged and went into the bathroom.

On one side of the door she was thinking how easy it was to distract him. He was like a child.

On the other side Larry, who was not in the least like a child, having stopped being one quite a while back, was thinking as he scrubbed his teeth, that was a lot of bull about those parcels. Now just what did they contain? Cosmetics, probably, or some such expensive rubbish for which there would be a whacking bill in due course—still, what could he do? Nothing. He would never have dreamed of calling her bluff as he might have done—by waiting to see what was in them, for instance. No, she would open them when he was safely away at the office. She had often lied to him in the past. He didn't mind that particularly—after all it was a feminine trait. Women seemed to have a predilection for the tortuous rather than the simple when it came to getting what they wanted; they even told quite unnecessary lies—and yet often with an ineptitude that was surprising in view of the practice they obtained. Why Milly should bother to lie to him he had never been able to understand. He only wanted what she wanted, that she should have whatever she desired insofar as he could, within the means at his disposal, provide it. What worried him far more than the lies themselves was the prospect of inadvertently finding her out in them, an embarrassment he was prepared to go quite a long step out of his way to avoid. Anyway, let her lie away to her heart's content so long as she did not lie about the important things—and this business of the parcels was not one of them, he decided, starting to scrape his chin.

" By the way "—he put his head round the door—" someone from the Embassy's coming down to-day. Routine inspection, they call it."

" Oh lord! One of those? "

" Yep. I've never met him—some old dodderer . . . quite high up, though. Admin. King of Eastern Europe. Name of Cantrell. Colonel Cantrell."

" Does that mean dinner? "

" 'Fraid so. Can you manage it? "

" I suppose I can. I'll have a shot, anyway. Cantrell . . . Admin. What about beetroot soup and crayfish? That ought to do him. Or d'you think I should put in another course? Admin., you see."

He came out, looking grave.

" Hm. Tricky. Feed 'em well and they carve you right down, and yet if it's not good enough they start wondering what you're up to. I dunno. I'd say that was about right. Tasty but modest. God, I'd

178

rather dine the Wigan Labour candidate or a couple of Maltese D.B.S., or even H.E. any day. It takes genius to strike an absolute bang-on medium."

" Not really," said Milly demurely. " I thought tinned fruit salad to finish up with."

" Milly, you've got it! That's it—that's just it. Good as butter on his paws—he'll know where he is and no funny business. I must say the crayfish had me a bit—better see the plates are cold, though."

" Never mind about that. You take care of the wine."

" Oh, the NAAFI's taken care of that, don't you fret. It's just perfect—medium as can be. Still, Wragg's got some of that local black-currant liqueur, I might borrow a bottle, just in case. Should damp down any unexpected culinary triumphs. So we're all set, are we? Operation Cantrell."

" All set." She held up her face and he kissed it. " And we can go to that party in Slavnik? "

" What, Schwelling's? " He looked surprised. " All right, if you really want to."

" Yes," said Milly. " I do."

When he had gone she poured herself another cup of coffee, opened all her parcels, and then lay in the snug nest of her bed, staring at the heap of wrapping paper at her feet. Why had she bothered to get the stuff for Antoinette? Kindness, was it? Or laziness? Certainly it would have been a bore, having to refuse. Weakness, then. Why hadn't she told Larry about it? I really don't know, she said to herself, but it's too late now, anyway, and began thinking about the American dinner-party, instead. That meant a new dress. Not because she didn't have dresses, but because—well, she *felt* like it. And also a length of stuff had arrived. Black velvet. She had ordered it some weeks back, having passed by the antique shop window so many times, and each time seeing that lace, old and fragile and costly, and simply crying out to be worn on black velvet, worn by her in a black velvet gown, that is to say. So the velvet had arrived—and it was quite a coincidence, really, that it should arrive to-day, together with the invitation. Then she must find a dressmaker. Antoinette must know of one. Antoinette must help —that was only fair, considering. Considering? She kicked the packages away, down to the end of the bed, and thought about the dress instead. She knew just how it would be—rather plain, medieval, because of the lace (if one had the lace), cut very low . . . possibly even long tight sleeves. . . . She sat up rather crossly as Miss Raven breezed in.

" I heard the parcels come," said Miss Raven, as if she had heard the brushing of wings or the patter of tiny feet. How she could have heard was beyond Milly's powers to imagine. Still, Miss Raven's glance had swept over the eiderdown on which was confirmation of the news, however it had travelled.

"That cough mixture I told you to order for Dermot—have they sent it?"

"No," said Milly slowly. "I don't think they have. How long ago was that?"

"Two weeks now." Miss Raven gave her a look. "You did order it, didn't you?"

"Of course I did." She thought, that's funny, now how did I come to forget?—and added quickly, "It'll be in the next bag, I expect."

"Oh, will it?" said Miss Raven. I wonder, was what she meant.

"We're having a guest for dinner to-night. Someone from the Embassy."

It worked like magic, to her relief. After a pause Miss Raven said, in quite a different tone: "That's nice. It'll do us good to see a new face. One of the dips., I suppose? I'll take your tray, shall I?" she added, unbending so far as to do so at the prospect of the evening's entertainment.

"Oh, no one wildly exciting, I'm afraid. One of those dear old duffers who goes around checking up . . . what was his name, now, wait a second. Cantrell. Colonel Cantrell. Why Colonel?" she mused, "that's odd."

Odder still, it occurred to her, was the behaviour of Miss Raven, who, on the way to the door with the tray in her hands, had suddenly stopped in her tracks. Putting the tray down carefully on a side table, she stood quite still, brooding over it, apparently lost in thought.

Milly, who wanted her to go, said brightly: "So you'll put on your best bib and tucker, won't you, Miss Raven?"

"Yes," said Miss Raven. "Yes, of course." Then she went out, quite forgetting the tray, which was left on the table.

Milly got out of bed and wrapping herself in a dressing-gown began a note to Antoinette Rapovska. "Dear Princess, the things you asked for have arrived . . ." She paused, crumpled the paper into a ball, took a fresh sheet and started again. "Good news has arrived from England." That was better. She chuckled. No call signs. Then it struck her that even the word England might be indiscreet. She tore it up and stuffed the scraps through the grating into the glowing heart of the stove. She also poked about in the wastepaper basket, found her first attempt, and threw the screwed-up ball of paper in as well. It did occur to her, as she watched it flare up, that this was the way criminals behaved. Then she trailed through all the various rooms to the kitchen-bathroom, where she found Gisela stirring a pan of beetroot soup. She poured some into a cup for Milly to taste. It was clear crimson, piping

180

hot, pungent. "This was the favourite soup of Mr. Simpson," Gisela observed rather sentimentally. "His hangover cure." Milly raised her eyebrows but forbore to comment, as almost any comment would have sounded priggish, let alone the one that was on the tip of her tongue. Instead: "Well, now, Gisela," she began, in such an elaborately casual tone that Gisela, contrary to recent practice, immediately dropped what she was doing and turned to give her full attention to her employer, even going so far as to remove the cigarette from her lips and place it carefully on the edge of the sink. She had taken to smoking quite openly whilst at work in the kitchen. Milly wished rather feebly that she herself had not been so weak-minded as to overlook it the first time she had seen her at it; it seemed hardly worthwhile complaining now that it had become an established practice, although she could not remember exactly when it had been initiated. So she merely frowned at the cigarette in lieu of verbal protest, and began again: "Later on, Gisela, when you've finished here, I want you to . . ." She was interrupted by a gentle tapping at the kitchen door.

"Blast," she muttered, and went to open it. Outside was Sophie, in her usual bus conductress rig, but carrying an offering of some sort, a flower pot, it looked like.

"Darling . . ." she began, as always, but her smile faded at sight of Milly's stiff, unwelcoming face. "Oh, I've come at the wrong time! Of course, I know that it's not my time, but I just thought . . ." Her voice trailed off. "Look——" she thrust the package into Milly's hands. "I just had to bring you this. I saw it—and knowing your love of plants, flowers, indeed, of anything beautiful, I——"

"That was very sweet of you, Sophie. Well, you'd better come in, don't hang about out there. How nice," she went on, unwrapping the pot. She did quite like flowers, but she detested them in pots, or rather the type of flowers that go in pots, cyclamen and so on. She had been afraid that this might turn out to be a cyclamen and had wired up her smile accordingly; lucky, in a way, because what was merely an aversion regarding cyclamen amounted to a horror, or phobia, in the case of what the pot contained, a cactus; like a caterpillar, preserved but still life-like, its looping progress checked, a band of yellow spines bristling up its grey-green dusty pelt.

"Isn't it a little beauty?" exclaimed Sophie.

"Yes," said Milly, "isn't it?" and quickly put it down. "Sophie, you don't happen to know of a dressmaker, do you?"

"A dressmaker, darling? You want one? Why, of course. Wait—I'll put my thinking cap on. Yes, of course I do. There's the one who made my confirmation white—quite a dear, she was, in her way. But that's rather a long time ago, now. And I believe I did hear she'd gone a bit blind. Still, I could ask her—shall I? But now I come to think of it," she was frowning deeply, " I must say it wasn't what you might call a succès fou, that dress. Shall I ask, darling? We could go together whenever you like . . . I dare say she might manage it—if she's not blind, that is."

" No, don't bother, Sophie. It doesn't really matter."

" Darling, how pretty you look in your négligée." Sophie touched the sleeve in wonder. " Easy to see this came from England."

Milly jerked her arm away. " Well, it didn't," she said, rather rudely, but she was irritated beyond endurance. " It came from America. We're rather busy, Sophie, this morning. We've got a dinner-party to-night."

She felt guilty at once, Sophie looked so crestfallen.

" Milly, darling—of course tell me if I'm in the way—but can't I help? Peel potatoes or something like that? I'll only stay for a minute or two." Milly relaxed slightly, although by now she knew what Sophie's " minutes" were, and the latter, immediately sensing this change of mood, began happily bustling about: " So, just tell me what. Come along, anything . . . Gisela, give me a knife—see—a little sharp knife, and I'll do the potatoes—yes, and a bowl of fresh cold water——"

" The potatoes are already done," said Gisela dryly. Three made a crowd in the kitchen, and now Clarissa and Dermot filed in, rather with the air of coming to stay, Clarissa carrying a book and Dermot a model vehicle; when Clarissa saw Sophie she threw her arms round her neck and dragging her down, kissed her hard on both cheeks. Sophie looked gratified by this attention but Milly, whose due it rightly was, said sharply: " Good morning, Clarissa. Why aren't you on your walk?"

" Because of Miss Raven, Mummy. She's——"

" Die Nanny," Gisela explained in her flat, sardonic voice, " is sick. Suddenly. After eating the hot salt meat and fried eggs I always prepare for her breakfast and two of those large biscuits in milk and a few buttered rolls and——"

" Oh dear." It was difficult to pretend surprise. " I'd better go in and see her."

" She doesn't want to see anyone, Mummy. She's drawn the curtains and she's lying in the dark."

" Her monthly pains, perhaps? " Gisela suggested charitably, with an uncharitable little smile.

" Poor Milly, how terrible for *you*," said Sophie, grasping the real point at issue which had escaped the rest. " I tell you—let me take the children for their walk. What about that? "

182

" Sophie—would you really? But won't it be a nuisance? "

" No, darling, of course not. I have one or two lessons, it's true, but I'll cancel them—where's the telephone? No, dash it, they aren't on the telephone. Never mind. So it's settled. I am your nanny to-day, Clarissa—how do you like that? "

" Oh, Sophie! " Clarissa embraced Sophie's tweed girth. " My angel dear . . . I love you best in all the world, I think . . ."

Milly looked rather cross, and then remembered that her own liberty depended upon Sophie that day, so all she said was:

" Now don't bother Sophie, Clarissa. It's certainly very kind of her. Well, Dermot," she went on, turning to her son, " how about you? Are you ready to go out with Sophie? "

Dermot's attention was elsewhere. Apparently fascinated by the cactus, he hung over the flower pot, his nose touching the rim.

" This is a nice little thing," he observed, with a deceptively casual air. Then, as no one made any comment, he added in distinct but gentle tones, " I would rather like to have it for my own." Remarks like these, in his experience, if tossed ever so lightly into the air, had a way of falling on good ground and occasionally of bearing fruit—at least they brought rewards as often as Clarissa's more strident demands. As it so happened in this instance he was quite right. "So you shall have it, my little dear," his mother promised him under her breath.

" The water boils," said Gisela. " I am to attend to the crayfish, yes? "

" Not *crayfish*! " exclaimed Sophie, jumping up from the bath. " Well, what a lucky chance! That's dashed lucky, Milly, I must say, that I happen to be here." She was already tying an apron round her hips. " No, no, Gisela—*I* am to do it, thanks. Now you just watch. I have my own country way, these being a speciality of our district. First, the cauldron. It must be of sufficient size. Ah, yes, that's good. The water boils? That's it—so, where are they? "

Gisela lifted the lid of a large basket in which several dozen well-developed crayfish were nestling, fairly comatose, in a bed of rushes.

" Aren't they *sweet*! " crooned Clarissa. " What dear little claws."

" Don't touch, Clarissa, for pity's sake! "

Sophie, appraising her victims, hesitated. They seemed larger than the ones she remembered from her youth.

" What are you going to do? " said Milly, seized at Sophie's manner with sudden disquiet.

" Cook them," murmured Sophie abstractedly, and picked up the basket. The crayfish, jolted out of their stupor and inspired possibly by some premonition as to their fate, anyway no longer lethargic, began scuffling about rather fast, creaking at the joints; in their panic even

183

rocking the basket. Gisela retired to a corner where she began to giggle.

" Oh, look," said Dermot. " There's one poking out."

Milly had gone rather white.

" Sophie—*please*! You're not going to boil them *alive*! "

Her quivering burden held at arm's length over the cauldron, distracted by the note of anguish in her friend's voice, Sophie glanced round. Her expression resolute, in tones of Slavonic doom she cried: " IT MUST BE, MILLY! " and tipped the basket towards the cauldron just as Clarissa in uncontrollable excitement hurled herself at Sophie, tackling her from behind. Losing her balance, Sophie dropped the basket, a shower of reeds fell over the top of the stove, Milly screamed and Dermot jumped up and down.

For a second or two, owing to the screen of rushes, it was not easy to gauge the extent of the disaster, but it was soon evident that only a handful of the little beasts had actually met the end prepared for them; several of their luckier brethren were already perched on the edge of the stove and there was a crackling in the rushes as reinforcements emerged.

" Dear God," muttered Sophie under her breath.

" Sophie! " shrieked Milly, jumping on to a chair. " *Do* something! They're all over the place! "

Indeed, this was the impression to be gained from the scene, as one by one and then in batches, the frenzied but gallant crustaceans launched themselves into space, landing each with a plop, or thud, rather, on the stone floor. Armoured to withstand all natural hazards, like a highly trained paratroop battalion they collected themselves and scuttled for their objectives—the dank dark crannies under the bath.

" Quick! " yelled Sophie. " After them! " The children, infected by her excitement, screamed and fell on their knees, fearless in pursuit.

" Oh Christ," said Milly.

" They do nip," said Dermot, proudly displaying his finger from which a shiny black shape depended. Tugging himself free, he nonchalantly threw it into the cauldron. His mother closed her eyes.

" Catch them by the throat," muttered Sophie, the sweat pouring down her face.

" Mine don't *have* throats," said Clarissa. Making her own contributions to the cauldron, she was absorbed in watching the resulting chemical change. " I do believe they die *almost* at once, Mummy. And they turn a most heavenly pink."

" I am afraid some have got away," said Sophie at last. She sat down on the bath, mopping her face.

" Six missing," said Gisela laconically, ladling out the rosy corpses. " The biggest, of course. They went too fast to catch."

184

" And just what do we do about them, Sophie? " said Milly with a touch of acerbity in her voice. She was still pale and still on the chair.

" Well, Milly, I really don't know," said Sophie frankly. " But I think they will be all right."

" Oh, I *do* hope so," said Clarissa. " We could put out bits of food for them so they wouldn't starve. Name them, even? "

Milly looked at her daughter and sighed. She climbed down from the chair.

" I think you'd all better go for your walk now."

" Yes, Milly," said Sophie meekly. " That is best." She shepherded the children out.

" Gisela," said Milly without any preamble, as her morning seemed rapidly to be getting out of control, " please would you slip along to Princess Rapovska's now and ask her if she could spare the time to come round—to-day, perhaps."

" Certainly, gnädige Frau," said Gisela without argument and without any evidence of surprise. She had after all seen the sack of parcels arrive.

" And I wondered—do *you* happen to know of a dressmaker? "

" A dressmaker . . . well, if I were you," said Grisela kindly, as one woman to another, " I would ask the princess. There is a dressmaker, but you have to have an introduction."

" I would like a *good* dressmaker." Rather dubiously, Milly ran over in her mind's eye the princess's wardrobe as she knew it.

" This one is good. Very capable. She made for Mrs. Simpson." Her hand on the door, Gisela added, her eyes on her employer's face, " Mrs. Simpson was *very* chic." She smiled ever so slightly and drifted out.

Downstairs, passing through the hall, just for a second Gisela hovered, caught like a piece of thistledown, at the porter's desk.

" Good morning," she murmured.

" Good morning. And what was the cause of all that brouhaha? The housekeeper heard it, passing your door."

" Nothing," said Gisela, " only some shellfish which escaped."

" Ah so," said the porter, clearly disappointed by the humdrum nature of the explanation. " The children have a new nurse, I see."

" Yes. The old one is sick. She's nice, the Bielska. She's prepared to do anything for them, it seems."

" A good friend," agreed the porter, " is worth his weight in gold."

" Please tell the housekeeper that the wash-basin is stopped up again."

" If I tell her, you know what she will say. When one cooks in the bathroom—washes dishes in the hand-basin—that is what happens."

185

"The gnädige Frau told me to tell you."

"I will pass it on." The porter shrugged. Then, in the same monotone: "I shall see you this evening?"

"Not this evening. There is a guest this evening. To-morrow will be better than to-day. Now I am off to the Princess Rapovska."

"Ah yes, of course. What a big sack came to-day. Poor Vladek, he will soon be asking for extra pay. All those stairs. Well, good-bye."

"Good-bye, then. Till to-morrow."

*   *   *

The summons was answered by the arrival of the princess in person, as prompt and full of bounce as a returned pingpong ball.

"Chère Madame Milly!" She clasped Milly's hands, pinioning her, as it were, whilst her baby-blue eyes fluttered round the room. There were no packages in sight and the sugary smile visibly "set," hardening as if it had been subjected to a cold water test.

"'Ow are you?" she said, and releasing Milly's hands trotted over to her favourite arm-chair, where she sat looking so sulky that Milly had to laugh.

"How are *you*, Princess? Your medicines—they've come."

She brightened up at once, clapped her little pink jewelled paws together. "Fine. Ow, that's fine. Clever girl," she added encouragingly, as Milly made no move.

"Will you have some sherry?"

"No, not to-dye—I 'aven't time. . . ." Her heels began to tap the parquet. "I 'ave to go at once, yer see, now that the medicine's 'ere . . . pore Andrew, yer know . . ."

"Andrew?"

"Yes," said the princess impatiently, "Andrew, the one for 'oom the medicines are. Yer know, I explain all about 'im, 'ow they 'ave given up 'ope."

"Ah, of course," said Milly slowly. "I remember." It was true that she did remember. She lit herself a cigarette, thinking, now that's funny. The ailing young relative for whom the medicine had been requested had been named Paul—she was certain of that, because she herself had had a brother called Paul and this small coincidence had, ever so slightly, weighed with her at the time. Then in that case . . .

"How is everybody?" she asked sweetly. "Your sister Irène, Paul, and the others?"

"Irène? Paul?" The princess shrugged, puzzled. "Très bien, comme toujours."

"I'm so glad." Milly sat down on the arm of a chair. "I wondered,

186

dear Princess, whether you could recommend me a dressmaker? I hear that the one Mrs. Simpson——"

" Oh, that one," said the princess hastily. " Well, I don' know. Hm—per'aps I 'ave the address in my bureau. I look—sometime. Now—you think they are the *right* medicines? "

" Oh yes, indeed they are." Calmly she went on smoking, thinking to herself, now I want that dressmaker, I really do . . . *so*—" About the dressmaker, Princess. I'm afraid it's rather urgent."

There was a silence. " Well," said the princess glumly, " I will send the address."

" I was wondering whether you would introduce me personally? It would be most kind. We might go together, perhaps—to-day? "

" *Together? To-dye?* " The blue eyes opened wide in horror. " Ow, my poor dear—yer don' know . . . what you ask that's quite impossible . . . natch'rlly I would like, but . . ." Her protestations died away. Evidently reading from Milly's expression what was certainly in her mind, an inflexibility of purpose that matched her own, the princess capitulated with a professional grace that would have done credit to a Smyrna merchant. " Okay," she said gaily, rootling about in her carpet bag, " I write this little note, see, an' you give it 'er . . . that's the best wye . . ." she muttered, scribbling, " she speak French, ver' nice, 'ere, already done, fine . . . now you give it 'er, '*erself*, Madame Bérénice, understand . . . and don' mention my nyme whatever you do, no! Discretion, please. Now I go." She stood up.

" Thank you very much," said Milly. " So where did I put—ah! " She picked up the sofa cushions; the little packages that were Antoinette's reward lay strewn beneath.

No sooner had the princess gone than the telephone rang.

" I'm sorry, darling," said Larry. " I've just had a signal. That bloody man can't come."

" Who? Oh—can't he? "

" You aren't livid? " He sounded relieved. " I thought you would be, having it all laid on."

" No, I'm not livid," she said. She had forgotten all about it.

" Damn' cheek, at such short notice. So sorry, sweetie."

" Never mind."

" I'll ask Abe, shall I? Better than wasting all the grub."

" Much better," she agreed.

So that's all right, she thought. I'll go to the dressmaker this afternoon. No, dammit, there's Miss Raven, I wonder if Sophie——

And at that moment Sophie came in. " Look, darling, if it would be of help, it occurred to me," she began rather timidly, " as you have a thousand things to do and entertaining is a worry, I know, shall I come this afternoon and take them out again, the children? It's hard for you, with that fool sick "—anyone who inconvenienced Milly was a fool—" and, well, it gives me pleasure, if . . ."

" Oh, Sophie, it *would* be a help. But do you think——"

Milly's tone was so warm, so unexpectedly friendly, that Sophie was quite beside herself with joy.

" My pet, of *course*. Easy. Now, you're busy, so I'll go. I'll come back early, very early. Leave them to me, the dears. Don't worry your head in the least."

Milly thought, that's very nice of Sophie, but then she's fond of the children and it's probably quite fun for her—quite a break, in fact. I suppose she *has* got her other work, lessons and all that, but she doesn't seem to bother about them very much—so she can't be in *such* a bad way. I dare say Abe was exaggerating. Of course I can't *pay* her, it's quite unthinkable. And we really haven't had a proper lesson for days, have we? She just comes and chats. And it would be an insult to offer her money for that. It's really very nice that she likes the children so much.

This afternoon, then, the dressmaker. Really, she felt in quite a good temper, considering what a troublesome morning it had been; so she poured herself a glass of sherry before lunch.

Chapter Two

IN THE afternoon she set off by herself, and following the directions given by the princess she found the dressmaker's, which was in a tall old house in a street of tall old houses on the far side of the main square, an apartment on the fourth floor, up a dark wooden staircase which creaked at every tread. There was no name on the door; she rang the bell and waited and presently an eye glittered through a spy-hole in the door and then after some whispering she was admitted. The apartment smelt like all Central European apartments, of moth-balls, beeswax, sour cabbage, damp woollen underpants, at least one tomcat, geraniums, prayer books and mice. A tall young woman, rather masterful in manner and with a fuzz of hair on her upper lip, looked blank and then rather amused as Milly explained, first in German, then in French, the object of her visit. Shaking her head as if determined not to understand, although her black eyes gleamed, she led Milly down a long dark passage to a waiting-room where she was left with two other clients who had arrived previously. There she remained for some time, sitting on a shiny horsehair sofa, flicking through back numbers of *Elle* and *Marie Claire*, aware of two pairs of inquisitive and hostile eyes focused on her every movement. They might have been twins, these two ladies, except that they sat on opposite sides of the room and were clearly unacquainted. They wore identical coats of blanket material, the cut of which, Milly did rather hope, was not the work of Madame Bérénice; both were shod in brand-new Bata shoes and their sticky red fingernails clutched identical plastic handbags. Their expressions, manner, too, bore a sort of family resemblance; they sat there, one on each side of her, eyeing her grimly, avidly, and yet if she looked up and chanced to catch the eye of one or the other, each would look away, furtively shuffling her feet, as if fearful of some unwholesome contact. Now and again the dark young woman peeped into the room, the odd trio of clients apparently amusing her and others vastly; each time she shut the door on them cackles of laughter could be heard from what must have been a workroom at the back. Milly began to wish she hadn't come. After three-quarters of an hour or so one of her companions was summoned away, and then after a similar interval, the second, and she was left alone.

She was already accustomed to the Slavonian tempo of life, but **it**

189

was not altogether restful, she decided. It afforded too many opportunities for meditation, for day-dreaming, even for second thoughts, so that an operation could be conceived with determination and zest but by the time it came to carrying it through one's mood, irritatingly enough, might well have changed. She had been in the waiting-room two hours, nearly, and the room was growing dark. The stove gave out a stuffy heat, the surface of the tiles glimmering, and musing to herself, she experienced that odd recurrent feeling of unreality, of herself being a disembodied ghost, wandering in this or that unlikely spot—why here, for instance? A queer sort of half-way house—the mezzanine floor between one stage and the next; or perhaps just the breathing space before taking the plunge off the board? Was that what it was? Scarcely. Two hours was rather long for that. Now she wished very much she had not come, and was just about to get up and go when she saw that the dark young woman was standing in the doorway. She switched on the light.

" Madame Bérénice will see you now," she said gravely, in beautiful French. " Please come this way."

Down some more dark passages, eventually Madame Bérénice was tracked to her lair, a small bright parlour, where she was seated at a bureau engaged in her accounts; without turning, she motioned to Milly to sit down, and presently she pushed aside her books and rose from her desk, taking off a rather striking pair of tortoiseshell-rimmed spectacles. At sight of her Milly at once experienced a mild shock. For the first time since she had left London she herself felt at a disadvantage—that is to say, she was at once reminded that a nail on her right hand was chipped, that she had not put on her best set of underwear, and that it was three months since her hair had been professionally set. Madame Bérénice, on the other hand, was as well groomed as if her sphere of activity were the Rue St. Honoré. A small plump woman, trim and neat, because, Milly guessed, splendidly corseted beneath her navy-blue grosgrain suit, her nylon stockings were immaculate, and fluffy curls of palest blue clung, tapered by no Slavonian shears, to her small round head. As she came close Milly recognised " Amour Amour "—her own favourite scent, of which, it occurred to her, she was now out of stock.

" Madame? " She smiled sweetly, expectantly; she had very clear sharp grey eyes, and her voice was soft, scarcely more than a purr. Milly handed her the note from the princess. Madame Bérénice put on her spectacles and read it, holding it in her little white paw. Her nails were perhaps a trifle too long, Milly thought; with them she might, certainly could, scratch. When she had finished reading, she tore the note into small pieces and put them in the stove.

"Any friend of the princess . . ." she murmured, tentatively unfurling her tape measure. "So you are—American?"

"No. English."

"Aaah . . ." With an ever so slight waning of enthusiasm Madame Bérénice paused to gaze reflectively, and with evident misgiving, on her client. "Ah-ha." She draped the tape measure round her neck and sighed, as if, pending settlement of one or two points, she could go no farther. "And what was it you required, chère madame?"

"A dinner dress. Not a ball dress. A simple dinner dress. I have the stuff with me."

"Hm . . ." The dressmaker spread the velvet over a chair, stroking her chin dubiously. She still seemed undecided, certainly quite unimpressed.

Milly watched her, puzzled, and was driven to play her last card. "I hear you made for—for Mrs. Simpson," she said, the invocation of whose name was never, she had learned, to be without effect: this time it was electric.

"Ah, *you* are a friend of Mrs. Simpson! But now I understand, of course. Well, by all means, delighted . . . vraiment . . ."

All smiles, she fetched a great book, and opening a fresh page scribbled on it. Over her shoulder Milly read: *Mme X (amie de Mme S)*; and then she began flinging the tape measure round vital measurements, chattering away in such a friendly manner that Milly asked herself, not for the first time, what was it that Mrs. Simpson had *had*—she must have had *something*—but *what*?

"Perfect figure . . ." Madame Bérénice rattled on, "Americans, English, etcétera, all perfect figures . . . poor Princess Rapovska . . . these hard times . . . she was so chic once, you would never believe . . . before the war, madame, everyone so chic . . . Slavnik was a little Paris . . . I remember, imagine, before luncheon everybody en marron, de rigueur, and then, for the five o'clock, black, black, black . . . and now . . ." She offered Milly a cigarette and fitted one for herself into a long holder. "Sobranie Balkan, you know them? I prefer . . ." she said simply; then, "You have a design? . . . I have *Vogue*, 'Arper, now we choose . . . ah, in Slavnik I had such a clientèle, and then the war, tellement désagréable, vous savez, so I moved here . . . but they still come, the clients, the old ones, but how to make for them? However much I make adjustments, they still would not be able . . . and I must live, évidemment. . . . So . . . now, I have *that* type of person!" She tossed her curls. "You saw just now, out there . . . coming to *me*, Bérénice, imagine!" She laughed rather unpleasantly. "I am *forced* to take them, with their great hips, great bopos, great boom-booms . . ." her hands behind and before, in gestures not the
191

most delicate, illustrated the proportions of her new clients. "They are pigs . . . the wives of pigs . . ."

"But—*who* are they?" Milly asked in bewilderment. The description was so emphatic, so malicious, that it conjured up a farmyard of clients all paying through their snouts.

"The wives of party bosses, my dear, of *big bugs*. If I say no, I don't want, then they tell their husbands . . . and that would make it hard for me." She put her head on one side in a kittenish way, made a little grimace. "Because, you understand, in the autumn and the spring, twice a year, I have to go to Paris—or I go mad. Folle, tout simplement."

"Oh," said Milly, "do you really? How awful for you, I mean . . ."

"Yes. It is—awful. What horrors it involves—what miracles of patience . . . but then it's worth it, because I adore Paris. Still, you don't know how I suffer. 'Madame Bérénice' "—she mimicked a whine —" 'tell me, please, do I wear gloves for the cocktail . . . a hat? a train? A *train*! Should I sit down, shake hands, tip the servant, where to make pee-pee?' My dear, I tell you, I earn those trips."

She turned away to write in her book.

"About the price," Milly began nervously, "for this dress. Could you—well, make a special price for me?" She smiled, feeling very ill at ease. The dressmaker nodded, smiling too, a mechanical and far from reassuring smile, and with it still on her lips, without the least hesitation or effort at calculation, named her price.

"Excuse me," said Milly, "just while I . . ." As she tamed the rows of noughts into sterling, Madame Bérénice stood by, humming a little tune, casually buffing her nails.

"I'm so sorry," said Milly at last. "To have wasted your time. I mean—I simply can't . . ." she began rolling up the velvet in its paper.

"It's too much? Tiens!" The dressmaker gave a little tinkling laugh, patting her curls in front of a mirror. "All sewn with silk," she murmured like a litany, "American zip fastener . . . hooks, eyes, rustless . . . all finished off inside . . . still——" She abandoned her own reflection with a sigh and then quite briskly she turned and said: "If it's too much we can arrange, I dare say, some other way."

"Some other way?"

"Quite frankly," observed Madame Bérénice, idly stabbing pins into her pin-cushion, "I am not interested in money—not at all."

Astonished, Milly pondered this statement. It struck her not only as original, but in the context of the demand preceding it, positively paradoxical.

"You see," she went on, in her soft sad little voice, "money has no value, after all." She paused. " It's pretty, your tailleur." Meditatively, she stroked her fingers over the cloth. " Prince des Galles, it's always nice. Eh bien, it's like that . . . we could . . . systématiser . . . you know, the price. Hm . . . quelques bouteilles de veeskee, peut-être ? "

" Whisky ? Oh, I see . . . but I'm afraid—well, we only get one bottle a month . . . it's—well, it's been *rationed*, you see."

The explanation sounded not merely unconvincing, but thoroughly mean and sordid. It was evident that this was the way it sounded to Madame Bérénice, too.

" Le veeskee! *Rationed?* Tsst!" She screwed up her little nose in sympathy and distaste, as at the mention of a slightly vulgar disease, pinkeye, say, or ringworm—a disease contracted by one's inferiors, generally speaking, as a result, in part, of their inferiority—but when, as now, afflicting a dear and hitherto reputable friend, well then, better called by another name. Certainly her manner implied that the tidings might have been broken less harshly.

" Brandy, perhaps ? " Milly suggested dubiously.

" Perhaps." Madame Bérénice looked dubious also. Plainly making a concession, she said: " *If* cognac, then French of course, with those little stars, hein ? And a few hundreds of these nice Sobranie . . . coffee . . ." she went on, picking up her pencil, deliberating, as she might in giving an order to a grocer. " The American kind, in tins."

" I don't know about that," said Milly miserably. " What about tea ? "

" Tea ? Tea . . . let me see . . ." She tapped her pencil against her teeth. " No, I don't need—I have enough. But *if*—then the Lord Grey, it's delicate, I like the flavour. Soap, yes . . . Chanel is the mark I prefer—the scent of verbena, you know ? I like it best, don't you ? "

" Yes, I do, as it happens."

" Bravo. You have good taste." She bared her sharp little teeth in approval and continued.

At last Milly said: " But how shall I—well, get these . . . er, *things* to you ? "

" My dear, it's not *far* . . ." Madame Bérénice reflected, but not very seriously. Clearly the matter of delivery was the problem of the supplier, and it occurred to Milly that all this must have happened before.

" Could you not," she suggested, " bring it . . . c'est à dire, them, les articles . . . in a little *sack* . . . one evening, perhaps? Yes, evening would be best." She laughed merrily. " From all points of view, n'est ce pas? Tr-rrès bien . . . then everything's arranged very well . . . yes, next week . . . au revoir." She clapped her hands daintily together, and Milly was escorted from the room.

*   *   *

She hurried across the square. It was already dusk, and during the afternoon it had become much colder; there was a smell of snow in the wind. The shops were lighted up. Nightmarish under the greenish-white glare, the packets of detergent, the rows of square-toed brown boots straight off the assembly line in the Bata factory, paraded across the windows, uniform, hideous, fulfilling their purpose merely by filling up space, without, however, camouflaging the interior; one could still see inside. This deliberate and desolate transparency was a characteristic of all the State shops; one could see in and who was there and what they were up to, one could see it all, through and through to the other side, and one was seen seeing it, and now she saw, as usual, the queues shuffling forward. Those people at the tail ends who were still in the street blew on their mittened fingers, peered at their newspapers or at those of their neighbours but not a one ever looked to see what he might buy; even the women stared straight ahead, brooding or muttering out of the corners of their mouths to the one in front, the one behind.

"If I don't go to Paris twice a year I go mad"—and Sophie, and those greedy scarlet claws clutching plastic handbags and the queues of people huddling in the wind—"none of it makes sense," she muttered, pulling the fur collar round her neck. "None of it feels *real* —and nor do I." Once more the thought came to her, crossing the square, "I am just a shadow . . . but it's not true," she told herself fiercely, "I'm *real*. I know I am. I've never felt this way before, any-where else. It must be this town . . . it's depressing . . . it always seems to be evening. Dusk, or dark."

The sound of singing drifted towards her on the wind. The doors of the church on the corner stood open; the church was always crowded but this evening the people overflowed down the steps into the street, kneeling pressed together, women mostly, all in black, black shawls thrown over their heads. In passing she glimpsed the altar, a blaze of candle-flame and tinsel against the shadows, mysterious, remote, set apart from the seething black mass of worshippers, magnificent as a medallion on velvet, untouchable behind stout wire mesh: a dream, not for the possessing, and better so, better sighed over, prayed for, dreamed of, better at a distance, to remain a mystery, a legend, in order to be of real and permanent comfort in distress. At the tinkling of a bell the people on the steps swayed, dipped all together in the wind. That's all very well—gloomily she paused to watch them

194

—boots and saints' days and detergents—it may be enough for them but it's not enough for me. If they are crying out, as I am, for something real and they get served up with all this instead—the plate glass and nothing behind it, the singing and the sound of this little bell and all the paraphernalia they can only see or hear, but can't touch, or *have*—well, if they imagine that to be reality, if it does for them, then they are the shadows, not me. It doesn't do for me. I'm real and I know what real things are . . . oh, yes, I do, she insisted stubbornly, her thoughts having strayed to her mink coat in the cupboard, and finding that even that reassuring symbol of rock bottom reality did not, as it usually did, come up to scratch.

Suddenly her mood left her. She was nearing the hotel and there was a light in the antique shop window, a single bulb lying in a shell; warming the interior of the shell the light spread over the fluted rim, shone through a veil of gossamer that was the lace. " Ah, *that's* real," she whispered, looking at it with intense pleasure, the desire to possess it stronger than ever, and which was the reality, that or the lace? was beside the point, because she had cheered up.

*   *   *

Feeling cold and longing for some tea, she went straight to the kitchen, where she found Miss Raven for whom, it was plain, the kettle was on the boil, and the teapot arranged on the tray. Perfectly at her ease, certainly by no sign revealing herself caught short, Miss Raven in her camel hair dressing-gown was engaged in transferring chocolate biscuits from a large tin to a subsidiary and private one. She said, snapping the lid firmly on the latter and placing it on the tray: " Just making myself a cup of tea." With an economy of action to suit her words she did just that, then switched off the electricity and began to fill the hot water-bottle with the remaining contents of the kettle.

" How are you feeling now, Miss Raven? " Refilling the kettle, Milly brought out the early morning teapot for her own use. " I'm so sorry you felt so rotten."

" Ah," said Miss Raven, pressing the bottle to her chest and expelling the air from it, " there's never any knowing with me. Still," she added, with just a hint of martyrdom in her voice as she watched Milly rooting about vainly in the parent biscuit tin, " I hope *you* have a nice little do."

" A nice little—oh, I see. No, that's been put off. He can't come."

" Colonel Cantrell? " said Miss Raven quickly. " You mean he's not coming after all? "

" Yes. Nuisance, isn't it? " She gazed at the saucepans, covered dishes and so on. laid out. " We've had to ask Mr. Schulman instead,

195

to help us out. Pity you aren't feeling up to it, Miss Raven. There's such a lot of food." She smiled encouragingly at Miss Raven, and for once, greatly to her surprise, Miss Raven smiled back.

" I did feel groggy," she said, " that I must admit. But I've an idea it's going off. All of a sudden. That's the way it is with me, come and go." Her spirits equally mercurial, it seemed, Miss Raven, with rather a lively air looping her bottle round her finger, bore her tea-tray away.

So then, losing no time since it had to be done, Milly went off to the salon and took paper, pencil, her account books and the current NAAFI list and set to work. The operation was by no means so simple as it might appear, because on the basis of a certain premise which she preferred not to define, in adjusting the usual list to her present requirements she had also to furnish herself with an explanation for these adjustments. Not all; no need, for instance, to worry about reasons for increasing the orders for tea, soap, and so on; like medicines, these were her province. Other things could be ordered separately from London, sent out by bag, and paid for out of her own money. Still, one mustn't lose sight of the fact that they would arrive. That was the worst of it, she thought ruefully, the fact of their—well, their *bulk*. She felt unpleasantly like a would-be murderer planning his deed; there was little doubt that once the body was disposed of, so would the sense of guilt be, too, and all would be plain sailing. The sense of guilt troubled her scarcely at all—as yet; that followed on the crime, surely? But one couldn't shut one's eyes to the fact that the body was a damned awkward affair and the problem needed some thinking out. Never mind, she told herself, sufficient unto the day—she could invent something in the meantime, no doubt. The main, the immediate problem was how to order those items which were not in her province, the brandy, the wine, and the cigarettes.

It was a singular and most remarkable feat that she achieved when as now her mind was fixed on a certain purpose; sheer concentration enabling her, whilst aware of the broader implications of what she was in fact about, to shut her eyes to any such as were a potential hindrance to her as if they did not exist. When circumstances demanded, that is, when she wished her train of thought to race full steam ahead and with maximum manœuvrability, she would, with such technical skill that the operation was almost unconsciously performed, slip those coaches which were an encumbrance—in any case they were always rather to the rear—shunt them into a siding and leave them there. Then the train, getting up steam, moved up and down exacting gradients very fast indeed; but because the space was circumscribed by various factors, because there was such a maze of tracks, it was in fairly constant

196

danger of taking the wrong turning and inadvertently running into that line of track on which those stationary coaches stood; yet, although it sometimes swerved perilously close, it was obviously in the hands of an expert driver—a collision never did quite take place. Because a collision would have been fatal, as the driver, even if only subconsciously, knew very well; only a collision could so have shocked her mind as to integrate it, so that the whole appraised the whole—which was, above all things, what she strove to avert.

But all at once, in the middle of her calculations, she did stop short; the pencil fell from her fingers and she sat staring at the paper in her lap. Perhaps because she was tired, perhaps because she had taken a dislike to Madame Bérénice, perhaps, too, because the affair had progressed, it was no longer a matter of a fib here, a bit of bargaining there—now action must be taken, she must calculate, write orders, send cheques—whatever it was, she did experience a moment of weakness, even a premonitory pang of guilt. Who was the enemy? Whom were these elaborate explanations intended to deceive? Deceive—it was an express train now almost out of control, one would say, the way it rolled, veering dangerously close—deceive? An unprepossessing word, too plain by half. But who is it, Milly, the enemy? Who? The voice nagged her, not to be stifled, and the answer seemed to sidle up to her elbow, jostling her until she was about to turn upon it angrily, confront it if only to be rid of it, to tell it to be off, and there is no knowing whether the course of events would have been altered had she done so —but at that moment Miss Raven came in.

" All alone? " she said. " What a busy bee." Seeing the curtains undrawn, she went to draw them, and Milly's eye was caught by a flash of colour as she passed.

" That's a very snazzy outfit you have on, Miss Raven."

" This? " Miss Raven bridled. " It's a bridge coat."

" Ah! That's what it is."

" It came from Pekin." She seemed to hesitate. Then, loudly, " I say," she said. " I feel much better."

" Good."

" Ever so much." The bulletin, Milly thought, eyeing her, was superfluous—indeed, Miss Raven looked on top of her form.

" You'll stay up for dinner, then? "

" That's what I thought," she agreed. " You won't forget to come in to the children, will you? "

" No, I'll be along." It was true she had forgotten the night before.

" I'll send that countess in to you, shall I? I'd like to get them off now, and anyway, I expect she wants her drink."

" Soon, Miss Raven. Not just for ten minutes or so." Frowning, she shuffled the papers on her lap. Miss Raven, taking the hint, sniffed and went off through the bedroom.

" Someone's overdrawn at the bank," she said to herself, pausing in Milly's bathroom to admire herself in the glass. " See that a mile off." She gave her hair a teeny spray of lacquer. " Bet *he* doesn't know. Little bitch." She passed on. She had no very high opinion of her own sex and the mothers of her charges she treated with a special mixture of dislike and contempt in equal parts.

So really, muttered Milly, reapplying herself, it's an economy to do it this way. The interruption had allowed time for her resolve to stiffen.

Fifty per cent, at least. What *she* asked in the first place just for the making—what the . . . the *things* would cost—well, the difference was almost exactly half. Fifty per cent, she repeated, pleased with its business-like ring.

When Larry came in she said with an air of fatigue blended with conscious virtue, " I've done the NAAFI list, darling. Razor blades, shaving cream, I haven't forgotten a thing. You can't complain I don't think of you."

" I don't. This it? " She sealed up the envelope and put it into his hand. " I say, this *is* service, what's come over you? All ready to go off? "

" All ready."

" Sweetie. That's saved me a lot of trouble. Give me a kiss." She gave him a kiss, so light was her heart.

" She's a brick, isn't she? " Sophie beamed fondly on her pet, sipping her third gin. " A real brick. You are a lucky man."

" I know," said Larry.

In the bath, all the grubbiness of the interview with the dressmaker together with those little dark stains of guilt on her peace of mind were washed away. It had been done, he had accepted it. Well, accepted the envelope, anyway. A fuss—a fuss about nothing. Lying in the water, she remembered the lace. Somehow, after what she had been through to-day, there was no longer any doubt about the lace. She must have it—it was as simple as that. A ha'porth of tar. Though I doubt it'll be a ha'porth, she thought rather uneasily, and turned on the hot tap. Magnificent, the tranquillising effect of hot water. All one's cares melted away. Perhaps she had never at any stage from the moment of setting eyes on the lace truly forgotten its existence nor left it out of her calculations, nor ever doubted that one day it would be hers. You are *naughty*, Milly. She giggled. Naughty was a word she rather enjoyed as applied to herself or her actions; entirely acceptable,

198

implying femininity, coquetry, innocent misdemeanours to be forgiven with a loving kiss—it covered so much.

*   *   *

Sophie's family were at table, waiting for their supper, when they heard a crash from the kitchen.

" Another heirloom gone west," Ludovic remarked. " Lucky we've got plenty."

Sophie came in holding a tin of fish, a handkerchief wrapped round her hand.

" The Dresden," she said, " dash it." She went over to the dresser and reached down another plate and turned the fish on to it.

" Third this week," said her brother.

" Naturally," said the aunt, " it goes in threes."

" The tin-opener was blunt," Sophie explained. " Shall I give you some, Singe? Not export, I'm afraid. One has to wait so long and I hadn't time."

" And how is your pupil getting on, Sophie? Ah! how well I remember those first few lessons—in that book of Miss Brownlow's. You're using that one, eh? " Tilting his chair, his eyes fixed mockingly on his sister's face, Ludovic recited: " Lieutenant Grant is a lieutenant. He is not a soldier—how right, how true—he is an officer. Mr. Jan is a lighthouse-keeper. He likes to read the foreign papers. From the Spanish newspapers—why *Spanish*?—he receives tidings from Europe. Lucky fellow. Times have changed, haven't they? He'd be in the salt mines if he did that now. Ah well, at least Miss Brownlow never learned a word of that subversive stuff. I wonder—what does Mrs. Chose make of it? Perhaps you haven't got as far as that? "

" Can't you see that Sophie is tired, Ludo? Let her eat."

" Did Father Joseph come, darling? " Sophie turned to her aunt. She had not spoken to her brother for many days now.

" I met Mrs. Tonovska in the street," Ludovic went on. " Hm, these are terrible, these fish. And she asked whether you were ill, Sophie. Her children, curious as it seems, are anxious to recommence their lessons. So I said you were pretty well but rather busy. I hope I did right."

" It worries you, does it, Singe, this taste? " Sophie said to her aunt.

" I don't mind," said Singe. " It's apart—one acquires it gradually." Holding up her bread she nibbled it, like a squirrel, her bright eyes shifting from brother to sister.

Ludovic put down his fork. " I wonder, now," he mused aloud, " just what the British are having for supper to-night? Not these dear little sprats preserved in a by-product of petroleum, I dare say. I should

199

have thought Sophie could have provided for us better, Singe, with her contacts."

Sophie raised her head and looked at him. " Just what do you mean by that? " she asked in a low voice.

" Ludo," said Singe. " I have already asked you to be quiet. Can't you see Sophie's tired? "

" Tired, is she? La pauvre Sophie. With a face as red as a beetroot, smashing up the place—you know what I think, Singe? " He giggled. " She's not tired, she's drunk . . . tiddly, stinko . . . the way she's been every evening ever since . . ."

" How dare you speak to me like that? " Sophie flashed at him. " You who never raise a finger to help—the day you bring some money into this place, honestly earned, Ludo, then you can talk. Meanwhile, just *shut up*! "

" Children, stop it, please . . . I can't bear it. Don't shout."

" We're not shouting, Singe." It was true they were not. The habit of whispering was too deeply ingrained in them for that.

" You know what, Sophie? " Ludovic went on. " Antoinette Rapovska cut me in the street two days ago . . . so to-day I went round to ask her why, and she said—she was very nice about it— that in public that was what she must do because I'm *your* brother . . . and because of that, I'm dangerous to know."

She snorted with contempt. " That's all you care about, you and your ' smart set '! . . . afraid they'll *drop* you . . . and you'd do anything rather than risk that, snivelling and toadying the way you do . . . I've seen you, Ludo. Much I care about the Rapovskis . . . they're a no-good bunch, and I am ashamed to own that I am of the same race and class as they . . ."

" You're a fool, Sophie . . . you're a crazy middle-aged country frump, and they laugh at you—do you know that? A country cabbage, that's what you are, and as green as a cabbage. You're riding for a fall, my dear . . . prancing in and out of the Grand Hotel as though you owned the place, visiting and drinking with your British friends—how long do you think that's going to go on? "

" Antoinette herself goes to the Grand to visit the British—what about that? "

" She goes discreetly . . . you flaunt yourself."

" *Discreetly?* You mean she comes and goes by the back way? Ha-ha. I rather imagined that was how she did it. Well, let me tell you that I am not accustomed to go in and out of back doors, like a servant or—or a *thief* . . . I am not afraid, and I am not ashamed, on the contrary I am *proud*—d'you hear—*proud* to be their friend—and I shall continue to go there every single day just as long as they want

200

me . . ." She flourished the breadknife, her eyes sparkling with fury, and Ludovic recoiled. " And what is more, I don't believe anyone or anything can touch me, because—because," all of a sudden her anger seemed to leave her, she put down the knife, and said, very low, staring at the table, " because what I am doing is good, and God will protect me. My conscience is clear, Ludo . . . I love them and they need me."

" That's very nice," said her brother after a pause, looking at her strangely. " Very convenient. But if anything happens—if God should slip up, take his eye off the ball—where would you be, Sophie? Who would do anything for you then? Not your British friends, my dear."

" You can't frighten me," she said quietly. " I'm not going to give them up just for you, and don't think it. My mind is made up."

" Then you might do it for Singe," he said, calmly lighting a cigarette.

" Singe knows I must do what I think right." Rather gloomily, Sophie eyed her aunt. " Don't you, darling? "

Singe folded up her napkin. Her little face was quite screwed up with misery, but her jaw was hard as a golf ball, round and hard and set. " I don't like to hear you both quarrelling." She spoke sharply, looking from one to the other. " And I *don't* like," she turned with spirit on her nephew, " *your* way of talking, taking the name of the Holy Lord in vain. I don't know what has come over you. I've heard it once or twice lately, Ludo, and I will not have it, at least not in my presence—do you understand? "

Ludovic stared at his aunt in surprise. He opened his mouth to retort and then thought better of it. " All right," he said sulkily, " I understand."

Singe got up from the table and went to sit on her bed. She began pushing sawdust into a felt shape, making a brown sausage, a leg. " Sophie is older than you," she went on, " and she must decide for herself. She works like a slave for both of us without complaining— and we are a heavy burden on her shoulders, you and I, never forget that."

" Darling . . ." Sophie jumped up, knocking aside her chair, and threw her arms round her aunt's neck. " It's not that. I would work my fingers to the bone for you."

Her aunt smiled sadly, then her nose twitched. She sniffed with interest.

" What is it, Singe? Is it my breath? "

" Yes." Singe giggled. " It smells funny. Sour—I can't think what it reminds me of. What is it? "

" Gin, I expect," said Sophie airily.

"What is that? A British liqueur? It must be delicious."

"Oh, it is. But it's not a *liqueur*, exactly . . . more a sort of light potato wine, I think."

"Only about seventy per cent proof," Ludovic remarked, getting up from the table. "Nice and light." He strolled over to the door of his own room and shut it behind him. Sophie made a long nose in the direction of the door as it shut. Then she laid her head on her aunt's lap and began to laugh.

"Mind the sawdust, Sophie. It's getting in your hair. Are you happy, darling?"

"Oh, Singe . . . wildly happy! To go there, every day . . . and to-day I was there all day, except at lunchtime, when I had to go to those wretched Kovalskis . . . because I had missed two or three times . . . and the tram never turned up and I had to walk and it was raining . . . I'll need new soles, Singe, soon . . . and the Kovalski children were at their worst . . . you know how they can be . . . and they forgot to give me coffee, and of course there was no time for lunch because I had to get back . . . *there* . . . once there, of course, it's always a little bit of heaven. They are so wonderfully kind, there's no end to their kindness. I love them all. But I am so afraid for them—though I wouldn't tell *him* that . . ." she grimaced at the direction of her brother's door. "They are so innocent . . . so blessedly unsuspecting . . . they *need* me, Singe."

"Yes," said her aunt sadly, "I expect they do."

"But then to come back here and find him like that . . . well, it's too much."

"Don't bother about it, Sophie. He is upset. He means well, at least I think he does. He was talking to me before you came in—it seems there may be a job for him."

"A *job*?" Suddenly wary, she stiffened. "A *job*?" she repeated, frowning, then leapt to her feet. "For *him*—for Ludo? What sort of a job?"

"I don't know, darling."

Sophie paced up and down, thinking hard. Suddenly she went over to the door of his room. In front of it she paused. Then, her mind made up, she knocked.

"Come in." Ludovic was standing in front of the glass, tying his tie.

"Going out?" she said casually, leaning against the door.

"I am." Smoothing his hair, he examined the effect of the tie from all angles, without a glance at his sister.

"Where to?"

He flicked his shoulders, picked up his coat and came towards the
202

door, still without meeting her eyes. "It's no business of yours," he said as he passed her in the doorway. "As I am frequently reminded, you pay for the food I eat but I'm damned if you own me body and soul." He paused to put on his coat.

She said in a level voice: "What is this I hear—about a job?"

Ludovic buttoned up his coat, took from the pocket a thin gold cigarette case which had belonged to his father, selected a cigarette and tapped it on his nail.

"Oh, yes." His tone was amiable. "I was going to tell you—in fact I was even going to ask your advice—but from what you have said this evening I can see that it would be a waste of time. There is, or appears to be, a job going—for me. I have been undecided whether to accept it or not—because, really, that depended on you."

"Hadn't you better explain?"

"Well," said Ludovic, savouring the first few puffs of his cigarette, "it's like this. It seems—I may say that I did not know of it myself until to-day, when I visited the Rapovskis as I told you—that Paul, Antoinette's grandson—you know the one?—has a job. You didn't know either? Ah well, he has. In an office." He smothered a yawn. "And he has put in a word for me, that's all."

There was silence. Then Sophie burst out:

"But how can *he* have a job—without a permit? I don't understand."

"My dear, I see that you don't. Not *without* a permit, oh dear me, no." He smiled sweetly. "On the contrary—*with* a permit, and a lot of other perks as well." Amused, he studied her face.

"You mean . . . no! I don't believe it . . . but does his grandmother know?" Swiftly she crossed over to him, grasped the lapels of his coat, "Ludo! Tell me . . . *does she know that?*"

He brushed her hands away, laughed shortly: "The old girl? I rather fancy so. It doesn't upset her—so why should it upset you? What's sauce for a princess should be . . . eh, Sophie? And, you see, as you persist in this madness, I must think of myself. I have no scruples, my dear—two fools in the family would be just one too many. Ta-ta, then . . . Good night!" He waved to his aunt, tilting his hat jauntily, and went out.

"Darling!" Singe called to Sophie under her breath. "Darling—don't look like that. Please."

She was leaning against the door. All the colour had drained out of her face. She looked as if she had received a mortal blow.

"Sophie . . . *please!*"

She stumbled across the room and fell at her aunt's feet, clasping her hands. Singe felt Sophie's hands cold as ice.

203

" Tell me he's not serious, Singe," she whispered. " It's not possible, is it? Tell me he wouldn't do that. He can't mean it, can he? "

Singe stroked the head on her lap, pulling bits of sawdust out of the bright curly brown hair. Presently she said, " I don't know, Sophie, about him any more. He's changed. I think he does mean it, perhaps."

Chapter Three

THEN THE snow came. Not a white world overnight—nothing so sensational—but the following day and the next, the temperature dropped, dropped, until it was too cold for snow, they all said, although the bitter wind held the taste and smell and promise of snow, and the clouds, urged by the wind, were clumsy with the weight of the snow; and then for a while the wind dropped, the sky sagged low over the town, and a few flakes were squeezed from the heavy billowing bosom of the sky, where it was pierced by the church spires, grazed by the tops of the surrounding hills; but this snow when it fell in the town was mashed into the cobbles, it did not lie; dusting the shoulders of the hills, it froze there. It was too cold for snow. Then the wind got up again, more ferocious than before. The people crept through the streets, slinking under the arches out of the teeth of the wind, their faces yellow and pinched beneath the arc-lamps which hung swathed in icy yellow fog; they crowded into the coffee-bars where there was coffee of a sort, corrected, for that was the word, with vodka, where there were no chairs, and the chromium plating glittered cold under the merciless strip lighting, but where at least if one edged away from the swing doors, there was no wind. The price of wood was soaring, Sophie said; it would never come down. And old people were being carried off right and left.

" Carried off? " said Clarissa, agreeably startled.

" Died," said Milly.

" Passed away," said Miss Raven.

" It will be better," said Sophie, " when the snow comes." But the wind continued, holding off the snow. " Soon they will ration vodka," she said. " It seems vast quantities have been consumed in the past week. People staggering in the street——"

" Yes," said Milly. " I have seen that too."

" They drink all day—a nip here, there, to keep themselves warm. Because their clothes," she explained, with for her unusual under-statement, " are not of the first quality, not to withstand this cold. I think they are a bit drunk all the time. And '*they*' "—it was always '*they*'—" encourage it up to a point. The fault lies of course in the vodka. I fear that it is not of the first quality either, and then there are hangoverskis "—Sophie had had one herself recently and christened it thus—" and then they don't work next day and production falls off."

" Ah," said Miss Raven, as a dictator, ruthless, " then they *ought* to ration it."

" It is already forbidden on Saturdays," said Sophie, " besides, it is a risk to remove the one pleasure of the people before ever the winter has begun."

Then one afternoon, while Milly was at a fitting and Sophie was waiting to give her a lesson, they were roasting chestnuts on the grating of the nursery stove.

" In the park," said Clarissa, " I blew my nose and what do you think? My handkerchief was frozen stiff before I put it back in my pocket."

" And if you were to cry," said Sophie, " out there in the park, great peas would roll down your cheeks."

" No! " exclaimed Miss Raven, affronted at this trespass into her own province.

" It happened to me," said Sophie mildly, " in the park, one winter."

" Remind me," Clarissa enjoined her brother, " oh, remind me to cry in the park to-morrow! "

" I told you the truth, Clarissa," said Sophie, " there is no need to go out of your way to prove it. Besides, it is too late. It has stopped freezing—don't you notice it?—and the wind has dropped." She moved to the window and drew aside the curtains. " Look! "

They all three came and stood beside her, and gazed out, at first uncomprehending. Then one said, breathed it in a whisper, because somebody had to say it first: " Snow." And they each said it, savouring the word, whatever it meant to each of them, chilblains and changes of clothing and extra work to Miss Raven; high-priced fuel, the necessity for a coat for herself, bronchitis for Singe, to Sophie, who knew how long the winter would last; and to the children untried but legendary delights—yet now, in the event, it was they who proved exacting in respect of the phenomenon, disparaged its appearance, criticised its performance.

" It's not falling nearly fast enough," said Clarissa. " And what small flakes."

" Not even *white*," said Dermot.

" It always starts this way," said Sophie, " the real snow."

It snowed all that night and for three days and three nights after that. Then it stopped and the sun came out but the sun made no impression on the snow. Glare as it might, it had lost its powers, and the snow lay basking in the harmless glitter of its light, defying the sun whilst exploiting it to the last, scintillating beneath it, transformed by it into a miracle of beauty, so that everybody said: " Just look—look

206

at the snow!" and the sun that had worked the miracle, humiliated, retired in a huff, vanished for days behind the clouds which swept in from the mountains and more snow fell.

It was to outlast many, not only the aged and the ailing—some of whom may have had a premonition of it—but also the visitors, that first snow, the first to fall that would be the last to thaw. After only a few days it was hard to remember the town as it had been before the snow came.

* * *

"The car," said Wragg, "was due to go into workshop to-day."

"Oh, was it?" said Larry. "Well, one day either way won't make any difference. It can go in to-morrow."

"We're short of petrol vouchers—they didn't turn up this month."

"I meant to tell you, but I clean forgot. They came by the last post yesterday."

"You'll need chains if you're going to Zagranyza."

"Mm, I thought so. I've just told Vladek to put them in the back."

The office stove roared softly. Wragg unwound his long body from the table where he had been laying out press cuttings. Against the light, Larry could see his Adam's apple working in the throes of some emotion; anger, as it turned out to be.

"Simpson," said Wragg, "always let *me* do Zagranyza."

"Well, that's fine, I've no objection. You carry on. But I'll be in Slavnik at the end of the week, and I'll have to make a report, so I thought I'd better show my face there once, just for the record. Wouldn't it be a good idea if you came too?"

"Oh, no," mumbled Wragg, "one of us must stay."

"I don't see why. Nothing's likely to crop up. Schulman'll be in soon—he can answer the telephone if there's anything vital."

Wragg reared his head in a way he had, seeming to lay back his ears. "I don't think that would be advisable at all," he said with indignation. In its way, Wragg's face was an expressive one; he was able to register certain emotions—indignation was one of them—as unequivocally and effectively as an actor, though not with an actor's range; having mastered the art—like an actor—partly by practice and partly with the help of certain natural advantages. His face was so narrowly constructed that his eyes, which in fact were large, dark, and fine, from a head-on view almost seemed to meet; for this reason he would often regard his interlocutor sideways on, with a single eye, swivelling it round like a hen. This trick conveyed degrees of anger, affront, pique, disgruntlement and plain astonishment wonderfully well; how it reacted with the more saccharine emotions no one had yet discovered; it wasn't

207

often put to the test. Still, he performed it now, one eye rolling at the impropriety of Larry's suggestion.

"Oh, come now," Larry said mildly. "The Yanks are meant to be our allies, you know."

"It wouldn't do at all." Wragg's voice quivered. "We'd have to lock everything up——"

"My dear chap, Schulman's got the free run of our files just as we have of his."

"All right." Hunching up his shoulders he turned to gaze out of the window, clearly intimating that he, Herbert Wragg, washed his hands of the whole affair.

"I'd like to make it perfectly clear," he added, as if he had not, "that the responsibility, in that case, is on you."

A little taken aback, Larry considered the hind view of his colleague, pondering on which of the five or six different ways of dealing with this remark, and with the speaker, he should choose—which was the right one, the one that would not further widen the breach that existed, undeniably, between them and that he himself deplored, and at the same time which would maintain his own authority, although he cared least about that, and yet might encourage old Wragg to be a shade less prickly. He made up his mind within ten seconds, which was one of the few things the army had taught him, and said gently: "You know, Herbert, funnily enough that's one of the few points I'm quite clear on, actually. The responsibility, I mean."

Pale as death, Wragg turned round to be met with Larry's unruffled smile.

"Yes . . . I'm—I'm sorry." He gulped. "I realise—it sounded—well, in that case—if I'm coming, I'll have to phone Mrs. Wragg."

"Ask her to come too. Why not?"

"Good lord, no!" He looked thunderstruck.

Larry scribbled a note for Abe Schulman and went to put it on his desk in the adjoining office. He opened the door.

"Abe! I didn't know you were here."

Abe was taking his ease at his desk, his feet up on it, blowing smoke rings at the ceiling. His eyes were closed and remained so. Larry grinned.

"You must have overheard. So sorry."

"Not at all," Abe replied in a sepulchral voice. "It was most revealing. Everything comes as grist to the artist's mill—my mill, that is. Anglo-American Relations Behind The Curtain. I was going to do it anyway—and now I'm in the mood—mewd, as Wragg would say."

It was true that Wragg betrayed his Midlands origin in his pronunciation of this word. Larry laughed.

" All right, in that case here are the keys. You might need additional material."

" Thanks very much." Abe, with a lordly gesture, spurned them with his toe, pushing them off the desk. " I've got all the material I want—*right here*." He tapped his forehead. " Hm. I doubt, somehow, I'll waste time fixing you both up with pseudonyms. After all, I'm covered. Hirelings of H.M.G. you can't sue, can you? Ha!" He snorted. " So it'll run something like this—I favour that intimate, damning style—wait . . ." He intoned: " Rumour has it that Britain's ace-propagandist, blond, gangling Lawrence Purdoe——"

" Gangling? What on earth's that?"

" James Stewart. Take it easy—it's not a compliment . . . and his co-Slavophile, balding 'Wrazzle' Wragg—get the alliteration?—are ganging up on *Transat's* veteran newshawk, Schulman (Joe Soap, as I now discover he is known to his friends) . . . wait, I haven't done . . . ' Quoth Editor Purdoe—" Whisky " to *his* friends, if he's got any——' "

" Quoth is good," said Larry.

" Whisky, though, that reminds me. Any Scotch in your room?"

" You were on late last."

" You mean to say you've omitted to refuel since then? Really, Purdoe, I can't be expected to do everything, can I? Too bad . . . simple little detail like that . . . Milly's downstairs, by the way . . ."

" How d'you know?"

" I just been talking to her." Abe smiled blandly. " You won't need chains. Now scram. And for Chrissake keep Wrazzle on the straight and narrow and, above all, *bring 'im back.* I'll tackle anything else for you but not Olga Wragg."

Wragg muffled himself up. He was still furious, in a way; that is, he was furious with himself and only with Larry in so far as the latter had left him high and dry without a grievance. An impatient hooting on the horn of the car came from the street below.

" My wife," said Larry. " She's driving."

Wragg's long skinny neck twisted up out of the muffler, his bright hen's eye brighter with alarm.

" Aren't we . . . can she—I mean, aren't we taking Vladek?"

Intended to sound bold, his voice as usual turned traitor; reedy, it sounded—he could hear it himself, the ignominious quaver in it, as if he were fearful as to his own safety.

" She's not a bad driver," Larry said gravely. (So it *had* sounded like that. He raged inwardly.) " Anyway, I thought we'd economise. I hear there was a bit of a fuss about Vladek's subsistence the other day—that picnic."

Wragg felt himself flushing. So he knew about that.

209

"There's a difference between business and pleasure," he said stiffly.

"Oh, I don't know. It's sometimes hard to draw the line. Let's go."

Scowling, Wragg followed him downstairs, the scowl being assumed to conceal his satisfaction, not because *she* was accompanying them, on the contrary; because her presence provided him with the necessary grievance.

"Ha*llo*, Mr. Wragg." Milly stuck her head out of the car, her face sparkling in a bundle of fluffy white fur. "You coming too? What fun!"

He grunted in reply. He could do no more, struggling against the familiar sensations that the sight of her infallibly produced in him; pounding heart, clammy palms, furred tongue, this last being additionally afflicted by a spasmodic paralysis which tied it when all that was required of it was a civil answer to a straight question, and, in contrast, unleashed it to go bounding off with reckless garrulity merely to maul what might otherwise have been a healthy little silence; but as if all these more or less private symptoms weren't bad enough, the blatantly conspicuous had also to be endured; the freakish distortion of his limbs, the evidence of his great clumsy feet, ditto hands, having now mysteriously become blown up to cartoon proportions. Avoiding her glance as if it were the evil eye, he grunted again and got into the back of the car.

So they drove to Zagranyza. Milly drove faster than Vladek, and, even Wragg had to admit it, quite as well. Watching her sharp lifted profile, he was nagged by the suspicion that she was enjoying herself; what nagged him even more was the thought of Olga, and what she would say when she found out. Would she find out? Better not underestimate her—better assume that she would. Then how to mention it? Casually, glossing over it?—"now I come to think of it, yes, she was, drove us, in fact—an economy, really"—no, he decided he could never pull it off. Well, then, not refer to it at all? And then if—then appear surprised?—"it never occurred to me that you would —a mountain out of a"—no. He couldn't do that either. Why hadn't he told her on the telephone?—because he hadn't known then, had he? Would she believe that? No. Oh Christ, thought Wragg miserably, and tucking his head deep into the breast of his overcoat, he breathed into headquarters, his craven soul, little warm puffs of encouragement to be relayed to the outposts of his gaunt and ridiculous masculine frame. Milly, catching sight of him in the driving mirror, began to giggle, then suddenly aware that in the folds of the muffler one eye, beady, baleful, was fixed upon her, sneezed instead.

His life, he told himself, a shade melodramatically, was in her hands.

210

After a bit, fascinated by the sight of the hands themselves, in brown gloves, placed rather lightly on the wheel, now and then snapping knobs and things on and off with tremendous efficiency, he discovered that his opposition to this state of affairs had mysteriously melted away. His only objection might have been that the hands themselves seemed too small for the magnitude of the responsibility. Ah well, he reflected, gazing out at the snowbound countryside whizzing by—an appropriate background to a pleasurable gloom—his life wasn't all that important. Plenty more like him, he dared say—although secretly he was not perfectly convinced of it. At least they didn't *talk*, these two . . . What was he up to, Purdoe? Ah-ha. Ximenes—same corner had floored him, too, had it? He wouldn't get that in a hurry. Experiencing a momentary satisfaction, Wragg sat back. What has *he* got—the thought, unoriginal, inconclusive as ever, popped up again—that I haven't? Of course, Olga's right, I do dislike him and I know he's a type—a type they turn out of the sausage machine—but I wish I could dislike him *more . . . rely* on disliking him all the time. That "Herbert" for instance; it still rang in his ears . . . a surprise, more, a shock, and a curiously pleasurable one, to discover that Larry—Purdoe, that is— had bothered to find out his, Wragg's, Christian name. Still, bet he doesn't get Nine Down. Larry's pencil moved and against his will Wragg leaned forward. Don't say he's got it . . . he has . . . but he hasn't got Eleven Across. Hm, a teaser if ever there was one. Now he remembered the clue perfectly . . . should he?—no, I'm damned if I'll tell him Eleven Across, he snorted, giving his familiar, apparently taking time off to-day, a moral kick up the backside. Between them they usually managed to keep a nice little bonfire smouldering, stoked up with chips of resentment, disappointment, spite. Now, with attention, the fire flared up. Does she have to *hum*? He glowered . . . Blast, he muttered, catching himself out, humming too. Blast. That little pyre wasn't burning so well to-day. Pyre? A crossword addict and a stickler for usage, he corrected himself. However had he come to make a slip like that?

*   *   *

The town of Zagranyza nestles in the foothills of the Carpathians. Beyond the town, out of sight of it but not more than a couple of miles distant, bisecting the farther valley, its course elusive, invisibly defined, serpentine, weaving in and out up hill and down dale; fluid, rigid, imaginary, actual, non-existent except on paper, on maps and in treaties; of fluctuating significance, its exact delineation a yard to one side or the other disputed through the centuries with bloodshed; now become scarcely more than a symbolic barrier, although at any moment capable of reverting to its former state, to be blazoned in headlines, traced in blood; its position arbitrated by man, by generals and by common soldiers, by negotiators of power-politics, assassins who put paid to dynasties, prophets of sociologies whose gospels catch like tinder and set a continent on fire; man-made, not God-made, for the pine forests stretch uniformly black to the horizon; signifying this to one and that to another but never failing to signify, to cause a quickening of the pulse, to stir up a unique sense of defiance and pride, delight and sometimes fear in the contemplation of it, this proof of man's power to impose his will, parcel out the universe, arousing these emotions alike in the breasts of emperors and exiles, welchers and defectors, armament tycoons, Scandinavian businessmen, journalists and tourists, there it lay—the frontier.

*　　　*　　　*

" Before the war," Sophie had said, " you should have seen Zagranyza before the war. In Eastern Europe as famous as St. Moritz or Davos in the West. A Kurort, you know, a resort, the air being so fine that people recovered there from tuberculosis and those who did not died in such pretty surroundings and in the best of hands. The sanatoria and the great hotels are placed on eminences around the town—the town being deep in the valley—so that early and late their windows catch the gleam of the sun. At night, I remember, the air was so still that if you were out for a stroll in the town you could hear the music from all the ballrooms of the hotels around, jumbled up, streaming out, all the different tunes and all very sweet so that the air was quite full of music. In the town itself there were always four night clubs, one just opened, one going bankrupt, and two doing decent business; also tearooms, the Carlton, and the Lord Byron, coiffeurs and chemists. The *pensions* for those who could not afford the hotels occupied the back streets where also were the shops selling skis and sheepskin jackets and authentic local products. We went there every winter. Our hotel was the Krystal. You will see it is the biggest, if it is still there, God knows. It was very grand. They used to change the pillow-cases every single day and on the arrival of a new guest, quite often they even changed the sheets. That is something, you know, in view of what those swine called our famous ' slavonische Wirtschaft.' And such bathrooms! On arrival, Miss Brownlow would cover the bidet with a big towel—even the sight of such an object upset her; a sign of immorality, she said—and yet there in that very hotel once, in my night-table drawer, I found a sign of immorality she had overlooked, and I asked her what it was and she didn't know, naturally—so I showed it to Ludovic and how we laughed. Of course, later, in the

212

time of 'those swine,' we used to pick them off the hedges," she added with sophistication.

"So did we," said Milly, "but not off the hedges. There are no hedges in Grosvenor Square."

"No? Funny, I pictured it with hedges. And in her splendid English way, the very first visit, Miss Brownlow got the maids to scour out the bath. That made us memorable, I can tell you. After that first visit—for they strove to please us, one family, two great suites—there was never any trouble.

"Well, there were fleas in the beds but you could have French champagne served there if you needed it, and all the menus were in French and dinner up to two or three in the morning but never, which made Miss Brownlow very ratty, before nine in the evening. Gipsy bands and a lot of meat—because we are rather coarse eaters, you know, as a race—birds, pigs, oxen, whatever you wished. What else? Sables, and champagne, as I said, and acres, lakes of parquet, and the noise of silk, metres of it, rustling down a staircase, and men's shoes, narrow, elegant, made in Budapest, and the *strangest* couples "—she giggled— " the evening was always fun to see who would appear together. The women awfully pretty, most of them, but you didn't see them in the morning, not to ski, of course, because most of them were on the run and they didn't want to break any bones, especially vital ones. You see," she mused, " there was nowhere so pleasant to run to as Zagranyza . . . a charming spot, but not *irrevocable* . . . because to cross a frontier, that means a decision, doesn't it—or at least a situation? "

"Well, yes," said Milly cautiously. " Perhaps."

"Whereas to stay within it," Sophie nodded, worldly-wise, " then, of course, it's still just a week-end. So—Zagranyza being, well, only Zagranyza, that was the place. And the evening was the time."

"And you? "

"Me? Oh, I see. Well, I hated it—for myself, I mean. I am not the type. Mama was very beautiful, much admired. I had a dress, too tight under the arms, taffeta, a certain pink, the choice of dear Miss Brownlow, I'm afraid. And when I danced with my cousin Andrew, with whom—although only he and I knew it—I had not been on speaking terms since the age of eight, he held me in such a way—I sweated heavily—so that they all saw and I could have died with shame. Oh, Milly! I wouldn't be young again for all the tea in China. I always sweated heavily and my skin had a natural shine—and nowadays, young girls, they don't have to suffer in *those* ways at all. I was gauche, too, always this cursed shyness, like a cat with a tin can tied to its tail . . ." She pondered, then, knocking back the contents of her glass, " Where was I? "

"Zagranyza."

"Of course. So you see what I mean, do you? What it was like?"

"Yes."

"Well, it is not like that now."

Nor was it.

*   *   *

Zagranyza had become a rest camp for the proletariat. The great hotels, the sanatoria, were situated on the summits of the slopes around the town, just as Sophie had described, but no longer were they set in splendid isolation. From the valley up to the very walls of the imposing edifice at the summit each slope was covered, as if it had broken out in a rash, with rows of wooden huts or châlets. Identical as rabbit hutches, varnished treacle-brown, innocent of curtains or window-boxes or indeed of any feature that might disrupt the uniformity of the impression, they were systematised to an identical plan; fanning out symmetrically in semi-circular tiers, the lowest tier enclosing an open space, or parade-ground or whatever it was, in the centre of which was a flagstaff flying the familiar scarlet flag. Each encampment was surrounded by a high wire fence.

"Well, I never," said Milly. "Aldershot—or Auschwitz?"

"No, more like a holiday camp," said Larry. "More or less," he added, for they were passing the entrance to one of these camps at that moment.

"Oh, look!" She pulled up. "Aren't they sweet?" Above the entrance in the fence hung a large white sign with black lettering. "What does it say? Mr. Wragg, please translate."

Clearing his throat, sheepishly Wragg complied: "Railway Workers' Children! Health and strength are your Birthright ... Devote them to the glory of the New Slavonia ..."

"Crumbs," said Milly. "Poor little mites."

Around the totem poles several squads of children, aged between nine and twelve, were being put through their paces by a few beefy young women in overalls. The impression immediately gained was two-fold: that discipline was exemplary, and that the little mites, abnormally diminutive in uniform, their faces pinched between knitted earcaps, appeared to be thoroughly aware of their responsibilities. They looked scared out of their wits, straining to fill each minute with sixty seconds' worth of holiday fun.

Farther on, a dilapidated sign announced the Hotel Belvedere, a hundred rooms with running water, French cuisine and dancing nightly, and then they came upon it, the hotel—its terrace crammed with army transport, the snow in the drive pitted with the bright yellow

214

rain of urine, and on its hundred balconies soldiers in various states of undress lounging about, listlessly Blanco-ing, polishing, preforming the essential function required of soldiers the world over, that of killing time, of whiling away yet another afternoon. Past the Belvedere, in yet another establishment behind a wire fence, the mothers of Coalminers' Children were busy accruing health and strength to the glory of the New Slavonia. From a glance it would seem that they had indeed been kept very busy doing the washing of the military gentlemen next door, the evidence stretching away on either hand round the corner of the hill and out of sight. A team of lucky ladies was engaged in clearing snow from the paths under the command of a young person with a whistle, and more mothers, some not young and most rather heavily built, all of them lightly clad in bloomers and blouses, were limbering up around the flag. Farther down the hill members of the Steelworkers, Union, fathers, probably, but there was no knowing, the state of paternity being what it is, undetectable and usually under-publicised, were having a good time, too.

"Reminds me of Happy Families," said Milly.

"Really? I'm afraid I'm not quite with you there," said Larry. He felt unaccountably depressed.

"Well, I mean—where are the coalminers' *children*? Or even the coalminers, come to that? We've only scored the mothers so far. And where are the *mothers* of the children up the road? Mr. Wragg, do explain."

Wragg jerked himself out of his trance. "Not *here*," he said, with sinister emphasis. "They wouldn't be *here*, you see."

"Oh, I see," said Milly, although she did not.

Across the valley Sophie's hotel, the Krystal, brooded over the town, its windows, blinking in the sun. It looked very empty.

"V.I.P. hotel," said Wragg. "That includes foreigners."

"*Us*, you mean? We could stay there, could we?"

"I suppose so," he said, "if you wanted to." He made it sound as if it were the sort of damnfool thing she would want to do, and so she didn't say any more. Realising it had sounded that way, he blushed.

No longer restricted to a merely seasonal popularity, the town was permanently *en fête*. Red bunting fluttered the length of the main street, and the orthodox accompaniment to pleasure, the noise of several loudspeakers braying in concert, echoed and re-echoed across the valley. Fleets of open three-tonners, the cargo space laden with holidaymakers conscripted, according to placards displayed on each vehicle, from diverse professions and the most distant points of the New Slavonia, proceeded majestically down the main street. The stream appeared to be never-ending, but as Milly discovered on endeavouring to insert the Austin into the procession, the impression was created on the principle of the endless belt or circular pantomime stage.

" Get a move on, Milly."

" I was just waiting," she said timidly, " for that old bozo with the textile workers to come round again. He had a kind face."

" Here he is—in you go." Bravely she swung into the stream.

The lorries, thus economically deployed, served admirably as " floats " to stimulate a carnival atmosphere, the reactions of the living cargo, who were equipped with little red flags and singing fairly hard, being visible to all and an encouragement to many, notably to the queues of less fortunate pleasure-seekers on foot. These latter, converging tamely enough on specific points, the single cinema, the picture-postcard kiosks, and one or two bars, co-operated manfully in the spirit of the thing, keeping up a pretty continuous cheer, and skipping out of the gutters as the lorries splashed past.

The traffic moved in fits and starts. The lorry drivers, after a morning on the circuit, were becoming acquainted with the route and, urged on by their passengers, were seeking to enliven it by a mild form of speeding; indeed, there was no good reason why the village street should not have resembled the Nurberg Ring—but for a single hazard. This was the " local colour " squad, a posse of young persons (some even authentic peasants of the environs) rigged out in the costume of the district, marching ten abreast. The front row contained some good-looking girls with noble busts and stalwart young men to match, all in piercing voice and fine fettle; these were the professionals. The other ranks, locally recruited, tended to fall short of the standards set, like all amateurs preserving a sort of dilettantism which proclaimed them as such; shambling along in no sort of step, ba-baaing hopefully as they went, casting shifty glances at the queues, they were clearly embarrassed in their role of colour-merchants. It was quite a formid-able obstacle, nevertheless, as Milly realised when she tried to rush it; eventually at a curt signal from the leader the whole detachment swerved and she was allowed to pass.

" If we're going to eat," said Wragg, " we eat here."

" Why? "

" Don't be silly, darling," said Larry. " You can see why if you look."

So she parked the car and they went in where everybody else was, because it was the time of day at which everybody felt like eating, and because there was only one place to do it in, namely, this restaurant, the Slavonia, which had seating accommodation for about half the number of people who were hungry; thus automatically an atmosphere of conviviality and comradeship was created. Really, Milly couldn't help

216

reflecting, standing at the door and looking round—the familiar smell of roast pork, boiled cabbage and humanity like a blow under the belt —it was a very good wheeze. Infallible, almost; Lady Mendl had sworn by it as a recipe for a party, although she might have chuckled to see it adapted thus.

The vast pine-panelled dining-room was set with long tables, and the diners were packed on benches, fifty a side. The constriction would have made individual service impossible, even had there been any; accordingly plates were passed down from the top, and the stacks of used plates, glasses, etc., formed a unique decoration, or barricade, between the opposed teams on either side. The tables were covered with sheets of paper, tacked down; appetites being robust, the style in table manners vigorous rather than refined, large areas of these coverings were already transparent with grease and in general the worse for wear. Strings of red flags were strung across the ceiling and decked the tables, too; in any case most of the guests possessed their own as part of their regulation equipment. Dance music, the same that was being relayed all over the town, lest any of those present were hard of hearing, blared from loudspeakers set at the four corners of the room. A picturesque touch was provided by two ancient and decrepit waiters; their dress, a reminder of a bygone age, albeit conventional to their profession but clearly appearing in the nature of carnival costume to the eyes of the New Slavonia, attracted gales of laughter. Bleary-eyed, rather dazedly aware of having some sort of entertainment value, the pair shuffled about like a comic turn; the actual service, that is the link-up between the kitchen stoves and the tops of the tables, being in the hands of a few black-browed, sour-faced and authoritative young women, the objects of much sycophantic attention from the crowd. The intense heat from the kitchens which opened directly on to the dining-room, the animal warmth of the feeders engendered by the nourishing slabs of meat and the vodka which was being freely consumed, made for a snug atmosphere in contrast to the cold outside, and what with the flushed cheeks, raucous laughter, bursts of song and so on, the scene was one of the wildest gaiety; the spirit of bacchanalia was definitely abroad.

Standing there in the entrance, Wragg, happening to glance down, caught sight of Milly. It struck him how perfectly incongruous her appearance was against that background. Like the waiters, she seemed an apparition from another world, conjured up to provide contrast; her hands stuck deep in the pockets of her fur jacket, her eyebrows slightly raised, whether in bewilderment or criticism or dismay he could not tell; perhaps rather as if she were highly amused by it all.

"Come on," said Larry, "we'll have to squash in."

217

Against his will Wragg found himself admiring her as she immediately set off in the direction indicated, self-possessed, impervious to the stares and comments her appearance aroused, like a grim little tugboat dragging the pair of them in her wake. She's got a nerve, he thought, normally a term of disapprobation with him, but it was difficult to temper his recognition of what it was that she had got with the necessary degree of disapprobation, as he would have liked.

Pressed close one against the other, the three sat at the end of a bench. Not by any physical withdrawal on the part of their neighbours, because that would have been impossible, but nonetheless sensing a withdrawal, a veiled hostility around them, they were transformed at once into a unit, however insignificant—solid, and to be reckoned with, just as the presence of the smallest rock in the sea must be taken into account even by ocean liners; isolated, they became an island. The Purdoes, thought Wragg, were very likely unaware of it; they probably took solidarity in the way they took so many human comforts, for granted—but he himself did not. He suddenly experienced an utterly novel sensation. He was—well, almost enjoying himself.

" Did you bring that flask, Milly? "

" I did."

" Well, hand it over. Now's the time." Larry, as if his mind were elsewhere, poured three equal tots of whisky, pushed one to each of them, and began slowly sipping his own.

Wragg almost never drank whisky, yet he felt oddly flattered to be treated in this way, as one of a trio, without any pandering to likes or dislikes, or preliminaries, even. Olga, for instance, would have said " Blue Skies " before crooking her finger and sniffing her glass. No, it was assumed that he would want the whisky because, and there was no doubt about it, it was the moment for whisky; it warmed and soothed, just as the sharing of it—without comment, as a matter of course—had the same effect. Never having had brothers or sisters, he imagined it must be like this—doing the same thing at the same time because it was the logical, necessary thing to do, placed in the same situation all together, all reacting in the same way to it. And if that happened regularly—not necessarily between brothers and sisters, he amended—well, he simply could not imagine the sort of relationship that must grow from that. Indestructible, he would have thought—and blushed at the presumption of these conjectures—but he couldn't help it, he did have a sudden vision of how it must be with *them*. It occurred to him that they were not over-polite with each other, more like brother and sister, and this seemed to poor Wragg the most enviable of relationships, this teasing friendliness with its stamp of diffidence representing the very sweets of marriage. Indeed, a less

218

naïve observer than Wragg might have been struck by this aspect of the Purdoes' relationship, and, having pondered it, whilst agreeing on its singularity, have drawn quite other conclusions from it.

"Take their time, don't they?" Larry poured more whisky.

A space had been cleared at the far end of the room and people had begun to dance. Presently Milly said, "There's a waiter," as the more venerable and infirm of the pair hobbled into view. Wragg, pale with determination, rose without a word, thrusting his way between the benches, and they watched his progress, his beaky profile and narrow glossy head travelling like a periscope above the sea of heads.

Milly giggled. "Give me another tot, quick."

"I'm getting quite fond of him," said Larry. "He's not such a bad old stick."

"Oh, dear." She sipped greedily. "But I wish he'd come off it. He makes me *nervous*."

"Don't be silly. Can't you see he's the one who's nervous? He'd like to come off it, if he could, but he can't."

"I never thought of that."

"Didn't you? It sticks out a mile. Look out—he's coming back. Got hold of a waiter, too."

Towering over them, Wragg announced with an air of triumph: "I've ordered pork—and barszcz!"

"*Wonderful*," said Milly.

He sat down. "It was all there was," he added truthfully.

"Why, they've even brought it. Dynamic."

Wragg blushed as red as the barszcz. Again he had experienced that curious twinge of pleasure.

When they had eaten Larry said: "Best we split up, isn't it? I'll do the mayor and the newsagents, if you'll take the car and do that other village, will you, Herbert? Not far, is it?"

"No, not far," said Wragg, all of a sudden at his shiftiest. "Along the lake."

"So the problem is Milly. She'll have to stay here . . ." Dubiously Larry took stock of the scene, in regard to which in a matter of minutes orgy would be the appropriate descriptive term. "Or come with me. But that means a lot of walking and hanging about." At the prospect of these alternatives Milly looked depressed.

"The only thing is "—Wragg cleared his throat—" I'm afraid . . ." He met Larry's eyes with a terrible frown and blurted out, "*I can't drive*."

"Then that settles it. Milly must drive you—best thing, isn't it, darling? Give you something to do."

Wragg twisted his neck around uneasily this way and that, as if

219

preferring to gain confirmation of the worst by some more oblique method than by meeting it face to face, rather as an earthworm, surfacing, first surely investigates the portents of ugly weather on its own level, without so much as casting an eye at the sky.

She said after a pause: " Along the lake, is it? That's good." There was a new note in her voice and suddenly daring, Wragg glanced her way. To his astonishment she had brightened.

" Why? " Larry, too, glanced at her, her manner being so airy as to put him on his guard.

" Because I rather wanted some smoked salmon, that's why. I should think I'd get it cheaper there." The waiter, who had taken a fancy to their party, happened to be drooling over her shoulder as she spoke. " Ask *him* if you can get smoked salmon along the lake, Mr. Wragg. There's a dear."

Obediently Wragg put the question, to which the waiter, his eyes filming over in nostalgic memories of other days, nodded, and went on nodding.

" You see," she said, pleased. " Just what I thought. *Smoked?* "

" That's what I asked him," Wragg replied stiffly.

" Fine." Larry got up. " So everybody's happy. You be careful, Milly. No dicing, now."

*   *   *

In the car Wragg sat up very straight beside her.

" I shall have to go slowly," she said, slithering into gear, " because of the ice. I hope you don't mind."

" Mind? Good lord—I mean, you *must* . . . Me, mind? " He laughed, and it sounded all wrong so he stopped. " I—I rather *like* going slowly, in fact."

" *Do* you? Fancy that. *I* rather like going fast." She glanced round at him, fluttering her lashes in genuine, or mock, surprise. Mock, he decided. She had an infuriating trick of taking one's lightest rejoinders, conversational inanities which only God and he knew what it cost him to make, quite literally and replying with a gravity which— as she must well know—rendered them twice as inane as they had sounded fresh from one's lips. Which was saying something, he reflected. " *I* rather like going fast," he repeated to himself, viciously. " *Do* you? " he would say. " Fancy that! " Side-splitting, wouldn't it be? Everyone holding their sides at her expense and she—well, she'd just have to curl up and die, wouldn't she? He didn't see it, somehow, even if he could have managed the right inflection in his voice. Anyway —he disentangled himself from the web of futile conjecture—most people did like going fast.

220

They took the road out of the town which led in the direction of the frontier and had once even led over it. Leaving the town and the valley behind, it wound through the mountains in to the next valley where there was a lake and then ran along the lake shore. The pine forest stretched right down to the water's edge, the trees overhanging the road. Every now and then, as the car passed beneath, a clot of snow slid off a branch and the branch, released from its weight, shot up, powdering the windscreen with snow. There was no sound except for the crunch of the tyres over the snow; no sign of a living thing nor of human habitation. The winter's afternoon was utterly still; in detail as sharply drawn, tinted as delicately as a Chinese painting on silk, lacking only the small figure on a bridge, the rowers in a tiny boat. All colour had withdrawn from the sky, leaving it light, the colour of steel —colourless; the lake, black under the shadows of the trees, mint-green in the broad sweep of it, smooth and shining as glass. There was not merely the familiar sensation of having entered a dream world; the farther they went the more the suspicion grew upon her that they were themselves part of the landscape, themselves the puppets, the car, even, the symbol chosen by the artist to link his conception with reality; and robbed of free will and identity alike, they had been set in a frame the dimensions of which were beyond their powers to perceive—which was all very well and not too unpleasant but along with it there was the distinctly unpleasant sensation of having been cut off, trapped in that valley, and diminishing, with every mile they covered, the prospect of return; the lake on the left, the snowy road ahead, the slopes masked by the laden trees.

Presently Milly said: " Give me a cigarette."

Wragg fumbled in the dashboard and held one out to her. She took it and stuck it in her mouth and after a while she said: " Match? "

Fumbling again, he found them, struck one and she slowed down. Head bent, she sucked at the flame. " Look! " she whispered. " Don't move—but look! " It was difficult to obey both commands but easier for Wragg than for some; he performed his swivel-trick with pride.

" Don't you see it? A baby deer."

Stare as he might, he could see nothing beyond the trees and then all of a sudden he did see it, the young deer standing among some saplings, snuffing at the shoots; now and then, its mouth overfull, champing, it turned to gaze at the car with the mildest speculative interest, its soft eyes focussing with an effort, in the manner of a lush young thyroid blonde viewing her newest protector over a dish of grouse in cream.

" I *must* have a photograph." Milly switched off the engine and

221

dived beneath the seat. The deer, alarmed by the sudden absence of noise, tossed its head and lolloped away.

" I'm afraid——" Wragg, at a loss how to break it to her, looked down at her as she squinted into the lens, adjusting levers. " I'm afraid it's gone."

" Oh, blast, has it? It was so pretty." She tossed the camera into his lap. " You hold it. It's set. There might be another. I'm always missing things, or they don't come out—it's complicated, the setting."

" I had a Box Brownie once," he remarked, adding tactlessly, " you didn't need to set it. You just took snaps."

" Oh? How nice. And did they—how were they—the . . . er . . . snaps? "

She was at it again. He wasn't such a fool as not to know that. What was wrong with " snaps "? Snaps? Snaps? Perfectly good word. He shrugged. " They were all right," he said, and then, just to let *her* know that he *did* know that she was laughing at him, and in any case unable to resist the advantage offered: " They always came out." Observing from her silence that he had scored, he immediately recognised himself for what he was, an unchivalrous beast, and sat speechless himself, worsted once more.

At last they came to the village, a handful of cottages scattered on both sides of a deep gully; a footpath leading down to a patch of flat ground by the lake side. There was no one about. Wood smoke drifted from the cottage chimneys; here and there at a window, a face, a white shape swimming in the dark behind pots of geraniums, peered out.

" Please stop," said Wragg.

" I have. Is this it? What are you going to do? "

" My job," he said gravely, in a tone of rebuke. He gave her a sharp look, but her expression was meek, her nose blue with cold. He relented. " That is the newspaper shop we were talking about, where we have contacts." Breathing heavily, he reached over, assembling all his material, posters, leaflets, dispatch case and so on, then ramming his hat on his head he got out. Milly watched him as he strode up to the door and knocked.

She had a feeling there would be no reply and she was right. After a bit he stumped round to the back, over icy flags, through a desolate garden where a few frost-bitten shrubs stuck up out of the snow. The moment he was out of sight she allowed herself the laugh she had been saving up. She could hear him pounding away at the back door so she had a nip out of the flask, too, and had smoked a cigarette through and lit a second before she saw him turn the corner and come down the path. He looked terribly upset, distracted, even, clutching his armful

222

of leaflets and junk, one end of his muffler trailing down behind; a ridiculous figure, on account of his size, perhaps; atop the huge frame his narrow bony white face engulfed in a black hat.

Then all at once, in the way they had, nowadays, two thoughts came to her—one familiar, the other an utter stranger, they stepped out of the crowd of half-thoughts with which she was accustomed to treat and presented themselves. The first, the familiar one, was: Why am I here? What has led me to this particular spot, this particular afternoon?—and behind it, as if it were followed by a retinue of lesser thoughts which must also be presented: And if that had to be, why should I have for companion this fantastic unlikeable creature—and why do I suspect that this incident—was it that? or coincidence?—no, that was just it, it wasn't a coincidence—fits into some scheme somewhere? Although what or whose or where it fits—that's impossible to say.

But on perceiving the second, the stranger, the first was swept out of her mind. In appearance it was so arresting, and its retinue, she could see, so much more impressive than that of its predecessor, that she hesitated before receiving it at all; she had a fancy that it and its followers might cost her a lot of trouble to entertain; nevertheless it forced itself upon her. Quite suddenly, as she watched him standing there in the snow, she had the extraordinary feeling that she *was* Wragg —or at least, she had a glimpse of what it must be like to *be* Wragg. There he was, sombrely eyeing the street, aware of having failed in his mission, of her watching him—making up his mind—or rather (*and she knew it*) at his wits' end what to do next. All at once she became conscious of the knife edge on which his equilibrium was balanced— how he might, at this very moment, for no less trivial reason than that she was watching him, or that a peasant's door had remained latched, be *literally* at his wits' end—how it might well be that it needed no more than a chance remark of hers or Larry's—instantly several came to mind—to make mincemeat of him, of the guts of the inner man, of Wragg's soul. Oh, crumbs, she muttered to herself, staring ahead at the gleaming water, what have I done?

It was as if she saw for the first time not her customary view of life, a gentle upward gradient splashed with patches of sunlight which she was ascending at her leisure, but rather, having reached a certain point, a knoll, and pausing to look back the way she had come, to her surprise the downward slope appeared quite different, in shadow and much steeper and full of hazards; here and there crevasses, even, which from her vantage point she could see, but the figure who was the object of her attention, who was toiling up in her wake, could not. He was not enjoying the expedition, she could tell; he was progressing slowly, with many halts for breath, not coming up as she had done, straight, in a bee-line for the top, but weaving rather, making heavy weather of the minor obstacles, large boulders and rough ground which seemed to bother him, whereas she herself hadn't noticed them at all; but he could have no idea of the crevasses, and she wanted to cry out, to warn him—although he was too far off to hear—because she could see and he could not. " Why," she said to herself in dismay, " I had no idea it was so difficult." Indeed, it was difficult. There was no fixed path; you had to pick your way for yourself, depending on your own judgment which in turn depended on how it appeared to *you*—that was the trouble—because now it was plain to her that almost any of the ways, and certainly any one he might be likely to choose, could lead to disaster. " But I never saw that," she whispered, " on my way up." And reminded that she was not yet at the top herself, she looked ahead and it was quite a step and it occurred to her: " Supposing it is not as it appears (the upward view looking as it had always looked to her, inviting)—supposing I, too, am blind to what lies in wait—there, or there, or round the corner? Then even I . . . *I* . . . might—well, come a terrible cropper." Momentarily she felt shaken. " Now I know," she said to herself solemnly, " what it's like to be Wragg," and so saying, exorcised the alien spirit.

As a first essay at empathy, she hadn't done too badly; had been distracted from the subject that habitually preoccupied her for the best part of seventy-five seconds. " I'll carry on just as I am," she told herself sharply. " Look where it gets you otherwise. Just ruins your nerve and a waste of time into the bargain. And if anyone, why *him*? Why not Larry, or Abe? At least they're *men*—and the sort I like."

The silence was so profound, here by the lake, her mood so strange, that at once she realised her mistake. Questions were answered.

" Why not? Because each of them is complete in himself—each has as strong a will as you, if not stronger. That is what you like about them. But try as you might you could never approach either as closely as you would like—because neither is part of you nor you of them."

" That doesn't explain why it has to be that twerp, that shivering ass on the path over there. What have I to do with him?"

" Everything, *now*. You can't escape him, Milly . . . because of what lies between you."

" And just what lies between us, may I ask?" She was full of resentment, but fascinated, too. " We are as different as can be! "

" That lies between you—the difference. You are poles apart, different as love and hate, midnight and noon, sadness and joy—that is, not different at all, but opposites; inextricably mixed. Ah-ha, you'll never be rid of him now. He is, to you, the obverse side of the coin."

224

" Well, in that case," she argued smartly, " it stands to reason we shall never meet."

" But you *have* met, my dear," came the silky whisper, " that's what's so remarkable. That's just the trouble. And it's too late to do anything about it."

"Good God! " she muttered, not at all taken with this idea and its implications, and leaning out of the window, shouted: " Try next door! "

Wragg, coming out of his daze of indecision, winced at the sound of her voice as if she had flicked him with a whip. Still, he took her advice and wheeled off up the street. Even from his back view he looked, as ever, in a huff. He knocked at one of the doors and waited; began chewing the ends of his gloves. In lieu of fingernails, she supposed. An old peasant unlatched the door.

She got out of the car, and the cold jumped like a judo-expert, fastening on vulnerable points. As she came up the path Wragg said: " We're out of luck. He says everyone's gone to Zagranyza—to a funeral."

" Oh," she said, not much interested, the news being irrelevant to her purpose. " Ask him where I can get this smoked salmon." She blew on her fingers. " What a nice old man."

Wragg curled his lip in disdain, but he put the question.

" Well, what does he say? "

" He says farther on. He—er—wants us to come in and try some mead."

" Really? How *very* sweet of him! What fun."

" But—I say," he stammered, " I mean, we ought really to be getting back. . . . Besides, you won't like it . . . the mead, I mean . . ." His voice trailed away. He had not the faintest idea how to control a woman like Milly.

" How do you know I won't? " she said rudely, and swept past him and shook the peasant by the hand. Bloody little duchess, thought Wragg, following her in.

It was warm inside, the air thick with wood-smoke and stuffy with the sweetish smell of milk, and a richer smell from a huge black cauldron sizzling over the log-fire in the hearth. Crouched over it, an old woman was stirring the cauldron with a long spoon and poking bits of wood underneath to keep it on the boil. Two cats and a kind of bull terrier lay stretched out on a rag mat in front of the hearth, their paws on it, but keeping their distance from the sputtering cauldron. In one corner there was a big shallow pan of milk, the surface all crusted and grimy with ash. Away from the fire the room was rather dark owing to the low ceiling and the smoke-blackened rafters; some wintry daylight filtered in through the leaded panes. Bunches of herbs hung from the ceiling; apples were spread on the brick window-sill between flower-pots, and dangling down, like a bead curtain, strings of dried mushrooms. In the darkest corner a shaded oil lamp burned below a picture of the Madonna and Child; the kind of picture sold in the market, quite cheap, but lavishly done, sprinkled with silvery dust in the right places so that it shone. There were framed photographs of young men round the walls; bits of yew were stuck behind these; even so, the faces all wore that unmistakable look which the dead wear in their photographs, the features fuzzy, the expression resigned, the look which overtakes the image almost at once at the passing of the soul.

The old woman straightened up and bobbed a curtsey. Like her husband she had bright inquisitive blue eyes. Their sheepskin jackets, the embroidery faded, stained with grease, bulged where they bulged like a second skin, as if they slept in them, and why not, thought Milly, very cosy. Good-humoured, a shade guarded, the old pair stood waiting with a natural dignity, allowing time for the strangers to orientate themselves and to make the first move; a courtesy to which Wragg responded by scuffing his feet to show that he deprecated the intrusion, and Milly, who did not see it as such, by rising to the occasion.

" Look! " she exclaimed, crossing swiftly to the kitchen table. " Herbert, come and look! " Dizzy under the shock of this intimacy, the second that day, like a somnambulist Wragg approached. Milly's eyes sparkled, and the peasants came up and stood beside her, smiling at her pleasure. There was a large amount of meat on the table, neatly arranged on newspapers all sodden with blood. " You see, they've killed a pig! " He did see. The pig's head was on the table, too. He turned away, feeling sick. The old man bustled about, bringing a bottle and glasses. He set these on the table amongst the portions of the carcass. Wragg, who was slouching about examining the photographs, came when he was called. He looked unhappy but he accepted his glass. They stood over the table sipping the mead, which was sickly-sweet, like cough mixture.

" Pretty filthy, isn't it ? " said Milly, with a charming smile at her host.

" I told you you wouldn't like it."

" So you did." Cheerfully, she accepted another glass. " Why are you looking like that ? "

" Like what ? "

" Well—ropey."

" I—I don't know." Because I hate the sight and smell of blood,

226

that was the truth, but he couldn't say it. Not with the pig's head there in front of him. Its eyelids fastened down, the lashes fanning over its fat white cheeks, just the suspicion of an eye glinting beneath; its expression meek, but cynical round the lips: " I'm as good as you," it sneered, " if not better . . ." holding its own and a bit more, even in death.

Milly said, admiring it too: " They're awfully clever, I believe. They are supposed to *know*." Wragg shot her a look of hatred.

The woman came in through the back door with a washtub and set it on the floor by the table. Her hands were clean and wet, but there were bracelets of dried blood round her wrists. In the tub was what looked like a bundle of wet grey stockings, all tangled together. She began sorting out the heap, cutting it into lengths.

" Even rabbits have twelve feet, I believe," murmured Milly, deeply interested. " And we have twenty-two. I've no idea what a pig has, have you? " Wragg made no reply.

The peasant filled his pipe, took a swig of mead, and with his pipe in his mouth worked his great fist into a heap of chopped meat whilst his wife sprinkled it with peppercorns and bits of garlic and coarse salt; the operation looked haphazard, but there was the impression that they knew, as a team, just what they were doing. Then, when the meat was properly mashed up the woman grunted, and the old man dived into the tub and, selecting a length of stocking, knotted one end and began stuffing it with the paste.

" Goodness! " whispered Milly. " Look at that. I do believe it's salami." At that the old man let out a cackle of laughter; nodding, rocking with laughter, he went on prodding, poking the meat down tight.

" Oh, dear, I would like to buy some," she said, licking her lips. Not because she cared for salami; she didn't. " Could I? "

Wragg looked at her with distaste. " No, you could not. He wouldn't sell it anyway—it's the greatest delicacy. Besides," he moved away from her, " it's illegal . . ." He waved his arms in a desperate gesture to include everything, the blazing fire, the hospitality, the pig's head and their chuckling hosts. " It's all illegal, the whole thing."

" I see," said Milly demurely, doing up her coat. " You mean we ought to be going? "

Immediately a great fuss started. Wragg, hovering on the doorstep, fretting to be gone, thought he had never seen anything like it. " It's a knack," he told himself grimly, " just a knack, that's all—a knack which, thank God, I haven't got." Milly had rummaged in her bag and produced slabs of chocolate; the old man presented her with a bottle of mead, they filled her bag with apples, the wife picked a sprig

227

of geranium and stuck it in her coat; the good-byes, the compliments, the handshaking, all took time before at last they were allowed to go.

" Where did they say I could get this salmon? "

" Farther on. At the dam."

" What dam? "

" Just a dam. I rather think I've heard something about it, but I can't remember what." Ever since the old man had mentioned the dam something he half-remembered having once heard about a dam in these parts had been teasing him, but his brain was stupefied with the whisky, the cold and the mead. " Damn and blast," he muttered to himself, and then woke up to the fact of having made a little joke. He would like to have passed it on, but decided she might not think it was funny.

The lake, narrowing, curved like the blade of a scimitar, the mountains closing in. The steel colours of the sky and the snow had softened; the trees and the shadows of the trees on the water merged soft and dark as sable, a sable trimming along the edge of the lake. The water still glimmered, but the green had faded to grey, and thick mist obscured the farther bank.

Round the next bend a large, newly painted signpost stuck up out of the snow on the roadside. In red letters it announced: ROSNOM. The sight of it caused a little flash in Wragg's brain, as if two wires had brushed but failed to connect.

" What a big signpost," said Milly as they swept past. " Don't do things by halves, do they? First one we've seen." She was humming away to herself. Presently she said, pulling up and switching off: " I'm cold. Where's that flask? "

He passed it to her. She took a gulp, wiped the neck of it with her handkerchief and passed it back to him. " Go on, have a go. Do you good. I say, look! " Wragg, the whisky trickling down his throat, choked. " That must be the dam."

He looked, and saw that there were indeed some sort of installations on the farther bank; at the same moment the whisky repaired the faulty connection in his brain, establishing contact.

" Go back! " he cried. His voice, hoarse with terror, stuck. " G-go back *at once*, Mrs. Purdoe—please! "

" What on earth? " She began to laugh. He was fumbling with the screwtop of the flask, his hands trembling in his excitement. She took it from him.

" You see—I've suddenly remembered. *This is Rosnom*."

" I saw. It was on the sign."

" Yes, well——" he gasped. " It's all my fault, of course—but it's

228

secret—I remember now . . . it's a military zone . . . we've got to go back, Mrs. Purdoe . . . *please*, quick as you can."

" Oh, lord." Just to show that *she* wasn't excited she took another nip. Unwisely, Wragg caught her arm, and she shook him off, looking very cross.

" Listen," she said. " *Don't* get in a flap. I can't bear people who flap," and she took another nip, just to teach him, then screwed up the flask and gave it to him to hold, smiled at him kindly and switched on the ignition. " You see . . . take things calmly and you get there just as quickly in . . ." she frowned, as the engine whirred, grunted and then stopped. She tried again and went on trying whilst Wragg, too cowed to speak, his expression mutinous nevertheless, gazed at the dam across the lake.

" That's that," he heard her say after a bit. He whipped round to find her lighting a cigarette.

" What d'you mean, that's that? "

" It won't start. Perhaps we've run out of petrol," she added placidly. Her smile irritated him to a frenzy.

" But—but surely—isn't there some way of telling? "

" Oh, yes, there's the usual gauge. It says nil."

He wrenched open the door and flung himself out into the ditch. Standing knee-deep in snow he took great gulps of icy air. Milly got out herself and stamped up and down, chuckling as she watched him prowl round the car, stooping to pinch the tyres, prod the bonnet; for two pins he might have kicked it—or her. Finally he leaned up against it and put his head in his hands as if in despair. Really, she thought disgustedly, he behaves like a woman. Her own phlegmatic reaction to the situation struck her as commendably unfeminine; apart from the situation itself—the business about forgetting to fill up.

" Listen! "

Wragg raised his head. As yet still far off, but approaching along the shores of the lake they could hear the rumbling of wheels and voices singing.

" Saved! " said Milly, diving into her bag to attend to her face.

At each bend of the road the sound of singing blossomed and died and blossomed again, and at last it came into view on the crest of the hill, a three-tonner packed with grey shapes waving and singing; poised it seemed to hover for an instant and then came careening down the snowy slope towards them. Wragg saw Milly leap from the bank into the road and stand there, her arms spread out, and in the same second he saw the flashes on the mudguards of the three-tonner, by then close, and the number-plate and its passengers, who were not holiday-makers as he had expected but in a uniform he recognised along

229

with the flashes and the number-plate, and he had time to think, bloody little fool, and to shout, although he never knew he shouted, because the next thing he knew was that he was in the road scooping up an armful of fur and another of rather taut thin legs. The three-tonner glided to a stop with a yard to spare.

Still holding her, he blurted out: " Bloody little fool."

She twisted her head angrily. " Put me down! "

He obeyed so promptly that she staggered.

Soldiers were swarming over the sides of the three-tonner; they were rowdy and excited and there was a lot of horseplay as they dragged their weapons out of the back. Then they began to close in, looking sheepish, but forming a tight circle round their prisoners from which there was no escape. One or two, Milly could tell from the suppressed giggling, were beginning to make remarks. She hardly dared to glance at her companion, expecting him to be in a state of total collapse. When she did, to her astonishment his bearing greatly exceeded her expectations; having, for once, surrendered himself to a single emotion (anger, it chanced to be), he was transformed by the capitulation; he looked impressive, formidable even; certainly thoroughly angry. A sergeant had pushed his way through the soldiers; he was holding, she noted, a smallish but solid weapon, a sort of gun. Prudently she edged nearer Wragg.

" Ask him for a lift," she whispered, and quick as lightning the sergeant spun round at her raising the arm with the gun. As a gesture it struck her as rather rude, and she decided to ignore it, by way of rebuke reaching in her bag for a cigarette.

" *Milly!* " Wragg began hoarsely, but the sergeant had already seized him by the arm and was propelling him towards the lorry. Milly, a soldier on either side of her, was jostled along behind. The soldiers gathered round, disposed to be playful, as first Wragg, then she, climbed up into the cabin of the vehicle. She was conscious of a single emotion to the exclusion of all else, relief that she happened to be wearing ski-pants. A man with a tommy-gun crowded in on her other side. As they moved off she saw that a guard had been posted round the Austin.

" That is kind of them," she murmured to Wragg, " isn't it? Larry says a CD plate *always pays*."

" You bet." He snorted. " Right now I should say that one's worth its weight in gold." Remnants of his recent grandeur still clung to him, she noticed. She didn't mind him when he was like this—formidable, abrupt. It rather tickled her, in fact. One could forget his dripping wetness underneath. Then his remark struck her afresh. She was still pondering it when they reached the end of the lake. It had become dark.

230

" D'you mean," she whispered, seeking to phrase with all possible delicacy the outrageous fancy which had just occurred to her: " You don't mean that they're . . ." a cluster of lights sprang out of the dark, " *RUSSIANS*? "

" Oh, shut up," mumbled Wragg, sick at heart. A dig from the tommy-gun made her shut up.

They passed through a check point and were kept waiting as the soldiers in the back dismounted. Then the three-tonner rattled down a steep slope and drew up in front of a group of Nissen huts. Some soldiers came out of the main hut with an officer in charge, and he marched them up to the truck; they stood around as the officer threw open the door nearest Wragg and shouted something.

" We're to get out," said Wragg. Unwinding himself he clambered down, but tripped—he would, thought Milly—arriving on hands and knees in the snow at the officer's feet. The officer, looking very embarrassed, quite a nice blond young man, she noticed, helped him up, and exploiting the confusion to her own advantage she dismounted herself. Arc lights marked the boundaries of the camp, shedding an unhealthy greenish glow over the snow, illuminating, too, barbed wire entanglements, pillboxes, and some sentries walking about. The odd part of it was that the very ground seemed to shake beneath one's feet and there was a vibration in the air the cause of which was not immediately identifiable until one realised that one's ears were deafened by the low steady roar, ferocious yet controlled, of falling water.

They were marched into the largest of the huts and left in a guard-room, empty except for a bench and a stove; the officer and others disappeared into an inner room and shut the door. Milly smoked three cigarettes and was about to light a fourth when Wragg, who had appeared to be dozing, said:

" You'd better keep those. Unless you've got an inexhaustible supply."

Thinking it over, she decided he was probably right. She slid up the bench towards him.

" Tell me one thing," she began in a cosy, almost flirtatious voice. " Why did you rush into the road like that? "

Why indeed? He saw it still, that scene—he thought he would see it all his life.

" Because I thought the truck wouldn't stop," he said. Let her laugh, he thought, let her bloody well laugh, and she was just about to laugh because he looked so fierce, when the door opened and a guard, with a jab of his weapon, indicated that they should pass through into the next room.

The blond young officer with two others was sitting behind a large

231

desk on which were a few papers, several used glasses of tea, all Wragg's precious "material" and Milly's camera. Knots of soldiers hung about round the walls, whispering. Standing at the officer's elbow was a lanky young man in civilian clothes, unshaven and without a tie; recognisably a Slavonian in contrast to the rest.

A bench had been placed in front of the desk and the officer without looking up waved to them to sit down. Milly and Wragg sat down side by side, and then the young man in civilian clothes cleared his throat impressively and said, in English:

" Sit down, please, sir and madam."

The officer took off his cap and placing it in front of him, began to speak softly, inclining his head towards the interpreter; his voice went on and on, his pale eyes roving over the room and sometimes over his prisoners, the interpreter nodding blandly from time to time. Then he stopped. The interpreter took a deep breath.

" Passports," he said, getting to the kernel of the thing as only interpreters know how.

Wragg produced his passport and handed it over the desk. The officer, with an expression of the frankest cynicism, studied it from every angle, becoming engrossed with the pages to the rear rather than with the more personal and useful data contained elsewhere.

" Oh, dear," said Milly, smiling nervously at the interpreter. " I'm so sorry, I forgot to bring mine."

The interpreter failed to respond to the smile but performed his duty instead. As the situation was being put to him, the officer glanced up, his eyes flickering over Milly's face. He nodded at her almost approvingly, as if he sympathised with her plight and could readily understand it; even, as he went on nodding, seeming to suggest that her open admission of negligence reflected to her credit rather than otherwise—at least as against an attempt at passing off a bogus document, such as the one he now held in his hand. Then he talked to the interpreter for a long time.

" You are," said the latter, getting into his stride as soon as he was able, " of course aware that this is a military zone and that you have exploited your diplomatic priviliges for the purpose of disseminating bourgeois-nationalist propaganda. . . ."

" Bourgeois? " Milly exclaimed, much affronted.

" Equipped also with a camera." Certainly all the evidence of guilt confronted them on the table. Open, uppermost on the pile of seditious literature lay a two-page spread illustrating the mating habits of seals in the Hebrides. It does look pretty black, thought Wragg, examining it upside down in a new and sinister light.

" The captain demands to know the object of your visit."

232

"An excursion," said Wragg. "A picnic."

Translated, this reply was received by a wry smile from the officer and sniggers from the men. The former, leaning lazily across the desk, waving the interpreter to one side, addressed Wragg direct.

"Mari?" Her jerked his head towards Milly.

"N-non," said Wragg, and then, as if on this point at least there were no need for shame or equivocation: "Oh, *no!*"

The officer turned to Milly, to check up. He seemed to have taken against Wragg. At any rate there was a trace of insolence in his expression as, indicating him, he inquired of her: "Femme?"

"Non!" she rapped out, getting her own back. The officer murmured something and the soldiers burst out laughing. Even the interpreter grinned. She and Wragg exchanged looks of loathing.

"The captain," said the interpreter, after another long colloquy, "is tired of jokes. He wishes you to explain the *true* object of your visit."

Milly sat up straight. "Oh, well," she said, with engaging candour, "it's perfectly simple, really. We came to get smoked salmon." The interpreter looked rattled. "*Saumon fumé*," she explained helpfully, as the captain leaned over, frowning.

"*Qu'est-ce que . . . ça?*"

"*Saumon*," she repeated in a bright governessy manner, wiggling her fingers in imitation of a fish. "*Fumé. Pour manger avec le cocktail.*"

There was a pause whilst the captain put two and two together in his own style. Never taking his eyes off her, he spoke rapidly. He had been caught napping. She was sly, this one.

"The captain says there are no salmon here," said the interpreter.

"Oh, but there *must* be—with all that water . . ." she sprang to her feet and something clicked behind her. Wragg's long arm shot out and he pulled her back on to the bench. For the second time that day he discovered himself to have acted long before his brain had apprised him of anything at all, let alone a situation. Anyway, she was back on the bench now, as cross as two sticks, he could tell. She peeped round behind. A guard was watching her, holding a sten in a business-like manner. She slid up close to Wragg.

"He couldn't *shoot* me with that thing, could he?"

"Yes," said Wragg. "Easily." She sighed and looked very meek, contrite even. As for him, he glowed with his new-found confidence. It occurred to him that other men—manly men, a category to which hitherto he had been thankful not to belong—went about doing this sort of thing habitually; acting first and thinking afterwards. On women it did seem to have the most extraordinary effect. Glancing at Milly's aggrieved face he almost laughed. Of course one shouldn't make a

233

habit of it, but now and then . . . Olga, for instance? Yes, but would mastering Olga give one quite the same sensation of—would it be quite so much fun? Was there any point in mastering Olga? He was inclined to think not.

There was a long wait. The captain, so far as could be seen, was filling in the time doing noughts and crosses. In reality he was trying to break this new and ultra-fishy code. Meanwhile, the interpreter was poring through Wragg's stuff. After another lengthy briefing, eventually the latter sighed, as if preparing himself for a full-scale wrangle:

" For the purposes of the charge to be brought against you the captain wishes to know your diplomatic status."

" I have no diplomatic status," said Wragg.

" You have already been warned," he was told, " we are tired of frivolity. You were travelling in diplomatic vehicle No. . . ."

" I repeat, I have no diplomatic status. I am merely the—go on, tell *him*—the assistant editor of the newspaper *Voice of Britain*." Then, as the interpreter demurred, " VOICE OF BRITAIN! " Wragg cried out loud and clear, as if in truth his voice were it. The officer glanced at him and grunted and all three officers put their heads together.

" You goat," whispered Milly. Wragg could see she was pleased.

" That's foxed them," he said, rather pleased himself.

The ensuing confusion justified this boast. A wooden chest in a corner, which housed the archives of the establishment, was unlocked and its contents showered over the floor. Some of the other ranks were set to stacking the papers in heaps, others to brushing out and polishing up the chest. The officers, suffering the penalty of their literacy, were rather overworked. There were a great many papers and it would take some time to sift through the lot. The interpreter, who was clearly not on the TOP SEC. distribution list, ordered fresh tea and sprawled over the table devouring Wragg's material, a weekly feature—Photocrimes—capturing his interest from the start. The intimacy between him and the prisoners had advanced almost to the stage of pooling their deductions when the captain returned, his gravity scarcely concealing his satisfaction. He instructed the interpreter who, with his mind only half on the job, sulkily gathered the *Picture Posts* together and with a sigh addressed Wragg:

" You are a spy," he began gently, and scratched his ear, his attention distracted by a headline FABIAN OF THE ——, but recollecting himself, he pattered on. " There is no assistant editor of this capitalist journal *Voice of Britain*. There is only the Editor, an Englishman named Simpson. So you see," he concluded rather apologetically, as if he might coax Wragg into an admission of the fact, " you are an

impostor and a spy. And," he added feebly, with even less conviction,
" the woman, too."

" Well, really! " said Milly.

Wragg flushed scarlet.

" Tell the captain Mr. Simpson left Slavonia three months ago.
It's not my fault if his records "—here his glance flitted over the
soldiers who were cramming the papers back into the box—" are not
up to date. Let him telephone to Grusnov. He will find that the present
Editor is a Mr. Purdoe, P U R D O E, this lady's husband. And
whatever the captain says," Wragg went on, quelling interruption with
a fiery glance, " I *am* the assistant editor of the weekly journal *Voice
of Britain*."

" So there," said Milly under her breath.

" Yes, of course," said the interpreter soothingly, thereby robbing
Wragg of some of his effect, and began to translate, after which the
captain said something genial and apparently final because everybody
laughed and the officers stood up.

" What does he say? " Wragg asked belligerently.

The interpreter looked baffled for a second, then he churned it out:
" The captain is of the opinion that if you are the assistant editor of
the journal *Voice of Britain* then he is a Greek."

Wragg's expression—when he had worked this out—of incredulity
and outrage was such that Milly had to suppress a giggle. In doing so
she caught the captain's eye. He, too, seemed not unamused. So,
seeing that they were all going to be friends, she said chattily to the
interpreter: " I should think that must have been tricky to translate,
wasn't it? I mean, I wasn't quite sure whether you meant to be nice
or nasty, just at first. I must say, I think you speak English awfully
well."

" Thank you." He bowed and continued, " Before taking the
summary action permissible in cases of this kind the captain is putting through a telephone call to headquarters informing them of the
facts. It is a transparent straightforward case of espionage to be settled
simply. For the time being you will remain in the next room under
guard."

" Well, do please thank him very much," said Milly. " I'm sure
he's doing everything he possibly can." She beamed encouragingly
at the captain, who, it struck her, now looked rather hot under the
collar; bashful, almost. " There won't be much *delay*, will there? "

" Delay? " The interpreter frowned. He was not bound to answer
every silly question put to him—still, he thought they were very brave,
and if the truth was all that was required of him it might even cheer
them up.

235

"There is always—*delay*," he said sombrely. Even by Slav standards it was a good exit line. Collecting up his papers he stalked off.

So back in the guardroom, on the bench in front of the stove, Wragg sat at one end and Milly at the other. He looked, she thought, more than ever like a great sick bird, sick or wounded, on a perch. He was huddled into his overcoat, his head on his chest. She thought, it'll be a very interesting experience *afterwards*, but goodness, it is boring now. The soldier who was guarding them was bored, too. She felt sorry for him. He was fiddling about with his sten, adjusting gadgets, now directing the barrel her way, now at the light bulb, sometimes even peering down it himself, rather mystified, like a child with a toy he does not understand, at once too complicated and too expensive for one of his years. Every so often he achieved a click that made her jump, a reaction which clearly afforded him such exquisite entertainment that she stopped feeling sorry for him. At length even he tired of this sport and leaned over, nursing his weapon in his arms, and fell asleep.

She slid up the bench. "I say," she whispered, "I want to go to the loo."

Wragg stirred.

"I want to go . . ."

His nearside eye flickered coldly. "I don't suppose there is one."

He saw her face crumple as though she might be going to burst into tears. Heaving a sigh, he settled himself again. He washed his hands of her. Let her fix it, since she was so smart.

Which, of course, she did. He must have drowsed off, because the next thing he heard her say was: "Est-ce qu'il y a une toilette," and raising one eyelid he saw the captain, tunic unbuttoned and half asleep, leading her off. The moment she had gone he felt deeply ashamed. It was strange. The sight of her irritated him profoundly, yet once out of it, as now, he wanted her back, desperately, so that he might make it up to her and explain—or was it simply in order that he might, with justification present, continue to be irritated? I could have asked where it was, he thought wretchedly. That was the least he could have done. Besides, he might need it himself before long—then he *would* look a fool. He stared at the stove, seeing her as he would always see her, standing there in the road; tiny, yes, she was that, reckless, and that, and a bloody fool—and yet, not *quite*. . . . Of course it was all her fault, the whole thing, but she hadn't grumbled, not once. Take Olga, for instance, similarly placed. He could imagine her arguing with the officer and putting his back up—she would still be arguing now with the buffoon opposite—demanding to know the conditions of service in the Russian army if he knew her, *and* taking notes. If it

236

had been Olga, there would have been no telephone call, no reprieve, and any action, even the most summary, would have been excused by the overriding necessity for silencing that voice. And he himself would have found it in his heart to forgive the captain. Oh, yes. He had often felt that way himself. Whereas, although Milly Purdoe did get on one's nerves, it was not in *that* way nor on *those* nerves. He couldn't imagine her nagging—partly because she had a very pleasant voice.

In view of all this, when she came back he was moved to say: " Did you find it? "

" Yes, I did! " she snapped. " No thanks to you."

He revised his rosy dream.

The stove gave out hardly any heat. She slid up next to him and held out the flask. In silence he took it and swallowed a mouthful. Then she dozed, leaning a fraction of her weight against him. He watched, with a compassion which quite melted all his resentment and came near to melting even the marrow in his bones, as her head tilted sideways, jerked up, and tilted again; eventually, and he went half-way to meet it, it rested on his shoulder. Now there was nothing to be seen of her except a bundle of fur and the top of her shining head. He sat rigid, staring in front of him. Once or twice, to ease his neck, he turned his head this way and that. Her way, the smell of her hair jumped into his nostrils. In between sniffs of it he thought it had a tang all its own, aromatic, a shade medicinal—a bewitching smell which provoked him to battle with himself, to delay turning in order to smell it again. How it teased him, that smell, reminding him—just before he, too, dozed off, he remembered—of the smell of Wendy's hair, ten years ago. Herbie, she had murmured, rubbing her nose into his neck, pressing her full beautiful body against him—Herbie. He slept.

* * *

Miss Raven was creaking about the salon. Larry, stretched out on the sofa, wished she would go away. Much as he would have liked to know what she was doing, it wasn't worth the risk of raising an eyelid to find out. He could think of nothing for which he felt more disinclined at this moment than conversation with Miss Raven. Now she had stopped moving about—there was a faint chance she might have gone off. Cautiously he opened one eye, and it was just another black mark to be chalked up against the day that she should be standing motionless at the foot of the sofa, looking down at him.

" Oh, Mr. Purdoe—I didn't wake you up, did I? " She smiled her bright " nursey " smile. " Now I want you to be a good boy and have something to eat. I know how you feel "—did she? he wondered— " but you must keep your strength up. The girl's out " (Miss Raven

237

always referred to Gisela as "the girl"), "I don't know how many evenings she's taken off lately . . . I was going to speak to Mrs."—here she checked herself tactfully, as if Milly were already laid out on a mortuary slab—"anyway, there's a nice bit of pork pie, look."

He saw what she had been doing. She had laid the small table in front of the stove.

"I don't want anything to eat, thanks.".

"Oh, but we mustn't talk like that—it won't do us a bit of good, will it? Now I'll just cut——"

"Not now, Miss Raven. Truly. It's kind of you to have gone to all this——"

She had already cut a large slice of pie and put it on a plate. "Oh, Mr. Purdoe, you are being naughty!"

"Miss Raven. Look. *I don't want anything to eat.* Understand?"

For a moment he half-hoped that he had wounded her to the point of her taking herself off, but it seemed that she was not at all put out. Simpering, she cleared the plates away.

"So what *can* I do for you?"

"Well," he wanted to say, go away, but he hadn't the courage. "You can pour me a whisky and soda, if you would."

"Now," she handed it to him, "I'm not going to leave you because you'll be mopey and lonesome and that won't help matters, will it? I know exactly how you feel."

If that were really so, he thought, she would be out of that door like greased lightning.

"So we'll put our feet up and drink our whisky and read *The Times*—here—and try not to think about it at all. And I'll get on with my patience—I shan't disturb you, I promise."

She sat down opposite and began dealing out the cards. Presently she said: "How long did Mr. Schulman say he'd be?"

"He didn't know. He's got to get hold of the Chief of Police who's a sort of pal of his. Then there'll be some telephoning."

"Ah," observed Miss Raven shrewdly, "it won't be a matter of five minutes, then, will it?" This was a statement rather than a prediction and redundant at that, Abe having already been gone two hours. She had stopped laying out her cards. Now what? thought Larry, rustling *The Times* in defence.

"It's not like England, is it?" she said gently. He put down the paper. "I mean, there's no one to turn to—that's what one feels, doesn't one?"

Yes, one did. At least he did, but then it was his pigeon; the others shouldn't feel like that—he was supposed to be the person for them to turn to and look what had happened to him. This is where contacts

238

count, Abe had said. You leave it to me. Unwisely omitting to reply to Miss Raven, instead he closed his eyes, thinking of Milly in a snow-drift, Milly in the lake, Milly in one of her scrapes, without him, and with—to make matters worse—that incompetent ass, Wragg. Miss Raven peeped round the corner of *The Times*.

" Headache? " he heard her whisper.

" A bit."

He heard a creak as she moved, and suddenly he froze with horror as he felt the touch of her hands on his forehead; she began stroking. Where was she? Craftily he plotted her position from the sound of her breathing. Somewhere behind his head, blast her. One had read about this treatment, he remembered, this laying on of hands; so, it would seem, had she. It was always supposed to work wonders—certainly reaction was pretty well instantaneous. At this rate he would be reduced to a state of gibbering frenzy within sixty seconds. Gritting his teeth, he bore it for half that time, and then sat up. Her action arrested in mid-air, she looked grotesque, but pathetic, too. For maximum safety he stood up.

" Tell you what, Miss Raven. You have a drink. I'm going to have another." He went and poured them. When he came back she was sitting over her cards.

" Thank you," she said quietly. Her dignity made him feel a brute. It also occurred to him that she must be awfully used to rebuffs. He stood looking down at her, vaguely wishing to make amends.

" Come on, Miss Raven. Let's see you drink it up. It's been a pretty grim day all round."

" I was just thinking," she murmured, " it's my birthday."

" Good lord, is it really? You shouldn't have kept it a secret—we'd have done something about it." Although what, he couldn't imagine. " Well, here's the very best and . . . plenty of them, all that kind of thing." Forgetting to be on his guard, his voice and his smile were kind. " That's the girl. I'll get you another."

Poor old geyser, he thought. Rather rotten. What a birthday. Yet she wasn't so old. Older than he was, of course. He had never even asked himself how old she might be. Milly would know. And it would be in her passport, of course, which he held. He must look, just out of interest. When he brought her glass, she was sitting staring straight in front of her. Her knobbly cheek, he noticed, was beginning to be flushed. He could not have said why, but he had the feeling that her mood had changed, and he hesitated; fleetingly the memory of that incident at the picnic returned. Then with extreme caution he put her drink on the table and backed away. She began to speak, and it seemed to him that even her voice had altered, become dreamy. She was about

239

to launch off into reminiscence; Ireland again, he thought—still, it is her birthday.

"On my birthday," she murmured, "when I was a little girl, and oh, right up till I was in my teens, my father would have the gardener pick a mass of flowers"—he looked at his watch. Abe had been the helluva time—"and my old nanny used to make a wreath, a garland, you know, of the flowers, freesias, anemones, violets, all sorts"—she tossed her head, as she summoned the gardener, the nanny to mind. He stared at her fascinated. It was true, the lines of her face had changed, become blurred; there was an odd little smile on her lips. He even had the idea that the atmosphere in the room had changed. For one thing, it was stifling.

"Stove gives out a good heat, doesn't it?" he said nervously, but she took no notice.

"Then I wore it all day. Just imagine. Funny, the little things one remembers." Larry did as he was bid, sketched in his mind's eye the image of Miss Raven in a wreath of flowers, and decided that such a vision had he ever beheld it would have gone straight into the unforgettable class. Then he said, teasing her: "Freesias and violets, at this time of year? You must have spent your youth gadding round the South of France."

Miss Raven seemed offended. "Certainly not," she replied coldly, carefully, too. "I have never visited the South of France." She went on, warming to it: "But they grow in Cornwall, you know . . . at least, we grew them quite easily, that is to say, the gardener did . . . in the sheltered nooks and crannies . . . the garden stretched to the edge of the cliffs. We had a wonderful old house, in Cornwall." She sighed. "That was where I spent my youth, you know, until"—Larry, half-mesmerised, was tempted to complete it for her—"until the crash came. I must show you the photos some day."

He said, taking a cigarette: "Yes, you must. Did you—so you were born there, were you?"

"In Cornwall? Yes, I was." Rather coyly, she leaned forward and helped herself to a cigarette.

"I'm so sorry, I didn't know you smoked." He lit it for her. "It's a part of the country I don't know . . ." He hated himself for pursuing the subject. I may be mistaken, he told himself, I must be. "Lovely, but lonely, I should think. Still, you were a large family, I expect."

"Oh, no." Meeting his eyes, she gave him a gallant little smile. "I was an only child." Then—and he could have sworn it was due to no change of expression on his own face, which was rigid—he knew which one he was wearing and it fitted very tight, the one Milly jeered

240

at, had christened " the Monster of M.I.5 "—he thought he caught a flicker in Miss Raven's eyes—a fraction of doubt, did it, for an instant, slip in?—he was never to be sure, because at that moment the telephone rang.

" Abe? "

" Yeah, me. It's all fixed. I been waiting for confirmation. Jeezus, do I feel stewed—you owe me a bottle of Scotch, Larry—it took two of bourbon to fix it up. Still, they're on their way. Yep—under escort, everything hunky dee. Saved from the jaws of "—he laughed—" oh, sure. No kidding. They'd landed up just where I said, blundered right in, and there was some young lunatic in charge up there—anyway, tell you when I see you. I'll be right round."

Larry said, coolly, so far as he could judge: " She's all right? "

" *All right?* " Abe snorted, and the telephone bucked in Larry's hand. " She is *now*—she won't be soon. Just let me have a coupla minutes with that gal—no, maybe I'd better leave it to you."

" They're on their way, Miss Raven," he said, trying to tether the balloon which threatened to go soaring up, up through the top of his head to the ceiling where it had no business to be, the balloon being his heart.

" What a good thing," said Miss Raven.

" Don't you wait up." What had they been talking about? He came up to her chair. She was sitting quite still. " Please, there's no need . . ."

" I *like* waiting up," she said jerkily. Her eyes, he saw, were filled with tears.

" Miss Raven," he said gently, putting his hand on her shoulder, " what is it? What's the matter? "

" You're so kind to me," she mumbled, and as if with these words she had pressed a trigger, the tears shot out. That is to say, they did not overflow, or spill or trickle or merely fall—they popped out as big as peas, like peas from a peashooter, exploding on his hand, his trousers, the hearthrug, and her lap.

He hated tears; all tears, no matter who shed them, he hated them in every way, shape, or form. He hated them in prospect, the quivering lip, the sighs, the twisted handkerchief, the slow welling-up; he hated the aftermath, the blotches and hiccups and shininess; he hated them near at hand, snuffled into one's own clean handkerchief or damping one's shoulder, he hated them at a distance on the cinema screen. He hated the threat of them, the secret weapon concealed about each female person to be employed at the least hint of an attack; he hated them for the efficacy with which in seconds they could reduce him or any man to the rank of bastard, and whilst hating himself for the bastard he indubitably was, he hated the tears that washed it home to him far more. He hated them as the outward and visible signs of self-pity, as the preface to chapters of remorse which must be ploughed through, which they would freely punctuate before an evening might be considered well and truly spent. Most particularly he hated those tears whose purpose was to provide " relief "; through a vale of tears one would be frog-marched beside her, the weeper, still humbly wishing to do her a service, acknowledging oneself to blame—whilst " something in the oven " burnt to a cinder or one's own passion grew cold —and when one was permitted to clamber up the other side, panting, when the river of woe had run dry, she, the Niobe, the source of it all, would perk up and say brightly: " Now I could do with a sandwich " —or—" You know I'm always this way about this time. . . ." Tears of rage, of fatigue, frustration, petulance, jealousy, boredom; tears for the act of love (shed, at least, after it), tears to accompany a welts-chmerz, at the sight of the moon, say, or as an agreeably salty appetiser to a re-hash of old letters; tears with a thousand uses, as a threat, an excuse, an outlet, useful in prevarication, provocation, useful all round the clock—God, even in dreams!—buckets and buckets of crocodile tears. How he hated them. But he had never in his life seen any quite like these.

He stood over her awkwardly, waiting. Then, as the jet seemed to have been turned off, he ventured:

" Happy birthday, my dear," and she lifted her face. Her cheeks and throat were flushed bright red; where the lipstick had worn off her lips showed dry and cracked. Because she looked piteous, pitying her, he bent and kissed her forehead. Instantly he felt her arm round his neck; like a grappling iron it clamped him into position; her breath rasped in his ear as her lips travelled over his face, dragging at his flesh like a vacuum cleaner devouring a strip of carpet, until they found his own lips and fastened there, glued tight and moist and gelatinous as a sea anemone—and in those seconds he really did identify vacuum cleaner, sea anemone—then with a push that nearly winded him he was sent staggering and Miss Raven was no longer in the chair, no longer in the room.

It took him a minute or two to collect himself. He rubbed his face where she had mauled it, flexed his jaws, stroked his bruised lips; then he went over and filled his glass with whisky, swallowed it neat and poured some more. His lips smarted at the touch of the spirit. " Well, I'll be damned," he kept muttering under his breath, " well, I'm—well, I really am . . ."

He lit a cigarette, and kicking open the door of the stove, smoked the cigarette through. Staring thoughtfully at the glowing embers, he

242

examined his emotions. He was shocked, yes, deeply—but there was more to it than that. He wriggled his neck—he could still feel the pressure of that iron arm round the back. Why was he shocked? Not because a plain woman, employed as a nurse to his children, undoubtedly suffering the disturbances of a certain age, had attacked him? No, certainly not. Surprise, embarrassment, those were the reactions to *that*—had it been just that. Then what was it that had so shocked him? Clumsy as it had been, the embrace, mismanaged and thoroughly uncomfortable, its peculiar flavour lingered—crude, earthy, a taste so fundamental that it failed to repel him as it should have done, indeed, at all. Rather it was as if a wind had scorched over him, as if he had felt the earth tremble beneath his feet—his heart was still pounding—but an earthquake, a sirocco, these were natural events; a human being was not *repelled* by natural events, any more than he had been repelled by that incident just now.

No, it was something else—and for some reason it seemed important to define in his own words what that something was. The shock had been the revelation—that was more like it—the revelation that a force which he had immediately recognised but whose veritable existence he had doubted, imagining it to be some shameful element peculiar to his own nature—in consequence of which it lay smouldering, hidden away within himself—did, in fact, exist; that is to say, in another human being (surely the accepted proof, anyway good enough for him, of the fact of existence?)—and it was not at all like a bonfire smouldering in the corner of a field under a November sky, half-heartedly incinerating last year's leaves—no, more like a blow-lamp's flame, white-hot, blistering, a flame to kindle even old timbers, however damp and solid, into a blaze; and to go one step farther on this hypothesis, if his were not, as he had thought, the only flame—if flame and flame should ever meet, become one, then how awful the resulting conflagration would be. So it exists, he said to himself. Passion.

He brooded over his own little clutch of memories. Twelve and a half minutes in a brothel in Haifa. A WAAF who had enticed him into the fastness of Moncrieff House and in whispers behind a curtain had bargained with and bullied her room-mate (whom he had glimpsed on entering and was much more desirable and knew it) into vacating the premises for just that sunset hour when the notes of the muezzin's call circle the rooftops, and plummet to their prey, the believers in the coffee-shops shuffling their amber beads. Then, a few days later, the room-mate herself, who had obliged in the back of an Ordnance truck in the Mena House car park—an incident memorable for the roll of barbed wire in the corner on which he had barked his shins and she had discarded her nylons, and her wistful ultimatum: " It's a piece of

cake taking things off—I'd *marry* the man who put them back on . . ."
And the elderly woman with the poodle he'd run into in the black-out
near Portland Place—her splendid flat, her coyness at the initial
intimacies constituting a hold-up that had made a bypass imperative,
explained, as he discovered later, by the novelty of her hairy nipples and
the incident itself all too thoroughly explained, although he had ducked
all explanations, by the spine-chilling array of barbiturates on her
bathroom shelf—and that was the sum of it, apart from Milly. Then
what must have happened? It was there—it still smouldered, but at
some stage along the line of years the flame had been blown out; or
systematically doused. Curious, that he should feel so ashamed.
Passion. He should have had his glut of it by now—enough and to
spare, enough to have been honestly repelled by—enough, at any rate,
not to feel shame, and envy, yes, envy, now. That old girl—who would
have thought it? Her blood ran hotter than his. " God bless my soul,"
he murmured, unconsciously reverting to an expression of his father's,
marvelling at Miss Raven.

*   *   *

" They should be here any minute," said Abe Schulman.
" What can I get you to drink, Mrs. Wragg? " said Larry.
" Nothing, thanks. I'm not thirsty."
" Well, do sit down."
" No, thanks. Quite happy as I am." She had taken up an uncompromising position on the hearth rug, as if determined, so far as
possible, not to risk contamination from her surroundings. Larry
sighed. He would have liked to sit down himself. Olga Wragg wore
her lounging kit, the tight velvet trousers and the wisp of a blouse,
both of which emphasised the robustness of her frame; strings of
beads and long ear-rings jangled like the accoutrements of war. She
had been experimenting again, too, with a new sort of woad; the main
effort devoted to the eyes, already by nature conspicuous, and their
environs, the supporting features dwindled into comparative insignif-
icance—comparative, because there was not one that was not forceful,
not one that on its own account could not have redeemed a lesser face
from insipidity. The two men, maintaining a certain distance, stood
by sipping and smoking, both, in the silence, aware of a deepening
respect for their absent colleague, Wragg.
" We mustn't worry," said Larry feebly. Somebody had to say
something.
" *I'm* not in the least worried," Mrs. Wragg snubbed him crossly.
" I'm surprised, that's all. It's not like Herbert to get himself into a
mess. He's not that sort," she added, scowling at the man and the girl
244

on the back cover of Milly's *Vogue*, as if to indicate precisely which sort Wragg was not.

" How's the story, Olga? " Abe skipped away with the glasses. " Olga's writing a novel. It is fiction, isn't it, Olga? "

" You could call it that," she replied haughtily. " It's fictional, certainly—but it has a historical background."

" I've often thought I'd write a book," said Larry, with a malice quite foreign to him, " if I had the time." As though he had tweaked the string of a marionette, Mrs. Wragg turned her face away to hide a smile.

" Guess what," said Abe, " they're here."

*   *   **

Dishevelled, blue with cold, they shuffled in together and stood together, dazed, in the doorway; even to the uncritical eyes of their next-of-kin a certain resemblance seemed to have sprung up between the pair—superficial, of course.

" And how were the salt mines? " Abe pushed a glass of whisky at each. Larry was taking Milly's things. Mrs. Wragg plucked the glass from her husband's hand.

" Sorry and all that. Herbert's better off without spirits, they upset him. Supper's waiting, Herbert, now come along." She turned in the doorway. " Camomile tea, that's what I'd advise . . . that's what I'm going to give *him*, hot and strong."

Abe laughed. " Poor old Wragg. I bet that's how he gets it too. Hot and strong. Rocket to end all rockets."

" Talking of rockets——" Larry paused, his arms full of things.

" Well? " Milly sat crouched in the arm-chair, doing the waif, and with a professional touch to-night.

" You do deserve one, darling," he finished, carrying off her coat.

" So you do," said Abe.

She pouted. " I'm not taking it from *you*, Abe Schulman."

" If it hadn't been for Abe," said Larry at the bedroom door, " remind me to tell you about it sometime." He disappeared.

" Did you *save* me? " she said, getting up and leaning against the mantelpiece and looking up into Abe's face, " did you do that? "

" Aw, boloney. I just happened to have contacts."

" I see. So you did save me. Well——" she stopped doing the waif and did Scarlett O'Hara instead, " you *can* give me a rocket, if you like." It would not be at all disagreeable, she thought, to receive it from him.

" Oh, I can, can I? I guess I'll leave all that to Larry. He's had the worry."

245

" You mean—you didn't worry? "

He stubbed out his cigarette, picked up his overcoat and hung it on his shoulders before he turned round to look at her. Then with his forefinger he jerked up her chin and grinned broadly into her face.

" No, Milly," he said, chewing over the words in a way he had, " I'm afraid I did not."

It was the grin that annoyed her. Of all facial expressions to be assumed by man, a grin, was the one she cared for least. What could you tell from it? Nothing at all—and while you wasted time examining it the ball had already bounced once in your own court. She was only starting to move up into her advanced sulks position when the door shut behind him.

*   *   *

" Fancy going without your scarf."

Wragg laid his overcoat carefully over a chair, cuff to cuff, tail to tail.

" I said—whatever made you go without your scarf, Herbert? "

" Oh, I see. Sorry. Nothing, really. I mean, I didn't go without it."

" Well, where is it? "

" I lent it—to Mrs. Purdoe."

" *Lent* it? To *her*? " Mrs. Wragg snorted. " Whatever for? With all her furs. I can't understand what she was *doing* there, anyway. That's what I can't understand."

Understand my foot. As if she needed to understand, when all she had to do was what he could see she'd already done—donned her seven-league boots and made light of a vast tract of boggy territory— in which he had rather hoped she might become bogged down—and here she was, already sniffing at the fringes of the dark, certainly dangerous, but not, unfortunately, impenetrable jungle through which at some time or another—but not this very night, surely?—they would both have to pass. He said in desperation: " I wouldn't mind something to eat, if there's anything going."

" There's stew. Vegetable stew."

" Oh, Christ."

" Pardon? "

" I said, oh, Christ."

" I thought that was what you said." She had assumed her quiet, telling voice, so that he didn't dare make the obvious retort. " You know it's Thursday as well as I do," she went on. " So what did you expect? " Wragg went off into the bathroom. When he came back, she said, " I said, what did you expect, I should like to know."

246

She had *not* said all that, he fumed to himself. If just once she could be brought to report herself correctly . . .

" I'm sorry, Olga. I suppose I forgot it was Thursday." He had. He sat down at the table. " Well, let's have it, whatever it is."

She levered the dish out of the oven. The contents had dried up a bit, so she added water, swilling it round. It was odd, she thought, how, with vegetable stew, one ingredient tended to predominate in colour and in taste. Quite a gamble, really. This time, luckily, it was the potatoes; these being putty-coloured and neutral as to flavour, the result wasn't too bad. Last week, for instance, the beetroot had got the upper hand. For some obscure reason she was thankful that she had been guided to omit the beetroot to-night.

Wragg ate in silence. Olga sat opposite, fiddling with the beads round her neck. When she could bear it no longer, she said: " Whatever were you doing on that Rosnom road? I mean we don't usually go there, do we? "

He wiped his mouth and carefully folded his napkin; he was particularly wary of this, her " bon copain " approach, which she had originally mastered, along with the details of his job, as an alternative —the only one—to her superficially more formidable style of direct supervision. So he said guardedly: " I wanted to look in at that newspaper shop in the village. You know the one."

" Oh, did you? And how's distribution? "

" I—er—didn't find out. The place was shut."

" *Shut?* You mean you didn't *see* anyone? All that time and petrol, well, I don't know . . ."

" I saw the man next door. He asked us in."

" You and?—oh, I see. Asked you in, did he? Whatever for? "

" Mead, actually. They'd just killed a pig. It was quite interesting," he added brazenly.

" A *pig*, Herbert? *Interesting? Mead?* " Her beads all rattled. " Well, honestly, Herbert, for once I'm just *not* in the picture."

" No? " He stared at her. For once she was not in the picture. Which picture was that? There were any number of pictures—certainly it was a fact that she did not figure in a single one.

" Sounds to me like sheer waste of time." She snuffed the air, scenting some kind of head-on engagement ahead. " The pig, and so forth. You've never gone in for this sort of thing before, have you? "

" What sort of thing? "

" Well, prancing all over the countryside, dropping in on peasants, hobnobbing with every Tom, Dick and Harry. . . . *Your* job is public relations, Herbert—and you'd far better stick to it, the way you've always done."

Wragg pushed his plate away and got up from the table.

"And then, after that, what did you do? Mistook the road, I suppose?"

"I'm sorry, Olga. I suppose I forgot it was Thursday."

He sat down at the table. "Well, let's——"

She leaned over, helping him to vegetables from the big brown bowl with vegetable stew, one of those fierce economical stews, the nourishment of these being put in, as it were, from the top, the only nourishment here superficially.

"Whatever are you smiling at, Herbert?"

"Ever been along on that Remson road, I mean two-thirds of the way to——"

"Whatever for?" She had risen and was clutching the edge of the table; her great white arms taut, her great dark eyes hooped with pencil, she was like a barn owl poised on a rafter, taking the measure of a giddy young mouse. "Whatever *for*, Herbert?"

He leaned his head back against the stove, watching her under his lashes.

"Smoked salmon," he said.

"Smoked *salmon*?" For an instant she was seized with a terrible thought—he was making fun of her. He had never made fun of her, to her knowledge, yet. "Whatever for?" she said faintly, back-pedalling faultily in her dismay.

He took a step forward, just to show he could do without the stove at the back of him, and laying his hands on the table he gripped it so that the dishes clattered. "Olga, don't keep saying *whatever for*!" He towered over her, his eyes glittering. Then he stalked across to the bedroom door. Reaching it, he turned: "What is it that *really* bothers you? What do you want to know?"

"The smoked salmon," she whispered. "I don't understand. What *was* it for?"

He smiled slowly, disagreeably, and there was no doubt about it, she caught a gleam in his eye.

"Pour manger avec le cocktail," he replied, and went into the bedroom, shutting the door behind him.

"You'll pay for this, Herbert Wragg," she muttered to herself, sweeping the plates together. Or someone would pay for it; whoever was at the bottom of it, that one would pay. She would see to that. He had been making fun of her all right.

*　　　*　　　*

Miss Raven sat crouched in front of her dressing-table, gazing into the glass. He kissed me—her thoughts sang—he kissed me—our lips have met. She glossed over the manner of their meeting. It was cold, sitting there in her nightdress, but when she was all set to soar above the confines of reality her dressing-gown, a drab uncompromising garment,

248

hampered her in the tricky initial stages, tethering her to earth; nor was it in any case the fitting costume for romance.

She stroked the gossamer frills round her shoulders. " Yielding to ungovernable desire he bent over the young governess . . ." The Duchess and Lady Featherstone faded into the background; old and trusty friends as they had been, she could afford to drop them now and she did, without a twinge of regret; hers was a different aristocracy, in which a governess was so near the throne as to take pride of place. " She turned with a little startled cry as his burning kisses rained upon . . ."

" Miss Raven, are you in bed? "

She sat quite still. " No." Her voice was a whisper. She tried again. " No," she called through the door, " not yet, Mr. Purdoe."

" Miss Raven, I wonder . . . if you're not . . . would you mind awfully . . . my wife would love a cup of tea. She's gone to bed . . . she's terribly cold and tired."

" All right," she called out, " shan't be a tick."

She made the tea and carried the tray through the children's room. If the bathroom door happened to be unlocked this was the quickest way into the bedroom. It was unlocked. The lights were very bright and at first she was blinded by steam. Then she made out a topknot of dark curls and a rosy shape, slippery, gleaming, twisting about in the water. She stood holding the tray, staring. She had no wish to stare but she was unable to drag her eyes away.

" Miss Raven, you angel. Look, put it there." Miss Raven put the tray down on a chair. " Be a sweetie and pour me a cup. Such adventures . . ." Milly submerged, giggling. " Children been good? " There was no reply, and she looked up, puzzled.

Miss Raven was bent over the tray, clasping the teapot; now, quite suddenly, she put it down. " I—yes—that is—good night."

She blundered towards the door and fled. Once in her own room she stripped off her dressing-gown, jumped into bed, turned off the light—and there in the dark, waiting for her, was her refuge; a world of her own, complete, furnished with a passionate lover and faithful friends and all that her heart could desire. More, she understood that this world of hers would never forsake her now. For the first time, the occasion being one of unprecedented emergency, it had been ready and waiting for her to step into—no more struggling with the chrysalis to be enabled to spread her dazzling wings and fly—that was a thing of the past. Now she might enter at will—or better, perhaps, never leave it; adopt it as her element for ever. He had kissed her—passionately. Theirs was a love affair. Snuggling down, stretching her chilly legs, she was at once enfolded in a comforting embrace; at last she was where

249

she belonged, safe in the arms of fantasy, reality being as it had ever been, treacherous, not to be borne.

*   *   *

" Darling . . ." Milly began tentatively. She was sitting up in bed with a little leather case on her knees doing her nails. " Darling . . ." she repeated, more firmly, employing the word as a barometer, only one of its many uses, thrusting it between them. She waited, but in vain. It failed to register anything whatever, which was ominous, and with a flutter of dismay in her heart she searched amongst her bottles for a sympathetic shade.

Larry was laying out his clothes for the morning. When he had finished he came to stand at the foot of the bed. With a steady hand she went on with her work.

" I want to ask you something."

" Mm ? " She gave him a smile which faded at sight of his face, and she hastily assumed one of Dermot's expressions, allowing her lips to droop. " Oh—a rocket. I see. Can't it wait ? "

" No," said Larry. " Whose idea was it—to go round the lake ? "

" Mine, of course." She flapped her newly-decorated hands.

" Of course." Larry began walking up and down. " Well, it's made a helluva lot of trouble all round, d'you see ? "

" I never thought—I mean, it just seemed the *natural* thing——"

" I dare say, but that's not the point."

" But they were so *stupid*, darling . . ."

" Milly, do please listen to me. Don't measure the situation up to what you think it *ought* to be—accept it as it is. I dare say they are stupid, but that's not all they are. They're also suspicious and frightened, which makes them trigger-happy. This little jaunt of yours might have ended in quite a sticky do, do you realise that ? " He glanced at her; her head was bent. " You know perfectly well you can't behave here as you would anywhere else—good heavens, I *know* it was the natural thing to do, but what seems natural to us may appear quite otherwise to them—and so, do you understand me ?—it becomes foolish and foolish behaviour is just as bad as—well, anyway, we can't have it. You see, darling, everything you do here has consequences— I mean it's *serious*, not just a game."

" Oh, lord." Heaving a sigh of boredom, she stretched out her hands on the sheet. " Finished ? "

" No, not quite." He stood beside the bed, looking down at her. " Now, listen," he went on quietly, " I want you to be perfectly clear about this. Our job here is simply to lie low and not give them any cause for complaint. We're not wanted here—not any of us—but

250

they've got to have us because they've got to have their people in London. So every time they can prove one of us—well, unsuitable, they take a trick. They keep a dossier on each one of us, don't forget that. And however well you behave they can still fix it so that you slip up. They're experts at getting two and two to make five. And it may not even be you who carries the can—they'll frame it around whoever it is they want to chuck out. For instance—well, take Abe. It would be a real feather in their caps if they could get him out—he knows they've been trying to do that for years. So when he went around to the Chief of Police this evening he was sticking his neck out—on your account, Milly. He was there for hours."

" For hours, was he?" A smile creeping round her lips, she appeared to be giving all her attention to the application of the second coat. She was finicky in her movements as a cat. Watching her, he was irritated by her painstaking devotion to each glittering claw, her unruffled complacency. He had never before felt this particular sort of irritation, not in the whole history of their relationship. It had something to do, oddly enough, with the colour of the varnish she was using; she knew very well that he detested crimson nails.

" Do you understand what I've been trying to say, Milly?"

" Well, I suppose I do. Yes."

" So long as you do. All I'm asking is that you should be very, very careful. Just watch your step all the time. Don't do anything at all—well, unusual. Not that you've much chance, I admit. And don't *trust* anybody—except Sophie. Sophie's all right. But not Gisela— nor, incidentally, Antoinette."

" Antoinette?" She had started at that.

" Least of all Antoinette," he said grimly. " Abe's heard that one of her grandsons is in the O.P."

" Damn." That single involuntary movement had ruined her handi-work. " Now I'll have to do them all over again."

" Understand, darling?"

She glanced up at him, her hair falling round her shoulders, her face pink, younger without make-up, her eyes quite candid, and, lest he miss it, the candour, open wide. " Oh, yes, Larry," she said meekly.

He went into the bathroom and turned on the bath. Lying in the water he was oppressed by the gloomiest of thoughts. Ah, he murmured to himself, why do I have to know her so well? She's been up to some-thing—he knew that—but what? The chances were he would never find out. There was a hopeless element in dealing with Milly when— he was going to say " moral " but changed it to " serious "—serious issues were at stake. Sometimes, even, he was forced to the conclusion that he himself was to blame in asking too much. He sighed, and then smiled ruefully to himself, because this sense of despair, of helplessness, reminded him of an incident years ago, and he had to smile, remembering it. Once, in the early days of their marriage, out East, someone had given them, as a present, a young monkey straight out of the jungle. Convinced that patience and firm handling were all that was required to tame it into an agreeable household pet, he, Larry, had enthusiastically set about the task, and indeed was rewarded with success—up to a point. The point had been quickly reached. For a week or two, the little fellow had trailed him about, conscientiously aping his every gesture, and Larry had felt highly gratified. It was true that now and again he had had his misgivings; now and again, when he caught sight of himself mirrored in those vacant eyes, perhaps an irrepressible titter, or a suspicion of insolence in a skilfully imitative grimace, would cause his heart to sink at the nature of his task and he had been filled with depression; he remembered it well, recognising that same depression now.

"Why don't you leave the poor brute alone?" Milly had said. "You're making him miserable as sin."

"Nonsense," he had replied, cheered, doubtless, by some freakish token of progress in the education of his pet: "He's a very lucky monk—and what's more, he knows it. As for sin—that's one thing I've taught him, the difference between right and wrong."

"Have you indeed," she had said sceptically, with a scepticism that was all too soon justified. That very evening they had gone out to a party leaving the monkey—he's on parole, said Larry—with the free run of the bedroom. The havoc to which they returned had been wrought on a Jovian scale—as impartial as it was thorough, magnificent, meaningless. They discovered the culprit—or rather the sinner, for such Larry in logic had to admit him to be—in a cosy ball on top of the mosquito net, a grin on his face, in a coma from which they guessed he would never awake, a half-empty bottle of sleeping-pills still clenched in his hairy fist.

"It's all your fault," Milly was in tears. "Messing him about. His poor little brain couldn't take it. Mind you, I think he did take it—with a pinch of salt. I often caught him laughing at you behind your back. Couldn't you *see*, Larry—he just didn't *have* a sense of right or wrong. And now look at him."

Feeling pretty low himself, Larry, cradling the recumbent form in his arms, had carried him down and laid him on his deathbed in the cupboard under the stairs, and after a night sleepless with remorse, he had gone out into the garden at dawn and dug a small grave under a banyan-tree. Then with a heavy heart he had opened the cupboard to find, not a corpse, but his little pal as fit as a fiddle, having had his

252

nap out, and gibbering with glee. They had passed him on to someone else after that.

Without making any closer comparison between the woman of his choice and the monkey, he was well aware—and he'd discovered it long ago—that in her make-up, too, there was quite simply a gap where a moral sense should have been; what was more, she also seemed to lack what might have served as a substitute, a code of behaviour such as he himself possessed. Had she had such, in however shaky or feminine a form, once he'd cracked it he'd have been able to gauge what she might do next. Still, she didn't have it and there it was.

His own code of behaviour was the very fibre of his being. Initially thrust upon him, it was that of most Englishmen of his class—infinitely flexible, adaptable, despite its ramrod appearance, it served them all—bullies, hypocrites, megalomaniacs and plain maniacs, swindlers and honest men; it was a very good and reliable code. Unconsciously, over the years, he had adapted it to fit himself, so that it had become in his case the code of a kindly, a perceptive, and a modest man. It rarely let him down.

In default of any such stern and comprehensive directive, for Milly there was desire. She was ruled by her own desires—desire and gradations of desire; that is to say, when disturbed by the conflicting forces of rival desires she was sometimes compelled to choose between them—to back one against the other, subdue one in order to gratify the other—even to abstain from one course of action in order the better to pursue another. It was crises of this sort that provided him with his only opportunities of exerting influence over her; then, by suggesting that one course might yield greater satisfaction or be more convenient to pursue or in general suit her book better than another, he might persuade her to act accordingly. Impervious to all other forms of persuasion, she was still to be swayed by considerations such as these; she was, he admitted it, in some ways as greedy and comfort-loving as a cat.

Now, for some reason feeling thoroughly uneasy, suspecting that some such crisis threatened yet prevented from questioning her, partly because, according to this code, it was not done to question one's wife, and partly because if he did question her it was highly unlikely that he would be met by the truth, and, further, his presumption in so doing might well cement her intentions into action in deliberate defiance of his wishes, he could only trust that his plain speaking would have its effect; that perhaps, appreciating the hazards of their present position, she might also appreciate that what he had said had not been said lightly, that it had been in the nature of a warning and that if she disregarded it, he would be deeply upset. That was reducing the matter

253

to its simplest—Clarissa, even, would have been able to understand the situation put like that; more readily than her mother, it occurred to him. So surely there was a chance that now she would act with discretion, because it was preferable from her point of view to have him in a good temper, at peace and so on, than not? Surely?

Possibly no man, but almost any woman could have advised poor Larry—told him not to bank on it, because it was a pretty slender chance.

*   *   *

Now, she thought, admiring her manicure which was really quite professional, if I were alone I'd go on such a wonderful beauty bender —eyebrows and blackheads, a mudpack even, and peppermint creams and a novel by Elspeth Cowen and all. I'm just in the mood, and imagine what bliss—a night in a bed on one's own. As it was . . . she considered whether or not she should get out of bed and go to the dressing-table drawer, weighing up the prospect of the slight but immediate inconvenience as against postponement, which would entail —although possibly not inevitably—more serious inconvenience later; no, she decided, she would take a chance on it. Besides, he would see that she was very, very tired.

She sighed, nestling amongst the pillows. How fragile her hands looked. She regarded them pensively, turning them this way and that. You wouldn't think they could *do* anything, such little hands. Tipped with crimson, laid out on the billowing crimson quilt, it was true that they did appear undersized, although not exactly incapable; as if resting, rather. The sound of the bathwater gurgling away and of Larry brushing his teeth reminded her, not of him, but of a certain disquietude in her own mind in connection with him. Her thoughts instinctively flew to various small and as yet unconfessed bills, because the bag had arrived —but it was still unopened so it couldn't be anything to do with that; in fact, the bag had been the very first thing she had seen on entering the salon with Wragg—she had been on the look-out for it, of course— and there it had been, in the corner. And very thankful she was to see it, because if the bag had come then so had the NAAFI and she was relying on them both—for to-morrow.

To-morrow she must pay for the dress; the day after to-morrow wear it. Now she was getting warmer, approaching the source of her disquiet. What had he said? Watch your step—don't do anything unusual. *Unusual?* She was merely going to pay for a dress in the currency most acceptable to the dressmaker. What of it? It was an established practice all over Europe, and the currency just depended on where you happened to be—in Greece gold pounds, in Yugoslavia an old pair of shoes, in Italy connections, recommendations and so on; only in England, alas, in cold cash. Here, luckily, it seemed that almost anything would serve as currency. There was nothing *unusual* about that—it was just lucky, that was all. Anyway, he *knew* about the dress —that is, he knew it was being made; so that was all right. Whatever it was he had been hinting at it couldn't be that. For one thing, he didn't know about—well, about the *arrangements*. What was more, he never would know and she would never do it again. Here and now she could faithfully promise him that—except as regards the lace. Because the lace would involve—she had known it from the start—another little bit of this and that. The very last time, though. Anyway, she had to have the lace, to go with the dress.

If he *is* cross—she watched him walk in and over to his dressing-table where he picked up his nail file from precisely the spot where he expected to find it, where he had last laid it—if he *is* cross then why doesn't he come straight out with it—whatever it is—or beat me, or something? Revenging herself on him for his silence, his preoccupation with routine, she thought—that's what Abe would do, beat me, most likely. There'd be none of this pretence that the whole thing's a game of cricket in which we're both on the same side.

Then she caught sight of his face bent under the light, the profile stern, unhappy-looking, and her heart smote her—oh, but I'm a beast, a beast—what can I do? He's much too good for me. He really does expect too much. If it were—Abe, for instance, he wouldn't expect anything, except possibly the worst, and so I wouldn't be always disappointing him. Oh, what can I do? The last, although accompanied by a sigh, was purely rhetorical, merely to provide cover for illicit fancy which, pursuing the direct path so soon as this had been indicated, had outstripped the humdrum respectable thoughts that were still plodding along the conventional and more devious route. But fancy couldn't get anywhere on its own, so she made it pause to give the others a chance to catch up, and soon they met, brought up short on the same spot. What would it be like—an *affaire*? A *real affaire*—which would mean? . . .—yes, of course; in short, an *affaire*. With, for instance? Abe, for instance. Yes, with him. She explored the possibilities of this notion—for the first time appearing as a possibility—until the light was put out.

He took her into his arms.

" Why, you're as warm as toast."

" But I'm *not* . . . I'm *frozen*."

" Just you wait." Holding her, he soon began to want her. Drowsy, with the by no means disagreeable sensation of his arms about her, she had been thinking about love happily enough, but now the restless

255

movements of a body suddenly become hard and on the alert to an advantage disturbed her flow of thought, snatching her from the gentle rhythm of the tide on which she had hoped to drift to sleep.

" Don't," she whispered, " I can't breathe."

Sighing, he released her. He should have known better than to hope that she might, just for once, consent to be spurred on by the moment, and nothing more. Milly thought far too much and too seriously about love ever to take it so lightly. And to conquer that resistance—kittenish or shrewish, how well he knew it—to whip himself up to the point of ignoring her little half-uttered half-meant cries for mercy, thereby making an occasion of it, sufficient of an occasion at least to merit a response that would in turn enable him to delude himself that she loved him, and would open to him as a flower to the sun—ah, no . . . no, no. *That* whole operation would demand more time, patience and effort than he could muster to-night. He put her away from him and turned over. Just as he was on the edge of sleep he heard her say, in a clear, wide-awake voice:

" Darling—how did *you* get back? "

" By taxi," he said, and smiled into the dark. Darling Milly. She was all of a piece.

Chapter Four

" Swine! " Sophie, as was her custom, was sitting on the edge of the kitchen bath, glaring at the glass of gin and orange in her hand. Now and then she would attack it with fierce little pecks, like a hawk demolishing its prey. Vodka ran in her veins deeper than she knew; she would never learn to sip. " Swine! " she repeated for the twentieth time. " Mongol swine! "

" Mm . . ." said Milly, on her knees, in front of the kitchen cupboard. She was checking the newly arrived NAAFI against a master list and another, subsidiary, list in her hand.

" My poor darling! I couldn't sleep all night worrying about you —I came round, you know, for news . . . then I heard you were safe. . . . But the shock of the experience! That's what kept me awake, the thought of what a shock it must have been, such an experience, for one of your breed and culture . . ."

" Sophie, do shut up, there's an angel. Just let me finish this."

" Of course, darling. Now I'm shutting up." Her mouth pinned tight, occasionally banging her fist on the edge of the bath, the word "swine" bubbling to her lips, she sat glowering at the enemy, the persecutors of her friend.

Milly had unearthed a sort of canvas holdall—Larry's, of the type known as valise, Officers' Shop, Cairo—this having seemed suitable to her purpose. Capacious as it was, it was unlikely that it could contain the stack of merchandise accumulating beside it. Fretfully she made piles of the packets of tea, tins of cocoa. Funny, the sheer bulk, per pound avoirdupois, of tea. At least, far from funny; not funny at all. And the actual *weight* of half a dozen bottles and the dreadfully indiscreet way in which they clanked together. Gold sovereigns had been child's play by comparison.

" Darling! " Sophie, having in the meantime mentally dispatched a whole herd of swine, woke up to the present situation. " I am doing nothing, and you are slaving! Let me help. What can I do? "

" Pour us some more gin, Sophie, that would be a real help. It might give me an idea."

" My poor pet." She snatched up the glasses. She knew how to pour gin now. " So, Milly—here. And where is that servant, that Gisela —she should be arranging your effects, no? "

" No. I told her to take the afternoon off."

Gisela, who was sitting on the camp bed in the little cupboard of a room that was hers on the other side of the wall, pricked up her ears at the sound of her name. She was darning her employer's socks. She darned exquisitely; it was no task to her, but a pleasure; the larger the hole the greater the challenge and the more satisfaction she derived from it. Mr. Simpson had possessed small neat feet, and occasionally she had had to resort to clipping a larger hole than the one that had originally called for attention, simply in order to display her art. In the case of Mr. Purdoe, she was given ample scope without any need for artificial contrivance. It did not perturb her in the very least that she sat on an unmade bed, and that her possessions were scattered in heaps around her; rags, old toothbrushes, magazines, broken coat-hangers—one never knew when these might come in handy. Irreproachably neat and methodical in her work, she was incorrigibly untidy, even slatternly, in private. She saw no point in keeping her room neat for the simple reason that no one ever came into it. Now, as she heard her name mentioned, she laid aside her work the better to listen. Her English was limited, but she could piece a conversation together fairly accurately from the tones of the voices alone. There was almost nothing, if she set her whole mind to it, that Gisela could not do.

" You get up, Milly, please. I will finish." Sophie stood over the litter on the floor, wrinkling her nose. " Hm. It's a question, then, of packing *those* things—into *that* bag? "

" Yes," said Milly, scrambling to her feet, astonished by this swift and practical appreciation. That was indeed the question.

" Ha! " Sophie had already plunged down on hands and knees. " In that case—newspaper, please. Plenty. Thanks. Otherwise the bottles will bang about and cause inconvenience. Now—see how I am tucking them all in? I know to you I must seem a duffer—to one of your intelligence—but for this sort of job my big silly hands are of use. When are you coming back from Slavnik? How I shall miss you, you don't know."

" Really, Sophie—we're only going for the *week-end*."

" Ah, the British week-end—one of your charming customs . . . but might it not last for three or four days or even more? "

" Certainly not. Whatever put that idea into your head? "

" I don't know," said Sophie humbly. " But somehow it seems to be there. Look! " she cried. " Oh, *look*! " She had caught sight of a tin of salt on the kitchen shelf. " Milly, may I look? O-oh! " She took it down, examining it, fondling it, rather. It was of the type with a bakelite chute in the lid. "Really, Milly, you know . . . it's *enchanting*." She allowed a few grains to trickle into her hand. " How white—how

258

pure—how it *runs*," she murmured, unconsciously supporting the manufacturers' claim.

" Sophie, you are a goat. Take it, if you like it—no, take a new one, here."

" *Take* it? " Sophie barely paused to flick a pinch of salt over her shoulder then slammed the tin back on the shelf as if it had been a hot potato. " *Take* your things? No, darling, never. Certainly not." She chuckled, and turned back to her task. " I was just admiring the *device*, that was all."

She went on packing in the bathsalts (gardenia, as stipulated), the soap (Chanel, verbena, ditto), the brandy, embellished sufficiently with stars, and the classily fragrant tea.

" Look, Sophie," Milly began uncomfortably, " if ever you do want anything—you know . . . I mean . . . *anything*, because you can't buy things here, I know . . . you've only to say." She did rather hope Sophie wouldn't take her at her word, but still . . . the offer, at least. Really, she need not have worried, she saw that at once. Sophie sat back on her heels, her work interrupted, her eyes beaming with love.

" Darling," she said. " Darling. You are the sweetest little woman in all the world."

Milly, who wished not for the first time that Sophie were not given to these extravagant terms of endearment—because it sounded so *funny* between women—although there was the excuse that she was a foreigner and didn't quite understand—edged a step away. How emotional she is, she thought, and to put a brake on these emotions whatever they were, and frightfully unhealthy, no doubt, she frowned.

Sophie thought, now what have I said? She was smiling before. Clumsy fool that I am. She, with her delicate sensibilities . . . Wisely she went on with the packing, because Milly had often criticised, quite rightly, the deplorable Slavonian habit of breaking off for a chat before a job was half done. But what had caused that frown? She hadn't mentioned England, had she? The subject of England was taboo— she had learned that. But it was so hard to keep a check on herself— somehow it just seemed to slip out, the word England. It was self-indulgence, of course; simply because she loved it so, that name, and to say it made her heart swell with pride—although that was nonsense, she knew very well, she being Slavonian. It was a joy, though, just to think of it, to know that it existed, that perfect land, and the god-like race who dwelt there, the men of unusual height with splendid limbs (although there had been Mr. Simpson but he had been of Wales, she had heard) and the women of unusual beauty (Mrs. Wragg must be a Jewess, she was so black), all, at any rate, happy as the day was long living in that heaven where—there was no need to tell her, she knew very well—the sun did not shine: but did the sun shine in heaven? *Did it?* No one, not even the cardinal, could give an opinion on *that*. Anyway, there it was, that island, the air above it rarefied, the sea that beat against those white cliffs not like any other sea, and so was it not— she dared anyone to contradict—heaven? Ah, but the rows there had been with Milly about that. Last week, when she herself had behaved like a dashed idiot and had taken a drop too much of this delightful gin, not being able to contain herself with the intoxicating word " LONDON " staring at her from the face of the bottle itself—she had forgotten herself so far as to quote a poem of Kipling's, a favourite of Miss Brownlow's, and Milly had been terribly cross. How modest they were—the English; the modesty of the truly great. So she knew better now than to talk about England and she felt sure she had not mentioned the word in any form—therefore the frown must be due to something else. Perhaps Milly had a headache; better not to ask, though. If she hadn't one, the question itself could quite easily give rise to one. Concentrating deeply, pondering by what means the frown might be removed from Milly's face, Sophie worked very quickly and skilfully and in no time at all the job was done.

" There! " She jumped to her feet, zipped up the bag and swung it in her hand. " Whew! " She really did say " whew." " You'll need a porter, darling—you know that? "

Milly appraised the luggage dubiously. The bag had rather long inconvenient leather handles. Although she herself had always managed to evade the experience of carrying it, she remembered that Larry had several times complained, referring to it as " that damn' sack."

" How it bulges! " cried Sophie, with glee. " One would say there were goodies in there! "

Milly looked at her coldly. There was no doubt Sophie could be extraordinarily irritating when she chose. Nevertheless she made an effort to control her irritation. She wasn't quite finished with Sophie yet.

" When do the shops shut? "

" The shops? Milly, darling, what is it that you want? The time, now—what is it, the time? Ah—so late. But then, it depends what it is you want. Can I get it for you? Let me dash out."

" No, Sophie . . . it's something rather—well, special. Cigarette? "

" Darling. Thanks."

" You know I'm—er—having this new dress—to wear in Slavnik? "

Sophie waved her cigarette. " Of course—and how charming you will appear! "

260

" Yes—I mean, no—but, well, it's like this. In that shop, the one just along the street, the antique shop . . . in the window . . ." she paused; with Sophie's great brown eyes fixed upon her it was really not so easy to explain: " In the window there's a piece of lace."

" Milly! " Sophie jumped up, tossing her head about, quite beside herself with delight. " You're going to buy it! Perfect, what taste! I say, what colossal taste! For the dress, of course—and I can just see it, how it will suit you. Darling! "

" You know the shop I mean? "

" Know the *shop*? Darling, I know the *lace*! Of course, who doesn't? It's quite a—how d'you say—Erbstück . . . pff . . . *family piece*. Point de Vénise—it belonged to—well, it doesn't matter, an arch-duchess, I think, but I am not sure . . . I don't know them, we never moved in that set, we were just rough countryfolk in comparison, but I should say they will be overjoyed." She smoked furiously, chuckling, every now and then glancing at this fairy-tale princess whose right it was to buy heirlooms as and when she pleased, as if she might vanish in the twinkling of an eye. " Anyway," she went on, " who it belonged to is not the point. Now it's going to belong to *you*. How splendid! How perfectly right."

Although identifiably an expression of her own thoughts, rather more succinctly summed up, Milly felt her way cautiously:

" I don't know about *buying* it," she said, " I thought one might ask the price."

" Then, darling, I will go and ask, shall I? That's what you'd like me to do? "

Milly nodded, Sophie's agility at interpretation again taking her by surprise.

" Hm. So I'll go now. That old man, I believe he is not at all a bad chap. He knows me—at least, he will know my name."

" Perhaps, Sophie . . . don't you think—perhaps it might be better not to tell him your name? "

" Not tell him my name? " Puzzled, the brown eyes searched Milly's face. " *Not!* Well, I never thought of that. Oh, perhaps you are right. My goodness, you are clever, I see now. What consideration —thought for others. Never mind, then—I *won't* tell him. But I will *bargain* with him. Ha! You wait." She grabbed her leather jerkin, slammed the beret flat on her head, scowling at herself in the square of glass above the stove. " I am not such a duffer as you think. I'll make him knock off quite a lot. Though "—she shouldered the satchel —" I'm afraid, darling . . . it will still be a bit . . . *dear*, you know. Now I go. I'll be back in a jiffy."

" There's no desperate hurry, Sophie." Her head was throbbing.

261

" There'll be plenty of time to-morrow. We shan't be leaving early. Let me know in the morning."

" Not to-night? Oh. But I can understand—after all that "—she gestured towards the valise that she herself had packed: " You are worn out, Milly, my poor one. To-morrow, then. In a way, better." She smiled at her own cunning, spreading out her treats like a wise child. " So to-morrow I shall see you again. To-morrow morning then, I'll bring news—without fail." She kissed Milly and went out.

Now that she was alone, Milly dragged the valise into the middle of the floor. She walked all round it, eyeing it—this lump of a thing which must somehow be moved from one spot to another. It was like a great toad, squatting there. How she hated it, but there was no going back; she must go forward, with this monster in tow. This represented the dress. It had been so easy to visualise the dress—but this she had always avoided visualising—that was also the dress. Now the moment had come—it was to-night or never. For no real reason—because, although horribly heavy, the thing was merely a bag that had to be carried across the square—she felt nervous and depressed.

She made sure the children were in bed and asleep and Miss Raven's door shut. Then, setting herself to it, she heaved the valise into the children's room, placing it just by the door which opened on to the passage. Her own bedroom having no direct access to the passage, this was where it had to be. Then she fetched a thick tweed coat from her room and threw it over the valise, covering it up carefully. She would just have to trust to luck that Miss Raven wouldn't take it into her head to visit her charges again. She went back into the kitchen and filled the shopping bag with the rest of the consignment, and then she locked the door of the store cupboard which she was always careful to do, slipped the key in her bag, finished her glass of gin and poured herself another. She was not a heavy drinker but she was beginning to feel as nervous as she had ever felt in her life. For one thing, she realised that she had made no real plans for the execution of the operation and on closer examination it seemed to bristle with difficulties; they were springing up like magic, thick and fast. She went along to her bath-room and ran a very hot bath. Lying in the water, she began to think it out.

Gisela looked at her watch, and then stretching the sock over her knuckles under the light critically examined her darn. It was the best she had ever done. Now that the kitchen was quiet she got up off the bed and put on her black dress and, after deliberation, a clean white collar. The collar was in honour of the occasion.

*   *   *

Always, on leaving Milly's apartment, Sophie would feel happiness inside her like a flame, warm, glowing, that would stay alight until the corner of the corridor, but when she turned the corner, it was as if there were, waiting there, a little puff of icy wind which blew it out. Afterwards, at home, she would relight it—but just there at the corner, every time, she knew it would go out. There was no reason why this evening should be an exception and it was not. It was there at the corner of the corridor that you could see into the well of the hall beneath.

She paused at the top of the staircase and looked down. Just her luck. There was that terrible housekeeper leaning across the porter's desk, whispering. Holding her head high she marched down the red-carpeted stairs and without so much as a glance at the reception desk, and although she was aware that both heads had turned to stare at her, without quickening her step, she crossed the hall. The whispering stopped as she passed. She would never have confessed to a soul just what it cost her each time she crossed that hall.

Once in the street she moved into the shadows and leaned for a moment against the clammy outside wall of the hotel. Getting her breath back, she swallowed a mouthful of fog. Gritty, it stuck in one's throat. The lights from the shop windows fell aslant the deep ruts in the snowy street. The snow on the pavements had been pounded into a hard, pebbly surface, like frosted glass. The passers-by were muffled up to the eyes in scarves. She had lost her scarf some months back— left it in a tram, or something. Really, she was very careless, Singe was always telling her that. Now one needed a scarf. Still, no time to bother about that. She went on slowly, her lips moving as she spoke her thoughts. She was not conspicuous on that account—nowadays many people were to be seen talking to themselves in the street. My poor darling, she was thinking, meaning Milly, how worried she was to-night. I would never dare to ask, of course—a woman of her guts would never sneak to me—but she was dreadfully worried. Fancy what it must be like for a person such as she is, so gentle and refined and accustomed to the best, to come to a madhouse like this. . . . Sophie shook her head, pausing to look at the sweet-shop window. The antique shop was next door.

She was glad to see that they had not forgotten St. Nicolas's Day —but then they wouldn't. This was one of those confectionery-fruit-shops which were still privately owned; little black caverns sandwiched in between the State shops, little black holes in the magnificent, shining façade which didn't really show (anyway, a few flaws here and there proved it wasn't false) and in any case which they didn't know how to stop. So there he was, the old boy, stately in his robes in amongst the lollipops and oranges, his sugar beard a bit dusty, melted even—dribbled on? Well, he was ageing, wasn't he? And there was the devil, such a jolly devil, how one loved him—more, even, than the good saint, although both were a part of one's youth. "It's strange," she murmured, staring at the devil who rolled his eyeballs at her, the same kink in his tail, brandishing his pitchfork (bent, she noticed) with the same exuberance—but look, he had lost a horn!—why, he must be as old as she was herself. "It's strange, how I see her surrounded by enemies. If only I could be of use. Still, what I can do, I will do." Bracing herself, casting a quick look up and down the street, she slipped in next door.

Presently she came out of the shop and went on her way and now more than one passer-by coming towards her glanced at her twice, so rare was it on a winter's night such as this, or indeed ever at all, to glimpse a happy face. At the corner of the park under the shelter of the trees there were the droshkies lined up. The horses between the shafts wore sacking to protect them from the cold; the drivers were gathered round a charcoal brazier, their fur caps pulled right down over their ears. Stamping their feet, swinging their arms, they sounded quite merry, although surely they could not have hoped for many fares that night. As she passed they called out to her. Sometimes she would have given a lot to have gone home in a droshky but there was no need even to tease herself with the thought of it—she was too happy for that. She waved to them, called good night and plunged down the street which led to her home.

Here the snow lay thick. There were no trams and no shops in this street, which was long and gloomy, the precincts of the university on the one hand, Government offices, museums and one or two churches on the other. Not a single window showed a light. The buildings frowned down upon her, grim and forbidding, whiskered with snow. In the fog the street lamps flowered like those small fuzzy yellow chrysanthemums, fading away in the distance. The light they shed glanced off the crystal surface of the snow. It was a pleasure to hear that surface crackle at every step, not such a pleasure to feel the snow seeping into her boots. She jumped aside as a droshky, suddenly appearing from nowhere, swept past. The horse's hoofs had made no sound on the snow, there was only the crack of the whip, a faint jingling, the creak of wheels as it passed, the shadow of a driver, the shadow of a horse, and like shadows they vanished in the fog. She plodded on. Goodness, the silence. Nearing the Church of the Apostles she heard the whirr of the clock, long before it chimed, and a shudder seemed to pass over the grave granite faces of the buildings as the hour was struck.

Now, at last, she could see the corner house that had once been

264

their house, and which was still her home. Heartened, she walked more quickly, resuming her dialogue with herself. " Ha—but it wasn't bad, that bargaining. I can just see her face to-morrow, like a child's—all smiles, it'll be. You know, you've missed your vocation, Sophie, my dear . . ." She chuckled. " You see, at heart you are a real business woman . . ." Onion soup, chopping onions for the soup. How she hated that—but Singe liked onion soup, only Ludovic complained . . . perhaps I don't make it right? But then it's awfully hard to cook well something that you don't like . . . still, that's all there is, so he will have to lump it . . . I haven't time, these days, to bother about him.

Anyway, I'm not a cook, or a teacher . . . my goodness, no, I'm a business woman! *What* a reduction—five per cent (whatever that meant). . . . She began to think what it did mean, which caused her to add under her breath, " Better not tell Singe, perhaps." She fell silent, because, although she struggled against allowing them in, one or two thoughts had put their big feet into the door of her mind, and there was no closing it to them. They were thoughts one could not speak aloud. Anyway, she told herself, Singe, who had been favoured with a hundred anecdotes concerning her new friends, could not expect to be treated to every single one. " But why particularly not this one? Because—well, better not. I am such a perfect fool, God knows, and I might let slip about the *price*—and it is none of our business—but it *might*, yes, it *could*, strike silly old Singe . . ." as indeed it had struck her, Sophie, who cursed herself for a mean pig and a peasant for having even *thought* of such a thing, that the amount by which the price of the lace had been reduced was precisely that sum which represented a month's wages to her, sufficing as it must for the needs of three. She herself had dismissed this fact as a coincidence—why, some time back, passing that last church—what of it? It had no significance. What was one thing for them was quite another for Milly. Only the best was good enough for her. All the same, she would *not* bother to explain all this to Singe; it might not be so easy to make it clear and somehow she couldn't *rely* on her silly old aunt viewing this odd little coincidence in quite the same light.

The house door still stood open. That was a bit of luck. If the porter's wife were in a bad mood it was closed early, before eight o'clock, and then one had to tip whoever opened it—either the porter, who would grumble whatever the tip, or his wife, who would pocket the tip without a thank you and stand at the bottom of the stairs shouting all kinds of remarks as one went up. But they were that sort of person and one had to make allowances. Now, coming up the steps, stamping the snow off her boots, Sophie could see the porter quite plainly through the crack of the hatch which had been recently installed in order that he and his wife might combine enjoyment of their home surroundings with devotion to duty all round the clock. He was sitting on his stool at the counter behind the hatch, the newspaper spread before him, his moustaches gathered up in one hand, cooling with his breath a steaming glass of tea. Going up the stairs, out of bravado Sophie called out good night. The porter, as was to be expected, made no reply. He merely slid open the hatch and poked his head through, the better to follow her progress. It was not his duty to greet the tenants nor yet to respond to greetings, particularly not from the likes of her. He watched her up the first flight and out of sight. Then, satisfied—for that was his duty, to watch those who came in and those who went out—he withdrew his head, readjusted his moustaches, and settled down once more to his tea.

* * *

As with almost any hazardous operation, however ill or well planned—and this one was scarcely planned at all—that which in prospect had appeared to be the principal problem, and an insoluble one, in the event solved itself, simply melted away, or at least became dwarfed by a whole chain of other problems, all unforeseen, all presumably having loomed so large and so high as to have remained out of sight until the moment of encounter, that is, at the moment of running slap into one or another as each stage was muddled through.

Quite obviously the main problem—which occupied Milly to the exclusion of all else as she bathed and dressed—was how to furnish herself with an explanation for going out into the town alone after dinner; or, alternatively, how to induce her husband to absent himself for a sufficiently lengthy period. There was no excuse for her to go out. Not only that, it was unthinkable that she should do so. It was not as if—and she remembered Larry's words of the night before—this were an ordinary place. There was nowhere to go, and certainly no one outside the hotel whom she might visit. She wished, now, that she had bothered more, earlier, about Mrs. Wragg. That might have provided her with a pretext—even now, perhaps? No. It was far too much of a risk—involving lies both before and after—a tissue of them, really. Milly was no gambler. Facing her problem as she made up her face, she thought how strange it was that she should not have taken any pains to make a proper appreciation of the enemy—nor even fully recognised him till now. Of course, it was her husband. Once his hash were settled—she used this phrase to herself, being rather driven and agitated—all would be plain sailing. Simply a matter of going down the back stairs and out into the courtyard where the cars were garaged —she had reconnoitred it that morning from the street—and in ten

266

minutes she would be across the square. Once that were achieved, she would then return through the front entrance having, apparently, taken a breath of fresh air before going to bed. The porter at the reception desk—well, too bad, he would have to admit to being fallible, that he sometimes slipped into the public bar for a glass of beer. That he did this she knew. She had seen him. No, all that was simple—even with the unforeseen complication of the weight of the beastly stuff—compared with the problem of Larry.

She was still turning all this over in her mind and no nearer to a solution when, over dinner, as Gisela was handing plates, Larry said: " I'm sorry, darling—but I'll just have to go back to the office afterwards." Catching the look on her face, in spite of Gisela's presence, he leaned over and took her hand.

" I shan't be long, I promise. I know how you feel, poppet."

Oh, did he? She felt quite faint, as a matter of fact. She would bet he didn't know *that*.

" It's all right," said Milly. " I mean, I don't mind."

Over coffee Larry picked up *The Times* and began the crossword. Milly smoked one or two cigarettes and then she said, getting up: " More coffee, darling? "

" Mm."

" Not hot, I'm afraid."

" Never mind. Just as it comes."

After a pause she said: " You're slipping. Seven and a half minutes, wasn't it, once upon a time—for *The Times*? "

" Was it? I dare say. It's not the same when they come in batches. You spin them out a bit," He attacked it once more as if she had thrown down some kind of challenge. So she had, of course.

She stopped pacing up and down and stood in front of the stove, drumming with her fingertips on the porcelain tiles.

" What time do you have to be there? "

" Where? "

She turned and faced him. He looked genuinely puzzled and she was seized with a sudden but most definite desire to hit him in the face; but suppressed it.

" At the office."

" No hurry. Tennish. Wragg's getting out' some figures. What's up? "

She had flounced into a chair. She snatched up a magazine and flipped over the pages.

" Nothing. Why? "

" Darling—you seem . . . I dunno . . . jumpy. What is it? "

She felt pettish, childishly spiteful. " Em-Wye-O-Bee," she

267

muttered under her breath—a retort sometimes employed by Clarissa and, her mother discovered, a satisfying one. Aloud, she said: "Nothing. I told you, nothing at all."

She glowered at the open page. *Mode*—why, as a schoolgirl, and long after that, she had thought it marvellous, the last word. Now—on one page a blonde with the face of a fairy doll modelled a crinoline like the Christmas tree itself, a bobbydazzler, alight with sequins, decorated by the junior members of the family who held strict notions on symmetry. Opposite, the original models from the " houses," here they were—" It's a Blessing if it's a Blessington "—" A Polly Fayre " —the indefinite article was good, she thought—to be *purchased* at Blights of Bournemouth, or even—my God, if one were ever there—in Weston-Super-Mare. So what's *happened*? she asked herself crossly, her headache worse—in between? Was *Mode* always like this—or has it changed—or have I? She knew the answer. She threw it aside and sat smoking instead. At a little after ten Larry went.

The moment he was out of the room she flitted across to the window and crept inside the curtains to watch him go. Presently she saw his shadow, mixed up with the swinging doors, and then he came out into the saucer of light just below her in the street. She saw him turn up his coat collar, stick his hands into his pockets and then he strode off into the fog, and no sooner had he stepped over that rim of light into the dark than his image was sponged clean out of her mind as though he had never been.

" Now," she said to herself, and moved out of the shelter of the curtains. " Now . . ."

The corridor stretched away ahead, deserted, gleaming under the dim light. Opening the next door along, into the children's bedroom, she groped inside for her coat. She put it on, as well as her gloves, and then picking up the valise and shopping bag, set off. She was prepared for the weight of the valise but not for its clumsiness; the handles were far too long, so that the bulk of it swung across her legs. She managed to shield the shopping bag under her coat. There was, of course, no shielding the valise. Eventually she let it drop, and stooping, humped it along the parquet. Nearing the kitchen she heard Gisela singing softly to herself some German song, mournful, familiar. Against her will, she paused to listen:

> *. . . da steht ein Lindenbaum;*
> *Ich träumt' in seinem Schatten so manchen süssen Traum;*
> *. . . schnitt in seine Rinde so manches liebe Wort . . .*

There, opposite the kitchen, was the baize door through which the

268

corridor branched off into the servants' quarters. Just inside, on the right, was the door which led down the back stairs to the courtyard.

. . . *Zu ihm mich immer fort* . . .
. . . *mich immer fort.*

Boldly she pushed open the baize door and, dragging her burden through, she unlatched the door on to the staircase, heaved the valise over the sill and stepped inside. She was searching for the light switch with her free hand when the door swung to, and she was left in darkness. Then, from the bowels of the earth, it seemed, she heard raucous laughter and voices, and she remembered that the servants' dining-room was in the cellars . . . boom . . . boom . . . the laughter echoed back through the vaults. What if one of the maids should come up now? She plunged down the stairs, which were of wood, steep and narrow, testing every tread in advance, allowing the valise to slide after her under its own steam. Her eyes becoming used to the dark, she saw that a faint light shone from far down below, enough to show up the banisters. There. She had managed it. She was on street level. This great studded door must be the one into the courtyard. The staircase continued down. She let the valise rest on the bottom stairs and dropping the shopping bag on top of it, took off her gloves and wiped her face. Then with her bare hands she felt over the surface of the door. There was an iron bar across, with a padlock attached; unlocked, however. The bar slid back quite easily, and immediately the door, being very heavy, swung towards her and the cold night air rushed in. Her objective almost achieved, now that she was so nearly in the street, she leaned against the doorpost, gulping the fresh air. It was a starry night—no moon, but the starlight penetrated the fog, so that it was not perfectly dark. It was something to see the stars.

" Now." Once more she collected herself and was just about to pick up the bags when she cast a glance to the right where her goal lay. Then her heart froze. It really did; or at least, it seemed to stop, whilst she stared, unable to believe her eyes; then it began racketing about in her chest. Instead of what she had expected to see, that side of the courtyard open to the street, she saw that it was enclosed by gates. But —how could this be? This morning there had been no gates and now there were gates as high as the gates to a fortress; the street lamps, almost on a level with the electricity conductors, scarcely shone over them. But—*how*, this morning—*how on earth* could she have missed see-ing them, the gates? It was this which caused her immediate concern, the revelation of her own incompetence. She should have reckoned with gates; *naturally* there would be gates. Then, in that case—she steadied

269

herself—there was bound to be a door in those gates. She was about to creep forward to investigate when from somewhere near at hand, on the opposite side of the courtyard, she heard a grunt and the sound of a match being struck. The flame blossomed and then died down to a steady glow as a lantern was lit. She stood back flat against the doorpost, absolutely still. The lantern was hung at the entrance to a stable—or garage, as it was now. Just inside, under its light, a peasant, a very tall old man wearing a sheepskin coat, began sorting through a bunch of keys. He had snowy moustaches and a bony nose; a squat roughish sort of terrier was stretching itself at his feet. When he had finally selected a key, he hawked and spat into the cobbles, took a slab of bread from his pocket and bit into it; munching, he broke off a piece and threw it to the dog which caught it in mid-air, bolted it and then sat with its ears cocked as smug as if it were already half-way to earning the next. The man began to roll himself a cigarette, close under the light, taking his time about it; then he gave a great yawn, stuck the cigarette over his ear, picked up the keys, unhitched the lantern and made off towards the gates.

So there was a door in the gates. She saw it as the lantern swayed, its light moving in widening circles over the yard. Yes, and he was going to lock it, that door—*now*! she muttered under her breath, and in the act of stepping forward instead stepped back, sensing, a second later than it had sensed her, the dog, a white shape hurtling towards her—and slamming the door to, she pulled the bar across and had the satisfaction of hearing the thud of its head against the wood. It recovered in an instant, whilst she was making sure that the bar was across. Fairly dancing with rage on the cobbles, it began to bark. It barked and barked. Kicking the bags to one side, she fled up the stairs. Arriving at the top step she stumbled, and at that moment the light was switched on, the door opened and there just below her in the service corridor, standing in the doorway, was the housekeeper; her hand, as to a dagger, instinctively reaching for the keys at her belt.

She looked up at Milly and Milly looked down at her. Neither, for perhaps a quarter of a minute, seemed able to say a word. The housekeeper's face was quite yellow with fright, bristly and moist, like the corpse of an old fowl recently plucked and washed in cold water.

" That barking," said Milly at last. " The dog."

" The barking? " said the housekeeper slowly. They both heard the key turn in the lock downstairs and immediately the barking stopped. " It woke the little ones—the barking of the dog? Then I shall——" she made a move to pass by down the stairs.

" No." Milly stepped down and shut the door behind her, con-fronting the housekeeper on the same level and even pushing her back.

270

Her eyes sparkled and her cheeks were flushed. She would—if nothing else—win this round. "It did not wake the children but it might have woken them." Not for the first time she was grateful for the impressive armament of German grammar—almost every word a potential Big Bertha and if correct, the bigger the effect. "Kindly speak about the dog in the morning because it is not the first time. Please see that it is the last."

"Yes." The woman was nervous, she could tell. "Certainly, gnädige Frau. My excuses." Her eyes lingering on Milly's face, she opened the baize door, allowing her to pass through from enemy territory into her own, then she passed through herself and scuttled off down the corridor out of sight.

In the kitchen Gisela, her back turned, standing in stockinged feet on the edge of the bath, was arranging the saucepans on the shelf. She was still singing.

> *Komm' her zu mir, Geselle, hier find'st Du deine Ruh'!*
> *Hier fin'st Du deine Ruh'!*

Milly sank into a chair. Time—what tricks it played. Had all that happened—had all that been sandwiched in between those two verses?
"Gisela."

At the sound of her voice Gisela, who in any case had heard her come in, jumped from the bath to the floor and wheeled about as smartly as a lieutenant should, as if she had only been filling in time, waiting for the sharp imperative, the crack of the pistol, the signal for the balloon to go up.

"Gnädige Frau!" Even shoeless, a triumph, really, she managed to stand to attention, alert, eager, her periwinkle-blue eyes on parade, too, shining dreadfully bright. Discipline did not extend to her lips, however, which twitched. She is laughing, thought Milly. I dare say she knew all along. And yet she could feel no resentment—she was conscious only of a sense of relief. Here was someone she could trust, an accomplice, and heaven knows she stood in need of one. She had never liked Gisela so well.

"At the foot of—*those* stairs . . ." Gisela nodded, and she went on: "There are two bags . . . one large . . . one small . . . they . . . that is, I . . . must——"

"The dressmaker? Madame Bérénice?"

"Yes. But . . ."

Gisela had already put on her shoes and was taking down her coat from the hook behind the door.

"But . . ." Milly repeated, with such determination that Gisela

271

looked round. " You see——" she met the girl's eyes unwillingly. " It's not so easy. The gates are shut . . . there's a watchman . . . and a—a dog."

" Pff! . . . That dog." Gisela buttoned up her coat. " I know that dog." From a plate of scraps by the sink she picked up a knobby end of salami by the string. She snapped it up in her hand, rattling it, with just that smile on her face, enigmatic, teasing, with which a gambler about to throw prepares his opponent for nothing less than a six. Then, leaning over the table, quite close, she whispered:

" *First*, gnädige Frau—and I could have told you—one should always . . . *get to know the dog*."

*   *   *

When she opened her eyes next morning, there was Gisela hanging up the new dress on the cupboard door. Milly closed her eyes quickly. Funny—now that the dress was hers, she could tell at once that she positively disliked it.

" Good morning, gnädige Frau." Primly Gisela approached with the tray of coffee. " You see the gown—how beautiful it is? "

" Yes," said Milly, " I see it. What time is it?"

" Oh, late. Quite late. But you were sleeping so sound when I came in first and your man said not to wake you. And then when the Bielska came——"

" The Bielska? You mean——" she had been going to say Sophie, but she stopped in time, and pressed her hand to her head. She had slept badly, dreamed—oh, what terrible dreams until . . . and then she had lain awake for so long, because it had been preferable to lie awake . . . until after the market carts had passed, and then she must have fallen into a deep sleep. Her head still ached. She sat up as Gisela poured her coffee. " So she came, did she, the Countess Bielska? And what did you say? "

" I said that you were asleep and not to wake you, as Herr Purdoe had instructed."

" I see. But she'll come back later? "

" I think not. She seemed busy and it was not worth while as you are leaving immediately."

" But we *aren't* leaving immediately." She frowned. Still, she couldn't help feeling a certain relief. Hating the dress, she was sure she would hate the lace even more. That was out of her hands, at least.

" I did not know," said Gisela meekly. But that's what she must have told Sophie, thought Milly, her headache not rendering her utterly dim-witted. " The Bielska left a message." Gisela dived into the pocket of her apron. " About this lace required for the dress."

272

Milly took the slip of paper, staring at the girl as she did so. Gisela had a wonderful talent for reducing the sensational to the conventional. " It seems," Gisela went on softly, as Milly pored over Sophie's hiero-glyphics, " that she was able only to obtain a small reduction and she was afraid that it would still be too dear, perhaps."

" I see." Milly crumpled up the note. That was certainly a précis of the contents. Damn Sophie, she thought, lying back and closing her eyes. Damn her. Fancy blurting it all out—fancy *writing it all down*. Really!

" Gnädige Frau."

She opened her eyes. Gisela was smiling down at her.

" You'll forgive me, I hope . . . but, you understand . . ." she did a big act with a gulp and a sigh, " I thought, what a pity to spoil the dress and knowing that old man at the shop, from the time of Mrs. Simpson —better even than the Countess knows him, I—well, look . . ."

Milly looked. It was there, spread on the crimson quilt—a thousand cobwebs blown together by the breeze; caught in the meshes, a butter-fly's wing, the imprint of the skeleton of a rose; strewn with forget-me-nots, true-lovers'-knots—roses, butterflies, true lovers and forget-me-nots all part of another summer, centuries ago. When she touched it, as she had to do, it crackled under her fingers like dead leaves.

" Schön," said Gisela softly. " Sehr schön."

Milly took a deep breath. " But—how am I going to *pay* for it? "

" If you want it, it's easily arranged. If you——" she glanced at her mistress, " want it, that's to say."

" *Want* it? " Yes, she wanted it. Anyway, she *had* it now, so really there was no argument. The thing was done. The lace lay there on her lap. As if she read her thoughts, Gisela smiled:

" I will arrange, then—while you are away." Then, casually: " Is it made, the list of meals for die Nanny and the Buben, gnädige Frau?"

" Yes. It's here, in my bag. Here."

Gisela took it without glancing at it.

" So I shall be needing the key to the cupboard? " She still wore that suggestive little smile, eyeing Milly as if she were speaking in a code that was shared privately between them. Which in a way she was.

" Yes," said Milly. " You'll need it." She had intended leaving the necessary stores out on the kitchen table, as she always did, locking the cupboard and taking the key with her, but really it didn't make much difference, did it? Or did it? She couldn't make up her mind. Gisela, who knew when to leave well alone, said, collecting the cups and stacking them on the tray:

" The old man mentioned something about a tea service. He remembered you—the pretty young lady, he said . . ." She made it sound just right, reporting the flattery quite impersonally as if it merely stated a fact that required no comment. " He has one, it seems. Meissen. Very nice—one saucer slightly cracked and therefore——" she hesitated, " very nice. I said we would let him know. The . . . er . . . price is not too bad."

" Certainly *not*! " said Milly, alarmed by the " we " as much as by any of the other implications: " On *no* account. I wouldn't dream of it. This—well, this lace is quite enough for the present, isn't it ? "

" Ach, die Nanny! " exclaimed Gisela, evading a direct reply, as Miss Raven's voice was heard from the nursery. " How she shrieks— I'll go and see. I come back for the tray." She slipped out.

When she had gone Milly got out of bed and turned on her bath. She was making a fuss about nothing—anyway, she was late, she wouldn't have time now to bother about those stores. She took the key out of her bag and laid it on the tray. There. That would mean ordering more NAAFI in Slavnik—well, what better opportunity than to-morrow when she would have the whole day free, on the spot? She went into the bathroom and shut the door. She had no wish to see Gisela again just at present. When she came out, the tray had been taken away.

*   *   *

It was when she was packing the hard-won trophies, the dress and the lace, that the familiar disenchantment set in. She jammed them both in the case, stuffing them with tissue paper. Of course the lace was absolutely lovely, but had it not been for Sophie, she told herself, she could have done without it. She had been *prepared* to do so, even —goodness, hadn't she made up her mind ? What could have possessed Sophie ? To be so indiscreet, to leave a note, open, like that, with the maid and blab it all out to her into the bargain—well, naturally she would never *mention* it to Sophie—but what on earth could have possessed her ?

And Sophie was thinking, off and on through the morning, which was quite unpleasant on its own account: " Oh, if only I could have seen her! But at any rate I did badger that girl—and how I dislike that girl—to bring an envelope, and I saw her face when I stuck it down. Ha! I'm not quite such a duffer. I hope Milly will be pleased—but now there's no way of knowing, for certainly I can never *ask*—it would seem like, well, *hinting*—and it's possible she may forget to tell me, the darling little scatterbrain, what in the end happened about the lace."

And Gisela, as she washed up, the key of the store cupboard safe in her apron pocket, was singing to herself and thinking: " It was a

274

risk—but if one never took risks? They will never mention it to each other, and I am so glad that she has both the dress and the lace, and when the Herrschaften have left for Slavnik, I will pass by the shop and tell that old chap—without doubt we shall be delighted to take the tea service, too." Gisela, unlike Milly, was not only a born gambler but quite a sound little amateur psychologist as well.

* * *

Later, sitting in the car outside the hotel, Milly was kept waiting almost ten minutes. The luggage had been stowed in. She was pleased that Larry was driving and that they were leaving Vladek behind. She had recently conceived an unaccountable dislike for the driver, And Abe, she wondered, when would he be leaving? His Citroën was still there in the side street. He would have to leave this afternoon or to-morrow early to be in time for the party to-morrow night.

A week-end. Well, that was nice. They certainly deserved it, all three of them. Goodness, what moody, disagreeable expressions they wore, these people in the street. How sick and tired she was of seeing poorly-dressed people with glum faces. How she wished—here he was. Now what? Something had happened—even she could tell that.

Larry got in, started up the car and they moved off.

" Darling—mind out! For heaven's sake, what's the matter? "

He let the tram live and moved on. Then he muttered, in a clear patch: " *Damn*' funny . . . I must say . . ."

" What is? *Mind!* "

On the outskirts of the town he took time off to explode: " *Damn*' cheek. . . . My *God*, what a nerve."

" Calm down, sweetie . . . cigarette? . . . Now, tell me what? "

" *Damned* impudence . . . thanks, okay . . . well, you'll never believe it . . . just as I was coming down the stairs, blow me if that old—witch, you know the one, I've never even spoken to her, only seen her once —remember, that time the sink got blocked up? Well, this old—housekeeper, or what have you, in the hall there, grabbed me and you know what she said? "

" For heaven's sake," said Milly, " that was a cart. Well, what? "

" She asked me for a bottle of three star brandy."

" *Brandy?* "

" Yep. Can you beat it? *Three star*, if you please—oh, she was quite clear about that. As a nameday gift for her brother, who, it appears, is the director of the hotel—doesn't that just take the biscuit? "

" You mean she expected you to *give* it her? "

" Oh, lord, yes. She had that much sense, luckily for her. I should have known how to deal with it otherwise. Just a little token of

275

friendship from me to her to the director. She was blathering some nonsense about a *dog*. The porter's dog."

" So what did you say? "

"Told her to go and boil herself, of course. Really, for sheer absolute unmitigated unparalleled—honestly, Milly, I just can't get over it."

Indeed, it appeared that the incident had affected him very deeply. He broke silence to refer to it three or four times on the journey and remained in a bad temper all the way.

About half-way, Milly said: " Where's Abe? "

" Abe? "

" Yes. I mean, when's he going to get on the road? At this rate he'll be late."

"Late? What for? Oh, I see. Didn't I tell you?—he's not coming. We've done him a kindness, he says, standing in for him with Schwelling. I thought you knew."

" No. I didn't."

They arrived in Slavnik rather late and went straight to bed, because in view of the pile of invitations waiting for them it looked as if there was a busy day in store on the morrow.

Chapter Five

So THE next morning Milly had coffee with the wife of the Chargé-d'Affaires (British), and both she and Larry went to luncheon with the Head of Chancery, and then Milly took tea with the wife of the Italian Commercial Attaché whom she had known elsewhere, and then they met at the Turkish Embassy, where sweet champagne flowed in honour of a national day and afterwards they went on to cocktails with the Swedes and at this function they were pressed to make up a party to to go on somewhere and dine, first of all by the French and then by the Danes, both of which invitations they were obliged to refuse owing to their already having fixed up to dine at the Bussemakers'.

" You're taken care of for dinner, I gather? " The First Secretary (British), whose cosy little residence—from which not a few of his seniors had attempted to oust him and failed—was situated between the Turks and the Swedes, poured them sherry. Then he poured some more into a porcelain bonbonnière and set it on the Aubusson carpet as an offering to a pair of dormant intermingled Pekingese who immediately woke up.

" *So* good for their coats, naughty little things." He crooned over them fondly. " But zey won't touch zere olives, will zey? " He had sprinkled a few of these appetisers on the carpet. " Nasty common olives with howwid stones. Surely——" he inquired, a querulous note in his voice, peering into the shadows. A fellow in a turtle-necked sweater masked rather unconvincingly by a man-servant's white jacket was lurking there, presumably in attendance. He stepped forward quite smartly; a brawny youth, hulking almost—something of the prize-fighter in his manner.

" Di'n'ge' ya—wha' was tha'? " Whatever else he was, he was a Geordie, from his accent.

" Olives," repeated the First Secretary, a shade bashfully. " Those teeny ones—stuffed . . . surely, haven't we . . . ? "

" Wha'? For them poops? Naaaah! . . ." Incensed, with an almost maternal indignation he swept the already bemused creatures into his arms. Making for the door, he turned and from under his lashes—he had very long lashes—shot a look of unequivocal content, familiarity mingled with contempt, in the direction of his master. " *Stooffed*? . . . Gar—wha'ever next? " In triumph he bore his babes away.

277

" That was Robinson," remarked the First Secretary wistfully as the door closed. " *Quite* a character . . . dear me." He sighed and got back on the job. " So you're dining with the Americans? Hmm . . . oh, but they'll *do* you quite well, I assure you . . . the *food's* first class . . . I had hoped to drop in on the Swedes, but I'm booked with the French, tant pis—who do one awfully well, too, of course . . . one can't go to everything . . . and how is dear old Grusnov? How's Princess thingummy? Charming old girl, isn't she? Quite a period piece . . . hmmm . . ." He was distracted, momentarily, by his own reflection in the glass over the mantelpiece. It was a fine, rocky profile so far as it went, that is down to the point where it crumbled away. He caressed these lower reaches meditatively, so managing to obscure them a bit whilst reassuring himself as to the rest of the view, then, turning to Milly, " Hm . . . Family quite fit? Good, good . . . no more brushes with the powers that be, Mrs. Purdoe? Never mind, these things crop up . . . so glad to hear it's all ticking over . . . not too lonely? You must come up more often—if ever you get to screaming pitch. Treat for us . . . delighted to see a fresh face . . . not at all, delighted . . ." His voice became tinged with enthusiasm as he helped Milly with her coat. " The Bussemakers . . . hm . . . you'll find them very friendly . . . everyone really, most friendly . . . co-operative . . ."

* * *

" D'you suppose they carry on like this every day? "
" I suppose so. They've nothing else to do."
" But mightn't it get a bit *tedious*? "
" Drive you round the bend, I should say."
The taxi turned into the Bussemakers' drive. The residence was ablaze with light.
" Lovely dress, darling."
" Like it? "
" Slinky as hell. Weakness of mine—black velvet. And that bit of frilling—it just sets it off."
Pleased with themselves and with each other, they arrived.

* * *

It was properly speaking a joint dinner party, that is to say that Mr. Schwelling and the Bussemakers were co-hosts, in consequence of Mr. Schwelling's status as a bachelor, and also as head of a department in the Embassy in which Mr. Bussemaker's position was a shade more lowly; it was therefore not only natural but expedient that Mr. Schwelling should entrust his share of official entertaining to the capable and willing hands of his junior's wife.

There were eight or ten persons standing around the Bussemakers' drawing-room, all, as Mrs. Bussemaker maintained with her first breath, patting the numerous little bows festooning her silvery curls, "perfectly lovely people and dying to meet the . . . ?"

"Oh my, *of course* . . . friends of Joe's? Ed!" she screamed, endeavouring to attract the attention of a gaunt stooping figure already engaged in conversation. "Joe's not here right now," she explained, "I guess he's been held up by those shooshkybarbs at the Turks . . . he'll be right over, though . . . Ed!" she repeated in a firm sotto voce, turning aside to snatch a couple of immense frosted glasses off a tray and pressing them on the strangers. "Friends of *Joe's*!" she hissed, and Mr. Bussemaker obediently turned round; an impressive figure as he loomed over them, rearing his head, snuffing out their where-abouts as if expecting to encounter them on his own level which was somewhat above the level of the common man; stumbling upon them, luckily, at his very feet.

"Mr. Purdom . . . doe . . . I do beg your pardon . . . a pleasure to welcome any friend of Joe's . . . and Mrs. Purdoe . . . well, well . . ."

Milly gazed up at him in awe. Although the eyes of the visionary burned behind the rimless lenses, and his skin was of a ghastly pallor, there was nevertheless not the least suggestion of the ascetic in his appearance as a whole; Mr. Bussemaker was too well nourished for that. The dew of perspiration which clung to his brow—a lofty one, time and the State Department having combined to set its margin fairly well back around the crown of his impressive head—suggested rather the bloom clinging to some exotic fruit, picked early, ripened in the dark bowels of a cargo vessel and then laid a shade too long on ice. His hands, too, were chilly and damp. A pervasive aura of mouthwash, talcum powder and other virile perfumes hung about his immaculate person, their combined fragrance so delicately impersonal, yet func-tional, as to hint rather at the embalmer's stock-in-trade. Here was a man, one would have said, who was of the earth, earthy—more, that Mr. Bussemaker had somehow slyly contrived to skip a base in what some are pleased to call the game of life; not birth, nor marriage, evidently—then perhaps that one reputed to be the most taxing—the very last? Certainly, as at first encounter with any richly upholstered, well-preserved man, one had the fancy—instantly to suppress it, of course—that although his might prove an uncommonly troublesome corpse to lay out, the worms were in for a treat.

"You all fixed up with a drink?" There was even an agreeably sonorous thrill in his speaking voice. "Fine, now we must get you all acquainted," he went on, commanding the attention of the company, "I wanchertameet . . ." and the Purdoes shuffled in his wake . . . "our

Attershay, Air ... Hadge ..." A broad, youngish man with a pleasantly wrinkled face grinned. " Coralie, his wife ..." a dark young woman in red, lying back in an arm-chair, uncrossed her legs . . . " Gaymer Adams . . ." a very young man with a crew cut blushed. " Gaymer's our pet demonologist," Mr. Bussemaker explained, " Janette, his wife . . ." An extremely pretty girl, her great eyes bulging with fright like a rabbit's, giggled. " And last, but by no means least, our Slavonian friend, Mr. Polevski. *The* Polevski," he amplified kindly, but without that one sensed the hush that had fallen upon the company, possibly in deference to the bearded gentleman indicated, or more probably as a tribute to Mr. Bussemaker's diplomacy in having snared this rare bird. " And here we have our good friends—British—Mr. and Mrs.— Purdoe ... from ... where d'ya say it was? Grusnov! Friends of Joe's," he added, as if it were unlikely that Grusnov would figure on every-body's map, whereas Mr. Schwelling surely did.

" Mrs. Purdoe! You're artistic, I *know*." Mrs. Bussemaker, switching Milly's glass, thrust a fresh Martini into her hand. " Don't ask me *how* I know . . . something just tells me here inside. . . . I'm like that, I just get a feeling and so ... so ..." She was steering Milly across the room at a great rate. " I want you . . . because you'll have a whole heap of things to talk about ... Why! " as if happening on her victim by accident, " Mr. Polevski! I do declare—hasn't anyone fixed you with a drink? Mr. Polevski's a *great* artist," she whispered to Milly, and bracelets a-jingle, bows a-bobbing, she was off with his glass.

Milly was rendered speechless, aware of Mr. Polevski's small shrewd eyes fixed on her face. After he had studied it at his leisure, he indicated a couple of straight-backed chairs:

" Siddown," he commanded, and Milly, allowing herself to fall into this old Continental trap, sank into a chair with resignation, Mr. Polevski with relief.

" You—you paint? " she said nervously.

" *Paint!* " His beard waggled at the effrontery of the suggestion. " No. I *play* . . . the pee-ar-no . . ." after a pause, darkly, " some-times . . ." He glanced round the drawing-room ". . . but not to-night."

" We-ell! " Their hostess, bearing Martinis aloft, beamed down upon them much in the manner of a Highland mother who, having engineered a bundling, awaits felicitous results. " Oh, I won't disturb you, goodness, no. You haven't had the privilege, Mrs. Purdoe, of attending one of Bell's musical evenings? Why, Mr. Polevski's the *star*." As if conscious of disloyalty she corrected herself, " and Bella, of course. Bella Gatch "—she sketched in a caption to the picture already conjured up—" is our Minister's wife . . . crazy about music

280

. . . how she finds time with those three lovely kids and all her social life, I just can't think . . . a beautiful player, isn't she, Professor?"

The great musician appeared momentarily depressed. "Very beautiful," he muttered, punishing his Martini in the manner of his race. At this point there was a disturbance in the doorway, caused by the entrance of Mr. Schwelling with a plump young woman in black satin on his arm. As if on greased wheels, Mrs. Bussemaker glided off to the centre of the storm.

"You ain't met the wife of the American Minister, Mrs. Gatch?" Mr. Polevski set down his glass with a bump.

"No," said Milly, who had just heard Mr. Schwelling say: "Only just arrived in town—such a lonely li'l girl . . . so far away from home . . ."

"Never heard her *play*?" The professor went on, dredging up a clawful of almonds, "Mrs. Bella Gatch?"

"No," said Milly.

"Lucky for you." Brooding, Mr. Polevski sucked his teeth. "Plays like hell. Like hell," he repeated, rising from his chair, ostensibly to replenish his cigarette case from a box on a side table, which he did; merely a blind, however, prior to making a beeline across the room. Mr. Schwelling's " li'l girl," already snuggled into an arm-chair, was engaged in deploying the resources of her brief costume so that its margins should enclose her nipples, without any repressive suggestion of permanency, and at the same time sheathe her thighs with the modicum of encumbrance to the knee-joints. She had, Milly reckoned, a fifty-fifty chance of success. Mr. Polevski was perched on the arm of her chair, superintending the operation, before ever Milly woke up to the fact that the wily old fox had left her flat.

"Joe," said Mr. Bussemaker in his gorgeous pulpit voice, " there's friends of yours present." He indicated Larry.

Mr. Schwelling, who was where he wanted to be, on the other arm of the chair which housed his protégée, reluctantly rose to his feet.

"That's right" he acknowledged, graciously enough. " Mr. Purdoe . . . Grusnov, wasn't it? A pleasure. Brought along your lovely wife? Fine . . . that was a great little party . . . How's Antoinette? Fine? Fine. Like a breath of fresh air, Grusnov, that's what I always say."

"That's right, Joe, you do." Mr. Bussemaker turned to Larry. " Breath of fresh air . . . fact . . . Joe always says that."

Mr. Schwelling, getting into his stride, went on: "You're privileged, y'know, Mr. Purdoe. *May* seem like being way out on a limb . . ." In the din arising around a tray of fresh Martinis, Larry caught a phrase here and there: ". . . ancient bastion . . . culture . . . freedom of thought

281

... privilege ... I can honestly say. . ." The tray passed on, "... honestly say . . . I'd throw up all *this* "—Mr. Schwelling with a comprehensive gesture indicated the present scene and company—"*to-morrow* . . ."

" Joe! " Mr. Bussemaker looked properly shocked. " Come now, Joe."

" I *mean* that, Ed . . . to-morrow . . . so's I could bury myself in that sleepy old town . . ." Another tray of drinks was fast approaching, ". . . heartbeat of the country . . . aristocrats like Antoinette . . . peasants like—well, like peasants, I guess . . . whereas, *we*, Mr. Purdoe, here in the capital . . ." Mr. Schwelling took a deep drag on his cigarette, his eyes, efficiently scouting in advance of the spoken word, darting over the room, and Larry sensed that barely detectable whirring in the clock-work which promised that the regulation span allotted him was drawing to a close. " In Slavnik "—Mr. Schwelling made a final spurt—" in this great little capital, could it be, Mr. Purdoe . . . that we're missing the vital message? Are we just, as one might say, treading on each other's toes? " Someone did say it, rather loudly, as, winding up his peroration and stepping back in order to avoid the waiter with the tray, Mr. Schwelling trod heavily on the toes of the Air Attaché. This was the man with the face of an utterly reliable well-worn boot to whom Larry had taken an instantaneous liking; the one who had been introduced as Hadge.

" I guess you could use one of these," said the Air Attaché sympathetically, altering the disposition of glasses on the waiter's tray. " Tovarich! " He addressed the waiter. " Now you better get some more and pretty goddam quick. Hired waiter," he explained to Larry. " He's everywhere, li'l pal to all the world. Third place I've seen him at to-day. Great guy, Tovarich. Hm." Suspiciously he sniffed his whisky. " No, it's okay . . . but you gotta watch out with these culture boys, Ed, Joe and so on . . . you never can tell. Now, we haven't met, have we? That's one opportunity for social blunder obviated in this town . . . either you have or you haven't . . . and if you have, it's likely to've been too goddam often. Up here for long? "

" Back to-morrow."

" Is that so? Schwelling's racket? "

" No," said Larry with a degree of vehemence.

The boot creased pleasantly, as one had instinctively known it would do. " Hell, I only meant—newspapers. You're a friend of Schulman's, I hear? "

" I am, as it happens . . . but how did you hear? "

" Oh, from Schulman," said Hadge calmly. " He's a friend of mine, too. And of my wife's. That's my wife."

The dark-haired woman who was lying back in her chair watching

282

them raised an arm in lazy salutation. She had a narrow and rather ugly face, likely to be memorable if only on account of her exceedingly mobile and full-lipped mouth, twisted now into a curiously masculine and cruel smile which accompanied her response to the introduction. Larry, happening to catch a glint of reciprocal malevolence in the eyes of her husband, immediately gained the impression, almost invariably disagreeable to the stranger, that here was a couple whose secret, shared delight lay in mutual torment. Even sprawled as she was in the chair one could not but be aware of her wonderfully shapely body.

" You gotta hand it to Joe Schwelling," remarked the Air Attaché who, waging his private connubial war and employing conventional long-range weapons, had turned to admire the young lady in black. " He can cer'nly pick 'em."

Mr. Schwelling having at that moment launched a small chunk of ice down the slope which led to the ditch in the bosom of the black satin dress, Larry inquired innocently: " Is that—er . . . *Mrs.* Schwelling? " Simultaneously it occurred to him that everyone present must have attended more than one social gathering that day.

The Air Attaché appeared genuinely amused by his question. " Bit o' frat," he explained when he had recovered himself sufficiently to speak.

The waiter rolled back the dividing doors.

" Whaddya say we go in an' eat? " suggested Mrs. Bussemaker.

The dinner table was a splendid sight with rosy shaded lamps and waterlilies floating in a central tank from which streamers of ivy trailed in and out of a crazy paving of dainty mats. The guests peered in amongst the ill-lighted thicket for the cards which would indicate their several fates. Mr. Schwelling, satisfactorily placed between his young lady friend on his left and Milly on his right, lost no time in whispering to the latter:

" That's our Attershay for Air on your other side, Mrs. Purdoe; very comical, you'll find, very comical indeed—real live wire," and quick to take a hint, at least one as broad as this, she turned to her neighbour whom she found in the act of disentangling his soup spoon from the undergrowth.

" Funny thing," he was musing aloud, " I'm actually paying cash to have my house stripped of this stuff right now. Where d'you women get these tips? No, don't tell me—I can guess. But it seems to me you oughta know where to draw the line."

" Me? "

" Oh, no, not you." He smiled at her, lavishing so much charm that she felt her blood tingle, at least down to her fingertips. " Nothing personal . . . just women."

283

" You sound—cross? "

" Cross? " He sighed. " Hell, no. Just constipated, I guess." He looked moodily around. His wife was murmuring to Larry, seated on her right: " Forty-five?... six? How come we never met up in Rome?" She gave a little low laugh. " Why, I met *Hadge*—that's my husband —in Rome just around that time." Far from being a non sequitur, this statement, if one took into account the tone of voice and the expression on the face of the speaker, seemed rather to imply the drawing of a comparison, or equally, if not a direct refutation of the Spanish precept that what must be must, of necessity, be, at least a hint that if it were it need not for ever remain so. Larry looked rather startled.

" Funny," he said, " I met my wife in Rome, too. Must be a fateful city."

" A fateful city, you've said it."

She had a number of little tricks in the bag then, and she was turning them out thick and fast, but this one he had met with before, the neat back-quote of the last phrase to leave one's own lips; a favourite with lazy and over-confident women. And very flattering it was up to a point—still, he hoped that she wouldn't perform it too often, the tricks of a parrot not inevitably endearing one to the bird.

Unlike the other ladies he had encountered in the course of what already seemed a protracted evening—all of whom had worn topless gowns, the bodices dependent upon a scaffolding of whalebone, the nipples, knobs of iron, set precisely apart, erected and sustained by some miracle of engineering—Mrs. Hadge, if one had to think of her as that, to give her her due was dressed with taste and circumspection in some gorgeous red clinging stuff, the top cut like a man's shirt, the effect not at all like a man's shirt with a man in it; moreover, at the wearer's least movement the eye was tempted to seek out the underlying causes of the difference. Yes, he thought, yielding to the temptation without much of a struggle, there was nothing for it, you just had to follow it all the way. He hoped, rather feebly, for the sake of his own peace of mind, that she might have terrible legs. He didn't put much faith in it, somehow.

" I was doing Red Cross——" She put down her soup spoon and sat up rather straight, so as to vary the temptation, but not, he reflected sadly, his own reaction to it; he fell for it all over again.

" At that hotel in that piazza—remember?—Barbareeny? Hadge —well, soon as we met—or pretty soon—we made up our minds. That's how it was."

He could see how it was—or most of it. How she must have looked in uniform with a cap on her dark smooth bob—worn short pigskin gloves driving her jeep—efficiently, of course; and how it must have been when, punctual to the minute, the first breeze from the sea fans through the oven-hot streets, in the darkened hotel room during the hours of siesta—the bars of sunlight through the slats creeping over the stone floor (or fairly waltzing across, depending)—and afterwards, after a shower, you ring for the waiter, and in between sips of Campari and soda, chew melon pips while the melon you haven't eaten thaws in its sweating silver dish, you decide where you are going to eat . . . and there you sit, wherever it is, in a daze, soft and quivering and vulnerable as a couple of turtles stripped of their shells, and you are still licking the sore place on your lip where she has bitten it and the touch of your fingers is lingering, very likely, for her to remember you by. He thought of all that as he finished his soup. Then, catching sight of Milly at the far end of the table, he knew by her gravely attentive manner to her neighbour that she had, by some masterstroke of unilateral telepathy, twigged. So with an effort he stopped thinking about it, Mrs. Hadge, Rome, and so on; there was no other way of fooling Milly.

There had been sherry with the soup and a decent Graves with the river fish and now there was a full-blooded burgundy and still two wine glasses remained at each place; like symbols of the unknown, empty, shining, full of promise, nevertheless indicating by their very shape the course the conversation must take. It had ranged from the flippant with the cocktails to the whimsical with the soup, the purely conjectural with the fish and was due to become philosophical with the brandy if not with the champagne; only the ultimate threat of the personal lurking unseen, the whisky glasses being still mercifully out of sight. But they were not yet so far. The hosts both had their talking points, and the arrival of the turkey, a massive bird and a challenge in itself, reminded them that they had still to unload the really heavy stuff.

In the discharge of his duty Mr. Bussemaker favoured either of two techniques: either by means of oratio obliqua, enlisting the patronage of eminent personages, e.g.: " As I recollect, it was Mr. Dulles who said, only last week, that . . ." or, with more daring, but on the whole to less racy effect, under his own steam, involving a laborious pressure build-up before he was enabled to shunt himself off, e.g.: " It's my considered opinion—don't quote me, though, this is off the record— and I can honestly say I've lain awake nights thrashing over the pros and cons . . ." Whereas Mr. Schwelling, in the majesty of his superior rank, preferred the Olympian approach to his task; would loose off the odd thunderbolt and sit back with splendid impassivity, allowing it to strike where and whom it would; there was this about it, his missiles brooked of no argument. Both gentlemen acted in such perfect accord that it was a delight to watch—when one led, the other fed;

otherwise—as may be judged from the following exchange, the instance of the single lapse—the dinner might never have been done.

" There can certainly be no question that when Joe Stalin was bargaining for his zone of influence he contemplated putting it under Communist control." Mr. Schwelling, possibly feeling that he was being made to shoulder more than his share of the burden, and in any case held up waiting for a second slice of bird, called down the table, " May we have your views on that, Ed ? "

Having betted on the certainty referred to by his chief so far as to commit himself elsewhere, Mr. Bussemaker was justifiably aggrieved to find himself caught short, dabbling in cranberry sauce. Casting a mildly reproachful look at his colleague, he adroitly passed the buck. " Sure, why not? But I suggest young Gaymer here might give us a few pointers on that . . . ? "

Gaymer Adams, who had been quietly at work on his plate, blushed and reluctantly laid down his tools.

" Well, Gaymer? Go on, son . . ." Encouraging as was his tone there was a sparkle in Mr. Schwelling's eye, an evident relish as he smacked his lips, suggesting not so much a paternal interest in the young man as the frankly voluptuous appraisal of his victim by the cannibal chief with the cauldron just on the boil.

" I don't see . . . I mean, Mr. Schwelling, why *me* ? "

Everyone laughed politely and Hadge whispered to Milly, " He had it, poor sap."

" C'marn now, Gaymer . . . you've got it right there at your finger ends. I chanced to glance through that report of yours, you know."

" You did? " A look of horror crossed the young man's face.

" I did." Mr. Schwelling wagged his head coyly. " These things go higher than you think."

" Well . . . as I understand the . . . er . . . question . . . Mr. Busse-maker . . ."

Mr. Bussemaker, now fed and apprehending his fledgeling's distress, graciously came to his aid, repeating—for it was no trouble to him, having as it so happened memorised the text of the original handout: " . . . that when Stalin was bargaining . . ."

" Oh, sure . . . sure . . . Well, now, I take it you mean around 1944 . . .?" Aware that he could hardly expect to receive support on a premise so boldly defined, he hurried on: " I would say, undoubtedly —but for a few glaring contradictions . . ." In the act of marshalling his thoughts Mr. Adams suddenly smiled, a sweet brief smile, catching sight across the table of the expression on the face of his wife. Her great eyes—their protuberance, size and quality due possibly to nothing more than the erratic functioning of the thyroid gland—were fixed on

286

him, shining with love and pride, in her regard an intensity, a childish
sincerity which caught at the heart. Indeed these eyes of hers, her best
feature, were so striking that they must have impressed even the casual
beholder; she was to die in childbirth within a year, when even those
who scarcely knew her claimed to have glimpsed the shadow cast before
the event; and although she was not otherwise a remarkable person—
there was no time for that, she died merely a junior wife—she had
many mourners; everyone remembering her for her eyes, their soft
yet searching light. Now, her face silly with youth, her moist mouth
slightly ajar, her knobbly hands clenched in her lap, she willed her
husband to win, and he spoke.

" Take Lvov," he said.

" Go right ahead," murmured the Air Attaché in Milly's ear, " I
don' want it."

" A Slavonian-Ukrainian city, that was Lvov. Surely it would have
been all the same to Stalin whether it was governed from Commie-run
Kiev or Commie-run Slavnik? Similarly—if he'd been planning
revolution for Eastern Germany why incorporate into Slavonia all the
German provinces east of the Oder-Neisse line? Why expel the entire
German population from those territories? It could only make the
Germans mad—and what about the demand for the liquidation of
German industry? Already, at Teheran, you recall . . ."

" Gaymer, that's a very comprehensive reply . . ." Mr. Schwelling
tidied up his plate, wiped his mouth, and took a sip of burgundy.
" Two points, before we go any further. As I understand it . . . correct
me if I'm wrong. . . . One, you suspect there *are* reasons for supposing
to the contrary? "

" That's right, I do."

" No . . . no more, thank you . . . quite gorgeous, but no more . . .
and B, Gaymer . . . B . . ." He paused, partly for effect and partly to
think up B, and Hadge observed in an undertone to Milly:

" Could be some advantage in a military education after all . . ."

Mr. Schwelling swivelled round in his chair. " What was that,
Hadge? " he inquired pleasantly.

" Well," said the Air Attaché, " it's all most interesting, fascinating,
really . . . and I'm not disputing one single little thing, oh, no, I should
say not! But isn't it perhaps just a shade—well, a shade theoretical?
Maybe I'm looking at it from the wrong angle but—now, don't mis-
understand me, Joe—what I'd like to know is "—Milly caught a gentle
jab on her ankle—" what *in actual fact* happened? I mean, did he, or
didn't he? That's what I want to know. Facts are facts . . . that seems
to me the crux of the whole . . . goddam fool argument," he added
under his breath as Mr. Schwelling nodded vigorous approval.

" Right on the ball, Hadge—as usual. Facts *are* facts . . . Now, Gaymer . . . ha-ha . . . where do we go from here? "

" But, surely . . . as I understand it, Mr. Schwelling, the question *was* theoretical . . . surely? "

" That's all right, my boy," purred Mr. Schwelling, ". . . you just carry right on . . . assuming it was . . ."

Where do we go from here? thought Larry. Her latest trick, the ultimate so far as his own dinner-table experience went, had involved a long silk-clad shank brushing up against his own. Pardon me, she had said prettily, and then it had happened again. She's a cool one, he thought, amused, watching her adjust the slant of her head to what must undoubtedly be a familiar and famous angle, pestering him, too, for recognition. She had all the assurance of a celebrity together with a provoking air which suggested that whatever it was she was celebrated for was only properly to be comprehended by the initiate and was certainly not for the likes of you, a stranger; some mysterious art which she herself had discovered and perfected, and which rendered all other pursuits tame and unrewarding by contrast. So her name was Coralie. What did she expect him to do? Call her by it? Not on your life. So where do we go from here? She'd allow—indeed, just love you to go crazy thinking it over.

" I don't *agree* . . ." Gaymer Adams was still arguing doggedly. " I *can't* . . . it just doesn't happen to be included in Marxist doctrine."

" Aw, c'marn now, Gaymer," coaxed Ed Bussemaker, as if with champagne and dessert already on the table he could surely manage to cram it in somewhere.

Baited beyond endurance, the young man cried: " These aren't *my* ideas, sir! "

" Ho, ho," laughed Mr. Schwelling, who was partial to champagne, and everybody thankfully joined in. " You can't shuffle out of it thataway, Gaymer. . . . Hadge here has just made a very, very pertinent contribution . . . will you repeat that, Hadge? "

The Air Attaché, diving for his napkin, muttered somewhere near Milly's lap, " What the hell's he wanta persecute me for," then, sitting up, said sternly: " *No*, Joe . . . I'm sorry . . . I can't see my way to putting that question again . . . it's withdrawn, absolutely. Matter of fact, I think it was irrelevant."

Young Adams shot him a look of undying gratitude.

" You play Canasta, Mr. Purdoe? " said Mrs. Bussemaker. Her dimples were for him, but not the light of her eyes, extinguished by a cloud of worry; nor her thoughts, which were scampering ahead.

" I'm afraid not."

" Bridge? " said Coralie in her deep voice, which seemed to hint

288

another fifty interpretations to the word, all relating to activities fifty times more pleasant. Stupefied, he could only think of one; he became aware that the pressure on his leg had started up again. Just then he caught sight of Milly, who was looking at him hard. Summoning all his fortitude he smiled fairly directly at her and to his surprise she smiled back. Stealthily he moved his leg away.

Mrs. Bussemaker, meanwhile, in the connubial language of nods, becks, winks and so on, had conveyed some intelligence of a gratifying nature to her husband.

" Joe! " he called down the length of the table during a lull in the conversation, " It's *not* Canasta! "

Mr. Schwelling, as co-host having the advantage in this respect over his guests, clearly aware of the significance of these tidings, reacted in no uncertain manner, his face more or less breaking up under the impact of some blow, or shock; after a second's disintegration it was rapidly rebuilt into an expression of the keenest anticipatory delight.

" And Gaymer here'll be our projectionist! " Mr. Bussemaker, excitedly ranging up and down behind the chairs, slapped Adams on the back, causing him to choke. His cup, though not his glass, had been full for some time and now it overflowed.

" You kinda sprung this on me, Mr. Bussemaker . . ."

" That's all right, Gaymer . . . I can trust you to be meticulously careful . . . besides, I got copies . . ."

" There's a treat in store for *you*, Mrs. Purdoe . . ." Mr. Schwelling licked his lips, chuckling, sadistic pleasure being better than none at all. " Ed and Amy have these gorgeous colour films of their trip," he went on, " I've seen 'em—they're just great."

" Trip? " Milly repeated in a daze.

" Oh, sure. Round the world."

" You mean—right round? " she said stupidly.

" Right the way round," confirmed Mr. Schwelling with glee, bent on extracting the last drop.

" Mama mia," moaned the Air Attaché on her other side.

" I just can't wait, Amy," squeaked little Mrs. Adams.

" Well, it's that or Canasta," said Mrs. Bussemaker inexorably, shepherding the ladies out.

* * *

" I just love your dress," said Coralie.

" Oh—do you? It's just something I had run up locally."

" Why, *no*? It's divine. But with your petite little figure anything would look good, I guess."

" *Your* dress is heavenly," said Milly, feeling a fool.

" Thank *you* . . ." Occupying the dressing-table stool, Coralie yawned at her own reflection. " It's just an old rag."

" Oh, *Coralie* . . ." Mrs. Adams giggled. " That's just the way she goes on. . . . Everyone knows," she turned to Milly, " Coralie's the best-dressed woman in Slavnik. My," she fingered the red stuff, " it's *gorgeous*."

" Phooey, Janette . . . it's real old! "

Amy Bussemaker, squinting like a hobgoblin, dodging this way and that in pursuit of a square inch of glass, at last succeeded in laying hands on her own powder-puff and applying it as best she might, remarked: " Where d'ya get it, Coralie? "

" Iddaly . . ." Good-naturedly she swung herself off the stool. " You better come here, Amy. If I had your skin, I'm not sure I wouldn't try a really deep rachel . . ."

" Oh, Italy . . ." little Mrs. Adams sighed. " Of course."

" I thought that's prob'ly where ya got it," said Mrs. Bussemaker, working savagely on her face. "Those li'l shirt waists are cute . . . I got one on mail order from Macy's coming out." She fluffed up her bows. " Not that colour—luckily. We wouldn't wanta look like twins, would we? "

" No . . ." Pensively, Coralie examined her long shining finger-nails. " We wouldn't want that."

Mrs. Bussemaker, picking up a bottle labelled " Apple Blow—Nature's Own Friendly Fragrance," directed vicious jets of liquid down her bosom and behind her ears. Mr. Schwelling's little girl—a typist in the Turkish Embassy, as it turned out—who had been hovering in the background now approached, tempted out of her own element, the dizzy vapours of Chanel, to sample that of her hostess. Sniffing, she wrinkled up her nose.

" You laike? " she inquired of Mrs. Bussemaker, innocent wonder in her voice.

" Sure I do," affirmed that lady gamely, " here—lemme give you a shot. It'll kinda freshen you up." To her astonishment the young lady skipped back out of range. " Why not, for heaven's sake? I got plenty."

Cornered, Miss Turkey wriggled. " *Ay* don' laike . . ." she cooed softly, but with telling emphasis. " Ay don' laike *at all* . . ."

Rather out of temper, what with one thing and another, Mrs. Bussemaker said crisply, " Come on down, girls," and led them all back to the drawing-room.

*   *   *

" Oh, Amy, what gorgeous cups! Look—aren't they just darling?"

" Meissen," said Mrs. Bussemaker, rather smug.

" But *complete*—why, I never saw one whole dozen before—where d'ya find them?"

" On Molotov," her hostess replied carelessly. " They're pretty nice, Ed says."

" Pretty *nice*—I should just say they were . . ." Mrs. Adams, unable to resist temptation, swooped on a cup and turning it up, examined its underside. Her face fell. " Oh," she said gravely.

" That's the mark," said Mrs. Bussemaker, on the defensive.

" Why . . . sure it is, Amy . . . but there's no date."

" There doesn't have to *be* a date," Mrs. Bussemaker's voice rose a little shrill. " Does there, Coralie? The salesman said it's better without the date . . . isn't that *right*, Coralie?"

Thus appealed to, the Air Attaché's wife herself leaned forward and picking up a cup, glanced at it, then put it down. Her eyes flickered over the round dozen laid out on the tray.

" Oh, sure," she said soothingly, " that's all right." Far from soothed, Mrs. Bussemaker shot her a suspicious look, and by way of calming her nerves began pouring the coffee into the cups.

" You interested in antiques, Mrs. Purdoe?" Coralie fitted a cigarette into a long holder.

" I—well, yes, of course—I think they're lovely. But they're awfully expensive, aren't they? I mean . . . er . . . aren't they . . .?" Her voice trailed off into an awkward silence. The American ladies, deeply shocked, politely averted their eyes as, her blush deepening, Milly realised that she had but confirmed, if confirmation were necessary, the accuracy of Napoleon's judgment on her race.

Mrs. Adams babbled on to fill the breach. " You must let me have that receipt, Amy . . ." and the Air Attaché's wife sauntered across and sat down on the arm of Milly's chair.

" Tell me," she began casually, " you know Abe Schulman, is that right?"

" Yes. You know him, do you?"

" Know him?" Coralie smiled as she lit her cigarette. " Uh-huh. I guess I do." Her eyes rested on Milly's face. " Kinda cute, isn't he?"

Once more she found herself blushing under that cool stare. " He's very—very nice."

" Oh, he was just raving about you—and your husband—last time he was up."

" He—comes up here quite often, then?"

" Every so often," said Coralie, with a pleasant little air of mystery,

291

as if, had she so wished, she could have produced Abe from her pocket then and there.

"You've known him for a long time, have you?"

"A long——? Oh, yes . . . you know he had that terrible tragedy? . . . "

"Yes. I did hear about it."

"Oh yeah—well, we had to get him over that."

"And "—her breath was quite taken away—" did you? "

"Oh, sure," said Coralie easily, as if terrible tragedies were little low hurdles encountered in the daily run of things, and for her part she would kick them aside: "We got him over it all right. Tell me," she went on loudly, the conversation having died elsewhere, "do they still have those wonderful junk shops in Grusnov?"

"Grusnov, Coralie?" piped up Mrs. Adams. "That's where you got that piano, wasn't it—the walnut—remember? Do you still have it—that one?"

Coralie paused to reflect. "Yeah," she said at last, "I think I do. But I'm not so interested in pianos any more, Janette. They clutter up so. Hadge found me a spinet last trip—I'm crazy about spinets right now. Though one by itself's no good," she added.

"No, I guess not," said Mrs. Adams meekly.

"You're an expert, are you?" said Milly. "On antiques?"

"Sure, I'm interested," she drawled, with her slow attractive smile. "It's this way," she lowered her voice to reach Milly's ear alone, "I been here a coupla years now and I'm really starting to know what I want . . . all that, for instance," she waved her cigarette at the posse of cups lined up demurely on the tray: "That sorta thing's no fun any more, Mrs. Purdoe. I can't seem to get any kick out of a complay . . ." She sat up, her voice warming with enthusiasm. "Right now, my aim's to make up a coupla dozen *all different*, d'ya get it? Same period, same mark, naturally . . ."

"Naturally," murmured Milly.

"But *different* . . . colour, design, y'know . . . believe me, I'm having quite a search!"

"I should say that would make it much more—well, interesting . . ."

"Yep—that's so. Much more."

Milly laughed breathlessly; Coralie's enthusiasm was not merely infectious, it was intoxicating.

"But can you—I mean, just buy *one*—out of a set?"

"Oh, good heavens, no . . . you have to buy up the complay, naturally . . . then, what you don't want you send home . . . I do— as gifts. I'd be all cluttered up otherwise. They just adore that kinda stuff back home, an' Hadge gets it loaded on a plane. As for that

292

bozar restriction nonsense—we don't let them get away with that. Of course, Hadge's appointment helps, don't forget."

" Yes, I . . . er . . . imagine it would."

" So that's what I mean. You gotta be selective . . ." The men's voices came drifting through the open doorway and Coralie began rounding off her chat: " See what you want—pick it, and—then—we-ell . . ." she paused as the men came through, Larry amongst them, and added, her glance roving over Milly, " why, then—all you have to do is just get rid of the junk. Excuse me, I must go find my bag."

Tovarich was pinning up a white sheet.

*   *   *

" So—would you say you'd had your fling, darling? "

" *Mine*? I like that. Would you say you'd had *yours*? " It was scarcely a rebuke. Fatigue had drained her of all spirit, and in any case she had been thrown into his arms as the taxi hurtled through the streets.

The driver poked a mad white face through the partition. " English? "

Larry nodded.

" Aha! " Without slackening speed he turned right round to observe his passengers more closely, a diabolical grin on his face. " Me "—he yelled over the screech of the brakes—" Me—three one nine Squadron . . . Spitfires . . . Manston . . . You believe? No? " Turning back to the wheel he set out in his own way to prove it.

" Americans are funny, aren't they? " said Milly, after a bit.

" Fairly funny," said Larry.

" Margate? " The driver's voice was borne back to them on the wind. The tyres screamed rounding a corner. " You know Margate? " he persisted, over his shoulder.

" Yes." Larry leaned forward. " And I'd like to see it again! " he shouted, right in the man's ear.

He shrugged. " Okay." Still, he seemed to take the hint. Larry put his arm round Milly once more.

" Well, here we are," he said, as they came in to land. " Now watch him rook me." He had the notes ready, and getting out, he pushed them through the window. To his astonishment, his hand was brushed aside and the driver himself leaned right out, cleverly managing to rev up at the same time. " English! " he roared, louder than his engine. " English!—no damn' well pay! . . . no damn' well no . . . jolly good time, Margate . . . bye-bye, bes' luck, cheerio! " Describing with a flourish that once unequivocal gesture which has come to have an

293

alternative significance, of encouragement and hope, he took off into the night.

"Well, I'll be . . . " Larry stared after him, shaking his head; nevertheless, he felt strangely comforted. Then he went up the steps, following Milly into the hotel.

*   *   *

At some hour in the night she awoke. She had been dreaming—and in spite of variations on scene, company and time of day, she recognised the old familiar dream. She had dreamed that she was standing in the doorway of a room; a charming drawing-room in the English style such as you find in a country cottage, the ceiling white-washed, raftered, the rather smart wallpaper and chintz curtains giving a snug effect in winter, you would imagine, and the whole very well furnished, copper and brass ornaments gleaming, and so on; but now it was a summer's evening, the long windows leading on to the lawns stood open; there was a great vase of delphiniums in the fireplace and the room was full of people. These people were standing about in tight little knots, clutching glasses and cigarettes, their eyes bulging, shiny, their mouths opening and shutting rhythmically, like ducks' bills, quack-quacking, yet no single voice rose above the steady boom like the noise of surf which engulfed you if you came and stood where she was standing in the doorway. The last reddish-gold rays of sunlight struck across the heads of the crowd, lighting on a face here, there, so that it hung for a second or two, disembodied, all aglow like a ripe orange, encircled in shifting coils of bright blue smoke, the surrounding faces receding into shadow.

There on the threshold, judging the moment to plunge in amongst the crowd but first seeking the whereabouts of the person whom she must find, who she knew was present, she could not but be aware of the picture she made, young, eager, in a frilly dress, because there was a mirror on the opposite wall, and yet to her surprise nobody turned to glance her way; indeed the eyes of those facing the door slid over her as if she were not there at all. Then, catching sight of the one she was to meet, in a far corner with his back towards her, she started across the room in his direction, only to discover, with a sensation of pique which soon gave place to dismay, that she might have been invisible for all the attention she received. She glided between the knots of people, who were all exceptionally fat or exceptionally tall, tugging at their elbows, brushing against them, treading on their toes, and not one of them greeted her, although some were faces out of the past that she knew well; each one remained planted in his spot, impervious to her struggling progress and even subtly—maliciously, she suspected—

294

hindering it. Whenever she caught a glimpse of *him*, his shoulders, the back of his head, she willed him with all her might to turn round, but he seemed to be engrossed in conversation, and the corner where he was standing was enveloped in shadows that deepened with every second.

Here in the centre of the room the crowd was much more dense, and panic-stricken she began, within the limits of convention, almost to fight her way through. In despair of reaching him before the light waned altogether, she tried to call to him across the sea of heads but her voice made no sound, or else it was lost in the din. Then, just as the clumps of people hemming her in disintegrated, about to re-form, just as she was about to seize the chance to break through, she saw him, whoever he was, in company with two or three others, step out of the long windows and move slowly away under the apple trees up the garden and out of sight. At that, forced to watch him escape her, disappearing before her very eyes into the green twilight under the trees, she cried out, a terrible cry which rang out over the whole room so that everybody turned to look her way; suddenly everybody was looking at her, their faces shiny, flat and round, identical, like rows of pennies turned towards her, and she awoke with that cry still ringing in her ears. But Larry was still asleep. She could have made no sound.

She lay quite still, her whole being flooded with that familiar sense of joy, a sensation so unbearably sweet that she almost welcomed the no less familiar one of pain that accompanied it, was mixed with it in the same proportions, each seeming to alleviate and sharpen the other, and blended, becoming one—the sense of irreparable loss. She lay not daring to move for fear that one or the other, the joy or the pain, should stab her to the heart, or equally, that either should diminish. She had but the one desire, to sleep and take up her dream again, and yet scarcely was it formed, that desire, no sooner recognised, than the dream, the joy and the pain alike, receded; happiness had slipped through her fingers once more, not to be recaptured. She was awake and the dream had gone.

So she was awake. It was better to be awake. Heavens, what a dream. Always the same. Was she never to meet him face to face, the one who held her fate in his hands, who would prove a rock of strength and in whose arms she would find—what? She had no idea what. Everything, she supposed. As to whether he was fair or dark—impossible to tell. It was always in shadow, that figure, although always recognisable, from a distance; she had never yet been permitted to approach. There are signs to be read in dreams, they say, and I believe that, said Milly to herself, because now that it was gone, the dream struck her as being very romantic and suiting her very well. So who could it be? Who, of all the men she had met—apart from Larry—had shoulders so broad and was so tall as to stand out in a crowd? Well, there's Abe, she thought, because certainly the description fitted him—the description, that is to say, as she described it—so it must be Abe. It was unlikely to be some stranger whom she had yet to encounter. After all, my dear, she told herself in her funny, callous way, you are thirty-three—but we are most definitely not going to dwell on *that* at three o'clock in the morning. If it is Abe—and really I think it must be —what are you worrying about? You'll see him to-day, this very day —and, well, soon it'll be Christmas, and anything may happen.

So now she lay in the dark, quite cosy and cheerful, going over in her mind all that the American woman had said, starting with that about Abe, and remembering with perfect clarity the words, she had an equally clear vision of those eyes, cool, cynical, amused; and the conviction grew upon her that she had been slow, very slow, in having failed to grasp the significance not only of the conversation but of the expression in those eyes, and she was angry with herself for having been so slow to arrive at the obvious conclusion, only arriving at it now, in, the dark, where it all became clear, all that the expression in the eyes, the tones of the voice, even the words, had been intended—yes, she would give her, the bitch, the benefit of the doubt—intended to convey, became clear as day. Far from being repelled by the picture which this notion conjured up, she allowed herself—and even experienced a certain pleasure in doing so—to dwell upon every detail of it, even down to the appearances of the figures involved, with the result that the whole composition, so vivid as to be disturbing and so disturbing as to be stimulating, became etched on her mind. Well, that was that, and there was nothing to be done about it now. She guessed that it was over and done with—the past was the past and the future, unless she were very much mistaken, hers.

Included amongst her many talents Milly possessed, when occasion demanded, the hardy and thoroughly masculine one for appreciating a situation and, within its limits and hers, acting upon it. At the jolt of a personal crisis—such crises being, generally speaking, the occasions which demanded and received her full attention and encouraged the fullest display of her talents—it was truly astonishing the way in which her mental machinery, however long submerged in the whirlpool of her own ego, could instantly be set in motion, move smoothly without any signs of rusting up, dealing as ruthlessly with her own vanity as with any other impediment, and making short work of the slippery weeds of sentiment—which tend to clog most feminine brains, whether still or in motion—as it performed its task. In this respect she was like one of those rather junior officers, a flighty young subaltern, say, who although irresponsible and not outstandingly gifted in any way, never-theless on the field of battle when the day is going badly, and if there is some question of a vital emergency, will rise to almost heroic heights so long as the situation is presented to him as such. Himself incapable of apprehending degrees of emergency, having not the faintest idea of any manœuvres or dispositions outside his own immediate area of operations, nor of the course of the battle, its probable outcome or even of its primary objective—and only the most hazy and romantic notion as to the nature of the war—he is, notwithstanding, unsurpassed when it comes to moving *his* tank, with *his* men in it, over minefields and under fire from point A to point B.

Milly was like that—but she was not so favourably placed; a woman, she had to operate not merely on her own account, but alone —not against the background of war, nor with the feather-bedding which the army provides. So, given this faculty for assessing a situation together with the knack (courage, in the case of the subaltern) of blinkering herself to all hazards both in prospect and in retrospect which she did not choose to see, she usually did manage to get from A to B, but with no omniscient staff to guide her the performance appeared less heroic than foolhardy; achieved in a series of blind leaps, like a frog jumping in the dark. As for points A and B, it must also be admitted that A was simply where she happened to be at the moment and B was where she wanted to be.

Still, the manner in which she made her preliminary appreciation was beyond reproach. Now, bypassing the emotional tangle with which a lesser woman would have become involved, with the minimum of delay she stopped thinking about Abe and thought about Coralie instead. Coralie was—and she, Milly, humbly admitted it—a lovely person from the top of her smooth head down to her elegant feet; nobody could feel shame at stepping into those shoes. Coralie, she was willing to bet, didn't have " housewife " on *her* passport. And Coralie had exquisite taste. She liked Abe and other attractive things —what was more, she had thought it worth her while to go out of her way to acquire them, and now she had them—or had had them. " But then," Milly said to herself, " so have I—exquisite taste, in that case." Indeed, it followed. " As to being *pretty*—she's not pretty at all— and she must be older than I am by at least a couple of years. So why shouldn't I? . . . " Why shouldn't she what? That was where the blinkers came in handy. There was no need to define what. Heavens, if nothing else, one thing stood out right under her nose. Everybody did it. " Everybody does it," she told herself, " so it's all right."

In no time, then, she had the situation where she wanted it, coaxed into perspective; her conscience itself with its sly habits under control;

her doubts, her fears, of whose existence she had been aware although they were of fluctuating significance—just as that young man in battle may be aware of the enemy's projectiles, the noise and the smell of the explosions, without on that account allowing himself to be deflected from his purpose—why, there they stood, at the bottom of the bed, there and there, but now they were no more substantial than the bogeys which frighten a child in the dark—she had merely to laugh them away. " Why, what a fool I've been! " She laughed to herself in the dark, and they melted away.

The next morning, taking the car, she went by herself to the NAAFI and after that she collected the bag which had to be stowed in on the back seat because there was no room in the boot, and then she went to pick up Larry and before noon they were on the road home.

Chapter Six

" CONTINUITY," said Mrs. Kovalski—it was a favourite word of her husband's, who was a university professor just recently appointed. " Continuity," she repeated after a pause, " is essential to—for—young people studying a foreign language . . . what I mean to say is . . . (what did she mean to say? Well, yes, she knew *that*) . . . they've missed a lesson here, a lesson there . . . and last week none at all . . . and for the whole of the past month not so that you could rely . . . so whilst we appreciate the excellent grounding . . . other arrangements . . . always a pleasure . . . still, one's got to think of the kids . . . that is, for the good of the children . . . which must be put first . . .naturally . . . exactly . . ." The young Kovalskis, listening through the keyhole whilst their mother sacked the English teacher—whom they quite liked but a scene was always welcome, just to vary the routine—looked at each other askance. Their mother must be losing her grip. She had had that speech off pat last night.

Mrs. Kovalski twisted her hands in her embarrassment. She did wish very much that the Bielska would say something—anything; also she wished that she herself were not still clad in her dressing-gown, a garment which lent her no confidence. She blamed the Bielska and the dressing-gown equally, the Bielska for having caused the situation and the dressing-gown for robbing her of the poise and firmness of manner which were usually hers when treating with paid employees of her household. Definitely there had been something wanting in the delivery of that speech, which had still to be concluded, she reminded herself. The fact was that all those ladylike but purposeful phrases, and dear knows she was justified in getting rid of the woman, had now run clean out of her head, and yet generally speaking she was never at a loss for words—indeed, prided herself on having a sharp edge to her tongue, no scruples in speaking her mind, and poise enough and to spare, never being forgetful of her social position which, quite apart from her husband's recent upgrading, was better than most, her father being manager of the State Grocery Shop. In her embarrassment she found herself, to her dismay, polishing up the wax fruit in the bowl, the apples and cherries and pears, on the sleeve of her dressing-gown, She went on doing it out of sheer nervousness. Polishing the cherries one by one, she remembered a day, long, long ago, a hot summer's evening it had been, before the war—why, she could smell it now, the dusty smell of the street, rotting strawberries and horse manure—and she and her mother had shut up shop and were sitting on chairs on the pavement to enjoy the cool and watch the world go by when a carriage had gone by, in it a lady wearing a hat with a bunch of cherries on it and beside her a younger lady, quite a girl, and her mother had clutched her arm and said: "Did you see? That was the Countess Bielska—and the daughter. My, she's no beauty—they'll have a job to get her off—though, mind you, I've heard tell there isn't a horsewoman in the whole of the country to match her." For almost a year now, the Bielska had been teaching the children, and ever since the first lesson Mrs. Kovalski had been careful not to forget the cup of coffee, and more than once had brought it herself on a tray with a paper napkin—and the monthly envelope had always been secreted under the shabby felt beret on the hall table; she knew she could never have brought herself to hand the envelope over personally, although her husband would have laughed her to scorn for having such silly bourgeois inhibitions. Never mind; there were still some things one could not do. Now she was just praying with all her heart that the ex-English teacher would look up from the open page at which she was staring so intently, shut her books, get up, say a few words to show there were no hard feelings—and—go.

Sophie did all these things in that order just then. "Well . . ." she smiled. "Of course . . . I quite understand." She held out her hand. But, surely, there were tears in her eyes? Yes, there were tears, Mrs. Kovalski decided, but what could one do? In the first place her husband was quite adamant . . . having heard tell of some strange story . . . and in his position, naturally . . . and then, this, not turning up for the lessons. That was what it boiled down to—before, always so punctual, now, for the last six weeks, one simply could not rely on the Bielska turning up.

Indeed, there were tears in Sophie's eyes and once out of the gate she brushed them away. But they had been there all morning and not on account of parting from the Kovalskis, because that had come as a surprise. No, but what dashed bad luck, not to have been able to say good-bye to Milly. Perhaps she had felt a teeny bit hurt about that —which was silly, of course. A week-end. The hours, the days, stretched ahead like a desert. Passing the hotel in the tram that morning she had not been able to resist staring up at its stony face, identifying those windows—strange, how overnight it should have changed character; passing that way again she had turned her head away rather than see it like that—empty. Anyway, Mrs. Kovalski had put a stop to such silliness. There was no time to feel hurt or lonely, now this had cropped up.

Really, she had to smile. Here at the terminus, naturally, to-day of all days, there was a tram waiting. To-day, when she could no more think of taking a tram than a droshky; that was life. So now, she thought, setting off on the long walk home, to break it to Singe, about the Gobelins. Why, even if you put your thinking cap on (Sophie's term for the severest imaginable flagellation of the human brain) you could never foresee the odd tricks life would be up to next. Who would ever have suspected that dumpy Mrs. Kovalski, whose greasy hairpins, like pressed spiders, one dreaded discovering between the leaves of an exercise book; of whose presence, even when she padded up behind one in carpet slippers, one was warned by the distinctive personal odour which preceded and announced her; who would ever have thought that *she* would turn out to be the instrument selected by fate to deal them, the Bielskis, this mortal blow? Because that it was a mortal blow, that is, a matter of the Gobelins, had been apparent to Sophie as soon as ever Mrs. Kovalski had begun to speak—indeed, as if that lady had said: " It's the Gobelins, I'm afraid; I'm truly sorry, Miss Bielska, but there's nothing for it—you must dispose of those tapestries which hang around your aunt's bed."

It was not Mrs. Kovalski's fault, poor thing. She could have had no idea that her words were to be interpreted thus any more than she could have known that she was halving their income with her clumsy little speech. Thanks were due to her, really. One must look at it like that. It would have had to happen sooner or later. It had happened now.

Singe would be sad, for sentimental reasons, and because one develops a special fondness for the walls which provide one's only privacy. The tapestries had enclosed her bed ever since they had taken over the attic; hanging inside out, partly in order to disguise their worth from the eyes of intruders, partly in order that Singe, lying there, might have the benefit of their faded, legendary beauty. She would miss them dreadfully, but that couldn't be helped. Ludovic—well, she, Sophie, would have to handle *him*—she knew how. She ought to, by now.

Of the three, only she knew what those shreds of canvas represented, assessed them at their true worth, which far exceeded their commercial value, although that was very great. What price was to be set on them? In terms of the future, they were priceless. What were they, to her? They were everything, almost; the last remaining security; an insurance policy realisable in case of emergency; a provision for the other two in the event of her own death; a private clinic instead of the State hospital for Singe; an old age pension for herself and her brother; ready funds in case of the necessity for bail or bribes—nowadays one

301

never knew what circumstances might arise and one must be prepared; even—and the idea had occurred to her more than once—it was only a question, so she had heard, of the manner of the approach, they might prove the key to freedom for them all. What were they, indeed? Rather, what were they not? the last rations, the last round of ammunition, the last hope and the last prayer between them and the besieging enemy at their gates.

Now, when she must lose them, she realised what a measure of comfort she had derived from their presence in the room; how, when making her aunt's bed, she would brush against these hangings tenderly, as if the figures depicted within were the living figures of friends; how, in conversation, she would stand fingering the rough-grained exterior, the canvas powdery with dust but still sturdily resisting the centuries, the final disintegration into dust; and how, sometimes, when she was tired or depressed, she would sit inside the tent herself and, switching on the light, gaze at the jostling procession. There they were, the riders, with hooded falcons on their wrists, their calm, pale faces all wearing the same satirical expression round the lips, their cold eyes beneath drooping lids seeming to regard her with mildly critical surprise; and she, in return, could not but criticise their horsemanship—unnaturally stiff atop their mounts, some appeared to be propped up in the saddle, others to be sliding off. I could give them a tip or two, she had often chuckled to herself: in particular to the lady with the long thin nose, dangling a scarlet flower in her hand, her long thin feet in blue satin slippers (most unsuitable, in Sophie's opinion) but not in the stirrups, so serve her right when she ran into the unicorn that lay in wait round the very next bush—but that she was not the kind of woman to take a word of warning you could tell at a glance.

Somehow, the longer you looked, the more you felt you were there with them. You could smell the October morning and the taste of it lingered on your tongue; it tasted of mist and smelt of the forest— not a breath of wind to rustle the leaves. And when you saw the spaniels frisking in the grass between the horses' hoofs—and how mettlesome they were, the horses, reined in but ready to be off—and the larks and eagles commingling in the upper air, a boar and a good deal of mixed game co-operatively displaying themselves in a not very thick thicket, why, then—your heart simply had to rise with joy because— because . . . *what a rare day that must have been for a hunt!* " Courage," she would whisper, her eyes flitting from one face to the next, enlisting them all in her support, the whole gallant procession: " Courage— the Devil is dead . . . and I still have *you*! "

So that was that. She began to step out faster because already she was late. Really, it was startling, the way in which with a sudden

302

change of circumstance one's whole viewpoint changed, even the most ordinary things appearing in a new light. She would never have realised, for instance, had it not been for Mrs. Kovalski, how convenient it was, that tram—although she had cursed it time and again—and how far it carried one for that really modest fare—and yet she had always reckoned the fare excessive, again because she had never fully appreciated until to-day the distance into town. A tram was coming up behind her at that moment. " What a splendid thing it is! " she murmured, stopping to admire it as it passed. It halted just ahead. " And look at the people—how proudly they mount! As if it were a chariot bound for Paradise. . . . Goodness, I'll never be able to get on a tram in the ordinary way again—it'll always give me a thrill after this. But walking is a pleasure, too, I suppose, and Singe, once she's used to it, I dare say, will come to like the horse-blanket almost as much as the Gobelins, because now she'll have to make do with that instead."

*   *   *

" Roses! " exclaimed Miss Raven, stepping into the salon. " Fancy that."

" Rote Rosen! " Gisela heaved a sentimental sigh, snapping off the stalks. " Rot, für die Liebe. Lo-o-ove," she explained, eyeing Miss Raven sardonically as the latter approached.

Miss Raven sniffed. " I understood you the first time," she said coldly, picking up the card that went with the flowers.

" Herr Schulman," said Gisela, as the card was tucked into an envelope and Miss Raven seemed to be hesitating. " Schön, nicht? " She began working on the petals, turning them inside out, as she touched each petal chanting under her breath: " Er lieb mich—vom Herzen—mit Schmerzen—oder—ach, Pech! Noch eine! Los. Er liebt mich—vom Herzen . . ." Darting a sly look at Miss Raven, who was watching her in astonishment, Gisela giggled. Miss Raven had never seen the girl so cheerful. In the ordinary way this would have irritated her beyond measure, but not to-day; she was feeling pretty cheerful herself. The week-end was over and in an hour—or less—he would be back.

" Y'know," Gisela began softly, her head on one side to examine the effect of her vase or, equally, of her words on Miss Raven: " I zink . . . Herr Schulman . . . lo-o-ove . . ."

" Love? " said Miss Raven vaguely, as the word, like a homing pigeon, flew in to nestle amongst her thoughts. " Love? "

Gisela nodded, indicating the card and then the flowers. " Lo-o-ove . . ." she grinned, " Frau Purdoe."

" Tst . . . you silly girl! " Miss Raven snorted. But something in those mischievous eyes made her pause; very bright, they held her own. " Why? " she went on, articulating clearly. " Why do you think that? "

Her shoulders shaking with laughter, Gisela brushed together the stalks and leaves.

" I *zink* not . . ." she murmured. Suddenly she leaned over the flowers, thrusting her face close to Miss Raven's own. " I zink not . . . I *know*! " She nodded several times. " I also . . ." she went on in her teasing sing-song voice, " *I* also . . . lo-o-ove . . . I—have—ma-a-an . . ."

" *Man*? " Miss Raven recoiled. " What d'you mean? "

At sight of the expression on her face, Gisela burst out laughing. " Las' night . . ." she drawled, rolling her eyes.

" You disgusting little . . ." Miss Raven took a quick step round the table. Before she knew it she had grasped the girl's shoulder; it felt sharp and brittle as a chicken-bone under her hand. The blood was pounding in her ears. " How *dare* you . . . how dare you . . ." She dug her nails in. " Where? . . . Go on, tell me that, *where*? " Gisela wriggled away.

" Here . . ." she cooed, " here, naturally . . . in hotel . . ."

" I shall tell Mrs. Purdoe." Miss Raven could hear her own voice, shrill, harsh, horrible—she might even be shouting, but she couldn't help that. " I shall tell her the moment she gets back . . . understand? " She stood away, panting. Suddenly, catching sight of the lashes fluttering over the periwinkle-blue eyes, the thin lips twitching, she knew that the girl had been making a fool of her.

" Who? " she asked quietly.

Gisela bubbled over with merriment. " *Nice* man. Porter—downstairs. See." She stretched out her hand, encircling the ring finger with a rose leaf to make matters perfectly clear. " *Verlobt*. Las' night."

So that was it. No need to have blown up like that. The girl's got a boy, that's all—she wasn't getting at *you* . . . as though she could possibly be interested, let alone guess . . .

" Oh, the *porter*," said Miss Raven and, unwisely, she smiled. Gisela shot her a wicked look.

" He is—ma-a-an . . ." she murmured.

" I hope you will be very happy." With dignity Miss Raven picked up the mending basket, which was what she had come for in the first place, and was half-way to the door when Gisela called out: " Fräulein Nanny! I forget . . ." She was swaying with laughter over the flowers. " Ach . . . I laugh . . ." she put her hand to her heart: " You want know somezing? "

304

" No," said Miss Raven, stopping in her tracks.

" Komm' . . . Komm' mal her . . . Picnic . . . Also! Herr Schulman . . ." Gisela formed her lips into the shape of a kiss and smacked them, waving at the flowers. " Frau Purdoe! Is true," she added softly, awkwardly, almost. She had stopped laughing.

Miss Raven was standing stock still, staring at the roses as if she had never seen them until that moment; as if she were seeing them, these roses, or whatever it was that she saw, for the first time.

" Is *true*," whispered Gisela in her ear. " No kidding." Peeping into Miss Raven's face, she uttered a little cry of alarm and fled from the room.

* * *

" It's interesting," said Singe. " Before, it was like being in bed in a museum . . . very comme il faut, but a bit . . . chilly . . . even my dreams were *correct*. Now it is like a stable . . . very cosy. I dare say we Slavonians are more at home in a stable, that's why. Did you know, Sophie, this blanket—which of course you have washed many times—still smells of *horse*? "

" Does it? " Sophie looked up, frowning. She was totting up figures. She had been totting up figures for the past two days. " Ah, *that* one. Well, I expect it does. It was Beorut's blanket, the darling, and he was a *very* powerful horse."

" Oh, that's quite another matter, then," said Singe, settling in, like an Arab, and surrounding herself with bits of felt. " If it was *Beorut's*, I don't mind. One just prefers to know where things come from, that's all. It's Father Joseph I'm worried about. He may think . . ." she faltered.

" What? "

" Well, those fleshy-nosed men, funnily enough, not like eyes or ears, you know, Sophie, have a specially keen sense of smell . . . and what I'm afraid of is he may think—from the smell, you know—that we've come down in the world."

" Really, Singe, if that's all that bothers you, you've only to keep him at a distance. There's no need to ask him in to bed with you."

" Sophie! " Singe giggled. " The idea! Though I remember "— she stopped her snipping—" when he was a young man . . . before, naturally, he became . . . well, he had the post of tutor one summer . . . not so far off, and I must admit, all of us girls . . ." she sighed. " When you look back, you'll discover this . . . it's strange, when it's so long ago, you can't remember the kiss, nor even whether there was a kiss . . . but I do remember the smell of hay and the lights on the drive and that it was Midsummer's Night, and his eyes . . . black, very

305

bright black eyes . . . I believe there was a kiss, now I come to think of it."

" So, Singe." Sophie got up. " That's what's between you and Father Joseph. I've often wondered."

" Don't tease me, darling. I mean, it's strange how *regulated* life is. If I did kiss him, it was my first kiss. But if it was my first . . . it's strange, I mean, how *few* people there are in one's life, and those one returns to again and again—not that you want to, perhaps, and not even the people you expect—but there they are, to the very end. Of course, I don't mean *men*—or only by the by. But it just so turns out . . ." She began snipping again, so that her words were scarcely to be heard. " He'll probably be the last."

." The last to kiss you? You stupid little aunt—what thoughts you have." Sophie threw herself on her knees in front of the bed. " Listen. With this money—we might even . . ." Her eyes sparkled. " All three of us. What d'you say to that? It's only a question of "—she dropped her voice in homage to the password—" dollars."

" I couldn't," said Singe.

" You mean you wouldn't? "

" Darling, what does it matter? I couldn't and I wouldn't. But— if you feel like that—*you*, Sophie, must."

" Not without you." She sprang to her feet and began moodily pacing up and down. " It would be nothing without you. It's all three or nothing. Understand? "

" Have you *got* it yet, darling? The——? "

" Not yet. This evening. In a little while. You see," she said rather grandly, " he had to examine them. It's not just a matter of twopence halfpenny, after all."

" Be *hard*, Sophie—be very *hard*."

" Hard? What do you take me for, a fool? I'll be hard like nothing on earth—except that he's an honest fellow, you know—remembers us all. Now I must go because I see it's later than I thought." She scrambled into the leather jerkin and smashed the beret on her head. " Hm . . . it's risky, carrying large sums in the street. Then the question is, where to hide it? It must be hidden very safely somewhere. Only I mustn't tell you where . . ." She looked around the room, knitting her brows, concentrating as only she knew how.

" The loose floorboard," suggested her aunt. " It's the only suitable place."

" Really, Singe," Sophie turned on her, " I shall get ratty, I warn you . . . please try and co-operate . . . I'd just that second thought of it and now I'll have to think of somewhere else . . ."

" Ssssh! "

Whistling, Sophie adjusted her beret in front of the glass as Ludovic came into the room. He mumbled good evening to his aunt. At sight of his sister he stopped short.

"Do you want supper?" said Sophie politely. "It will be a little late because I have to go out." Frowning, she dabbed powder on her nose, then turned round. "Well?"

He had come up behind her. He was smiling in a way she didn't like.

"Of course I know you have to go out. Frankly, I didn't expect to find you here. I was looking forward to one of those tête-à-tête suppers with Singe."

"What do you mean, Ludo?" Her brown eyes had become quite black with anger. "How do you mean—you *knew* I would be going out?"

"Mean? Nothing, my dear. Except that they are back, aren't they? Your benefactors, employers . . . whatever they are?"

"Back?"

"Yes, back." He shrugged. "At least, I saw their car in the street outside the Grand a couple of hours ago. Madame never sent to inform you? Tiens! Perhaps—who knows?—they hoped to have a free evening just for once—en famille—without you, eh, Sophie?"

"Ludo," said his aunt in a clear high voice, sitting up straight and scattering her felt scraps on the floor, "go into your room. I shall call you when supper is ready."

Surprisingly, he went.

Sophie bent to kiss her aunt. "I must hurry now, darling. He's a nice old chap but he won't wait all night. I'll be back in a jiffy. I won't go and see *them*, I promise. All the same," she smiled unhappily, "I might just give her a coup de téléphone."

When the door closed her aunt sighed and bent to pick up the pieces of felt. It scarcely seemed worth going on, sometimes. She had once more reached that crucial stage between finishing one doll and starting the next. Nevertheless, she went on, and started the next.

*   *   *

"I will go along Minska Street, although it's a little out of my way . . . snowing again, dash it. Never mind, the walk will do me good . . . there's a telephone booth at the end of Minska Street, so this will be a kind of test to prove how strong-minded I am. Then straight to his shop and straight back by the short way . . . there it is, the booth! Already? Heavens, how quickly I've come. Ha, there's a light—it's occupied. Well, that's all to the good perhaps, although I know that I could have passed it. I have that much will-power, I should hope.

307

Still, better walk on the opposite side, just in case. . . . How it glows, so warm and friendly. . . . Stay in, my good fellow, that's right, I shan't disturb you—go on chattering for as long as you please. Ah, but look! —he's come out. Drat him! He'll go back . . . no, he's going off. What an excellent notion that was to come over on this side, now I'll not take the trouble to cross . . . certainly *not*. Besides, I haven't time. . . . It's a test, my dear, and you're doing splendidly . . . don't look yet . . . you haven't passed it yet—*don't look!*—ah, what did I tell you? I'm sorry, Sophie," said Sophie to herself, " it was too much to ask of me," and crossed over the street to the telephone.

*   *   *

" Oh, lord," said Milly, " who on earth can that be? Abe, another drink? Pour us all some more, be an angel. It's only Sophie, I expect. Be *quiet*, children, I can't hear myself speak. Hallo? "

Sophie heard music and laughter before she heard that voice.

Milly put her hand over the receiver. " Turn that thing down a bit. Hallo? Sophie? I guessed it was you." She made a little grimace. " Yes, of course we're back . . . oh, early . . . about tea-time . . ."

(All that time ago, whilst she had been picturing them on the road. How could she not have known—she had thought she must surely feel it in her heart the moment they arrived. The music, what was it? A gramophone? How gay—it sounded almost like a party. She could hear the children's voices, the dears. How happy they all were. Now, if Milly asked her to come round—well, she must refuse. What an intrusion it would be—Milly was like that, too kind, and one mustn't take advantage—so she would refuse—oh, *definitely*.)

" Mmm . . . heavenly . . . one mad rush, of course . . . we're worn out . . . no, *no*, fit as fiddles . . . just worn to a frazzle . . . oh, *no*, my dear, just too many parties, that's all . . . one after another . . . oh, *thoroughly*, of course, quite wonderful . . . dear old Grusnov seems as quiet as the grave after all that . . . I'll tell you all about it when I see you . . ."

(Oh, now you must be strong—Sophie, be strong! You *can't* go, d'you hear? You must refuse . . . but I could just manage to slip along for a couple of minutes, couldn't I? Just to greet them? Why not?)

" News? . . . No, I don't think any at all . . . oh, yes, there is! Apparently there's some idea that we *might*—it's not by any means certain, but it's on the cards—that we might be moved up there . . . Where? To Slavnik, of course . . . yes, permanently . . . what's the matter?—you sound funny . . . goodness no, I wouldn't mind . . . might be rather fun . . . (Larry, do come and get rid of her for me . . .

308

she's just babbling on . . . sounds a bit off-net, actually . . . oh, all *right*, meany). . . . well, Sophie, my sweet, I'll tell you all about it when you . . ."

(No. But only a couple of minutes, mind. Just dash in to say hallo and dash out.)

"When am I going to see you? . . . (Clarissa, will you be quiet?) How about to-morrow? Tea-time . . . wonderful . . . sweet of you to ring up . . . anything special? All right . . . fine . . . to-morrow it is . . . 'Bye . . ."

Milly put down the receiver. "Phew! Talk about the hind leg off a donkey. Now, what *is* it, Clarissa?"

"Was it Sophie, Mummy? I haven't seen her for two whole days, and I wanted to speak to her *badly*."

"Oh, sorry . . . I didn't understand. You were quite welcome to, I assure you," she said dryly. "Anyway, you'll see her to-morrow. Now for my drink—I've earned it."

"What did she want?" Larry gave her the glass.

"Oh, heavens, nothing at all . . . just wanted to pass the time of day, you know what she is. I must say I'd hoped to give her the slip just for this one evening. Abe, those roses are absolute heaven. Did I say thank you?"

"I don't recall—did you?"

"Well, I'm saying it now." She smiled at him across the room. "In a way, it's wonderful to be back." She bent and dropped a kiss on the top of her daughter's head and Clarissa looked up in astonishment. "Like your present, darling?"

"Mm." She was squatting on the floor over her present, a box of glass toadstools, each nestling in a compartment lined with tissue paper. She fondled them lovingly. They were of the type *Amanita muscaria*, the fairy-tale ones, red with white spots. "I knew Daddy would bring me these," she said, her eyes shining up at her mother. "They're just what I wanted."

"I don't see how you could have *wanted* them, Clarissa," said Milly with an edge to her voice. "You didn't even know there were such things."

"Oh, yes, I did. I—I *dreamed* them," said Clarissa, hastily retrenching in territory unencroachable even by her mother. "A Christmas tree"—she dug herself in properly while she was about it —"all covered with them, that's what I dreamed."

"A slight case for Freud, I should say," murmured Larry.

"I didn't dream my snowman," said Dermot. "I couldn't of."

"Darling." Milly stroked her son's hair. "Of course not."

Clarissa flushed. Still her ammunition was by no means exhausted.

'It was you chose our presents, wasn't it, Daddy?" she persisted, with a loving smile for her father. Abe, over by the drinks, gave a little snort, or cough, and Milly looked across.

"While you were about it, Larry, I wish you could have found something for Sophie."

"As a matter of fact, I did . . . just a bit of nonsense. You give it her to-morrow."

"Darling, you are angelic, you think of everything. I couldn't see anything to buy, else I would have . . . all those little squatter huts in a mass of rubble . . ."

"There was a market and I just happened to stumble on it . . . it's time you brats were in bed . . . where's Miss Raven?"

Both children eyed each other and began to giggle.

"She's been hanging up her present." Clarissa choked, scarlet in the face. "She's hung it on her looking-glass." She caught her brother's eye again and they both dissolved into giggles.

"So Miss Raven's got a present too, has she?" Milly's eyebrows were raised. "You've really excelled yourself, darling. And what was it?"

"A—a fairy doll," Larry grinned at Abe. "Most suitable, I thought."

"Oh, she likes it *very* much," said Clarissa gravely. "Dermot saw " —she gulped—" saw her *kissing* it."

"Good God," said her father. "Fancy that."

"Just fancy," said Milly, giving him a curious look.

"Oh, she's always kissing *me*," boasted Dermot, adding complacently, " she seems to like it. She doesn't kiss Clarissa at all."

"Because she knows I *don't* like it," retorted Clarissa. "Kissing's soppy, *I* think."

"You don't know what you're talking about," said her mother snappishly, and both men laughed.

* * *

Sophie's business took a little while to settle. When she arrived home her aunt and her brother were finishing their supper. She put her satchel down by the foot of her bed, took off her gum-boots and then she came to the table.

"Ah, my dear—so there you are," said Ludovic. She saw at once that for some reason he was now in the highest of spirits. " We have a real treat for supper to-night—you'll never guess what . . . look, we have kept some specially for you—delicious sprats. This bread, too, that's something special . . . excellent in this state, good for the teeth and the jaw muscles . . . bread, to be at its best, must be at least a week old. And cheese—let me give you some . . . ah, what can compare with our pure Slavonian cheese—what's this, by the way—pure goat or pure sheep? Who would wish for Emmentaler or Camembert—or Stilton? Remember Miss Brownlow, how she adored her Stilton? Pah! Let them keep their foreign cheeses—give me the present cheese of our country! See—even a nice black thumbmark. That shows it's authentic! "

"Butter, please," said Sophie.

"You saw them, then, your friends? No? Funny, I guessed it somehow from your face. But after a long trip, you know how it is . . . I dare say they were tired and they have probably been—what is the expression?—burning the candle at both ends." He tittered. " Poor things—it must seem quiet as the grave to be back here."

Sophie glanced at him. She decided that this was a shot in the dark, a coincidence, merely; he was naturally gifted that way.

"If you want to smoke, Ludo, you should go away from the table," said Singe. " Sophie is eating."

"My dears," he got up, folding his napkin. " I am going, almost at once. I have an appointment."

He strolled round the room, finishing his cigarette, eventually and apparently inadvertently, coming up against the blanket which hung round Singe's bed. Singe cast Sophie a warning look. Ludovic paused, standing in front of it in an attitude of exaggerated admiration.

"Mais comme c'est élégant! " he exclaimed at last. " N'est-ce pas, Singe—tes nouveaux rideaux? Vraiment, ma soeur," he turned to Sophie, who, with her head bent, went on eating, " c'est une idée merveilleuse . . . tout à fait d'avant-garde—joli, pratique—en même temps," he giggled, sniffing, " nostalgique! Est-ce que je sens "—he sniffed vigorously—"ah oui, un parfum exquis, raffiné . . . de?—de?—c'est ça—une forte odeur de—tu te souviens de Stendhal?—enfin, de cheval? Hmm . . . tu aurais dû devenir interior decorator, Sophie . . . dommage, mais enfin tu as encore le temps." With a dazzling smile for both his relations, he approached the table, murmuring, as he passed by Sophie's chair, " Déjà vendus, les autres? "

Sophie went on cutting up her bread into small pieces. She made no reply.

"Tell me "—his very pale green eyes roved over her—" tell me, Sophie, you got a good price? "

She looked up. " I got a good price," she said quietly.

"Alors, c'est très bien. I only ask—because somehow I don't see you as a commerçante." He stood there, examining his nails, humming under his breath. " Tara-ra-ra . . . madame la Marquise . . . tara-ra-ra . . . tout va très bien—tout va très bien . . ." He finished with a flourish,

311

rapping on the table with his knuckles, then remained where he was, staring down at her with a smile.

"Well." She pushed her plate away. "Let's have it. What's worrying you, Ludovic?"

"What's?—ah, Sophie, but how quick you are, there's no concealing anything from you. Tst—well, to be frank, there is a small point that bothers me. On whose authority did you dispose of those—enfin, those miserable bits of canvas?"

"On my own," she said sharply. "They were mine to sell."

"Ah, come now, Sophie."

"It's true, Ludo!" His aunt was crouched in her chair, her eyes fixed on him, and for once her voice was shrill. "Your father told me before he—why, we all know that—that they were Sophie's . . . not mine—not yours . . . *Sophie's*!"

"Sssh! . . . Tante Singe . . . ssh! Don't upset yourself . . ." He spread his hands. "I am not disputing *that*. Oh, no, it is just a tiny point of law that troubles me." He sat down and took out his cigarette case and lit a cigarette, then went on with mock pomposity, "Now I have this job, I have to understand the new laws . . . and, well, I am afraid that our poor Sophie may have got herself into a terrible mess. You see, by *law*, ma chère Singe, *present* law, that is—those *things*, dirty old things they were too and I for one never liked them—horribly old as they are, cannot and do not belong either to her or to me or to any private person. You understand, Singe? Sophie understands, don't you, my dear?"

Sophie got up from the table, and Ludovic got up, too, at once. She still stood above him, and he moved a step back.

"Sophie, I didn't mean——"

"Shut up, please." Her voice was low and clear, without a trace of expression. "Now *I* am going to speak. We will forget the subject of the Gobelins for the minute. Don't worry," she added with a direct look at her brother. "I shall return to it later. So, Singe, Ludo, please listen." She began pacing up and down, as her custom was. Suddenly she stopped in her tracks, and turned to face them both, her head high and, to their astonishment, a smile on her lips. "I have decided," she announced, "to give a party."

"A *party*?" Stunned, Ludovic looked at his sister as if she were out of her mind.

Unperturbed, she nodded. "To-morrow."

"Sophie, darling!—but—but what *sort* of party?"

For a moment Sophie seemed taken aback. "Why—I . . . I don't know." She smiled at Singe, then went on breathlessly, "A party—in the old style, I thought . . . let me see now . . ." Frowning, she strode up and down. " Music and dancing and plenty to drink—oh, Tante Singe, it *would* be possible! " She moved swiftly to her aunt and kneeling beside her, caught her hand. " We will have some hens roasted at the bakery, cut up cold, with what—you remember?—Sauce Tartare, eh? And I know where to get export vodka—and we will make a huge potato salad in the old way, if you still have the recipe? "

" Yes, oh, yes." The old lady giggled. " Of course I have it. And I can ask Father Joseph and the Reverend Mother? "

" Darling, the Cardinal himself—only I fear he will be unavoidably detained . . ."

" And the British? " suggested her brother. " You are asking the British, Sophie? "

" The British? " Sophie turned to look at him, then threw back her head and laughed merrily. " Why, Ludo—you say *I* am quick— I am sorry I cannot say the same for you. Have you missed the point? Who do you think it's for, the party? Why, it's *in honour* of them— the British." Then turning back to her aunt, she rattled on: " And we will have canapkis, all sorts, roast eels and a stuffed fish, perhaps a hare or two—and—why not?—Hunter's Stew? If you have the recipe, Singe . . . it all depends on you."

" Naturally I have the recipe, darling, but there is no time for Hunter's Stew—it takes four or five days to prepare . . ."

" This is an emergency stew," said Sophie inexorably. " It will have precisely twelve hours to prepare. Don't worry—it'll respond. Then —for the dancing we have the gramophone and the records——"

" *My* gramophone," murmured Ludovic, " *my* records."

Sophie said, over her shoulder, " If you don't mind, Ludo, I will attend to all that in just a minute. As I was saying, Singe, for the dancing we have the gramophone and the records . . . and then songs, perhaps. What about it? Just for one evening . . . like old times? " her soft brown eyes shone. Her brother had come up behind her; he stood looking down at them both. His eyes, thought Singe, were cold as stones.

" I have to go out, Sophie. You had something else you wished to say, I think? "

She sprang to her feet. " Quite right, I have. Is *he* "—she jerked her head—" in the bathroom? "

" I don't know . . . no, I don't think so." A shadow of alarm flickered over Ludovic's face. " Why? "

" All right. In that case, I suggest we go next door, you and I." Swiftly she crossed the room and stood waiting at the doorway for him to follow. " Excuse us, Singe," she winked at her aunt behind his back as he passed through. " It's better you don't hear."

"Now," she said to her brother, stepping into his room and closing the door behind her, "how much do you want?"

*   *   *

Later that same evening Kazimierz, the porter, on duty at the reception desk in the hall of the Grand Hotel, finished writing up in the book provided for that purpose all the comings and goings he had witnessed that day, blotted the page and locked the book away. He had taken rather longer over his task than usual, partly on account of his hangover from the night before, which was only now beginning to lift, and partly because Gisela, in a free and easy manner that he privately considered unbecoming, was hanging around his desk. It occurred to him, and a very disturbing thought it was, that the liberties Gisela was taking with his time were not unconnected with certain liberties he had himself taken the night before—which he remembered, more or less hazily, but as to whether or not he had committed any verbal indiscretion as well? He was beginning to have his suspicions. He knew himself, unfortunately, and not for the first time he cursed the elixir of his country, export brand; his head ached like mad and he longed for a beer.

He looked at her worriedly. There was certainly something rather sinister—proprietary, almost—in the way she was hanging about him. Any other night he would have had no scruples in telling her to be off, but to-night he didn't feel up to it. No harm in probing about a bit, and finding out just what he had let slip, if anything. She had dolled herself up, too . . . she wasn't bad; no, she wasn't bad at all. That's got nothing to do with it, he told himself sternly—just you keep your eye on the ball.

"So you see, Gisi," he continued their desultory conversation, "there's no *future* in the provinces. Here am I, stuck in this dump, where you only get a handful of foreign permanents with about as much temperament as mice in a cage, and not worth the trouble, in my opinion—it's all routine, sheer routine, and I was never one for that."

"Naturally not," said Gisela, "you're a man of action, that sticks out a mile."

"In Slavnik, now, there are bigger hotels, foreigners galore and bags of opportunity . . . so," he added dreamily, "I might try for a transfer when all this is over."

"A transfer?" Gisela fluttered her lashes. "But I'm all for that, too, Kazimierz . . . after we're . . . you know . . ."

The porter made no reply; he simply rattled his pen over his teeth. So that's what he'd said last night. The trouble was he needed her, blast it. Not in *that* way, anyone would do for that—but much more specifically, her. No one else. Until this affair was settled, anyway.

"When were you thinking of going?" she said.

"When? Oh, nothing definite . . . it's by no means definite . . . hm . . ." He turned his back, ostensibly to check the pigeonholes, flicking the keys hanging on the hooks, just to show that he *was* on duty and by the time he turned round he hoped to find her gone. Not a bit of it. She was leaning farther across the desk.

"I was thinking about arrangements," she whispered coyly. "After last night—we'll have to be making arrangements, won't we?"

"Arrangements?" he murmured, with his finger easing his collar round his neck. With the movement, he could feel that his shirt was sticking to his armpits, too. "Arrangements? Ah, what a business they are, to be sure. But you know . . . things have a way of arranging themselves . . . in time, all depending . . ."

"Depending?"

She certainly knew how to make the most of herself, and like this she was at her most appealing—all eyes, lower lip quivering. Still, he did hope she wasn't going to make a scene, but at that moment he noticed that the hatch between the office and the hall had slid open. The housekeeper sat in there in the evenings and if bored this was what she did; she slid open the hatch. Reinforced, he said briskly:

"Oh, very much so, Gisi. Depending, of course. Hmm." He coughed. "A little cash, a little hope, a little time—and who knows?"

"You see," she smiled shyly, "I'm ordering the dress."

"A dress? That'll be nice. What colour?"

"White, of course. It must be white."

"Ah?" In his tone amusement and tolerance were nicely blended to show that a man of action could not be expected to follow the reasonings of the feminine mind; or, at the very least, to make it clear that he simply did not connect. Gisela tried again.

"The dressmaker is very busy, but I said it was urgent. You see, it's only a few weeks to Lent."

"So it is . . . how time rushes on. No sooner New Year than it's Lent," he agreed, and too late, cursed himself for a fool.

"Well," she said quickly, "New Year, then? What about it? That's a nice time. Darling," she murmured, giving him the Marlene Dietrich smile that was like evipan, almost, in its effect. The porter winced, struggled, and would have gone under had he not caught sight of the housekeeper's face looming through the hatch. Once again he blessed the old cow. Fancy, a little thing like Gisi, an orphan, no background, nothing to offer, all of a sudden to be so presumptuous, so brazen! Still, he risked stretching out his hand to pat her cheek.

She was a pretty little piece, if only she wouldn't keep trying to pin him down. She must learn that a man of vision and enterprise was not to be pinned down—at least, not until he was caught.

" We'll see, Gisi, we'll see . . . hmmm . . . what the New Year will bring. Hey, look who's come in! " The distraction was surely heaven sent. " Poor old Vladek! I say, what a load. You ought to be running along now, what do you think? "

" Yes." Gisela watched Vladek dragging the sack over the carpet and up the stairs. The hatch had slid farther open, too. " I'll go and wash up the dinner things," she said, " and then perhaps I'll come back. I might even have something for you . . . something you like. You'll be free in a little while? "

" I'm always free for you, Gisi," the porter responded gallantly. When she had gone he unlocked the drawer and once more took out his book. It was tedious, this routine, just when he thought he had finished. Heaving a sigh at his lot, he added a postscript to his record of the day's events.

*　　　*　　　*

On going into the kitchen, Gisela was startled to find the light on and her mistress sitting at the table, her large crocodile handbag on the floor beside her, two or three exercise books, or account books they might be, spread in front of her. She was chewing a pencil, deeply absorbed, and for a second did not even glance up.

" Gnädige Frau? "

Then she looked up, but with such a bright, charming smile that Gisela instantly thought, now what? In view of the dinner things, stacked in the bath, yet to be attended to—puzzled, she took down her apron from the back of the door and tied it round her, instinctively feeling in the pocket for the key of the store cupboard. Yes, still there —foolish of her to have left it in the pocket—but then the gnädige Frau would never——

" Well, Gisela . . ." She seemed very nice, still smiling, reaching down into her bag for her cigarette case.

" Well, gnädige Frau . . . I'm sorry about the washing up . . . but I had to slip out for a minute . . ."

" That's all right . . . of course. Cigarette? I hear that we are to congratulate you? "

" Oh, gnädige Frau . . ."

" No, it's splendid . . . why, you're blushing! I'm sure you'll be very happy." She's certainly tarted herself up, thought Milly, not displeased to note that Gisela was one of those girls who are prettier in uniform than out of it. " When is it going to be, the wedding? "

" Soon . . . I don't—don't know yet."

" And who is the lucky man? "

" The porter," said Gisela, rather subdued. She was puzzled by her employer's manner.

" One of the porters? Very nice," she pronounced, meaning, very suitable. A porter? Vaguely she considered men in striped jackets who carried luggage, or the funny little gnomes who danced up and down the corridors in felt slippers. Of course there was also the night porter—horrible old man; no, it couldn't be that one. Whoever it was, she wasn't much interested, really—it was none of her business.

" You must let us know what you would like for a wedding present," she went on. " Think it over . . . perhaps we might order something . . ." Her smile seemed to tighten just a fraction, Gisela noticed, watching her intently. " Well, and so how has everything been going? "

" Everything went fine, gnädige Frau. I cooked my best . . . die Nanny, she has complained? "

" I'm sure you did. Of course she has'nt complained."

" And—everything else," Gisela went on with diffidence, carefully choosing her words, " well, that has all been arranged."

" I see. That's good. All squared up, is it? "

" Oh, yes. You would like to "—she fingered the key in her apron pocket—" you prefer to check the—cupboard? We do it now, yes? "

" No," said Milly, " don't let's bother—there's no point in doing it now . . ." There was no point, in fact, because she had just finished checking the remaining contents of the cupboard before the girl came in. I'm glad, she thought to herself, that I put the key back in her pocket—it was the tactful thing to do. Otherwise she might have been offended, and I don't want her to be offended. Still, I had to check, didn't I? I had to know. And it was quite expensive, that lace. Quite. But then it was expensive lace.

" Besides," she went on, flicking open her notebooks again, " I've got rather a lot to do, Gisela, and I was wondering if you would help me—that is, if you are not tired? "

" Tired? " She stared in amazement. The English, she thought, they're crazy. There's just no knowing with them. " I'm never tired, gnädige Frau." She laughed. Then, eagerly: " What do you wish me to do? Unpack? " She gestured to where the sack that Vladek had carried up lay sprawling behind the door.

" No," said Milly, rather shortly. " No. Not to-night." Then, remembering that she couldn't afford to be short with her, smiled. " Cigarette? Oh, you've got one. First of all, I thought we'd have a little . . . er . . . talk."

317

"Ah." At last Gisela was beginning to understand. "One minute." She tiptoed to the door into the passage and opened it abruptly. Then she closed it. "All right."

"Hadn't you better—sit down?"

She shook her head. "No, it would look funny." She perched herself on the edge of the bath.

"First of all," Milly began calmly, "I've decided to have that tea service. Remember?"

"The——? Oh, yes, of course I remember." Stunned, she was thinking, but this is too good to be true . . . be careful, Gisi, be careful, now.

"It's a bargain, as you said—and I've thought it over. I think we can manage it, but of course we must work it out. I thought we'd do that now."

"Yes," said Gisela, who, having got over the shock, was thinking very fast. What was it due to, this sudden change of tactics, this new approach? In its objectivity it surpassed even that of the dear departed, Mrs. Simpson, and she herself was all for encouraging it—but, on the other hand, might there not be some other reason behind it? Might it not be a trap? She had to decide quickly, now, at once, using her judgment—and in doing so she took into account everything that she had learned from experience about the British. She was well aware of the stumbling-block, the trait inherent in her own race which often led to defective judgment, the propensity to be over-suspicious, to credit this particular brand of foreigner with ulterior designs when in fact none existed; if they existed they were not usually concealed cleverly, and very often not concealed at all. How often she had shaken her head over the British—intrigue, conspiracy, these being the breath of life to her; no, she had had ample proof in the past that they were not the stuff of which conspirators are made. So, she decided, it was very probably nothing of the kind.

"You see, Gisela"—her mistress held out the exercise book to show her—"I've arranged it all in four columns. Another cigarette? Yes, well—now look. Here's the stock, we'll say, on the left. Then this next column shows the actual—I mean, the NAAFI price, per kilo, bottle and so on, and the *third* column I've headed, as you see, G." She smiled brightly. "G stands for Gisela—meaning, Gisela's price. And the fourth column is the difference between the two. That's clear, isn't it?"

"Yes," said Gisela cautiously. Indeed, it was clear; formidably so. Herself, she was trying to keep from smiling, having glanced at the clock on the wall. It said two minutes to midnight. "So that's it," she told herself. "It's happened. My luck's changed. This was my unlucky day and to-morrow, too—but now, at midnight, it's changed. When that happens—it's very rare, but it can happen—I must look it up in the book—it's a sign of unusual good fortune and of great events. Well, fancy it happening to me. But I think it has. It looks very much like it."

"So here at the top," Milly went on briskly, "we'll write down" —*our* target, she had been going to say, but it wasn't "our," exactly, was it?—and "my" sounded crude—"what was it he wanted for that tea service?"

They giggled, heads together, like a couple of sisters, checking the noughts which rambled across the page.

"And now," said Milly, "we'll just fill in your column. You sit over there on the bath and I'll read out the items, one by one, and you tell me what you can get for each. I've arranged it all in alphabetical order, so it won't take long. Right? Off we go. Hm . . . A . . . A is for . . . where are we, wait a second . . ." she shuffled amongst her papers, "yes, here we are. A is for Aspirin, per bottle of 100 tablets . . . Gisela," she rapped out, "your price?"

"Really?" she murmured, frowning as she wrote it down. "Goodness me, I'd no idea what a luxury a headache could be."

*　　　*　　　*

Meanwhile the porter was picking his teeth over an American periodical. This was the second time it had passed through his hands, in transit, as it were; it was to be returned to the room of the journalist Schulman that evening, lest its temporary absence give rise to complaint. The jangling of keys warned him of the housekeeper's approach.

"You saw what I saw—the driver with the sacks?" she hissed across the desk. You could smell her fusty black clothes a couple of yards off; at closer proximity, her breath. He backed away.

"We are neither of us blind," he replied diplomatically.

"You don't need to see more than that, do you, to know what's going on? What's to be done, that's what I want to know. You seem to me to be on the slow side, young man—yes, rather slow."

"My dear lady," he murmured, glancing round. The hall was empty. "It's a slow business. For example—I see luggage being carried upstairs—but as to what it contains I can only guess. We may think our guesses are not far short of the mark—but that's no proof, is it? And as to what is or what is not proof—well, that depends on what is to be proved, doesn't it? So that's not for us to worry about —oh, dear me, no, wiser heads than ours are engaged on *that* score. My job is to provide the detail—but to do that I must rely on co-

319

operation." He gave the housekeeper his gimlet-eyed look. He had been rehearsing it in private, and was pleased to note the effect. " For instance," he continued, on the strength of it, " if you'd come to me straight away the other evening about that—incident—on the back stairs, instead of waiting until the next day—until the matter of the cognac being refused . . . eh? One would have been in a stronger position . . . by then, of course, it was too late." The housekeeper seemed about to speak. " No, no," he went on, relaxing his severity of manner somewhat, " it was quite natural, I understand perfectly . . . but it hinders, you know . . . it hinders. I only mention it because your complaint is that I'm slow. Think of it like this. Imagine it's a factory. What happens here? " He thumped his desk. " We take in the raw material. It may be routine, but it's of vital importance, my job at this desk. What happens afterwards? It's processed, of course. So although I know nothing of what happens beyond that door you see there, into the street, nothing at all of the processing, I can appreciate that skilled work takes time and patience. Slow? Of course. But it's just like the mills of God, I assure you. How does it go?—langsam aber sicher. And in a complicated little affair . . ."

The housekeeper licked her lips, and the porter thought, no, better not elaborate on that, but he could not resist impressing her and confusing her and something had just come into his mind which sounded vaguely apt, enigmatic and gentlemanly all at the same time:

" How can I put it? There's a saying where I come from: if you should start up a hare when you're out for a boar, leave the hare alone; you'll take it later, with any luck, or another one. Hares are common. Understand? "

" No," said the housekeeper. She looked bewildered, as well she might.

" Just as well," said the porter, with an air of mystery. And it was just as well, too—it had been no more than idle speculation on his part, but it suddenly occurred to him, supposing it were true? No one ever told you anything.

" So," he went on, winding up his homily, " don't forget, co-operation—and detail; not one that has not its own importance, but only *relative*, you see, relative to the main object. And what *that* is—that's not for us to know . . . but rest assured they aren't fast asleep with their eyes shut, the ones who do know."

" I don't want to *know*," she moaned, wringing her hands, " I don't want to *know* anything—it's only on account of the manager, my brother, who's fretting himself into a decline. You see, this has always been a most *respectable* hotel."

320

"Calm yourself, gnädiges Fräulein . . . excuse me, but you know as well as I do—no hotel is respectable that has Westerners in it."

* * *

"P is for penicillin, per capsule . . . pepper, ground, white . . . R . . . razor-blades, in plastic dispenser case, ten to a case . . . raisins . . . and rice . . . S—oh dear, what a lot comes under S! . . . "

"Cigarette?" said Gisela.

"Thank you—and you? Shaving soap, brushless—never know what that means . . . shampoo . . . sherry . . . shoe-polish . . . sultanas . . . and now T—well, T is for tea, isn't it?" Gisela smiled politely. "This pound and kilo business is just too *maddening*—per 415 grams —ridiculous, they should pack it like that in England and be done with it . . . and toothpaste . . ." They worked steadily on.

"That's the lot," said Milly at last. "There's W, of course, whisky, but we only managed to get two bottles—one for us and one for Mr. Wragg."

"Mr. Wragg doesn't like whisky."

"Don't be silly, Gisela, of course I know that. If he'd wanted it he'd have put it on his list. As it is, I should think my husband and Mr. Schulman are three-quarters of the way through his bottle by now."

"What a shame!" said Gisela, genuinely moved. "Best of all, whisky—with regard to Column G, I mean."

"Shame?" Milly sniffed. "It's worse than that—it's downright disgusting. Absolute waste." She collected her papers together. "Now you go off to bed. By the way, the key to the cupboard——"

"Yes, you want it?" the girl broke in quickly. "I'll go and get it, shall I?"

"No, not now." She paused. That's funny, she thought, but concealing her surprise went on: "To-morrow will do. Just leave it here in this drawer, will you, with the account book, before you go to bed? Then if you're out to-morrow I'll know where to find it. Sweet dreams, Gisela. Good night."

Milly, who never went back on an exit if she could help it, passed through the children's room into her own. After a long hot bath she lay in bed doing her sums. She could hear the men's voices through the door; they were bent, it seemed, on finishing Wragg's bottle. It was fascinating how, after the tedious donkeywork of addition, multiplication, and so on, the rows of noughts in the totals satisfactorily cancelled each other out. So the tea service at least was hers, with a margin to spare if she took into account the parcel of drugs which had come by bag, and which she had kindly, far too kindly, ordered for

Antoinette. Well, that was going to be put a stop to right away. It was disgraceful of Antoinette. She'd had three or four lots already and heaven knows what she did with them. Something illegal, I bet, she murmured to herself. So from now on I'm not going to be involved in it, and I'll tell her so. Besides, she reflected, there were the candlesticks. Very nice they were too, Venetian, the like of which were not to be found in Venice these days, search as you might. She had happened to see them in the window on the last occasion she had stopped to admire the lace. " What a ridiculous lark," she told herself, tucking her notebooks deep down into her bag, and snuggling under the quilt. " I almost wish I could tell Larry. Razor-blades, tea . . . perhaps it might even be a bit sordid if one didn't treat it, as I do, as a joke. The candlesticks will be just right. I'll have them on the dressing-table there. Perhaps I could say they were a present from Sophie? " Then, just before she fell asleep, something that had been at the back of her mind wriggled its way through—what was it? Some detail that had struck her as odd. Oh, yes, about the key. It wasn't so odd, really. Perhaps Gisela hadn't realised that she had it in her apron pocket all the time. Very likely not. Except that it wasn't a very *small* key. Oh, what does it *matter*? She dismissed it impatiently, and almost at once fell asleep.

*   *   *

Gisela, alone in the kitchen, smoked a cigarette through, deep in meditation. Once or twice she gave a dry little laugh, thinking of Milly. What a business woman. A woman after her own heart. But her thoughts were not primarily concerned with her employer. When she had finished the cigarette she took the key from her apron pocket and turning it over in her hand she muttered under her breath, " Really, there's very little risk. It's usual, ten per cent, although apparently she has yet to learn that. But she's in a good mood and clearly she's no fool; she must realise that from now on she depends on me. And it just so happens that it might make all the difference, now, to-night. That lousy so-and-so." Gisela was referring to her betrothed. " Does he think I don't see what he's playing at? If there were one single solitary other man to whom I could turn—but it's coming to an end here, that's the point—he let slip that much last night, the drunken clown—and I must look to myself. Imagine a job in an office, or a factory? Thanks—not for me. I'd die of boredom. Ah . . ." She stretched out her arms, feeling the excitement tingling down to her fingertips. " This is what I like—not knowing what's going to happen next. I have the feel as if my luck's changed. And he wasn't too bad last night. Fiery—the vodka, perhaps. But then so am I—fiery . . .

322

and I don't need vodka to be that way." She gave herself a sharp look in the mirror and smiled grimly. "We're six of one and half a dozen of the other, he and I. I'll see he doesn't have it so easy, later on." She swung herself off the edge of the bath and stood pondering, staring at the key in her hand as if she was still undecided, as if she were still to be swayed by this omen or that; in reality, and she knew it, her mind was made up. "No, there's no risk," she murmured. "No real risk. Ha, and what if there is? If the worst comes to the worst—well, what then?" She gave a hard little laugh. "I'll trust to my luck."

She had slid into that state of mind that was second nature to her, the reckless state of mind verging on lunacy that from time to time afflicts the psychopathic personality—criminals, gamblers, and other desperate persons; a trance-like state, in which the sufferer, the one possessed, whilst hypersensitive to trivial details, highly receptive to oracles, seeking and of necessity finding omens in every haphazard arrangement of stick or stone, swayed by the position of the planets, the forecasts of soothsayers, the pattern of tea-leaves in a cup, or simply by the pricking of his thumbs, is, nevertheless, deaf to counsel, blind to danger, and incapable of balanced judgment or of counting the cost. It is symptomatic of this state that although he is in full possession of his faculties—indeed, they are sharpened, even at their sharpest—and so cannot fail to be aware of all the factors in his situation, he will properly apprehend only those which suit him, and disregard any that are distasteful to him, that is, which might conceivably thwart him in the achievement of his purpose—because these bouts usually occur when he has some objective in view, often criminal, almost invariably anti-social, something that requires just this self-induced state of trance for him to see it through. Then nothing can deflect him, nothing is allowed to stand in his way: even if there would appear, in the light of common sense, an obvious risk, he will not see the risk; not see, likewise, all unpropitious omens, not see even the very face of danger itself if it comes between him and his desire; he will be truly blind to all that, as if his brain, possessed, had perfect control not only over itself but all five senses as well, anæsthetising those sensibilities which, by giving the alarm, might deter him from accomplishing what he has set out to do.

There is a further symptom of this curious state of temporary near-madness; indeed, it is one of the initial symptoms. At the onset of the attack, the subject, or patient, or victim, being only human, and before he becomes, as in the later stages, inhuman, will be conscious of the need for some reassurance, some support outside himself; and he casts about and finds none. Then it will occur to him, being desperate, and his plans being desperate and very likely his situation, too, that what he really needs is an alternative—an escape-route, as it were, should his other plans miscarry. He must have a way out, but where, or what? No sooner has the thought crossed his mind than he is supplied with what he requires; in a flash the answer is there—in a flash because it has had no distance to travel, because it has always been there, lying low in his brain—yes, this is it, the solution, the only true one for him, desperate to match himself. He recognises it at once and with relief, deriving such a measure of comfort from its presence that he wonders how he ever did without it. It is quite indispensable—the answer to so much. Instead of restricting it to its proper function, for use in an emergency, he allows it to develop into an all-purpose theory, a precept ample and comfortable enough to live by, and before long it is dictating his actions; it has taken charge of the operation and of him.

As to what it is, this formula, which reduces all problems to simplicity, dwarfs all fears, and by redistributing light and shade, and altering the slant, alters beyond recognition the picture of a situation, it may best be summed up as he who adopts it so gladly would sum it up: " To-day I shall live and to-morrow, if things go badly, I can always die." So then he lives, acts accordingly, with this assurance firmly fixed in his mind—the assurance of there being always this exit, no matter how impossible things may become. With that in reserve, it is scarcely surprising that he sees neither risks, nor contrary omens, and can laugh even in the face of danger itself.

Gisela's temperament was such that she was well acquainted with this state of mind, although with her it did not take an aggravated form; instead of short sharp bouts she suffered a milder visitation, but nevertheless subtly clinging and persistent. She was seldom entirely free of it, nor was it ever very far away, so much so that she had become addicted to the pleasurable sensations of excitement it produced. To her it was a way of living—indeed, she had never known any other—and her taste for it was formed. As for the escape-device principle, there was nothing new in that; her own nature, circumstances, and events had produced situations that were often grim, but never complicated with a profusion of possibilities; in fact, she had never found herself in a situation that offered any alternative but this one. Still, by reason of her looks, wits, and a certain gambler's instinct, things had not, to date, gone as badly for her as they might; she would herself even have said that they had gone fairly well; her life had not been dull. Things had never gone so badly as to have caused her seriously to contemplate the alternative, but had she done so, it would have been without emotion, at most with a little shrug. She reckoned with it, however, even if unconsciously, and had she ever analysed her

324

rules of conduct, she would have acknowledged that the fact of there being no alternative but this one (which in prospect did not frighten her) lent considerable piquancy to the pleasure she extracted—and was determined to go on extracting, until circumstances should decree otherwise—from life.

So, her course of action decided upon, she took down from the back of the door a large haversack which she sometimes used for marketing, and kneeling in front of the cupboard, opened the door and removed what she considered was due to her, her cut. A shade over ten per cent—and quite justifiably she calculated in terms of the more advantageous price, the NAAFI one—made an appreciable difference to the appearance of the stock, already depleted, on the shelves. She began rearranging large worthless packets of cereal to fill the gaps and then remembered that it didn't matter in the least what the shelves looked like, her employer not having had time to examine the cupboard as yet. She stuffed the goods into the haversack, combed her hair, put on more lipstick and went out.

Once having fallen into that fatal mood she was past caution, capable of the strangest mistake. She had interpreted omens to suit herself. She had even felt her luck change when it did not. She should have respected and abided by those previous omens which had advised the utmost discretion in her actions for the present; for the present, for that day and the next, her luck being most definitely, conspicuously out.

*   *   *

" You're a smart girl, Gisi," said the porter kindly, when he had been prevailed upon to accept the haversack on his side of the desk. When he had listened to all she had to say he seemed even better pleased.

" Well, that's fine," he said. " Facts are just what we want. A list like that—in the handwriting, of course—and then the rest's easy, I should imagine. I wonder if I ought to slip up to headquarters now and give them a hint—it's tricky . . . I can't explain . . ." He rejected the boar-hare parable as not being for Gisela's consumption—she was altogether too sharp.

" Not yet," she murmured. " Don't go yet." Her eyes were brimming over with love.

" All right," said the porter, yielding after a surreptitious investigation of the contents of the haversack, which he locked away in his personal drawer. " Tell you what "—his voice was injected with enthusiasm, if not gratitude—" we'll have a coffee in the bar." No one can pretend, he thought to himself, that I'm a mean man. On the other hand he was, and he never pretended otherwise even to himself, a weak one; on Gisela's maintaining that she preferred vodka to coffee, the only gentlemanly course was to follow suit.

Thus it came about that Gisela, when at last she did go to bed, went in a happy frame of mind. They had talked over the possibility of New Year's Day. Really, one might say (and the next step was to say it, all over the hotel) that the date had been fixed. To-morrow morning early she would go to the dressmaker. Leave the breakfasts ready—anyway, what did it matter now? White satin, with puff sleeves —and even a little train. She knew a pawnshop where they had a length of such satin; that was easy. She went to sleep and dreamed, not of nuptial rites, but of her father's hut in the forest and her mother screaming in childbirth, and the younger children, made fractious by the noise, all squabbling for a place near the fire—she herself kneeling in the firelight, over the cauldron, alternately cuffing the children and stirring the blackish potion of bark, herbs and berries that had been her father's recipe for easing her mother's pain.

326

Chapter Seven

SOMETHING TICKLED Milly's face, and a voice chirruped right in her ear: "Wake up, sleepyhead."

Without opening her eyes, she groaned.

"Milly, Milly! What is it! You're suffering?"

Reluctantly she opened her eyes. "What are you doing here, Sophie?"

"Darling, I've been here since eight-thirty o'clock! Waiting for you to wake up."

"Only you didn't wait," Milly snarled ungraciously, moving her foot from beneath a heavy object. "What on—Sophie, put the tray on the table, would you? Where's Gisela, for pity's sake?"

"She's gone out, dear. So I made your breakfast. Now you sit up and I'll make you comfy."

"Sopheeee . . .!"

"Oh, I'm sorry, darling. But put this round your shoulders . . . why, now you look like a teeny flower. My pet!" Milly heaved a rebellious sigh, glanced at the breakfast tray, glanced again, screamed, and lay back on the pillows, her fingers over her eyes.

"Milly—Milly . . . what have I done?"

"What's in that glass?"

"Eggs, Milly. A la coq. The English way, darling, isn't it?"

"No, it isn't. And what's that—that mess? . . . "

"I cut it into fingers, I'm afraid."

"I'm perfectly capable of doing that for myself. And what—what the hell, Sophie—the hell, I repeat—is this *rose* doing on my plate? Is that part of the diet, too?"

"No, dear. I—I read it somewhere. To—to make it dainty."

"I see." She sat up. "Now, look . . . Just remove the entire shambles, will you—no, leave the coffee—just put the tray anywhere, so long as it's out of sight—and put the rose back in the vase where it came from—and then come and tell me all about it."

"You've done the coffee very well," she said, when Sophie came back.

"Really?" Sophie's face lit up. "I see now I was off my rocker about the egg, Milly. Can you forgive me?"

"Forget it. Now sit down—not on my *feet*! God, I've got a headache."

" A little bit of a hangoverski, perhaps? "

" Nothing of the sort," snapped Milly, who had just at that moment identified her indisposition as such.

" Well, now to tell you." Sophie drew up a chair. In her earnestness she leaned forward, knees apart, hands clasped.

" Sophie! " Milly chuckled. " What superb bloomers! "

Sophie blushed, adjusting her position. " A joke, yes? I know they're not dainty . . . but practical . . ." She might have added that they were all one could buy. " Stop it, darling . . . is it so funny? I know it must seem strange to you, you sweet little fairy, that one can wear such horrors . . . oh, dear, now I'm laughing myself . . . it's a good joke, I agree. But now, *listen*."

" Yes, Sophie."

" To-night—oh, you'll never guess . . ."

" Sophie, don't let's have guessing games at *dawn*, please . . ."

" No, all right . . . It's a surprise, you see, and I don't know how you'll take it . . ." She twisted her hands nervously.

" Sophie, *get on with it*, or I'll throw the coffeepot——"

How charming Milly was, thought Sophie, always joking. Still, she decided to take the plunge. " I'm giving a party! "

" Oh, really? "

" Yes. That's it! To-night, in our flat. And we'll be so happy to see you, and Larry, and—and Miss Raven, it's too late for the children, I suppose—but—well, Milly, what about it? You'll come? "

Milly, with visions of cocoa and biscuits in a slum, said slowly, " I'll have to ask Larry, Sophie. I don't know if——"

" Milly . . . oh, *Milly*! " Sophie sprang to her feet. " Darling— you *must* come . . . you see . . ." She looked and sounded dreadfully agitated.

" *Must?* " said Milly gently, just to tease Sophie. She lay back on the pillows. " *Must*, Sophie? "

" Well, yes . . . how can I explain? You see, it's *for* you . . . it's all for you. Please, Milly."

" It's very sweet of you—but, I mean—what *sort* of party? "

" An evening party," said Sophie grandly, beginning to pace up and down. " With music, dancing, singing perhaps, and fun. Some people will turn up." She added, under her breath, facing the window, " I hope." She went on, " I was on the telephone at seven a.m. to give notice. . . . Grass doesn't grow under *my* feet, darling," she boasted. " First I rang up Schulman."

" What, at seven a.m.? " Milly giggled. " That was a good start."

" Yes, he was quite delighted," said Sophie gravely. " He will come.

328

Others, too. So now I'll be off. Shall I fetch you a hot bottle? Your tootsies are frozen, I should think. Oh, Milly, don't get ratty, I'm sorry—perhaps my English is deserting me, I'm always saying something wrong. I'll go now. So—if you'll excuse my not coming this afternoon—it's a question of preparations. But if you need me specially then of course I'll come." She frowned, her lips moving, muttering silently to herself. " I've so much on my mind, it's possible I might forget one or two items—donkey that I am." She approached the bed and suddenly smiled one of her sweet smiles. " Oh, darling, you'll come, I *know* you'll come . . . you little rose-petal thing—let me give you a kiss."

Milly gave her a certain look, which caused the smile to vanish at once. " D'you mind, Sophie . . . I'm in a nasty bad temper . . . please just *go*."

" Of course. You dear. I understand. Well, now I'm off."

And she really was.

" God, what a trial she is." Milly yawned, and took another cigarette. " Now, what do I feel like? A long lazy morning. Lunch? It'll have to be out of a tin. Unpack the NAAFI, check it—oh, lord, though, not yet."

Lying in bed, she became aware of whispers, giggles, a shuffling and banging in the salon next door. At last, unable to bear the racket any longer, she got up. Pulling a dressing-gown round her, she opened the sliding doors. The furniture in the salon was all topsy-turvy. Two or three little creatures were performing their reel on the waxed parquet. Another appeared to be dismantling the stove. A couple of maids were beating the upholstery in clouds of dust, and there were two men on step-ladders hammering at the pelmets over the windows. All were laughing and chattering together, but as first one and then another saw her standing in the doorway, each stopped in his work to gaze at her; their voices died away, and all the other noises too. In the hush, out of sheer bravado, she crossed the room to her desk just as the housekeeper sailed in through the open passage door, her appearance setting the clockwork figures once more in motion. The housekeeper swept straight over to Milly. Her face, Milly saw, was pale cheese-green in the morning light.

If I had lipstick on, she thought, if only I had lipstick on, and snatching up the vase of roses and a box of cigarettes she moved off to the sanctuary of her bedroom. The housekeeper, however, was planted directly in her path.

" Good morning." Her glance raked Milly over from head to foot, her tone by no means over-polite. " You'll be vacating the bedroom in a few minutes? "

" Why? " Suddenly defiant, she looked the woman in the face. She was fiddling with her keys, her eyes averted.

" It's the custom of the hotel," she muttered, " an overall turnout every so often. In twenty minutes the servants will require to go in there." Why doesn't she look at me? Milly asked herself. All around her, she could tell that, although the servants were working, they were also watching.

" All right," she said quietly.

The housekeeper turned on her heel and stalked off. She herself withdrew into the bedroom and fancied she caught the sound of a giggle as the doors shut. Setting the vase on the table by the bed, she lit a cigarette. Pulling at a flower here and there, she stood thinking, puzzled. She could not help contrasting that scene with the scene just after their arrival—three months ago, was it, or four?—when that same woman had—well, *fawned* over her, almost. Just now, her tone, her manner, had been rather as if—as if she, Milly, were a housemaid caught out in a theft. I don't understand, she thought. And really she did not understand. What a horrible creature she was, that house-keeper. Perhaps it was because—perhaps it was Larry's fault, refusing to give her the brandy. Better to have given it her. Still, the affair of the brandy would certainly not have been made public, did not account for the way they had all stopped work to look at her—she shivered, remembering that hush . . . as if . . . as if . . . She was still standing there, lost in thought, when she heard a tapping, or scratching, on the bathroom door.

" Come in," she called out crossly, thinking, if it's that woman again, or even Sophie, either or both I'll eat them up. It was neither. Antoinette Rapovska sidled in, her carpet bag clutched in her hand.

" Sssssh! " Miming in the style of the old school of Victorian melodrama, the princess tiptoed across the bedroom, her finger to her lips, patting Milly's cheek in passing, and after listening for a second at the keyhole, turned the key in the lock. Her eyes starting out of her head she whispered: " They are *cleaning* in there! "

" I know."

" Hst! " She paused, her ear cocked, then, in the same hoarse whisper, approaching on tiptoe: " S'very *clean* hotel . . . very, very *clean*, yer know . . ."

" I think we can safely speak up," said Milly. " Sit down, won't you? I'm sorry . . ." She waved towards the unmade bed.

" Ow, never mind—don't excuse—in these days one makes allowance . . . I place myself 'ere, yes? " She sat on the bed.

" Cigarette? "

"Ow, never." Her eyes, wandering round the room as their custom was, brightened at sight of the tray. "Coffee—yes."

"I'm afraid it's cold."

"Ow, never mind, never mind." She was disposed to be gracious, it was clear. "The sherry will do very well." She put on spectacles and began rummaging in her bag. "Vraiment," she said encouragingly, happening to look up and perceiving that her hostess was still standing there: "Vraiment, chère amie, I can tolerate it, le sherry . . . ce n'est pas mauvais, du tout."

Gathering up her skirts, Milly unlocked the door and crossed the salon once more. Once more it was as if she had surprised a team of leprechauns at work. Silent, still as statues, they watched her as she picked up the bottle and glasses and, with her head high, marched back into the bedroom.

As the door closed: "On dirait "—observed Antoinette, placidly jigging up and down on the spring mattress—" they're 'appee 'ere, les servantes? "

"Certainly they seem easily amused," Milly agreed dryly.

"Ah . . . c'est très bon, vous savez . . ." She smacked her lips over the sherry. "Comme vin léger . . . matinal . . . comme apéritif . . . enfin, tout court, il me plaît." She set her empty glass on the carpet. "Alors—to bizi-ness! I am razzer short of time—and what pain I've 'ad to pay my respects todye—c'est formidable . . ."

"I'm sorry." Milly stooped to refill the glass. "Don't let me keep you."

"Oh, s'nothing—je vous assure—a pleasure to spend a little time with you—un petit plaisir pour vous aussi, n'est-ce pas? " She whipped off her spectacles. "What's come? " If the words were like bullets, then suddenly turning and meeting the eyes of the princess was like looking down the muzzle from which they had been fired.

Milly sat down suddenly.

"I'm afraid—I—I don't quite understand," she said, fingering an object which happened to be under her hand on the dressing-table.

"Ah—regardez-la! " The princess let out a little scream of joy. "Mais regardez-la—la petite boîte! Comme c'est jolie! Elle vous serve—pour les lozenges, une mille de choses? Au moins, maintenant je vois bien qu'elle vous a plu! " Her joy was so intense, and so protracted at re-encountering the little snuff-box, it occurred to Milly to wonder how she could ever have brought herself to part with it. Herself, she never wanted to see it again. Reaching for a cigarette, she was surprised to find that her hand was shaking. She huddled herself into her dressing-gown. She was shaking from head to foot.

"Vous avez froid? " The princess chafed her own stubby fingers.

331

" Moi, non! Toujours le sang chaud, moi. Tant mieux avec ces prix pour le chauffage central énormes . . . Alors . . . what we talk about? I forget—Ah, mais oui . . ."

" I said that I didn't quite understand you, Princess."

" C'est ça! " It tinkled creditably, her laugh. " Vous n'avez pas compris. J'ai dit "—she leaned forward, speaking as to a cretinous child—" Any-zing arr-rrived? "

" Arrived? When? " No sooner had she spoken than she realised her mistake. The princess merely glanced at her with amusement, and shrugged.

" Enfin—las' night," she drawled, as Milly hesitated. " Alors—didn' come? "

" No," said Milly.

" Nozzing? " Her eyebrows disappeared into the bush of curls on her brow. " Tiens, the order not come? "

" Princess, what order? " Irritated beyond measure, Milly looked up. " What do you mean? The order for what? "

A second's pause, then the princess, reverting to her kittenish self, put out a little velvety paw, patted Milly's lap: " Ah, je vois bien," she said softly, forgivingly, " you don' understand? Maintenant c'est tout expliqué . . . you didn' understand it was an order regulaire? Je vous en prie . . . pas un mot . . . peut-être la faute était la mienne . . . neow, s'all explained and the next time . . . eh? S'my fault, but I thought you understand . . . Silly me! Neow, I must be trotting." She got up. " I 'ave to visit a friend—très ennuyeuse—the niece of the Archduchess—very old, cripple . . . to whom some good fortune 'as arrived. You met 'er? No? She 'ad some wotchercall—dentelles, lace, an old piece, nothing much, but point de Venise, yer know . . . two or three darns but not to notice . . . and it's been sold! Imagine! One never thought she would arrange it—and at a price—my dear! I don' know 'ow she 'ad the courage to ask that price. Still, now she dies in peace. One 'as pleasure when affairs go well for a friend. N'est-ce pas? Maintenant, je prends mes adieux . . . no, no—I won't 'ear a word . . . I understand . . . next time . . . all okay, eh? " She turned, about to go out through the bathroom, and gave another of her little screams. " Mais, regardez—les roses! Qu'elles sont belles, ces fleurs! " She buried her nose in the vase of roses, her delight perhaps heightened by her delayed reaction to their presence, the vase having been at her elbow during the previous half-hour.

" Hmmm . . ." she squeaked, snuffing. . . . " Je me rappelle . . ." she shut her eyes, " now it's like in Molly's time, 'ere . . . Madame Simpson, vous savez . . . I don' know where 'e gets them, Mr. Schulman, it's 'is secret . . . but yer know, when Molly was 'ere . . . everywhere you smell these roses . . . but everywhere . . . before your time, natch'rallee . . . So—off now! I come again—let's say, fifteen days, eh? Bye-bye." She poked her head round the bathroom door, roguishly wagging two fingers, " Et n'oubliez pas . . . *regulairrrre* . . . ! "

Now there came a rapping on the double doors and when Milly slid them apart there were the servants, standing all in a row, armed with their tools, gazing up at her. Meekly she stood to one side and they flocked into the bedroom; swooping upon the bed they began tearing it apart, tugging at the furniture, swarming up the curtains. She knew when she was beaten and she left them to it, pausing to swallow a couple of aspirin as she passed through the bathroom into the nursery, where she found Clarissa crouched like a frog on the red plush sofa in front of the stove, her nose literally in a book. On her way through, she was about to greet her daughter when the latter raised her eyes and said: " Good afternoon."

She altered course abruptly. " Is that meant to be funny? "

" N-no."

" Well, let me tell you that it's very rude." She stood frowning, at a loss. As a rule she would have followed up this rebuke with some supporting argument, but she didn't feel up to it.

" Sorry." Clarissa, eyeing her mother, decided that she looked more *feeble* than cross; a correct diagnosis. " I'm so glad you've come," she went on diplomatically, " there's something I want to ask."

Milly softened. " Go ahead."

" Well, what I was wondering . . . you're past your first youth, aren't you? So——"

" Just say that again? "

" What? Oh . . . it's all here . . . wait, I'll read it . . .' She was a woman past her first youth, say twenty-six or -seven years old but still comely . . .' So what I was wondering was——"

" What book is that? " said Milly weakly. " You know, you read too much."

" It's one Abe lent me . . . and *he* says I can't read too much. I haven't got into it yet. In fact I've only got to the first page."

" Quite far enough, I should say."

" *Anyway,* Mummy, how many youths does one have? *I'm* in my first, aren't I? "

" You're a child, Clarissa," she said crushingly. " Childhood has nothing to do with youth. At least, they're by no means the same thing." She cheered up, feeling rather pleased with herself. There was no doubt that for the first time that morning she had scored. " Where's Dermot? "

333

" In with Miss Raven."

" Doing what ? " said Milly suspiciously. Goodness, she would have to think about Miss Raven some time. Not to-day, though. Later.

" Talking, I suppose. He talks to her while she does her hair." Clarissa added, thoughtfully, " She allows him great liberties."

" *What do you mean?* "

" She lets him take her alarm clock to pieces. I wouldn't. But then they're on the best of terms. Dermot," his sister observed, with more than a hint of implied criticism in her voice, " likes to be liked—and Miss Raven likes him because he's like Daddy . . . *I* think."

" So he is," said Milly, too bewildered fully to appreciate the shrewdness of this triangular appraisal.

" Personally," Clarissa went on, because it was seldom that her mother stopped to chat, " I go in for *dis*liking."

" Why? " said Milly wretchedly. " That's not the right attitude," adding, in a voice which robbed her of the last shreds of authority, " or so I believe."

" *Isn't* it ? " She stared up at her mother. " Liking people is nothing but a bother and it's awful—I mean, it must be awful, I should think," she put in quickly, " if they don't like you back. If you dislike them, then they leave you alone."

" Of course they do. You wouldn't like to be disliked yourself, would you? "

Clarissa shrugged, her lank fair hair falling over her face. She had flushed. " I don't mind," she declared, her chin stubbornly set. " I don't mind at all. Disliking and being disliked—what's the difference? "

On an impulse Milly brushed back a lock of hair and felt the child quiver at her touch. Nervy little thing, she thought.

" What nonsense you talk," she said lightly, and went on her way into the kitchen.

*   *   *

From the disorder in the kitchen it was apparent that Gisela had not yet returned. The breakfast trays had been placed on the floor, there being no room for them on the table on which was the tray from the night before, also glasses, ashtrays, empty whisky bottle and so on; even the dinner things—a point which had escaped her notice the night before, how, she couldn't imagine—were still unwashed, stacked in the bath. She put her hand to her head. The aspirin seemed to be remarkably slow in taking effect. " Where in God's name *is* that girl? " she muttered. " Goodness, I'll tell her where she gets off." She filled the kettle, composing, as she did so, a reprimand for Gisela. Just then

334

she heard footsteps in the corridor outside. " If there's a knock on that door now," she said under her breath, about to place the kettle on the electric plate, " I'll scream! " In the same instant there was a knock at the door and she did scream, but not on account of the knock.

The door opened and Mrs. Wragg loomed in the doorway. " Excuse me, Mrs. Purdoe. . . . Funny . . . ay thought ay heard a scream."

" Yes." Milly was leaning against the dresser. " You did."

" Oh . . ." Mrs. Wragg laughed rather strangely, having sighted the contents of the bath. " Well . . ." she went on, more at ease now that she had, as it were, identified the sound track with the film, " what was the mattah? "

" I've just had quite a nasty electric shock, that's all. Won't you come in? "

" Ay was just on my way out—as a mattrofact, ay was going to leave a message with your girl—it was for you, of course, the message, only ay didn't want to trouble you." She was still hovering.

" Cigarette? "

" No, thanks awfully. Ay smoke heavily—but not in the street. Ay've a thing about that. Oh, well, just for a second, then. May ay? "

Mrs. Wragg came in, seeming to fill the bathroom. She was very smart in a new tweed suit—it's a dream, the advert had said, and Milly, recognising it, decided that really it was; to match it, a felt hat, a " classic," and brogues, the whole costume (closely modelled on one of Milly's own) having arrived by that very bag and in which the wearer, albeit proud and pleased, looked about as much at home as a Hottentot in a kilt. In her way Mrs. Wragg was no mean actress; even her accent had been remodelled to fit her present part, and, indeed, her make-up struck the only jarring note; the effect would have been striking even on the stage of the London Palladium—on a grouse moor in Scotland it might have poached on the preserves of the guns.

" Ay—well, ay came about the whisky, ayercktually."

" Ah. Do sit down. Do you mind if I do? Well? "

" It's rather tricky to explain. *Ay'm* no spirit drinker, myself . . ." Here Mrs. Wragg, to emphasise the point, happened to lay her large gloved hand on last night's tray; the glasses rattled merrily and the dead man fell over.

" Oh dear, oh dear . . . empty? Lucky—had me worried for the moment . . . as ay was saying, *Mr*. Wragg, too, only touches "—she shot a grave look at Milly—" IT—now and again . . . but we do from tayme to tayme invayte guests, university folk and so on, to coffee, and he feels—*ay* feel, too, mind you—that one should have something to *offer*—something *else*—if you see what ay mean? "

335

" Oh, yes," said Milly, who saw all too plainly. " I couldn't agree with you more."

" And in—er—view of the recent circular as regards the Nayerfi . . ."

" You mean you want your whisky ration ? "

" Oh, *well*," Mrs. Wragg smirked at this blunt way of putting it, " not *want*, exayercktly—but it *maight* come in handy, and . . . what ay wondered was, as you were up this week-end, had you perhaps . . . had they, that is . . . well, what ay thought was, you *maight* have collected it—er—automayertickally . . . as it were . . ."

" *Automatically?* " To her intense annoyance, she felt herself flushing.

" Oh, we know it's our fault. It wasn't on our list. In fact, Mr. Wragg only mentioned the mattah to me—oh, quayte recently . . . but if you *haven't*—ay mean, it's perfectly okay, Mrs. Purdoe . . . just so long as it's clayerified . . . he'll write up to-night and they can send it . . . after all, fair do's for all, no one can deny us that . . . oh, *here's* the Nayerfi! " she exclaimed, taking a step back and tripping over the larger of the two large sacks. " Not unpayercked yet ? "

" No . . . it's . . . rather a long job."

" Oh-ho, ay can believe that . . . pity they couldn't payerck our frugal order separately . . . it would never fill one of those great sayercks . . ." Edging towards the door she gave the impression of being forced out by the combined weights, personalities, of the sacks. " So now I must be dayershing, Mrs. Purdoe . . ."

" Look. I've suddenly thought—if . . . if you want the whisky *urgently* . . . there's no need to write for it . . . I can let you have . . . I mean I think I've a bottle to spare . . ."

" Oh no, ay wouldn't *dream* . . ."

" Yes, please. I mean, I'd rather . . . it's in that cupboard . . ." She rooted in the drawer for the key. Take it easy now, she told herself, don't get flustered . . . " I can't—can't seem to find the key . . . the maid must have it . . . I tell you what, Mrs. Wragg . . . I'll find it and send it along—the bottle, I mean . . . or better still, bring it along, shall I? Bring it along myself? " She broke off, and looked round. She thought that Mrs. Wragg, who was already out in the corridor, was staring at her very oddly. Her face was all steely, the features were all steeled to do double duty; one was reminded of an express train just before the whistle blows—the wheels still, but the wheels within wheels already turning.

" That's okay," she said quietly. " Quayte okay, Mrs. Purdoe." Then she plunged off down the corridor. Milly stood there gazing after her, when Miss Raven came clattering in through the other door, a tray in her hands.

336

" Hall-*lo*! " she remarked, pausing to reconnoitre for a spot where she might lay her burden: " So you're up. We are in a pickle, aren't we? Oh, well, have to go on the floor . . . needs must when the Devil drives, eh? " Milly looked rather coldly at Miss Raven. It struck her as a curious summing-up of a situation which all too clearly revealed the suspension of any motivating power and the absence of any kind of driver, let alone one likely to be as dynamic as Old Nick himself. Going over to the dresser, she began rummaging frantically in the drawer.

" Where *is* Gisela, Miss Raven? "

" That would be telling, wouldn't it? " Simpering Miss Raven adjusted her waistband with the aid of the kitchen mirror.

" All the same, I wouldn't mind being told."

" Oh, we must make allowances, Mrs. Purdoe." Miss Raven, who could afford to be tolerant, chuckled. " After all, it's love that makes the world go round . . . I've lost three pounds in the last ten days. Hm . . . Slim's all very well, but soon I'll be just skin and bone. Notice the difference? "

" I can't say that I do." Indeed, Miss Raven's frame, in the overall view, was like a landscape so rugged and so liberally scattered with unalterable freaks of nature, knobbles, saddles, sharp declivities, craggy protuberances, that any swelling or diminution of the gentler contours might for long have passed unnoticed.

" That Gisela," snorted Miss Raven, a personal aspect of the situation at last striking her, "she knows I've got to have my hair done at three so she'll be back by then, I should hope."

" Before, *I* rather hope."

" So what are you going to wear? Long or short? "

" Long," said Milly. " What are you? "

" Ballerina."

" Oh," said Milly, rather staggered. She hadn't thought of that. She glanced at Miss Raven. She was perfectly solemn; meant what she said.

" With my Pekin jacket. The countess is a scream, isn't she? Going to be quite a slap-up do, she was telling me. Funny—I never knew she had means." " Means," the evidence of, had apparently caused Miss Raven to review Sophie's status. She was no longer " that countess."

" Dunno how to have my hair done," she rattled on. " You've got yours in the new style, I see. Must be a bit of a trial to wear."

Already subdued by the suspicion that this was not her day, and that the morning at least was dead against her, Milly was stunned by Miss Raven's manner, suggestive of an intimacy existing between them,

337

of a chat between two equally attractive women; this tugging at the bonds of what, so far as she was concerned, was a purely fictional comradeship, came near to irritating her more than any other single event of that irritating morning.

" Why? " she asked curtly. " Don't you like it? "

" Oh, I think I might." Miss Raven was rather clever in her use of the conditional, employing it to qualify, ostensibly to moderate, in reality to barb and promote to insult level, not a few of her remarks. Suspending her judgment on this equivocal note, she added: " I say, what's for lunch? Time's getting on."

If Miss Raven only knew—that if now, this minute, this morning, she were to open her lips and call me madam I'd double her wages on the spot—I wonder if she would? No, thought Milly despondently, I don't believe she would. Miss Raven would never call her madam.

" Not a thing, unless I can find the key to this cupboard."

" Lost, is it? Oh, I expect it'll turn up. Not room to swing a cat, is there? " she remarked good-humouredly, having trodden in the tray on the floor. " Case of too many cooks, I'd say, wouldn't you? "

" No," said Milly, goaded, " that's just what I *wouldn't* say . . . what about the washing up? I got a fiendish shock just then, putting the kettle on. Look, it's boiling . . ."

" So it is," Miss Raven concurred, observing the chemical evidence with the air of sober detachment, as it might be, of one scientist to another. " Well, there's Dermot! I must fly. If you take my tip you'll switch off before you pick it up. Really, I'm quite thrilled about tonight. . . . Remember this? Bit of a back number, but *you*'ll remember it . . ." Suddenly, in the small space available, she twirled in a waltz, carolling, in her deep and not unpleasant voice, full of trills and undercurrents:

> " Lay-dee . . . dressed in jayde . . .
> " Iyer'll—meetyew at—the mask—kerrayde . . ."

Not a moment too soon, if she were bent on keeping any sort of appointment that evening, she twirled herself out.

Milly crossed over to the kitchen mirror. Did it—or didn't it suit her? True, she'd had doubts herself. One couldn't judge without make-up . . . surely it couldn't be *that* time already—twelve o'clock? In a panic she snatched at the drawer of the dresser, and pulling it out bodily, hurled its contents on the floor. There was another drawer and she treated it the same. A great many lost objects bobbed to the surface, but there was no sign of the key. Quite frantic, she knelt down in front of the cupboard and tugged at the door, inserting a knife-blade into the crack. She broke the blade and a fingernail and then, happening to glance up, on the rack above the cupboard she caught sight of the meat pestle. It was an excellent instrument, made of steel and very heavy, and she wielded it with a will, taking three vicious swipes at the lock. The wood was already splintering and she was about to deal a final blow when she became conscious that the door behind her into the passage had opened, and someone was standing there watching her. She turned round. It was the housekeeper who stood there, gazing down at her in astonishment, whether feigned or not she could only guess. Not, she decided, becoming sensible to the spectacle she herself must present. The pestle dropped into the folds of her dressing-gown. If I'd put lipstick on when I got up, she reflected angrily, none of all this would have happened.

"I heard the banging," said the housekeeper.

On her knees, at bay, summoning all her powers, Milly retorted: "I'm not surprised. I can't open the cupboard. It's locked."

"There is no key?"

"There is a key—that is to say, a key exists, but I do not happen to have it. *Had* I the key," the heavy guns of that splendid ally came thundering in to her aid, "I assure you that I the door not down-battering would be. Unfortunately, Gisela has the key."

"She is not here?" The housekeeper muttered a scowl but Milly guessed that the counter-attack had shaken her.

"That's obvious, I should have thought."

As if this news constituted an invitation, the housekeeper stepped into the kitchen and sniffed about, her eyes kindling with delight. "She's a dirty girl, that one . . . tea leaves in the sink. . . . Wait till my brother hears of that, he'll have a crise . . . Pah! And the electric current wasting—the kettle overboiling . . . Tch!" In one stride she had crossed the kitchen and grasped the kettle. The current was notoriously erratic but it had its moments and this was one of them. With quite a loud shriek she jumped into the air like a beheaded hen, and, keys, beads, crucifix, all her ironmongery a-jangle, shot out into the corridor and that day, by Milly at least, was never seen again.

"There," she soothed herself. "It's the law of averages, high time too. I was beginning to think I was in for a really bloody day." Greatly cheered, she scrambled to her feet and suddenly, high up on a shelf over the sink, she saw the key poking out from beneath a saucepan. Gisela sometimes left her account book, small change and so on in this spot. Certainly it was not where she had been told to leave the key, but on the other hand she would have had a reasonable excuse for so doing—which was, in fact, exactly how Gisela had calculated.

Almost crying with relief, Milly snatched it up, and kneeling down once more in front of the cupboard, she unlocked the door.

* * *

Larry came back rather late for lunch, which was customarily a light meal laid out for the parents in the salon, Miss Raven and the children taking theirs in the nursery. There was cold meat, and Russian salad out of a tin, but he ate fast and made no comment, although it occurred to him that Milly had probably had one of her bad mornings. There was usually some fresh salad and cheese served as well.

" I've got to rush back," he said. " Should be rather fun this evening. But how on earth can Sophie afford to push the boat out like that? That's what Abe can't understand, nor can I. What do you think?"

" I haven't the least idea," snapped Milly. " I couldn't ask, could I?" It had never occurred to her to ask.

Larry looked up. She seemed upset, he thought. She hadn't touched her plate.

" What's up, darling? Feeling under the weather?"

" Rather a headache." She got up to light a cigarette. She never smoked with a headache, he remembered. She didn't come back to the table but paced up and down. Just as he was finishing, she said hurriedly: " Larry——"

" Well, what is it?"

" I want to get a message to Sophie. It's rather—well, urgent. Could Vladek take it round and then bring her back here?"

" Is there any coffee?"

" Oh—no . . . I'm sorry . . . there isn't . . . I can go and——"

" Never mind, I've got to go, anyway. Yes, he could take it round —after he's dropped me, that is—but I don't think he'd better bring her back. I'm quite sure Sophie wouldn't want to be seen in the car."

" I never thought of that. I—just thought it would be quicker."

" Well, as long as it's ready, darling, the message." He was already putting on his coat. " I can't hang about." There was a note of impatience in his voice. He hated mysteries and he sensed one brewing, and he did like coffee after lunch.

" It won't take a second." She went over to her desk. She knew him in this mood, without knowing what caused it, without suspecting

340

that it was a reaction to an atmosphere created by herself. She put it down to a masculine dislike of interference in routine, of being kept waiting. At such moments he could be cold and brusque and quite unsympathetic.

With the pen in her hand, aware of him standing behind her, chafing to be off, she was suddenly at a loss for words with which to convey her message to Sophie.

" Dear," she wrote, and then crossed it out.

" Come on, Milly."

" Darling," she scrawled over the word " dear," there being no time to start a fresh sheet, " Darling Sophie, can you come right away? I need you "—no, your—" your help. It's urgent." She underlined the word " urgent," without thinking dashed off the signature, and with her back to her husband, her hands shaking, sealed up the note first in one envelope and then, on an afterthought, in another.

" Ready," she said, turning round with a rather bright smile and handing it to him. In the car he remembered the smile as she gave him the letter, and the touch of her hand as it had brushed his own, how cold it had been. It was only after he had gone that it struck Milly that perhaps it had been a mistake to put her signature. No call signs. Nonsense, she told herself, you've got the wind up, that's all——anyway, too late now.

*　　　*　　　*

Sophie's kitchen was full of noise and bustle. Three or four elderly women were working round the table, one chopping onions, another rolling pastry, and so on; in a corner a couple more were squatting over newspapers, one plucking birds in a cloud of feathers, another disembowelling them as they were plucked. There was a smell of burnt feathers along with that of onions and other strong smells. The air was thick with steam, and the women's faces were crimson, their voices shrill; a bottle of vodka stood in the middle of the table and a communal glass with which from time to time they refreshed themselves. Singe was sitting propped up in an arm-chair, a shawl round her shoulders, her private recipe book open on her knee, intoning gently to herself. Sophie, with her sleeves rolled up, a handkerchief tied round her head, brandishing a wooden spoon, was standing at the stove; her eyes, keen as those of a general, darting over the table, like a general she barked her commands.

" *Lightly*, Marya—that's not a sledge hammer you've got in your hand—heavens, you can't have forgotten? Your fish patties that used to melt in the mouth . . . the lungs, Jasha, for pity's sake, scrape them out with your nails—one doesn't eat lungs, not yet, at any rate. Leda,

341

the mayonnaise, watch out! Oh, you who used to be a cook and what a cook—Holy Mother of God!"

"Sophie!" said Singe.

"Sorry," said Sophie, leaning over to snatch the vodka bottle off the table. "Not another drop till the mayonnaise is thick . . . look, you'll need another yolk—Leda, *careful*—that's olive oil, you know, in other words, liquid gold. Steady . . . down the side . . . it's easy to spoil . . . yes, now the lemon, that's a lemon, by the way—the only one in Grusnov, I believe . . . ha, you see, it thickens . . . stir, woman, STIR! . . . Oh my God!"

"*Sophie*," said Singe, "keep calm!"

"Calm!" she replied in English, moodily surveying the scene. "What donkeys these women are! How is it possible that in just a few years they can have forgotten—that one there, famous, actually, for her pastry, Singe—and now appreciate the nature of the disaster she is turning out. But it's not their fault. I've forgotten," she muttered, "we've all forgotten—because it seems these are things one forgets . . . how to cook, to eat, to talk, to live!—not like beasts, but like human beings. To think that these idiots worked in Mamma's kitchen once upon a time. Look at their finger nails! And look at mine! Ah," she shook her head in despair, "at bottom we're just a race of potato-gobblers, that's what they called us, and for once those German swine were perfectly right. The bell, Singe! Did you hear?"

"The bell? Oh, Sophie!" Her aunt looked scared. "Perhaps—for—*him*?"

"No. For us, I think. I'll go." She untied her apron, a worried frown on her face. She put the vodka bottle back on the table.

"Help yourselves," she said absently. "But hush your voices a bit. I have to answer the door."

*　　*　　*

Vladek, the driver, after delivering his employer to the office, at once drove off on his errand, not, however, by the most direct route. Parking the car in a side-street, he investigated the contents of the note, chuckling over the two envelopes, a device which, although a failure as a precautionary measure, proved that the sender of the message recognised the necessity for caution, which in turn implied that a certain transformation in that person's outlook must have taken place. Vladek had a soft spot in his heart for the English, as has already been said, but, like Gisela, he held a low opinion of their capabilities in certain respects; they were no more fitted for subversive activities than were babes in arms. He was, too, fond of his employer, and had the message borne the latter's signature, he would have been

342

inclined to ignore the call of duty and to deliver it as he had been instructed, direct. As it was, he had no reason to be fond of the person whose identity was established by the scrawl at the foot of the page; he had a long memory and the affair of the champagne still rankled—and so he was relieved that for once the performance of his duty involved no uncomfortable tug-of-war within himself, between loyalties. Still, this dodge with the two envelopes tickled him; for that reason he saw to it that the message was still in two envelopes when it was delivered, after a short delay and a detour, to Sophie.

*   *   *

When Sophie came back into the kitchen, crumpling the note in her hand, her expression was so altered that the women stopped what they were doing to stare at her curiously. For a moment she scarcely seemed to know where she was; then, suddenly conscious of the inactivity round her, she came to herself.

" Get on," she said. " Has it thickened? Good. Put it away, outside the window. Now chop parsley, please. For the stuffing. Mind it's chopped fine." She crossed over to her aunt.

" Look here, Singe, I've got to go. You're in charge. Here's the list. Watch that stuffing—it's dashed tricky. And the oven must be hot for the patties, hot like hell. Here's the brandy. Keep it here, see, between your knees. They can start roasting. First smear each breast with brandy, put a match to it—well, you know how. Look for lungs, tendons—don't let them use a speck of any other fat but butter. You know what the English are—so sensitive they would immediately taste the filth that we . . ."

" I know," said Singe meekly. " But not even pork fat, Sophie? "

" *Pork* fat! I should think not! No, butter. And the vodka, keep it under your chair. When they want more they must ask you. Wait, I'll explain, to them." she did so. " There you see, they understand perfectly. They're good souls at heart. So it's up to you now, Auntie. Keep order, mind. I shouldn't be so very long, but I don't know when I'll be back."

" Darling," Singe clasped the brandy bottle between her wrinkled little paws, her muzzle twitching. " Sophie," she whispered, " tell me, what is it? What's happened? "

" I don't know," said Sophie, scowling as she struggled into her gumboots, " but I think she's in trouble."

*   *   *

It seemed that Sophie would never come. Pacing up and down, lighting one cigarette from another, Milly found the waiting so unbear-

343

able that at last she telephoned Larry at the office. Her voice, he thought at once, sounded strange, as if she were out of breath.

" That's funny," he said. " I sent him—oh, an hour ago, I should think. She's busy, I expect. Don't fret, darling. What's up? You sound as though you'd been running." He could hear her breathing and then it stopped and he realised she must have put her hand over the mouth of the receiver. He was no sooner irritated than contrite. " Anything the matter, Milly? "

" Yes. I've had rather a do with—well, with Gisela."

" With *Gisela*? "

" Yes. I've had to get rid of her."

" Get *rid* of her? "

" Yes," she said impatiently. " I've given her the sack."

" But—Milly! Was that wise? "

" Wise? " Her voice, out of control, floundered into another key. " *Wise?* What else could I have done? "

" I don't know—I mean, it's so sudden. What's the reason? I know you don't like her much, but what for? You must have a reason." He laughed nervously. He felt nervous. When she got the bit between her teeth—but why in heaven's name hadn't she consulted him first? So that was what had been the matter at lunch.

" I've reason all right," she snapped. " None better. Dishonesty."

" *Dishonesty?* "

" Yes. There's stuff missing. From the store cupboard. I discovered it this morning. Including a bottle of whisky."

" *Whisky?* I say! " This reliable bombshell burst with its own peculiar effect. " But does she—admit it? "

" Oh, she admitted it, of course."

" But, darling, look . . . you haven't thrown her out without notice, have you? I do wish you'd told me first . . ."

" Of course I haven't *thrown* her out. I've simply told her I don't want to see her again in my kitchen or anywhere else. I've been perfectly fair. I've told her she can sleep in that room of hers for one week as from to-day and I've given her a fortnight's wages. At least, I "—she seemed to hesitate—" I left them on the kitchen table."

" Ah," said Larry. " You mean there was a row."

" She did make rather a scene," said Milly evenly. " But, for heaven's sake, tell me what else I could have done? "

" No," he said, " in that case, I think you've done quite right." Whether right or not it was done, that was clear, and if those *were* the facts, then why did he feel this disquiet? For one thing it was unlike Milly to bluster, to sound so angry and at the same time so aggrieved:

344

generally speaking, these were signs that she was lying, or, at the very least, knew herself to be in the wrong. Still, if the girl had admitted to it, dishonesty—*whisky*, too . . . He sighed.

" What are you doing now? " he added feebly, as if by holding her to the telephone he might restrain her from further acts of folly.

" Waiting for Sophie," she replied in a dreary little voice, all the bombast drained out of it, and the click of the telephone as she put it down, severing the frail connection between them, severed, too, something that was even more frail, whatever control he might have imagined he had over her, cutting him adrift, leaving him helpless in the dark on a very strong current. Now that he felt himself to be really in the dark, his perceptions all at once became sharpened, and like a blind man, without the distraction of the gift of sight, he seemed to sense by some other means the presence of the various hazards—banks, weir, cataracts, shoals, and so on, and there was no need for sight or daylight to feel the tug of the current and tell the speed at which he was being swept along. Alone in the office that afternoon, the stove roaring softly, the click of a typewriter through the door, he sensed more keenly than ever before in his life the presentiments of disaster. And yet, after smoking two or three cigarettes, he consoled himself with the thought that if this were in truth his position, that he was helpless, then in all likelihood it had always been so—although he had been blind to it until now; and, he thought, hearing Abe come into his office next door, if it has always been so, it has never yet ended in disaster. The situation only gave the impression of having deteriorated, of having become, not merely precarious, but truly perilous, because at last and with the greatest reluctance he was forced to recognise that he had never had, and very likely never would have, any control over Milly. These thoughts depressed him so much that he left all his work and went in to have a chat with Abe, who had been in the country so long that he seemed to know instinctively when to lay on a special vintage brand of gloom and doom that was guaranteed to cheer one up.

*   *   *

Milly had put down the telephone because the door had opened, and there was Sophie, standing in the doorway.

" Sophie! " She sprang to her feet. " Oh, I thought you would never come! " and she burst into tears.

Sophie, who had come prepared for anything and everything, including, of course, the worst, stepped forward and, greatly daring, enfolded her friend in her arms. Holding her, stroking her hair, whispering words of comfort and, eventually, comforting her, took

345

some minutes, precious minutes, the memory of which Sophie was to treasure all her life.

*   *   *

" It's a pity," said the porter thoughtfully. The news had flustered him. " Here—don't, Gisi, not here at the desk. It looks bad. Take my handkerchief. So what did you say? "

" Naturally I said I would make trouble."

" That was not very wise."

" *Wise?* " Gisela exclaimed, much as Milly had done. " What else could I say? Then *she* said, but I could see she was a bit nervy, where is the whisky—meaning," she shot a look at the porter, " that bottle I gave you last night."

" Tch! "

" And then she said, ' That is stealing and . . .' "

" And so it is, Gisi," the porter put in earnestly, lest there be any mistake on which side he was on. " So it is. The law's the law. Such a pity that you—er . . . took—you know . . . one or two things in advance. I didn't say so at the time——"

" That's right," she interrupted with spirit, " nor more you did . . ."

" For fear of hurting your feelings," he continued smoothly. " It's the old tale of the boar and the hare . . . when you're after a boar and you start up a hare . . ."

" Huh? "

" I mean," he explained, sacrificing the subtleties of allegory in order that the issue should be made crystal clear, " I would've preferred that list you spoke of to a whole crate of whisky—but, well—never mind." He considered her. Her eyes were magnificent, brimming over with tears. A pair of eyes like those, they could spell ruin to a man. If he didn't look out—he decided to take a firm line. " So what will you do now, Gisi? " he went on, in a tone of mild, almost avuncular interest. " Now that you're without a place, where will you sleep, I wonder? "

Gisela looked at him from under her lashes. The low-down dirty scum, she was thinking. " There's a week's notice, so I shan't be moving yet. I'll sleep up there in my own little room—you know, the one you came to, remember? "

" There's the Bielska going up," said the porter hastily, diving for his book.

" And after that," she murmured, coming closer, " it'll only be a week or so to New Year. Or, it occurred to me, we might even put the date forward . . . make it for this day week? What about that? "

346

The porter, who was recording Sophie's entrance, pretended not to hear.

"And so, once we're married," Gisela persisted, stretching out a hand to cover the page on which he was writing, an unprecedented impertinence: "Did you hear me, Kazimierz? Married, I said." He stopped writing and mopped his brow with his handkerchief. The hall seemed overheated to-day. "Then," she said softly, "then there will be no problem at all."

"Not so fast, Gisi." He reached under the desk, groping for his horn-rimmed spectacles, and in desperation put them on. They were quite new, having been left behind by a traveller the week before, and made a startling alteration to his face. Anyway they startled Gisela, he was thankful to note, who drew off her fire, temporarily at least. "You see, Gisi, I've got my reputation to consider, and that's just the pity of it." He shot her an owlish look. "I'll be frank with you because I'm a frank sort of fellow. You've lost your place—that's to say, been dismissed. For theft, too—we mustn't mince words—and it does reflect on me, being a Government servant, you might say. Apart from that, I'd been relying on your co-operation, as I explained to you, I thought; and, well, Gisi, dear, forgive me, but you seem to have bungled it a bit. It was proof we needed and nothing but proof will do. Now—oh dear, now that you're no longer in what one might call a key position—it may take ever so long. It's a thousand pities you fell to temptation. Tst . . . what did she say?" He didn't want to dispense with Gisela and then find her reinstated; she was a proper little twister, he knew. "Tell me exactly what she said. Don't go into the kitchen again, or something?"

"She said——" Gisela kept her eyes fixed on him, and he fidgeted under the desk; how could he ever have been deluded into imagining that those eyes were soft? "She said, 'never let me see you in here again.'"

"Ah. You see. That makes it very tricky . . . hm . . . very tricky indeed . . . ha-ha, you must have had quite a row, eh?"

"Quite a row. Listen, Kazimierz," she went on quietly, "you say you want proof. If I can bring you proof—because I know what is going on and I can guess what is going to happen—by to-morrow morning . . . or perhaps even earlier . . ."

"Ah," said the porter, giving her a strange look. In his agitation, he had flushed, and she observed that the smallpox scars did not take the flush but blazed out dead-white against it, and what's all this for, she asked herself, just to go to bed with this creature for the rest of my life, to be tied to him? No, she answered herself, I have to be tied to him in order to get out, that's as it always was, but now it's also a

347

question of being tied to him the better to teach him a lesson; one he won't forget.

"Ah-ha," he said, ruminating. "That would be a very different matter . . . the proof. So long as," he added, wishing that she would go, "it was real proof. In writing, preferably."

"Of course," said Gisela, leaning across the desk, not seeing what the porter saw, the housekeeper approaching. "In writing. In exchange," she smiled up at him, "for something else—also *in writing.*"

"Oh, yes, Gisi—well, I'm sure that can be arranged." He smiled, too, with relief. "We'll see, anyway . . . ah! Gnädiges Fräulein, good evening."

The porter, reflected the housekeeper, receiving the benefit of his smile, was not at all a bad young man. He was wasted on Gisela, in her opinion, and it was on this subject that she wished to give him a friendly word of advice.

"That girl." She turned to watch Gisela disappear up the stairs. "I heard a rumour . . ." she tittered, "ridiculous, I dare say . . . that you and she . . . were actually *engaged*! "

"Did you now?" said the porter, taking off the horn-rimmed glasses, which, although they had protected him from one sort of onslaught, were not an all-purpose defensive weapon. He moved out of range. "And who told you that?"

"A little bird."

"You shouldn't believe everything you are told," he replied gaily. "Little birds can lie."

"Ah." The housekeeper drew back her lips in an approving snarl. "That's what I thought. You've a head on your shoulders. She'll be in trouble before long, that girl. You'll see."

"Maybe," he murmured, scratching his nose. He was not going to commit himself. Still, he decided to slip along to headquarters that very afternoon to apply for the transfer. He didn't at all fancy the way things were shaping.

*   *   *

"I never liked her, darling." Sophie patted Milly's hand. "I never trusted her. Oh, but it's too much! To steal your beautiful whisky and things—and from *you*, a foreigner—I'm ashamed, Milly. I feel it here, you know." Sophie tapped the solidly upholstered front of the leather jerkin. "And she—wasn't *she* ashamed? Here, take my hanky. Did she admit it?"

"Yes, she admitted it." Milly sniffed. "No, I don't think she was ashamed. It was all frightfully unpleasant." How very unpleasant it

348

had been, now she came to think of it. She had been shaking ever since with—with anger, of course. Certainly, anger.

"You mean"—Sophie hesitated, "forgive me, darling, but it's a way they all have nowadays—you mean she turned *nasty*?"

"Exceedingly nasty. She—well, it sounds fantastic—but she even *threatened* me."

Sophie snorted with indignation.

"Threatened *you*? My poor innocent. And with what, I should like to know?" Rather taken aback, Milly reached for the cigarette box. With what, indeed? Her hand, she saw, was still unsteady. It was hard to think of a reply, so she made none.

"Thanks, pet." Sophie puffed away, breathing fire and vengeance on Gisela. "That's the way it is nowadays, you see. The disease has spread. Have they no decency? To *threaten* guests, foreigners?" The verb had already assumed, in Sophie's eyes, a broader significance. "A girl like that," she went on, frowning horribly, "a simpleton, a peasant—she's picked it up, d'you see; it's a bug, this way of behaviour. The shame of it. And you did quite right, Milly, quite *right*! I can understand what a shock it is to you, darling, with your English manners, your high principles, your kindly behaviour to servants, friendly but firm—yes, yes, Miss Brownlow was very keen on all that, absolute discipline but in the nicest way, and loyalty, too . . . the nanny, the housekeeper, the footmen, right down to the kitchen maid . . ." She rambled on, her eyes bright with distress, and happiness, too, being allowed to continue, wonder of wonders, patting Milly's hand.

Milly scarcely listened. The patting irritated her, but Sophie's gentle voice thrilling with indignation was, on the whole, soothing, and the very bulk of her presence seemed to provide the shelter of which she was in need.

"You mean," she said at last, beginning to feel better and drawing her hand away, "you wouldn't take it—*seriously*?"

"My little Milly!" Sophie, seeing her little Milly scowl at that, and as ever on the alert for such danger signals, went on quickly: "*Seriously!* Pah! for me, well, I suppose that would be a different matter. Anyone can make trouble for me. But for you—innocent as a babe unborn—ah no, she is crazy, my darling, and what's more, I fear—*she's a rotter!*" Having delivered herself of this expression of judgment, than which there was clearly none more pejorative, she stubbed out her cigarette. "Don't worry about it any more. We'll find somebody else—oh, easily. I tell you what!"

"What?"

"I'll put my thinking cap on!"

"Oh." Milly sat back with a sigh.

349

" Oh, yes, I will." Sophie could not help, at that moment, allowing her thoughts to stray to her own household and the activities in progress there, but reproving herself sharply, she concentrated on the immediate problem, the tragedy of her friend's position, bereft of a personal maid, for at least a day, in a hotel. Gallant little soul, thought Sophie affectionately, how she is facing up to it, wishing but not daring to press her hand, but it seemed—heavens, as if that were not enough—as if Milly had something else on her mind. And yet she, Sophie, had had a kind of presentiment all along of there being more to come.

" The thing is, Sophie," Milly was saying, " that's not all. There's something else I wanted to ask your advice about . . . the main thing, actually."

" I knew it! " she exclaimed with a little scream of ecstasy. " Darling," she added, sitting bolt upright, her ears pricked, her eyes fixed on Milly's face.

" It's hard to know how to put it." Indeed it was hard, confronted by those glowing trustful eyes.

" Something I can do? "

" Perhaps. I'm in rather a spot, you see. Now Gisela's behaved in this way."

" Yes? " Sophie smiled eagerly. " Ho-ho, and I can understand that, I should think. With all these hungry mouths to feed—you'd like me to come and work? "

" Don't be *silly*, Sophie. Just let me explain, will you? You know that we order—that's to say, we *have* to order our own supplies of—well, everything . . . from England . . ."

"Ha, I should think I do know. Your perfect gin, whisky and so on—you need them in a pig sty like this, such dainty mortals as you."

Milly stared at her, unaccountably vexed. The way in which Sophie tumbled to one's meaning was almost indelicate sometimes. Still, remembering how she herself was placed, she composed her features.

" Yes, well. I find I've—I've rather too much—of, well, certain things—and what I was wondering was . . ."

" But, Milly, darling—you could sell them, you know! "

" Could I? " she said faintly. " That was what I was wondering."

" But of course! Splendid! I'll help. What fun. Is *that* what was worrying you? Oh, darling——"

" Yes," she laughed, " that was it." Was it then really so simple? Was it all in her own imagination, all that—the anxiety, the sense of guilt? " You see, now that Gisela——"

" Gisela? " said Sophie timidly. Then, seeing that Milly was happy now, she laughed too, to hide her bewilderment. Gisela? What had Gisela to do with all this? No, that's beyond me . . . that's something

350

I can't fathom and that's because I'm a dunce, she told herself, and always have been. There's some simple connection I dare say . . . anyway, Milly knows, the darling . . . something very obvious, probably, dunderhead that I am. She went on, with enthusiasm:

" Listen, darling, there's nothing to worry about. It's such luck, you see, that I'm perfectly placed. I know—personally, that is—let me see, *several* people who would dearly like to "—she flinched at the word " buy "—" like to have the chance of such goods. Wait—yes, there's one old professor, I'm rather a pet of his, by the way, who regularly—and he makes no secret of it—*every month*, Milly, actually buys a whole quarter of a kilo of "—she had been going to say " black market " and changed it—" *foreign* tea! "

" Ah," said Milly bleakly, thinking of the twelve pound packets to be disposed of.

" Oh, I'll get you a good price. You don't know—I've become quite a commerçante, latterly. Shall I take it now and see what I can do? "

" There's . . . er . . . more than one thing."

" Naturally, I should say so," said Sophie loyally, " the splendid things you have. Then shall I come and get them—another day, say, and take them away? "

" How? " said Milly, after a pause. " How would you do that? "

" Why, stuff them into this faithful old satchel, of course! " Sophie stroked it with glee.

" It's not so easy," Milly said slowly. " There's a porter downstairs, who watches . . ."

" Oh, *him*! "

" Besides "—she raised her eyes to Sophie's face—" they wouldn't —the things, I mean—they wouldn't go in."

Sophie took a deep breath.

" You mean—darling—that there's a—a *certain amount*? "

" Yes. That's what I mean. A certain amount. . . . But I think I've got an idea."

" You brainy pet." Sophie giggled fondly, surreptitiously glancing at her watch.

" I tell you what I'll do. I'll pack all the stuff up and bring it to-night, to your party. You see, we want to make a contribution, anyway." She had only just thought of this, and really it sounded very nice. " And in the confusion, you see . . ."

" Milly—*brilliant*! " Sophie clapped her hands. " What a brainwave! Indeed, I see now that would have been the problem—that cheeky young idiot downstairs—and this way—ah, perfect! Who but you would have thought of it? " She gazed tenderly at her friend.

" I think it is a good idea," Milly murmured modestly. " And it

351

saves you coming back and forth. Now what about the party? What do you want me to bring?"

"*Bring?*" Sophie hugged her and jumped to her feet. "Nothing—at all. Just yourselves. Now I must fly. Oh, you don't know how happy you've made me—this morning, you see, I thought . . . well—now you're actually *coming*!"

"We're certainly coming," Milly smiled.

"This morning . . . duffer that I am . . ." she crammed the beret on her head, quite beside herself with joy, "I thought . . . just for a second, you know . . ."

"This morning . . . here, your satchel, Sophie . . . I was in a bad mood . . . a lot's happened since then."

"A bad mood . . ." Sophie gurgled, "of course . . . you little angel. Who doesn't have them? I know I do. Now I'm off."

At the door she turned. "Milly . . ."

"Mmm? . . ." She was lighting a cigarette by the stove. Sophie, in the doorway, shuffled her feet.

"It's suddenly struck me . . . don't think—*please* don't think I'm a—a cowardy custard, Milly . . . and don't be cross, darling . . . but, to-night, you know. . . ."

"Yes, Sophie?" said Milly patiently.

"Could you . . . as you enter . . . with the—er—things, you know, be just a teeny bit careful of my porter, too? He's not over-nice."

"Sophie! *Your* porter?" For a second she had thought Sophie had been going to back out. Now she laughed very pleasantly. "Why, my dear, *of course*. I must say, I'd no idea until now that porters could be so important!"

"I know," said Sophie gravely, swinging her satchel, awkward as a schoolgirl. "And you must excuse me for mentioning it . . . but . . . well, of course, you simply couldn't have any idea how important porters can be."

*   *   *

"It's too early for tea," objected Clarissa, as her mother swept in with the tray.

"No, it isn't," said Milly crossly, "it's the one meal you can have any time—whenever it suits you." Aware, too late, that this was the sort of remark likely on some future occasion to come home to roost, putting the tray down in front of the stove, she added grimly, "And it suits *me* that you have it now."

"Oh, it suits me, too," said Clarissa. "Cake *and* biscuits! What a funny day. No walk—no rest—it's been quite one of the nicest days I've ever had."

352

" We've been all alone," said Dermot, unwilling to let authority off scot-free. " All alone for ages and ages."

" Yes, I'm sorry. I forgot. Miss Raven went to have her hair washed for the party. Have you been good? "

Clarissa glanced at her brother. He was quite quick off the mark, considering his years. " Oh, yes," she sighed lugubriously, playing it his way, " considering."

" Considering what? " said Milly sharply.

" Considering nobody's bothered about us . . . but it doesn't matter, Mummy," the little heroine added bravely, easily maintaining a stiff upper lip, " I kept Dermot amused."

" Yes, I was amused," said Dermot, ably partnering his sister, allowing his lower lip to quiver.

" Well, darlings, just for *to-day*—— " Milly retreated, vanquished by the sense of her own guilt, " be extra specially good. Please. Give him his tea, Clarissa. I'm busy in the kitchen, but I'll come back in a little while."

" Can we have cake *and* biscuits? "

" Yes," she said weakly. " You may. Just this once."

Clarissa winked at her brother. When their mother had gone she said: " I'm putting it all in my knickers. Look. You'd better give me yours too."

" Not *all*," he pleaded. " Let me have *some* now."

" Don't be such a baby, Dermot. D'you want a feast or don't you? "

" Yes, I do, but—— " He sniffed. " I'd like some *now*, too. Last time it got all . . . ma-a-ashed . . ."

" You can't have it both ways," said Clarissa firmly, making a clean sweep of the plates.

" Don't take it *all*! " Her brother watched, horror-struck. " She'll notice! "

" Oh, no, she won't." Clarissa was stuffing the goodies away. " She's not in the mood."

*   *   *

She locked both kitchen doors and got down to work. There was not very much time because Miss Raven might return at any minute.

Two portable parcels, she had decided, were better than one mammoth one. Therefore she divided the groceries into two piles; the bottles would have to go separately, they were too difficult to pack, and she could carry them herself, loose, in the shopping bag, ostensibly as a contribution to the party. The drugs were best split up, shared between the two parcels, so without hesitation she snapped the string of the package containing them—ridiculous, after all, to have any scruples about it, to feel it did not belong to her—it was addressed to her, wasn't it? How enchanted Sophie would have been by the wrappings. The little phials nestled in cotton wool. There seemed to be three different sorts. Injections, she thought vaguely—but at least with none of those idiotic and rather pompous labels, personally addressed—what a discreet and sensible chemist; an excellent firm. Then she made a list of the contents of each pile, writing in block letters for clarity and against each item the price, calculated in the currency of the country, which according to Gisela represented the value of the goods. After all, it was better to have it on a business-like footing from the start. It so often tended to be awkward, dealing with friends. Sophie herself would undoubtedly prefer it this way, and when it came to checking up at the end each would know exactly where she stood. Besides, the price, Gisela's price, here clearly set down, would act as a sort of guide for Sophie, a target figure. If ever she were at a loss when hawking pepper, sultanas, insulin or rice, commodities she might conceivably have no commercial experience of, she would have merely to turn up this list and find the catalogue price.

As she made up the two parcels, laying the appropriate list in each, wrapping them in thick paper, securely knotting the string, Milly could not but reflect what an accomplice she had lost in Gisela—Gisela who, she now realised, had known not merely the ropes but all the likely knots as well; Gisela, who had never once complained, was never to be stumped by a British trade name, however obscure, who spirited a load away and spirited back the reward and always with such a good grace, as if it gave her pleasure—she spirited the stuff away all right, Milly reminded herself grimly. But her back was aching and her head too, and her fingers were bleeding where the string had cut them, and in her heart she knew very well that she bitterly regretted having got rid of Gisela. Not only on account of her aching head and bleeding fingers; now that the parcels were ready she stood back and stared at them, loathing them as they squatted on the table, bulky in their wrappings, in some awful way belonging to her, as if she had given birth to these twin monstrosities; there they would sit until she moved them, or made plans to have them moved. They were her responsibility, hers alone, and there was no Gisela now to relieve her of it.

And there were still the bottles. Three of brandy, five star, one of whisky. Then she remembered Mrs. Wragg. No, not the whisky. It was all the whisky they had—this bottle they had brought down yesterday, Larry's ration—still, it would have to go to Mrs. Wragg, to keep her quiet. What about Larry? Well, she was covered there— Gisela had taken it. Oh, lord, she thought, is there no end to it?

Now, something for the party. Nuisance, really, but she had half-promised . . . She peered into the cupboard. Sherry? No, she was rather fond of sherry herself, besides, it wasn't really suitable for a party. Wine. Of course, that would do very well. The cooking wine? *Cooking* wine—nonsense, a very decent little light wine, and Sophie would never know the difference. Three bottles—generous . . . she paused. *Three?* Well, really, it wasn't as if they were expecting an *orgy*—perhaps a couple would be—what *was* the price of wine, anyway? She was getting confused in her prices, and small wonder; three different sets to keep track of would have taxed even the brain of a Selfridge. As she replaced the third bottle of wine in the cupboard, suddenly she caught sight of the aspirin. There they were, the white packets containing bottles of a hundred tablets each, ordered not from the London chemist but from the NAAFI. She had overlooked them. " Blast," she muttered. How could she have been so stupid? It worried her, this proof of her own carelessness. Had there been time she would have unpacked all the parcels and checked them over again. There might be other mistakes. But at that moment someone tried the kitchen door. She snatched up one of the packets and stuffed it into her handbag, snapped the bag shut, closed the cupboard door, glanced around to see that the table was tidy, and unlocked the kitchen door.

" Locked yourself in, had you? " said Miss Raven. " What's all this, Father Christmas? Sorry I had to dash off—it was my hair, like I told you."

" That's all right," said Milly. " I gave the children their tea."

" Oh, you needn't 've done." Miss Raven removed her scarf and stepped over to the mirror to admire the results of the afternoon's labours. " I told the girl to see to it. Where's she gone now? Dashed off again, I suppose? "

" Not exactly. She's . . . gone."

Miss Raven, who had heard that tone in the voice of an employer more than once in the past, often enough to diagnose its import correctly, turned round. " Ah," she said, giving Milly one of her rare direct looks, and just for an instant it was as if those opaque milky eyes shifted, as if a lens had clicked. Meditatively she rubbed her blunt dogfish nose. Already, in the warm, it had reddened. " Can't say I'm surprised. Found someone else, have you? "

" No." Frowning, Milly searched for a cigarette in her bag, pushing down the aspirin packet which rose like a body to the surface. " Not yet."

" Gosh! " said Miss Raven admiringly. " On the spur of the moment, was it? You will have a time! " Turning back to the mirror

355

she fluffed out the kiss curls with which she had been lavishly adorned. " Decided not to do it your way after all. Filthy dirty place—terrible dryers they have, don't they? Bangity-bang and pick the hairpins straight up off the floor. Still, I will say he was quick on the uptake. In the R.A.F. too—so he said. Might have been, at that." She smiled reminiscently. " I just showed him a photo in *Vogue*—that last one you had—he copied it and—well, here we are! "

" Very nice."

" Now I've got my skirt to iron." She picked up her bag and gloves and glanced vaguely round the kitchen. " I mean, what about the washing-up and that sort of thing? There was a smash this morning and no mistake. It mounts up."

" Yes. That's the trouble."

" Oh, well," Miss Raven flashed a smile of sympathy, " won't be for long, I dare say. Surprising what you can do when you're pushed. Did you give Dermot his Choc-Lax? "

" No," said Milly. " I did not."

" S'ppose you couldn't have known. Never mind, I'll do it. Want the iron? Okay, I'll take it, then. See you later."

* * *

Gisela, with pins and needles in her foot, cautiously shifted her position on the camp-bed, where she had been crouched for the last couple of hours. The daylight had long since waned and the room was quite dark. There was no stove and it was very cold, but she was oblivious to the dark and to the cold; every nerve in her body had been concentrated on listening.

She was glad now that the rustle of paper had stopped. She couldn't have borne it much longer. That continuous rustling had tormented her in the way that a whiff of cigarette-smoke is torment to the smoker in the first days of abstinence. Pepper, sultanas, rice; Gisela's thoughts roamed over these mundane commodities; their very names to her spelt romance; peacocks, sandalwood, pearls from distant Ophir, were nothing to these. How she loved translating these foreign goods, some in frivolous wrappings, into money—worthless money as it was; how she loved running here and there through the back streets of the town, transacting her business in whispers, in holes and corners, and always with the element of risk attached. And then there were the other things too, that were contained in neat little tubes, in flat little boxes, easily concealed about the person; most of all it gave her pleasure to dispose of stuff like that. Because then she had to have her wits about her; she had not merely to know where to go, but to know each customer and his circumstances, and then, depending,

356

the price was simply the price that she herself set. There was no price but her price—for those articles people would pay anything—but she was never unreasonable because with that class of goods it was better to have a steady clientèle than make the odd sensational coup. There was also some additional element in these transactions, apart from the risk which was profoundly satisfying to *her*. She derived what was almost an emotional pleasure from the bargaining because the goods themselves were bound up with the desperate emotions, not only those of the customer, the barely disguised emotions of fear, anxiety, relief, but her own, too; and as she exacted her price on what might mean the difference between life and death, but more often pain or release from pain, a night of wakefulness or of dreamless sleep, she had the triumphant sensation of revenging herself upon life. Yes, above all things Gisela preferred to deal in drugs. Oh, how she regretted her stupidity. She would have given anything to be there now, just so that she might handle the goods for herself, sort them out, tie them up. But all that was over. Instead she must wait.

Mrs. Simpson, Mrs. Purdoe. What a pair. Funny, it was not hatred she felt for Mrs. Purdoe—any more than it had been love she had felt for Mrs. Simpson. No, Mrs. Simpson had been goddess, protectress and boss—a relationship profitable to them both, and only Gisela knew to what extent her professed hero-worship of that lady had been tinged with contempt. And yet this situation would never have arisen with Mrs. Simpson. No, because it wouldn't have suited Mrs. Simpson's plans at all. She had been a very different sort of woman from Mrs. Purdoe, greedy, and vain (like Mrs. Purdoe, only more so) but sentimental, too; although the main difference between them was the fact that about Mrs. Simpson there had clung an aura of success. Big, and bullying and lethargic, too, she had been as confident, and as impervious to life's shoves, as a plump tabby cat on top of a garden wall. You could no more imagine her coming to grief than you could imagine that cat going unfed. Whatever it was that had happened to Mr. and Mrs. Simpson, Gisela was convinced that at least in the eyes of the latter it had not figured as disaster. She had left, taking with her a very nice load of stuff—enough, as she had herself remarked, to keep both Mr. Simpson and herself in comfort for years, and leaving behind her a watch, a pile of old clothes and a fat pourboire for her devoted little maid—who would eat her heart out for a while— gratifying, that—and then recover, because that was life and Gisela was a sensible little thing. Gisela smiled to herself. Mrs. Simpson need not have troubled on that last score—Gisela's heart was the least of her worries.

And poor Mrs. Purdoe—when she came to counting her spoils what

357

would they amount to? A few knick-knacks from the market and that mouldy piece of lace. But it was her own fault. She went about it the wrong way—head down, like a chicken with its beak to a chalk line, losing sight of the main objective in the effort to follow one path. And if you compared the two women, not only were they different in themselves and in their choice of methods, but also in their attitude to the objects they appeared to desire so much. Mrs. Simpson had known the value of china, silver, glass; she had even ordered a big book on the subject and studied it. She had wanted to possess such things not because they were pretty but because later on, in England, they might be turned into cash. Mrs. Purdoe, on the other hand, was like a child. She saw something that took her fancy—because it was pretty, or because someone else had one like it—and she felt she had to have it too. Thirty years earlier she would have screamed for it, ten years earlier grabbed it; now she had to scheme for it—but she was still just a child at heart.

But Gisela had a soft spot for children. She would have liked to have gone on helping poor Mrs. Purdoe. In a way she had come to be fond of her, in spite of the row that morning; curiously enough, it had made no difference to her feelings. She saw something of herself in Mrs. Purdoe—at least their situations weren't too dissimilar, she thought.

The Nanny was still blundering about, humming to herself, now and then bursting into song. First the ironing-board, then the iron—would she never go? At last the door shut and there was silence. Gisela was just about to creep out when she heard voices at the end of the corridor. Herr Purdoe, Herr Wragg, back from the office. Herr Wragg striding past to his own apartment. His shoes squeaked. Speaking to Herr Purdoe, just then, his voice had sounded quite lively, almost unrecognisable. Now his steps seemed to slow down to a shuffle as he approached his own door. No wonder. Frau Wragg. Like a man, that one, only not so interesting. Then the housekeeper rattled past, checking the passage lights, twitching the curtains. Then silence. Her own concentration in the silence was so intense that it was as if the whereabouts, the movements, even the thoughts of each member of the family were signalled to her brain. She knew to the instant when the bathroom tap was turned on. That bath was for *her*. She was dressing for dinner. She didn't usually dress—were they having guests? No, only Herr Schulman, of course. But how early to dress —no, she was nervous, she still had things to do. The children were going without their baths to-night—the steam might damage the Nanny's set. Where was *she* off to, the Nanny? Why had she had her hair done? Old fool, thought Gisela. *He* wouldn't look at her even if she dyed it pink. He was in the end room, the salon, pouring a drink. The children were in bed.

She slipped out into the passage. With her hand on the kitchen door she felt her heart pounding. She turned the handle and went in, closing the door behind her, leaning against it. She had never felt so frightened in her life. In the dark she heard the tap dripping, the electric plate creak as it cooled off, a scuffle under the bath. For three years until to-day this had been her home, her domain; here, in Mrs. Simpson's time, she had reigned supreme. Now she was a trespasser. Anyone might challenge her right to stand here. She dared not even turn on the light. Instead she struck a match. Yes, there they were, just as she had visualised them. Two. Quite right. Just what she herself would have done. She stepped forward, her fingers itching to touch them, but this she dared not do. There was nothing she could do, yet. She had seen them, that was all. She smiled sardonically, appraising the squat shapes much as Milly herself had done. Frankly, she was puzzled as to how Mrs. Purdoe intended getting them out of the hotel. If she managed *that*, she would be a worthy adversary— more, a magician. Probably late to-night.

So, thought Gisela, one thing's clear, my fate is linked with them. The match had burned down to her fingers. She let it fall to the floor, where it glowed for a second and then went out. In that second she had caught sight of a crumpled piece of paper. She struck another match, and bent down. Yes, the distinctive olive-green paper with the cream label, used by that London chemist. She grinned to herself. So —they were tucked away in there, too, were they? Quite right—the Rapovska was greedy, too greedy. She had been going to suggest that very thing, funnily enough. Really, she and Mrs. Purdoe would have made a magnificent team. She took one last lingering look at the table. All in all, she couldn't have done better herself. Then she crept out, closing the door behind her.

Regaining her lair, she lay down on the bed. Ah, but it was awful, this waiting. One could move so far and no farther. Well, nothing could happen yet. She gave a great yawn. How tired she was. What a day. But she mustn't sleep. She couldn't afford to sleep. When might she sleep again? Not until . . . not before . . . not unless . . . She was already asleep.

* * *

Milly herself was puzzled on that score—as to how to get the beastly things out. It irked her that she could light upon no comprehensive plan. She detested a complicated operation of this sort, involving so many different stages and processes that it was impossible

359

to proceed with dash from start to finish; one was forced to grope one's way, and in any case merely to react as and when factors, setbacks, opportunities, presented themselves.

Once the things were out of the hotel—that was the first stage, obviously. Then what? She had no idea. Then she would have to think again. Still, once out of the hotel, the battle was half over, so far as she was concerned. Then the matter would be in the hands of Sophie, or fate. All the same, she felt far less confident than she had felt before the affair of the dressmaker. She had, to some extent, lost her nerve. Her heart still quaked, remembering that experience with the night watchman; once or twice she had even dreamed about him and his dog. She never now descended the main staircase without first glancing down into the hall below; sometimes, on the way to the market, overwhelmed by the sensation of someone following behind, she would dive down a side street. She remembered, long ago—three months ago, but it seemed longer—Abe saying: " You'll change. We all do. Best thing is not to jump at shadows. Get to know them. Yep. I know mine—I'd feel lost without him. Alby's a pal—he knows I know and he knows I know he knows that I know . . ."

" Stop it, Abe," Larry had said. " You'll make the girl nervous." But it was true. She and Larry had both changed and their habits with them. Why, she never kept letters or bills now; she threw them into the stove and even stayed to watch them as they burned. Her handbag was never allowed out of her sight; she took it with her even into the bathroom; at night it was under her bed. She had developed a photographic memory which automatically recorded the position of any article, book, hairbrush, keys, as she laid it down. As for Larry—look how he had changed. Why, even she noticed it. Take for instance to-day, his manner on the telephone. And he hadn't her *worries,* had he? Nothing like.

So before he arrived she had two quick drinks to restore her self-confidence. The drinks were a great help. She was dressed and had almost finished her face when he came in.

" How do I look? " she demanded, smiling.

" Very nice." He himself looked tired. " By the way, what about the children? "

" The children? What about them? "

" I happened to see Miss Raven dressed up to kill so I take it her plans aren't altered. Fixed up for anyone to look in on them? "

" Well—er . . ." She took a deep breath. His manner flustered her. " Not exactly. I mean, I think they'll be all right."

" I see." He went out, to pour himself a drink, she supposed. He was gone a little while. When he came back, glass in hand, he said:

" Wragg's asked their maid, Helga, to keep an eye on them. I've said she can sit in the salon."

" Oh, that's good," said Milly brightly. She gave a nervous little laugh. " Well, I mean, it's lucky, isn't it ? "

" Yes," he agreed shortly. " It is, isn't it." He took his drink into the bathroom with him.

And so they would have been all right, she argued to herself. It's a hotel, isn't it? How funny he was sometimes—still, he'd get over it. And why shouldn't he fix things occasionally—especially when she had so much on her mind? She dismissed it forthwith.

What with the small amount of alcohol churning cosily in her veins and the sight of herself, really very pretty—Sophie, she felt sure, would take it as a compliment that she should *dress*—the thought came to her, supposing all this is a fuss about nothing? Keep calm, and think it out. Supposing those parcels were perfectly ordinary parcels—containing supplies for the office, say—who would Larry get to carry them out to the car? Who was the only person who was not under suspicion, *whose job was it to carry parcels*? None other than the person who had delivered them, of course. Vladek. There you are, she told herself. Certainly it was rather—audacious—but Vladek was reliable, Larry had often said so, and as for the party, he would be driving them there in any case, so he knew about *that*, and what could be more natural than that she should wish to make a contribution? At least by this means the parcels would get as far as the car. Then she would have to think again. After that—she could see it looming ahead—the problem would revert to its familiar shape: Larry. Still, one thing at a time. Really, it all fitted in wonderfully. Honesty, she told herself, brushing her eyebrows, *is* the best policy. Honesty and generosity combined.

When she was quite ready, she called through the bathroom door: " Darling, I promised Sophie some bottles and things to help out. So if Vladek's waiting downstairs I'll get him to take them down."

" All right," he called back.

She telephoned for the driver to come up. He came at once, and she was waiting for him in the passage, her fur wrap round her shoulders, her large handbag in her hand. She smiled graciously by way of greeting and led the way down the corridor. Opening the kitchen door, in silence she simply indicated the two parcels, Vladek picked them up, and she herself took the bag of bottles. It was as simple as that. As they went down the passage together she murmured to Vladek, " Miss Bielska, party, to-night! " and Vladek, who was staggering a little under the weight of the parcels, merely nodded and grinned in the way he always did. He was all for a party himself—and if the

361

weight of these was anything to judge by, it should be a good one. Miss Bielska was a favourite of his—she wouldn't leave him to sit out in the cold without a glass or two to keep him from freezing to death.

Following him down the stairs, Milly paused to glance below. Abe Schulman was standing by the porter's desk, his back to the stairs, reading a letter. He was in his overcoat, his hat pushed back on his head. She thought he looked pleasantly big and solid, and momentarily she experienced a little thrill of excitement, childish, almost—well, almost, because childish wasn't *quite* the word—at the thought of the evening ahead. Allowing Vladek to go down the stairs alone, which in any case was advisable, she herself hung back, unable to forgo the pleasure of savouring the moment, having spotted it. I shall remember this, she thought, all my life—and chalked it up. Poor Milly. In the matter of moments her powers of discrimination were slight; her fancy might have been termed the housemaid's choice. Still, she was not so absorbed in savouring it as not to notice that Vladek's progress through the hall and out through the swing doors had, by some strange chance, gone unremarked by both Abe, who was engrossed in his letter, and the porter, who was bent behind his desk, locking a drawer; and the housekeeper's hatch, for once, was shut. So honesty really *is* the best policy, she told herself wonderingly, and went on down.

As she reached the bottom stair, Abe glanced round.

"Hi, there." He gave a low wolf-whistle. "Milly, Milly. The things you do to me. Don't forget I ain't seen a white woman in— why, I could eat you up, every little bit, you luscious morsel, you . . ." He stroked her under the chin as he would a cat.

"Stop it," she said, fluttering her lashes. He stopped it at once; too suddenly, in fact.

"I was going to call you up," he went on.

He had this odd trick of paying her an elaborate compliment, or of teasing her (flirting with her, *she* would have called it), and then, for no apparent reason—that is to say, not because her husband had suddenly turned up at her elbow—but quite unpredictably, of switching his manner, tone of voice, to that of mere friendliness, sometimes even of formality. Disconcerting as it was, this trick, it was part of his attraction for her. You never know where you are with him, was how she expressed it to herself. She had long since overcome her original feeling of irritation on this score, having long since convinced herself that these were simply the rather baffling tactics he preferred. Now, for instance, she knew that had she interpreted his last remark as signifying that he had intended to telephone her personally she would have been very much mistaken. The pronoun " you " when

362

employed by Abe might, maddeningly enough, equally well be intended as a plural " you " to be shared between her and Larry.

" I hear the Wraggs have been invited. I guess old Fräulein Lorelei's going too, is she? "

" Yes," said Milly, giggling.

" So I thought," he said, " someone might be wanting a lift."

And that was the way in which it came to her. Quite suddenly—and in the nick of time, too—it just dropped from the blue; the plan, perfect, and perfectly simple, that would see her through.

She looked up at him, giving him her pussy-cat smile which had seldom been known to fail. " Me," she said softly, " *I* want a lift. You'll give me a lift, Abe, won't you? "

He looked a little surprised, as well he might.

" Sure, okay. Fine."

" Come along to us, then, when you're ready. We'll have a drink waiting. Remember, now," she laid a hand on his arm, " *I'm* the one who's going with *you*."

She tripped out into the street. The office car, the Austin, as was the custom when it was to be required later, was parked in the side street round the corner. Abe's small Citroën was parked just behind. Vladek was groping around in the back of the Austin, she could see the glowing cigarette stub between his lips; probably clearing a space for the parcels, which he had put down on the pavement under the street lamp.

" Vladek! " she called under her breath, coming up behind him. He emerged, and seeing her, threw away the cigarette. He was punctilious in his manners always.

" No." She shook her head. " Not *there*." Indicating the parcels, and beckoning him to follow, she walked round to the back of the Citroën and with perfect confidence flipped open the boot. There. Somehow she had known it would be open—and it was.

She nodded, smiling, and watched as he stowed them in. " *I* "—she paused; it seemed to her that some explanation might not be out of place, but her Slavonian was not up to much—" *I*," she repeated with deliberation, ". . . er . . . Mr. *Schulman* . . . understand? "

Vladek had looked up and was staring at her in astonishment. She caught his expression under the street lamp. Then he grinned and slammed the boot shut. " Thank you," she said prettily, and tossing the bag of bottles on to the front seat of the Citroën, she tripped off.

He watched her round the corner, chuckling to himself. *Understand?* She was a cool customer and no mistake. He understood all right, but fancy telling him in so many words! He wondered if his employer were aware that his wife was the American's mistress. Very odd they were, the English. No natural jealousy, or not so that you'd notice; a deficiency in the national character he had himself exploited more than once during his own sojourn in that country. He went to sit in the Austin, still pondering over this aspect of the private lives of the three foreigners; then, quite naturally, his mind turned to that same aspect of his own. A party. What better excuse to stay out? His old woman would have to lump it. The night was young.

PART THREE
THE LAST FORAY IN
SLAVONIA

And I was there among the guests and there
drank wine and mead;
And what I saw and heard I wrote, that all
of you might read.

ADAM MICKIEWICZ: *Pan Tadeusz*

"The way I look at it is"—Mrs. Wragg resettled her black satin skirts on the bed—"it's a great privilege to be here at all." Apparently the guest of honour, with five persons hanging on her words, she was in her element. She had been in it now for—Sophie glanced at her watch—one hour and thirty-five minutes. Father Joseph stirred his tea, blinking at Mrs. Wragg. He was terribly afraid of falling asleep and, in that event, of falling off the bed.

"You have not living-rooms like this in your country? Is that it?"

"Oh, I wasn't referring to the interior dec., Father—I think we can probe a bit deeper than that. No, the fact is we haven't advanced quite so far as you in our experiment . . . but when the day arrives, as it undoubtedly will, I dare say we shall find the initial period—the settling-down stage, you might say, a bit trying to . . . Now, at least," she went on brightly, rallying the other poor old man on her right, whom she had been at great pains to draw out, "now at least it's the same for everybody, isn't it? Running water, and all that?"

"Running water?" replied old Prince Mischka, rather dazedly. He had come on the dot, as Sophie had asked him to do, so that he too had had one hour and thirty-five minutes of this sort of thing and a hard day's bicycling into the bargain. Surreptitiously he stroked the tendons round his ankle joints. The lady was not at all his type. But in such a small company, three of them on a bed, you couldn't very well, unobtrusively, that is, move your place.

"Quite a step forward, isn't it? There's running water in all the new blocks, I read the statistics only yesterday. It's by no means the case even in England, I can assure you. . . ." She laughed, and because she didn't look quite so fearsome when she laughed Prince Mischka encouraged her, although he hadn't the faintest idea what the joke was, and their laughter woke up Father Joseph, who joined in, and Ludovic giggled because he had been dying to for some time, and Singe gave a cackle, catching Father Joseph's eye, and Sophie laughed quite spontaneously, thinking she had heard footsteps on the stairs. Only Wragg went on looking glum. When Sophie realised her mistake she stopped laughing abruptly, and so did everybody else. It was exactly as if they had all of them set to at once and stamped out a very small heath blaze.

"Possibly you may consider a word of advice from an outsider just the sheerest impertinence. . . ." Olga Wragg smiled graciously at the old man. Herbert should've been a dip, she was thinking, meaning that she, Olga, would've made a dip's wife. " But what you must realise is, that critics such as myself, that is, holding liberal views, deplore the reactionary spirit—private enterprise and all that—as a waste of time. Not a step *forward*, but a step *back*. See what I mean? In other words, from what you've told me about your job, I'd say you were just swimming against the tide. Mind you, that's plain speaking, still . . . swimming against the tide, that's it." The prince looked helplessly over at Sophie for guidance. If it was plain speaking it wasn't plain to him. Running water, swimming against the tide, the lady seemed to have water on the brain.

Olga, fixing the prince with a fairly powerful beam from her black orbs and leaning back on the bed, fitted a cigarette into her holder, well pleased with herself. They would remember, later, that she had talked with them thus, shared their problems, helped clear away the lumber of bourgeois principles with the incisive hammer-blows of reason—and yet shown herself warm, human, sympathetic—she had that genius for making you feel that *you*—no, what was it—a personality which attracted others willy-nilly like bees around a—not *jampot*—well, around a flower then? No, not flower. One mustn't descend to clichés . . . bees—peas . . . sneeze . . . fleas—she murmured to herself, a means she was accustomed to employ when searching for rhymes at the bidding of Tiny Tim and Co., or, more frequently, when stuck in her literary labours and prospecting for a snug little creek up which a shoal of thoughts might be dispatched on an exploratory jaunt, and, if it suited them, spawn there. V. Woolf must have employed the very same device, she was convinced, else how explain the fact of another feminine brain, a decade and a half later, tossing off passages of prose so lyrical and baffling and thoroughly inconsequential as to be indistinguishable from those of the maîtresse? Still, these dear people *wouldn't* remember unless they were told, in due course, of her success. She must be her own propagandist, remember to send them—what would it be? Probably a two-page spread in *Picture Post*—that would be best, because of the pictures. . . . She could see it all so clearly, their delight, the reverent murmurs—" She sat there "—etc., that she was a little disconcerted on looking round her to find no evidence of corresponding premonitory emotions on the faces of those present. They all looked tired. She smiled, a peculiarly radiant smile—of promise, really, did they but know it—a smile which prompted Wragg, who had been following, and, thanks to the dreary privilege of intimacy, interpreting, the play of expression over her features, to stir his tea widdershins; the single outward ritual, designed as a vent, he permitted

368

himself on occasions such as these when the voice of the inner man rose up within him, yapping, clamorous, in the past merely gibbering incantations which latterly, however, had become canalised into a priority personal call to the gods for help.

" Swimming against . . ." murmured Singe, as no one else volunteered to speak. " Oh, you're quite right, I think. It certainly does feel like that."

" I'm not sure you've *quite* got my meaning . . . now, you, for instance——" Mrs. Wragg turned to the old prince once more. " Let's approach it constructively. Your hours of work, travelling time, and so on . . . seem to *me*—and by any standards, I should have said—excessive."

" Ah," said Prince Mischka. " You would say that? "

" Yes, I would. Surely—wouldn't it be better to—I mean, there must be a trades union in which—toys . . . toys . . . manufacture, distribution of—let me see . . . now what would that come under? "

" Luxury goods, perhaps? " Singe suggested timidly.

Mrs. Wragg, apprehending the dimensions of the pitfall to which agreement would lead her, shook her head. She had not been secretary of the Finchley Road Branch all those years for nothing.

" Selling well, are they? " said Father Joseph, who was faint with hunger, but cheered to notice that Sophie had slipped out of the room.

" Oh, like hot cakes." Prince Mischka smiled. " *Now*. Aren't they, Singe? "

" Yes, *now*! " squeaked Singe. " You see, *now*, Father, I've learned to put the hair on. It's made all the difference, the hair."

" Hair? " Not having contributed to the conversation for over an hour, as per usual Wragg's voice played him up, emerging on a booming note. He clattered his spoon in the saucer to mitigate the effect. All the same, he did want to know. In a bronchial whisper he persisted: " *Hair?* "

" Why, yes," said the prince with pride. " Undoubtedly the hair's done the trick . . ." He broke off, knitting his brow; then leaning forward and tapping Wragg on the knee, added solemnly: " Not *real* hair, you understand."

" Oh no," muttered Wragg, feeling uncomfortable. " Of course not."

" Ah, but then you see," said Singe humbly, " they're not even *real* dolls."

Ludovic escaped into the kitchen where his sister was feverishly dismembering the roasted carcasses on the table.

" Sophie, look here." There was a truce between them that night. " How long is this to go on? It's *awful*, that clerk and that ghoul of a

369

wife. Qu'elle est moche! That's the seventh hen you've cut up and so far we've only four guests. Please, Sophie. Tell me, whom else have you invited? Anybody at all?"

"Everybody," she replied haughtily, wiping the carving knife and starting to remount the dismembered limbs on to the vertebrae, a trick of presentation at which she was very skilled. Her brother, when her back was turned, filched a drumstick from the plate. He was about to start gnawing it when she turned round.

"Put that back," she said. "I'll be a leg short otherwise. If le bon Dieu couldn't manage to prop up a bird with one leg, neither can I," and Ludovic did as he was told.

"But listen, Sophie . . . for what *time* did you invite?"

Singe also had crept into the kitchen. Sophie banged away with the carving knife and the pestle, severing joints, splitting breast bones, as if it afforded her a special relief.

"Darling," said Singe. "*What* time did you say?"

"Six o'clock," she replied curtly. She paused. "At least, I think I said six."

"Mais évidemment, ma tante," said Ludovic, "pourquoi tu demandes ça? Ne sont-ils pas arrivés—les deux—à l'heure précise?" He went on, turning to his sister: "But for *to-day*, Sophie, did you invite?—or for to-morrow?"

"Shut up," said Sophie. Her hands had begun to tremble. Surely she had said six? Or, at least, the evening—that she remembered—but, *to-day*? Dear God, surely she had said *to-day*?

"You see, darling," murmured Singe, "it's this way . . . you know you invited the Rozinskis? Well, apparently she told Father Joseph this afternoon that it was impossible to come . . . I'm sorry, but we didn't dare tell you, neither he nor I . . ."

"Ha!" Sophie gave a snort. "The Rozinskis, eh? And *why* can't they come? Any reason? Any excuse? A previous engagement, I suppose?"

"She did say something like that . . . but you know as well as I do. Once they hear there will be British—well, then, not everyone can come."

"Whewww . . ." Sophie straightened up, dashed her hand across her eyes. "*What* a race!" For once she spoke in her mother tongue. "What a *noble* race we are!" She had the carving knife in her hand. Suddenly, with all her might, she plunged the point of it, like a dagger, into the table top. She stood back, glaring at her relatives, the blade quivering between them. "So *this* is what we've come to! I must say, I'm *proud*." The scorn in her voice was terrible to hear. "What nerve, what heart, what fibre! Why, *these*"—with a sweep of her arm

370

she indicated the corpses on the table—" these had more *guts* than we have! "

" Sophie, darling," pleaded Singe.

" I won't hear a word, Singe, I warn you! " Nevertheless, she relaxed somewhat. " You know I asked the Liehas, the boy and girl who always seemed nice, but oh no, now *they* can't come—having heard, I suppose . . . and the Karolyskis, I didn't dare tell *you* that . . . *they* can't come either. I got the note a little while ago. Previous engagement again. I must say I hadn't realised until this evening what a whirl of social activity goes on in this town of ours. But *never mind*! " she muttered, withdrawing the carving knife from the table, as she had to get on, " I've arranged a party and a party it shall be! "

" Listen," said Ludovic, seeing that the worst of the storm had passed, " tu l'as arrangé parfaitement, Sophie. All *this* side of it's excellent. But without people, ma chère, it's impossible. It's not a party."

" *Not* a party? "

" Supposing your British should arrive now? They'll go away again thinking they've come to the morgue by mistake. *We must have guests.*"

" He's right, darling. And a little vodka soon, perhaps. Even Father Joseph is getting sick of tea."

" And *she's* off again," said Ludovic.

" Oh, no! "

" Yes. Now, co-operatives," said Singe. " She wants to start a regular discussions group."

" Crumbs," said Sophie, and crossed herself.

" So shall I go and get the Rapovskis? " urged Ludovic. " I happen to know they're free."

" *Never!* " she cried. " I won't have them in my house."

" Oh, but they wouldn't mind coming, Sophie . . . they'll put up with anything, you know."

" Ah, so they will, will they? That's decent of them, I must say."

" Don't go off the deep end, my dear," said Ludovic, " I only want your party to be a success. Of course, I'd still have to coax them a bit, you know."

" Tell them there'll be whisky," his aunt suggested. " That'll fetch them."

" I'm sorry," said Sophie. " I've told you, I won't have a Rapovski in my house. Auntie, you agree, don't you? "

" Darling, I—I don't know . . . you see, there's such a lot to be eaten, and that room—well, it does look bare . . . and just for the *noise*,

371

you know—it might be as well. At least they are big, and, well—noisy . . ."

They watched her erect another whole carcase in silence. Then she looked up and caught her brother's eye.

" Well, Sophie," he stammered, " what shall I do?"

" *Do?* " she stormed at him. " What are you waiting for? Go and get them! If we've got to have them let's get it over quickly."

" But—how . . . how *many* of them? "

They had never seen her in such a rage. " *How many?* Enough to furnish the place, I suppose. No, wait . . . if we have them at all we'll do it properly. . . . Get them all. Let's have the whole "—she hesitated, an expression of Milly's coming to mind, an expression that would have horrified Miss Brownlow but now, if ever, was the moment . . . " the whole—damn'—shooting—match! " Singe gasped. Ludovic had already scuttled out.

After that, of course, in the next five minutes or so, everybody began to arrive at once.

*   *   *

Abe had made a detour by way of the florist to pick up a bunch of roses he had ordered for Sophie, so that the Austin was already parked outside her door when the Citroën arrived.

" Okay, out you get." Abe leaned across Milly and opened the door. " You go on up—it's right at the top. I shan't be long."

" But——" She stared at him blankly. " But—I don't—where are you—what are you going to do?"

" Go park the car."

" But you can leave the car here, Abe. There's Vladek just in front."

" That's just precisely why I'm going some other place. Go on, Milly, do, it's cold."

She pulled the door to, remaining where she was. " But I don't *understand* . . ." she wailed.

He sighed. " Look, sweetheart, do we have to have all this argument? I don't want to be brutally frank, but doesn't it ever occur to you to think of anyone else? It just so happens that this isn't London, Paris, or New York, and Sophie's sticking her neck out quite far enough without our complicating things for her. One car looks fairly funny, two would look positively bee-zarre. Understand? So be a good girl and do as I say. . . ."

" But where will you *go?* " Everything had run so smoothly up to now. Too smoothly, of course.

" Oh, I'll find a place."

372

She slammed the door shut. "I'm coming too," she said obstinately.

He heaved an even deeper sigh. "Listen, *dear*—you just *can't* walk through the snow in those ridiculous shoes." They were of the glass slipper variety. There was nothing to them, that was what had made them so expensive. First time on to-night. It cut her to the heart but there was more than a pair of shoes at stake.

"I'd rather come too, if you don't mind," she said coldly.

"*Okay* then, come. You asked for it." He let in the clutch. "*Jeezus*! What a gal!" He cruised about the snowy silent streets until he found a convenient side turning.

"This'll do," he said and switched off the engine. Milly made a move to open the door, but he caught her arm.

"Not so fast, my dear, if you don't mind. Cigarette?" She shook her head and he lit himself one. He smoked in silence for a minute or two.

"Well?" she said, feeling unaccountably nervous.

"Well . . . perhaps you'd satisfy my curiosity on one point? It's like this. You're the first woman I've ever met who's actually gone out of her way just so she can walk through snow in evening slippers. New, aren't they?" He looked down at them. "Very pretty—and pretty destructible. Interesting. Now if you had a passion for walking through snow on a cold night, well, I'd say, eccentric, yes, but not screwy, not necessarily—because I guess you'd still have brought overshoes, wouldn't you? Oh, yes, you would. You wouldn't be that screwy. So, I may be just naturally suspicious but it strikes me, Mrs. P., there's more to this than meets the eye. D'you mind telling me . . ." He turned towards her. She was sitting staring straight ahead, the light from the street lamp aslant her face. He turned right round in the driving seat, putting an arm along the back of the seat in order to look at her. "Would you mind, Milly," he said softly, "telling me what all this is about? Just what goes on?"

She made no reply. She was a little frightened. She had an idea he would not be as easy to handle as Larry.

"H'm. So you won't talk, eh? Well, well." He leaned right forward and looked at her close. He was puzzled and he really did want to know the answer. "You know, Mrs. P.," he murmured, "you ought to say cheese more often. That's a pretty mouth you've got but that expression just ruins the shape . . . cm'arn, now. Try saying cheese. Just once." In order to make her turn her head towards him he brushed his lips against her cheek. She turned her head.

"Cheese," she whispered, and smiled because you have to smile, and then the smile faded away, as all at once it occurred to her that there was a way to stop him badgering her with questions. Some

373

instinct told her to tilt her head back, and as she stirred a warm delicious smell reached him from the interior of the bundle of fur and quite without his own volition his arm moved round her; when he discovered, too late, that this had happened, he was already kissing her mouth. She did not flinch away, as some women would before a party, scared of having their faces mussed up. Her lips opened. She had been waiting for it all right—he simply registered that without stopping to work out what it meant and right away forgot it; he forgot to think, forgot what had started the whole thing off; for a while everything went clean out of his mind. He let her go when he realised that she was fighting for breath. She recovered, though—and quickly, too, while his own breathing still seemed to rock the car. He took a cigarette out of his pocket and lit it. Then he took out another and passed it to her.

She shook her head. She was busy re-doing her mouth. If she hadn't been doing that, she'd have been smiling. He could tell.

" You ought to be ashamed of yourself," she said. She sounded very cool, very sure of herself now.

" That's it, baby. Right on cue. Somehow I knew you would be."

She was stretching her lips, rubbing the stuff in. Her movements were mechanical, fastidious, thorough, yet somehow indicative of recent gluttony; if she had begun to purr, he wouldn't have been at all surprised.

" Well, aren't you? " she repeated, putting her tools away. " Ashamed? "

He said quietly, " It's none of your business if I am." His tone was so much altered that she looked round at him, startled. No, he wasn't being funny. He didn't seem to be in the very least amused.

" Abe! "

" When you're ready."

" Oh . . . sorry, yes, I am. Abe, what is it? You are . . . *odd.*"

" Odd? Who—me? " He had picked up her hand and was turning it over, frowning. " Yeah, maybe I am." He held the fingers bunched together, examining the nails.

" What's the matter now? "

" Funny." He sighed. " You don't seem to have those cute little furry jarbs "—he exaggerated his accent with effect—" y'know what I mean. . . . *Can't* you sheathe them, Milly? " He tossed the hand back in her lap. " That's too bad. All the others can."

" Really! " She was really cross, and he laughed.

" Women . . . women. Remind me some time and I'll give you my opinion, my frank and honest opinion, guaranteed unabridged, uncensored and unbowdlerised, on the whole goddarned bunch of
374

you." He jerked open the door. " Cm'arn—it's all yours, baby. You asked for it, and I'm not carrying you—I got the bottles an' they're vital."

Her inner glow of satisfaction had worn off considerably by the time they arrived.

*   *   *

" It's lovely, the colour of your dress," said Prince Mischka, who, as an old and experienced courtier, adhered so far as possible to the truth where compliments were concerned. " What colour would you say it was? "

" Jade," said Miss Raven, blushing.

" Jade, of course. Now, to drink this vodka, let me teach you. Look. This is the way. You gulp, and then you eat—you must always eat too. Take a bite of herring, of pastry—these are just right for vodka—that's it. Now gulp it down. Watch your husband over there —he knows how to do it."

" My husband? "

" And what a fine-looking man," murmured the prince. " Isn't he? " He turned to smile encouragingly at her, the Englishman's plain and elderly wife, and stared, unable to believe his eyes. Why, he must have been blind. She was no beauty, certainly, but she was far from plain. Her face was transformed. With love, he supposed, noting how her eyes lingered on the tall figure in the far corner of the room. It was touching to see. Prince Mischka was not at all a cynical old man.

" He's the real English type, one would say, isn't he? "

" Yes," Miss Raven agreed, turning a deaf ear to the entreating voices, faint, ever fainter, of the Duke, J. Mason and the rest; wail as they might, they had lost her now. Dimpling like a young girl, her eyes shining: " He is, isn't he? " she said.

Then through the crowd they saw the door open and Milly and Abe Schulman came in, Milly carrying a great bunch of red roses in her hand.

*   *   *

" Oh, Milly! " Sophie buried her face in the flowers.

" They're not from me, Sophie. They're from Abe."

" Oh, Abe! " said Abe. " Just let me hear that note in your voice, Sophie."

He was such a tease. She blushed.

" Thank you, Abe. I've never had such flowers before in my life."

" La pauvre Sophie! " chipped in Princess Rapovska. Her hair

375

was carefully arranged in a froth of curls, her small stout person blazed with jewellery; the background to this magnificence being the familiar woollies, plus boots. Doubtless she had decided that in view of Sophie's status as a poor relation any more basic change in her attire might have appeared ostentatious. " Mais tu sais, Sophie, Mr. Schulman, 'e gives all 'is lydyfriends these splendid flowers . . . n'est-ce pas, Madame Milly? "

" So I've heard," said Milly, and both women glanced maliciously at Abe, who, to their satisfaction, looked momentarily taken aback.

" I've brought one or two bottles for you, Sophie," whispered Milly.

" Come into the kitchen, darling," said Sophie, interpreting correctly her meaning look.

" Dites, Schulman "—Antoinette tapped him kittenishly on the arm with her lorgnette—" qui est donc ce monsieur là-bas, vous voyez? Mince, assez élégant, avec cet air de mélancolie? I never see 'im before."

" Where? Oh—you mean that sad-looking guy in the tuxedo? "

" Mais oui . . . bien sûr . . . c'est justement ce que j'avais dit."

" Don't say you've not met *him*, Antoinette? Oh, my, that's too bad," he said gravely. " You go right over and introduce yourself." He bent low and whispered in the princess's ear, " That's Mr. *Wragg*, the British Ambassador."

*　　　*　　　*

" There's a bit of Spanish blood, too," said Mrs. Wragg, " on my mother's side. But of course I'm a Celt, really."

" A Celt? " said Father Joseph. He had no idea what that might be, but he could well believe it. She was a very strange lady.

" The Celts have all the artistic temperament that the English lack. Imagination. Second sight. Intensely passionate—hot-tempered. Oh, we have it all. We're wild as wild."

" Ah? " Father Joseph looked a bit alarmed.

" Actors, musicians—and, of course," she cast down her eyes modestly, " the great bards, the story-tellers—all Celts."

" So? And Shakespeare too? "

" Oh, *Shakespeare*—well, I dare say he had Celtic *blood*."

" Very interesting. So then they are not English, all such? "

" Oh, yes, *English*." She told herself that he was rather a stupid old man, but that was the Church for you, blinkers, Dark Ages, all those peasants and no contraception. She could have lectured on that—in fact had done so once. " But basically, *Celt*. You could recognise it, of course, in my looks. I'm very typical."

376

"So?" To himself he pictured an island, mercifully remote, peopled by a savage race whose archetype was Mrs. Wragg.

"Black, black hair. Pale, pale skin. Dark, glowing eyes," she went on, romanticising her own appearance rather.

"And your husband? He's one too, I suppose." Father Joseph was suddenly struck by the appearance of the husband, now talking to a young woman in white. Certainly, now that it had been pointed out to him, he could identify the dark glowing eyes.

"My husband?" said Mrs. Wragg sharply. "Oh, no, *he's* not one. Definitely *not*." If the discussion group idea came off, she might rehash her notes and give that lecture again. They needed someone to clear the cobwebs away, and who better than she?

*   *   *

"So, Mr. Wragg," said Milly, "you'll know me next time, I should think."

He jumped. "—I'm sorry . . . I . . ."

"Well, what's the matter?" The small white teeth, one of them uneven, bit her lower lip. That uneven tooth—why was it? All the charm of her smile seemed to depend on this one fault. She was twinkling up at him, and he took a deep breath.

"You see, I'd—I'd never thought of you . . ."

"You'd never thought of me?"

"I mean——" The words came out as they usually did, as if he'd inadvertently unpenned them, and like the Gadarene swine they rushed out headlong and threw themselves over the brink. "I'd never thought of you in a white dress."

He knew she would laugh and she did.

"Don't you like it?"

"Oh, yes," he said stiffly, listening fascinated, resigned, as the last few thudded on down, "it's very unusual, I think."

"Come and dance. You do dance, don't you?"

"No. Well—that is, in a way." That tea dance at the Metropole in Bournemouth, on his honeymoon. They hadn't stayed there, of course. They'd stayed in a boarding-house for students where there were cut-up sheets of the *Daily Worker* in the lavatory, which had upset him, it still being the Gospel, as it were, and Olga had been upset because no one had really believed they were married; he'd left her crying one afternoon in a shelter on the sea-front in the rain, and gone and had tea at the Metropole all by himself and watched them dancing, and had thought how easy it looked—dancing, that is.

"Well, come on."

"All right. Just a sec." He couldn't dance before wiping his hands

377

on his handkerchief. The palms were quite wet. He turned his back to conceal the gesture from her. The trouble was, being the only man in a dinner-jacket. " It's a brand-new dinner-jacket," he muttered, " and be damned to them all." Whereupon he turned round to face, and grasp, Milly.

He swung her out into the middle of the room. Terrifying, the intimacy of the position; there ought to be a law against it. Cornering, he could feel the bone of her hip against his thigh, and there was a mole, a very small velvety one, rather far down on her right shoulder blade, and an overpowering incense rose up out of her hair. How awful it all was. Everybody was watching, of course. He manoeuvred her sideways on to get his hen's-eye view of the room. No one was watching, no one seemed in the very least bit interested. Even Olga was in a similarly compromising position in the arms of Sophie's brother, swinging in a sort of Valetta, adapting it to the tune. But then Olga's movements, her relations with her partner, compared with those of his own partner, were altogether more fluid, more majestically impersonal, ballroom dancing being to her but a corruption of folk-dancing, for which she had an acknowledged preference.

" *Relax*," whispered Milly. Rigour seized him in the attempt to obey; then, to make matters worse, he perceived that a slender white arm was creeping up his numbed shoulder like a snake on a bough. He shivered, averting his eyes from it, as it stole farther up and eventually settled around the back of his neck. True, its presence did make synchronisation of movement astonishingly much easier, giving her a sort of halter hold on him, but he wondered, his heart in his mouth, did she always dance like that?

Milly did always dance like that—that is, with particular regard to the position of her left arm, ever since an old rake of her acquaintance had instructed her in the portents to be read from the position of that limb. Accepting his theory (adequately supported as it was by chapter and verse) and its implications, namely, that eighty-eight per cent of her countrywomen were doomed for all time to dance with waving flippers, she had then and there plumped for, and trained, the business-like claw; whether or not the underlying inferences were applicable to her only she could testify to that, and it was preferable to have at least the appearance of belonging to the minority, as small as it was select.

Wragg gritted his teeth. At least Sophie didn't have long-playing records. He supposed he could just manage to bear it. Just.

*   *   *

" Sophie darling," said Milly, going into the kitchen, " I only wanted to say—whatever's the matter? "

378

Sophie was standing stockstill, gazing at her.

" You look so—lovely. It makes my heart turn over just to look at you."

" Oh, don't be *silly*," said Milly shortly. Sophie was always spoiling things with this kind of remark. " Old hag like me. Anyway, it's a *heavenly* party, Sophie——"

" Honest Injun? Oh, I'm so glad! They're all getting tiddly? "

" Well on the way. Sophie, what I wanted to explain about was—where's that bag of bottles? "

" Yes, here . . . darling, yes, explain, please. I'm all ears . . . put it on the table . . ."

" First of all, these two of wine—they're for you, for the party."

" Milly! Oh, you're too generous—your exquisite wines, how well I . . . thanks, oh, thanks, darling . . ."

" Yes, well . . . we'll put those on one side . . . then, let's see, there are three . . ."

Abe burst in, followed by Larry.

" Sophie, my duck, come and dance! You mustn't stay out here, everyone's asking . . ."

" Where is she? Sophie, you're dancing with me. Go on, Schulman, get out. Can't you see the lady's engaged? You'll have to wait your turn and you're pretty low down on the list."

" Don't you dance with him, Sophie, you'll get your feet mashed to pulp. You come along with me."

" Abe, don't, please. Larry, go away," she giggled, delighted. " I tell you I can't dance with anybody till I've finished—Abe, you dance with Milly."

" No, Sophie, hell, you don't understand. I can dance with Milly any old time."

Milly's face was a study. Larry laughed.

" What *is* that, Sophie? Strawberries and cream? "

" Cold crayfish soup. It's a speciality."

" Holy Mike! We're not starting to eat all over again? "

" We haven't even *begun*," said Sophie in a shocked voice. " Those were only the canapkis, the hors-d'œuvres."

" There's food for five thousand, Sophie, darling, but—er—well, the Rapovskis seem to have swigged a coupla bottles of Scotch already so what we were wondering was——"

" Oh, Abe! I'm sorry, so sorry . . . you want more to drink? There's any amount of vodka, any amount—and look here—may I, Milly? There's this wonderful wine that Milly brought. Look! "

Larry looked, studied the label.

" I can't wait," he said, with a glance at Milly.

" My, my, my," said Abe, who was prowling round, " but that's not all. See what this wonderful little woman has brought, Larry? Boy, what a treasure trove! Milly, I kiss your feet! "

" I say, darling, this is more like it. Brilliant—full marks."

" I didn't know you could get five star," said Abe.

" Nor did I," said Larry. " Well, what are we waiting for? "

" Corkscrew, Sophie."

" Oh," said Sophie, in distress, not daring to look at Milly. " No, don't let's open it. *Please*, Larry."

" Not *open* it? What do you think it's here for? "

" I don't know," said Sophie miserably.

" What d'ya say I open 'em all while I'm about it? " said Abe. " Save time, won't it? We're going to need every drop. Slip the Rapovski gang a Mickey Finn all round and then get down to it. How about that? "

" Go ahead. Glasses, now. Right." Larry sniffed appreciatively. " Just the job. Here, Sophie—here you are, Milly. Why, what's the matter? "

" Looks kinda stunned, don't she? " said Abe kindly.

" Drink up your nice brandy, sweetheart. You've done awfully well to think of bringing all this . . . come on, now. No—wait. We must drink to something. To Sophie? "

" No, not to me," said Sophie, smiling at them all as they stood round the kitchen table. " Because then I can't drink too, you know."

" Yeah, that's so. Wait," said Abe, " I got an idea. I'll tell you what." He grinned, looking round at them; then the grin vanished as, with his eyes on Sophie, he raised his glass: " Ladies and gentlemen, I give you a toast. The Last Foray in Slavonia! "

" Oh, Abe! " Tears rolled down Sophie's cheeks. " Why did you think of that? I'll remember it all my life."

" Cheer up, honey, we ain't even drunk it yet. Cm'arn now—all together! THE LAST FORAY IN . . ." The shout died away as they perceived a strange figure standing in the doorway; a large man wearing striped pyjama trousers, a suède jerkin and a cloth cap pulled down over his ears; the most forcible impression amongst many conflicting ones being that he was unshaven. He grunted, but not by way of greeting, and they watched in dead silence as he strode straight across the room, kicking a saucepan out of his path before passing out by the far door. The door slammed and the key rattled in the lock. In their amazement they had put down their glasses untouched. It was Abe who broke the silence. He said, his eyebrows raised: " Graf Dracula, I presume? "

" König Kong? " suggested Larry.

380

" Or Big Brother himself, eh, Sophie? "

" Sssh . . ." Sophie was giggling weakly. " He *lives* here."

" Ah-ha! Demon Lover. Just what I'd suspected. And you were saving this marvellous cognac for that fellow? What's he got that I haven't got? "

" I should have thought that was obvious," said Larry. " A three-day beard, for one thing."

" Sssh . . . please, dears, ssh! He's the—*the Occupier*! "

" He is now," said Abe, " if that place in there's——"

As he spoke there was the sound of the chain being pulled violently. " So now he'll come back, will he? " he whispered excitedly.

" Oh, no," Sophie whispered in reply, " not yet. He'll stay there for a while."

" Ah! " Abe poured more brandy all round. " Interesting, very. The proper study of man is man . . . travel broadens the mind and it takes all sorts to—well, well. When does he quit *occupying*, Sophie—generally speaking? "

" Oh, sometimes not for hours. Oh dear."

" You've said it—oh dear." His face had clouded over. " Must be suggestion or something. I mean, I might—well, do I? Yes, I think I do. Oh my. What do I do about it? "

" Abe, really, it's very embarrassing but I'm sorry—you'll have to, well, *wait*."

He rolled his eyes, hissing through clenched teeth: " What if I just *can't* wait? " He grinned, seeing her distress. " Don't fret, sweetheart. I'm a big boy now. I was only joking."

" It won't be a joke for long," murmured Larry. " It's freezing outside."

" Oh, why did this have to happen? " Sophie was wringing her hands. " To-day, all day, they've been so good and quiet. I gave the wife a whole box of chocolate creams, too."

" Maybe she didn't split 'em with him."

" Oh, dash it! " Sophie was near to tears. " I must put my thinking cap on."

" No, Sophie, just leave it to us. You girls scram, we'll fix it. Go on, out. You cramp my style."

" Abe, what are you going to do? Don't offend him, please."

" *Offend* him? Don't worry—I'm goin' to entice him—draw him forth—my honeyed tones will be the lure . . ." Adjusting his cuffs in the manner of a conjurer and flexing his fingers, he advanced towards the bathroom door.

*   *   *

381

He is certainly young for an Ambassador, thought the princess to herself. But he has truly le bel air.

" You like it, our vodka? " she purred. " Really, you like? "

" Yes, I do, quite," said Wragg, rather surprised. He knew who she was, old thingummy-bob Rapovska. Another old girl was crowding in on his other side.

" I present my sister, Irène." He bowed uncomfortably as they whispered together. Then they began cooing and fluttering round him like a couple of old pouter pigeons.

" Vous êtes venus en voiture, naturellement? By car? "

" Non," said Wragg, " non."

" Dans le train alors? "

" Non."

" Par avion, peut-être? " The one that was the sister chimed in. Some kind of long-winded Continental joke, he supposed.

" Non." He pointed to his size eleven evening pumps. " Comme ça." He gave a little snort which sounded like a laugh, just nerves, really. Both the old ladies practically fell over backwards with delight.

" Tiens! " they tittered, " rigolo, à pied . . . entendu, Irène? rigolo, vraiment . . . ha-ha-ha . . ." They were tickled pink. It was most gratifying. He had never experienced such instantaneous success in his life.

There was more whispering.

" You prefer we speak French or English? " the old princess broke off to ask.

" I don't mind," said Wragg, " that's entirely up to you." It was, too. He was planning to move off, anyway, but seeing this the old girl put a detaining hand on his arm.

" One day soon, you promise "—she waggled her rings in his face —" you come to us, eh? We myke all this kind o' thing, but bigger, better, too, yer know "—she indicated Sophie's arrangements—" for *you*. You come? " She sounded quite keen, you could tell; she was even sort of cuddling up to him.

" Well, er, thanks very much." Jolly nice of her, he thought. Funny, he'd always heard that she was a bit of an old dragon, rather snobby and all that . . . really, she was extraordinarily friendly. Couldn't be nicer. Which all went to show, didn't it?

* * *

" It's not at all bad, Singe, your apartment." Antoinette settled herself on the bed. " I'd heard you were in such straits, pictured to myself rats, no light, window-panes all broken, and so on. Instead— hm! C'est commode, assez propre, pas du tout mauvais."

Singe, who did not consider anyone but a blood relation entitled to the privilege of using her nickname, said frostily, " You'd like some whisky, Antoinette? "

" A little drop. Oh, that's enough—or I'll be tipsy. How they dance, the young ones. I've been talking to Mr. Wragg."

" Yes, I saw you."

" If I'd known the sort of company you had invited I could have lent you our old servant."

" Thank you, but it doesn't matter. As you see, it's very simply arranged."

" That was Sophie's idea, the buffet? Very nice, very adequate, considering. Ah, what bad luck to lose all those beautiful things. Well, I warned your brother at the time, Singe, you know. I said —to leave town at such a moment and go into the country, that's madness—on vous volera tous. They were all begging me, all the grandchildren—go into the country, they said, run away—ah, not me! C'est magnifique, ce veeskee. And—look at me! " She indicated her breast where a few drops of the British elixir glistened, outshone by the dazzle of the really heavy stuff. " Me, I haven't lost a thing! Même pas une cuillère de café! " She swung her little fat legs up on the bed.

" Of course "—Singe discovered that her voice was trembling— " you'll recollect, Antoinette, that at the time of which you speak, my brother, all of us, were already living in the country. There was no question of running away——"

" Ma chère Singe! But did I say that—I never said that. No, you misunderstood. I mean that I—indeed, all of us Rapovskis—have been singularly *lucky*, that's all."

" The English have a proverb—what is meat to one man is poison to another." She added, dryly, " I did hear that your grandson has had the luck to find himself a good job."

" That *was* lucky," Antoinette nodded, not in the least discomposed.

" So you haven't lost a single coffee spoon and he has a good job. As you say, lucky . . . but perhaps—could it be?—both due to the same stroke of luck? "

Antoinette, because they were old enemies, she and Singe, returned the flinty little smile.

" One thing leads to another, certainly. For instance, Paul is such a good fellow, always thinking of others, he shares his luck, and that has led to this job for Ludo. It's nice, I think, that they work together in the same office, the two cousins. It's not at all bad for the young to adapt themselves to new conditions. It's their world, Singe—their future. Life is not what it was, heaven knows, but they must make the best of it as it is."

383

Irritated at receiving no reply, she went on, " Look at Sophie, for example. Poor Sophie, with her mania for these British—don't you think she'd fly off with them were it not for you? There's no life for her here—an unmarried girl, and no longer such a girl, I'm afraid." She sighed, looking smug. " One mustn't clip the wings, you know, Singe, just because one has no wish to fly oneself."

" You've become quite a philosopher, Antoinette." Singe spoke softly, looking down at her hands in her lap because, as the other guessed, her eyes were full of tears. Satisfied, Antoinette laid a plump little paw on these hands and, doing so, gave a cry of horror.

" Singe, vos mains! Regardez! But they're torn to shreds, my dear . . ." The old prince, who had been watching the pair of them, came up to sit beside Singe on the other side.

" Ah, Mischka," Antoinette greeted him vivaciously, " how are you? Yes, it's a long time—I hear you're a great traveller these days. What I am saying is, look at the hands of our poor little Singe here— all cut to ribbons . . . I'll send you round some lotion, my dear, I have some excellent lotion from England. . . ."

" I have lotion, thank you," said Singe.

" It's all your fault, Mischka, you naughty old man! " Leaning across, she tapped the prince coquettishly on the knee. " You're a slave-driver with your wretched doll factory—oh, I've heard all about it—and she's quite ruined her hands, working herself to the bone." She fluttered her own, which were pretty and white.

" Ah, Princess, but there I'm afraid I must disagree." Gently Prince Mischka picked up one of the ruined hands and raised it to his lips. " For me, they have a special beauty, these hands. You know why? Because "—he paused, his eyes very blue and bright—" because," he went on softly, " they bear—honourable scars."

" Alors . . ." Princess Rapovska shrugged, and with a rather uncertain little laugh slid off the bed. " Excusez-moi—je vais chercher encore des excellents canapkis de Sophie," and she trotted off.

A tear had fallen on the hand that was in Singe's lap.

" Dearest," he said tenderly. " Dearest Singe . . . nothing she might say could ever deserve one of your tears. Don't. Here. Save them for something worth while."

*   *   *

When Gisela awoke, for a minute or two she had the feeling it must be morning, so strong was her sensation of having overslept. Then there were the trays, the tea, the rolls to fetch, the coffee to grind . . . ah, but she felt tired, she didn't want to get up. How dark it was, and how cold . . . so cold. She put out her hand, searching for the

384

quilt, then she realised that she was lying fully dressed on top of the bed and all the events of the terrible day came back.

She sat up at once and switched on the light. The time—what time was it? Her heart was beating so fast, so loud, it choked, deafened her. Her watch. Half past seven. That couldn't be the time. She ran to the window. No, the streets were silent. It was black night outside. Whether morning or evening it was not half past seven. She put the watch to her ear, rattled it. Yes, it had stopped. But how could that have happened? The watch Mrs. Simpson had given her, that had been her own; solid silver and worth a lot—that it should have played her this trick put her in a panic as nothing else could have done. An omen, for sure.

She moved about the room, stumbling about, knocking into things. "What am I doing?" she muttered under her breath. "Hurry . . . wash your face, comb your hair." She dashed cold water on her face but then there was no towel. At least, there was a towel but she couldn't find it. Her face all wet, blindly she grabbed the edge of the bedspread and dabbed it with that. Then where was her comb . . . lost, of course, like the towel. Not a sign of the comb. Lipstick? No time for lipstick. Time. "Be calm," she told herself, "think. Sit down." She sat down on the edge of the bed, but she was unable to think; she felt stupefied, as if her brain, inert, were lapped in a pool of warm mud. Presently she became aware of the ticking of the kitchen clock next door. The sound came through the wall as clearly as if there were no barrier of lath and plaster between. Tick-tock. Tick-tock. Night, it must be night. Or morning? Dawn, perhaps. There—a tram. The last, or the first? One or the other. It had that rather embarrassed rumble common to both that was aggressive, and priggish, too, as if aware that whether early or late it outraged the propriety of all honest citizens, but, however unpleasant, the duty must be performed. At the hour she would hear the bugle call. The hour? That was no good. She might have woken on the hour and have to wait another hour, whereas if she could but see through the wall and find out the time, then—if she knew that—she would be able to gauge the dimensions of the gulf between herself and reality, the rift caused through her own negligence, having overslept, and widening every minute—and then she would bridge it. Somehow she would manage to bridge it.

She should never have fallen asleep. That was it. As she sat there in the silence, unable to think or to move, the little room in disorder, the disorder reflected in the black shining window-panes, listening to the tick of the clock, the drip of water from the tap, she was seized by the dreadful conviction that she herself was the only proof of her existence; that her hold on life depended on the slenderest of threads, these threads resting in her own two hands, and if she were to relax her conscious grip, then they might slip or even be tweaked from her fingers; so she should never have risked falling asleep. Asleep she was, to all intents and purposes, no more. All those hours whilst she had lain unconscious on the bed—what might not have happened? The wonder of it was that she had ever woken at all. There was no one to awaken her—not a soul in the whole world who cared a fig whether she was awake or asleep, alive or dead; she was utterly alone. Clocks chimed, telephones rang, dinner-gongs were struck—for others, but not for her. Eat, don't eat, get up, you'll be late, stay in bed, you're not well, how d'you feel, come on, hurry up—they all had someone to say that, someone who expected them somewhere, urged them to do this or that whether they liked it or not—for their own good; and they, the ones to whom it was done, performed the same functions in return because otherwise—well, otherwise it wasn't to be borne, was it?— this loneliness.

Then what is it about me, she asked herself, that makes me different from everyone else? Truly, if I had died here on this bed just now, they might have found me after a week, perhaps, needing the room; not before. As a situation it strikes me as unnatural—although it's not strange, it's always been like that—for me. But why? I'm only twenty-three. I'm cleverer and prettier than most, yet all my life I've had to struggle tooth and nail just to keep alive. Then what is it that I lack? Roots. That's true—I've no roots. Because of the war? No, she went on, inexorably honest in her way, that's too easy. It's something like that but there's more to it. I've no roots because I'm not intended to flourish. Like a weed, that's what I am. Pretty and clever and scrambling around, working as hard as anything just to survive— but anyone is free to throw me into the ditch to wither and die, and anyone who does so can feel he's done a good job. And although weeds often have very pretty blossoms and even in a wicked season flourish where flowers die, yet they're only weeds and remain so. A weed can never hope to become a flower. What do I want? I've never asked very much of life—less, I think, than most. It's always been a question of knowing that this or that I had to have in order to live—and of getting it. Just the very next thing. I wonder where it started to go wrong. Perhaps it never did start; perhaps it was always this way. I'm so frightened, she murmured, able, now, to say it, now that it was no longer the truth as it had been a few minutes before.

After this week—supposing it didn't come off, her plan—where was she to go? She could never now return to village life. Besides, to which village could she go? Certainly not to her own. Slavnik, then—alone? She knew Slavnik, certain districts of it, the only parts in which she would feel at home, but again she could never return there—on account of—ah, well, she smiled ruefully to herself, I learned *that* too late. To leave places as you find them. Otherwise, sooner or later, you find yourself running out of places to run to; her trouble now.

She picked up the watch, gazed at it for a moment. " Of course," she told herself, " you forgot to wind it up this morning. But I couldn't have forgotten that. Oh, yes, you could—look at all the things you've forgotten lately. You'll forget your own head next."

Smiling rather grimly, she got up from the bed, found a fresh white collar and put it on. There was the comb—it had been staring her in the face; where it should be, for once, on top of the chest of drawers. And there was the towel, on the floor. She glanced at herself in the mirror; dabbed lipstick on her mouth, rubbed in a little rouge. Still she looked a sight. Never mind. She went out into the passage. How quiet. Then it must certainly be early morning. Now, in a second, she would know.

She tried the handle of the kitchen door. It was open and she went in boldly and switched on the light, her eyes seeking the face of the kitchen clock as if it were the face of the judge upon whom her fate depended. It was half past eleven. She had to lean against the wall to steady herself, so great was her relief. She stood there, her hands to her face, quite sick with relief. Then the gap was not unbridgeable— three or four hours at the most—and all the rest had been her stupid fancy running riot. Now she could pick up the threads and carry straight on. Laughing under her breath, adjusting and setting the watch, she realised how frightened she had been. Why, after all that, she had not even overslept. Overslept? What a silly word; meaningless, even. She was her own mistress now. Overslept? She frowned. It did still mean something—didn't it? Only then did she remember what she had come for, what it was all about. Only then did she look up; and she saw that the parcels were gone.

As she ran along the passage and down the stairs, a voice hammered in her ears: " Keep very calm—don't panic—it's not too late—because you're *awake*—ah, *now* you're awake! " Whatever her failings, she was a most courageous girl.

*　　　*　　　*

" Olga, there's someone wants to meet you. Don't worry about the cap, it's the intellect beneath that counts. You'll find you have many, many ideas in common. May I present Mr. Karloff? Call him Boris, Olga, he'll respond—this, Boris, is the celebrated Mrs. Wragg." They bowed to each other and Abe bowed to them both, and then he went on gravely: " I've just had the opportunity, Olga, of a discussion with Boris here—superficial, naturally, my Slavonian isn't so hot—but he gave me the impression of having a very deep, subtle mind. So plumb it, dear, it's all yours. I'll leave you both a drop of Scotch to help ease things along." He was as good as his word, putting down the bottle on the window-sill. " My little chickadees," he murmured, looking from one to the other, and left them to it.

" Abe," said Sophie, " you devil. How did you manage it? "

" What? Oh—that. It wasn't hard," he replied airily, " we smoked him out, you might say. Had a little talk on dialectics through the hardwood door—what finally broke him down was the heady perfume of a Havana cigar puffed through the keyhole. In token of delights to come."

" I've never, *never*, seen him like this before."

" Shouldn't think his wife has either—and what about the cell-members? We got to work on 'im in there—zipped up his shirt-front, put his cap on straight and so on. He's pretty handy with the vodka bottle, but my, oh my! you should see him with good old capitalist-brewed Scotch! Strikes me this way you could start a counter-revolution."

" Dites, Schulman, zis drink you give me "—the princess wrinkled her nose—" c'est du vrai veeskee, ça? "

" It cert'nly is. Good heavens, Antoinette, that's a very special blend . . . I only produce it for someone really deserving like you. What does it taste like? " he asked, with genuine curiosity.

" Razzer—quee-er . . ."

" Queer? " He looked offended. " Is that *all*, Antoinette? Just—queer? "

" No. Ver-rry queer."

He snorted. " Oh, if that's the way you feel, obviously it's wasted on you. Here, give it me. I can appreciate it."

" Ah *non*! " She clutched her glass stubbornly. " If it's veeskee, I drink—I don't give awye . . ." She had put up her lorgnette to examine, across the room, Mrs. Wragg deep in conversation with her companion. " Oh, la la . . ." the princess giggled. " 'E's funny, Schulman, 'oo's 'e? From the zoo, one would sye? "

" No, Antoinette," he rebuked her mildly, " one wouldn't—unless one were a roaring snob, that is. You mustn't judge so hastily—the gentleman has a heart of gold."

" Mais ces pantalons? "

" What's wrong with them? I got some like that. You must come up and see them some time."

" Vraiment? Ow, you notty boy! Je vous comprends très bien. 'E

388

is notty boy, Irène—come 'ere. You want some veeskee? 'Ere, try mine—c'very nice, very queer."

"No," said Abe hastily, "don't give it to Irène." He quite liked Irène. "I'll pour her some fresh. What are those two talking about over there?"

"They don' talk," said Irène. "The lady is telling 'im things."

"What things?"

"Co-operatives. The lady knows much about co-operatives."

"So why doesn't he respond? Is he happy? Gosh, I hope he's happy—he's my responsibility, you see."

"'E's 'appy, I think. 'E says nothing, but 'e drinks."

"Seen Larry?" said Milly. What was Abe doing, she wondered, wasting time with all these old women?

"Yeah. B'lieve I did," he replied, deliberately mysterious.

"Where? What's he doing?"

"He's out on the balcony, I guess." He added maliciously, "Holding Miss Raven's hand."

Although it could have no foundation, the remark, as it was calculated to do, annoyed Milly beyond measure. She glanced towards the balcony, all the same. Somebody *was* out there. There was a draught from the half-shut door. She went straight over to investigate, and Abe smiled to himself.

There was scarcely room for two people on the balcony, which had a wrought-iron railing round it; banked underneath were Sophie's window-boxes. Larry filled the doorway, preventing her from coming out on to the balcony as she wished to do. He turned his head as she opened the door behind him, nodded, but did not move aside. He seemed to be shielding Miss Raven from the public view whilst she gazed, apparently spellbound, into a box of earth. As Abe had predicted, Larry was holding her hand.

Milly said sharply, in a voice which would carry past him, as she couldn't very well push him aside: "Miss Raven! What about the children? I think it would be a good idea if——"

"That's all right," said Larry quietly. "I'm taking Miss Raven home in just one minute."

"Surely there's no need for that—I mean, for you to go? Vladek's waiting, isn't he? You can get back by yourself, can't you, Miss Raven?" Dodging round his elbow, she caught a glimpse of Miss Raven, who had not stirred. "Can't you, Miss Raven?" she repeated shrilly, almost stamping her foot.

"No," groaned Miss Raven.

"Go on in, Milly do. Leave it to me."

"But——"

" Do as I say, will you? " It was rarely that she heard that note in his voice. She went inside. Abe was still there by the door. He waved to her and she went across to him. As she reached him, Antoinette whipped up her lorgnette.

" Ow! " she squeaked. " Look over zere! "

There was evidence of some kind of disturbance in the far corner of the room, accompanied by a rather loud shrieking, or howling noise, and a lot of people were clustering round the spot where it was plain a scene of some sort had been perpetrated. Abe craned his neck. The howling, which had been inhuman, had now become identifiably feminine, the short sharp yapping of a woman in hysterics. They saw Wragg, head and shoulders above the rest, glide swiftly through the chaos to the spot.

" But what happened? "

" Lidy 'as been insulted," said the princess excitedly. Overcome with emotion, she drained her glass.

" Mrs. Wragg? " murmured Milly. " Insulted? "

" Impossible," said Abe.

" No, I assume you, Schulman, I see it 'appen. Look, she comes."

Olga Wragg was sweeping towards them, Wragg trailing in her wake. They had a glimpse of her scarlet face and flashing eyes as she rustled past. Abe flung open the door for her and she flounced out.

" Herbert," said Abe, as Wragg went by, " what happened? Was it—was it Karloff? "

" Karloff? " Wragg paused, eyeing him. Then he smiled faintly. " Oh, yes, I see. Your friend? Yes, I suppose it was."

" Didn't do anything—wrong, did he? "

" Oh, no." Wragg seemed rather dreamy and detached. " No, not really. Smacked her bum, that's all. Good night."

" For Chrissake," said Abe, " where's old Karlyboy? I gotta get him outa here. He's in a spot."

" I don't think *he* thinks so," said Milly. " He looks quite happy."

The gentleman in striped pyjamas was sitting in the middle of the floor, beating time to the music with an ecstatic grin on his face.

" You know what *I* zink," said Antoinette, clinging to the edge of the buffet table like grim death and peering muzzily through her lorgnette: " *I* zink, zat man—'e's *dronk* . . " and they were the last words *she* spoke that night.

* * *

" Sssh! I heard you, Gisi, the first time."

" You didn't seem to be paying attention. I tell you I saw them as plainly as I see you now."

" I've been here all evening." He smiled patiently, humouring her. " They couldn't have been spirited away by magic, could they? Or could they? They may have been magic parcels, perhaps? "

" What do you mean? Don't make jokes, please. I tell you one minute they were there, and then when I went back——"

" Ah," said the porter gravely, " you ought to be careful, you know. That would look very bad if anyone were to catch you in there after all that's happened. Trespassing, you see, and with intent——"

" I know all that," she said, drumming her fingers on the desk.

" Just so long as you do," he observed smoothly.

" Listen, Kazimierz, you're fooling with me. What are you——"

" Now, Gisi, Gisi, don't get in a state. What am I going to do about what? Ah, yes, these famous parcels. I'll put it to you this way. How do I *know* there were any parcels there at all? "

" Because I've told you ten times."

" Gisi, you mustn't lose your temper, dear. I mean, how would it sound if I reported it? Somebody thinks she saw . . . Where are they now? they'll say. What did they look like? What—most important of all—did they contain? I don't know, I say to all that. You see how silly it sounds? "

At that moment, as he paused, some part of her brain did flash her a warning and had she not been in a state, and tired into the bargain, because it had been such a long and terrible day, she would have heeded it; as it was, she brushed it aside. You couldn't suspect everybody all the time. He as well as she stood to lose or gain, so that they would stand or fall by each other, surely, at least on this occasion. So she said: " I can tell you what they looked like, if that would help."

" Well," he said kindly, as if pandering to a child, " so what did they look like? "

With her finger-nail she was tracing out the grain of the wood on the desk, her brows knit together; he could see—and admired her for it—that she was concentrating hard. " There were two. Both half a cubic metre, about. I don't know how heavy. Very, I should say, but I didn't pick them up. One square, neat, as if it had boxes inside. The other not so neat, knobbly. Thick dark shiny paper—grey—no, perhaps——"

" Brown? " he murmured, his eyebrows raised to show that he was amused.

" No—not brown. Dark grey. That was it. String—plenty of string. Ordinary string." She looked up and saw how amused he was.

" Ordinary string. That's excellent. No sealing wax, I suppose, with the impression of the signet ring? "

" No."

"H'm. Very unusual parcels, those. Dark grey paper, ordinary string, large, square. That'll be a great help, that information."

"Stop it, Kazimierz, please. Don't try and be witty. This isn't the time."

"My poor girl, I'm only trying to make you understand. As the contents—unspecified, I suppose? Just anonymous boxes and bottles, eh? Really, better to say, 'contents unknown: but heavy, and definitely incriminating.' Don't you think so?"

For a moment she remained silent, and he availed himself of this respite to reflect that whilst he admired her powers of concentration and her sincerity, no woman, however pretty, and certainly no one as sharp-featured as Gisela, should permit the evidence of either quality to appear on her face.

"Groceries," she said at last, in a low, mechanical voice. "All sorts. I could give you a list. Tea, pepper, cocoa and so on. All the usual—everything that's short here. And chemist's stuff—razor blades, soap and all that. Also—drugs." Even at this moment it cost her an effort to say the word, as if she said it against her better judgment, but by now she was bereft of any powers of judgment at all. "Three or four kinds of drugs," she murmured, so intent that she missed the flicker of excitement which crossed the porter's face. "Penicillin, certainly. Insulin, and two others, one new, I forget the names."

The porter stroked his jaw. When he spoke his tone was as jocular as ever. "That all sounds very nice, I must say. *You* could give me a list, you say. Well, I'm afraid that's no good, is it, Gisi? What about this other famous list you were going to get hold of?"

"I couldn't get it. That's all."

"I see. H'm." He scratched his head, thinking fast. "I don't see how you'll manage to get it now," he said gently.

"I don't understand," she said. He didn't at all care for the change that had come over her face. "You don't have to have the list to tell them about the parcels, Kazimierz. They exist without the list, I can assure you of that."

"Gisi, dear, without that list how, I ask you, can I go and tell them this fairy tale? Who told? they'd say. A girl, I'd say. Which girl? A maid under notice—because you know it would come out right away—they've only to look up the file. Ha, they'd say, we're busy men, d'you mind—and laugh for a minute or two, at me, of course. And what would I get? A black mark for wasting their time. I told you all along—it's *proof* we want. Without proof we can't move hand or foot."

She leaned her head in her hands. "I might still get it," she whispered, lifting her eyes to his. She looked distracted, he thought, really quite far gone. He reacted accordingly; according to his nature, that is.

"You've a hope," he said in a brutal voice, "if you're found in that room again—you know what'll happen? They'll take you to prison. Where you ought to be, I dare say. I shan't lift a finger to stop them. You've brought all this on your own head, Gisela. You're just a petty pilferer—a common little thief."

"What you're trying to say is, it's all over."

"Listen," he went on more gently, because he never liked rows and there was no point in not parting friends. "We came to an arrangement, didn't we? Like a business arrangement."

"Not like one. It was one."

He glanced at her suspiciously. Her eyes were cast down.

"I'm glad you see it that way. In other words—if you did one thing I—although greatly to my disadvantage as it might be—I would, in all probability, do something in return. Was that what you understood?"

"Yes." She was staring at him. Her eyes had always frightened him and never more than now. He found himself stammering.

"I've come to the conclusion—I don't think we're suited," he blurted out.

"Ah. I see." She seemed—confused; anyway, strange. It bothered him, her manner, and he made good resolutions thick and fast. Let it be a lesson to you, Kazimierz, he told himself sternly, but she had started off again, mumbling, almost. "If I'd known earlier . . ." She spoke softly so he could scarcely hear. "I mean, what you wanted . . . the list—that's neither here nor there, really, is it? You want to get rid of them, don't you? . . . The way you got rid of . . . the—the others. Yes, I see now." She sighed. "Well, if I could still . . . somehow or other . . . get you what you want . . ."

She was off net. Quite off net, he could tell. No fear of any bother from her. He felt immediately, now that the threat was withdrawn, excruciatingly bored. It was *over*—surely he had made that clear? He could have yawned in her face and did, in fact, stifle a yawn.

"If . . . if . . . my dear, how does it go? If ifs and ands were pots and pans . . ." A double vodka after this, and by heaven, he deserved it! "So, for the present, Gisi . . ." In that Western film recently there'd been this very line, "I'm afraid it's good-bye . . ." He stretched out his hand across the desk and then added hurriedly, which was not in the script, "Quick, get out, someone's coming."

The swing doors burst open and in strode Mrs. Wragg, followed by her husband. Without a glance at the porter's desk they swept across the hall towards the stairs. Mr. Wragg, the porter checked automatically, looked pale and sullen, just as he always did. Mrs. Wragg, with a fistful of skirt in one hand, the rest of it rustling behind her, her face as red as a turkey cock's, was gabbling over her shoulder; this was not so usual. But Kazimierz had had enough of routine just for that night. Besides, he had better things to attend to. He did, however, permit himself a second's worth of emotion: commiseration with Mr. Wragg.

Gisela started up the stairs after them. She was in such a state of exhaustion that all her powers were concentrated on getting up the stairs in order to reach the haven of her room, but she had to slow down to avoid stepping on Mrs. Wragg's trailing skirts. All she wanted was to lie down in the dark and think, or just to lie there in the dark and not think—leave the thinking to some other time—good-bye—thief—prison—won't lift a finger—no, she couldn't think of all that now. Instead, oddly enough, she was much more interested, but genuinely interested, indeed, quite *fascinated* by the sight of the dusty voluminous folds of the hem sweeping the stairs before her eyes. How it twitched, that hem, like a living thing! Yes, think of that, Gisi, urged a voice in her ear, knock off for a bit, take a breather, just think of that in front of you—you'll do better that way.

Oh, she was angry, wasn't she, old Ma Wragg, as they called her, the hotel staff. What a voice—like a man's—or like a primus flame—hissing, choking, the words bubbling out, and Mr. Wragg not saying a single one. There were two flights. Twice Mrs. Wragg stumbled and Gisela had to step back to avoid treading on the black slippery tail. Now they had reached the landing. Now if you can just manage to keep up with them, she told herself, you'll get to the top. Otherwise . . . According to her mind Mrs. Wragg was always angry nowadays . . . for a time she had been nice, lah-di-dahing around—how they had carried on, imitating her in the servants' hall—then all of a sudden—and how everybody had laughed because they all knew why—she had changed from one day to the next, had become angry and remained so . . . oh, she couldn't get her breath after that row downstairs but they were nearly at the top . . . yes, remained so . . . in a shocking bad temper ever since . . . how could one stay angry for three months? Apparently Mrs. Wragg could . . . ever since—how it hurt to get one's breath . . . ever since, Gisela repeated, as an excuse to pause, for no other reason, just as an excuse to cling to the banisters for a second, pressing her hand to her heart where the stitch was, when suddenly she stiffened. She stood quite still as if turned to stone, clutching the banisters, allowing the Wraggs to go on ahead. " Why," she murmured, watching them go, watching the folds of stuff, shining but soiled, ragged in places, jerk up the stairs and out of sight, " why, I'm no better than poor Mrs. Purdoe . . . as stupid as a hen with its beak to a chalk line . . . getting in a panic when really——" She took her hand off the banister rail and stared at the patch it had left on the shining wood; she rubbed it with her forefinger—it was quite wet. " When really . . . it's all as simple as—" What were things as simple as? She shook her head. She couldn't remember. First she must go to bed.

She started to creep up the last few stairs, stopping once more to chuckle. What was it she had thought of? Oh, of course. The answer. Which all the time had been staring her in the face, like her comb. First, though, bed. There was no hurry. There were some people whose emotions you could rely on staying the same—Mrs. Wragg's, for instance—the porter's, not. Yes, to-morrow would do. Because this really was the answer. Nothing phoney about it—it had the feel, the taste, the ring. All wool, real cream, pure gold. What was more, it would keep. Until to-morrow, at any rate. She went on up.

*   *   *

The porter, in the meantime, was on the telephone, crouched in the cubby-hole to one side of his desk. He spoke softly, urgently, his hand half over the mouthpiece. Whilst he was speaking he saw the other Englishman, the tall blond one, come in through the swing doors with the nurse on his arm, and both went upstairs. His brain scarcely registered the incident, strange as it was; as he gobbled into the telephone, his gaze, which followed them up the stairs, was dreamy and preoccupied, clouded with greed; he was indifferent as a cat which sees a familiar person enter but is busy gobbling milk. " Two," he was saying all over again, whilst someone wrote it down. " Yes, certain. Dark grey paper. String. Large. One square, neat, the other not so neat. Oh, everything—ha-ha, everything you can think of. Yes, those too. That's the point. Yes, I thought you might be. Oh, not a shadow of doubt. The driver hasn't reported it? That's very strange. He's been ferrying them about all evening. You'll get on to him—of course." He paused, and then his voice changed; he almost clicked his heels there behind the desk. " Oh, that's very kind. Thank you. Oh, no, nothing at all," he coughed modestly, " oh, no, just routine . . . merely a matter of putting two and two—yes, exactly . . . oh, not at all. Thank *you*. Good night."

He put down the telephone, preening himself a bit, when, to his horror, through the swing doors he caught sight of the Austin. He frowned, scratching his head. That's what they'd been blathering about, the Austin and the driver. Well, that was a bit much. Oh, no, he wasn't having any of that sort of thing—not on his salary. Let them sort it out for themselves. Far better not mess around with a system.

395

Besides, if he didn't look out, Vladek would be muscling in and getting a cut off this—that had been the sheerest grind. Or rather, if he did look out. So he decided not to. He unlocked his drawer, and took out an American paper and began reading what Miss Louella Parsons had said. As a further precaution he put on his horn-rimmed spectacles, too, and not until the Englishman came running down the stairs and he heard the Austin drive away did he take them off. Thus he couldn't possibly have claimed to have seen the Austin at all.

*   *   *

" It's not good enough," said the Chief of Security Police to his second-in-command, who was winning at whist. " Here's this little bit of red-hot info. and the vital part, the connecting link, is missing. Where are they? Obviously, in the Austin. Now you say they can't even find the driver, let alone the Austin! Ha. This incident to my mind simply shows up what I maintain is a very great fault in our system. A lack of co-ordination. It's all very well the right hand not knowing what the left hand doeth, et cetera, but it encourages each man to concentrate on his own little square of the puzzle and when he's solved it he thinks he's solved the whole thing. All right up to a point but it means he works in blinkers, as it were. So what does that lead to—you'll have to go and look into this, by the way—*lack of co-ordination*. You don't know what that is, I suppose? " he said, interrupting his opponent who was checking up the score.

" No," said the second-in-command. The Chief of Security Police had a way of hearkening to the call of duty just when you had a run of luck.

" Well, there you are. Co-ordination—co-operation, much the same thing—my friend, are what I'm supposed to be able to rely on from all of you when I haven't got a hunch." He brooded. " I haven't got one now. I can't believe that in this small town—because small it is compared with Minsk, I can tell you—they can't find that driver. Now you go and rout out that fellow what's 'is name, Bielski, Ludovic —been sitting on his arse for I dunno how long fleecing all the clerks at poker, it's time he earned his salt; and the American's ' chum,' Albovski, get hold of him—get hold of them both, *separately*, mind— ask them if they've got anything to report and if not why not, and put the fear of Big Brother into them and come right back—and don't lark about . . . Hey! "

" Yes? " said the second-in-command, at the door. Old bastard, he thought. Doesn't even bother to ask what he owes me. He'll light his cigar with that score-sheet once my back's turned.

" Not a word, mind, to either of them. Don't give them so much as a hint as to what's going on. Don't start putting them in the picture whatever you do . . . anyway, you don't know what the picture is yourself yet, do you? "

" No."

" No. Exactly. Neither do I," he muttered to himself. " So just get them on the hop, report every hour and all that, and they're on twenty-four hour duty from now on . . . and so far, tell them, I'm very much displeased. Right? Now you see what I mean by co-ordination. So off you go."

He called to his orderly for some fresh tea. The only other lemon in Grusnov was sliced up to float in it. The aroma from the pale gold beverage stole up into his nostrils, clearing his brain. Co-ordination. A nice long pretentious word but so far as he was concerned it didn't mean a thing. At least he'd got rid of that jackanapes and rescued the remnants of his own pay.

Co-ordination, indeed. A lot of inferiors sticking their fingers in the pie. No, no, that wasn't his way, the Russian way. He was the Lone Wolf of Grusnov as he'd once been the Lone Wolf of Minsk. And he'd have a brainwave, he was willing to bet, any minute now. A cold night. It needed a bit of lacing, this tea. He leaned down to the bottom drawer of his desk and unlocked it. There was the bottle of bourbon the American had given him that time those two had got themselves in a jam out at Rosnom. Quarter full. There weren't enough Americans about, in his opinion. Just these British with their eternal Scotch. There was a cigar as well. He unwrapped it carefully and lit it from the stove, using the score-sheet to do so. One up to me, he chuckled to himself. Then he stretched himself back in his chair to wait for his idea, meditatively scratching the back of his neck, which was solid and bristly as a prize porker's; the Chief of Police took particular delight in fondling the necks of young girls, just for the difference in sensation, which was marked. The whisky fumes uncoiling in and out the cells of his brain, he savoured the rich flavour of the cigar; enjoying the gifts of the American, he quite naturally turned his thoughts on him. He liked the American—as a man, that is—but what dull reading it made, the American's file. And yet he'd been here longer than any of the others, with more opportunities than most for mistakes. Fly, he was; very, very careful. But then apparently he had a reputation at stake—he was famous in his own country, so they said. A rare bird, the American. Worth five of those pestilential British any day, in every way, shape and form.

Way . . . shape . . . and form. Yes. He sipped his tea gently, not gulping it, because although the idea had already appeared, conjured up in the clouds of smoke, it was flirting a bit as they always did and he didn't want to risk scaring it away until its outlines, which were still a bit hazy, had become defined, as clean-cut as a proper idea's should be, until it had come close and perched itself on his desk, and he could satisfy himself as to its neat little shape, its modest simplicity—for, like women, in his opinion, those outsize unkempt loose-knit ones were a waste of time, never did anyone any good—well, when it did that and he saw that it was a little beauty, as trim as could be, he pressed the bell and called for the files and another glass of tea.

Prudently, however, he forbore to lace this second glass with bourbon because he had another subsidiary little hunch, an offshoot of the main one, that this bottle of bourbon might be the last he was ever to see.

*　　　*　　　*

Although Miss Raven had unhesitatingly and without discrimination accepted and consumed every glass of liquid refreshment offered her, a mixture of vodka, whisky and cheap white wine in quantities which would have dispatched under the table a seasoned young subaltern in the Guards, she had an iron constitution and was herself seasoned, in a fashion; she may have felt decidedly peculiar for a moment or two on the balcony but not so peculiar as to be unable to relish her situation, the sympathetic presence of her Prince Charming and the manner in which he had protected her from the jealous little thrusts of his wife. By the time she found herself in the car all tremors of indisposition had passed, but she was not obliged on this account to move her head from Mr. Purdoe's shoulder, where it was comfortably accommodated, nor to permit him to withdraw his hand from her own which he made one or two feeble attempts to do. On the contrary; she relaxed and enjoyed herself, as a sensible girl is supposed to do, covertly admiring his profile by the light of the street lamps. The sight of his lower lip pushed out, his stern, almost gloomy, expression, was enough to make one's bones melt to water. How handsome he was. Brooding, that's what he was doing. Over that flighty little bitch, his wife? Not likely. Job, probably. Ah, what a mouth!

In fact, she was quite right, up to a point. Larry *was* brooding over a certain problem, and Miss Raven would have been flattered to learn that it concerned herself. He was debating which, of all the courses open to him, would be most advisable to take—whether he could himself give her a fireman's lift—if he could only remember what that was—and transport her up the stairs that way, or whether it would have to be a head and feet job, involving Vladek, or whether it might not have to be a head, bum and feet do, involving the porter as well. Whichever course he decided upon he was sensitive to the fact that the operation itself, if observed—and really it was not, by its very nature, likely to be inconspicuously achieved—could scarcely reinforce the already shaky prestige of the Western bloc. He even toyed with the notion of a basket and rope, a large jar, Arabian Nights stuff, or— brilliantly apt—might it not be possible to smuggle her up in a diplomatic bag?

What was really germane to a solution of the problem, and which, giving her the odd nudge in order to do so, he had been trying to ascertain, was her weight. With a woman of her build it was virtually impossible to estimate. All muscle, of course. Was it muscle or fat that weighed so heavy? He couldn't for the life of him remember. Better make no allowance for sex, then, in her case. Well, take an athletic man, approximately her height—a boxer, say. But he had no experience of carrying a boxer—although once he'd had to carry a boxer dog, not even fully grown, up the stairs from the District Line into the Earl's Court Road—and that had practically killed him. Well, take something one knew the weight of. A sack of potatoes. Say, a hundredweight sack? He glanced at Miss Raven, who merely nestled closer, in another attempt at appraisal. No, she'd be a bit more than that. He was fairly sweating blood over it by the time they got back, when to his astonishment and relief she nipped out of the car on her own two pins. His esteem for her went up by leaps and bounds.

He grabbed her arm, fearful of a relapse, and steered her inside, escorting her past the porter—the chap was on the telephone—but in any case there had been no need for panic, she beetled up the stairs under her own steam and it was all he could do to keep up with her. It was at the top of the stairs, along the corridor, that the situation became dicey. She'll pass out here, he thought, and then I'll have had it. He tried to coax her down towards the kitchen door but her condition seemed to deteriorate as they approached. She ricocheted from wall to wall; sometimes he would manage to get a grip on her, when she would slump, slide out of his grasp and go hurtling off again like a cannon ball, until she came slap up against a wall, which would send her off in the opposite direction. Once he'd mastered the technique of fielding her, dodging on in front instead of ineffectually trying to guide her, treading on her tail, they got on pretty well. In no time he'd shoved her in through the kitchen door and, opening the next one, contrived, in the same stroke as it were, to put her bang in the pocket, because there she was, in, or rather on the threshold, of her own room. He was holding on to her with one hand, feeling for the light, when she did one of her Bertram Mills stunts, loosened all her joints and slid to the floor.

He left her where she was and strode over to the bed, switched on

399

the bedside light, turned back the covers of the bed, paced the distance from the bed to the door and, setting his teeth, with his hands under her armpits, heaved her across the floor.

" There," he said, looking down at her kindly. She was sitting on the edge of the bed with her head in her lap. " We've made it, Miss Raven." He took out his handkerchief and wiped his brow and hands. He patted her shoulder. " Now just you jump into bed like a good girl. You'll be in bed in two seconds and asleep in three. Won't you, Miss Raven?" he added, with less confidence. " You can manage now, can't you?"

" No," said Miss Raven flatly, sitting up straight. " Oh, no, not possibly. You see, I'm afraid I may have taken a drop too much." She raised her eyes to his. The light was rather dim. She did look strange. Her face was—what was that ghastly expression?—*working*.

" Well, I don't know," said Larry awkwardly. " We all do, sometimes. It depends whether you're—what you're used to, I mean . . ." His voice died away as, to his horror, he saw that she was trying to extricate herself from the tunic, bodice or whatever it was that encased her torso.

" You'll have to help me," she said distinctly, " as I'm drunk."

He helped her tug the thing off. Her fingers, once started on the process of dismantling, seemed unable to resist going the whole hog; she'd be stripped right down to the chassis if he didn't—in a frenzy he looked around for a suitable covering, coat, quilt or blanket, with the same feeling of impotent embarrassment he had used to feel in the morning rush-hour as a young man, whenever his bus had been held up outside a department store window where, behind plate-glass, men like himself were chucking round limbs and torsos, casually slapping up a batch of delectably lifelike feminine frames. Seizing her dressing-gown, he smothered her bare shoulders and her movements with that.

" You just take it easy, Miss Raven," he muttered, swinging her legs up on the bed. He tucked the dressing-gown right up round her neck. She didn't seem to object, as he was afraid she might. You could almost say, as in murder stories, she'd gone limp. But her eyes were wide open, staring at him. He knew that, but he didn't dare look. When he'd covered her up he stood well away from her, fingering his cigarette case because he wanted a cigarette at that moment more than anything in the world, and said:

" So now, Miss Raven, as you're all . . . safe and sound . . . I'll say . . ." Suddenly, he couldn't have told why, he did look at her. Perhaps she was willing him. Anyone, he admitted it, merely by raising a little finger could have willed him just then. She was still staring up at him. Then he took a step forward, in order to look at her more

400

closely. His mind, that is, his thinking brain, a quite highly developed mechanism that worked independently of his emotions and masculine reactions to a given situation, had become, heaven knows how—by accident, very likely, the accident of a certain light in her eyes— switched on again and was now ticking away like mad, making up for lost time. He took out his case and automatically lit a cigarette as he stood there, puzzled, his eyes on her face.

Lying flat on her back, Miss Raven had assumed the position which, because it serves to erase the lines from the face, is generally recommended for those occasions on which it seems important to appear at one's " best," that is, five if not ten years younger and, in consequence, " different." However that may be, and certainly no one in their senses would wish to minimise the desirability of such a transformation, the achievement does not (alas, for such is life) invariably produce the desired reactions in the beholder, nor even results which conspire to the ultimate advantage of the owner of the face. The transformation in Miss Raven's appearance under the rosy light, prone as she was and also exceedingly confident, caused the scales to fall from Larry's eyes. Really, he had to pinch himself in order to make sure that he was not dreaming. For one thing was quite clear—Miss Raven was, in no manner of speaking, drunk. He judged that she had perhaps been a little drunk and then had got over it. In that case all the fun and games in the corridor had been a hoax. Well, all right. He allowed himself a spasm of annoyance but he was too much interested to become diverted by anger. He was already moved to speculation, and to further investigation; like a man who has over a period of time and in all good faith acquired from a certain antique dealer additions to his collection, but eventually one day—the light being exceptionally bright or a guest having smiled in a pitying, knowledgeable way— discovers a flaw in that thing most recently bought—or the first he ever bought, it's all the same—because then he re-examines his whole collection, item by item, in this new light, and whatever his findings he never goes back to that particular dealer again.

Her milky-blue eyes stared up at him, the sandy lashes fanned back, and he asked himself if she had made a fool of him once, just now, then how many other tricks might she not have played? That incident in the salon several weeks ago, that he had pushed to the back of his mind, his only explanation for it having been that it was due to a momentary loss of control on her part which had probably caused her some suffering to recall; now he considered it afresh. Not so very long ago, idle curiosity had prompted him to take her passport out from the bunch of passports in his keeping and glance through it. It had revealed nothing, nothing at all, except her age—which excused

401

her oddities, he supposed—and that her birthplace happened to be, not in Ireland nor in Cornwall, but Huddersfield, Yorks. The discovery had not struck him as being of any significance—he had no idea why people should bother to lie on such trivial points but the fact was, they often did, and he had put the passport away and thought no more about it. Until now. The deliberate twofold contradiction appeared different now. What sort of woman was she? Perhaps there was more than one Miss Raven; certainly it would seem so. Rather grimly he examined her face as she lay there. Her lips were parted. There was a smile, even, on her lips. This woman was not the Miss Raven he had known, who had aroused his pity, even his affection, and whom he would always have been inclined to treat with consideration as he would treat any person who so obviously needed and responded to kindness. That pathetic hotch-potch of emotions, that other Miss Raven, a plain Jane with a heart of gold, for so he had—all too misguidedly, it seemed—judged her, that woman had had the power to touch his heart and had touched it; this stranger not at all. He liked to be liked, but he loathed to be made a fool of.

He went over to the washstand, filled a glass with water, opened the medicine chest and found some aspirin. " Take a couple of these," he said, setting the glass down on the bedside table. " You'll be as right as rain in the morning. I must go now." The sandy eyelashes flickered, she murmured something and wriggled.

Standing well away, for fear she might grab hold of him, he gave her one last keen look. Perhaps he'd been wrong. No, he was damn' well sure he wasn't wrong—but he wasn't right, either—not quite. Strange, he couldn't even visualise that other funny old Miss Raven now. This one's smile was positively—sickening. Then how many were there? Certainly two—but what if there were more? And which was the true one? Perhaps one was no more real than any of the others—all false as they were true. Just let me get the hell out of here, he told himself, then I'll work it out.

" Good night," he murmured, backing away towards the door. She never moved and her eyes never wavered from his own. Then he got out.

*   *   *

Miss Raven lay shivering with excitement for some while. Then she poured herself a little nightcap to calm her nerves and sipped it, cosy under the quilt. He'd carried her to bed. Yes, pretty well. Then he'd undressed her. Had he or hadn't he? Who else had taken off her Pekin jacket? He had, of course. She stroked it, smiling to herself. Although he had had to control himself. Unbridled passion—that was

402

all very well, but she'd never seen any sense in spoiling good clothes. And then, at the end, how solemn he'd looked. Couldn't seem to take his eyes off her. For two pins she'd have given him a bit more encouragement—but better to come from him, all that; he was the manly sort. Well, if not to-day, to-morrow. How will it end? she murmured, and put out the light. She had no doubts about how it would end. When, that was the question. Enchanted by the whole evening, she took herself through every tiny incident from start to finish before she fell asleep.

*   *   *

" You've got this extraordinary idea that it's a heaven on earth, when I can assure you it's nothing of the sort. I wonder how you'd really feel about it if you went there."

" I should love it," said Sophie obstinately.

" You don't know what it was like before, so I suppose you might. But we didn't love it when we went back after three years. We were very thankful to come out here."

" Milly! She's joking," Sophie explained to her aunt, " she often makes jokes like that."

" Cm'arn now, Milly. Let's have it. What've you got against it? I must say I didn't care for it, but I'm certain our reasons don't coincide. I'll tell you mine, my main one—where's the bottle, Sophie?—no, don't put on the light—which was, that I conceived a very definite antipathy for a certain species of my countrymen who've settled down there . . . know what I mean? Gotten themselves little beejew cottages in Chelsea, the kind you don't pick up for a song; original accents pruned back to resemble the Oxford dialect; special blazers to wear Saturdays, sniffing around for bargains in silver in the King's Road; take and read the *Tatler*, educated themselves to be choosey about invitation cards— some go on the chimney-piece and some don't—oh, but they *go* to everything, just the same, oh, my, yes; burn genuine apple logs in the fireplace, serve you warm beer when you ' drop in,' blush pink with pleasure when some English débutante coos, ' I'd never have taken *you* for an American.' What with one thing and another that bunch makes me very, very tired. I wouldn't put it past them to have their mail sent poste restante, they'd be so mortified to own those letters with the nasty common stamps on the doormat as letters from home. Funny, now I'm getting hungry again—no, Sophie, don't get up, I need your lap, dear. Just reach me a leg of that corpse over there. Gosh, I'm sorry, Father, I thought that was Sophie's hand."

" Not at all, I assure you. It was a pleasure—although I had suspected for some time that you were deceiving yourself."

403

" So, Milly, tell us more. What's happened to the old country in these last few years? "

" It's changed."

" Ah-ha, so that's it. Has it really changed—or have you? "

" Oh, no, I haven't changed. That's *my* ankle you're stroking, Abe."

" Uh-huh. That's what I'd figured."

" Well. Take coffee bars, for instance. There never used to be any of those. There's a craze for them now—supposed to be Continental, they all have bogus Italian names—but they're nothing like Italian coffee bars of course—which are as slick, and about as cheerless, as operating theatres."

" *Italian*," snorted Sophie loyally. " They *would* be, of course."

" But an English coffee bar—how to describe it? They're all alike. There's this hideous machine for one thing, hissing in the background, and a kind of bamboo fence between you and it, and a cloud of steam and cheeky young men with dirty beards washing up and a manageress with a cigarette in her mouth bossing them, and the owner glooming behind the cash register, and posters on the walls, perhaps, or queer daubs done by the owner's wife who left him the week before, but perhaps not for good and that's what worries him, and it's all rather expensive and the coffee's foul so most people have chocolate which accounts for their spots, and . . . and there are one or two girls with greasy hair sitting with young men in duffle coats right in the window and they've all paid for themselves and dislike each other for that reason, and there they sit, mooning out of the window for hours on end wondering if this is really life, and of course for them it is, I'm afraid."

" That's nice," said Sophie. " I can just see it, can't you, Singe? Those delightful English coffee bars."

" Sophie, my sweet, you've missed the point."

" No, I haven't, Abe. It sounds charming. And the young people too—though greasy hair, that's nasty, I admit."

" They don't *all* have greasy hair," said Milly shortly. " There *are* exceptions, I dare say."

" So that's all, Milly? "

" Of course it isn't *all*. That's only a *sign* of the times—but it's all *like* that. Then there's television."

" *Television?* " Singe and Sophie breathed in reverent chorus.

" Not that *we* ever—I don't even know the expression—*looked in*."

" No, no, of course not," said Abe. " You must be quite an authority, then."

" You're just trying to get me mad, Abe Schulman, so shut up.

404

No, I mean, everybody has television, and when they've nothing else to do they switch it on and sit goofing for hours——"

" Oh, I should think so," said Sophie enthusiastically, " I would, I can tell you."

" Well, it's very *bad* for people—especially for children. They don't read any more and they're not taught to amuse themselves—they're just spoon fed. Nobody even goes to the cinema nowadays—they're too lazy even to do that."

" Then the cinemas are empty? "

" No, not *empty*, exactly. You mustn't take me so literally, Sophie. All I'm saying, is, as an influence television's bad."

" Television's out, girls," said Abe.

" Oh, dear," said Sophie, " we always thought it sounded so nice and convenient. If you're tired, you know, or poor."

" Or old," said Singe.

" No, Singe, Milly means perhaps that it is only possible to hear one point of view, like in this country. That's why it's so bad—only one politician allowed to speak, you know. . . ."

" As a matter of fact," Milly's voice came coldly out of the shadows, " I believe that's not the case. But it doesn't alter my point. It's *dope*. Like football pools. Gambling, you know, on fooball results. A lot of people do that every week."

" Of course," chuckled Sophie. " How delightful! Gambling! The English are sportsmen, you see, Singe, just as my father always said, remember? And football, that's their game. Every week, just think of it! It must be rather exciting, I should say. You don't need to know the rules of football, you just gamble? "

" It's pure chance," said Milly tartly, " if that's what you mean. You know, I think I should like another drink."

" Here. You're doing gallantly, my dear. Oh, God, we've come round to vodka again. Never mind. Just carry on. Sophie and Singe and the Father here and "—he peered round, where various shapes were reclining comatose in the background—" and others, are getting a wonderfully comprehensive picture of the Welfare State."

" Well, anyway, you can tell England's changed without even going there—by the sort of people who go abroad these days. *Everybody* goes abroad for their holidays."

" Everybody? " Singe and Sophie whispered together. " Anywhere they like? "

" Yes, I suppose so—but that's not the point. I mean, thousands and thousands of people who would never have dreamed of going *before* —well, they go now. So wherever one chooses to go oneself, one's dogged by these fearful charabanc loads of British proles—in Italy, last summer, goodness, we simply had to get out. It was unbearable. They swarmed all over the place, really behaving like lunatics, as if they'd never been abroad before, flocks of them everywhere, in churches and art galleries——"

" Oh, so I should think," murmured Singe.

" Guzzling cream cakes and sozzling sweet liqueurs—screaming at each other in English——"

" English? " murmured Abe. " Tst . . . tst . . . that certainly *is* odd . . ."

" And oh, so often, you saw them eating the wrong things, or you heard them being diddled by those pestering beggars who sell souvenirs —honestly, it made you want to curl up and die. It was just sheer misery."

" You mean they weren't enjoying themselves? " said Singe, her voice full of concern.

" Oh, dear, poor *things*," said Sophie, a ready customer for misery, other people's, every time.

" Oh, *they* were enjoying themselves, all right."

" The Italian people, Milly means, Singe. Try to understand more quickly. They were miserable, doubtless, to have these strangers all around."

Abe chortled rudely. " Go on, Milly, explain. *Who* was so miserable? "

" Well . . . not the Italians, of course. I didn't mean that, and you know it. The Italians were overjoyed, naturally." She put down her glass and gave him a kick. " *I* was miserable. How do you like that? "

" Better. Much better. At least it's honest."

" But what about London? " Sophie asked wistfully.

" London? " Milly frowned. What about London? " Well, the main thing about it is, everything's so—for instance, you can't *set foot* inside a taxi."

" Good heavens! " said Sophie. " But that's truly awful. Why ever not? "

" So far as I remember," said Abe, " because there weren't any."

" Ah, of course," said Sophie, " all destroyed in that swinish bombing. You see, Singe, *there aren't any taxis*."

" There *are* taxis," said Milly crossly, " but . . ."

" Verminous? " said Singe, in a low voice.

" *Singe*, tais-toi—there's nothing of that sort in *England*. Milly means politically—it looks bad to go in one——"

" When there are so many poor——"

" Or the drivers are—you know what . . . h'm—h'm . . . like here, I dare say . . ."

"All I meant was," Milly exploded, "that you can't go in a taxi because it's too damned expensive!"

"There," said Sophie, "what did I tell you, Singe? Just like here."

"Larry! C'marn in, boy. You look busted. Sophie, tell ya what, we'll go cook ham and eggs?"

"Oh, not yet," pleaded Sophie. "I want to go on. I love this intellectual conversation."

"Intellectual *what*?" He laughed for a whole minute. "Why, I even got an idea for a story a few minutes back, and that's awful, that rules it right out as intellectual conver—Jee*zus*! Sorry, Father. Sophie, you must learn, dear, how to distinguish intellectual conversation. One, first person singular disallowed, it's dull and it's dangerous—but you make up for it with a helluva lot of *names*—nick, for contemporaries, and for the old-timers—well, the grander the vaguer the better, and no explanations for either—you've gotta find your own way about. Maître, for instance, well—could be Voltaire or Schlegel or Proust or Schopenhauer, depending, could even refer to the best-selling novelist living in the next bungalow provided you didn't like him enough—and two, it must be sterile. Barren. God, how barren it must be. That's the beauty of it. Positive sterility. Could I be getting tipsy?"

"No," said Larry, fresh to the scene. "I should say that awkward transition stage has definitely been passed."

"Oh." Abe went on undeterred. "So, as I was saying. If, in the course of all this chit-chat, one single idea crosses your mind—not even that, if it flickers just so that you catch it out of the tail of your eye— then you know that the conversation isn't really one hundred per cent intellectual, Sophie; you know it isn't really *dead*—repeat *dead*— serious. And that won't do, see. What's more it must circle. It can go off at a tangent, that's okay, but you begin to worry when it doesn't start coming back. It must come back, time and time again, right back to the starting point—another name or two, a shade higher, lower, don't matter, round and round it goes, but one thing you can be sure of."

"What?" said Sophie.

"It'll go round once too often and then it'll snap. Snap, so everybody can hear it. And once it's snapped there's nothing to be done except——"

"Oh, *what?*"

"Change the drink."

"Oh, Abe. Let's *do* that. You mean—it snapped, just then? It's *finished*?"

Abe scrambled up from the heap of huddled shapes lying on the f oor round the open doo of the stove. Snatching up the vodka bottle, brandishing it, he cried: " I should say not! That's what I been telling you—it hasn't even *begun*. Why, we ain't even started on the death wish yet. C'marn! "

All the Slavonians, Sophie, Singe, Father Joseph, Prince Mischka, appearing from nowhere, and even Mr. Karloff, sat up at this challenge.

" Good old Karlyboy." Abe ruffled Mr. Karloff's hair; during his slumbers he had lost his cap. " He's a true Slavonian—he just couldn't resist that."

" If we are to discuss the death wish," said Singe, " then I should hope he couldn't—I can't think of anyone who could resist that."

" There's a lady," said Larry, " in the kitchen. She's mislaid a husband, it appears. She's resigned, but she's been there some time. She has two little boys. Rather big little boys. When I came in, Milly, they were going through your bag." He passed it over to her.

" Milly, darling—if there's anything missing . . . they're naughty boys, those . . ."

" Don't panic," said Abe. " Don't, whatever you do, turn on the light. Bright lights cause my mood to snap as nothing else. Here, Larry, take him. Give him back to his nearest and dearest—watch out, he weighs a ton. Dear old fellow—just fix him up a bit, willya—see, tuck his shirt in, brush the seat of his pants . . . I wouldn't want any harm to come to him. Still, think I could keep his cap—just as a souvenir? "

" No," said Larry, " give him back his cap. He's going to catch it pretty hot as it is."

Milly was diving into the large handbag by the light from the stove. How *could* she have left it in there? The precious notebooks, yes— make-up, yes—all the usual things were there. Really, she couldn't remember what she had had in it—something did catch at her mind, but she couldn't worry about it now. The notebooks had reminded her of what still had to be done. She got to her feet, and realised that she was just the least bit drunk.

" What happened to you? " she said to Larry. " Haven't you been away for hours? "

" No." He grinned; Mr. Karloff, like a friendly bear, clasping him round the neck. " Not *hours*, Milly."

" What's an hour? " said Abe, coming promptly to his rescue; in this sort of emergency he was exceedingly experienced and right on the ball; had probably never in his whole life wittingly let any man down. " What is time? " he went on. " A tumpity-tumpity in thy sight are as an evening gone . . . don't *you* go, honey, I'm just getting into my stride."

He had her by the ankle. "Let *go*, Abe. I shan't be long."

She slipped out into the passage, snatched up her fur wrap and crept out of the door, down the stairs.

A single unshaded bulb lit each flight. Her heels tapped on the bare boards. She would have taken off her shoes but the stairs were too dirty, although it must have been a grand staircase once. What a strange house. There was a queer smell, too, a sour smell of dirt and damp. The walls were grimy, splashed with slops and scrawled over in places with chalk, the banister rails slimy to the touch. So this had once been Sophie's house. Milly thought, how can she not *mind*?— it would just break my heart.

In the main hall the light was much brighter, too bright. As she opened the outside doors she heard a creak behind her, as of a cupboard door, or hatch, sliding to one side, and she glanced back over her shoulder. There was a hatch, but it looked shut. She slipped out, holding the heavy street door so that it fell to without shutting, and stood in the shelter of the portico.

It was a bitterly cold night and there was an icy wind blowing. Little gusts of snow whirled round the street corners under the lamps. She looked up and down the snowy waste that was the street. It stretched to right and to left, long, straight, silent, deserted. But where was Vladek? Extraordinary, how she had expected to see, in fact, absolutely *relied* on seeing the office car parked there, a black squat shape, the friendly glow of Vladek's cigarette inside—but there was no car, no Vladek. Abe's car—she knew where it was and she had intended to direct Vladek to it, but it was all of five minutes' walk away. She could never manage that—not carrying things as well. What time was it? Three—four o'clock? She would have to go up again and get Sophie to come and help. In despair she glanced down the street once more.

Then suddenly, quite near at hand, on the same side of the street, in the shadow of a doorway, she heard a sound which by association alone seemed to freeze the marrow in her bones; the sound of a match being struck. A late home-comer fumbling for his latchkey, a courting couple—none of the normal explanations jumped to her mind. She at once recognised the sound for what it was, proof that there was somebody on vigil in that doorway, somebody who had lit himself a cigarette. She was about to step forward, because she had to know who it was waiting there, when two figures, men, swung round the corner of the street. She flattened herself back against the pillar, heard a low voice call to them and saw them turn in at the doorway a little farther up. She heard the murmur of voices, and after a minute or two, prompted now by a quite ungovernable desire to know, to identify these shadows,

409

she moved out from the shelter of the portico on to the top step. Yes, there they were. Two—no, three men. At that moment one of them detached himself from the others and ran down the steps. He turned to the right, along the street, and turned again, just as she had known he would, and came swiftly up the step towards her. She stood her ground. She was not even very frightened now. Whatever happened, she must *know*. When he was quite close, he looked up and saw her. There was enough light from the street lamps for them to recognise each other. It flashed into her mind that he was quite as startled to see her standing there as she was to recognise him as Sophie's brother.

He recovered himself quickly, but no quicker than she did herself. He was holding a lighted cigarette and tossed it away. " Mrs. Purdoe —but what on earth! Ah, you're looking for the car? " he said at once, which was strange, she thought.

" Yes. I—I was."

" It's not here." He seemed excited, talked very fast. " You don't know where it is? That's funny, isn't it? I've just been saying good night to some friends "—he pushed open the door—" Come in, you'll catch your death—some friends," he repeated, looking down at her in the bright light of the hall, as if curious to see how she would take this explanation. His eyes were pale, clear as water, not like Sophie's eyes at all. They seemed to slither all over her face. " Now, what about the car? " Apparently he was really upset about the car. " What are you going to do? How are we going to find him, the driver? " He dived into his coat pocket and produced his cigarette case. " Cigarette? "

" No, thank you. It doesn't matter, really. It was only something I'd left in it that I—a coat."

" Oh, yes, a coat." They went up the stairs together. He was talking very fast all the time. " Sophie's been asking for me, has she? No? I had to go some distance, you see—first to take the Rapovskis home, it was a business with that old lady—I thought she had a good head, how we all laughed, I can tell you, ha-ha . . . they're still here, everybody? That's good. I'm sorry to have dashed out—you won't think it rude, I hope? And now—I'll go out again and look for the car, shall I? Shall I do that? Your husband perhaps knows where the driver——"

" Look," said Milly. They had reached the door of the attic. " Let's not bother about the car. I've said—it doesn't matter a bit."

" No? " He seemed disappointed, paused as if at a loss, as if for two pins, had it not been for the faint note of annoyance she had allowed to creep into her voice, he would have pursued the matter further. Apparently, however, he did not dare—which was wise of him—risk a rebuff; he held the door open for her and they went in.

The smell of liquor fairly hit one in the face. Someone had put on the gramophone again. She could hear Abe's voice booming from the darkened room; they were dancing in the dark. I don't understand, she thought to herself, hanging up her wrap, I don't understand one bit. There was only one thing she had learned for sure, in that moment under the bright hall-light (but she couldn't see that it had any importance, or where it fitted in), that for some reason—although he had never met her before, had scarcely even spoken to her that evening—Sophie's brother had conceived for her personally a very definite dislike.

Anyway, now that she thought it over, it was clear what had happened to the car. There was not the least mystery about that. So that there should be no mystery, she was impelled to say to the young man, who was still hanging about in the passage, " Sophie's in the kitchen. Let's go in and have a drink."

" Beet leaves," Sophie was saying earnestly to Larry, who was drying glasses, " but young, you know, tender, just the shoots, chopped up fine—Milly! Don't tell me, they're screaming for glasses . . . here, coming! "

" Did you send Vladek home, darling? " said Milly casually.

" Good lord, yes," said Larry. " Hours ago. Why? "

" Isn't that just like you two," said Sophie fondly. " Always thinking of others." She turned to her brother. " You're back, are you? Well, just carry these glasses in, please. And don't drop them."

*   *   *

It was so comfortable, dancing with Larry, like relaxing into an old, old arm-chair; dancing with Abe was like relaxing into an arm-chair, too, but one in which the cushions weren't arranged quite right; just as old, if not older, but it didn't give just where you expected it to give—it wasn't *quite* so comfortable because you couldn't exactly go to sleep, for finding out where the uncompromising spots were; it was old all right, but it was new to her. So one of the Rapovskas had revived? There was no *counting* the guests—some disappeared for ever, some got their second wind and, disconcertingly, bobbed up again. Irène, or Rose, was it? The lean haggard one, dancing with Larry now? Dancing? That was one word for it. Oh, well, who cares. The old priest was muffling himself up in the hall. The light was so dim, all you could see in the glow from the stove were pinkish calves weaving in and out, the toes of shoes that winked. Zara Leander. Abe dropped a kiss—or she thought he did—on her hair. Zara Leander. All the records were of that vintage.

Unter den Dächern—wenn die Sonne versinkt . . .
Bin ich—mit neiner Sehnsucht allein . . .

He was in love with her. No, perhaps not that, but he—well, he *wanted* her. She tried to respond, to inject some life into her body, but it had taken it out of her, all that—don't think about it now. She yawned on his shoulder. Out of the frying pan into the fire. No sooner was one problem solved than another cropped up. Or perhaps there was only one but it was certainly hydra-headed. What was it all about, anyway? What was the point of it? That was the trouble, one kept forgetting the *point*. Better not tell Sophie about those men down there in the street. She'd get in a flap. Later. Later. Everything could be arranged later. In the morning, if need be.

"Abe," she murmured, "just for a minute—let's sit down."

"She'll be okay. She's just tired. Sophie, don't *fuss*."

"Wait—my pillow. She must have my pillow."

Soft and cool. Linen. Fine old linen. Nothing so nice. Some embroidery, too; bumpy, to be avoided. She avoided it, cuddling down.

Jus' once ferawl—time . . .
Let forchewn greechew . . .
An' lead the wer-hay . . . to Par-rur-rur-rur-rur-rur . . .

"Ludo!"

"Coming." A click. Then, triumphant still, the voice:

DISE!
Jus' once ferawl—time . . .

"Very beautiful legs, Lilian Harvey." Ludovic. Funny, she'd thought he must be one of those. The only explanation that had occurred to her for that look—the look they always gave you, a woman, when they knew that you knew.

"These discs?" Ludovic again. "No, from a German officer. *Given?* No, rather not. Poker. I was surprised he didn't take them back."

"One must admit, some of them were honourable, the swine."

Bay-ay-ay-ay-sin Street . . . tum-ti-tum . . .
Where the light and dark . . . meet . . .

"Oh, oh, oh." Abe. "You'll have me sobbing next. Where'd he

412

get this one, I wonder? Negermusik. He couldn't 've been one of Poppa's boys. . . ."

"So *that* was it! Abe, what would I not give to have your faultless Western brain? It never occurred to me—but I dare say—you know, Singe, what?—I DARE SAY HE WASN'T! It puzzled me, always, the way he used to come out to the kitchen with those bones for the dog."

"But then, Sophie, in the end he took the dog."

"That doesn't prove him to have been a *Nazi*, Singe, not necessarily. That just shows he was a *German*."

"Oh, yes, I see."

"One must be *fair*."

"Of course."

And the next time.

"Oh, the wind," said Sophie, "without doubt."

"Mais non, mais non, Sophie, je t'en prie." Prince Mischka. So *he'd* lasted out. "C'est plutôt banal, tu sais. Le vent, tout simplement. Qu'est-ce que ça va dire?"

"At night, I mean. Like wolves, howling. In a storm."

"Banal, quand même," he muttered stubbornly.

"Objection overruled. Let it go. Larry?"

"Oh, that's easy. The rather oily well-lunched voice of Mr. A. J. Hancock, Number Four desk, Boyd's Bank, Piccadilly, calling down the speaking-tube for my statement—and, equally, the squeaky, disembodied, callously cheerful voice that replies: 'Yes, Mr. Hancock, right away.'"

"You're not entering into the *spirit* of it, Larry; *that's* just superficial."

"I can assure you it isn't."

"The English sense of humour," said the prince. "It's a terrible handicap. I know what you mean exactly, Mr. Schulman. Shall I tell you mine?"

"Sure, go ahead."

"Pssssssssssssssssss . . ."

Everybody burst out laughing.

"Dis-moi, Sophie—why do they laugh?"

"Because . . . oh, never mind . . . of course, it's the pneu—the what is it? the tyre. Oh, poor Mischka, and we *laughed*. I'm sorry."

"He's hurt now, Mischetchka . . ."

"I can assure you," said the old prince, on his dignity, "that to *me* that is the most terrible and sinister sound."

"It seems, then, that everybody has his own?"

"Oh, you *donkeys*," cried Sophie. "I mean, *I* am the donkey,

413

perhaps. I see *now* what it is. Each has his own—that strikes *him* as being so, but others, not so much. Well, but if it is the truth—if it is really the most sinister—then it will be *universal*—so that the true one, once told, will strike everybody, contain all theirs in itself, all at the same time. Ah—look, I haven't made myself clear."

"Yes, you have," said Abe. "That *is* what I meant."

"Well, then, yours. Tell us yours."

"I think . . . it's got to be the truth, eh?"

"Yes, yes . . . nothing but the truth now."

"Well, then—hell, why is it the truth's so hard to put? Well, then, when you—er—happen to be placed so that you can hear the heart-beat of a person . . . your ear to the heart, yes . . . of a person . . . h'm, it's not so easy . . . with whom, put it this way—you have just recently shared, at any rate, the—feeling of . . . er—being alive . . ." Murmurs of admiration for his delicacy reached him on every hand. "Well, you hear it beating, bang-bang, not too loud, not at all steady, seems to skip a beat, flutter, and then it goes on—and it sounds so pitiful you wonder it has the impudence to go on. Almost any other noise drowns it—and yet it's the most important noise in the world, that steady old bangity-bang—and you know it'll go on, just as you know that one day it'll stop and you won't be able to stop it stopping, it'll go on or stop quite independently of you—yeah, that's mine, I think."

"Oh, yes," said Sophie, "yes. That's a *very* bad one. Now I'm crying. If I'd ever heard that I should have felt it, I'm sure."

"Oh, Sophie," said Larry. "you put your finger on it every time."

"She does, doesn't she?" said Abe.

"You mean, it's not quite?" she said. "That's true. It's wonderful but it's not quite. It must be something everybody hears, at one time or another, a commonplace sound—which means nothing to some people, and then, when you've heard it once a certain way, *that* way, for ever after it's a sound to chill your heart. Now I've thought of one—can I?"

"No," said Prince Mischka. "You've had your turn, Sophie."

"Oh, dash it. Then there's no one left to tell it, if we can't have second turns. I can think of three or four now. Ah, there's Singe, though. Go on, Auntie. Our whole reputation depends on you."

"Oh dear, on me?" They saw her face in the glow from the stove, screwed up, creased, knotted like a ball of latex. "Well," she began timidly, "I thought—although it seems you have to understand the question—and yet I thought I knew exactly what I would say the moment I heard it—wait . . ." They waited. "Well, I would say—in

414

summer, in the country, a hot day and it's after lunch, everything very still, yet quite gay, you know, cheerful, what with the sunlight and the bees and a dog barking in the distance and the voices of them hay-making in the fields . . . and you drowse off under the trees, in a—a—*chair*?"

"Deck-chair?"

"Hammock?"

"No, *chair*—it doesn't matter, don't stop me now—under the trees. You drowse off and then you wake. You think—what was that, that woke me up? Oh, you're quite wide awake—but you haven't heard it yet, that's the point. Why is my heart beating so fast—you say—why are the shadows so hard and strange? They've moved, everything seems to have moved, the garden itself has changed. And you don't hear the bees, or the voices, or the dog barking—it's silent, all dreadfully silent, d'you see, because—because you're listening for one thing—the sound that woke you up. And then you hear it. A cock crowing. Such a—what was it, your word, Sophie? Such a *chill* sound—like steel slipping between your ribs. Oh, it's horrible, *I* think—the crowing of a cock in the afternoon."

"Singe, my darling little Auntie Singe . . . that's right, kiss her, Mischka . . ." They swooped down on the small figure hunched up by the stove. "Oh, she's done it, you know," cried Sophie, " it's *right* . . . you've saved us, Singe . . . isn't it so, Abe? That's what you wanted—oh, yes, it's right, I feel it *here* . . . now can we have it all over again—I've thought of a million more——"

"No, Sophie, please, dear—not just now, we'll think of something else later. Could we, in the meantime, d'you think have another bite to eat?"

Most of them sound certifiable, thought Milly, as they all trooped off to the kitchen, leaving her alone in the shadowy room. She turned over, away from the glow of the stove, and almost at once began to dream. She was in Boyd's Bank, waiting to cash a cheque, when suddenly high up in the roof, or so it seemed, a cock crowed, very shrill and clear; everybody heard it, the porters, the clerks, the typists, the clients, and they all looked up in mortal terror as though it signalled the dawn of Judgment Day; whereas she, who happened to be standing in front of Number Four desk, at once identified the culprit as Mr. Hancock himself, looking demure, not particularly cocky, con-ventionally rigged out for the 8.10, only his beak through the grille gave him away and he was having trouble, in that confined space, with his rather luxuriant tail plumage—but catching her eye, perceiving himself discovered, he winked at her *very* cockily, and she turned over again and muttered fretfully, " I haven't been asleep for one second,

415

what a noise they are making out there in the kitchen, yap, yap, yap," and immediately fell into a deep sleep.

* * *

The sun was shining into the room when she awoke. You could tell from the hoar frost on the window-panes that it was freezing outside. One or two of the panes were missing; instead, the spaces had been filled with plywood. The sun sparkled through the hoar frost so gaily that after a bit, lying there, you ceased to notice these boarded-up parts, or rather you saw that they were essential to the picture, the window, which was raffish and enticing but not in the least sordid, and fitted in admirably with the whole picture, the room. Anyway, that was how it seemed if you were lying there with time to appreciate it, and with a headache, the way she was.

The stove crackled at her feet. Someone had put a quilt over her in the night; it smelt of feathers, home-cured; quill points were sticking through the sateen. It was amusing to draw them out one by one, to see the way each unfurled, springing into shape as good as new, the webbing between the ribs like stockinet, silky, close-woven, even durable, you would say, but you only had to brush it up with your finger-tip the wrong way and there it was, the feather bedraggled, quite spoiled. So this was where the party had taken place—no, surely the room had been bigger? They had closed the doors now—there were two rooms, of course. Just then, in the next room, someone put "Tales from the Vienna Woods" on the gramophone. She could guess at which point the record would be likely to stick and she waited for it with interest. When it came, and the record stuck just as she had forecast, she chuckled to herself. Of course you could never hope to get anything *done* in this atmosphere: what time was it, for instance? Where were they all? But it didn't seem to matter, somehow. What did matter was her headache. She reached for her bag. There was, she remembered, aspirin in the bag. She must look a sight. Before she could find the aspirin, she became diverted by the pocket mirror. She didn't look too bad after all. The sleep had done her good.

She got up, waltzed a few steps to the music and sat down. Really, how pleasant to wake up in a strange room with this odd cheerful feeling. Sad in the morning. She had never understood why Mr. Hemingway laid such peculiar stress on that—never permitting his heroes to be that way inclined. It was natural to be sad in the morning, natural to the human race, to her, and, she suspected, to Mr. Hemingway himself. If only in order that mornings such as this one might be accorded their due as rare events.

Someone had spread a clean white cloth on the table and laid it

416

with knives and forks. Holding the quilt round her she inspected it.
" Why," she murmured, and giggled, " if I came across this table
anywhere in the world I'd know at once that Sophie had laid it."
There was pumpernickel, still in silver paper; a tin of herrings, open;
a very small knob of butter and a very large hunk of cheese; a plate
of cold meats, a single small sausage on a saucer and some sliced
pickles. She picked up the sausage and nibbled it in her fingers; it
seemed to her that nothing had ever tasted so good. Munching, she
drifted over to the chest of drawers. Sophie's relations. The banquet
in the snow. Those hats. And the books. She pulled Hans Andersen
out of the row. Clarissa hated fairy tales. Why was that, she wondered,
turning the pages. Gerda—the Snow Queen. Ah, now, she remembered
that one, and it was frightening. A splinter of ice in the heart. She
shut the book, and shivered, although the room was warm.

What a strange room it was—untidy, dreadfully shabby, but one
would not have it otherwise. It was friendly, it had personality, an
atmosphere that had worked on her as she slept, soothing her so that
when she awoke it was to find herself in this wonderful mood; but a
room couldn't have so much that was positive on its own account;
no, of course not—the personality, atmosphere, both were Sophie's.
All at once she felt the need for reassurance. She could hear voices
coming from the kitchen, and crossing the room she opened the door
softly, and slipped out. She stood in the dark passage, where they
could not see her, but where she could see them, through the upper
portion of the kitchen door, which was of glass.

The kitchen window faced north; there was the gaunt skeleton of
an iron staircase and, beyond, a view of snowy rooftops dazzling in
the sunlight; in contrast the kitchen appeared chill and sombre, full
of bluish shadows. At first she could scarcely make out who was in
there. Abe, yes, sitting at the table drinking beer. He held a great
glass mug of beer in his hand, and there were some bottles on the table.
He was talking and waving the mug about. The aunt was leaning
forward, her chin in her hands, listening. She looked very spry, not
at all as if she had been awake all night. Sophie was standing by the
kitchen stove in a dressing-gown with a curious turban, a towel,
perhaps, round her head; she was stirring a saucepan with one hand
but listening too, you could tell, concentrating with all her might. She
looked very large in the dressing-gown—uncorseted, that was plain to
see—but calm, cheerful, self-possessed. It gave one pleasure to look
at her. Why, thought Milly, seeing her like that for the first time, all
Sophie needs is *space*. They all three looked absorbed, perfectly
content, not in the least tired, and as if they had been there for
hours. She didn't want to listen—not yet. She didn't even want to

go in to them yet. She gazed at them for a minute or two longer and then smiling to herself she went back into the other room, where the sunlight was bright, and helped herself to a fairly large slice of cheese.

No, she would not go in to them yet. For the moment she was quite happy as she was, nibbling cheese, pottering about. When I do go in, she said to herself, they will still be talking and I shall still be happy. It had never before occurred to her that life might be as simple and pleasant as that.

*   *   *

" I can't see that it can ever do any harm. It just takes getting used to, that's all. Once you've got used to the idea, it adds such a spice to life. You don't want to pursue it to the point of morbidity, which would be easy to do, like increasing the dose, you know, until it starts having no reaction and then even goes into reverse."

" It's different for us Catholics," said Singe.

" Of course. The dose is prescribed, isn't it? And the pill gilded. It's arguable that he went the absolute limit—even cutting it pretty fine, but who's to say? He was a genius, you see—lucky for him—and he had all that vast reserve of creative imagination to draw upon so that what might in the case of a lesser man have become almost a disease, anyway unhealthy, choked up, with him it flows out and it's not unhealthy at all. He could afford to steep himself in gloom and doom with scarcely any danger of overstepping the mark because he could distribute all the surplus amongst his characters—in fact, he had to feel it for them all. That's why he doesn't leave you with a nasty taste of hopelessness, despair, what have you, because although he never forgets it for an instant himself and never allows you to forget it—after all, he'd had this awful experience, you know, he was tied up waiting for the firing squad, a matter of minutes from his account, and that's not the sort of thing you forget in a hurry—with him it acted as a stimulus, it was part of his inspiration—and so he used it to the glory of——"

" Of God?"

" Life, I was going to say, but it doesn't matter, it's the same thing. In fact—he's for life. Although he can, I agree, make you see it as gloomy and nightmarish in a way no one else has ever done, you can't deny that you do get an impression of a tremendous force sweeping you along—to destruction, possibly, but that's life, too, isn't it?"

" Miss Brownlow said he was very depressing. She liked cheerful books."

418

" A great many people do. That's just what I'm saying. It's because they can't bring themselves to come to terms with *that*—they will persist in averting their eyes from it in order not to have to recognise it. Funny, really, because it's the only bit of truth we are all permitted to grasp, which stares us all equally in the face from the moment we are born, and which, and this is what I was aiming to say, is *not* something to be disregarded, to be pushed as far as possible out of mind— oh, no. Naturally, you can't hope to lessen the terror that it holds for you, because it *is* terrible—but . . . Let me see if I can put it another way."

" Yes," said Sophie. " Another way, being such a dunce as I am. More beer. Here."

" Well, think of a very wide swiftly flowing river. It's so goddam wide you can't even see the other side—so you don't even know there is another side, but that's not the point. Well, you're put into a canoe —*put*, I repeat; you're given a paddle of sorts and a shove off the bank and you just naturally start heading across. But before that you're told two things, both newsy items calculated to inspire optimism, and it's all that you are told, too—one, that you won't get across because no one ever has and come back to tell the tale, and two, that somewhere in that water there's a rock—they don't say where—your own personal rock, and you're going to founder on it. Yeah. So once you're under way, you think to yourself, well, this is a damnfool journey but one thing sticks out a mile—or it ought to—*the crossing's the thing.* You're meant to enjoy it, see. But there's that old so-an'-so of a rock. Now you don't want to come up against it before you have to—nobody does—so what do you do? Well, you do one of two things —roughly, I mean, there are all sorts of ways of doing those two things, can't go into that now. Either you try to forget about the old rock and go on as if it weren't there—but sometimes even so, if you're not concentrating, you may just catch a glimpse of its snout poking up above the water which gives you a terrible scare—or, and this is the other way, see, the way I'd recommend, you take account of its being there right from the start, accepting that it may bob up any time— but that doesn't make you glue your eyes to the water, oh goodness no—on the contrary. Now and then you stop paddling to admire the view and dare the old bastard to show up while you're doing it— and really you get quite a kick out of the fact of its being there; it makes the crossing a helluva lot more fun. If you do it on the ostrich principle, well, it's not nearly so amusing and you may run slap into it sooner than you think. You will anyway, of course, but at least if you keep it in mind it can never be sooner than you think. *Just so long* "—he leaned forward, putting down his mug with a thump—

" and it all boils down to this and *he* said it too, much better—*just so long as you don't know the precise moment it's going to turn up.* But keep it in mind—then, that's the salt in life! "

" What is? " said Milly, who for a while had been listening outside to this discourse, and was, reasonably enough, unable to make head or tail of it. She came in, trailing the quilt behind her. " What is, Abe? "

" Why," he looked up and grinned, " a sense of mortality, my dear."

" And what's that? "

He took a long swig of beer. Then he said: " Being aware—bah, not good enough, *knowing*—that is, never letting it escape you for one waking second that to-day—or to-morrow—or whenever it will be, you—and I—and each one of us must die."

" Oh, dear." She stared at him, bewildered. Timidly, she came a step nearer. " Oh, dear. But that's so—so *sad.*"

" SAD! " A great bellow, it made her jump. " SAD! " he roared, thumping the table so that the bottles rattled. Then there was a pause. They were all watching him; you could have heard a pin drop in the silence, as he seemed to gather himself together, to crouch before he sprang. Then his voice, magnificent, filled the room:

> *O temps, suspends ton vol! Et vous, heures propices,*
> *Suspendez votre cours!*
> *Laissez-nous savourer les rapides délices*
> *Des plus beaux de nos jours!*

There was silence. Then Sophie, dropping the wooden spoon, suddenly turned to face them; the tears streaming down her cheeks, she whispered:

> *Mais je demande en vain . . . quelque moments encore . . .*
> *Le temps . . . m'échappe . . . et . . . fuit . . .*

Unable to continue, she shook her head, and Singe, in her high tinkling voice, went on for her:

> *Je dis à cette nuit: " Suis plus lente "; et l'aurore*
> *Va dissiper la nuit.*

" But—it's terrible," whispered Milly. " Terrible."

" Aw, boloney, Milly," said Abe, and all three burst out laughing at sight of her face.

" May I—go into the bathroom, Sophie? "

420

" Of course, darling. I am going to boil some eggs," said Sophie when Milly had gone. She lowered a quantity into the saucepan as she spoke.

" Oh, Sophie, why? " Abe yawned.

" In case." She shrugged. " You may want to eat them. It's round about the time."

When Milly came out of the bathroom Sophie said: " Did you find the towel? Was it all clean, darling? Sometimes they leave things in there—horrors."

" Oh, it was quite clean. Only a corset—pretty volksy, but I didn't look too closely."

Abe said quickly, " You know, I've got a wonderful idea. Let's all go off for the week-end." Sophie, with a red face, was banging about with the saucepan, the eggs clashing merrily against the sides. " How are you doing those eggs? "

" A la coq," said Sophie.

" Timing them? "

" Of course I am. Three minutes each. They'll be ready in—in twenty-seven minutes from now."

" Fine. Could I have mine underdone, though? " said Abe. " I'm funny that way."

" Milly, have I been a dunce once more? "

" No," said Milly, deeply regretting her last remark. " You just do them, Sophie, your way, and they'll be all right. Abe, where's Larry? "

" He had to go. Poor guy, he suffers from that occupational disease of the British Civil Servant—gets jittery on account any minute the sun might set."

" But it's high in the sky," objected Singe.

" That don't make no difference," Abe growled, shaking his head, " not to them." He looked up. " But what a lovely day. C'marn— we're off. Just let's finish this—wine, is it? Sophie, can you come? Miss Singe? We'll get Larry and go on a picnic—say, we'll go to Zagranyza—there'll be fresh snow . . . stay the night at the Krystal— come right back." He stopped, and there was silence. He looked round. " Can you come? " he said, in a different voice. " No, I guess you can't."

" Abe, you know how we'd love it, but it's impossible. You know that too."

" Of course. I'm sorry. It just slipped my mind."

" We would come if we could."

" I know that, Sophie." He put his hands on her shoulders. " You don't mind our going? You see, we have to go. We'd have

421

to anyway, sooner or later. But thank you for a lovely time." He bent and kissed her.

"Take a piece of sausage," she said. "The eggs, look, they'll go in your pocket. Milly, did you enjoy it, darling?"

"Of course. It was wonderful." She kissed Sophie, a quick darting peck on the cheek. "I'll remember it always."

"They're gone," said Singe. "They did enjoy themselves, you know. They loved it."

"Did they?" Sophie was gazing out of the window; the sun had moved round; the rickety staircase made a pattern of rungs on the snow. "How quickly they went."

"How else could they have gone, Sophie? It's the best way, when it comes to the point. What did you expect?"

"Nothing. Only I wished it could have gone on for ever. Now I must go out. There's a lesson. I think he won't pay to-day or else he'll say he wants to stop. I wish "—she turned away from the window —"I wish, Singe, that these last twelve hours—well, I wish that *that* could be life and that *this* were the dream. Why is it—when you're with certain people—they twist it around to make it seem possible? It's a strain to adjust yourself when once you've seen it the other way round. Oh, well . . . ta-ta, Singe. There won't be so much to clear up and I'll do it when I come back."

"Good-bye, my precious." Singe kissed her. "You know, they *did* love it. And they'll remember it—and so shall we."

"Oh, *that*. Remembering?" She sighed, lingering in the doorway, twisting the door handle, as if she had lost all sense of purpose, as if it were an effort to depart. "You see," she looked up and her aunt thought, she's dreadfully tired—"the trouble is, Singe, I'm becoming greedy. I'm wondering whether *memories*, by themselves, will prove satisfactory. I'm wondering whether they'll be—quite enough?"

* * *

Singe was still sitting there at the kitchen table thinking about Sophie, and what she had just said, when the lady they customarily referred to as Mrs. Nosey Parker came in. She was in curlers and a cotton dressing-gown with a woollen shawl round her shoulders. She looked worried, even as if she had been crying.

"Your young lady's gone?" Whenever she spoke to Singe, whom she rarely saw, she treated her as if she were Sophie's housekeeper.

She was a youngish woman with broad cheeks, small eyes and a muddy skin, but not exactly plain, nevertheless. Being vigorous in her movements and large-boned, she was not the sort one might easily be tempted to feel sorry for; also she had something in her manner which, because it had never occurred to them not to dislike her, they had mocked at as uncouth. Now, because one could see that she was worried, this certain roughness in her manner seemed—although the word was incongruous—to Singe, at least, rather appealing; no, that *was* too much, appealing; or perhaps it *did* appeal; it was not so much rough as direct. She stood there nervously, plucking at her shawl, one hand wrapped in it.

" Did your husband "—Singe smiled—" did he—enjoy it, last night, d'you think? I mean," she added kindly, " it was so nice that he came." To her surprise, she found herself saying, " It was a pity you couldn't be there too."

The woman laughed shortly. She seemed pleased, nevertheless. " *Him*—oh, he *enjoyed* it—I should say so. He was singing in his sleep, even. Now he's gone off to work. I don't know how I got him up, but he was still in a good mood. He's awful, usually, when he's got a head. But it wasn't that I wanted to—see you about. I'm glad the young lady's out. Because I want to explain." She was muttering, rather, in her nervousness. Singe had to lean forward to catch her words, which anyway were in dialect. " It's those boys of mine," she went on. " They're a handful." She was unwinding the shawl from around her hand. " They found something in here last night—thought they were sweets, I suppose. They didn't mean any harm."

" Of course not," said Singe, puzzled.

" But when their father—well, he gave them each a box on the ear —he was very angry, I can tell you, when he found out. And he told me to—although I would have done anyway, mind you—bring these back. I would have done anyway," she repeated, scowling, the fringe of the shawl tangled with what she had in her hand, " because I don't want to have anything to do with it. It's foreign stuff. But you won't tell the young lady, will you, madam? " she added, to the astonishment of Singe.

" No," said Singe. " Not unless—but what is it? "

" Here." A glass bottle, dusty white inside, empty, a printed label on it; an empty white carton printed with black lettering, a twist of cotton wool, and a piece of paper from an exercise book screwed up, these things she put down on the kitchen table in front of Singe. As if they were all imbued with the properties of black magic, she stood back and heaved a sigh of relief.

" But I don't understand," said Singe.

" In the paper," said the woman and Singe unscrewed the paper.

" I see," she said.

" There should be a hundred." The woman spoke as if she had rehearsed it. " The trouble is, he felt so bad, my man, he took one, because he knows what they are and he said, the young lady won't mind. Tell her, he said, that I've taken one and be sure to say, too, that I enjoyed myself, and I don't think she'll mind. So now there are ninety-nine. Count them, please."

Singe spilled the tablets out of the paper into her lap.

" Oh, I'm sure there are ninety-nine." She stared at the little heap with distaste.

" So it's all right?" She looked very anxious, Mrs. Nosey Parker, and Singe smiled.

" We won't say any more about it. But tell me, where did they find them?"

The woman turned to fiddle with the saucepans on the stove. Clearly the question embarrassed her. " I think," she muttered, her dialect thickening, and her voice owing to her embarrassment—and Singe understood it was due to that—becoming harsh and abrupt: " I think they found them in the foreign lady's bag. You know how it is, they're inquisitive at that age—youngsters." She flounced round. " I dunno . . . it's hard to explain. I'm glad it's you, not the young lady. He said this morning—my man—they're good people, their hearts are in the right place . . . Jasha, he said (that's my name, Jasha), it's worse for them, d'you see? And I enjoyed myself, he said, in a way I haven't done for I don't know how long and now *you*—he meant the boys— *you* let me down. And then he let out with his fist—ho, in a way they'll remember. Not because he was drunk. He'd got over that." She paused. Singe waited, not saying a word. The woman—she was not much more than a girl, but from the north, that type—rather sullen-looking, you never know with them, Sophie would say—had reddened. She had something else on her mind.

" What I want to say is," she began, slurring her words, as if inviting you to throw them back in her face all in one fistful, " for my part, I've done my best. It's hard these days . . . out at work all day, as I am, and they learn things at school—well, we were always brought up strict, both him and me, and we wouldn't touch anything not belonging to us—not only that, but we wouldn't "—she glanced at Singe—" we wouldn't ever, although you may find it hard to believe, go out of our way to speak out of turn. Know what I mean?"

Singe nodded.

" Yes, well, but what do they do to the young people nowadays, I should like to show? It's not my authority that counts—nor yet their father's—we even have to be careful in front of them, the kids. Ah, that's a fine thing, isn't it, to have to mind your p's and q's even in front of your own kids? These days it's such a rough and tumble . . . if I had time, I'd bring them up the way they should go—but as it is . . ."

424

She sighed. " Still, let's hope that a good slap will do something. He should have slapped them before, I always said."

" Don't worry," said Singe. " I'm sure they're nice boys at heart. It's not as bad as you think."

" It's not bad at all," she retorted, scowling terribly. " Don't think *that*. What I wanted to say was—just because it's so obvious what *you've* lost—you won't repeat this, will you?—don't think *we* haven't lost things too. We come from very decent families, my husband and I."

" Of course. I'm sure of it. And my niece thanks you very much for letting us have the free run of the kitchen yesterday. That was very kind."

" Oh, that was nothing." Truculent, ungracious, she tossed the shawl over her shoulder and moved towards the door. At the door she turned and smiled; intended to be pleasant, it was the smile of a woman who knows she has bad teeth, lopsided; a snarl, almost. " You won't tell her, will you? About—that?"

" No," said Singe, " never."

When the door had closed she shook all the tablets back into the bottle and screwed up the top and put the bottle into its carton and tucked in the flaps and then, with it held tight in her hand, she hobbled off into the other room.

She felt very tired—she hadn't had a wink of sleep all night—and sat down on the bed. The sun streamed in. Sophie had cleaned up wonderfully well in those dawn hours. But no one had eaten the breakfast. Never mind. It could all stay there; it would do for lunch. She sat thinking for a long time. Then, still deep in her thoughts, which were mostly to do with Sophie, still having the package in her hand, with the instinct of a squirrel which tells it that nuts mean the approach of winter and must be hoarded away, she bent down and undid the hasps of the brass-bound chest and hid the package inside, in the only private place she possessed.

PART FOUR

Unlike are we, unlike . . .
Unlike our uses and our destinies.
Our ministering two angels look surprise
On one another as they strike athwart
Their wings in passing . . .
           . . . What hast thou to do
With looking from the lattice-lights at me,
A poor, tired, wandering singer, singing through
The dark, and leaning up a cypress tree?
    E. B. BROWNING: *Sonnets from the Portuguese*

Chapter One

" I'M DUSTING your dressing-table," said Clarissa, starting to do that.

" So that was what you were doing? I thought you were spell-bound by your own fatal beauty. Still, do carry on. It's kind of you."

" That's all right. I'm doing it because of Gisela, who's gone, you see. Did you know?"

" Yes," said Milly, moving around fast, throwing things in and out of drawers.

" I even helped Miss Raven wash up."

" Really? Then the world must definitely be coming to an end."

" I don't know about that, but it is an emergency, Miss Raven said, if not a catter—catters——"

" Catastrophe?"

" Yes. Is that worse than an emergency? I do like emergencies."

" Do you?" Milly sat down at her dressing-table, and, as her daughter happened to be there, hugged her lightly. " Of course you do." She got busy with cream and things. " I remember," she said, slathering the stuff on, still in a very good mood and this all fitting in, " when I was your age, just about, there was a terrible flood and I prayed all night that the bridge would be washed away. Prayed and prayed."

" Did you *really*?" said Clarissa, drawing away a little and regarding her mother with intense interest. " That doesn't sound a bit like you."

" Oh, doesn't it?" said Milly curtly. Extraordinary the way this child fastened on the intermediate details of an anecdote without having any apparent interest in, and certainly no flair for appreciating, the finale. Other people's children weren't like that. *What* didn't sound like her, anyway? The act of prayer? Clarissa was lacking, utterly lacking, in objectivity. The point on which she had been about to give satisfaction—and surely it *was* the point, whether or not—was that the bridge had not been washed away.

" Children revel in disaster," she said rather stuffily instead. " All children do. I can't think why. I suppose because they don't have to cope."

" Sometimes they do. I had to. After all, I *did* wash up."

429

" So you did. Funny-face."

" Do you think I'm pretty? " said Clarissa, falling for this.

" In your own little way," said Milly kindly, and saw her daughter look rather crestfallen. Well, that would do her no harm.

" *You* look pretty this morning." She leaned up against the dressing-table, watching her mother at work. " Although you were out all night, weren't you? "

" Mm." Her head on one side, judging the overall effect, she decided to ignore the "although." She decided she could afford to. " Yes. Do you disapprove? "

" Goodness, no. Not at all. It's just what I shall do the moment I grow up."

" Then don't be surprised, my darling—just pass me my bag—if your father and I postpone that moment for as long as we are able."

" You are funny, Mummy, this morning. I wish you were always like this." Milly was rooting about in her dressing-case, packing things in. " Where are you going? "

" Into the country."

" Who with? "

" With whom. With Abe—and Daddy, if he'll come."

" I suppose you're going to stay out the whole of another night, are you? "

" Well," said her mother, frowning. It certainly did sound odd put like that. " We may . . . again, we may not. You wouldn't mind, would you? "

" Not in the least," said Clarissa accommodatingly. " So long as it's an emergency. I dare say it is, isn't it? Do you think—I mean, *if* it is—d'you think I could have—just a little bit? " She smiled cunningly.

" Oh, all right." Milly sighed. Clarissa was not completely lacking in objectivity, after all. " Here, you can have this old one. Now, look, Clarissa—it's not just for fun. More for education, really. Don't let your father see you with it on. Don't scrawl on the lavatory seat with it, and don't—I repeat *don't*—beautify Dermot as you did last time. That, more than anything, was what made Daddy so cross."

" It made him look scrumptious, I thought."

" That's not the point," said Milly hastily. " At least, it is in a way, but you're not to do it, all the same. You'll understand when you're older. Lipstick is strictly for girls and be thankful that there's something that is."

" Mink is, too, isn't it? " said Clarissa, leaning her elbows rather heavily on the dressing-table and leering up at her mother.

" It is really beyond me," said Milly coldly, " *where* you pick these things up. Is that Miss Raven crashing about in there? Go and see, darling—oh, hallo, Miss Raven. Good morning."

"Good morning," said Miss Raven, in the doorway. "Going off again, are you?" she added pleasantly. Although this last was a classic Miss Ravenism, a studiedly trite observation calculated to drive the subject of it into a state of frenzy, it was a new Miss Raven who uttered it. The party, Milly thought, must have done her a world of good. With no trace of a hangover, there she stood, smiling, rather well groomed, showing quite nice teeth.

"Mr. Schulman—we, I mean—thought we'd go for a picnic." Briskly she slammed things into the lower compartment of the case. "The trouble is" (make-up, new nightdress, yes, the new one—oh yes, make it the new one, thought Miss Raven in sympathy)—"the trouble is," she snapped the case shut and faced Miss Raven, paused, and then it all came out in a rush, "would you be kind enough to give my husband this note—I couldn't get through to him—or even, if you're not too busy, could you ring him up? But if you'd give him this anyway. It's to tell him where I'm—we're going, and that we'll expect him to—to follow. It's quite easy—it's—it's all written down."

She put the note on the dressing-table as if she expected Miss Raven to pick it up. As if it were a wager, almost. Miss Raven did no such thing.

"Well——" Milly gave Clarissa a brilliant smile. "I'll be off. It's all quite—*clear*, is it, Miss Raven?"

"Oh, yes," said Miss Raven. "Quite okay by me."

"Good-bye, then, pet. Be an angel child. Won't miss me, will you?"

"No," said Clarissa gravely, and Miss Raven smiled to herself. Suddenly the little girl put her arms round her mother's neck and, dragging her down to her level, whispered fiercely in her ear, "*Come back* . . . oh, mind you *come back!*"

"Muggins," said Milly, quite fondly, although rather surprised; disengaged herself, and picked up the dressing-case. "So you won't forget, will you, Miss Raven?" Somehow she did wish Miss Raven had picked the note up. It looked like a scrap of wastepaper, there on the table top. "Well, good-bye."

"I've done what I could," she told herself, going down the stairs. "What more could I have done? Now, it's up to her. Supposing I'd telephoned and he'd said he was too busy . . . no, better to leave it like this; to chance, or to Miss Raven, which came to much the same thing.

*　　　*　　　*

431

" So you are coming, are you? " said Abe. " I was just beginning to wonder whether you'd changed your mind. You got through to Larry? "

" Yes."

" He'll be along? "

" Yes," said Milly, getting into the car and snuggling down. " Just as soon as ever he can."

Once they were off, almost immediately she was seized with misgivings as to what she had done. Nothing, she told herself. Nothing at all—certainly nothing wrong. Nothing I can't get out of, nothing deliberate—only a shadow of a teeny-weeny lie, that one, just now, to Abe. Nevertheless, it took the edge off her pleasure, somehow. She would have given a lot to be able to recapture the spirit of the early morning. On the outskirts of the town, when he suggested that they stop for vodka, she agreed. They ate Sophie's eggs with the vodka and after that, although it wasn't quite as splendid as it had been, her mood, she felt much better. What was done was done. There was no altering it now.

*　　*　　*

Little bitch. She hadn't even *tried* to phone him, Miss Raven dared say. Well, then, no more would she. He should have the note when he came in for lunch.

At lunch time she opened tins, laid the table and really behaved in the manner she would have described as " going out of her way," when the telephone rang. He couldn't come back to lunch. He was too busy. Could he speak to his wife?

" She's not here, Mr. Purdoe. She's—she's gone out."

" Oh, well, never mind." He sounded harassed, almost cross. " I can't come back for lunch anyway. It would mean walking, because Mr. Wragg's taken the car. Will you tell her that? "

" What about your lunch? " she said, and his heart warmed to her. It was a point that would not have struck Milly.

" Don't worry. I'll get something sent up."

*　　*　　*

After a long squint at their identity cards, the young police guard at the check-point walked all round the Citroën, examining it dubiously from every angle. He looked rather unhappy. Eventually he put his head in through the window.

" Is this an English car? " he asked.

" An English car? " Abe exploded with rage. " I should damn' well think not. This, my friend, is a Citroën. Kindly note its points—

432

bodyline and so forth—appreciate them—take your time." He did as he was bid. " Now—I trust you'll know better in future."

" Yes," said the guard, blushing.

He had no talent for vehicle recognition, he knew that. Somehow he couldn't whip up any enthusiasm, having no hope of ever possessing a motor-car himself. Women, now, that was different. He could appreciate a pretty face without any trouble at all. This foreign woman's, for instance. He saluted and gave her a smile as he waved them on. Then he ran back to his hut, where the field telephone was ringing again.

The orders of this morning were countermanded, he was told. He was to forget about the Austin and concentrate on a Citroën. He listened attentively to the description of this brand of car. By the time the Austin turned up at the check-point, which it did within the hour, the young man had assimilated sufficient information as regards a certain model of Citroën to enable him to recognise it, even should he meet it in hell. Which was where he probably would meet it, he reflected, having deemed it prudent to suppress the fact that just such a one had recently passed.

On a day like to-day, Vladek, at the wheel of the Austin, was thinking to himself, Mr. Wragg as a passenger had his points. At least he never opened his mouth. Looked pretty browned-off, too, didn't he? Browned-off was the expression Vladek used in his thoughts, it being one of his favourites. Old Wragg had his own troubles, doubtless, just like he had himself—well, not *just* like. He probably hadn't got a hangover; he hadn't—although you could never tell with Mrs. Wragg —had his wife screaming abuse at him, nor, for certain, had he just received a wigging from the Chief of Security Police. What a morning!

It had started off badly and gone on that way. She'd rooked him, that girl, that was the first thing. Well, she'd written herself off as far as he was concerned—the nerve, raising the ante for a double duffy! This was Grusnov, not Slavnik, as he'd pointed out. And she'd been a nice simple girl once, when he'd first . . . h'm . . . still, it would have been worth it if it hadn't made him so late, and then this temperamental bitch of an Austin getting bogged down in the rubbish dump, where he'd parked in the dark, and half the spivs in the neighbourhood flocking round to push him out. That was the way the lolly went. Then to go back home with his story all carefully buttoned up, when all he'd wanted was a bite to eat and a shave—and what did he get? Fireworks from the wife, a message from Police Headquarters—*and* another message from the office informing him that he was required to drive Mr. Wragg to Zagranyza at twelve o'clock sharp—what a morning! He didn't mind about Zagranyza—he was thankful to have the chance of spending the night away with the old woman in that mood. No, it had been the Chief of Police who'd put the wind up him, a bloke that he, Vladek, had never even seen before, and never wished to see again, either.

Co-ordination! That was a new one. Why hadn't he reported last night? Why this, why that, nag, nag, nag . . . well, if they were so smart and knew the whole story, as it seemed they did, why the hell did they have to ask him? What did it matter in which car those parcels had been put? How could he know what had happened to them? He couldn't drive two cars at once, could he? And where was the American's car, they'd said. " Now? " he'd said, to gain time. " Over the frontier, for all I know "—and then they'd all gone mad, shouting, waving their arms, all except for this velvet-arsed bloke behind the desk who'd spoken in a very low nasty voice—" putting things plainly," as he had called it.

One thing, it turned out then, certainly was plain—that they weren't trying to catch him out; they didn't know themselves where the American's car was, either. It didn't seem to occur to them that even if they tracked down the car there wasn't an earthly chance of finding the stuff still in the boot. It stood to reason, didn't it? He had pointed that out, and then wished he hadn't, it all became so much more unpleasant—and that was saying something. What particularly un- nerved him was when this bloke suddenly called for his, Vladek's, file, and when it was brought he began looking through it, frowning, making a spiel with his eyebrows and so on, and then started reading out bits, jabbing at certain paragraphs with his hairy finger, and with every jab he'd dig up another chunk out of his, Vladek's, past. Then he began hinting things, this v-a'd bloke, about counter counter counter, and he'd muddle himself and have to start again—counter counter-espionage. Ha-ha. One thing at a time, please. Just simple counter-espionage was quite dicey enough to satisfy yours truly, thanks all the same.

Still, there it was. He'd now got to prove himself, they'd said: they were sure that if he really set his mind to it he could find the Citroën, or the parcels, or both, or even, best of all, the Citroën with the parcels inside it, and the American driving it! They had a hope.

" What about my Dienst? " he'd argued. " I'm on Dienst now."

" You'll have to combine it," the v-a'd bee had said. " Co-ordinate in order to co-operate, that's what you'll have to do." Very mirthful, that, very witty indeed. Was that all?

So taking it by and large he was glad to be driving away from Grusnov with Mr. Wragg beside him. Anything for a little peace. It's their job to find the Citroën, he argued. As for the parcels—why don't they search the Bielska's flat? He nearly bit my head off when I suggested that. I know why—because it wouldn't suit them to find the stuff there. They've other fish to fry. They can knock off the Bielska any time.

Still, it does strike me that they're not nearly as streamlined as they'd have you believe—for one thing, they don't seem to have any kind of plan; they act as if they just make it up as they go along. Nor so lynx-eyed, either. After all, it wasn't *they* who found *me*, this morning; I turned up. And yet the theory is they can nab you at any hour of the day or night. They had a whole squad out looking for me, so they said. Interesting, that. So it might not be impossible—if it comes to that, and it may do . . . He mused to himself. He'd liked Yorkshire. There was a girl in Hull who had really been, and therefore, he was willing to bet on it, would still be—a nice simple girl. But one thing at a time.

Never mind. I'm taking these few hours off. To-day is Dienst— I told them that. So it's Zagranyza and Mr. Wragg and there'll be a night's subsistence and the Krystal isn't bad, and Mr. Wragg'll be snoozing in bed by nine and then I might come across that little brunette in the tobacco kiosk who was there last time . . .

" What I certainly shall *not* come across," he told himself, and really the thought cheered him, " is the American, or his car, or the stuff that's supposed to be in it—so they can put *that* in their . . ." By way of relief to his feelings he trod hard down on the accelerator. " I'll get drunk to-night. Why not? May be the last chance. And as it looks like being the end of my career in the service let's make it a pretty sticky do."

In all of which Vladek was mistaken; and the Chief of Security Police again proved right: it being one of his pet theories that although there may be all sorts of ways of conducting an operation where there is a fixed objective to be gained, when in Slavonia, Slavonian ways are best.

*   *   *

" Cold, Milly? " Abe hadn't spoken a word all the way until now, although he had been singing, off and on. They were already in the mountains.

" Yes, I am."

" We'll stop for a quickie in the next village. There's a pub of sorts, I seem to remember."

When they came to the village he turned the car in through an open gate into what looked like a farmyard. A man was milking a cow in a shed. Off the flagged pathway the midden was churned up, the surface powdered white, crackly with frost. Some hens and geese scattered in front of the car, squawking.

Abe glanced in the driving mirror. " Looks like I've given Alby the slip to-day. Perhaps he's getting the jeep fixed. Steering's been all haywire for quite a spell. I've warned him about it."

Milly laughed. " D'you call him Alby to his face? "

" Sure, why not, he's democratic. He's a nice guy—hell, we're pals, even. One time—well, he'd been keeping up okay, right on my tail, then I missed him. On the homeward trip I found the poor guy in the ditch with the kingpin gone. So I had to give 'im a tow. Gosh, though, he lost a lot of face over that incident. So—here, come on, Milly. It's round the back."

They walked down the flagged path to the back door of the farm-house. Inside there was a low-ceilinged room filled with smoke, and peasants sitting on benches round the walls. They might have just dropped in for a drink after work, but from the state some of them were in, their faces a rich purple, their eyes glazed, their voices raised in argument, it seemed likely that they had spent the winter's day in more convivial fashion. Not one of them took the slightest notice of the foreigners, and Abe led the way through the room to an alcove round a corner. The farmer, or publican, brought vodka and put the bottle and glasses on the tiled window-sill. He was a young man, rather surly, with beautifully polished high boots. His wife came and peeped at the strangers from the kitchen, her hands sticky with dough. Milly smiled at her, and she vanished at once.

" They're jittery," said Abe, " probably no licence. They don't mind us but they can't figure out where Alby's got to. They wouldn't like having him in here. Try this—it's more like Schnapps. Home-made."

She tried it. It was fiery, but without the synthetic taste, a hint of petrol, of the shop vodka. In fact, it was quite nice.

" Would you say we'd been drinking all day? " she asked presently.

" Sure—why? "

" I just wondered. It sounds so terrible."

" Does it? Not to me it doesn't—and it *isn't* terrible—is it? "

" No—rather fun, really. I mean, if it's like this, why don't people do it all the time? Why is it considered—well, terrible? "

" Those are two quite different questions. Who considers it terrible? A lot of phoneys who've never done it. That disposes of that. As to why people don't do it all the time—I prefer not to go into that, because if I'm reminded of the obvious reason I might be craven enough, or prudent enough, to stop now, and I don't want to—so, let me tell you that a surprising number of people all over Europe do.

Drink all day, every day. Take a North Italian contadino—in the Red Belt, say, anywhere from Bologna to Milan—one of those guys with a face like a ham, wrapped in a green cloak, you find arguing in any market-place—he's probably never sobered up since the day he switched from mother's milk to grappa. In France—well, I don't have to go into that. In Jugoslavia, too, they're tight as ticks all round the clock —encouraged to be; from the State's point of view those rose-tinted spectacles are cheaper and more to the purpose than real ones. The Swedes are natural soaks—they wouldn't need those laws otherwise. Though it beats me how they can be so dull on it."

" There are exceptions, Abe. What about the Swiss? "

" The *Swiss*? Milly, I sometimes wonder whether you really follow my train of thought, dear. I don't give a goddam about the Swiss. For the purposes of argument they're neither here nor there, except to act as a yardstick to prove the rest of us human and fallible and reassure us all that that's the way we want to be, just as the sole raison d'être for Switzerland, at least as far as I've ever been able to discover, is its geographical position, which enables the traveller to enter Italy in the right mood, *i.e.* with joy and thanksgiving in his heart—like that horrible super-chlorinated, ultra-hygienic puddle you have to dabble your toes in before they let you through to the pool."

" I get your point."

" You do? Where was I? Guess I drifted off. These peasants— not only these, here—all over—why do they do it? Because it takes the edge off life. And if life is unbearable—and if you've ever watched 'em dredging up sand all along the beaches of Calabria under that sun, or ploughing with a couple of oxen on a hillside like a scorched bit of paper, you'll know what I mean—you see, Milly, I'm expanding on the theme—but there's no need to expand, maybe, when all I want to say is, let 'em soak, poor bastards, they sweat it out, they absorb the alcohol to keep themselves going and their bodies sweat it out— whereas we, *we*, the loafers, that is, *absorb it into our brains*."

" Well? " She began to giggle, which seemed to annoy him. He said shortly: " Well, brains don't sweat. The good and the bad elements of the alcohol go in—I'm putting it in words of one syllable, dear—and there they stick, see? And the bad wins. Partly because it almost always does, and partly because its methods are not too nice —insidious, you might say. It don't give you a chance to make a decision. By the time it occurs to you that there is a decision of some sort hovering—well, you realise you made it long ago. Alcohol "—he lowered his voice and his eyes rolled—"*rarts the brain*."

" Oh *dear*."

" Yeah," he chuckled grimly, " awful, ain't it? But it's not as bad
437

as it sounds." Meditating, he scratched his ear both inside and out, then poured out the rest of the bottle.

" Let me tell you how I see it. Imagine a lumber yard, sawmill or what have you, on the outskirts of a town. Does this bore you, Milly? "

" Not yet."

" Okay, I'll make it snappy. Spoils it though. See it, that lumber yard? Smell of shavings, healthy, *tangy*, all that wood lying around, most of it sawed up. Some of it's quite good quality, nothing special, but useful, for doors and so on——"

" Doors? "

" Doors or drawers, I don't mind . . . then a helluva lot of it's reject stuff, but useful, oh very useful, for rags, paper and all that. Then there's a quantity of high-grade stuff, imported usually, seasoned, expensive, and a lot of trouble's been taken in the growing of it, and they'll use that for the top-notch jobs—to panel some Generaldirektor's office or some similar nonsense. And then there's some even better stuff still—really *rare*—going to be carpentered and polished, carved probably, and it's so rare they've catalogued each piece, custom-made furniture, that's what it's destined for, altar-screens, treasures for some Fifth Avenue shop, anyway each chunk of it'll end up as a thing of beauty and a joy for ever. So you got all that wood, see? All neatly stacked, cheap stuff in big stacks, then the higher the price the fewer, all nice and neat and clean, and each of those blocks is going to be useful, see, going to do its job in the world, whatever it is; going to wipe asses or have big black lies printed all over it, or maybe going to be carved into cunning little masterpieces or cunning little fakes of little masterpieces, or going to make ships and bungalows and playpens and gallows—it'll be processed so you just won't recognise it—but what's *wrong* with it, Milly, all of it? In spite of its goddam usefulness, what's *wrong*, eh? Taking wood as wood, you understand."

" I don't know." She laughed nervously because at that he turned on her, quite savage.

" It's all *dead*, my dear—that's what it is! *Dead!* An' you've only to take one step outside this establishment—did I say it was near a forest? —only one step, and ya trip over a log—some tree or other, struck by lightning maybe, or maybe it just decided to lie down, and here's this old log, see, and it's rotting, it's rotten as hell, but by God, it's *alive*. Why, it's a sorta breeding ground; there's moss and ivy and stuff clinging to it, and mushrooms growing out of it, may even have one or two little green shoots of its own—and it's hospitable, too, a lot of happy little woodlice crawling under it and maybe a mole or a badger as house guests . . . and though it's lying in slime and tangled over with
438

briars and so on, and that's why ya tripped over it, it's not dead—far from it. It's so rotten it's alive! Why, it's so alive with rottenness," he snarled, squinting horribly, " *it probably even shines!* "

" Abe! " She giggled. He did look a little mad.

" Get me? About brains and drink an' all that? "

" Yes. I think so. Yes, I get you."

" Yeah." He brooded for a bit, then sighed. " Unfortunately it's not the whole story. There's more to it than that. Wanta hear? "

" I suppose I must."

" H'm. I gotta mix my images now. The old log won't quite see me through. Don't forget it, though. So you've got this old brain, see, all sodden and rotten but teeming with life, et cetera . . . so far, okay. Now you gotta think of it as a machine—easy, eh? " He grinned. " I admit, Olga Wragg couldn't 've put it better. A machine—doesn't matter what the hell it's supposed to do—and it's highly complicated, this machine, gadgets galore, but only two items really count. One, inside it there's a little needle—like a compass needle, static, though, which points due north, plumb centre—you know, it *indicates*—get me? The other—and they're connected, see—is a kind of compass arm which swings out—and that's what it's meant to do—oh, in such dizzy arcs and the looser the nuts and bolts the dizzier the arcs, and that's fine. They can be dizzy—they *gotta* be dizzy—but you gotta know how dizzy they are—and that's what the needle's for. Well, doesn't matter what's wrong with the rest of the machinery, whether it's rusty or there's a few screws loose don't matter at all, it can still go on doing its job, better even, that way—anyhow, it's practically indestructible—though I admit a bullet could finish it—no, *that* isn't what you have to watch, Milly, *how* it works—let it hum, let the little cogs and so on slow down or run riot, let that arm keep swinging around, just so it all keeps on humming—it don't matter what's happening so long as you can check up when you feel like it and see how far off course, mad, bad, etcetera —and you do that from time to time. D'ya get me? Well, okay. Then one fine day when it's all ticking over haywire as hell, as always, the way it's meant to be, the way you've gotten to like it to be, there comes a moment, dear—or there *may* come a moment—nothing dramatic, though—maybe you feel a little tap, jolt, hear an odd creaky sound—something you've never felt or heard before—and you getta kind of suspicion—don't ask me how—and you make your routine check, and you look and you look again because you can't believe this could ever happen, see——"

" What? What happens? "

" That needle, Milly. *The needle shifts!* It's not pointing due north, plumb centre—oh, you can tell right away, it's out of true. It don't

439

indicate any more. You can aim to fix it but once it's that way you might as well throw your hand in. That old compass arm'll go on swinging around, very likely, till it swings itself off—in fact, that's what must happen because it isn't connected any more. See? The gauge is broken so the whole works are broken. Yeah, broken. For good an' all. Know what can break it like that?" He paused. He looked so serious that she thought he might be about to say something serious. "Liquor can," he said, and laughed. "So you understand, Milly?"

"No. I'm afraid not."

"That's fine. Then there's just a chance I may be quite wrong." He took a big gulp of vodka, smacked his lips and put his glass down.

"Abe, really. I believe you are a drunk. Are you?"

"Why, cer'nly I am," he agreed, "potentially. I admit I haven't got my fraternity pin, as yet. I drink, sure I do, but those excursions are still more or less limited to when I'm in the mood. I don't, more's the pity, bask in that glow of perpetual optimism so I know the very next shot'll see me there—in the mood. No, I don't figure on attaining the state of Nirvana so easily—nor do I have to be in it all the time."

"It must be awful to get into the habit." She sniffed rather priggishly into her glass, thinking to herself, with just a twinge of disappointment, he's a nice man at heart. He gave a rude snort of laughter.

"How old are you, Miss Prue? No, don't tell me. Let me tell you something. You don't even begin to *form* an unbreakable habit before the age of thirty-one. Just chew over that. So you ain't seen nothing yet, baby. Anyway," he filled her glass from a new bottle, "you don't seem positively to hate it yourself."

"That's only to-day," she said, furious.

"Uh-uh . . . that's what they all say . . . you'll be on the slippery slopes before you can——"

"And what about you?"

"Oh, just sliding surely but steadily down. But then it's my vice." He smiled, very cheerfully.

"What's mine?"

"How you do remind me of my wife, the way you can wrench a conversation round to the most fascinating subject in the world. She'd have admitted to any vice provided you gave it a double-page spread first——"

"That's not like me."

"No," he said, "I only said it to catch your attention."

He had caught it, in any case. Although she masked her expression

440

with sympathy, she was in fact intensely curious, so much so that her nose twitched.

" She's—dead, isn't she? " she murmured, with delicacy.

" Yeah," he replied. " She sure is. Dead." From his tone it would seem that the delicacy had been superfluous. " Who told you? "

" Mr. Schwelling—ages ago. And someone called Mrs.—Hadge."

" Oh, Coralie . . ." He champed his jaw in a way he had and there was a glint in his eye. " I never knew you met her."

" She's a great friend of yours, isn't she? " Milly gave him a coy look.

" Great friend of mine? She tell you that? Well . . ." He champed more furiously than ever. " Hadge is a great friend of mine . . . known him for years . . . but Coralie? If she says so, I guess I'd better feel flattered. And she told you about—my wife? Very interesting. And what did she say? "

" She said that——" She looked doubtfully at Abe. It didn't seem to her in the best of taste to invite discussion on the matter. " That—it had been a great tragedy—that you missed her terribly— that you had been desperately unhappy. Mr. Schwelling said the same."

" Really? Big words. What experts our friends—if that's what they are—prove to be on the subject of our most sacred emotions. Far be it from me to rob them "—he was snarling again—" of any vicarious pleasure they can pick up . . . scavenge . . . . filch . . ."

" You mean that you *don't*—miss her terribly? "

" Who? My ever-loving? Oh, sure I do. I'm continuously and consciously grateful to Almighty God, Providence, the three Fates, et cetera, that the little darling is no longer tripping by my side."

" Abe! You mean you didn't love her? "

" Oh, gracious, Milly! Does it really sound like that? "

His sarcasm and the conclusions it forced upon her were disconcerting in the extreme. It had always fitted in so well—why, it was an integral part of her own picture of Abe—the deep mourning band around it, in respect of a beloved wife. The circumstances had from the first appealed to her, satisfying her insatiable appetite for romance, the aura of tragedy transforming what might have been a mere flirtation with the dignity of a serious love affair. Death, in its proper place that is, the death of a stranger two years before, had a wonderful hallowing influence which served to erase any slightly sordid smudges on the bright picture of the present.

" No," he said slowly, with the tip of his tongue searching his teeth, as if for raspberry seeds, his whole face mobile as always when he was thinking. " I didn't love her. I can't think why I married her. I was

441

sorry for her, in a way, but that wasn't the reason. I've thought and thought and I can't think why I did that."

" Why did she marry you? "

He looked surprised.

" For the passport, naturally. You couldn't have a more excellent reason. She was a Slavonian, didn't they tell you that? I met her just after we all got to Slavnik—you know, after the battle. How did it happen? Let me think. We were all rooming in the Hotel Slavonia in those days—where I saw you first, remember? British, American correspondents, Quaker Relief and so on—the whole lot. She was an interpreter—oh, quite the rage. There weren't so many other girls. So "—he yawned again—" I had a room and we all had rooms and she came and slept in my room until after a bit of argument we got married—seemed easier in the long run; and then I went on sleeping in my room and so did she, most nights—and after a while just now and again—by no means all the time. There were so many *rooms*, d'ya see, she could afford to be choosey—and all sorts of other people arriving every day, Heads of Missions and so on, not just simple newspaper guys—they made us look like small fry—only we'd got there first—well, that's about it. That's what finally got her down. All those *rooms*."

" But how did she—I mean, then she *died*? "

" Yeah. So she did, that's right. Caught a cold one night in some room or other—I never found out which. There wasn't any too much heating in those days and sometimes—how shall I put it—when the fancy took her, she displayed rather exotic tastes." He caught sight of Milly's face and laughed, diagnosing with accuracy the cause of her expression. " What's the matter, sweetheart? Doesn't it fit in? You shouldn't've listened to old tomcat Smelling—I told you so, didn't I, at the time? "

" You sound so—*bitter*."

" *Bitter?* Honestly, dear—I'm not *bitter* at all. I was a sucker, admittedly, until I learned—it's a luxury to be a sucker and I paid for it. The way she paid for what she was, too. But *bitter*? God, Milly, where d'ya pick these words up? You listen to Smelling and you listen to Coralie——"

" Well, she certainly implied that she knew you very well."

" I take your meaning, dear, but we'll let that pass for the minute. As I was saying, you catch the odd rustle from the old grapevine and you start putting two and two together and you make a snafu of the first addition so you try again and the second totals up to *bitter* because that's the next best thing, isn't it? You see, they're all cooked up, your answers, cooked up to suit."

442

" Suit what? "

" Whom," said Abe, " in this case. You, of course. If you'll forgive my saying so, it's characteristic of all your dealings with every single human being—you see what you want to see, what fits in with your own ego. We all do to a certain extent but I've never in my life before met anybody who does it as ruthlessly as you. So it's not surprising that you miss the priceless treasures scattered at your feet."

" Treasures? Miss them? " she said, startled, " miss " having been the operative word. " What treasures? "

" Well . . . mostly to do with love, I suppose. You miss them because you don't choose to see them—why, you even tread them underfoot. You don't want them, *now*. You just wait. You will some day—when you do happen to glance down and see that you're walking over a desert, the desert that you've made."

" Why? I don't understand. Why some day if not now? "

" Oh, I dunno, Milly. Isn't there a law—if not there oughta be— of diminishing returns? That's it, I guess. So far, d'ya see, you've been lucky. You're one of those people—and it's luck, dear, not a virtue, so don't get me wrong—who's only gotta step out on a bomb-site for the flowers to spring up round your feet. But do you see them? No. You're for ever head in air looking up at the sky, searching the heavens for some sign . . . I dunno what."

" Well, what *ought* I to be doing? " She was mystified, also annoyed.

He laughed. " You might do worse than look where you're going, for one thing. Or you could look right down at those flowers, Milly —count 'em, if you have to, but anyway smell 'em and don't, *please*, tread on 'em—best of all you could go down on your knees every so often and thank God not only for those buckshee flowers, but for the earth and for allowing you to live on it, because it don't do you a mite of good looking at the sky, dear, you're earth-based, no one more so, and don't you ever, ever, try kidding yourself or me or anyone else that you're not." He sucked his teeth for a bit, and then suddenly he grinned. " Did you ever do algebra? "

" Yes. Why? I was quite good at it."

" I'm not surprised. How did you go about it—solving a problem? Wait . . . let me just recall the whole loathsome process. You examine it first, eh? You decide what you want for the answer. Then—am I right, Professor?—you let x stand for it. And then you start fiddling around. Oh, for a time I was stunned by the natty logic of it—the way you could equate the moon with the sun and prove black was white so long as you stuck to it doggedly enough—until I found out, to everybody's relief, I may say, that algebra, mathematics, et cetera,

443

weren't my mettiay . . . but, on the other hand," he whispered with such a snarl that she recoiled, " that human beings *were*, and they aren't and never can be adequately represented by those punk symbols a and b and x and y because whatever the combination you employ to get the required answer that's all hooey, dear, when the true answer is —as often as not—that they *won't* equate—*they just don't add up*." He took a deep breath, finished his glass, and the bottle. " Thank the Lord, because otherwise what a stinkingly dull mathematician's world it would be. Cm'arn, Einstein, drink up—and we'll go. So help me God," he glared ferociously at a small and shrinking plant in a pot, pushed behind the curtain, " I never could stand the smell of geraniums."

Milly went through the kitchen, where there were some day-old chicks in a box by the fire. The farmer's wife waved her down a flight of stone steps, at the foot of which there was an earth closet. When she came out, through the back door, she found herself in an orchard where there was a dog running up and down the length of its wire barking furiously, but not at her. She saw that the Citroën had been backed so that one wheel had overshot the edge of the flagged path and was sunk in the midden. A crowd of peasants was standing around the car, the man with the milk-pail, a few children and some of the men who had been drinking in the room, their faces ripe purple, bruised-looking like windfall plums in the cold sharp light. More were trooping out. Also Abe was standing there, scratching his head.

" Hi," he called. " You know what? I ran over a goose. Can one do that? I didn't think it was possible."

" I should say you've proved it," said Milly, seeing that there was a sort of plump white pillow propping up the back wheel of the car. The farmer in the polished boots was hanging about, looking pleased. He didn't interfere. Then the farmer's wife came out and the crowd made way for her. Poultry was a woman's business. If she turned nasty, certainly the crowd would turn nasty, too, or at least begin to take sides. Because there is never a second to lose when negotiating with a crowd, Milly smiled at the woman and Abe drew out his pocket-book and everybody round hushed as he spoke. He spoke in Slavonian and on that account and because of his atrocious accent they forgave him and the wife started to laugh, especially when notes, in the way they have, changed hands. He got into the car and moved it forward an inch or two and the children snatched the corpse from under the wheel and held it up. It was a big fat gander, not much mangled or even dirty; only it had stretched out its neck a bit too far.

The woman went indoors and came back with newspaper and wrapped it up and put it on the back seat.

444

"But I don't like goose," said Milly.

"Me neither. But we gotta conform. If a scorched earth policy is what they're used to, then scorch it we must."

They parted with their hosts, indeed, with the entire village, on the friendliest of terms. Cheering and waving, the crowd saw them off. Once out of the village Abe slowed down, leaned over and kissed Milly lightly on the cheek.

"What's that for?"

"I dunno," he said, "but I thought perhaps you might." He started to drive.

She was pleased by the kiss; what it was intended to signify, she had no idea.

Chapter Two

BY THE time they arrived at Zagranyza the sun was sinking below the rim of the mountains, gilding the outline of the peaks against the sky. On one side of the valley the snow still held a pinkish glow, on the other the slopes were streaked with deep violet shadows; a cold little night wind rustled down the length of the valley, and already lights twinkled in the town. The Krystal, sumptuous as an immense bombe glacée, was perched on the summit of one of the pink slopes, the ground-floor windows ablaze with light and the noise of its radio streaming out to mingle with the cacophony from the radios of all the hotels around; the windows on the upper floors were shuttered, and in spite of, or because of, the blast of music, the localised blaze of light, the hotel somehow gave the impression of being deserted.

Milly waited while Abe put the car away in the garage, then they walked up the steps into the foyer together. She was carrying her dressing-case, Abe a bottle of whisky and the goose, which he held by its feet; it had lost its wrappings. Although there were several porters standing about, no one offered to relieve them of these pieces of luggage. Festivities of some kind seemed to have taken place; recently, one would judge, but there was no way of telling whether that day, or the day before, or even last Saturday week. Waiters with brooms and dustpans attached to long handles were weaving about between the hall and the ballroom, idly scooping up whatever rubbish actually impeded their progress. They seemed disposed to be skittish with each other, even over-excited, anyway, red in the face and in spite of the nature of their work, happy in it.

Milly and Abe, ankle-deep in paper streamers, waded across to the reception desk, an imposing structure occupying a lot of space and all wired in, as in a bank. In the office part, at the back, some clerks were sitting at typewriters, plates of pork and beans balanced precariously on the ledges above the keyboards; they were eating busily, and drinking fairly busily, too; glasses containing a greenish liquid, possibly a local liqueur, acting as paperweights on mounds of files, bills, and so on. Underneath the chairs, desks, almost everywhere, really, were bottles. The receptionist himself, a deathly-pale young man with rat-like features, was lolling over the main desk, comfortably placed with his back against the grille, also eating pork and beans;

446

casting an appraising glance over his shoulder as Milly and Abe came up, he went on eating. After a bit, stacking his fork systematically and stuffing in a mouthful that would last him through, he turned round; chewing, he treated them both to a hot angry stare. Suddenly he shot an arm through the grille and snatched the passports that Abe had in his hand. Propping himself up once more, he began to go through these documents from cover to cover at his leisure. One or two of his colleagues, sensing a diversion, left their grub and crowded round. Presently the receptionist finished his mouthful and stuck his face up to the grille.

" Wait," he said, and waved the pair of them to one side, completing the movement by snatching up his glass of green stuff and draining it.

Abe and Milly moved off roughly to the position indicated, and stood waiting. There was nowhere to sit down.

" What sort of dump is this? " she asked at last.

" Showpiece. Best hotel in the country."

" Abe, look. The goose."

Its head dangled down and blood was dripping from the wound in its neck on to the marble floor. As they happened to be standing in a patch that had recently been cleared, this was embarrassing; noticeable, anyway. Abe shovelled up some paper streamers and made a sort of bandage for it which was soaked through in no time.

" Who'd've thought," he said, muffling it afresh, " the old bird to've had so much blood in him? Look, Milly, you take him. I'm going to raise the ante—make that jerk sit up."

When he came back, he said, " I've ordered six rooms with six baths."

" What did he say? "

" He was deeply impressed. You see. They'll be just falling over themselves any minute now."

After another twenty minutes or so, his prediction was fulfilled to the letter. The receptionist came out from behind the grille and stood there yawning until, a waiter happening to moon past trailing pan and broom, he stuck out his foot and tripped the man up; leaving him sprawled on the floor he returned to his post. The waiter got up, dusted himself down, and without any show of surprise or even of justifiable rancour, indeed, rather as if this were the normal summons to an abnormal task, shuffled over to the grille for his briefing, which was lengthy and whispered; eventually the receptionist swept a row of keys at random off the board and handing the fellow the whole bunch, resumed his former position, back to the grille, and poured himself another glass of the green.

447

Jingling the keys on high rather in the manner of a tambourine, the waiter with an arch look over his shoulder indicated to the guests that they should follow him, which they did, round the back of the foyer to an open lift-shaft. Here he stuck his head into the vault and yodelled into it, his hand meanwhile playing a tattoo on a cluster of bell-pushes. Suddenly, catching sight of the goose, he stopped yodelling and even took his weight off the knobs, so that the bells stopped ringing, in order to cross himself. Shyly he poked the goose in the breast; the shock of discovering it to be real apparently causing him to reassess the whole situation. With a strange cry he threw open a door and plunged up a dark wooden staircase. They followed, guided by the clump of his boots ahead, and at the top of the flight caught up with him, fumbling about with switches on a board. Seeing them in the gloom, he gave a sort of muffled squeak and brushed his hand over the entire board. Immediately the corridor became not merely illuminated but enlivened by the blast from loudspeakers, one at each end. Heartened by the familiar accompaniment he swung along ahead, rattling his keys, now and then stopping to make a pass with one or other of them at the keyhole of a door, then after a time lag of a minute or so, possibly sensing that this was a precision job which demanded too much of him, he would throw in his hand and flounce off.

In this way the trio toured the first-floor corridor and the second; at last, on reaching the third floor and having made his usual per-functory stab at a lock and by a fluke achieved instantaneous success, the waiter seemed to recognise that some link must be forged between eye, instrument and hole. Once he had mastered the knack, there was no stopping him. Summoning with a touch of the switch both light and music, he himself burst into song and proceeded in mounting voice and confidence, his charges hard on his heels. With a swift unerring flick of the wrist he opened doors to right and left, revealing identical chill shadowy chambers, untenanted and unprepared, until, some way down, he flung open a door in no way dissimilar from the rest and his new-found confidence received a setback. The room was occupied, and the occupant—who was athletic and disagreeable-looking, athletic in view of his costume, navy-blue bathing trunks, which contrasted oddly with the dust-sheeted furniture and the snow on the window-sills; disagreeable independently of extraneous factors—sprang off the bed with a low growl and padded towards them. The waiter slammed the door and bolted off down the passage, Milly and Abe after him.

Here at the end of the corridor there was a door in an alcove that led to what was obviously a turret suite, and this was where their guide packed it in. Unlocking the door, he gave Milly a gentle push over the threshold and withdrew. Leaning up against the wall, he took a pen-knife out of his pocket and began to trim his nails.

On the threshold Milly peered inside. It was a suite and a very grand suite; murky, though, and there was a strange fusty smell. Illogically, she was at once reminded of Torquay. Then she saw why. The strange greenish light, the smell, were due to there being such a lot of plants. She bawled at the waiter, over the noise of the loudspeaker, " Bath ? "

He looked up, adroitly touched a switch and silence fell.

" Bath ? " she repeated.

" Millionaire! " he parried with pride, as if this were a code word implicit with all the reassurance she might require.

Abe came and stood in the doorway; sniffing, he too looked around. Then he put the goose down on a table, where its head dripped into a conveniently placed flower-pot, and stepped up to the waiter.

" Hey, Bluebeard."

The man went on dreamily digging away at the quicks. Abe bent down and bellowed in his ear: " Nix gut, savvy? Noch eins—d'ya get it? "

Apparently he did get it; snapping the penknife shut, he picked up the bunch of keys from the floor, thrust them into Abe's hand and with a hospitable gesture that included the entire corridor, sprang into a kind of oubliette, a concealed door in the wall, and they heard him making off down the spiral staircase rather fast.

" Blotto," said Milly crossly. She felt cold.

" You're so perceptive, dear," said Abe, frowning at the keys. " Well, I'd best——"

" Abe! You're not going to—don't *leave* me! "

He turned. Something about seeing her against the background of tropical greenery must have struck him as funny, because he grinned.

" Don't panic, honey. I'm only going to pick myself a room. Be seeing ya."

She went in and shut the door. There were plants everywhere, in pots, buckets, hanging baskets, round the walls, climbing up the window-frames, forming, in lieu of curtains, a curtain of green; plants in varying conditions of health, some had succumbed, some writhed in a kind of death agony struggling to catch the drops of moisture from the panes of glass; one or two, notably the fierce desert type of cactus, had, regrettably, thrived. On her way to the bedroom she tripped over a hosepipe which lay in coils on the parquet, and followed it through the bedroom to the bathroom, to its fount, the tap in the bath, to which the end was bound securely with wire and a stocking. For some reason the stocking struck her as sinister, peculiarly so. The bath would have been unusable in any case owing to the encrustation of dirt round the rim, apart from the fact that it served to accommodate two or three sturdy date palms. There was a row of rubber-saplings along the window-sill, calceolarias in the bidet and a eucalyptus sprouting, as it were, directly out of the lavatory pan. More to raise her morale than anything, she transferred this last to the floor, staking her claim to that much Lebensraum, at least.

She went into the bedroom and switched on the light. It was a large room full of large pieces of mahogany furniture, the walls lined with yellow silk. There were no curtains or carpets; clearly any removable furnishings had long since been removed, except for the bedclothes on the huge double bed which lay in disorder, precisely, it was to be supposed, as the last occupants had left them. Fingering the sheets gingerly—they were exceedingly dirty—she disturbed one or two moths which fluttered about and then settled down in the new folds.

She wandered through the sitting-room, which had french windows leading on to one of the long wide terraces, set in tiers, which formed the façade of the hotel. It was still light outside. The terrace had been cleared of snow, more or less, and somebody was out there, pacing up and down. Milly went up close to the window and looked out. A woman, it seemed to be, with an Alsatian dog; now and then she would throw it a ball. There was something so unlikely about the woman's appearance that Milly, at first unable to identify what it was, rubbed her eyes. The next time the figure approached through the dusk she stared hard. Those chiffon draperies, hyacinth and pink—Balenciaga, wasn't it? And if that stole's not mink, she muttered, I'll eat my hat, and opened the window and stepped out.

The air was wonderfully fresh after the dank smell in the suite, and the cold made her eyes smart. She leaned up against the edge of the stone balustrade. The mountains seemed to have closed in; the snowy slopes, huddled together, glimmered like swans in a backwater at dusk. The sky was varnished clear apple green. Later there would be a moon.

" Tartuffe! " Just behind her, the stranger called to the dog. Milly turned and smiled, and the lady, encouraged possibly by a reciprocal curiosity, approached. Definitely, yes, it *was* the Balenciaga, in all its glory. And the stole was mink—and the ear-rings were real, too. The wearer was dark and plump, with a long hooked nose, her eyes melancholy with make-up. Shivering, but determined, she came up

450

alongside, clutching her stole about her. Heaving a sigh, she eyed Milly just as Milly eyed her. They might have been two strangers who, after the funeral of some mutual acquaintance, had gravitated together, each with relief having descried the other, the only possible person present, across a large room.

"C'est épouvantable, ce pays, n'est-ce pas?" observed the lady, after brooding for a split second over the impressive view. She added, "Styin' 'ere?"

Milly nodded. From the pronunciation of these two words in her mother tongue she instantly recognised the slovenly vowels of the international vernacular as spoken by Antoinette and her kind; in the single French sentence, however, there had been the equally identifiable twang of the Levant.

"Ha . . ." The stranger smiled dismally. "You won' stye long." Delivered thus, the words gained in effect, the bald statement being more sinister than a prognostication, and infinitely more sinister than a simple question. Milly said quickly: "No—only until to-morrow."

"Plye breedge?"

She shook her head.

"Tant pis." The lady seemed quite resigned. "I been 'ere," she went on, "ten dye. On account my boy 'e convalesce from ze cheeken . . . but to-dye I phone my 'usban'—if you don't come fetch me queek, I tell 'eem, I go convalesce, too, chéri—à Paris . . . tha's wot I tell 'eem . . ." She gave a snort, the lugubrious snort of a horse kept waiting in a fog. "I zink 'e come pretty damn' queek now," she added.

"You come from—Paris?"

"Neoww . . . from Anka-rrha! You American or British?"

"British," said Milly glumly, hardening herself to withstand the customary reception of this news, but in so doing underestimating the good manners of the lady, whoever she was, who seemed prepared to treat an admission either way with a light-hearted impartiality, as a misfortune to be condoned with a smile and to be dismissed by a tactful change of subject.

"Tartuffe!"

The great creature bounded up.

"You like my dog?" She patted him, adding, a shade casually, "'E's very 'ongree . . ." She broke off as Abe came out on the terrace. She gave him a swift look, then, apparently satisfied, continued, including him at once in the conversation and allowing what had been the faintest hint of an undercurrent of tension to become unmistakable in her voice, so that her discourse could no longer be construed as merely frivolous in its intent, but more in the nature of an overture, even of a direct appeal. " I was just telling madame," she said, " my dog, Tartuffe . . . 'e's *'ongree* . . ."

" You mean," said Abe, staggering under the forepaws of the dog which it had placed on his chest, " he's not like this when he's fed? "

" Oh, not at all. Now 'e's *weak*—feeble, pauvre bête . . . My son, my dog," she turned to Milly, numbering the sufferers on her gleaming fingers, " même le chauffeur—we are all, all, *'ongree.* 'Ave you eaten 'ere? " she went on briskly.

" No. Not yet. Is it—er——? "

" Aw*fool* . . . mon dieu, but *awfool*! " Shrugging her furs round her, with a gesture for each syllable she said, " Peeg peeg peeg peeg peeg . . . alors—we are fed opp! " and looked it. " Le service n'existe pas. Downstairs—wait two hours. Up 'ere—rien du tout. My boy, 'e *was* seek—now 'e's seeker . . . parce que j'ai apporté "—she reeled off—" des marrons glacés, des confitures, des bonbons, des biscuits, et cétéra—vous savez—autrement . . ." She shook her head and went on: " Mais, madame, voyez vous, one 'as arrived at a certain point when one feeds marrons glacés to the dog! " Her voice softened: " Pauvre Tartuffe! Pour nous, ce n'est rien, mais pour les animaux? C'est bien autre chose. N'est-ce pas, Tartuffe? " She bent down to fondle the animal. " Il n'aime pas les marrons glacés, le porc encore moins. Pauvre bête . . ." Suddenly she glanced up and with elaborate offhandedness asked: " You don' 'appen, per'aps, to bring eet wiz you? "

" I beg your pardon? " said Abe.

" Food," said the lady simply.

" Oh . . . why, no . . . hey, though, wait a minute. Sure we did. Say, Milly, they'd better have Goostav, eh? Yeah, sure—we brought a goose."

" A *goose*? C'est à dire?—ah!—aaaaaaah! " The face, all its sombre ditches, arches, all suddenly irradiated. " But we cannot . . . oh no . . ."

" We don't like goose," said Milly. " We do rather like pork."

" *Vraiment?* Alors . . ." Teeth, rings, flashing, she stepped up to Abe. " Where is 'e? "

" Right here," said Abe, stepping in through the french windows and getting the bird. " Wait, I'd better carry him for you, though; he's not the goose he was." Careless of her draperies, the stranger had already seized the feet.

" Ah-ha, 'e's 'eavy! " She gave a throaty chuckle and lowering her burden, regarded it, knitting her brows, a little smile playing round her lips. " 'Ow you keel 'eem? " she asked at length.

452

Abe looked embarrassed. "Well—it was like this, see . . . I was driving—and . . . well, you know how it is——"

"La voiture!" She screamed in ecstasy. "Naturallee . . . la voiture? You crush 'eem under ze wheels? . . . Tiens!" She beamed on them both. "It's the best wye, y'know . . . they die 'ard, these birds"—she patted the goose—"like reech ole men . . . ha-ha! My old servant, in wartime, 'e' put the neck in the door of the cheep, then —crrkkk! An' one time, je me rappelle, in B.A., I 'ad as servant a li'l girl, Italian, sweet, fourteen years old, from Venezia—you know 'ow she do it? I tell you. With a needle—a needle de tricotage—'ere." She poked her own fleshy nose. "*Zey all 'ave a 'ole 'ere!*" With a shiver, glancing affectionately at her trophy: "'Orreeble, eh? It's the custom, paraît-il, en Italie . . . mais, enfin, zey 'ave zis somezing crool in the *character*, Italians . . . very crrrool people, y'know . . ."

"Oh?" said Milly doubtfully, involuntarily recalling everything she had ever heard about the Turks.

"So, bye-bye! Thank you ver' much—I go now. A bientôt!" She tripped off, dragging her booty behind her, the Alsatian sniffing joyously at her gold heels.

They watched her out of sight. "What's she stepped out of?" mused Abe. "Not Boccaccio, obviously. Could it be—don't tell me —the Arabian Nights?"

"As it happens," said Milly, who was shivering, "you're not far wrong. Please let's go inside. It's freezing out here. . . . Oh, Abe, it's freezing in here, too. These pipes aren't even warm, let alone hot."

"Really, dear? You surprise me. So they're not—not even warm, let alone hot. Now, don't get mad, Milly. Look, I got some Scotch."

"So I see. No, thank you."

A little later. "I guess Larry must've got held up or something."

"Yes. Oh, Abe, how can you just sit there *reading*?"

"Aw, come now, honey. There's nothing else to do. I'm just filling in time. You oughta know by now always to equip yourself with literature for this kinda trip."

"Really?" She stared at him. Then she said coldly, "What kind of trip?"

"We-ell . . . kinda rough shoot, would ya call it? No, obviously not," he went on hastily. "Now what can we find for you . . . here, look!"

There was indeed literature of a sort, used as a wedge under a bamboo table on which were some of the heavier plants.

"National Geographical Magazine, July, 1947. Why, you lucky girl. That should make absorbing reading. Just think of Wragg—or

Wragg's predecessor—sowing this seed of culture all those years ago and now—what's that line? You remember, out of Bette Davis by Villon——?"

"Yeah . . . In your field my seed shall thrive . . ." He began to laugh quietly to himself at sight of Milly's face. ". . . This is the end for which we twain are met . . . Gosh, I'm sorry, Milly. I guess I got a warped sense of humour. Whenever I'm actually forced to witness the British swallowing their own tails, I don't know why, it just kills me every time. Perhaps they had a puncture, or something."

"Who? Oh, yes . . . perhaps."

"I'll go order up some vodka. You look cold."

"I *am* cold," she said peevishly. "But I don't feel like vodka. Couldn't we—wouldn't they have—don't you think?"

"Champagne? Gracious, you're an optimist, child. I agree, though, it would be the only thing right now. One—even two—bottles would just—c'marn in!" he bawled, at the sound of a gentle tap on the door, and rose to his feet in astonishment as a man-servant in dazzling white jacket and gloves came in, carrying a small gilt bucket in which ice clanked around two bottles of champagne. The man bowed, handed Abe a small mauve envelope and withdrew.

"But—ABE!"

"*Wait*, will ya—just let me get the smoke out of my eyes." He stared at the bucket, at the envelope. "Hell, I didn't even rub my lamp, ring, or anything, did I? I just *wished*—remind me to try it again some time . . ." He took the card from the envelope, glanced at it, and whistled. "Ya know what did this? Goostav, dear old bird. Who'd've thought the old bastard'd've been worth his weight in—let's see—'45, I'll pass that—Perrier-Jouet—yeah, it'll do—demi-sec—now that *is* odd! I was figuring to myself just before the genie appeared. Take away your sec, your sweet—it's gotta be demmy or nothing to-day—what a gal! She's certainly cemented international relations all right."

"Who, Abe? WHO?"

"Her Excellency the Turkish Ambassadress." He flipped the card over to her. "From now on my number one sweetie-pie."

"Well, well." Not only pleased but immeasurably relieved by this timely intervention from a dea ex machina, she responded, touching up her lips. Putting her lipstick away, she saw to her surprise that Abe had sat down and was pouring himself some more whisky.

"Well?" She was smiling, puzzled. "Aren't you going to open it, Abe? For heaven's sake—my tongue's hanging out."

He put down the bottle he had been pouring from, took a cigarette, looked at her sharply, and lit it.

454

"Open it?" He was frowning slightly, she noticed. "Why no, Milly, I thought we'd wait."

"*Wait?*" She was really puzzled now, and forgot to smile.

"It's usual, isn't it?" He was watching her behind quite a haze of smoke he had blown up. "I mean, what about Larry? Best wait for him, I think."

"But"—exasperated, she blurted out the first thing that came into her head—"but that's silly! I mean—we might have to wait all *night!*"

No sooner had she spoken than she realised her mistake, not only because he was looking at her so strangely, but also from the way in which her own words rang in her ears. Yes, it had been a pity, that remark.

"Might we?" he said. Then, after a pause, "Might we have to do that?"

"All I meant was . . ." She felt herself blushing.

He got up and, with his glass in his hand, he came over to where she was sitting and stood looking down at her.

"He is coming, isn't he, Milly?"

Rather than meet his eyes, she got up herself and moved towards the window. She stood there with her back to him, looking out.

"Tell me," he came up behind her, pursuing her: "What did he say exactly?"

"He said he'd come," she mumbled. You couldn't see the mountains now. It was almost dark. "As soon as ever he could."

"Oh, he said that, did he? Well—in that case, he won't be long. Should show up any minute now, so I think I'll—so I'll go down and leave a message for him to come straight up. He might even be down there. Anyway"—he spoke softly, just behind her, at her elbow—"that's what I think I'll do. . . ." She felt him watching her. "I'll do that."

"But——" she began, and became silent, biting her lip. She couldn't turn round because he was still standing there. He stood watching her for another minute or so, then he went out.

*   *   *

He found his way to the main staircase, which was in darkness, and with his hand on the banisters ran down two flights. The last flight led into the lighted foyer. On the landing, in the shadows, he paused to light a cigarette; then he leaned over the rail and looked down.

The waiters were still pushing their dustpans about. The reception clerks had finished their meal; the plates were stacked in a corner on a desk, and they were getting down to the liquor in earnest; the stuff in the bottles had changed from green to red. Some holiday-makers had arrived at the reception desk; they were already lined up waiting to buy tickets for something. The receptionist, as if he had had his orders, was letting them wait. They looked depressed and resigned. They couldn't see what Abe could see, the receptionist on a stool beneath the desk reading a magazine and occasionally taking a swig from his glass. Now and then, jumping up with a snarl, he would push a ticket through the grille as if intending it as a personal affront, the recipient would shuffle off, the queue shuffle up, and—" Aw, the hell with it," he muttered to himself, taking the last drag out of the cigarette and lighting another. " Leave it alone, can't ya? Stop observing, Schulman—stop blotting up atmosphere. What d'ya think you are— Tolstoy or Fiddley Parson or Sourpuss Susie on the Ladies' Page? *You don't have to write this down.* What are you *really* thinking about? What's going on inside that big heavy box you call, God help you, your brain? What's *eatin'* ya, Schulman? C'marn now, give. Then we'll go right on down."

Because there *was* something eating him. That was how it always started—with a sort of eating process. A nibble, a twitch, a bit wrenched off, leaving that part ragged but the main chunk still intact, waterlogged but afloat in warmish water, and then a whole shoal of little shapes darting through the ripples—here they came, jaws snip-snapping—nip, nip, nip, quick, like quicksilver, silvery, here, there, those ragged bits torn off, tidied up—and that bit, too, a new bit— and you were the lighter for it, still afloat but in their charge now, not in your own; you felt it, being tugged against the current and then all of a sudden—they knew their job, these little bastards—into the current, but in which direction you were going you couldn't tell because you were still what and where you were, just a sodden old half-loaf being swept along. So there was no future to that and you got the hell out of it and you scrambled over the rocks and you climbed up—at least part of you did, the other part being left there in the water, that must be so, because you continued to feel that nibbling all the way up— nibble, nibble, goading you on up, through gorse and rosemary that pricked your legs, pines—they pricked, too, like hell—pines, a fig-tree or two, up and up, more pines, then a goat track, stony, but a track at last, so the going was easier, and you hurried on until you had climbed right up to where there was a flat-stone wall. When you put your hand on it, the stone was so hot from the sun it sent a shiver through you like an electric current; and you looked around and saw you were at the top, but you knew that anyway because just then the nibbling became truly ferocious and you felt the first tug of the real current, out beyond the headland, that would carry you away—and at that moment, too, you got the first whiff of what you'd climbed up to get—along with the view, which was a help but no good on its own —the smell.

Because there was always this distinctive smell. So what did it smell of? Well, it was a compound smell. Not of the sea, merely, though there was something salt and fresh in it like the smell of blood mixed with a tang which might be from the pines or equally from something Lanvin had cooked up—but like blood, sweet; sickly sweet, a sickly clinging smell like the smell of a rat or something bigger which has lain too long dead under the sun; and yet it clung the way that ether clings, heavy as ether but not quite disagreeable, teasing, tickling the nostrils, like the smell of a match struck, sulphur, that is; yes, definitely, because all that was mixed up with the smell of brown paper, dirty cotton rags, burning; anyway, of burning; and burnt-up air, bad air, the smell of a night-club you were the first signed-on member of as you go down the steps and one look tells it'll be for the last time, and the warm gusty clinging intimate loathsome smell from the bowels of the earth in the rush-hour which does more than claim acquaintance, hurling itself upon you—don't think you're not human, it breathes down your neck—you sweat, urinate, defecate, copulate along with the rest, and you can bloody well suffocate, too, while you're about it—and it was acrid, yes, a city smell; fog, soot, gasoline fumes, November dusk, along with the astonishingly alien smell of your sweetie-pie as she stirs from the nest she's woven in your bed over-night; and various other identifiable ingredients, sweet, sour, nostalgic, compelling—scorched hair and hyacinths and your secretary's Monday sweater and warm newsprint, printer's ink, and the first-class lavatory on the Belgrade-Skopje express, and the smell you smell when owing to excess you can't smell at all—the compound of all of which he smelt now at this moment, standing on the stairs, in the sweat on the palms of his hands; the smell which told him that something or other was about to happen.

There was the taste, too, of course, but by comparison it had no significance, depending as it did on the other, being simply the taste of too many cigarettes and the whisky which formed his diet once he had smelt the smell which was the operative sensation—that, and the nibbling, together.

They called it, whoever *they* were and whatever *it* was, having a nose for a story. It was far more than that, in his opinion. Anyone could have a premonition that a story was going to break without necessarily doing anything about it, or seeing their way to doing anything about it. No, this sixth sense—for that was what it was—

did a helluva lot more for you than that. It got you there—and back, too, usually. So far, that is. Here's something, it said, when your palms began to sweat—here's something big and somebody's going to get it and what's more, Schulman, that somebody's going to be YOU. And here's how. Now you do this, that, and the other, and just watch out there, brother, that's where you gotta be careful. So in effect what it did was to hand you a one-way ticket plus collect facilities—and usually, up to now, that is, the safe-conduct pass could be eked out to cover the whole expedition. It got you back. It had to have you back in order to come again.

And there was no knowing when it would come. Sometimes it came after long drinking bouts, sometimes in the middle of them, sometimes when the international sky was so clear, not a cloud in sight, that he had often felt personally responsible, even guilty when, arriving punctually on the spot where the assassination, revolution, or whatever it was that was scheduled according to his nose to happen, happened—within twenty-four hours, usually. Yet, by obeying it implicitly he had made his career; it had never yet let him down. For the sake of it he had badgered his way into the bad books of ambassadors, earned the title of Public Enemy Number One with countless Heads of Chancery, janitors of Press Ministries and similar fry; on account of it ignored the advice of eminent colleagues, weighty with prudence and inspired with envious malice; many times unreceived cabled ultimata from editors, cheerfully committed all the peccadilloes of his profession—forgery, perjury, plagiary, theft, as and when expedient; on the strength of it believed in face of all contrary evidence in more than one man—and disbelieved in more than one, too—and put the case for one or the other accordingly, so that the way he'd felt about it one day was the way quite a number of other people felt the next; and he'd taken airline tickets to places half across the world where in no time at all the corpses were only outnumbered by the rats feeding on the corpses, or hung on with his eyebrows in some place everybody else was getting out of, hung on regardless of the warnings, thrice repeated, of the Vice-Consul (British), and long, long after the Swiss had begun to feel overworked. Obeying it, he had dropped without a second's delay or regret whatever he had happened to be doing at the time—yes, but literally, though—*dropped; dropped* the *Herald Tribune* on the lid of the desk where he was invigilating an examination on the English Romantic Poets in a ladies' summer school in Santa Barbara, and *dropped*, or let lie, rather, on the ground, because that was where she happened to be at the time, an ex-senator's un-married younger daughter in a spinney at the bottom of a golf course outside Jacksonville, Fla.—and whether those ladies cheated or whether

458

they didn't and whether she ever met up with her pants again under all those leaves he never knew, nor cared, either—because he had gone . . . gone . . . GONE! And that was the time and that was the time and it had never yet let him down.

But because it was such a compound smell, with so much to tell him and most of it (owing to the nature of his profession) necessarily private, its message was in code. And now, although his heart raced and his major difficulty was to prevent himself plunging headlong down the stairs and out of the hotel and away like the wind to—well, nothing spectacular—back to town, to a typewriter, a telephone, a cable office, none of which were here, his brain remained calm, his hand as he lit himself a fresh cigarette was steady, and he paused, snuffing the air. That was not all his nose had to tell him; there were still some groups undeciphered; it was a more complicated message to-day. But not hard—not hard at all; for one who had trained himself to identify ingredients such as fog and hyacinths and Arpège and the W.C. on the Skopje train, it was child's play to identify the smell which to-day had absorbed and overpowered all the rest; the fairly familiar, rather repellent, but definitely analeptic smell of imminent personal danger.

So he waited, giving himself time to sort it out, and when he had sorted it out he went through it again in case of a slip, but there were no slips; no, it was quite plain. Plain, but incredible, illogical and contradictory; and for the first time in his life he was inclined to disobey, to discredit the validity of the instructions. So that was what he decided to do, to disobey, and so he made his mistake.

His—that is, his very own—mistake; because when it comes to the big mistakes, the real humdingers which, in retrospect, are like pegs driven into the ground, marking out the course—and they might just as well have been, possibly even were, driven in before ever you started for all the difference it would have made—the kind which even with the aid of a sixth sense are impossible to guard against because they can stem from strength, your particular strength, just as easily as from your particular weakness; the kind which, if you had your life over again, you would repeat in the same way at the same point, even knowing what you do know now, after bitter experience; in short, the kind which in some obscure fashion you *want* to make—there is no sharing the responsibility for these; as individual as handwriting, as a thumb's imprint, there is no disclaiming them; the fault, if fault there be, lying indeed in you and not to be attributed in whole or in part to any other factor, luck, friend, foe, or circumstance, in you— and nowhere else. So that was how it came about that Abe, although he had deciphered correctly the message received, found himself unable to correlate the various groups into sense. To him they made nonsense. He simply could not connect danger of the sort which threatened with a woman, any woman—least of all a woman like Milly.

" Aw, the hell with it," he muttered, back to where he had started from, frowning so deeply that the black eyebrows made a solid ledge of fur above his nose: " This time it's a phoney. If *that's* all it is, I reckon I know how to handle that baby." He glanced down, just in time to see Herbert Wragg, half-dazed with cold, dangling a rucksack, lurch over the threshold from outside.

*   *   *

It was while Abe was standing on the stairs deliberating, that Vladek, the driver, having left Wragg to walk up to the hotel, had taken the Austin round to the garage.

" Oh-ho, so we've company to-night," he had whistled in surprise, sliding in between the other two cars, in his headlights noting first, on his left, the immense Cadillac with the CD plate, then, on his right, the Citroën.

Switching off, he reached for a cigarette, his heart knocking against his chest. Although he had felt stiffness in his legs during the latter part of the journey, he now discovered that he wasn't over-keen to get out. He took a few more puffs of the cigarette. After a bit he got out, because there was no point in putting it off, really, and went round to the back of the Citroën. Sighing, he lifted the lid of the boot, which was open, of course, as he had known it would be. Schulman could've locked it, couldn't he? *Couldn't he at least've done that?*

Vladek stood there for a minute or two, shaking his head sadly over the parcels, which were, of course, still in the boot.

*   *   *

" What ails thee, knight-at-arms——"

Wragg jumped.

" Why, Herbert, you certainly are pale. What've you been up to? "

" Oh, ha-hallo ... er ... Abe. I've been—you know ... inspecting."

" Uh-huh. Have fun? "

" Fun? Oh no. It's too cold, isn't it? "

" Yeah, too cold. You're right."

Wragg blushed, blaming himself for having a preternaturally dirty mind. Very possibly Schulman never intended the half of what he seemed to imply.

"And here's old Vladek. Say, what's the matter with him? He looks pretty mothy too. Hi, Vladek."

Vladek smiled unhappily. "Hi, sir." He came to stand behind them in the queue.

"So where's Larry?"

"Larry? In the office, I suppose."

"He's not with you? I mean, does he know you're here?"

Wragg looked offended. "Of course he does. He sent me."

Abe scratched his head. "I'm sorry, Herbert, I'm just slow, I guess. What time d'ya leave?"

"I dunno. Oneish, I suppose."

"Gosh, that's odd. An' he didn't give you a message—or anything? I mean, we were expecting him, d'ya see—been waiting all afternoon."

"*We?*" As if the simple pronoun were a bob of white in the undergrowth, Wragg stiffened, quivering from muzzle to coat-tails like a pointer. He also seemed to go slightly green about the gills—at any rate, several shades paler.

"Sure," said Abe breezily, "Milly's here too."

"*Here?*" The news seemed to paralyse him for a second—then a reflex caused him to scoop up the loose end of his muffler and rewind it very quickly all the way up to his eyes, exactly, Abe thought, in the manner of a land-crab in a panic, shovelling up sand to camouflage its going to ground.

"Well, Herbert," said Abe, as soothingly as he might in view of the eyes, bright with terror, fixed on him over the top of the yashmak/muffler, "you'll be staying here—the night, I mean?" A nod. "You could do me a favour, then. I gotta scram, see. Right away—back to Grusnov. So I just thought . . . if I write a note for Milly—would you mind—in half an hour, say—just dropping it in on her? I'll give you the room number. Would you do that?"

Wragg gave a sort of shudder, but he nodded again. He seemed to be struck dumb. Just then the receptionist barked at him; he had reached the top of the queue. He handed in his passport, filled in the paraphernalia and took his key. After all that was attended to, he turned round.

"Vladek——" he began, but Vladek was no longer in the queue. He seemed to have disappeared. Abe had gone over to the far side of the foyer; he had taken out a pad and was scribbling up against a wall. Wragg, clutching his key and rucksack, drawn by curiosity, moved out of the queue to a position where he could watch him. Whatever it was Abe had written, it wasn't lengthy. He was glancing through it, rubbing his ear thoughtfully; a suspicion of a grin—but

461

you couldn't tell from his face what he was thinking. Fancy being like that, thought Wragg. Fancy being able to dash off a note on the spur of the moment without alterations, rough drafts, sleepless nights, the all too easily imaginable agonies that must surely be attendant upon the writing of even the simplest message to someone like Milly. Abe folded the sheet of paper into three, stuck one end inside the other, then scrawled something on the outside and looked up.

"Oh, there you are. Okay, Herbert, give her that, will ya? Thanks a lot." He grinned broadly. "You going up now? Have fun, boy. Be seeing ya."

He watched Wragg follow the waiter up the stairs. His shoulders bowed beneath the rucksack, his key clutched like a talisman in his hand, even making this prosaic ascent he had the air of a mountaineer, dedicated, or at the very least of one who is determined to take his pleasures seriously. Abe went back to the desk to check out.

"Mr. Schulman." Vladek suddenly appeared at his elbow. Poor little bastard, he certainly did look worried. Abe had known Vladek a long time now, and liked him.

"Uh? What's up?"

"You go Grusnov now? Can please give lift back—my wife sick."

"I'm sorry to hear that. Sure I can. Say, though, did you fix it with Mr. Wragg? How'll he get back? He can't drive, y'know."

Vladek hesitated. He thought: I'll give him one more chance. It would be worth it, just to cure this bad feeling inside. But if he swallows this one, then there's no saving him. So, with a perfectly straight face, he told the most unlikely whopper he could think of: "Mr. Wragg say okay. Mrs. Purdoe drive him back, he say. He likes better that way."

"Is *that* what he said?" Vladek's heart missed a beat, for an instant his hopes, absurdly, soared; were dashed, however, to the ground when to his astonishment the American threw back his head and laughed. Could anyone—even an American—be so stupid?

"Honest, is *that* what he said?" Schulman chuckled with delight. "That beats everything. The old bastard! Okay, then, Vladek, c'marn . . ." Still chuckling, he led the way out.

* * *

She put down the tools with which she had been working, brushes pencils, paint, and examined the result in the bathroom mirror; critically, and yet unable to resist showing it off to the best advantage, not as a piece of daubed canvas, inanimate, but injected with personality

462

and movement—not one but a dozen of the former and as many movements to each of those, the cream skimmed off a dozen film stars' facial tricks. She looked at herself in the way women do look at themselves when alone; the absurd phantasmagoric play of expressions that crowded in one upon the other was punctuated with snake-like darts, jerks, swoops of the head, eyes narrowed, watchful, little intimate adjustments, the current grimace currently relaxed—an eyelash here, a speck of tobacco on a tooth there—and then reverting, in deadly earnest, of course, no hint of a smile that was not The Smile, to the pose, the queenly tilt of the head, yes . . . or the gamine, like that . . . or . . . and so it went on.

The test of success, someone had said once, was to crick your jaw so that top and bottom seemed to dislocate, as it were, allow a second for the muscles to jell, then risk a blink—and if you felt like a horse, a well-bred bad-tempered horse, and looked like one too, then that was it. If that were it, then, she supposed, staring crossly at herself after the blink, that she had achieved it. Except for the eyes. The eyes, blast it. There was something very wrong with them. Well-bred my foot. " Oh, Milly, Milly," she said aloud, " why—why for pity's sake did you have to go and start messing around now? Why *now?* "

She sighed with disgust at the litter of open pots, bottles, in the lid of the dressing-case. A fine time to experiment when her heart was beating so fast and her hands were shaking and she felt slightly sick. And yet the minute he'd gone out of the room she had run to the dressing-case as if it contained remedies, restoratives, to save a situation, however desperate—when all it contained, the case, was the new make-up. The *new* make-up. She groaned. She had never in her life before tricked out her eyes with blue and silver paint, employing these long, slender and extremely awkward brushes for the job, pencils black and green, and *waterproof* mascara. Waterproof? Foolproof would have been more to the point—look what a mess! No, she had been used to make up her eyes rather conservatively and yet they had always been remarked upon, indeed, were remarkable. And now?

They were still remarkable—oh, heavens yes, you couldn't miss them, could you? They'd act as beacons even in Wardour Street on a foggy night. So why—she gave a little strangled sob—did you have to go and do this now? Experiment—in a *crisis?* Really it was like someone who, given the advantage of choosing the weapons for a duel, and himself a master with the foils, on a mad impulse plumps for pistols, never having fired a pistol in his life. It's so *like* you, Milly, she told herself bitterly, to do just this. *What* do you think you look like? I'll

463

tell you, shall I—what Larry would say? "You look like a—*tart*."
She nodded, fluttering her sticky lids. "What's more—an *old* tart.
So there."

A tart. Oh well. She pulled off her ski pants and sweater and
stepped into a black skirt. Take Madame Bovary, now—had *she* ever
felt like a tart? But then she'd had a different sort of husband—that
clumsy oaf who'd gobbled and snored—not a bit like Larry. And it
had all been so tragic for *her*—no doubt about it, tragedy helped. Still,
even Emma Bovary couldn't have known, could she?—so it could
scarcely have helped her much at the time. Perhaps she had felt like
this—just going from one thing to the next, because once started off
you couldn't stop?

She wriggled into the black sweater, which was tight. It had a zip
down the back. People took lovers every day of the week. There was
nothing to it. I mean, she told herself, tucking in her eyelashes, biting
her lips, and gingerly pulling the sweater over the façade, gingerly,
because *that* was something she could *not* do over again that night—
I mean, I don't think I'd mind if Larry—— She paused, struggling
to catch hold of the end of the zip. Wouldn't I, though? Would I
mind, or wouldn't I? Supposing—— It struck a chill over her, took
her breath away, the very idea—the novelty of it, of course. Supposing
—he *has*? Who? When? Where? Impossible. Even to think of it
made her—not *angry*, exactly, but she began tearing at the zip. It
went up a certain distance. "Yes, but—if *he* asked himself the same
thing about you, he'd say 'impossible,' too." It went up a bit more
and then stuck. This was what it always did, this zip. "Men are
different," she replied hastily. "Yes," said the voice, inexorable,
"they're worse."

These plants, she thought, tugging. They seem to take up all the
air. I can't breathe. The blasted thing *had* stuck, properly. This was
the point at which she was accustomed to say, with a fair amount of
impatience in her voice but controlling it wonderfully well, holding her
finger-nails out of harm's way, frowning though, because it *was*
irritating, the way it happened, infallibly, every time: "It's a perfectly
good *zip*, darling—hold the top parts together and pull—gently . . .
gently, Larry . . . I don't know why it is, darling," she would say coldly,
"but you're just *hopeless* with zips," implying, without *intending* to,
actually, but the implication was clear, that zips were not the only
thing he was hopeless at. And he would go on pushing and tugging,
and when he'd done it, achieved the click, he'd go off without a word,
looking sheepish and terribly relieved. He had encountered one or
two pretty bad zips in the course of his married life. "But *this* one"
—she spurred herself on, frantic—"isn't bad at all—in fact it's one

of the *best*, the most reliable . . ." It had been demoted by the time she got it up.

So, ready. On her way through the bedroom she paused by the bed. Really, it did look too sordid. Too sordid for what? Well, for words. She straightened the quilt and turned the pillows greasy sides down. Just to touch the linen made her shudder.

The ice had melted round the champagne. Well, then, no nonsense —the very moment he came in they would have it. If they'd had it earlier everything would have been all right by now. All right? She shrugged irritably, and sat down on a high-backed chair, releasing, as she did so, a long spray of maidenhair fern which, as if in answer to her question, sprang out, swishing across the back of her neck so that she jumped up in a fright and changed her place. There was a wooden seat built in against the wall by the door, screened from the door by a hedge of laurels in tubs; these plants were conspicuous as being amongst those that had thrived. One sat in a thicket, protected by rich glossy leaves, in a pleasantly obscure jungly light. After she had helped herself to one or two glasses of Abe's Scotch and still he did not appear she began to realise how much faith she was pinning on the very existence of the bottles, this one of Scotch and the two of champagne. They would fetch him back, if nothing else. But how long had he been gone? Rather too long. The champagne—she eyed it more frequently —had certainly assumed pride of place as a solution to all her problems. She had never opened a bottle of champagne in her life. " With a nail-file, I wonder? I bet I could——" and then there came the knock at the door.

" That was luck," she whispered, settling her skirts, her face, her nerves, and her own hash, as it so happened, by calling out promptly, " Come in."

If she hadn't said come in right away like that he had planned to push the note under the door and beetle off as fast as he could go. As it was, as she *had* said it, he came in. Disconcerted, he looked round. The room appeared to be empty.

" Oh," her clear fluty voice came from behind the laurels, " what a surprise." He peered through the undergrowth, through twisted stems. She didn't look particularly surprised—although he wasn't so much interested in her, he was merely having a shufti round the room —that was the impression he got.

" There's a note for you." Skirting the hedge, holding the note at arm's length he advanced towards her crab-wise, his head turned well away. He dropped it on the table in front of her. He was rather relieved to see out of the corner of his eye—not for the first time the abnormal setting of these organs doing him a service—that she didn't grab it or anything like that—because it *had* occurred to him to wonder . . . but anyway, she just let it lie. All she said was: " I'm so glad you've come. Could you, d'you think, open a bottle of champagne ? "

This question, or demand, which of course it was, really, surprised him so much that before he could stop himself he had turned towards her and seen her—properly, that is. As he wouldn't be doing it again he took a good look whilst deciding what response to make—a response which, if he were to follow the dictates of his conscience, *i.e.* truth, should be in the affirmative; if those of his heart, inclination, etc., ditto, but if those of *reason*—ah, well, that was a very different matter, it could lead to no good, could it?—and in consequence must take the form of a definite, even brutal, negative. The trouble was, having already observed that she was dressed all in black and looked very small, too small, really, and now, looking closer, seeing that her face was very pale, too pale, and her eyes in contrast extraordinarily large, shadowy, luminous, yes, they certainly were, lamps, or pools—he discovered that all these details although not strictly relative to the issue, somehow subtly contrived to reinforce the ayes so that they had it. Unanimously. In fact, he had never experienced such unanimity of mind in the whole of his life.

" Yes," he said modestly, drawing an instrument from his pocket. " I think I could."

The instrument or gadget, a fairly recent acquisition ordered by catalogue from London, had not yet achieved the status of a cherished possession; he was prepared to cherish it, but treated it with a certain reserve as being still on probation. Useful as it might be, he had a suspicion that it was useless to him—at least he had never yet had occasion to use it for any of the purposes detailed in the catalogue under the blanket heading of " everything "—although he had now and then used it for cleaning his nails. He had even pondered over the conclusion he had been forced to draw, that what were clearly little day-to-day occurrences in the lives of others, the removing of nails from horses' shoes, the mending of punctures, the clipping of cigar-ends and so on, featured as hair-raising improbabilities in his own. He had never stepped within the striking radius of a horse—there was one thing he did know about them, that they were reputed to be dangerous at both ends. He had certainly ridden a bicycle in his youth, but having once glimpsed himself in a shop window as a fully-grown adult, perched in the act, he had never done so again; he was ignorant, and thankful to be so, of all internal combustion engines, he never used pencils, he never opened bottles, he never smoked cigars and he never opened tin cans—which, according to Olga, contained poison—and he was not handy about the house, never having had a house. No, buses and a biro and the occasional beer—these were "everything" to him. Still, one must be tolerant. Opening bottles, he remembered, figured prominently in the established category. Now this funny little object was to be baptized in champagne.

"Steady," he enjoined it, kindly but sternly, kneeling down by the bucket, his back to her. She wasn't watching—she was reading Schulman's note. Well, she had to some time, hadn't she? "Steady," he whispered, "you're supposed to do everything—now prove it." He started to unwind the wire. The thing was to have a pop. He'd read about that. At Wendy's wedding they'd been popping all right. "If you don't make it *pop*," he muttered, "I'll—I don't know what I'll do—I'll send you back to Damages where you came from! Yes, that's what I'll do." He felt rather tense, he didn't know why. He went on unwinding the wire.

Abe's note said:

DEAR OLD EINSTEIN
TAKE MY ADVICE AND CHANGE YOUR METIER. QUIT ALGEBRA ANYWAY
—YOU'RE TERRIBLE AT IT. SORRY I'VE GOT TO GO NOW.

ABE

PS.—JUST FOR THE RECORD—REMEMBER YOU SPOKE ABOUT CORALIE?
LONG, LONG AGO I GAVE HER THE SAME ADVICE. SHE WAS LOUSY
AT ALGEBRA—JUST LIKE YOU.

The cork came out with a terrific pop which made her smile, and that was something. She was holding out the glasses, too, all ready; he wouldn't have believed that anyone could be so efficient, anticipating just what that champagne would do. Anyway, it frothed out straight into the glasses, looking absolutely right, as pictured up the walls by the escalators—he had always had a weakness for those charming little baby chamois, on crags, who enticed one to—or so he believed—this sparkling brew.

"What-oh," he murmured to himself, raising the glass to his lips, "Baby Chams."

"What?" said Milly.

"Nothing," he said, but feeling rather gay. For two pins he'd've —no, he frowned into his glass. This wasn't *everything*, after all.

So they sipped without saying a word, partly on account of the radio, which was going great guns; lucky, really, he didn't feel like talking, and then she poured them both another glass; he watched weakly, without demur—as they say—as she did it. He could have demurred, but it would have seemed rude, and the second for doing so passed so quickly. Besides, he was rather enjoying himself. Feeling sophisticated, he walked over to the window, right away from her, where there was a row of cacti in pots. He was rubbing their prickles up the wrong way, trying to think they were pretty which they were not, but if *she* liked them, well, then, perhaps they were rather unusual—when the radio stopped, and the room became—naturally enough—as they weren't talking and he was managing to force the gassy stuff down without more than a minor belch or two, quite quiet.

She was reading the note again, staring at it, rather. She looked up, as if the silence had impinged on her too, at last, and rattled the bottle which he now saw to be empty; leaning forward, she picked up the other from the bucket and held it out to him, smiling. He came forward and took it. Now, funnily enough, he felt more nervous than ever. For one thing it was so quiet, and for another, this bottle didn't look the same as the first. It was dripping wet and the label had peeled off.

" The second's never as good as the first," she said, in that voice of hers, serious, but with laughter rippling up and down behind the screen of gravity, like light, which made you long to pull it aside, the the screen, to let it in, the light, so that you too could see the joke. Still, the remark put him on his mettle and the second cork came out *better* than the first—why, it fairly catapulted across the room. Some-where, in the dimmest part of the jungle, in the far corner, they heard a smash.

" Broken a window, I should think," said Milly.

He went over to investigate, diving down beneath the dirty great leaves which rained a thick brown dust on his head and shoulders and down between his collar and his neck, but eventually he found it, the cork, in the wilderness, and was able to ascertain the damage it had done. On his knees, he stuck his head up above the boscage—like a giraffe browsing, did he but know it. She had to smile.

" Well? A window? "

He shook his head.

" Go on—tell me the worst."

" Only——" he stuttered, " b-b-bashed a b-b-begonia . . . that's all." But she wasn't even listening. She'd lost all interest, it seemed, all in a second. He scrambled to his feet. She'd turned away, she was staring at a spreading pool on the table; champagne was still seething languidly over the neck of the new bottle, down the sides, over the letter, plastering it to the table top, seeping into a packet of cigarettes. Well, that didn't matter, none of those things mattered, they weren't everything. He stood quite still, aghast at the expression on her face. Whatever had caused that was everything—to her. Oh yes. You knew it when you saw it, just as the face itself was everything to him. Then, feeling—what a word, but that was it, he *did* feel—that now he must act, do something, anything, to stop her looking like that—oh! let there be a dragon, he shrieked in his innermost soul—just one bloody great dragon! came the cry (silent, of course)—fingering his precious penknife, gritting his teeth, he took a step towards her and tripped over the hosepipe which happened to be in his way and so arrived pretty nearly at her feet.

He heard her give a short sharp yap behind him. Oh well, he thought, raising himself on his elbows, because he wasn't much hurt, not at all, in fact, but the funny part was that having stretched his length he'd ended up a great deal nearer to her, six feet three inches nearer anyway, more or less painlessly, a proximity which otherwise it would have taken him heaven knows how long to obtain, and if she was laughing at him—well, that was that; which she was, of course. So he levered himself up on to his knees, and any tall thin man on his knees looks like a praying mantis, he told himself savagely, that's not your fault, Herbie Wragg—and then he looked at her and discovered to his astonishment that she wasn't laughing—oh no, far from it. She had swivelled round so that her arms were stretched out along the back of the seat and her head was in her arms and her shoulders shaking, and some noises that she was making had nothing to do with laughter, they weren't even pretty; no, she was weeping; weeping as if—well, he had never had any idea that this was how one wept.

Being approximately on the correct level, and in the correct attitude, that is, on his knees, for approach, he saw no point in getting up. He shuffled a few feet over the greasy parquet and, more than ever like a praying mantis, reared his torso and put his arm round her. This was astonishingly easy to do. Astonishing, too, how far his arm went, how completely it encompassed her, could have gone still farther; something indecent about it, almost—like a Brobdingnagian assaulting a Lilliputian. On the other hand there was no denying that this element lent—lent, my foot—*was* part of the pleasure . . . making it a very special pleasure. Except that now she seemed to feel his arm round her her distress increased, so he levered himself up on to the seat beside her and covering her head with his hand, pressed it to his shoulder where she could go on crying in comfort and give them both pleasure. Her hair under his hand was unbelievably soft and springy; at first he was stroking it, he was almost sure of his motive, merely in order to comfort her, to induce her to stop crying, but in no time he began to be conscious of alarm lest she might stop. Then what? So, at any rate in order to

seal the moment, which was all he had, he bent down and pressed his
cheek to hers and miraculously, she softened in his arms—where by
then she was—seemed to crumple to nothing, like a small wounded
bird, he thought, or a small nylon parachute. She had even turned
towards him snuggling against his chest. He smoothed back her hair
and for a second studied that side of her face that was towards him,
that was his—an instant only, before he claimed it, made it his. Ear,
cheek, eye, chin, from point to point, lingering over the planes between,
his lips travelled as over familiar ground, with no sense of exploration
but of discovery, yes; that he knew and loved it so well. It was no
distance to her mouth. No distance at all.

What was worrying Milly out of proportion to everything else was
the sight of his bright brown index finger and other finger-nails as now
and then they flashed into view. If she shut her eyes, which she did,
she might enable herself to believe that this was Larry and that those
fingers belonged, not to a stranger, but to him; because her heart and
soul and brain were all crying out for him, for Larry, who had clean
finger-nails, and who did know, no one better, how to open a bottle of
champagne without the suspicion of a pop, and if this—*this* had been
Larry, then long ago there would have been clean sheets on that bed
in there—and she wouldn't have put it past him even to have had those
beastly palms thrown out of the bath and this headache she had, which
was awful, really, would already have become *his* headache, not hers:
he would have appropriated it and relieved her of it, because that was
how he was—that was Larry. A man in a thousand . . . ten thousand
. . . how many thousands . . . here she closed her eyes very tight the
better to imagine, count the tens of thousands of men who were not
Larry. If she closed her eyes tight and stopped thinking but went on
counting, then this nuzzling whispering thing which had approached
so close, which was rubbing its cheek against hers, might be persuaded
to take its proper place, recede, march along with the rest in that
parade—but it would not, it seemed, do that . . . it had fingers like iron,
yes, like iron, not at all like Larry's . . . just beneath her left lowest
rib . . . and then lips fastening down, not like his, oh, not at all, no . . .
no . . . but with your eyes tight shut it was extraordinary the way those
cries from heart and mind became faint, fainter, until they were
smothered altogether . . . the body, it seemed, was less fastidious—her
penultimate thought, as she was swung up off the place where she had
been sitting, in the arms of a tall dark stranger, and her last thought,
before everything came tumbling down—but there was no time for that.
It was dark and in the darkness there was a force which swept all before
it, shattering those barricades that had been so cunningly constructed
—but in the event, how flimsy they proved, all conceit and pretences,
470

twigs and straw—and like an avalanche rolled down, crashing over the last ditches that she herself had dug and had been dug deeper by the years and had looked, at least to her, and proved, at least to others, impregnable, but not against this, which was like an act of God; and then, briefly, it was like watching as a child, from a distance, an act of God, a catastrophe, magnificent, terrible, and she near but not too near, and then that, too, went—all that; the distance was being fast swallowed up, she could no longer preserve detachment because soon there would be no ground left to stand upon and any second now the whole establishment would crash down. Before that happened, however, she did have one last flicker of a thought, and she could have laughed with surprise: but this is an experience—this isn't *like* anything—it's an experience in its own right and *I'm* going to have it—*now*! And she could have cried with joy. She neither laughed nor cried. There wasn't time. It came up close—and she had it, instead.

*　　　*　　　*

" I wonder," she said, leaning up on her elbow, " if that's what he meant. Now I think I do know what he meant. A sense of mortality. Goodness—I'm *famished*! "

" There's nothing to eat, I'm afraid," said Wragg. " Would you like some more champagne? "

" It'll be flat. Well, I don't mind."

He went to fetch it.

" There's one thing—we've frightened the moths away," she said, when he came back with the half-empty bottle. She noticed what good shoulders he had. And there were no boils on his neck—she had wronged him there. He moved with grace, too, without self-consciousness, unashamed of his body; one of the minor but nevertheless conspicuous advantages that compensate for not having attended a public school.

" What's the matter? "

He was looking fearfully solemn. " I was thinking about what you said just then. A sense of mortality."

" Oh, I didn't say it. Not first, I mean. It was Abe who said it, this morning."

" What did he mean, I wonder? "

" Oh, don't ask me," said Milly impatiently. " It wasn't very amusing. About time—you know, being so short and all that—and dying. He quoted some poetry," she added.

" Did he? I bet I know what."

" I bet you don't," she said unkindly, " it was French."

471

Snubbed, he was about to retire into his shell when she took pity on him and smiled. Timidly, he said: "It might have been done in English too."

"What?"

"What we were talking about. In fact, I think it has been. Someone put it all—wonderfully. I know it by heart quite well."

"Go on." Then, seeing his whole face contorted in the effort to remember, "If you know it so well," she added, taunting him.

"It's gone out of my head," he confessed in despair. "It's fairly long, you see . . . oh dear, and it *does* sum it up so—but I can only remember the last two lines . . . which—which only tell you . . . well," he mumbled, with a shifty look of sheer misery, "*what to do about it.*"

"Better than nothing," she said, wanting to giggle. "In fact, rather to the point, perhaps. Go on."

"Thus," he began bravely, and then suddenly leaning over, he took the glass out of her hand and put it down on the carpet as if it disturbed him. She was too astonished to protest. Then, his eyes fixed on hers, he began once more:

Thus—though we cannot make our sun——

"I know that!" she cried out at once, "and I don't want to hear it—it's like the other—worse, even . . . all to do with being old and dying——"

"Oh no," he murmured, leaning right over her and grasping her wrist, "it's not. Not the way I see it . . . it's more to do with—well, with *being* . . . listen——" His fingers closed tight round her wrist and although she twisted her head this way and that to escape, he went on, shy, but dogged, too, in his determination, and it occurred to her that one would scarcely have recognised him for the same person:

*Thus—though we cannot make our sun
Stand still—yet . . . we will make him . . . run . . .*

He paused. Then he said softly: "And that's why—look at me, Milly—I'd—well, I'd rather like to do it again."

"You'd *what*?" She stared up at him for a second, unable to believe her ears. Then she burst out laughing. It was a fit of the giggles; she simply couldn't stop.

Presently she said: "I'm sorry . . . you don't mind, do you? My laughing like this? . . . I can't stop."

472

"Not at all," he said politely. "It doesn't make any difference."

Nor did it seem to. Soon she stopped anyway, as it was not easy to go on laughing and became less so. She had been proved wrong in so many instances that day that she had quite lost count. The second time, she had to admit, was just as good as the first.

Chapter Three

LARRY ARRIVED back at the hotel that evening cold and tired and
hungry. He had not had a wink of sleep the night before, and it so
happened that a great deal of unexpected work had come in during
the day, which, with Wragg away, he had been left to tackle single-
handed. He was already late when he left the office; then he had to
walk back across the town; it was between eight and nine o'clock
when he got in. He went straight upstairs thinking he would take a
hot bath and have dinner in a dressing-gown and go straight to bed.
Milly would be tired, too. They would all be tired. Yes, an early
night.

The door of the salon was ajar, as if someone had just slipped out.
He could hear the radio playing softly as he came down the corridor.
That was strange. Milly disapproved of the radio being played merely
as a background noise. He went in. The room was dimly lit, with a
pleasant flickering light. Then he saw that the dining-table had been
pushed up to the red plush sofa near the stove and on it there was an
ornate candelabra with four tall candles—not the NAAFI type of
candle, short and chunky, but the sort used in churches. The effect
was not so cosy after all; in fact, it was even chilling. He wriggled
off his coat, staring suspiciously at the table, then he edged up to have
a look at it. Milly never used a high candelabra; it got in the way, she
said. And there was a pot of cyclamen on the table, too, wrapped in
cellophane just as it had come from the florist. That wasn't Milly,
either—my goodness, no. She loathed cyclamen. Then who? There
were two places laid. Sophie? No, of course not. Oh, God, he
muttered, it's Miss Raven. She must have done it. What does she think
it is—a wedding anniversary? Well, she's got another think coming,
if she expects us to live up to it. I'm not in the mood, sorry. He called
outside the bedroom door, " Milly! "

There was no answer so he went in. The bedroom was in darkness.
He went through into the bathroom for a wash, and he was drying
his hands when he fancied he heard a sound next door in the children's
room. So that was where she was. He unbolted the door and peered
in. The bedside light was on between the two beds, there was a child
in each bed, but no Milly. Dermot's rosy face appeared above the
mound of quilt. He was wide awake.

" What's going on in here? " Larry said sternly, coming across the room. " What's this light on for? It's long past the time for you to be asleep."

" It's not *me*," said Dermot hastily; blame should fall where it was due and in this respect his sister and he were not as one, but two. " I didn't want it "—he grimaced towards the other bed—"*she* kept it on. She's blubbing."

Larry peered at his daughter, what he could see of her. The quilt billowed gently up and down; the storm was beneath it. He sighed and sat down on her bed.

" Clarissa." No answer. " Clarissa, what's the matter, you silly rabbit? "

She surfaced gradually, her sobs half stifled under the quilt. Dermot leaned over and eyed her dispassionately.

" She's been in bed ever since lunch," he observed with satisfaction. " She's been naughty."

" Clarissa." Larry turned her over gently. She lay staring up at him, her face quite swollen with weeping.

" She scratched Miss Raven," Dermot contributed, lest there be any miscarriage of justice. His father's tone had been undeservedly gentle. It altered now.

" Lie down, Dermot, and mind your own business. Now, darling," he stroked her hair, " what's the matter? Just you tell me all about it. Where's Mummy? "

" Don't—don't *you* know? " whispered Clarissa, her eyes fixed on his face.

" No, I don't. That's why I asked you. I've only just come back. Where is she? "

" She's gone." Her lips shaped the words, but no sound came from them.

" Gone? "

She gave a little nod, that was somehow touching, implying an adult resignation to an unalterable fact.

" Gone? " he repeated. " Gone where? Gone out? "

" No. Gone—away."

" Listen, sweetie—I'm tired and I want my dinner. Don't fool around like this—just tell me *where* she's gone and what happened and so on. She's gone out, is that it? When did she say she'd be back? "

Sensing his irritation, she began to tremble uncontrollably. He could feel that she was trembling from head to foot. He summoned all his patience, what there was left of it. " Well? "

Her great eyes, so like Milly's, seemed to cloud over, as if it cost her a terrible effort to put her news into words, and so make it reality.

"She's gone away," she began bravely, choked, and went on. "She —she won't come back. She's—she's never . . . coming . . . back."

He thought it must be because he was tired. He felt giddy, just for a second, as if a deep black chasm had opened at his feet. Clarissa must have glimpsed that fleeting look on his face because she put out her hand and caught his and pressed it. She smiled, too, such an elderly wise little smile. With an effort he smiled back, and seeing this, she flung herself into his arms, weeping once more.

"Silly chump," he murmured into her hair. "You let your imagination rip, that's your trouble. Lie down, darling, you'll catch cold . . . *Stop* it, Clarissa, you'll make yourself sick. Where's Miss Raven? What on earth's been going on round here? I'll go and find her."

"No, no, no, *no* . . ." Clarissa dug her fingers into the back of his neck, sobbing wildly.

"She scratched Miss Raven, you see," Dermot reminded him gently. He was vastly enjoying this emotional treat laid on by his sister.

"You shut up," said Larry. "Listen, Clarissa. Try to help and don't be an ass. Did you see Mummy this morning?"

"Yes. . . . Before she—went . . . I did."

"Where did she say she was going?"

"On a—*picnic* . . ."

"Well, there you are. What's funny about that?" Though it was funny, he thought. "Then she'll be back soon." She was sobbing and shaking in his arms; no, no, she kept repeating, no, no, no. He stroked her, thinking hard.

"Now, listen, darling. You're laying it on a bit, aren't you? Stop it, d'you hear? Stop it at once—because I've got a plan. Lie down— that's a good puss—there. Now I'll tell you what I'm going to do. I'm going off now to find out where she's gone and when she'll be back and all the gen—and then I'll come back here to you and make a report. How about that?"

"Yes, but—don't, please, oh, *please* don't ask Miss Raven."

He hesitated. He had pretty well decided that Miss Raven's authority was soon to end. However, that was Milly's job, properly speaking. All the same . . .

"Well, then, I won't ask Miss Raven. I'll go downstairs. There'll be a message with the porter, I expect. If there isn't, I'll—well, I'll telephone." She had stopped crying, anyway. Encouraged, he went on: "I'll find out, and I'll be back in ten minutes—with everything sorted out. I promise. You can keep the light on while I'm gone. On one condition. When I do come back in "—he paused, impressively,

476

to compare his watch with Clarissa's—" see?—in exactly ten minutes, or even before "—she nodded, deeply impressed—" and after I've proved it to you that—well, that we've got it all taped, then you, miss, go right off to sleep. Ack dum. How's that? "

" All right." He thought he detected a faint spark of hope in her eyes. Not very much. Well, what could you expect? He hadn't much himself.

" That's better," he said, not knowing quite what he meant. " Now I'm off."

She glanced at her watch. " Ten minutes," she said, in a funny little precise voice; not a trace of hope in it. She gave him such a shrewd grown-up look it startled him; as if she were keeping up appearances in order to comfort him, too. He got up.

" Hm." He grinned down at her. " Did you really scratch Miss Raven? "

She nodded.

" Bad puss. We'll have to clip those claws." She could tell he wasn't really cross. She watched him go out.

*   *   *

" Oh, Christ," he muttered, out in the corridor, " now I'm in a spot." There would be no message downstairs, he knew that. Telephone? Whom could he telephone? There was no one to telephone, no one who could help him at all. Still, he would have to think of something and what was more, think fast. It occurred to him that it would be difficult to fabricate evidence that would satisfy Clarissa. It would have to be a pretty good story, watertight as they come. Well, he was not a propagandist for nothing, although this looked like being his toughest assignment yet—to sell something to his daughter when she'd already been sold something else; yes, that was the point. Sold something else by someone else, and he didn't know what. But he knew who that someone was. She'd have to go. My God, she'd have to go and right away wasn't quick enough. Candles, cyclamen—he was passing the door of the salon, which was still ajar—could it be, he wondered, that by candlelight at last I'm beginning to see it—the light? And what was I supposed to be? The male sacrifice? But how on earth could she ever have *dreamed*—well, if she did, there's only one answer. The woman must be—he stopped short, all at once her face springing to his mind; he saw it vividly, just as he had seen it the night before when she had been lying on the bed, and once more he examined the peculiar expression it was wearing. " Good God," he whispered under his breath, and felt for a cigarette. He lit it and went on, down the corridor. He felt shaken. So that was it. No time now. They'd

477

have to sort that out later. First things first and first came Clarissa. Or Milly, rather. Of course, Milly.

Slowly he started down the stairs. There was no point in hurrying. He couldn't think of a way out; he simply had to think.

Milly first. Naturally. Obviously. Inevitably. Always. First, Milly. Which was all very well and he'd contrived, connived, to keep it that way for upwards of nine years, but there were other people in the world besides Milly. For instance, Clarissa. And if it hadn't been for this latest prank of Milly's—she could have telephoned, couldn't she?—better all round, and for her, too, he would have thought, if she had anything to hide—you're round the bend yourself, Purdoe, he told himself, what could she have to hide?—then none of this would have happened. Clarissa had been upset. Upset? That was one way of putting it—or would be, if you were given to understatement. He thought perhaps he could guess what had happened to Clarissa and what she had suffered. He had just had a taste of it on his own account —back there in the bedroom.

" What does she think people are? " he said to himself, voicing— to himself—certain thoughts for the first time in his life. Clarissa, Sophie—me, even—and there had been others. Clarissa, though. He had always rather admired Milly's handling of her daughter, assuming it to be based on a system of her own which was the result of a logical thought process; her aim being, presumably, to toughen her up, which necessitated putting her, too, her own flesh and blood, through that battle-course which she, Milly, had personally devised for all those raw recruits—a small army of them, to his knowledge—crazy enough to volunteer to serve under her colours; fanatics—or masochists, it occurred to him now that that was what they were—those who asked nothing better than to fall, having already fallen, for Milly.

And how they fell. Once they'd fallen they just weren't human any more; there they lay on the ground, having fallen as far as they could go, inviting her to ride roughshod over them. He'd taken good care not to make that mistake himself. Some instinct—self-preservation, probably, he thought grimly—had kept him from doing that. Once you lay down you automatically lost the will to get up. Why, sometimes —and however besotted he might have been, he had still noticed it— he'd heard her speak to people, that sort of person—Sophie, for instance —in a tone that made his blood run cold; but as often as he'd heard it he'd seen how the victim, Sophie, for instance, would cringe and meekly jump to obey or get out of the way, or whatever it was. And yet Sophie, fundamentally, wasn't a meek, cringing sort of person. She was a proper person in every respect—except in respect to Milly.

478

So he had always thought, hitherto, whenever he had thought about it—not as often as he ought to have done, he realised now—it's for Clarissa's sake that she's adopted the same policy towards her. She (the mother, after all) has seen the danger signal—and a bloody great red flag it is, she could hardly miss it—and so Clarissa's got to be put through the course, too, in order to survive. Somewhere towards the end of the schedule, he had assumed—he'd assumed far too damn much—if Clarissa went on doing as well as she was doing, *i.e.* giving as good as she got—she'd pass out and get her promotion and that would be that. Milly's methods would be justified by the results. I was lucky, he thought. Perhaps I wasn't raw, like the rest. I was seconded, already knowing one or two tricks. I may be wrong, but at least I do have the idea that I'm still standing up.

But supposing—and as he went down the stairs, which he was still doing, this thought, too, occurred to him for the first time, because there seemed to be no other valid explanation and any excuse, even stupidity, was better than deliberate wanton cruelty—supposing Milly *had* missed seeing it—that bloody great red flag? Supposing he had over-estimated her powers of intuition? Supposing her motives stemmed from greed and vanity and nothing more . . . or supposing she had no motives that could properly be called such—that she were thoroughly feckless and irresponsible? Was it possible that she could have misunderstood Clarissa's attitude to herself—that defensive stand, as gallant as it was pathetic? Supposing—no, but that *was* impossible —whatever else, Milly was neither blind nor a fool—but *just supposing* she were not aware, for instance, that her daughter worshipped the ground she trod on? Supposing that? " Then," he told himself, frowning down into the hall, " that would make her an altogether different person. And I should have been wrong all the way along—from beginning to end. But then I know—don't I?—I know she's *not* like that. Surely. Surely? " He gripped the banister rails. " *Don't I even know that?* " He plunged down the last few steps as if all the furies were after him, the question, now that it had been put, hammering in his ears—*how well did he know her—his wife?*

*   *   *

The porter was busy on the telephone. Larry waited at the desk, although he could see that his pigeon-hole was empty. There was only one car she could have gone in—Abe's. Well, then, she would be quite all right. He wondered whether, on this simple base, he could construct a story sound enough to present to Clarissa. He was a bit dubious. It would want a lot of dolling up, if only to disguise the base.

479

Why? It seemed rather shaky, that was all. He had no idea why it should seem so—but he knew that he didn't even dare touch it for fear it would shake. Clarissa would have no such scruples. She'd put her finger firmly on it, for that very purpose, to see whether it did or not. So it looked as though he'd have to do some pretty breathtaking arse-spinning in lieu of a few facts. If only he'd a clue as to what that old bitch had told her in the first place. Five minutes to go—funny, it seemed like a lifetime since he'd left those kids up there. Five minutes. Less.

Then Abe himself walked in through the swing-doors.

" Hi, there," he said, coming straight over to Larry and taking his arm and moving away from the desk towards the foot of the stairs and reaching for his pack of cigarettes and flipping it in Larry's direction and taking one himself and lighting it—all of which took about three seconds, the maximum Abe could allow himself, and that was stretching it in view of what he had glimpsed as he came in, the expression on Larry's face. He took a drag on the cigarette and thought, Jee*zus*, I must be losing my grip or is this old age at last, because all the way back he had been pondering over this encounter and now here it was, not merely slap on the dot but previous, and all he could think was, the little bitch. She didn't deserve he should lift a finger—but for Larry he was prepared to take quite a lot of pains—oh, yes, quite a lot. It was now or never.

" Say, didn't ya get Milly's message? "

" No."

" Uh-huh. So that's it, then. She thought you might not have, as you didn't show up. Too bad. She said to tell you she's staying over-night at the Krystal." He took another drag in case he was talking too fast. " She met up with the wife of the Turkish Ambassador—I gather they planned to have a spot of girlish fun. So I left them to it. She thought you wouldn't mind."

" *Mind?* No, on the contrary—I'm *delighted*."

Poor bastard. He certainly looked it. As though I'd handed him a million-dollar cheque. Meanwhile, it would be a pleasure, Mrs. P. —a pleasure, dear—to wring your little neck.

" I've just remembered." Larry chuckled. " Wragg's gone there. That should add to the fun."

" Fun? Say, that'll make it a riot."

" Anyway, good clean riotous fun." How they both laughed.

" Abe . . . look . . ."

" Now what's eating you? " No, it wasn't that. That was over. He looked serious, but not *that* serious.

" It's like this. I can't explain, but would you . . . that is, d'you

480

think you could do something for me? It'll only take a couple of minutes . . . if you'll come with me, upstairs—and then—well, then, I tell you what, we'll go down to the bar and I'll—if you'll do it, that is—I'll buy you a double vodka! What's the matter?"

"Ha . . . ha . . . ha . . ." A viler laugh it would have been hard to imagine. The leer that went with it was pretty vile, too. "And what would that be, eh? The famous Ischia-Tangier approach? Gosh, though—direct, isn't it? To a fault, I'd say. Personally I never got hooked up to that network." He simpered. "*We* were always more refayned on Annac'pree . . . Well, well, been nice knowing you, Purdoe . . . but . . . er . . ."

"Abe, look—I'm serious. Really."

"Sure, that's okay, Lawrence. Don't flap. And no need to go to extremes, my boy. I'll do whatever you want—just for the sake of a teeny-weeny Scotch by your own fireside after . . . if it's all the same to you."

"No," said Larry urgently. "It's not the same at all. That's just what we can't have—what we can't do. That's the whole point."

"Ah, so that's the whole point? Naturally. I get you. Ha-ha. Would it be bothering you awfully *much*," he snarled, "to put *me* in the picture too?"

"I was just going to do that." He grinned, because it had struck him then and there, at the bottom of the stairs, that he had never liked anyone as much as he liked Abe Schulman at that moment, that night. "Come on up." On the way up he explained.

*   *   *

"You only had half a minute to go," said Clarissa.

"A whole half of a minute! You mean we've rushed it? Why, there's time to go back for a drink. I'm off."

"That was Abe, wasn't it, Daddy?" squeaked Dermot. Then both children shuddered with delight as a strange creature re-entered on hands and knees.

"Abe, that's my hat. Where did you get it?"

"The Bla-a-ack Ha-at . . ." it growled, swarming round the room. Then it straightened up.

"Sneaked it from the chapel, of course," said Abe, sitting down on Dermot's bed, opposite Clarissa, the hat tilted rakishly over his eyes. "You shouldn't stare like that, young lady. We've met. May I smoke? Have one?" Dermot began to giggle.

"Where's my mother?" said Clarissa.

"Listen, goat." Larry sat down beside her. "You had it all wrong. Mummy's gone to the mountains. Abe says it wasn't a picnic at all." Silently, Abe concurred. " He left her there only a little while ago. She's staying in a hotel. With a Turkish lady," he added, spreading himself a bit, as a luxury.

" With a *Turkish* lady! " cried Clarissa, enchanted, as if the exotic nationality alone were sufficient commendation of a chaperon.

" And she's coming back to-morrow."

" How? " said Dermot.

" How? " Larry looked surprised, and Abe sat up on the alert. " By car, of course."

" In a *Turkish* car? "

" No," said Abe, heavily sarcastic, " I'm sorry, but it may have to be just a common Cadillac. That's the way it goes, young Purdoe. Too bad, too bad. My golly, you kids, you're *insatiable*. It's not enough to fix your mom up with an Arabian night—d'ya have to check the flight number on the magic carpet too? Why, I guess you're the sort to squeal for Peter Pan on *ice*! "

" Oh, no," said Clarissa, deeply shocked, " I should think not. It wouldn't work, anyway. What about Tinkerbell? And a big dog on skates would look rather silly."

" Sorry, ma'am," said Abe meekly. " Of course, you're quite right."

" So now, Clarissa, tell me one thing, will you? I won't be cross, I promise. Why did you scratch Miss Raven? "

At once they saw her face become stony. Larry lit a cigarette to give her time, and Abe reached over and plumped the black hat down on her head.

" Go on, Clarissa," he said in a hoarse compelling voice. " You're IT NOW—THE BLACK HAT . . ." He rolled his eyes in the way he had. " Yeah, and we're all *sworn to secrecy*! " He snapped round. " Did ya know that, Dermot? "

" Oh, yes," lied Dermot quickly, shrinking from the awe-inspiring figure that had been his sister, a reaction which had the effect of heartening the latter herself.

Abe, waggling two fingers in his mouth, produced an extraordinary, low, blood-curdling cry: " The Bla-a-ack Ha-at! Silence for the Bla-a-ack Ha-at! Speak up! "

Clarissa took a deep breath. " Well," she whispered, " it—it was because of the—of the coat."

" What coat? " said her father. " Now, *think*, Clarissa."

She cast him a piteous look.

" Oh, I am, truly I am. She—she wore it, you see. Mummy's coat."

" Miss *Raven* "—Larry found himself whispering too—" *wore*
482

Mummy's coat? My dear child, no coat of your mother's would have fitted her."

" Oh, but it did," Clarissa insisted, " this one did. *The Mink*, you see." All the members of Milly's family were in the habit of referring to this garment thus, reverently and with bated breath, much to her annoyance.

" You mean she tried it on in the bedroom? That's nothing special, Clarissa, just to try it on."

" Oh, *no*. I mean, yes, in the bedroom. But she didn't just *try it on*——" She hesitated, confused, but obviously the distinction she was trying to draw was quite clear in her own mind. " She *wore* it."

" But, darling, what's the difference? "

" Isn't there—a difference? " She began to snivel again. The hat had sunk low over her ears.

" There cer'nly is," declared Abe stoutly. " I've been in law courts and heard this argued out many an' many a time. But I'd like to have Clarissa's ruling, just so I know where I am the next time. Cm'arn, Black Hat. Here's a handkerchief." He tipped the hat back, and grinned. " Now shoot! "

" Well, she—she walked up and down."

" Ah! " Abe nodded approvingly. " So she walked up and down. Very neatly put. She walked up and down in it—in front of the mirror? As if it were hers? "

" Y-yes."

" And in front of you, I suppose."

" Well, yes—I mean, no, that is—— "

" Ah, of course. You were in—shall we say—temporary conceal-ment? Oh, don't let that bother you, you're the Black Hat, remember—you can skulk around."

" No." Clarissa smiled shyly, and clutched her father's hand. " I wasn't—not exactly. I was dusting. In the other room. At least, I'd been dusting, then I forgot. Because "—she sniffed—" my attention was caught by a—book. I don't know for how long."

" Say, Clarissa, what was the book? You mean you couldn't put it down? "

" No," she said carefully, " because I did put it down."

" Ha! " He snorted, pleased. " So it wasn't that good."

" I put it down and I went back to—the bedroom—and—well, there she was . . . in it . . . making faces, rather, into the glass . . . and —walking up and—down . . ."

" So you breezed in, did you, pussy, and—— "

" Oh, no! " She laughed nervously. " Not exactly. I'm afraid I— I more or less jumped out at her. She was—awfully surprised." She

483

smiled, but more to distract them, her inquisitors, than because she
was amused, even in retrospect. It was clear to both men, from the
way her lips were folded, that whatever it was that had happened did
not strike her as humorous in the very least. She looked from one to
the other warily, as if she already guessed what they purposed to find
out.

" So you scratched her? "

" I suppose I must have done."

" Why, darling? What made you do that? "

" Oh, nothing *made* me. Nothing special. I had to—that's all."

" Then what? "

" Oh, nothing," said Clarissa, taking off the black hat and running
her fingers through her ashy-blonde hair and then carefully attending
to the maintenance of the magic symbol on her lap; with eyes downcast,
she flicked off bits of fluff from the brim.

" Nothing? " Abe coaxed gently. " What, you ambushed her,
knocked her down, sliced her face to ribbons with those sharp little
claws and she said *nothing at all*? Not a murmur? Not a peep? "

" No—well, nothing—nothing much." She bit her lips as the tears
welled up and spilled over. Larry got up from the bed and began pacing
up and down. Suddenly he swung round.

" Where is the old bag, anyway? " he muttered to Abe, under his
breath.

" Old bag? " Dermot, charmed by the expression, pricked up his
ears.

" Miss Raven? " said Clarissa, smiling through her tears.

Abe nodded. Larry shot him a warning glance, but too late.
" Yeah," he drawled, " that's whom he's referring to."

" She's been cooking, I think, for Daddy's supper. Something
special."

" You don't say." He yawned, murmured, " You wanna watch
out, boy. Be Spanish fly in the stoo, I guess "—a remark that was
addressed to Larry, properly speaking, who laughed. The children also
tittered.

" She can take a running jump at herself, for all I care . . . well."
He bent over Clarissa. " Good night, precious. Go straight to sleep."
She flung her arms round his neck. " You know," she whispered in
his ear, " I'm so *thankful* you didn't go away too."

" Good night, Black Hat," said Abe. " If you'll allow me I'll just
park your emblem of office back on its hook. That don't mean the
magic stops, though. Oh, goodness me no. You're all charged up
with it—enough to see you through, anyway."

" What about *me*? " said Dermot plaintively.

484

"Why," Abe rumpled the boy's hair, "you don't need that kinda stuff, junior. You're not the sort things happen to. An' stay that way, too—you couldn't do better. 'Night, kids."

Clarissa watched them adoringly as they tiptoed out.

"Funny, weren't they?"

"Funny?" She sighed. "Oh, they were lovely, lovely . . . how I love them. I love Daddy and I love Abe, too. Goodness, Dermot, if she comes in now she'll smell the smoke. Wave it away your side, quick."

Too late. Miss Raven had come rustling in. She was very grand and glittering, rather like a dragon, Clarissa thought. The scaly brocade creaked as she approached, and one almost expected her to breathe fire from her nostrils, her face was so very red, but disappointingly there were no manifestations of this nature; she just stood at the foot of the bed, snuffing.

Clarissa, who was still sitting up, was fairly caught. However, due probably to the residue of magic working in her veins, she felt more than a match for Miss Raven in every way. Even the handicaps of size and years, usually so irksome to her in an engagement, had now become to her astonishment miraculously transformed into positive advantages; she glanced at Miss Raven pityingly, and the kindly thought flashed across her mind that Miss Raven would be advised to wear glasses, she was peering in such a funny way—as if she saw two or three Clarissas sitting up facing her, when one, if she did but know it, was going to be quite enough. Not angry, exactly—more as if she were puzzled, Miss Raven said: "What's the light on for?"

Now whatever you do you're not to feel sorry for her, Clarissa told herself, and accordingly hardened her heart.

"Because we've just had callers," she replied coolly, "Dermot and me."

"Callers?" Miss Raven came a step closer, then paused. "Who?" she said, staring at her charge in amazement. Clarissa, with an air of perfect composure, had spread her hands out flat on the top of the sheet as she had seen her mother do, usually to admirable effect, and was gazing at them reflectively, a secretive little smile playing round her lips. She was smiling because suddenly, just when she most needed it, the mood had come over her—a mood that she associated with her mother because it was when in argument with her that she had come to regard it as a trustworthy ally. It was a mood of sheer inspiration, nothing more nor less. Although by its very nature it was bound to be unpredictable, in that there was no telling as to when or in what circumstances it would appear, she recognised it at once whenever it

485

came; just for so long as it lasted, and so long as she submitted herself to it, she became invincible; that was how she recognised it, by the way she became. The secret was, not to think. Now, she told herself, don't think what to say. Whatever comes into your head will be the right thing so just say it.

"Who?" Miss Raven demanded more sharply. "Your father?"

"Yes."

"And who else?"

"Mr. Schulman."

"Mr. *Schulman*?" At this Miss Raven staggered rather, as if someone had biffed her between the eyes. If you're sorry for her now I'll kill you, said Clarissa to Clarissa. Just remember you can't forgive her, ever. Luckily Miss Raven herself made it easy by coming up close and hissing: "Mr. Schulman's away. You're lying, you know you are—aren't you, Clarissa?" She was breathing very fast. Clarissa could smell mothballs under the strong sweetish smell of scent. She looked up at Miss Raven.

"I'm not lying." This clear cutting voice sounded strange even to herself. "I know when I'm lying, Miss Raven," she said, with just a hint of emphasis that made Miss Raven blink. "Besides," she went on, indicating the ash-tray on the night-table, "Daddy never smokes those, does he?"

"Where's your mother?" Miss Raven bent down close; her eyes were a bit frightening, but Clarissa never flinched.

"In the mountains, like you said. She's coming back to-morrow."

"Did you tell your father about—about this morning?" Her breath, which was coming in short gasps, was not very nice, and Clarissa edged away.

"Yes, I did."

"Everything?"

"Nearly everything," said Clarissa with a maddening smile.

"So what did he say?"

"Oh, nothing." She shrugged. "He laughed, as a matter of fact. Mr. Schulman laughed too. We've all been laughing quite a lot."

"Laughing?" Then quickly, suspiciously, "Laughing at what?"

"Oh, jokes. I can't remember what."

"They were funny, too," Dermot chipped in. "The jokes. Flies in the stew." He chuckled.

Bewildered, Miss Raven turned to regard her favourite. Flapping his long lashes, Dermot cast her a wickedly languishing look.

"Oh, yes," Clarissa went on mercilessly, "that was one. Mr. Schulman told Daddy to look out because you'd put flies in the
486

stew. That was very funny, we thought. Have you *really*, Miss Raven?"

Miss Raven stared from one to the other. Then she said dazedly, " Put *flies* in the *stew*? "

" Oh, not *ordinary* flies," Clarissa explained earnestly, the fanciful detail being of the sort to captivate her imagination, " *Spanish* flies, he said."

For a second it seemed that her instinct had failed her, that she might have gone too far for her own good. Miss Raven's face which had been so red, had now become quite white. She stood there between the two beds, breathing with her mouth open in a very ugly way, then all the words came tumbling out as if they couldn't escape fast enough, a fire, or something, inside.

" You're dotty, Clarissa, d'you hear, you're a most abnormal child with a nasty filthy mind and I shall tell your father so, d'you hear, you're dotty—dotty—*dotty* . . ."

" Yes, I hear," said Clarissa gently. " I don't mind if I am—dotty. I'm not the only one who is, and anyway "—she leaned back against the pillows—" I dare say that *I* shall grow out of it. And you can tell my daddy what you like—he said *you* could take a run and jump at yourself, so there."

To her astonishment Miss Raven suddenly seemed to crumple up, all in a heap, on top of Dermot, who squeaked. Putting her arms round him she held him to her. She seemed to be blubbing or about to blub, so far as one could judge from her back view. Her shoulders were wobbling. Clarissa felt awful. This was her work. She had no idea which of her shafts had found their target. Her face felt stiff; the hateful little smile that had been such fun to wear now seemed to be gummed fast. She felt sorry, that was the worst of it—dreadfully sorry, yet she couldn't stop smiling. She might have blubbed herself if her face had allowed her to; as it was, she felt herself blubbing inside.

" Good night, Dermot," said Miss Raven in a chokey voice.

Oh, poor, poor Miss Raven, thought Clarissa in despair, what can I do? This was weakness, she knew; she had sworn never, never to forgive and yet . . . At this point, quite unexpectedly, it was Dermot who, snatching up the mantle of inspiration as it slid from his sister's shoulders, accepted with it the responsibility and the challenge and acquitted himself as to the manner born. As Miss Raven laid him back on his pillow:

" Old bag," he murmured tenderly, lavishing upon her the smile he had inherited from Larry. Miss Raven was out of the room before Clarissa had recovered from the shock.

487

"That was naughty, Dermot," she said quite severely, and turned out the light. Miss Raven had even forgotten to do that.

*   *   *

"Burns your guts out, don't it? Say, tovarich, is this export? Huh. Says it is. Potato fire-water. Two more doubles. Larry, you look all shot to hell, d'ya know that?"

"It's been that kind of day. Crowded to-night, isn't it?"

"Sure is," said Abe, looking round the bar.

"Telegrams back and forth. Our admin. king's coming down to-morrow night."

"That one that didn't show up last time?"

"That one, yes. Cantrell."

"*Cantrell?* That's the hire and fire guy, eh? Oh my, you shouldn't just blurt out his name like that. Simpson used to prostrate himself—allah allah—akbar—y'know. Didn't get him anywhere, though. But then he'd got himself in pretty deep."

"Deep?" said Larry. "D'you know, you've never told me anything about him at all."

"We know each other well enough now, Purdoe, eh, what?" The popular transatlantic version of a British accent always made Larry smile. "Wasn't his fault, poor bastard," Abe went on. "It was his wife. I *liked* them both. They were good fun. But I guess Molly did for him all right."

"Molly? His wife?"

"Milly—Molly . . . not much variety in your Anglo-Saxon names, is there? Yeah, that's it. Molly. Molly la reine." He laughed his horrible laugh.

"La reine?"

"Oh, sure. La reine . . ." he drawled, "doo Marshay Nwar."

"*Really?*" Larry thought this over, frowning. "I wonder why they—you know, it *is* queer, isn't it, that no one's ever told me a single —you mean, she—what's the word "—he fished around for it, delicately —"*dabbled* in it?"

"Dabbled my foot. Huh. She was in it up to her neck."

"Good lord!" Larry looked what he was, profoundly shocked.

"So that's how I know Cantrell—well, I only met him once and the occasion wasn't auspicious—he and I saw the Simpsons off on to the train. It used to be quite a tradition in the good old days—a year or two back, that is—this seeing off on to the train." He paused, remembering. "One or two of those occasions—the Simpsons was one—were what you might call impromptu. Twenty-four hours to git —and no heel-tapping. Champagne on the bahnhof, notwithstanding.

488

Not for the Simpsons, though—on account of this guy Cantrell. But departures can be more impromptu even than that—oh, my, yes. Some dear friends of mine have had to leave by aeroplane—special aeroplane —without champagne. Those were the days."

" It doesn't still happen ? "

" Once in a blue moon." He yawned. " But it's not a common-place any more—now it's an event—international repercussions and all that hooey. What was I going to say? Oh yeah—Cantrell. Just so you can't gripe about nobody tellin' ya anything, *I'll* tell you. Tall. Very light bright blue eyes, angry-looking, permanently adjusted to a point a coupla inches above your head. Beaky nose—Duke of Wellington to himself in his shaving mirror, I'm willing to bet—anyway, definitely a military man. Plus. That's what you gotta watch out for, the plus. All the rest—not *phoney*, exactly—though it *is* too good to be true—but the old conjuring technique; y'know, it's aimed to distract. It does, too. While you're busy falling over backwards with delight at having so astutely summed *him* up, he's untying your shoe-strings so when you come to you trip flat on your face and then *he* sums *you* up. They gotta nickname for him."

" Cantrell," mused Larry. " Yes, I should think they probably have."

" Two more, Tovarich."

" No, these are mine. All the same," Larry looked sheepishly demure, " I don't think I need worry this time. It's more or less a routine call, I fancy. In fact, they—well, they've been kind enough to say that they're not displeased, et cetera . . . and it's not impossible that at some not too distant date——"

" *Larry!* Say, well, I'm delighted! Yeah, I really am. That's *swell*. Hey, tovarich, noch einmal—gosh, isn't that wonderful? Mr. Am-bassador, your health! H'm . . . Tell me just one thing—and this'll be treated as quite off the record, Mr. Purdoe—taking a quick bird's-eye glimpse back over your career, early struggles, unpleasant stations and so on, and basing your opinion—and I'd like a considered one, please—on your wide experience, could you ever, ever visualise a situation ever, ever arising that *might*—taking into account any and every contingency, pestilence, war, famine blah-blah-blah—that *might*, I repeat, shake your masters into expressing themselves with a plain unvarnished affirmative ? "

" Good lord, no," said Larry. " At least to my knowledge nothing and nobody ever has."

"Very, very interesting. Just a minor technical point of phraseology, I take it? What do they say when they're *dis*pleased, though? In what terms, may one ask, do they couch their displeasure ? "

" Oh, that's easy. They merely fail to appreciate."

" Ah! So that's what they merely do? But that's genius! You gotta hand it to them." He shook his head in wonder. " Lisping at their mothers' knees those guys musta been majoring in double talk. We're just babes-in-arms by comparison."

" Talking of double talk, there's your friend," said Larry.

" Alby? Yeah. I saw him a while back. Seems kinda stand-offish to-night. Usually comes over to have a drink. Burned up I gave him the slip this morning, I guess. Besides, he's got one or two of his pals with him. Always makes him nervous."

" Where? "

" Oh, dotted around," said Abe, yawning. " Quite a gang of them just round the corner in the ballroom. I guess I'll call the whole bunch over for a drink. I like to know what's going on—and something is, I'd say."

" Message for you," said the hotel porter, handing Larry an envelope.

" Remind me to kick that slit up the backside," said Abe, when the porter had gone. " He's one I wouldn't buy a drink for, ever. Now what's all this? "

" Heaven, too, it seems." Larry passed him the note. Abe read it, frowning; then with a laugh he said:

" Boy, you're just a honeypot, ain't ya, the way ya draw 'em? " Puzzled, he scratched his ear. " Now what in hell can she want? " he murmured. " Urgent, underlined . . . my my . . . . I've felt that way myself, baby, but you don't have to put it in writing, a big girl like you." He glanced up. " D'ya want me to come hold your hand? I mean, I don't think *I'd* care to risk it on my own."

" No." Larry grinned. " I can manage this one. It won't be anything. Some bee in her bonnet, I expect—nut cutlets for the masses, as likely as not. I'll go up and see her now. Thank you, Abe, anyway —for everything, you know. Good night."

" Good night, Ambassador, and don't forget—if I don't see you before to-morrow—add the number you first thought of and go on adding and don't weaken—whatever else you do—*don't* subtract! "

" As long as I don't have to multiply."

" I didn't say he was that good, did I? He's not. At least he's not complicated—not at all. Still, I'll keep my fingers crossed. 'Night."

Larry moved over to the cash desk to pay his bill. Whilst he was waiting for the change he read Mrs. Wragg's note over again. He felt very tired. Shall I go up? he thought—yes, I must. This is what I'm here for. She may be in trouble. He didn't think she was, somehow. In trouble, real trouble, people almost never bothered to underline, let alone three times. More likely, that meant it was somebody else in trouble—Mrs. Wragg could fix that with no trouble at all. Still, he would have to go up.

He picked up his change and was about to pass through the swing-doors which led into the residential part of the hotel when he glanced back. Abe, at the bar, was already surrounded by his "pals," as he called them, Albovski and the rest. Albovski, who reached scarcely to Abe's shoulder, was speaking; Abe, his shaggy head bent, seemed to be listening intently, and Larry was struck by the look of dismay on his face. He wondered what on earth Albovski could be saying to make Abe look like that.

Then he went out through the swing-doors and up the stairs to find Mrs. Wragg.

Chapter Four

IT WAS all on account of there being no curtains. Given long, stuffy, velvet curtains, reaching from floor to ceiling, then her situation would have been different, anyway not precarious. She would have been able to have gone on sleeping, protected from what had been gradually seeping in through the windows and was now flooding in like poison gas, diluting, eventually to dissipate completely that which was an essential ingredient of her own element; as nitrogen to air so darkness was to evil, which was her element, and the daylight was steadily robbing her of it.

Because she breathed evil. Evil nourished her, housed her, encompassed her; here, under the quilt, she was wallowing in a little black pool of purest evil. If exposed to the light of day she would smell and taste of evil; it ran in her blood, it had melted her bones to a jelly, yet her own identifiable flavour remained, enhanced by the preserving fluid that was evil; as the heart of a tender young artichoke preserved in the finest olive oil tastes of itself and the oil, too, and is doubly delicious, so was her evil self—doubly evil. Yes, she was steeped—no, *pickled* in evil. A disgusting shape in a murky glass jar. And now she had been lifted out and the precious evil was draining away, leaving her high and dry and very soon she would begin to stink.

Because she was old. Goodness, how old? Very, very old. Oh, what an extremely ancient morsel she was. As old and grimy and dilapidated as a coelacanth. Yes, because this was a beach on which she was lying, just above the water-line where she'd been thrown up by the waves, rejected even by the sea, poor battered evil old thing—tears oily with evil and self-pity squeezed out of her evil old eyes at the thought—and when the sun rose high in the sky, which it was already beginning to do, she would begin to stink.

She twitched feebly, as the light poured over her. She'd been doing very nicely for the last couple of thousand years or so down in that dark grotto which had been her home. Then there had to be this storm, and she had to get washed up—and the sun had to rise. It was unfair. The tears soaked into the sand. Still—she sniffed—she was very interesting, wasn't she?—just as interesting as any beastly old fish. She'd have a lot of rarity value, she would say, it having occurred to her that the hand, claw, flipper or fin with which she was wiping her old nose was a part of her marvellously ancient frame. She regarded the appendage with a mixture of pride, complacency and acute distaste. Here was proof, scientific proof, of what she was. No wonder she'd had to live down there in the dark under the rocks—and what an outcry there would be when they discovered her, the oldest and wickedest thing in the world! You couldn't wish for older finger-nails than these—horny, chipped, yellow with age—why, they would be able to tell she was no fake simply by examining the deposits beneath. And her teeth—just let them take one look at her teeth! She explored them with her crusty old tongue. Actually, her teeth were rather a treat— deliciously furry round the back, slippery and nasty as rayon in front. They'd take one look and clap their hands for joy and cable South Ken. and in a brace of shakes that was where she would be—where she had always suspected might be her appointed resting-place.

They were coming now to fetch her. She could hear the beat of the tom-toms, the whooping cries of savages and the biologists' yelps of glee. Well, if they wanted her, by all means. She was not one to put obstacles in the way of science and indeed was scarcely in a position to do so. Just so long as they realised that she was a very valuable old piece. It was entirely up to them—the bother and the risk.

After a while, as the noise remained static in volume and her captors failed to approach, rather huffily she assembled a scratch team of old bones, together with such muscles, reflexes and so on, as would still work, and somehow managed to shuffle down into the shadow of the rocks where she nosed about trying to locate that particular black tunnel which led to her own familiar little grotto, and eventually stumbling upon it she crept in and made herself snug—whether for an evening or the next thousand years was entirely up to them, and they could sort it out.

*   *   *

The next time she surfaced it was to find no basic change in the conditions prevailing, daylight, noise (the radio, it was), a raging thirst, nausea, and so on, but a deterioration had set in nevertheless, their sum total now representing reality, and intolerable at that, she in the meantime unfortunately having regained sufficient strength to judge what was tolerable, and what was not. Her headache, for instance, was not.

She lay back and noted the various trends—that the daylight was now uniformly bright, that the music had become intensely loud, and that evil no longer hung irresolute in the air, a dim, lingering and on the whole agreeable presence; it had been vanquished by the daylight, as she had known it would be. But the evidence of battle, the relics of

493

occupation (like burned-out camp-fires, spent cartridge-cases) remained: an overturned bottle, pools on the table, a stocking needled on a cactus, and garments strewn over the parquet. But even with such disorderly details taken into account, the scene, the room as a whole, presented a positively monastic appearance as compared with the headquarters to which the erstwhile conqueror, evil, had been forced to retreat; the bed.

The smaller became its scope and the more docile in defeat it became itself, the more compelling became the need to define it more closely, to the nth if need be, to locate it, narrowing the map reference to a pin-point—anyway, she felt the need to do that. The bed was merely the headquarters. Evil itself had taken shape—a dual shape, hers and Wragg's. Furthermore, if it had to be to the nth, if it could be said to be concentrated in any single visible portion of either body, then it was so concentrated in Wragg's left foot which stuck out of the quilt at the bottom of the bed, and more particularly still, if determined to the ultimate figure in the map-reference, it was in the big toe-nail. In colour the normal yellowish grey, having been allowed to grow abnormally long it was transparent and frilly at the extreme edge; bore, too, curious brownish-purple markings in the insignia of skull and cross-bones—where someone had trodden on it, probably—so that in appearance (had it not been attached to a hairy toe) it was not merely reminiscent of, but identical with an Adriatic shellfish, not so widely known nor so costly nor succulent as scampi, called granchi—which, if freshly caught, may be sucked raw from the shell.

This last, although possibly the most repellent, was only one of the many thoughts that came to Milly as, having traced the root of evil, she lay staring fascinated at it; during which time it went on steadily growing inwards.

When she looked at her watch it said three o'clock. It was the next day, presumably. So it couldn't be three o'clock. She put the watch to her ear. Yes, it had stopped. Her heart almost stopped too, with relief. So what time was it? What time—time—time—echoed through all the empty corridors of her brain. She sat up. Time. That was it. Time. Fool, she told herself, fool. Time, that's it. She jerked round.

Wragg was lying turned away from her with the sheet pulled up round his neck. There was a greasy halo on the pillow round his head. His hair, which by day was glossy as a beetle's back, had become ruffled into spikes or quills, stiff with grease. She looked at him with revulsion. She could not bring herself to touch him, but she tugged the sheet round his ear.

" Herbert! " she whispered. Then, louder, idiotically, " Mr. Wragg! "

This formality of address succeeded in recalling him to consciousness. The craggy range under the sheet stirred and then subsided as he heaved over on to his back, where he lay with his eyes shut. It was horrible to have to look at him. although in fairness she had to admit that he didn't look too horrible. After all, she must look pretty horrible herself. It never showed so much with men. Such minor but invaluable advantages accrued to them as if by right.

Suddenly she realised that he was wide awake. His eyes glinted beneath rather long lashes.

When he opened his eyes, which he had waited to do, she was just as he had promised himself, as a reward for a minute's patience, she would be: kneeling up looking down at him, her hair over her shoulders. Against the light he couldn't make out her expression, but he had to smile, seeing her like that.

So he could smile, could he?—her accomplice in crime. He could lie there, without a trace of shame on his face, *smiling*? And what a smile. Lazy, bold, quizzical, tender—yes, no doubt about it, it was the smile of the triumphant lover. Disgusting. Even his eyes—how *dared* he?—*caressed* her. To her intense annoyance she felt herself blushing. She could even see the blush mottling her chest. Then it occurred to her that she was wearing a silk slip and nothing else; leaning over, she grabbed her skirt off the floor and flung it round her shoulders.

" Sleep well, Milly? "

" What's the time? " she snapped rudely. " That's the point."

" Haven't the foggiest."

" Well, look at your watch. Haven't you *got* a watch? "

He yawned. " No, sorry. Never wear them."

" Why not? " she said stupidly.

" I'm one of those people who can't." Leaning on his elbow, he explained with pride: " They just don't go on me. Play up, you know. Too much electricity, or something. I knew a bloke once," he chuckled in reminiscence, " he only had to pick up a watch for it to stop— stopped for good and all, too. Actually, I think it's something to do with——"

" Look," she interrupted, " I've got to know the time. Please get up and find out. And hurry—please *do* hurry."

" Okay," he said cheerfully, threw back the bedclothes and got up at once. She looked away, scowling. There must surely be some recognised rules of behaviour laid down for this type of situation; even if there were, she reflected, they were not likely to be recognised by Wragg. She heard him crashing about in the bathroom whilst she collected various garments, disgracefully dispersed in unlikely spots,

495

and scrambled into them. There was the noise of hammering and two or three cracking thuds and then the rush of water. After a bit he came out wrapped in the sheet and dripping wet. He looked pleased with himself.

" What on earth were you doing in there? "

" Oh, nothing much. Just smashing up the conservatory." He was rubbing himself down with the sheet. " You can have a bath now, if you like. Water's cold, of course." He began to whistle. This was the last straw, and she burst out, her tone so waspish they might have been a decade united in holy wedlock: " Herbert, *will you hurry?* "

" I *am* hurrying, Milly. Give me a chance." He added forgivingly, " I suppose you're hungry. I know I am."

" It's not *that*! " Her look would have withered him had he been looking; as it was she stalked into the bathroom with her make-up kit and slammed the door.

She washed her face in cold water and then started to paint it back to respectability, an icy little tune all the while tinkling through her head to a boring little refrain: adulteree, adulteree—you've committed adulteree—you, you, yes, you (bass)—fiddle-deedee, adulteree . . . " Oh, shut *up*," she sobbed, " let me alone, can't you? I can't bear it. Shut up—let me *alone!* " But it wouldn't let her alone. Teasing, inexorable, it persisted. She slapped the stuff on as fast as she could and got out.

She sidled into the salon, trying not to look at him, because she knew it would make her angry if she did. When she did, it made her very angry. He was apparently admiring the view from the window while eating biscuits out of a paper bag, and dunking them in a glass which held the dregs of champagne.

" Help yourself." He held out the bag, munching noisily. " Didn't know I had them. What a blessing, though. Olga must've put them in—she sometimes does."

" I don't know how you *can*! " said Milly, spurning the bag, this casual reference to his wife seeming to have touched on an open nerve, which throbbed in consequence.

" What—not gingernuts? " he said, incredulous. " Don't you like them? Funny, I always have. Remind me of school. Used to have them at break—on Tuesdays, I think it was . . . oh—sorry." He gave an insane sort of chuckle. " I've been downstairs. I say, we must've been shagged—worn out, I mean. Just guess what the time is."

" No," she said. " Suppose you just tell me."

" Two o'clock."

At that her heart really did seem to stand still. " It can't be."

496

"It jolly well is. We slept the clock round. Milly!" He came towards her. Although he was the last person she could spare a thought for at that moment, once more it flashed through her mind that he had changed. In some way. "Milly," he said, and paused, as if that were enough, as if in saying her name he had said all he wanted to say, really. Then, with a spark of genius, "Darling," he added, "darling."

"Look here, Herbert," she said, stubbing out her cigarette, "there's no time to fool about. We've got to go—now."

"Have we? Have we really? I mean—*must* we go back? Now?"

"Are you mad? What do you think this is—a desert island?"

He looked wretched at once—terribly crestfallen. "I wish——" he began.

"*Don't!*" she said fiercely. "I don't want to think about it."

"Don't you?" Stuffing the biscuits into the rucksack he mumbled, "I think—I'll never stop thinking about it," and gulped, looking down at her with the old Wragg look, perplexity and dismay mixed—yet again with a difference. At least almost at once he managed to smile —a bit rueful, it was true, but a smile.

"Oh, come *on*," she said, impatient with herself as with everything else. There was not the slightest need to feel sorry for him. "Come on."

"Coming," he muttered, and swinging the rucksack on to his shoulder, picking up her case, he followed obediently in her wake.

It took half an hour to check out and, after heated argument at the reception desk, to ascertain that Vladek had deserted them. At last a porter was unearthed who could testify to the fact that Vladek and the other foreigner, the one who had originally escorted the foreign woman (leering at Milly), had driven off together the night before.

"How very queer," said Wragg, thoughtfully, and it struck Milly as queer too. The hotel staff, notably the rodent at the reception desk, although obviously of the same opinion, were satisfied rather than scandalised and on the whole unimpressed. Queer it might be, but not in the sense of being mysterious, or surprising. One foreigner had brought the foreign woman and another foreigner was taking her back. The names on all three passports were diverse, as was only to be expected. So the two foreigners had shared the same woman. Here was proof, if proof were needed, that such was Western morality. Still, she must have stamina, the woman. Quite a small woman, too. The eyes of the receptionist flickered over her. Not his type. They behaved like beasts of the field, these Westerners. As though proof were needed. He had always known that. He had been told it often enough.

*   *   *

Then she couldn't get the Austin to start. The engine was cold or something. She tried again and again. Wragg infuriated her, leaning up against the neighbouring Cadillac, his hands in his pockets, whistling. It was a warbling, melancholy tune and one she happened to detest, connecting it with a young man in the Talks Section of the B.B.C. who, in a basement bed-sitter off Oakley Street, had played it on the gramophone as an overture to all three of his attempts to seduce her, and when eventually forced to acknowledge defeat, had remarked that it " did sometimes work," thereby implying, presumably, that there was nothing wrong with the tune—a point she would have been happy to concede him had he been man enough to tax her with it outright. His name and the name of the tune escaped her. But it was like Wragg to have picked on it now. If you spun out the key-word of her own refrain long enough it went to it very well . . . adulteree-ee, adulteree . . . but then it was such an adaptable word, with a lilt and a slur, you could make it fit almost anything. Take " kedgeree," for instance. Not much difference, basically, but it wasn't nearly so good.

" Blast," she muttered under her breath. She stuck her head out of the window. " Can't you *do* something? " Wragg stopped whistling and she remembered what it was called, that tune. " Greensleeves."

" Sorry," he said blandly, leaning in. " I'm no good with cars. Got everything switched on? "

With the ignition switched on, of course, it started. She played about with the choke for another second or so but she couldn't spare longer, even to save her face.

After five or ten minutes on the main road Wragg shouted: " I say, Milly, you will drive carefully, won't you? "

" No," she shouted back. " Sorry, not to-day. You'll just have to sit back and enjoy it. I'm going to drive fast."

He sat back and was not, in fact, unenjoying it when, from long habit glancing behind, he caught sight of the jeep. It was keeping its distance, about a quarter of a mile back. Milly hadn't seen it yet; she was concentrating on the road ahead. He decided not to say anything about it. As it was, something seemed to have upset her, although he couldn't think what.

*   *   *

" May I come in? " said Sophie timidly. " I've brought you a cup of tea, Miss Raven."

498

" Oh, hallo, Countess." Miss Raven was sitting at her dressing-table. Sophie came over to her and stood holding the cup as there was no room to put it down. The top of the dressing-table was covered with photographs and picture postcards and cuttings from glossy magazines.

" Half a tick." Miss Raven swept them into her lap.

" Feeling better now? "

" Right as rain, thanks. Felt a bit groggy—headache, you know. But it's worn off. I must say it was a lovely party last night, Countess."

" The night before last," said Sophie, with a smile.

Miss Raven took no notice of the correction. " Well, I wanted to tell you that I thoroughly enjoyed myself. It'll be a nice little "—absentmindedly she began shuffling through the pile on her lap, as if the word she sought were buried in it somewhere—" a nice little *memory*," she brought out finally.

" I'm so glad, and I was so sorry to hear you were ill. I thought you'd like to know—the children've been good as gold all day. I took them to the park and I've just given them their tea."

Miss Raven nodded affably, but without much interest.

" Cold out, was it? " She was flipping through the photographs in search of a particular one.

" Cold wind."

" Like to see a handsome man? "

" Well—yes, I suppose . . ."

" There! What do you think of him? "

Sophie peered over her shoulder at a large glossy print, a close-up of a swarthy face.

" Very—*dark*, isn't he? " she said cautiously. Then she added, for she had no wish to hurt Miss Raven's feelings: " Very unusual looking." Indeed, with a modicum of retouching the subject might have passed for a gorilla; nevertheless he had proved himself human by signing the portrait in one corner, a corner over which Miss Raven had her thumb as she gazed tenderly.

" That was James." She heaved a sigh. " See? " She uncovered the signature sufficiently for Sophie to ascertain that the brute might, in all likelihood, answer to the name of James. " Jimmy, I called him. My fiancé."

" Oh dear." Sophie cast about for something to say. Miss Raven's eyes, fixed on her, were so odd—swimmy, that was it. She is going to cry, thought poor Sophie. " What . . . why, I mean—didn't you? What happened? "

" It's a very sad story," said Miss Raven briskly, shuffling the
499

photograph to the bottom of the pile. " See this? What do you think of that? "

" Why, it's a—it's a mansion! " breathed Sophie. Here at least her enthusiasm had no need to be feigned.

" House where I was born. Lovely place, isn't it? "

" Indeed, it is lovely. Where is it? "

Miss Raven was squinting over the white lettering at the bottom edge of the postcard. That's nice, thought Sophie, to have postcards showing your house to send to friends. Only the English would think of a charming idea like that.

" Norfolk," said Miss Raven at last. " The Broads, you know. Yachting, and all that. We did a lot of yachting when I was young." She added, glancing at Sophie rather severely, " It's quite the best county, you know, socially speaking."

" I'm sure it is," murmured Sophie, at a loss.

" I must show you all these some time." She gathered them together. " All my friends are here."

" Do have the tea before it gets cold, Miss Raven."

She seemed not to have heard, to have fallen into a reverie. At last she said: " It's hard to come down in the world, isn't it? You must know that."

" Yes, that's true," said Sophie, " it's not too nice. . . . Look, Miss Raven, I'm afraid I ought to go now—if you think you're all right? "

" All right? " She looked slightly offended.

" I mean, they've had tea . . . I *could* stay and put them to bed— but I really ought to go . . . I thought perhaps they could put themselves to bed if you would just tell me about their supper. Mr. Purdoe's at the office . . . he's very busy, and I don't like to——"

Miss Raven snapped a rubber band round her souvenirs and stood up. She seemed almost square in her thick dressing-gown. She hesitated a moment, a pleasant, if vague, smile on her lips; her eyes, with quite an extraordinary intensity in their regard, searching Sophie's face. Then, as if she had come to a decision, as if she wished to impart a secret that was for Sophie's ear alone, she glided up close. Sophie, under the spell of those eyes, was transfixed.

" You'd never think," she whispered, spinning out the telling of her secret, confident of its sensational effect, " you'd never think, would you, *that I'd had such a life*? "

" N-no," said Sophie rather inadequately, and backing a step away. Realising that she might even have put her foot in it, feeling a " dashed fool " she floundered on: " Well, I mean . . . one can never tell, can one? "

To her relief, Miss Raven appeared quite satisfied.

" That's right," she agreed with wonder in her voice, as if struck by a new point of view which had instantly found favour, " that's quite right . . . you never can tell . . ."

" About the children, Miss Raven . . . their supper? "

She seemed to come back from a long way away. " The children? Supper? Oh, don't you bother about that." Suddenly she whipped round and slammed all her friends into a drawer. " I'll be dressed in two ticks. I'll put them to bed." She thrust the cup into Sophie's hand. " Just leave it on the kitchen table as you go out. I'll wash up. Off you go now. And thanks, Countess, thanks a lot. Cheerie-bye."

" Oh dear, how I wish Milly would come," thought Sophie miserably. Throwing discretion to the winds, she telephoned Larry from the desk downstairs.

" Miss Raven seems much better," she whispered. " She's up and –you see, I'm afraid I really ought to go now."

" Sophie, you're an angel. I can't thank you enough, you know that . . . wait till I see you, I'll give you a big kiss."

" Milly'll be back any minute, won't she? "

" Yes, I dare say she will." At once his voice had changed, become strange—quite hard and business-like.

" I wouldn't go, Larry, except that—well, Miss Raven isn't *ill* or anything."

" Don't you bother, Sophie, you've done quite enough for this family, now you run along. I'm a bit tied up just now, so . . ."

" Of course. I'll come round in the morning. Early. I hope everything is all right. Good-bye."

Everything all right? Heavens, everything was all wrong. She knew that. She had known it the moment she had seen his face that morning, when he came round to fetch her. Overnight, it seemed to have aged ten years. " Oh, my silly darling," she kept muttering under her breath all the way home, " my silly, silly darling. . . ." Meaning, of course, Milly.

* * *

" That was a bit of luck, wasn't it? "

" What was? " He had been gazing out of the window. Now, glancing at him, she thought he looked cold, subdued. Perhaps she had been rather beastly.

" That jeep turning up just when it did."

" I suppose so." He sounded wretched.

" *Suppose?* " She laughed. They were fairly flying along. " I thought we'd had it. There's been nothing else on the road, if you've noticed. Sorry I snapped your head off."

" That's all right."

" You see, I've never bothered about that sort of thing," she rattled on. " I've always relied on someone else being there to do it for me."

" Yes, I see," said Wragg. " I suppose that's only natural." He had resigned himself to the prospect of sudden death a long way back and her anger had caused him to forget it altogether. Now that she had stopped being angry, he found his thoughts reverting to it once more. She did seem to be driving faster.

So great was her relief to be on the road again that she began humming under her breath. It was only after a while that she became conscious that both words and tune had changed. You couldn't even call it a tune, now; it was no more than a rhythm, streamlined to fit the new words, which went: hurry, hurry, hurry . . . fast as fast as ever you can . . . hurry, hurry, hurry . . . How odd that, throughout the first part of the journey, with the original lyric on her lips, it had been in her mind that she would have an accident, that that was to be the end of it—the most likely, and indeed, suitable, end; and she had driven as she had never driven before in her life, daring an accident to happen. Will it be this corner—or that? Neither, as it had turned out, although both had been close shaves, but when others followed that were even closer and yet they still went on, after a while she began to wonder why the accident should be so long delayed. And then there had been the puncture. It was whilst the obliging young men in the jeep were changing the wheel and she was sitting on a milestone, watching—in fact, not until one of the wheel nuts rolled away so that they had had to search for it with a torch because it was already dark —it was then that she began to understand that there was to be no accident, that that was not to be the end of it; nothing so simple. No, whatever it was that threatened—*hurry*, she had entreated them, *hurry* —was connected with this intolerable delay, the fact that they were losing time, time, time . . . she must have known it almost from the moment of waking, that that was the important thing, but had allowed herself to lose sight of it, confusing it with the other, the adultery, which was a catastrophe proper, but could wait, whereas this, whatever it was, could not. Yes, that's the difference—and she smiled, thinking of Clarissa—this is an emergency; not a catastrophe—yet. That was it in a nutshell.

So now they were off again, but it was not so easy, driving in the dark. They had to pass through several small market towns and on the way in and out of each there were streams of peasant carts—the next day, she remembered, being market day in Grusnov. In the dark, these carts, twice as long as ordinary carts and almost never carrying rear lanterns, were a positive nightmare to the motorist; it was

502

impossible to judge their pace, sometimes the horse was spanking along, more often stumbling in its sleep. There were other hazards, too, more children, more drunks, more dogs, in every village, the closer they got to Grusnov. Now, however, that she had no doubts at all about what was required of her, that it was simply a matter of getting back fast enough as there was to be no accident—if she had been driving well before, now, inspired by these twin assurances, she drove with inspiration.

Six o'clock . . . half an hour, then . . . in half an hour . . . what was to happen in half an hour? *She* was the one who was making things happen—so that it depended on her, did it not? No, came the answer pat, it does not. It depends on whether you get there in time—there's all the difference in that. Ah, so it was an appointment, was it? So that was it. Poor Herbert, she thought, I daren't look at him—he's probably sick with fright. But then he couldn't know that they were perfectly safe just so long as this chant was on her lips—hurry . . . hurry . . . hurry . . .

She need not have troubled about Wragg. In that small space there was only room for one emotion as desperate as that which inspired Milly—and becoming infected by it, he willingly let it overpower him, or rather, shared it. He had no idea what motive impelled her, but it must be a good one; whatever she did was right. He wished for her sake that the car might sprout wings.

At the check-point they were held up, unexpectedly, by a whole squad of armed police who stamped round the car, clattering their rifles. They seemed particularly excited by the number plate. The nice young man with the smile was absent, and the quite senior-looking officer in charge seemed rather at a loss to know what to do. He waited, the papers of the car in his hand, looking embarrassed. She wondered what they were waiting for. Somehow she managed to keep a smile on her face. If she had stopped smiling she would have started to scream and gone on screaming. They were held up seven minutes by her watch and it felt like thirty. Then, once more proving itself their guardian angel, the jeep arrived. Really, it was most extraordinarily lucky. The police, it seemed, were unable to deal with two vehicles at once because no sooner had the jeep drawn up behind them than the Austin's papers were handed back and they were permitted to pass.

It was when they reached the outskirts of the town, where the tram lines began, that she lost her confidence. She had no idea how to get through the town, or even how to find the way to the hotel. All those precious seconds gained might well be lost, fiddling about trying to find the right doorstep.

" Herbert," she said, quite loudly, and then realised that he was sitting up straight close beside her; by some miracle he seemed to be with her, completely.

"No, Milly, no!" His voice was quite as urgent as her own. "Sharp right—that's it . . . now . . . yes, left, we'll cut off quite a bit. . . ."

"You just tell me," she said, "just go on telling me—but give me time, mind . . ." She screwed up her eyes, as it was difficult to see . . . damn and blast it, it had begun snowing again.

"Go on, over those lights . . . there's no one around—go *on*, I tell you!" He went on directing her. She was forced to halt behind a tram.

"What's the wiper on for?"

"It's snowing, isn't it?" She rubbed her eyes.

"Snowing? No. Come on, Milly . . . oh God!" He stuck his head out of the window. "Twot!" he bawled, and the old girl getting into the tram scowled.

"Cut out into the middle—cut out!"

"They'll take the number," she said, cutting out all the same.

"I rather think that's already been done," he muttered under his breath.

Now a long street, and a corner, and another long street and they would be there.

"Listen, Herbert," she said, as they raced down the street, and he noticed the needle and it made his heart stand still to think what they must have been doing out there on the open road, "I shan't have time to park, you know."

"No, you won't. Just pull up outside and nip out and I'll see to it somehow."

"You'll have to learn to drive one of these days."

"I know. I've already decided to," he said, and realised to his surprise that this was true.

She rounded the corner and crossed against some more lights and they were off down the home stretch, she still humming, when suddenly she said: "Sorry I had to go so fast."

"You needn't be," he said, "I enjoyed it." Afterwards he remembered these words; the last to be spoken between them.

There was the portico of the hotel at the end of the street. But what am I going to do? she thought, all of a sudden losing her nerve. "What are you going to do when you get there, Milly—have you thought about that? What's all this in aid of?" She pulled up in front of the hotel, right in the path of the tram lines—Wragg could sort that one out—and miraculously, at that moment, all her doubts were settled because all conscious thought ceased. Her brain, which

504

had been active throughout the journey, as if this were its rehearsed part in the stratagem now lay low, sucked a lemon, took a breather, as her limbs and all five senses, a formidable team, took over. They knew what to do. She wrenched open the car door, was through the swing-doors in a flash, raced across the hall and up the stairs. In the corridor, hearing what she would expect to hear at just about this time, half past six—the sound of shrieks and splashing from the bathroom—she paused; the lemon rind tossed aside, her brain leapt back into the fray because there was a split second, no more, in which to make the decision. Although the shortest route to the bathroom was through her own room, the bathroom door might be locked; she couldn't risk it—not only the delay but even rattling the handle; there was the door into the children's room, unlikely that it would be locked, but she daren't risk trying it for the same reasons—although had she stopped to consider she could have given no reason for this reasoning —so that left only one way—so—yes—now! Now there was no need to think—thought was an impediment; she flew down the corridor like a guided missile; a topnotch brain had contrived to make her marvellously accurate and swift—her own brain had done what was required of it, got her to the top of the stairs and taken the decision, and now that other, that superior mechanical force, that something which makes the whole works tick, now that was in charge. She flung open the kitchen door and was through like the wind, through the nursery, through the children's room and, pouncing on the handle of the bathroom door, she flung it wide.

The bathroom was very bright and full of steam. She could see Miss Raven, at least her big tweed behind, bent over the bath, and in the far corner Clarissa, pink and glistening, as if she were perched on a cloud, the lavatory seat, really; the steam eddied and she saw that Miss Raven was bent right over the bath, kneading away at something, like a peasant woman laundering, and most particularly she noted that Miss Raven's blouse had escaped from her waistband, and seeing all this took no longer than is needed to click a lens; steam swirled, she saw legs kicking in the bath, slippery legs, then all at once she heard, too—heard a queer chortling or bubbling sound, and Miss Raven grunting, and Clarissa's piercing scream of joy: " Mummee!— Dermot's—ducked—ducked—ducked . . ." and she had time to think, quite distinctly, seeing's quicker than hearing, before she sprang. She sprang like a tigress, claws outstretched, and her weight, although not considerable, had enough impetus behind it to sink those claws, which were sharp and pointed, deep into the flesh at the nape of her victim's neck; sufficiently deep for her, the attacker, to feel the other shudder, embedded deeply enough for her to drag her prey upright—whereupon

Miss Raven, swaying slightly, without the least resistance but seeming to take her time about it, toppled to the floor. Her head hit the tiles with a nasty little smack.

"Never mind about that," said Milly, scooping Dermot out of the bath. "Unlock the door, Clarissa, and go and get Daddy. AND PUT YOUR SLIPPERS ON! And stop *snuffling*, Dermot," she added sharply, "you're all right." With her free hand she let the plug out.

Chapter Five

" MY DEAR LADY . . . nasty shock, eh? Now just you sit down and let me help myself. I'm going to pour you one of my specials. You need something stiffish after that. Well, we've disposed of the body——" He coughed, and went on hurriedly: " Hefty lass, isn't she? They've found a doctor and he's giving her a knock-out drop. Your husband's getting through to Slavnik now—they'll send down the ambulance, we'll bundle her in, then they'll take her to the Embassy hospital. H'm . . . tst . . . tst . . ." He was clucking away over by the drinks. " What a dreadful thing." He came over to her, carrying a glass. " Never rains but it pours, what? "

Milly stared at him, fully in agreement, but wondering what had led him, a stranger, to voice her own thoughts so exactly.

" Here—you drink that." He patted her shoulder, looking down at her gravely. " Don't you bother about me—I've got mine. Young fellow all right? "

" Yes. Oh, yes."

" Amazing little beggars, children. Tough as blazes. You just can't ki——" she choked—" keep 'em down, can you? " That was even worse. He pressed on. " Too strong? Never mind, do you good. You're looking better already. I say, your daughter's a winner, isn't she? "

He leaned against the mantelpiece, twisting his wonderfully elegant waxed moustaches, smiling at her. Privately he thought the mother was a bit of winner, too. All the pretty wives somehow managed to get tucked away in these outposts. Still, he couldn't complain—made his job all the more agreeable. Pale, though. Strung up, you could tell. Only natural. H'm. H'mmm.

Downing the " special," which fully justified its name, she began to take him in. " Of course, you must be Colonel Cantrell. I hope you've got everything you . . ." She put her hand to her eyes. " I'm sorry, I——"

" Don't you worry your little head about me, my dear . . . H'mm . . . H'mmmmmm . . ." The colonel had a curious mannerism, that of punctuating his remarks, which were delivered in short staccato barks, with a resonant humming sound which, commencing fortissimo, continued diminuendo until it died away. It had originally been devised as a sort of game, or trap, and the sooner you, the colonel's interlocutor,

507

got around to it the better—for you; if some conversational response were not forthcoming before the humming died away, he would start barking again, having in the meantime chalked one up against you and thought up something fresh to bark about. Less noticeable in the company of women, who chipped in pertly enough, in the company of his own sex—who were usually his juniors, and almost invariably, for one reason or another, nervous in his presence—the humming was frequently protracted to several seconds' duration, on rare occasions extending even to a full minute. Like all mannerisms it was highly disconcerting to the uninitiated, and, as if the perpetrator were aware of this and were willing to play down to the stranger until he should get the hang of it, in the first few instances after encounter the humming was protracted almost unbearably. Still, the colonel was, on the whole, a chivalrous man and Milly in her present state was spared.

" We should have met before—wish we had," he added sincerely. " I meant to come some weeks ago, but at the last minute . . . er . . . too bad . . ." Nice young couple up in the north, he remembered. Another pretty wife. " Matter of fact, I'd only arrived a few minutes before young Miss—what's 'er name?—young woman in the bath towel——? "

" Clarissa."

"——Made her entrance. She's goin' to be ravishin', you know. She is now. Hmmmmmm . . ."

" Oh," said Milly, rather surprised. She certainly wouldn't pass that on to Clarissa.

Larry came in. " Well," he said, " that's that. You've got a drink, sir? Good. My God, I could do with one."

" Larry, how is she? " He hadn't kissed her yet, she noticed.

He replied without even looking at her, over his shoulder. But then he was pouring himself a drink. " Miss Raven? Oh, we've fixed her. Snoring her head off." He added, turning to Cantrell, " We locked the door."

" Quite right. Ambulance fixed? Good."

" What'll they *do* with her up there? " Milly asked.

" Ship her home in a strait jacket, I should think," barked the colonel, with rather a brutal laugh.

" You don't mean—she's——"

" Off her nut? My dear Mrs. Purdoe—the Ravin' Raven, a well-known harbinger of doom. Recognised her at once. It's a small world, I'm afraid. Excellent references, eh? "

" Oh, yes, dazzling."

" Ha-ha. Must admit I wrote one of them myself. Hmmm . . ."

Milly looked at him with dislike. He seemed to sense it, because
508

he went on: " She was a first-class *nanny*, you know. When we had
to get rid of her—well, my wife felt sorry for her, and so I decided least
said soonest mended. Hmmmm . . ."

" Whatever happened? "

" Oh, it was some years ago now—where was it, Budapest, I think
—when our brats were quite small. Of course, I was younger myself
then, too . . . Hmmm . . ." Glancing in the mirror, he stroked his
moustaches, no doubt a reminder of his heyday as they were, presumably, still in theirs, and Milly thought she caught him wink. " It
wasn't so much what *happened*, as what didn't happen. Fact is, she
got me—er—jumpy."

" *Jumpy?* " Good for her, thought Milly, and Larry looked at the
colonel with new eyes.

" Yes. Got on my nerves. I didn't feel safe. She was always nippin'
in and out—we lived in smallish quarters in those days, and—well, it
was most awkward. Then on one occasion my wife went away for a
day or two—and really, I—er—well, to cut a long story short, I had
to change my billet. Hmmmm . . . mmmmmm . . ."

" Gracious! "

" That wasn't the end of it. We found she'd consoled herself with
my driver. Used our bedroom, too, which was a bit much. Oh, she
was definitely queer that way—those people in Leopoldsville had
trouble, too. Something in her past—some very sad story, I believe.
She told us several. Of course she was a pathological liar as well, but
one puts up with a lot to get a good nanny. Still, there are limits.
The truth is," he added, rearing his head and allowing his eyes to travel
round the ceiling before bringing them to rest on Larry, " she'd make
a pass at anybody and everybody. That's to say, anything in trousers
. . . Hm." The colonel, without taking his eyes off Larry, grinned ever
so faintly, and Larry, suddenly reminded of what Abe had said, revised
his estimate, making a substantial addition very rapidly.

" Hmmm . . . mmmm . . . so, Mrs. Purdoe, if you'll forgive me, I'll
take myself off for half an hour or so. Just to fix myself up—and I'd
better get through to Slavnik on my own account. And after that
perhaps we could have a short chat, eh, Purdoe? And then I hope
you'll both do me the pleasure of dining with me—downstairs, eh?
Hmmmm . . . mmm . . ." Buzzing steadily, he buzzed himself off.

*　　　*　　　*

He came into the bedroom and stood behind her as she dabbed
dispiritedly at her face. She looked like the wrath of God—so she did.
She yawned, and saw him standing there. He put a glass down on the
dressing-table.

"Angel." She sniffed. "Bourbon? Goodness, how nice. Present from Abe?"

"Yes. Present from Abe."

Something in his voice made her glance round at him; one look at his face, and she got up from the stool and sat down in the arm-chair by the dressing-table, pulling her dressing-gown round her.

"Larry, do we have to talk about it now?"

"I'm afraid we do."

"But I'm so tired."

"Yes, I'm rather tired, too. But you heard what he said. We've only got half an hour. So let's get it over." He lit two cigarettes and put one on the ash-tray beside her, as if he knew that other-wise she would have had to refuse it lest he see how her hand was shaking.

"But what's he doing here, Larry, this man? Why's he come?"

"Mainly, though he doesn't know it yet, to accept my resignation."

"Darling!"

He seemed not to hear. In fact, he seemed for a minute or two to forget her completely, and it occurred to her that this was an old trick practised by authority on offenders. He had taken a sheaf of papers out of his pocket and was looking through them as if marshalling his facts; then he placed the whole bunch down on the table at her side. Her eyes, drawn to the pile out of casual curiosity, remained fixed upon it. Sandwiched amongst the papers was a wedge of pink slips, the counterfoils of NAAFI orders; those would have been sent separately —to him, of course; also one or two jottings in her own handwriting. She lay back in the chair, suddenly feeling quite sick; closed her eyes, and in her lap slipped her hands inside the sleeves of her dressing-gown so that each cold hand clutched a warm, throbbing wrist. Whatever he was going to say, she hoped he would get it over quickly. The silence seemed to go on so long, at last she opened her eyes and looked at him.

He had sat down on the bed and was apparently lost in thought. Her eyes travelled over his face, appraising it—perhaps on account of the expression it wore, which was certainly strange—as she would the face of a stranger. She noticed, too, that the fingers of his left hand were stained dark brown, that he could have done with another shave and looked as if he hadn't been to bed for nights. Then he looked up and his eyes roved over her, also, but without meeting hers, avoiding them, rather; and his gaze was cool, distant, critical, as if he were considering how best to tackle her, equally a stranger, but first and foremost a problem, one of his many problems, his duty being to assist, advise or reprimand her, whatever it might be. Seeing him thus in his

510

official capacity for the first time, that is, in relation to herself, her reaction to him, to this new personality, was quite new, too—transformed by a faint but definite thrill of excitement.

So this was her husband.

Now, supposing she were an adventuress—of the sort who at regular intervals spend hours and hours in consular waiting-rooms in the process of getting the chequered pattern stamped on their careers—how would she sum him up? Because she would know at once, wouldn't she, a girl like that? She would have come across them all in her travels —all those men behind desks, the incumbents of consulates, consuls plain, general, or vice? There weren't so many categories—half a dozen at most. She would distinguish and automatically discount the alert, prematurely pepper-and-salt worrier-terriers, the career boys from the Secondary Moderns; also the queers, of course, would be a waste of time to a girl like that, who would have learned that ambitions and inhibitions alike prohibit any response to what she had to offer. She would immediately identify the nice young man destined for great things, stern, awkward, and awfully helpful, who would stare at her legs for fear of meeting her eyes and then, blushing, meet her eyes in preference to having the thoughts that occurred to him in connection with her legs, and suddenly all in a rush invite her to lunch, merely in order, it would seem, to discuss his fiancée, and she would laugh to herself at the thought of him kicking himself after she had gone, wondering what went wrong. She'd know how to handle the portly old bully with a hundred cherished mannerisms who would bore his way and hers through a jungle of cricketing jargon in the effort explicitly to explain some piffling point, with a bluff twinkle in his eye which said: " We know what a bad girl you are, don't we, you and I? "—slyly pinching her behind as he said good-bye, doubtless regretting, not for the first time, that the horse-faced creature earning her pin money in the outer office was his wife. And the type found burgeoning, usually in the rich soil of culture centres, superficially a more likely-looking bet than the rest—but with her experience she wouldn't often bet—the decorative dreamer, rangily romantic, melancholy as a Jesuit, often not quite quite; in conversation inclined to the metaphysical, in appearance to dandruff and rather daring haberdashery, on encounter so shy, sensitive, over dinner proving himself capable of talking the hind leg off a donkey and very successful in talking his way into bed with her that same night—but not quite. She would see to that.

That virtually covered them all, thought Milly. And so this one, where did he fit in? Into any of those categories? No, he did not. She would know at a glance, that girl, wouldn't she?—that here was a man in a thousand, and she'd say to herself, wouldn't she?—*what a*

511

pity I can't have him. And then, the stamp being stamped, or whatever it was having been done, she'd go back to her hotel and, having nothing better to do, turn out her suitcases, inspect all the dresses she had, all flimsy, unsuitable for the climate—bought in the last place, paid for by someone she disliked—and wonder how it came about that although she was a clever girl, had done everything, been everywhere, there should always be a lack of such durable necessities as furs, bags, shoes, and so on, to go with the dresses, and never a scrap of jewellery —and unaccountably restless, sick of the sight of the shambles, she would wander into a bathroom flagged out with drying nylon, and removing the make-up, bravely face her face, and burst into tears at the pity of it—*that she couldn't have him.* And his image would come between her and a string of silly faces in taxis for a long time after that —and restrain her from one or two stupidities until it would fade, be forgotten, relegated to dreams, because a girl must live. Until—where did that sort of girl end up? In all honesty Milly had to admit, anywhere, almost; well, wherever she was, this girl, years later, married to someone in oil, or to a respectable solicitor, or even to a South American ambassador, or just going down and down, whatever that meant—eventually she would come across *his* name, in a newspaper, posted as something somewhere, something quite solid somewhere reasonably nice, and it would all come back to her, and she'd wake up in the small hours to the sound of the rain and through a haze of barbiturates the thought would return: " *What a pity I couldn't have had him.*"

If only he would get it over quickly.

She need not have fretted on that score. In the event he was quicker than she liked, brisk, methodical and thorough, now and then consulting his notes.

" First," he said, " we'll go over what Olga Wragg told me last night." As this was mainly concerned with facts which he had at his finger-tips, prices, lists of commodities, weights and dates, and as he contributed no comment of his own, the story gained from the manner of its telling, the whole presenting a black little picture indeed. When he had finished he got up and gave her another cigarette and took another for himself and stood looking down at her.

" You mean to say "—she thought she saw a chink in his armour —" you believed all that, without even waiting to—she's always been jealous, you know that . . . a jealous bitch, that's what she is, and you don't even give me a chance? . . . You're going to resign without even bothering to find out whether—it's true or—anything . . ." Her voice trailed away.

He sighed. " Oh, *Milly,* come off it. It's a waste of time. If you want to know, although as you can imagine it came as a bit of a shock and I had to think fast, also I'm afraid I did think it sounded like the truth, I told Mrs. Wragg that I was quite in the dark and before I could take any steps at all I must of course wait for an explanation from you. She had it all thought up because her answer to that was, that if I didn't resign within twenty-four hours she would get Wragg, or go herself, I think she said, to Slavnik, to the Embassy, and spill the beans. So I told her that as Cantrell was coming down anyway, the matter would be settled by this evening and she had to be content with that."

" But, Larry, you've decided *already*, you say. That's what hurts me, the lack of—trust . . . I mean, you *haven't* waited, have you? " She looked up at him, her great eyes swimming with unshed tears, a hint of tears in her voice.

He said impatiently, " Just listen, will you? I haven't finished yet. There's plenty more to come. Of course I would have waited to hear your version, explanation, what have you, if you had one —although it would have had to have been a rattling good one, wouldn't it, in view of all this——" He indicated the sheaf of notes. But——"

" But you've only *her* word—and Gisela's—no *confirmation*——"

" I was coming to that. Please don't interrupt. Unfortunately, you see, the confirmation, as you call it, turned up at once. Yes. Right away. I finished with Mrs. Wragg—or rather, she with me— about midnight. I left her and came along here and here it was."

She sat up; there was a prickling down the back of her neck. No tears now. " What? " she said sharply.

" If we had the time, Milly, I'd give you three guesses. As it is, the—er—confirmation was in the shape of a note." He spoke quietly, biting off each word; a new voice to go with a new personality. " A note from Abe. To say—amongst other things—good-bye. I found it tucked in amongst some bottles he'd left for us, magazines and so on."

" Larry! But where—what's happened? What's he doing? Where is he now? "

" Now? " He looked at his watch. " In the Press Club in Berlin, at a guess. With any luck, that is. Getting stinking, probably."

" Why? Why didn't he wait to say good-bye? Why go like that? So—so suddenly . . . *Please*, please tell me."

" Don't cry. I'm trying to tell you. For two reasons. Firstly he was in a hurry. He had to get the five o'clock plane from Slavnik this morning. He would just have made it, I think. In fact, he had to make it. The train wouldn't have left till the afternoon and it takes ten hours to get to the frontier, so that wouldn't do. Abe had to be out of Slavonia by—let's see, in just about an hour from now. Ten-thirty. So for his sake I hope he's made it."

She leaned back, closed her eyes. " You mean—he was given twenty-four hours? "

" Exactly."

" But why? " Her voice was faint. She felt faint. "What had he done? "

" My guess is, nothing at all. However, according to his note the police found two large parcels of black-market stuff in his car, which contained, amongst other things, drugs. You can explain away most things but not drugs—not in any quantity, that is, and not those drugs— what were they now? " He picked up a list and glanced at it. " Mm. Hard to explain those away. Gisela wasn't sure if this was complete —still, it's pretty bad as it stands. Incriminating from every point of view including the moral one. Abe's very lucky to get out at all. He might have been made to stand trial for this, you know—and then there would have been a first-class stink."

" But he's—he didn't *know*," she said wearily, " he's quite——"

" Innocent? Oh, I know that."

" How do you know that? I suppose he said so in the note. You believe *him*—and everybody else—but not *me*, oh no . . ."

" On the contrary. That shows how little you know him. In the note he merely said that these things had been found and that he'd been given twenty-four hours and that they'd been gunning for him anyway, and that Alby deserved the break, and che sara sara. That's all he said. So, coupled with his having gone off without saying good-bye, that was the confirmation, and pretty conclusive, too, I reckon."

" I don't understand."

" Don't you? It's quite simple, logical, even, if you know Abe. He was in a hurry, but he knew where to find me—in the Wraggs' apartment. He had time to pack and leave the bottles and write the note and all that. It would have been quicker and easier for him to come and find me—why didn't he? He didn't want to, that's why. More than that, he wanted to avoid me, to get away without seeing me and to give himself sufficient start, because although he didn't know what Mrs. Wragg had to say, he wasn't taking any chances. He knew he hadn't put those parcels in the boot of his car—but I bet you when they arrested him, he knew right away who had. Don't forget, he's no fool and trained to be observant—I dare say all sorts of little details tumbled into place all at once—the way they did with me, too. So off he went, knowing that if he'd waited to see me, I'd have prevented

514

him going, and if he hadn't given himself a start—he knew I hadn't the car—I'd have done what in any case I had half a mind to do, only it was too late, chartered a taxi and followed him, yes, right to the airport, to stop him getting on that plane and putting paid to his career all because——"

"Because of me?" She gave a little moan. Being angry, Larry misinterpreted both the moan and the question; he would have misinterpreted anything from her at that moment, he was so angry.

"Because of you, certainly, but not, shall we say, on account of your blue eyes. Just because you, my wife, had taken it into her head to branch out as a crook, that's what I meant." She flushed, not so much at the words, but the tone in which they were spoken. She thought she might be going to cry in earnest. Not that it would have any effect. She could see that. Silent, he went on looking at her until she could bear it no longer.

"You mean," she said in a small voice, " it's because of me—all this——" She made a little gesture as if at a loss for a word to describe what she had wrought, and Larry supplied it.

"All this? Havoc, you mean? I'm afraid it looks like it. Unless you—well, *is* there anything you can say?"

There was no point in crying, nor in lying, either. " No," she said bravely.

"That's what I thought. So now you understand why I have to resign."

" But——"

" Mm?" He had gathered up the papers as if it were all over. Curious, he looked down at her. " Well, what?"

"Larry, you can't say I'm a—a *crook*." Sniffing, she dug her knuckles into her eyes, " because I'm not. Not a *crook*. Because I "—she looked up at him defiantly—" I haven't got *away* with anything, you see."

He considered her, and she saw a smile creep round his lips; a very odd little smile.

"Too bad," he said at last, quite kindly. "Too bad . . ." Then, as if on an afterthought, "What, nothing at all?"

The silence was frightening. His eyes never wavered from her face. Unable to meet them, she looked away, down at her hands in her lap. She had been about to protest; now the remembrance of what had seemed of paramount importance not so long ago and which had gone clean out of her mind, because one cannot think of two things at once, suddenly swept back into it. Like a relation one is ashamed of, a bad penny, " Well, here I am," it said, bouncing and bonny, large as life and twice as natural, sniffing round the old haunts, taking possession,

" here I am—didn't expect me, did you—back as you see and back to stay this time, I shouldn't be at all surprised."

He couldn't *know*, could he, about that? Not unless she were to tell him. It stood to reason he couldn't know, because nobody knew. But then she mustn't forget that she wasn't dealing with the same Larry any more, who would give her the benefit of the doubt and not investigate too closely anything that seemed a shade dubious—in short, with the Larry who trusted her. No. Now he was worse than a—a *detective*. He filled in gaps with guesses and very accurate guesses they were, too. Once he started guessing, there would be no stopping him. Give him one fact, one single stone, and he'd build on it with guesses, build up a fabrication of guesses designed to imitate the way he guessed the original to have been—and the finished product might well approximate in the essentials to the way it had been. But the trouble was with guessing that *she* would never know how much he had guessed. What he had constructed would be invisible to anyone but himself; invisible, moreover, to the authority, the originator of the design, the one who should, but did not, hold the copyright—and who, although aware that the copy existed, would just have to fret all his life, chewing his nails in rage, unable to take action and without hope of redress; unable, even, to pacify his artist's conscience, confront the copyist, take the bull by the horns and say: " Look, it's done now— I don't mind, but here you've got it quite wrong and there it wasn't like that."

He had her there. So, unless she threw in her hand and told him, she would have to live with it for ever—this not knowing what he might have guessed up, coupled with the sense of guilt which was new-born, only a few hours old, but already more positively unliveable with than anything she had ever come across.

But it's so *unfair*, she thought. Because I doubt if I ever meant to —even with Abe—and cornered, almost fancied she could hear Emma Bovary's mocking laughter. Madame Bovary manquée. It was all a trick, she told herself, venting her indignation on circumstance because if she couldn't have it both ways, better to plump for one—a trick. I was caught, it all happened before I knew where I was—but what wouldn't I give for it to be undone? So long as I don't tell him, I'm safe—but how can I live with it all my life? I don't think I can do that, not all my life. It looked as though a decision had been foisted upon her. How she hated decisions. Still, there it was. Realistic as ever when in a tight spot, gloomily she appreciated how tight it was— that the decision was probably very important, perhaps even the most important she had ever been required to make and now was the moment for it. The moment? The second, rather. She must be quick.

Tell him now before it's too late? It's a terrible risk—but after all he loves me. Oh, what shall I do? Why can't I make up my mind? Quick, Milly, be quick. The trouble was, she was tired and so she paused. He's tired too, she thought, he won't notice the pause. It was the last time she was ever to under-estimate Larry.

Because love betrays itself, and carries within itself the seeds of its own destruction; love acts as spy, reveals the password, in broad daylight lets the drawbridge down, and even obligingly provides the weapons for its own execution. Because he had loved her, her face could hold no secrets from him; as she pondered, he read it as if it were an open page and from it learned what he would greatly have preferred not to know. So it was Abe, he thought. If it had to be anybody, better perhaps it should have been Abe. It never occurred to him, then or afterwards, to blame his friend, now that he knew Milly so well.

" I'll take the risk," she decided. " Yes, I think so. It's worth it. He loves me. He's always loved me—so surely he'll go on loving me? Yes, now . . . now I'll see whether I can tell him . . . it'll depend on how he's looking . . . now I'll see . . ." Her heart hammering, she took a deep breath, ready to speak, and looked up in time to catch the expression on his face; guarded, set, that same odd little smile on the lips. But his eyes—they were cold, quite cold . . . she had never seen it before, that cold light in his eyes which told her more clearly than words that there had been no need for a decision, that even had she resolved to confess in order to rid herself of the burden on her conscience and place it, as was her custom, on him—even this relief was denied her. There was no point in confessing, not only because he already knew, but also because the unbelievable had happened—he had ceased to love her. A pity, for it was precisely at that moment that poor Milly, perverse as ever, fell head over heels in love and for the first time in her life; with him.

Someone was whistling next door.

" There's Cantrell," said Larry. " I'll go. It may take some time. If you want something to do, you'd better start packing."

* * *

" So that," he continued, getting up out of his arm-chair, " is that, I'm afraid."

" Hmmmmmmmmm." The colonel tugged gently, upwards, at the tip of the right-hand moustache. Then, as if his equilibrium depended on their remaining symmetrical, he gave the left the same treatment. " Hmmmmmmmm . . ." Having started off at Strength Nine, this would take quite a while to peter out. Suits me, thought Larry, as there seemed to be nothing much left to say.

" Let me get you another."

" Another? Certainly. That is, if you're not short, eh? Ha! " He laughed, or barked, as if to signal that this was a joke, which, in a way, Larry had to admit that it was. He gave the colonel his drink.

" Thanks. Hmm." He pecked suspiciously into his glass. His nose was thin and shiny, mottled pink and curved like a beak. When he looked up, which he did after he'd swigged half, and opened his eyes, Larry, noting that they tallied with Abe's description, being a light fierce bright blue, was tempted to launch into an arithmetical progression in order to make up for lost time and catch up to what he now saw might approximate to the right answer.

" So what d'you expect *us* to do? " Cantrell shot at him irritably, taking him completely off his guard.

" Well," he stammered, " I mean, I thought—er—as I've *resigned* . . ."

It was as if the skep had been taken off a whole hive of bees. " Hmmmmmm . . . hmmmmmm mm . . . *as you've what?* " he rapped out, suddenly, unfairly, dropping the skep back into place.

" R-resigned," said Larry. " I thought . . ."

The colonel purred, lapping up the last few drops; and then, in rather a silky voice, " How long've you been in this show, Purdoe? "

" In the——? Oh, since the—the war." He counted up the years. A decade, nearly. So it was.

" Just what I thought! " snorted Cantrell. " Trouble with you temporary wallahs is, you're weak on procedure. Scamp your paper work. Shun it, even. See it all along the line. Slapdash. Think you can hop skip and jump over this and that—I don't know where we'd be if we didn't adhere to procedure. This verbal sort of nonsense won't do at all. Come now, d'you really think this is the way—idle chit-chat over a drink—to convey a decision of such a nature "—his voice dropped low—" to the *Department*? Do you really think you can approach them like *that*? "

" No," said Larry truthfully, and Cantrell, ever so faintly, smiled. " But I thought it might be an—an emergency."

" An *emergency*? " The beak became veined with scarlet. " Hmmmmmm . . ." The skep was lifted again, and very angry they were as they emerged. " Hmmmmmm . . . If *I* decide that an emergency, as you call it, exists which calls for action, then I shall take action. That's what I'm paid to do. As a matter of fact, I think you're probably right. We'll come to that. Let's get this straight first. You haven't resigned.

Oh dear me no, ha-ha. It's not as easy as that." He went on, his voice dangerously soft, caressing—almost: "You can't consider you've *resigned*, Purdoe, until the Powers that Be have *accepted* your . . . er . . ." he chuckled, "*resignation* . . . the intimation of which must first of all be submitted to me in triplicate—I think, triplicate—and then, if and when I see fit—well, the camel through the eye of the needle is a piece of cake compared with what happens after that—get it? Good. Of course," he added blithely, with a look which caused Larry, too, to add—noughts, at random, to what he'd totalled so far, "what usually happens is, they terminate your contract. Which they can do just like that. In triplicate, I dare say—but their carbons, not yours. With a month's notice," he concluded, in the manner of one providing a real straw of comfort.

"But, I don't see—I mean, I can't *stay*, can I?"

"Stay? Ha-ha "—a bark—" oh no, you certainly can't *stay*," he agreed with an alacrity that dashed Larry's last hope to the ground.

There was silence, Cantrell having produced a gold pencil and a diary from his pocket; yawning, he began going through the diary, starting with January.

"So . . . we'll have to go? . . ." ventured Larry at last, seeing that the colonel's commitments in May appeared to have been heavy, and might in June have become even heavier.

"So you will," he murmured. Still engrossed, fastidiously raising the fringe of the moustache, he tapped his right upper canine with the pencil; then he tapped the left one. He went on tapping for a bit, doing a thorough check-up all round. Selfish old bee, thought Larry. Typical admin. Who cares about his bloody teeth? I hope they give him hell.

"Tst." He shook his head, and pretty well automatically held out his glass. "Thanks very much." He looked up. "Quite right, you've got to go, my boy. Sooner the better. Train to-morrow evening? That charming little wife of yours—can she get packed up by then? Got no one to help her, poor girl."

Handing him his drink, Larry said, rather stiffly, he hoped: "She's getting down to it now."

"Good, good. Go by boat, eh?" he suggested kindly, mellowed by the first sip of his fourth or fifth glass, as if, had they wished for more exotic means by which to make their exodus, a caravan of dromedaries, say, he could have arranged it. "Don't worry, I'll fix that. Hmmmmmmmmm."

Larry thought viciously, go on humming, grinning, soaking up my whisky. Just make yourself at home, that's right. It's only me, a temporary wallah. Plenty more where I come from. Room for one here—Purdoe's out. Hm. Was that *all* he could say? A dubious hmmm . . . perhaps it was a suitable epitaph.

" Never met the Simpsons, did you? "

And one thing I do promise myself, if anyone, ever—and I don't care even if it's the Secretary of State himself—asks me that again, I shall open my mouth and——

" Ah, of course, I remember now," said Cantrell, with a lot of elaborate by-play to indicate that he had indeed been prodded into recollection, " left before you came, didn't they? " and then spoilt the effect—causing Larry to deduct in spite of Abe's warning—by remarking: " That was arranged expressly, of course. That you shouldn't meet. Hmmmmmmmmm." Dreamily he dug away at a lower molar before he continued. " Charming chap, Simpson. Easy-going. Very well liked. Pleasant wife. Hmmmm." (That buzzing—he'd identified it wrongly. It wasn't bees—at least it wasn't now—it was more like the buzzer from the bridge down to the engine-room to indicate the presence of shoals in the immediate vicinity, visible only to Cantrell himself, who was on the bridge at the wheel, and who would undoubtedly steer clear but wished (a) everyone present to recognise what a bloody good helmsman he was, and (b) to keep everyone on their toes.) " Been here for years, Simpson. Good old days, you know, just after the war. Dug themselves in. Even a bit deep, perhaps." He paused, and in the silence began tapping away at the lower molars again, one by one. They all gave out the same dull thud. Larry was reminded of the railwayman in *Anna Karenina*; anyway, the calculated effect was much the same, sinister. " Know why they left? "

" I didn't know until—well, Schulman did tell me something about it last night."

" Last night, eh? " He grinned cheerfully. " Had your eyes opened a bit in the last twenty-four hours, haven't you? "

Was it really to be described like that, what had happened? Well, perhaps. In that case, he certainly had.

Cantrell grunted into his glass. " So we can cut the watchamacallit and come to the 'osses." He really did pronounce it " 'osses," with a complacent glance at his long legs stretched out in front of him. He had, and it was clear that he knew he had, what is known as a good leg for a boot. " It was an experiment, d'you see? I mean, getting you here, chap without a clue—sorry, you know what I mean —and not briefing you into the bargain—(deduct for that, thought Larry)—an experiment, which I may say," he glanced over his shoulder as if the hidden microphones he feared were those that might be linked directly with Whitehall, " I, personally, was against. Hmmmm.

520

In my opinion, it was too much to ask. Hmmmm. Take Simpson, now. He'd've been all right on his own, but—BUT—he had—as most of us do have, ha-ha, thank God, hmmm . . . a wife. It's all right for the chap. He's got the job. But it's a different matter for the girl —I'm not talking about Slavnik, mind! Anyone who goes off the rails in Slavnik gets no sympathy from me. Too many ruddy parties. Too many wives—too much nattering over canasta, coffee, and so on. They all egg each other on—from the wives of Chancery Guards up to—well, I won't go into *that* . . . but if I find they're salting away their pay, not even drawing their allowances and still apparently chucking it about—any hanky-panky with the NAAFI or the bag, by God, they're out! Out they go, neck and crop, husbands along with the wives—if they can't keep them in order that's their look-out. And they can be the direct descendants of Charles James Fox and marchionesses in their own right, I don't care—I'll still get 'em out! I dare say I'll get you out. It may come to that. But in these smaller posts—the way I see it, it's a very different kettle of fish. For instance, take a place like this—isolated, not much to do. Take someone still young, neat, attractive, naturally sociable—like——" He had been about to say " like your wife," but he thought, hallo-'allo, something's up, something else, pity, not my business, and swept on: " See what I mean, don't you? Put her down here and—well." He shook his head, not for long. " Another point," he said, with a different voice for it, " and I'd like you to listen rather carefully," he added, seeing that Larry was not. " I dare say you'll think me very cynical. I've met Schulman. I'd say, definitely a good type. I understand how you feel." Ha!—got his attention now.

Do you? thought Larry, raising his head. Do you really, you old something you. Seeing that the glass held out to him was empty, however, he meekly went and filled it.

" But Schulman had had his run, you know—he couldn't've expected to last for ever. Besides," Cantrell went on, as pontifical as if his proper element were the Savile, his delight, post-prandial frolics with arm-chair-fellows Messrs. Allen & Snow, Snow & Allen and the like: " I gather his stuff's been falling off a bit. Maybe he *needed* something like this—a jolt, injection . . . fresh what's it and all that. This'll give him a gallop. Now he's been kicked out he can write a novel. That's what he *ought* to be doing. Ha! Not enough novels. Great reader myself—order 'em out by the ton—but not enough of 'em—know why? I'll tell you. They're lazy bastards, these writers. Loafers. Hmmm." He paused to brood for a second, in his eye the disgruntled gleam of the fiction addict who has the cash all ready to push down the right slot and in return expects no more than five minutes' time-lag, and, at the very least, that all machines shall be working. " Oh, Schulman'll turn up in South America or somewhere —you mark my words; just as soon as they go poppity-pop-pop-pop. . . . What's the matter? "

" I don't know," said Larry. " I can't look at it that way, somehow. You see, he was—well, he was happy here."

" *Happy?* " bellowed the colonel. " *Happy?* Good God, it's not his business to be *happy*—he's a writer, isn't he? Is he or isn't he, correct me if I'm wrong? " He added gravely, as if contributing the result of his own researches into the habits of a comparatively rare sub-species: " They can't write if they're happy, you know."

" Oh. No, I didn't know that."

" Fact. Hmmmmmmm. Anyway, neither here nor there—I'm afraid I have to look at it this way. Much as I liked Schulman, he is not, I am thankful to say, our responsibility. Joe Schwelling hasn't got so much on his plate at the moment and Schulman goes slap on to it because he's entirely his pigeon—thank God—and no question of carving him up. In other words, we can't have your departure tying up with Schulman's."

" But it will, won't it? "

" No, it won't," said Cantrell brutally. " Although it might've done if you'd made some idiotic attempt," he grinned, " as I dare say it crossed your mind to do—to get Schulman out of the mess—clean breasts at the airport and so on. Oh no, we can't have that sort of thing. We've had too many headaches lately caused by romantic tomfoolery—take that row six months ago, which involved directly or indirectly not only every single person in our Embassy but four departments at home including M.I.5 and also the French, the Americans, and the Swiss, all on account of some bloody fool who came swanning in to collect his bit of frat—couldn't even keep his eye on the ball doing it and fell into the harbour he was so tight. Well, they had him sitting on packed ice in no time and serve him right. A pain in the neck for everybody concerned and yet I suppose he thought he was a helluva chap while he was doing it. He's got bags of time to think it over now." He chuckled cruelly. " What I mean is, Purdoe, just such a row could flare up over this. They—the Slavonians— would be perfectly entitled, if they felt like it, to search all diplomatic bags from now on—ha-ha, then you *would* be popular. Packed ice in a Commie gaol would be a picnic to what you'd get when you got home. But don't worry—it won't happen like that. It's all worked out quite well, by a fluke. I mean, my coming down here to-day and so on." He puffed gently, visibly self-inflating.

" Yes," said Larry, wishing him at the ends of the earth.

522

" So you're getting out of here to-morrow night. You're going for two reasons. I don't care what the police know, they've got their human sacrifice and they can lick their chops over that. Ha! Ostensibly, you're going on transfer."

Larry looked up.

" Ostensibly, I said," purred the colonel, licking his own chops with delight. " I came down here expressly to tell you that. Get it? The other reason Miss Raven has obligingly provided us with. Very upsetting affair. We aren't quite heartless, you know." He smirked. " Your wife's very upset—change of scene wanted, etc. Well, she is, isn't she? Upset, I mean."

" Yes, I think she is."

" So no nonsense about resignation now. Don't go shooting your mouth off to anyone about that. Hope you haven't been? "

" No," said Larry rather stiffly. " There's no one to do it to."

" Good. You can't resign, d'you see, and then bugger off. That would give rise to—you can't anyway, of course, as I hope I've made *quite clear*." The blue eyes bored into him.

You had to hand it to the old boy—it hadn't all been pure waffle—there'd been something behind all that initial tirade, too.

" Now, hmmmmm . . . We come to the last point, or points rather. I feel I owe it to you—if you'll bear with me. . . ."

What the hell does he think I've been doing, Larry asked himself, plodding off on the familiar chore. Three-quarters of a bottle, he reflected, that's what it had cost so far, just to get the sack. What an outfit. When he came back with the glasses, Cantrell had risen and was standing in front of the mirror, yawning and stroking his face. At one time he must have worn sideburns; he looked as if he were seriously considering the advisability of re-embarking on the venture. " Baa . . . haaha . . . Where were we? Ah yes, thanks." He grinned. " Sorry you had to go and flog your NAAFI, Purdoe. That's bad—very bad, as I've been at pains to explain. Your—er—account—of your transactions, however, was not over-explicit. It occurs to me, for instance, to wonder why, after indulging in what must clearly have been a thriving trade, you should suddenly see fit to unburden yourself of your guilt—quite apart from any sentimental regrets you may be having as to the fate of the late Schulman. Hmmmmm . . . we've had all sorts of reports about you and one thing does stand out a—well, eschewing hyperbole, does stand out, that you have a head on your shoulders. I should say you were not—mind you, I don't know you—a chap given to sudden fits of amnesia. You'd be unlikely to leave—out of sheer carelessness—incriminating evidence lying about in a friend's car. I mean, if you're so rich, you must be smart, too, mustn't you? And

523

you certainly didn't plant it there on purpose. I'm inclined to wonder, d'you see, whether you ever put it there at all? Hm. No, I'm afraid— very much afraid—you haven't been entirely frank with me, which wasn't fair, you know, and unwise, too, because supposing I—and I'm the only one who can save your bacon now—had been as green as you clearly suppose me to be—I'd have been all at sea." The improbability of his ever being so placed caused him to smile modestly. Even Larry had to smile too.

" No. I fear how it strikes me is, that once more it's a case of— quite customary in my experience, I assure you—of . . . er . . . cherchez la femme." The colonel stroked the fertile itching flesh round his jowls. " Trouble is, you see, I'm not as green as I'm cabbage-looking . . . ha-ha. When I sloped off just then . . . after the—incident . . . I did think your wife looked upset, poor girl . . . well, while I was putting through a call to Slavnik downstairs at the desk, it so happened that I was waylaid—*waylaid*," he repeated, as if this were a word that he took especial pleasure in using, and encouraging Larry to suspect that the colonel had not been waylaid at all, " by a lady who—although I've met her before once or twice, always succeeds in putting the fear of God into me. Wife of your colleague. Mrs. Wragg."

" I see. You mean she told you? So you know all about it then— you knew all the time? "

" Oh, come now. Well, in a way, yes," Cantrell admitted, meekly, for him. " But wait a minute. Mrs. Wragg—Ethel, Edna, is it? Oh yes, Olga—she certainly did seem to be bursting with good news and so—as I'd already been up to see you and, I do hope you'll forgive me, one didn't have to be a Sherlock Holmes to get wind that something was wrong—especially as I'd heard about Schulman on the news this morning—I'm afraid I did accept her invitation to pop in for a—I forget what she called it but I know what I got. The courage of these amateur drinkers! I've noticed it before. Mrs. Wragg's notion of a pick-me-up was half a tumbler of gin sizzlin' with raspberry pop. Now gin's not my drink," he said. " I know my poison and I stick to it."

" Another? "

" Well, that's very kind of you. Luckily, I didn't have to lower much of this red biddy because she'd hardly got properly under way with her tale—though, mind you, I'd got the gist of it——"

I bet, thought Larry.

"——before Wragg himself appeared, bless him, with a bottle of the right grog. *The* bottle, as Mrs. Wragg said darkly—because we happened to have got on as far as that, you see." He smiled winningly. " But believe me, they were the last words I heard her speak. *Extraordinary* chap, Wragg—isn't he? I mean the way he's changed. Perhaps

524

you haven't noticed it? Well—we were in the kitchen, you see, because obviously what she had to say was private—and Wragg, if you please, simply picked up my glass of pink stuff and poured it down the sink. Then turning to me he said, we'll go next door, shall we, and turning to her, with a pretty chilling look, he said, I'd rather you didn't disturb us, Edna, or Olga, or whatever it is—and I thought, you know, now there's going to be some argy-bargy but not a bit of it. She came to heel all right. Banged about a bit in the sink but I dare say she always does that. As for me I nipped in next door sharpish. Funny, eh? She's not exactly my idea of a doormat. Is she yours?"

" No," said Larry.

" Bloody marvellous," said Cantrell simply. " The man's trans- formed, at least compared with when I saw him, which was on the occasion of—Simpson," he finished lamely. " So, there we were, Wragg and I, and I'm afraid I pumped him for all I was worth. Oh, lord, yes." He smiled his engaging smile. " It is my job, d'you see," he said gently, as if divining Larry's thoughts, " and I didn't know you were going to come clean, did I? Even Olga Wragg wasn't taking any chances on that—though I can't say I give her any marks for anticipating it. Besides, I don't like dealing with women, especially when another woman's concerned. So I worked away on Herbert Wragg—who, I judged from previous experience, would not be back- ward in coming forward . . . Hmmm."

" I see. And what—I mean, did he? Was he? "

With a dramatic swoop Cantrell clashed his glass down on the mantelpiece. " Got no change out of him at all! Not a single solitary sausage. In other words "—the eyes were awful, brighter, fiercer than ever, but just then Larry thought he caught a fleeting twinkle in them —" I was wrong! Of course, his wife had told him the tale, yet the extraordinary thing is that he maintained, and I believe he'd have gone to the stake for it, that it was all a monstrous concoction of lies. Now, in a parallel situation, when Simpson . . . er . . . Wragg was only too keen to give chapter and verse and I fear I took against him on that account. I made a mistake, if you like—another one. He was in the running for Simpson's job, d'you see . . . but I summed him up as a chap with a chip on . . . hmmmm . . . tricky post . . . no good on his own . . . hmmm . . . so—he didn't get it. But *this* time, I couldn't shake him—although I tried, of course. What's more, he expressed in no uncertain terms his admiration for you and the work you've done here . . . and really, my questions were leading ones and there was every opportunity . . . but what struck me most of all was his *manner*. It's not too much to say that I wouldn't've recognised him for the same man. The way he handled Edna—Gunga Din, you know and all that.

525

Remarkable. And the right grog produced at the right moment and that gutrot going down the sink. Well, one can't help thinking—that's the sort of chap we want. See what I'm leading up to?"

"Of course," said Larry wearily.

Cantrell let out a guffaw which he stifled with an ivory silk handkerchief, and began, unnecessarily, polishing up the bridge of his nose, groomed its scarlet-veined recesses with a decently swathed forefinger and tossed off the remains of his whisky—his last, Larry decided privately, that was to be.

"You do, do you?" he said, still chuckling. "Well, just to make sure we see eye to eye, because there are several ways of looking at things, I'll tell you how I see it—from the Admin. angle, that is. Because that's what I am, I'm afraid, Admin."

You don't say, thought Larry; the colonel looking rather coy.

"Wragg will take over your job—on trial, of course," he qualified hastily. "Still, that's neither here nor there. The point is, you." Larry tried to prevent a mild interest from displaying itself on his features. "Hmm. You. I see it this way. We get bags of chaps—eager beavers, you know, A1 at their jobs—but can they leave them? No. They like to think they're indispensable so they bloody well try and make themselves indispensable. The way they do it is, they don't delegate responsibility; they mug up everything they can from the files and after that they don't use 'em; don't trust 'em, see? Because any promisin' young whippersnapper might get at those same files and mug up stuff, too—so they keep everything locked up in their heads. In other words, they aren't prepared to see themselves as units in a team. Now if there's one thing I've learned it's this. No one is indispensable. And my marks go to the man who can produce, at the drop of a hat and from the most unlikely material—don't repeat this, of course—a successor. To do that requires patience and sympathy and—well, you've got to be able to *teach*. Hmmmm. So—as regards the present situation, which you rightly describe as an emergency, I've told you what immediate action I propose. Off you go and Wragg takes over. Apart from that I consider that you came here totally unprepared and ill-equipped for what you were asked to do. Your wife—of course I don't know her—but possibly more sinned against than sinning, eh?"

You silly old fool, thought Larry. Though he wasn't old if you looked closely. Perhaps there were no more than ten years between them.

"A toughish deal, anyway. In fact, there are in my opinion, Purdoe, extenuating circumstances. Now, very likely you're going to be out on your ear in a month from now. Just forget that for the minute—if you can. I want to ask you something."

526

He suddenly looked intensely serious—at least he stared into his empty glass without being reminded to ask for another. " Taking into account what I've said, also the fact that you are, from our point of view, not without your uses—that is, you get on with people, you bring out the . . . er . . . best . . . hmmm . . . and so on . . . and also taking into account the . . . er . . . other factors . . . women in the case, and so on—all this is quite a do, isn't it? Boiled up in a big way." He looked Larry straight in the eye. " Who do you think is to blame? "

" I am," said Larry, without the least hesitation.

" That's right." Cantrell nodded rather sadly. " I'm afraid that's true. Of course you know what I'm driving at, otherwise you wouldn't've answered like that. One could, and one might argue that one was justified, distribute the blame over a widish field so that only a negligible proportion rested on you, but I don't see it like that; nor do you, do you?—now. No. That's my point—my last, you'll be glad to hear. Personality's a very dangerous thing. To be administered in small doses. Funnily enough, the flamboyant ones aren't the ones who do the most damage; it's the charmers who corrupt. What people go for is sympathy—well, they shouldn't have it, not in large doses, because then they become addicts—unless of course, one's in a position to go the whole hog. In the long run—and especially with women— you've just got to be tough. Otherwise," he coughed demurely, " one's likely to get oneself into a fearful jam."

" You mean I'm responsible for Miss Raven, too."

" No, I don't say that. But I dare say . . . with a little foresight . . . not my business, that. It would've happened anyway. No, I wasn't thinking of her—entirely. At least, not so much. Funny thing is," he went on, as if afraid he might not have made himself clear, which he had, " women actually *like* one to be tough. Of course it's tough having to be tough. Find it hard myself, now and then—still, Gunga Din, you know, and all that."

Who *was* Gunga Din? That was one thing Larry was determined to find out.

" Still——" the colonel hesitated, casting a wistful look at his glass. " Oh, thanks very much. We'll go down to eat after this. You'll be off to-morrow and I wouldn't say this unless—well—thanks—you know, one's inclined to get things a bit out of focus in these parts. So don't brood on it too much. Just wait till you get the first sniff of the breeze from the Kiel Canal. You'll know what I mean, then. By the way, expect a signal from me on board. Oh, and now I come to think of it—I gave you the wrong gen just now. I believe it has to be in *quin*tuplicate . . . hmmm . . . hope you're well supplied with carbons . . . ha-ha. . . ."

527

He was chuckling when the door opened and Milly came in. Larry, who barely glanced at her, saw the colonel's chuckle change to a smirk. Well, that was Milly. She'd have old Charon smirking as she waited to cross the Styx. She would always manage, come hell or high water, to look very nice.

All the same, he wondered about the chuckle that had gone before. In a way Cantrell was right; he had to hand it to him. And as for Cantrell himself, it made a pretty alarming total, even done by simple addition; only at the start had he been tempted to deduct. Yes, Cantrell was right—so far as he went. Nevertheless, Larry had a suspicion that the whole business wouldn't stop there; although neither he nor Cantrell might be able to go further than the point now reached, it might go much further than they would ever know—at any rate, further than that.

Chapter Six

MILLY AWOKE at dawn to the familiar sound of the carts coming into market; the rumbling of wheels, the creaking of harness, the whine of an unoiled axle, now and then the crack of a whip and a shout; one by one they went past beneath the window, like an army on the move, in endless procession. These were the same carts she had passed the evening before, fifty miles away. Still half asleep, she remembered that this was the last day; she would never hear them again. Instead of burrowing down into the warmth under the quilt she got out of bed, tiptoed to the window and pulled the curtain aside.

As always, a yellow haze of fog clung round the street lamps. The town still slept and the sky was dark as night. She could see the whole length of the street under the dim glow of the lamps, and she rubbed her eyes in amazement. The street was deserted, except for a single cart grinding its way towards the hotel—and yet the sound was the same as ever, the sound of a long stream of carts in procession. Almost at once she understood the reason for the misconception. As if the cart were passing through a deep canyon, the rumbling of the wheels was echoed by the stone façades of the buildings that towered on either side of the street, so becoming exaggerated, distorted, to give the impression of many where in reality there was but this one, moving at a snail's pace, the peasant and his wife huddled together, welded into a solid mass up in front. Passing beneath the window, the peasant twitched the whip and grunted to the horse; these sounds, instantly magnified, were echoed down the street. She watched the cart turn the corner out of sight, but the rumbling of wheels was loud as ever, and glancing the other way, she saw that another had already appeared, travelling in the same direction as the first with the length of the street between them, and already the commands of the driver of this next cart were audible, ringing down the street. And so it was with the next and the next. Although barefoot, shivering, she stayed to watch, because it seemed important, for some reason, to have proof that all along she had been under a delusion. A trick, she whispered, that's what it is, just a trick. Now she knew the secret—and yet, how strange; if it hadn't been the last day, she would never have troubled to get up and see for herself, and so very likely would have continued to imagine what was not, a vast procession.

From far off she heard the rattle of the first tram as it approached and then she saw it, the other side of the square, looping the corner like a jewelled centipede, smoothing itself out, sliding to a halt; and at once a covey of shadows flitted over the snow towards it. A man on a bicycle skimmed down the street, past the hotel, pedalling as if for dear life. A woman with a shawl over her head ran across the street right in front of the cart that was passing; the horse dug its heels in, reared as if it had seen a ghost, and the driver, disentangling his shape from that of his wife, leaned forward and brought the whip down with a crack on the horse's back, and as the crack echoed, cracked and cracked again, the first notes of the bugle call floated out, high above the town, high and sweet—a call to awake, a call to arms, a call to stir each living heart; up, up, it soared, wild, unearthly, and yet triumphant —as if the bugler, in that instant before the arrow pierced his throat, had glimpsed beyond the invading legions, victory. Up it soared, and stopped; and the town slept on.

Six o'clock. The last day had begun. Wrapping herself in her dressing-gown, she put on the bedside light and got busy with lists. There was so much to be done.

*　　　*　　　*

Gisela, who had slept through the whole of the preceeding day, had scarcely slept at all that night and now at dawn she, too, was listening to the carts coming in. To-day, she thought, many things may happen. To-day she would know. Mrs. Wragg's maid, Helga, was keeping her informed. To-day, come what might, she must venture out—to buy food, for one thing. She had eaten nothing for the past forty-eight hours and she would need her strength. Also she must make arrangements, depending on the news she would receive. She was almost certain, from the commotion in the kitchen late last evening, tins being pulled from shelves, paper rustling, the sounds of packing, that things had gone well. If that were the case, then she must act at once—immediately set about claiming her reward. Immediately? That wasn't soon enough—low-down scum that he was.

And otherwise? There was no otherwise. She had gone into all that. In the meantime, this room was her fortress; only here was she safe; but once *they* had left, if they were going, there would be no one to defend her rights. Particularly she must beware of the housekeeper, who was her enemy: later, when she went out, she must manage to leave unobserved. There was the back way. She had plenty of English cigarettes. If the gates were shut she would have to bribe the old fool with the dog.

530

She switched on the light, wondering why it was that she should be filled with dread at the thought of the day to come. Above all, she dreaded the thought of leaving this room—even for a short while. Although its walls had been those of a prison during the last two days, it had become home to her; a homely prison. But she must dress and make herself especially neat and go out—after the maids had done the rooms, after the housekeeper had been on her rounds. Towards midday, then—or even later? Later, perhaps, because by midday her luck would have changed.

Reminded of this, she reached down under her bed, pulled out her box and took from it her father's tattered book. She spread it open on her knee, under the light. Here were all the secrets of his craft, written in his spiky hand, arranged in orderly fashion; first the formulæ for spells, and spells for undoing spells cast, and then, listed under the various symptoms, cough, fever, flatulence, and so on, the corresponding remedies for each, the required simples, or recipes for tisanes, purges or sleeping draughts, and listed by name in cross-reference the different herbs, berries, roots, their therapeutic and/or toxic properties and precisely, most being bi-functional, to what extent each was each, and in the case of the latter, the toxic, the appropriate antidote—all this data was carefully set down. But by far the greater part of the book was devoted to the principles of astrology and of palmistry, and the interpretation of omens. Gisela possessed a further treasure, bought from a travelling salesman in the Kanetta market; this was her personal calendar for the year, plotted according to the hour and date of her birth. After consulting both these authorities, she interpreted their joint verdict (that was in opposition to what every instinct, every nerve in her body, cell in her brain, seemed to be telling her) as signifying that the omens for the day were neither propitious nor unpropitious; that there was nothing whatsoever to suggest that this day that was dawning promised great events before its close, or would prove remarkable in any way at all; in short, nothing that appeared to distinguish it from any other. The authorities being what they were, absolute, yielding easily to their persuasion, she lay down and fell into a light, troubled sleep.

*   *   *

As the effects of the injection began to wear off, Miss Raven became more restless. Struggling from the coils of nightmare, she awoke in a sweat to the sounds outside her window, the cracking of a whip, a rough voice raised in a shout, so that she felt herself to be still in her dream, these sounds being part of it.

She had dreamed that she was a girl again, that she was back in the

531

grim little kitchen in the slate-grey semi-detached, two up and two down, which was part of Arcadia Villas in a street of identical slate-grey semi-detacheds which was Arcadia Terrace, in the slate-grey city of Huddersfield, Yorks. And she had dreamed of her father, a strict Wesleyan and a big burly man, who, partly because his wife, a colourless uncomplaining creature, had one day upped and left him for someone else, and partly because of his status on Sundays which denied him the pleasures of other men during the week—pubs, dogs, football were not for him—had often been bored; especially on Saturday afternoon. She had dreamed that it had been just such a Saturday—when he would work himself into a slow mounting rage as the grey afternoon wore on, until the grey dusk fell and the curtains were drawn. Then they would give him his tea, she and her sister, with a bit of bacon, perhaps, to soothe him—and the way they handed it to him they might have been pushing it through bars—and when he had finished and was sucking his moustaches, he would only have to hear the footsteps slapping down the wet grey pavements, the footsteps of his colleagues at the works, off to enjoy themselves, for him to feel the need of a little enjoyment, too—of the only sort that was available to him, nevertheless of the sort that he had come to fancy. So that if the tea were not scalded to his liking or the bacon had been fat, not lean, or lean, not fat, or failing any of these failings there were the housekeeping accounts —whatever it was, it would all end up the same way, a routine. Unbuckling his belt, he would growl to one or other of them to get upstairs, to the dark icy bedroom with the texts on the walls, where one or other of them would lie like a sack across the bed; even now, in her dream, if it was a dream, she could feel the slippery art silk coverlet under her fingers, hear her own whimpering and the belt swishing through the air and his harsh breathing and the way it would slacken off when at last he would find, as eventually he always did find, after recreation of this sort, some spiritual peace.

They had one prayer in common, she and her sister, that on reaching the climax of one of these treats he might one day drop down dead—and yet when he had been killed in an accident they had buried him in style and both of them had wept. Now, in the dark, she recognised the whimpering, and the other sounds too, and the terrifying thought sprang from the place where all those years it had lurked, reigned supreme over an underworld where all things crawled, crept or lurked—from the back of her mind to confront her —he was not dead. That harsh excited breathing, she'd know it anywhere . . . even—no, especially—in the dark. He was here. He was somewhere in the room.

Turning her face to the pillow, she willed herself out of reach, escaped to that refuge which she had found no other being in all the world, only she herself, could provide.

*   *   *

Clarissa, too, had been awakened by the sound of the carts, and when she heard the jingling of the harness and the clickety-clack of the hoofs over the patches that were bare of snow, now and then a whinny, she put her head under the bedclothes because these sounds brought her and her dilemma face to face.

As yet she had taken nobody, not even her father, into her confidence. She was quite sure that as yet they none of them suspected —but what would they do when they found out? They'd find out any day now; there had already been all sorts of veiled allusions to it, threats of what had become a permanent threat. Yet surely it must have occurred to them to wonder why she had learned to read by herself; had learned how to add and subtract, although she hated it, and she could spell very well, they all said that. If they didn't connect these things up, then they were stupid; if they didn't suspect the truth —that she was a girl who couldn't go to . . . S-C-H-O-O-L. . . .

She herself had accepted the fact as soon as she had discovered that it was one, last summer, when she had gone to stay with her cousins, Jennifer and Jean; but from various bits of gossip let slip she had an idea that the adults in whose charge she was might not accept it in the same phlegmatic spirit. They might, when confronted with it, argue—but no argument would prevail. They might even attempt to coerce her—but if they did anything so foolish she would simply run away. There were other promising possibilities as means to evasion, but on closer inspection it seemed that whichever way she looked a lifetime of deception confronted her. A weak heart was the thing. She tested this organ now, briskly rubbing her bony rib-case on the left-hand side. It wasn't beating at all: which could only prove that she was dead, which she wasn't. Besides, even if one felt a beat, how could one tell if it was a *weak* beat? Only by comparing it with Dermot's and he might object, or sneak. It would have been the best bet, the heart, but it was by no means the last hope; not a bone in her body but might be conscripted to serve.

The main thing was, never, never to breathe a word, a hint, as to the real reason why she couldn't, etc. . . . because the moment they divined what it was that *really* made you feel sicker than anything else, like mutton fat, or of what *really* it frightened you to do more than anything else, like getting up on top of a horse, automatically they made you eat it, or do it. It was a way they had. There was simply no trusting them with confidences of that sort.

533

Her cousins, although silly and dull in every other respect, had been quite right about *that*—about YOU KNOW WHAT. When she had asked Jennifer—who was thirteen and wore steel-rimmed spectacles and pretended it was on account of these that she couldn't jump from the hay-loft to the granary floor and yet swanked about them and her visit to the oculist and the things he had said so that her piggy eyes formed her only other topic of conversation—*why* she liked IT—Jennifer, looking more owlish than piggy, owing to her precious aids, had replied: " Because we ride."

Well, she might have known it. Because that was the other topic of conversation, the primary one, between the two sisters, and one which excluded their guest: intimate revelations concerning the characters, performances, details of toilet, foibles of diet, of one's Moppet and Betsinda, who, it turned out, were not *people* at all, but a brace of these hateful brutes. Jennifer even had a photograph of one of them over her bed, astride it a plump and pig-tailed unknown. " Betsinda," Jennifer had explained and, blushing, added something else which sounded like " andsmithcauliflower." Clarissa said, " what?" and Jennifer replied crossly: " She's a *prefect* and it's a *double barrelled name*! " It was then that Clarissa had had her first suspicions as regards the nature of the whole project, and she had asked, casually, she hoped: " At your—er—I mean, do you *have* to ride? " And Jennifer's eyes had clouded over strangely. " I don't suppose you *have* to," she had said, " but everybody does. The ones who don't have a pretty beastly time."

Then it had all been confirmed, of course, in print. She had been very cunning in her choice of reading matter, gleaning her facts where she might; from several school annuals, two Angela Brazils lent by Sophie, and a batch of magazines sent down from the Embassy library as being suitable for one of her sex and years, all of which she had enjoyed enormously, except that in each and every one, on almost every page, there was underlined the basic reason why she herself could never go . . . to . . . The golden-haired games' mistress was a passionate horsewoman; the head prefect, cornflower blue eyes and almost invariably d-b name, was constantly throwing her shapely limbs athwart sorrel or chestnut steed and nipping off cross-country with a maniacal disregard for personal safety; and the shy, persecuted new girl (brought up on a ranch, but this revelation withheld until the last page) became overnight The Most Popular Girl In The . . . on account of having volunteered in the nick of time to understudy for some damaged colleague in the Gymkhana—which only left Mona, a dreadful scholarship girl with spectacles—rather like Jennifer, actually, from the illustrations—who, in addition to a weakness for pinching valuable bracelets from people's lockers, couldn't or wouldn't ride, or fell off when she was on, or was too miserably poor to afford the proper vestments, or acquitted herself in some otherwise discreditable manner vis-à-vis the sacred beasts.

" I'm not going to be a Mona," said Clarissa stubbornly under the quilt. " I don't see why I should. But I'm not going to ride either." Although far from impervious to the charms of games' mistress and head prefect, she was no nearer to a solution. " Oh, well," she thought, " in that case, I just can't go—to——" She slept a little after that but the jingling of the harness persisted through her dreams.

*   *   *

And Singe, too, heard the carts, and welcomed the sound. She had been awake for a long time. She never slept now after three or four in the morning, because it was just about then that the pain, which remained quiescent in her finger-tips during the night, began to wake up, too, and to shoot all the way up her wrists as far as the elbows, and no matter how she twisted and turned she could not drive those five separate pains in each arm, ten in all, back to their customary quarters, the finger-tips. It was the cold that brought it on. Each winter seemed colder than the last. Each day of this winter seemed colder than the day preceding it. Each dawn was colder than the day that followed, and yet the next dawn would be colder still.

It had been a major disaster when, at the very start of the winter, the rubber hot-water bottle, fifteen years old, from the Army & Navy Stores, had sprung a leak. Now she had to make do with the stone bottle, Bols, it had contained, which the Germans had thrown on the rubbish dump. Sophie despised her for using it, very likely. Certainly it was not nearly so comforting as the other had been. If it became any colder she didn't know what she would do. She couldn't ask Sophie for another blanket because there were no other blankets, which would mean that Sophie would give her the blanket from her own bed and use her outdoor jacket for herself instead—or perhaps Sophie might think, why doesn't Singe use Beorut's blanket which makes the tent? No, it would never occur to Sophie to think that, the dear child; she knew that her aunt would rather freeze to death in privacy than be warm under a mound of blankets and still have nowhere to hide her face.

Instead of thinking about blankets, then, which was a waste of time, she indulged in a flight of fancy, as had become her custom at dawn since the real cold began, allowing her thoughts to dwell on a tantalising picture which, in the initial moments of conjuring it up, warmed her as if by magic from top to toe; a picture of an actual

535

picture, it was, that she had seen in an Army & Navy Stores catalogue, a recent one, which Ludovic in the way of his job had somehow acquired. She had wished so much to cut the page out but that would have meant asking Ludo, and Sophie was angry with him and with good reason, Singe considered, so that would have been disloyal to Sophie. So she had to try and remember how it had been, this marvellous thing.

You could have it in any colour. That was magnificent, a joke in a way. What did it matter, the colour? It was an electrical appliance, and you had it by your bed. Well, there *was* a plug near her bed, as it happened, only of course, nothing to plug into it . . . oh, go *on*, Singe, she told herself impatiently . . . well, then, there was a clock and a kettle and a teapot all on a tray, all matching, very dainty, and you filled the kettle the night before and set the clock and at the required moment—now, for instance—the alarm went off and you found that the kettle was *already boiling*—no, surely not?—and all you had to do was to pour the water on to the tea—or did even that happen by electricity? No, of course not. All the same, it was incredible, such luxury. Now, for instance, to be lying here sipping tea and listening to the carts as they went by; to feel the warmth, a *real* warmth, steal over you, down to your toes, coaxing the pain back into your fingers . . . you would sniff the steam—her nose wrinkled, sniffing—and your eyes would water with the heat of the tea and the sharp fragrance of the lemon drawn out by the tea——really, now she could almost believe she had drunk it, this tea. She had caught a whiff of it, certainly—that delicious smell—but now it had gone. How cold it was. The blankets were heavy and hard as boards; you might be warm under them only if you had warmth in your body, but there was no warmth in hers; it was stiff and cold and brittle and old. She put her hand to her cheek and found it cold and wet, and although she scolded herself she couldn't help the tears which came now. And yet how strange; one would expect these, at least, to be warm, whereas they fell cold as rain. She hunched herself into the smallest possible space and thought, when will it be light? Nothing was ever so bad in the daylight. Others have suffered, really suffered, and here am I crying like a child, all for a glass of tea. But if ever I had to give advice to the young, this is what I would say. Don't live longer than you must. Don't live longer than you ought. At the end it goes much slower than you would think. Soon, surely, it would be light? Light itself was warmth. But it wouldn't be light until all the carts had gone by, and they were still coming in.

So these were five who lay awake that winter's morning listening to the sound of the carts coming into Grusnov market; and although on the face of it, it might appear that they had nothing in common, they had this—that none of them was to hear that sound again. A sixth, Sophie, who was to hear it many, many times more, slept on.

*   *   *

Dressed in her best in a tweed coat Mrs. Simpson had given her, and high-heeled shoes, Gisela wandered through the streets during the dinner hour with no fixed purpose other than that of killing time; not only were most of the shops shut, but also there was no point in returning yet because the porter, Kazimierz, would be downstairs having his food.

It was one of those mid-winter days that scarcely seem to dawn, being wrapped from the start in a gloom which merely intensifies as the hours glide on towards night. The coat was of light-weight wool, intended for the spring, and she shivered, dragging it round her. She was not accustomed to walking in high heels; they skidded on the slippery pavement. The air was quite still, yet damp and raw with a cold which did not have the clean bite of frost but hung in the air almost solid, and if you felt you could touch it, you felt you could smell it, too; it had a smell all its own. The sky was a blackish-grey. Very likely there would be more snow. The buildings had a blanched appearance, almost ashen in contrast to the sky.

She had been dressed and waiting in her room ever since midday, but Helga, Mrs. Wragg's maid, had not appeared until nearly one o'clock, although Gisela had already guessed, from the excited chatter of the maids in the corridor and from the noises in the kitchen and the peremptory manner in which the housekeeper had rattled the handle of her door, what news Helga would bring. "This evening," Helga had whispered, her eyes agog, " yes, the whole family. By the evening train." And it appeared that the Fräulein Nanny had been taken away in an ambulance all the way to Slavnik because she's—and Helga had, with a gesture, indicated what ailed Miss Raven. There again, that was no surprise, Gisela could have told them that die Nanny was " ein bisschen verrückt." And Frau Wragg was pleased because once they had all cleared off she planned to move into Suite Nine. Silly creature, Gisela had thought, can't she let well alone? Surely she must realise that Suite Nine has a " Pech " on it? Frau Wragg should stay where she is, and be thankful to do that. But there had been no time for more gossip. Getting rid of Helga, she had waited until the coast was clear and then had slipped down the back stairs.

The courtyard gates were shut, as they sometimes were during the dinner hour, but she had not been dismayed on that account: she had come prepared. The old porter was eating his soup out of a tin basin at the entrance to the stable, his fat dog beside him, but on seeing Gisela he had wiped his dripping moustaches and come out in quite a friendly fashion. This amiability in itself was unusual; yet even more strange had been his manner when she had offered him, a normal transaction between them, a packet of English cigarettes. No amount of persuasion could move him to accept them; not only that, he had not so much as glanced at them, although on other occasions his eyes would light up at the sight and to-day there had been two packets in her hand, not one. He unlocked the little gate for her, explaining that he had developed a cough and didn't care to smoke that type any more, and whilst she knew this to be a lie, it was the fact of his geniality, of his having bothered to tell the lie that had planted the first little seed of anxiety in her mind. Half-way down the street she had glanced back, and seeing him standing there looking after her she had waved to him, but without responding to the gesture he had quickly stepped back inside. She had decided not to worry about it. One couldn't hope to have an explanation for everything.

So there she was, wandering around the town. She had plenty of money. She could have eaten in a restaurant had she so wished, but she preferred to be alone. Like this, walking through the streets, she was free as the wind; knowing nobody, unknown, lonely as a ghost. Still, she was hungry. She went into a sweet shop which, being of the better sort, was open, and bought a bag of expensive liqueur chocolates. The assistant, a girl of about her own age, glanced over the counter at the high-heeled shoes and heaved an envious sigh. You never saw heels like that nowadays, and yet surely no race of women ever stood in such dire need of the illusion created by them as the Slavonians.

Coming out of the shop, seeing that she happened to be in a street near the market-place, Gisela set off in that direction. No sooner had she turned the corner into the square than, her eyes alighting upon the tiny figure bent over her barrel that was one of the traditions of Grusnov market, she knew at once what she had come for; she felt a desire that was not just a fancy, but a terrible longing, for pickled cucumbers. She must have, not one, but two—or even three.

The cucumber woman was so shrivelled with age that she reached no higher than Gisela's elbow; for all that, she had a cackling laugh and a tongue that was feared by the peasants who kept the stalls round. Now, stooping over the barrel, she was swilling the milky fluid around with a long spoon, all entangled with trailing dill stalks.

" Good day, Granny," Gisela greeted her politely. " I would like two or three." The old creature, who could see Gisela's feet out of the tail of her eye, ignored her, and went on stirring and a few shapes bounced to the surface. After a bit, as the feet did not take themselves off, she mumbled, " All finished go away all done to-day." But Gisela, whose mouth was really watering by this time, was not so easily to be put off; seizing a second spoon which lay nearby, bending over the barrel herself she scooped up three fat ones with no trouble at all.

" There! " she said, smiling. The old hag, still muttering, sullenly gave her a piece of paper to wrap them in, staring, as Gisela got out her purse, in that malevolent, dazed way that old people have at the high-heeled shoes, and when the money was put into her hand—she must have been very cross indeed—with a darting movement of her head she spat, viciously, like a snake, on the coins in her palm and hurled them on to the cobbles. They bounced away and two or three women standing near laughed.

Her cheeks flaming, Gisela stalked off, which was difficult to do with dignity over the cobbles, but once on the pavement she fell into her light loping stride; soon she would be in the park. Why had that had to happen? Bad, she thought, it's very bad, and then, correcting herself, or at least it would be bad if I didn't *know* . . . otherwise—she shivered, it was so cold—then certainly it must have been an omen. The second. And in her father's hand it was written: " *When three come together for good or ill—beware.* " Nonsense, she rebuked herself sternly. To-day is to-day. Nothing can alter that.

There was not a soul to be seen in the park. It was scarcely the weather for sitting about. She found a convenient bench behind a thick yew hedge, under one of the beech trees that spread its skeleton arms against the ugly, swollen sky. There, she fell at once upon the bag of chocolates. She stuffed them into her mouth two or three at a time, scarcely waiting to peel off the silver foil; she simply couldn't devour them fast enough. Suddenly, fickle in her greed as a child, her appetite for them vanished, was transferred to the package containing the cucumber. Scrabbling away the paper, she pounced on the largest, a bite into the rather tough outer skin releasing a flood of juice; acid, pungent, sweet and sour, it flowed down her throat, cleansing it of the sickly taste of the liqueur. How delectable it was, the flesh of the cucumber; cool, tender, yet resilient; she admired the grooves made in it by her teeth, before swallowing it almost whole and starting on the next. She was clever, that old witch, at pickling cucumbers. She frowned, not wishing to think of her, yet she had to give credit where it was due. No onion. Quite right. Only people who knew nothing about the job put onion in to conceal their mistakes. She ate all three so quickly that under her coat even her lean stomach noticeably bulged.

She looked at her watch. Better give him another ten minutes just to be on the safe side. How quiet it was. The cold seemed to deaden every sound; even the noise of the trams as they whined round the corner of the park was soothing, like the sound of waves on the lake shore, or of the wind in the pines. Moisture was seeping from the trees. Great drops fell plop, plop, on to her hair, pitting the surface of the snow. So it was not freezing after all. That didn't stop it being cold.

All at once she saw that she was not quite alone. Some yards off the branches of the naked snowball bushes stirred and an old man, the one with the sack and the pointed stick whose job it was to keep the grass free of litter, poked his nose out. Just a bundle of rags and a bristly beard, he looked like an old badger, snuffing this way and that before venturing out on to the snowy lawn. He couldn't have seen her sitting there, because now he blew his nose on his fingers, vigorously, a thing he never did in the ordinary way. He was carrying his sack, not on his back as in summer, when it was full, but in his hand, swinging empty. She watched him rootling about under the trees, prodding with his stick in the snow. Nearby, some children had made a slide. He went up to it, examined it for a minute or two with a disapproval that was almost comic, poking the ribbon of ice and shaking his head. For two pins, Gisela thought, he might have tested it out. All the while, close on his heels, a small and cheeky bird, a robin or something like that, unnoticed had been following him and now it hopped up right under his feet. Suddenly, catching sight of it, enraged, as if scenting mockery, he lunged at it with his stick, and the bird, just to tease him, fluttered a couple of yards off and began unconcernedly pecking at the snow. Two or three times this happened, the bird plaguing the man, the latter becoming quite wild with rage, and the bird quite insufferably cocky, until really, she felt she must burst out laughing. How funnily people behaved when they imagined themselves to be alone.

Still, she had taken a fancy to him, this angry old fellow. Unlike the cucumber woman, who had seemed to be consumed with a personal spite directed against her, this one's anger appeared to be directed against the whole of life. She could sympathise there, herself. Now he was approaching. There was one chocolate left. Fascinated to see what he would do, mischievously she screwed up the paper bag with the chocolate inside it and threw it on to the path. She waited, a smile on her lips, as he came nearer, mumbling to himself, now and then swinging round to make a jab at his tormentor twittering along behind. For some reason she felt quite tense—wished even that she had not taken the risk. In a matter of seconds it became of the

540

utmost importance to her what he would do when he found the paper bag.

He caught sight of it when he was still a few paces away. As if unable to believe his eyes, he began to stalk it, sidling up to it as if it, too, might fly off; even his sack seemed to inflate at the prospect of this unexpected titbit. Eventually impaling it on the stick, he picked it off the point and began to smooth out the ball. She heard him chuckle when he felt something hard inside the paper. He wore mittens and his movements were so clumsy she thought he would never come to an end, but at last uncovering the small oblong shape, he held it up, peering at it in the same way that he had examined the slide—with wonder and a sneer of disapproval, too. Then, to her astonishment, instead of unwrapping the chocolate and eating it, with a sudden savage gesture he squashed it between finger and thumb, and the sticky red stuff oozed out. He shook it off in disgust, as if it were a slug, and wiping his hands on his tattered behind, slouched away down the path.

Gisela had not stayed to see him go. Already she was out of the park gates and running down the street towards the hotel.

She pushed open the swing-doors and entered the hall and saw at once that it was a stranger who stood behind the porter's desk. She had anticipated almost every eventuality but this, and she hesitated; as she did so, behind her the housekeeper's hatch opened a shade wider and then, stealthily, it was pulled shut.

The new porter was bent over the desk, busy writing. As she stood there, undecided whether to approach him or go back into the street or on up the stairs, he glanced up. It was merely the flicker of a glance and then he resumed his work, but something told her that he knew very well who she was.

Then it was no use approaching him. Best get back to her room where she was safe. Deep in thought, she crossed the hall towards the stairs. Her foot on the bottom stair, she looked up. The housekeeper, in a rather dramatic pose, her arms outstretched, was barring the way. She was smiling, even licking her lips, which were pale and full and reminded one of slivers of fat on mutton chops.

" Where is he? " said Gisela, her voice very low.

The housekeeper, placed to advantage two steps up, leaned forward. " He's gone," she whispered. " Gone."

Lest her expression betray her, and afford the other some satisfaction, Gisela glanced down. She noticed that the carpet was fraying badly on this bottom stair. They ought to get another, but they never would. Irritated by her apparent composure, the housekeeper added, bending still lower: " You won't see him again, you know. He's been transferred."

541

"I see." She raised her eyes, said coolly: "Then I'll go up and get my things."

"There's no need." The housekeeper stared down at her, triumphant. "We've had your bits and pieces packed up. They're all ready for you to take. Come." Rattling the keys at her waist, she swept past, and led the way towards her sanctum, the small office behind the hatch. Throwing open the door, she motioned Gisela inside.

"There." She pointed to a corner where, stacked up, were a box, a sack, and a bundle wrapped in newspaper. "Take them, and go." Picking up a paper knife she began tapping with it on her desk, watching the girl who stood, as if in a dream, looking down at her worldly goods.

"I think "—murmured Gisela—" If you don't mind . . . I'll . . ." The tapping distracted her so that she couldn't think. She noticed, for instance, that in here, where she had never been before, there was an over-powering smell of cats. On the wall over the hatch there was a stuffed satin heart, edged with a lace frill, a Valentine, of all things— the satin much faded and the lace grey with dust. The tapping stopped.

"So, if you don't mind——" she interrupted the housekeeper, who had been about to tell her to hurry up, "I'd rather leave them here." She frowned at the junk in the corner. "For the moment."

"H'm." A sniff. "As you like. Of course," the housekeeper went on disagreeably, "you realise that this is the residents' entrance. Still, if you care to give me a tinkle when you want to collect—all this . . ." she indicated the disreputable heap, "I dare say I could arrange to have you let in . . ."

"Thank you," said Gisela quietly. "If—if it's not bothering you I'd like just to repack one or two things."

"By all means." The housekeeper sat down at her desk, to enjoy the spectacle in comfort.

Gisela took off her new coat and her high-heeled shoes. There was a hole in the toe of one of her stockings, which were not over-clean. She was always a slovenly piece, the housekeeper thought. Gisela didn't care what she thought. Kneeling on the floor, she undid the mouth of the sack and found her old winter coat, stuffed in anyhow. She dragged it out, and beneath it were her thick boots and a woollen scarf; she took these out and bundled in her new coat and shoes in their place.

"Tst!" exclaimed the housekeeper, seeing the good coat going in like that. Gisela paid not the slightest attention. Humming under her breath, she tied up the sack and then she undid her box and rummaged about in it until she came upon what she was looking for, her father's book. She took it out. Underneath it was the calendar. She took that out, too, and sitting back on her heels, examined it with a smile. Now, strangely enough, it was apparent to her that the calendar had been more cunningly devised than she had suspected; although it gave the impression of having been plotted for the individual customer, in fact it might be adapted to suit anyone and everyone. It just depended on the way you looked at it. So this precious oracle of hers was after all nothing but a splendid—and expensive, she remembered—hoax.

"Tell me," she said pleasantly, looking up at the housekeeper, who was watching her with intense curiosity, "in which month were you born? What date?"

"August," replied the housekeeper, somewhat taken aback but easily falling into the trap, easily seduced by the rare pleasure of receiving a personal question, and even seeking to prolong the enjoyment. "August," she repeated, and told her the date.

"Ah. Well, then, let's see." Pursing her lips, Gisela scrutinised the calendar, and was pleased to see what she did, namely, that all the portents encouraged her to leave the little matter of vengeance in the capable hands of fate. "Hmm." She nodded, giving the housekeeper a grave, kindly smile.

"Why, what's the matter?" asked the latter, understandably made nervous by the smile.

"Oh, nothing." She shut the box and got to her feet, put on her boots, then her old coat, and wound the scarf round her head. She kicked the pieces of baggage into a heap, picked up the book and her handbag, put them under her arm, and the calendar she laid on the desk.

"Here," she said, "you might like to have this. A present from me. It'll bring you luck."

"Thank you," said the housekeeper, surprised into civility for once.

At the door Gisela turned. "Thank _you_," she replied with a little bow towards the stiff black figure who sat motionless at the desk, the calendar staring her in the face.

Outside the hotel, she turned to the right, retracing her steps to the market-place. She moved differently now, with a purpose, and she looked different, too, unrecognisable as the young lady who had been loitering about earlier on. In her thick coat, the scarf round her head, she might have been taken for a peasant girl come to town for the day, except for the book she carried and her new handbag. Passing the gates of the park, she took out a handkerchief and scrubbed off her lipstick.

543

It was now the time of the afternoon—in winter, that is—when the peasants, their midday meal finished, dismantle their stalls preparatory to going home. She paused, her eyes travelling up and down the rows of stalls. She knew them well but sometimes their sites changed. Then, having picked out the one she was looking for, a certain poultry stall, she went over to it. The peasant woman who kept it was squatting on the ground, tying up the live ducks left unsold, in couples by the legs.

"Good evening," said Gisela. There is no afternoon greeting in the Slavonian language. "I hear you're from Bialy Kun." She had always kept in reserve the knowledge that the owners of this stall came from her part of the country. The woman, struggling with the ducks, looked up and grunted.

Gisela gave her a nice smile. "So I was wondering"—she went on, and stooping, held the ducks down with her free hand to make it easier for the woman to tie them up—"I was wondering, if your cart's going back this evening, would you give me a place?"

"It's going back now." The job done, the woman stood up. "Just as soon as my man comes out of the pub." She looked at Gisela rather hard. "Why should you be wanting a lift to Bialy Kun?" she asked, a shade suspiciously. They were a suspicious lot, the wealthier peasants, these days.

"It's my village," Gisela declared boldly.

"Who might you be? I don't know your face."

"No? I am the daughter of Tadeusz. The late Tadeusz, that's to say."

"I don't recollect . . . well, just give me a hand with these . . . Hop in now, at the back. Here he comes, my good man. Got your pass, by the way?"

"My pass? No, I'm sorry. I've forgotten my pass."

"Never mind," said the woman good-naturedly, rather taken with the girl's pleasant manner. "Pull your shawl over your face when we get to the check-point and I'll speak for you."

The peasant clambered up on to the driver's seat and gathered up the reins. One could tell he had taken a drop too much.

"Who's that?" he growled, jerking his head over his shoulder.

"A girl from our village who wants a lift."

He wiped his moustaches and spat over the side of the cart. He didn't feel like arguing; having to negotiate the kerb was bad enough.

"Who's the girl?" asked the young man at the check-point.

"A girl from our village," replied the wife. "Here, I kept a fat duck for you and your captain. Don't forget us next Friday, same

544

time." She handed over the indignant bird. The man grinned, saluted, and the cart lurched on.

"Who's the girl?" the peasant asked again, much later. Owing to the cold wind from the mountains, against his will he had begun to sober up.

"I don't rightly know," said the wife. "I don't recognise her, anyway. Still, she's very nicely spoken. Daughter of Tadeusz, she says. Tadeusz that was."

"Tadeusz?" Growling to himself, he tried to puzzle it out, then gave it up. After vodka, names became like wood-pigeons, hard to get; no sooner sighted than gone, but the whirring of their wings went on long after, as if they beat in his head.

"Come on, old man, or we'll never get home to-night."

He flicked up the horses so that they plunged off at a great rate, and Gisela was thrown about amongst the crates in the back. The lantern light jigged up and down over the snowy hedgerows. There were no other lights anywhere to be seen, only the dim radiance of the starlight on the snow. Now, coming up to the top of the pass, you could hear the pines gnashing together in the wind and smell the freshly-fallen snow. At the top of the pass by day you could see for miles; now even the starlight vanished, and leagues of velvety blackness stretched away to the horizon, to where it was rimmed with a reddish glow. Over in that direction was Gradovice, a town where they manufactured small arms; she knew that this was what they did there, although she had never been. It was many miles off.

Anchoring herself between sacks of meal she lay back and gazed up at the stars. After a bit, just as they were about to descend the other side of the pass, the peasant shouted at the horse and with a jerk the cart stopped. Gisela sat up. The horse stood sweating and shivering in the wind. The man, swearing under his breath, leaned forward and unhitched the lantern; then he turned right round, holding it high over the back of the cart so that it shone down on her face.

"Hey, you!" His eyes were still glassy from the vodka, and his moustaches webbed over with frost. He was swaying a little, and the wife, who had turned round too, clutched him so that he shouldn't fall. "You say you're the daughter of Tadeusz?" He had a bullying voice. "There's no Tadeusz in our village now, my girl. That's bad luck, isn't it? And as I don't know you I want to know who you are."

She kneeled up in the cart, the scarf falling away from her face as she lifted it to the light. "You don't know me," she said, in her high ringing voice, "but I know *you*. Your farm's at Pine Knoll corner, isn't it? Yes, and my father came to treat your father—ten, eleven years ago, now—when he had the gout. He got better, your father. Remember?"

At that, the lantern wavered and dropped lower; two pairs of eyes glittered down on her, two mouths gaping like round black holes. All at once the man swung the lantern back on to its peg, whipped up the horses, and the cart rattled off into the dark. When they had reached level ground and were going at a steady pace, he shifted the reins to his left hand and crossed himself, not once but three times. Startled by this gesture on a week-day as by nothing else, his wife nudged him: "What's up?"

"Shurrup," he growled, but very low. He drew the blanket up round them both as if glad of her company. Presently he muttered, first casting a glance over his shoulder, "Ssssh . . . listen . . . Tadeusz, the necromancer, remember? The one the Germans shot—who——"

"Why, yes," she whispered excitedly, "of course. I remember. Wait—wasn't there some story? Wasn't he the one who—oooooh!"

"Shurrup. You remember. That'll do."

"And *she*—that's his daughter?"

"You'd know the devil, even by lanternlight, wouldn't you? That's her, right enough." He brooded, in great perplexity, it seemed. "Tell you what. I'm going to put her out a bit farther on. I don't want her in my cart."

"You can't put her out in this cold," the wife objected. She had been thinking, if the devil chose to appear in that sort of shape, not only had he very good taste but one couldn't be blamed for having been deceived; horns and a tail were what she had been brought up to expect. "Take her as far as the turning," she pleaded. "You can't do less than that."

When they turned off the main road the farm dogs heard the cart rumbling down the lane and began to bark. Gisela recognised the knoll of pine trees as they went past; here was the farm. The man drove in over the cobbles, into the yard. Climbing down from the cart, he swore at the dogs who were leaping about in a frenzy, whining and rattling their chains along the wire. Unhitching the lantern he stumped round to the rear of the cart and unfastened the back, which fell with a clatter. Then he held up the light. Her white face glimmered over the sacks.

"So now what are you going to do, missy?" His tone was menacing, but she could tell he wasn't too happy about her. She kept silent, and he went on, gathering courage: "We've no room here, so don't think it. Where will you sleep? It's a step to the village, through the forest all the way—as of course you know, none better—

but off you'll have to go," he added, working himself up, " and good riddance."

The woman was on the doorstep, unbarring the door.

" No," she called out. " She must have a cup of soup or something —you can't turn her out like that . . ."

Gisela sprang down from the cart. She was light as a cat, he noted, or a fairy, and haughty as a princess. He didn't care for her sort, the kind that appeared in dreams. " Go on—get moving . . ." He made a grab at her but like a fairy she eluded him and was already on his threshold. " I shall sleep in your loft to-night," her high sweet voice reached him. " Don't worry—by daybreak I'll be gone."

She disappeared inside, and he aimed a kick at the nearest slavering dog. He'd take the crucifix to bed with him to-night.

" That's right, dearie." The woman shut the door. " You come in and warm yourself. Don't mind him, he's a good man—but on market days . . . you know how it is, after a few tots . . ."

It was warm and quiet in the kitchen. Outside, the dogs were still whining, clanking their chains on the wire; the man was relieving himself against the wall. The woman had thrown some faggots on to the mound of ash in the hearth; already they were beginning to catch. She stopped blowing and sat back on her heels. " There's some nice cabbage soup," she said, looking round at Gisela. Disregarding her, Gisela went straight over to the ladder which led to the loft. " With a bit of bacon," the woman called after her, quite loudly, coaxingly, almost, " how about that? "

Reaching the foot of the ladder, Gisela turned, and saw that the woman had stood up and was staring at her, a strange expression on her face.

" I'm not hungry," she said curtly. " I'll go up now and sleep," but instead she paused, watching the other until, as she had known would happen, the woman took a step towards her, as if drawn against her will approached. Gisela had grasped the ladder, her foot was on the bottom rung, but still she waited, allowing her to come up close. She came up close, breathing in a peculiar way, as if she were excited; a queer flush of excitement mottled the potato-coloured face. Gisela, who had seen that look on villagers' faces before, raised herself on the rung, so that she towered above, a foot and more, and holding the other with her eyes, spoke softly:

" My father cured his father," she said, " so no thanks are owing from me. Still, you've been kind . . . whatever you find up there "— she nodded to where her refuge gaped above her—" in the morning . . . well, you may treat it as yours." The face below her that had been flushed all at once became deathly pale. So she remembered now, did

547

she? Very likely the whole story had come back to her mind. With a scornful little laugh Gisela sprang up the ladder and vanished from sight.

Up in the loft she lit a cigarette and sat down in the hay. What a smell it had—she took up a great handful and buried her face in it, snuffing. Ah, now that she was back in the country, the forest no more than a stone's throw away, she felt at peace. This was home; here everything was to hand. Although it was not the season for flowers and berries, there were stalks, roots, evergreens, hemlock and wolfsbane and yew, or she could grub for mushrooms beneath the snow; she remembered the place where those mushrooms grew. Luxuries were scattered all about in such prodigal style, there had been no real need, even, of the book. But which? That was the point, which? Whilst she smoked the cigarette she toyed with a dozen possibilities. Hemlock —water hemlock? No. Once—she shuddered—she had seen a dog— no, anyway, the pool would be frozen over—until, lighting another cigarette, beginning to smoke in earnest, she realised that she had merely been passing the time, flirting with her real choice that had been made earlier out there on the high road at the top of the pass; when she had spoken of her father as having cured the gout.

Although she knew by heart what she would find, she snapped on her lighter and searched through the book. Gout. Yes, cross-referenced here. An infusion of the flowers of the Meadow Saffron —sometimes known as Flowering Arsenic, Colchicum or Autumn Crocus. Then the quantities. Then, beneath, in his spiky uncompromising hand, her father had written: " Administered in the above proportions its efficacy is infallible; to wit, if no effect, diagnosis incorrect." And below that, in big black letters across the page:

> *Beware—Too little, no cure*
> *Too much—suffer no more.*

She grinned. That had been his idea of a joke. Snapping off the light, she lay down in the hay.

Through the forest, over the brow of the hill, there was a sloping meadow where those flowers grew; where, in the spring and in the summer, in contrast to the fields around, there were no flowers to be seen; instead, covered with fleshy leaves, it was uniformly green. But by September the meadow would have become a lake of melting colour, a flood of salmon-pink shading to violet, coral, rose, set off, not by leaves, but by the green fields round—this being the peculiarity of the plant, that the blossoms appear when the leaves and all other law-abiding flowers have perished, even the seeds being set to mature

548

in the ground during the winter, after the blossoms are gone—a programme, she thought, so thoroughly topsy-turvy, so slipshod and contrary, it might have been designed expressly to suit me. There they were, the pursefuls of seeds, hoarded away under the snow, containing all that the flowers contained, and more. Now it wanted only the light of day. Well, that would come. Meanwhile it was pleasant to stretch out like this; the hay tickled her face and she heard a faint rustling by her ear. Almost at once she fell asleep and slept soundly. Not even the mice could keep her awake.

* * *

In the hollow in the hay the peasant's wife found a leather handbag and a tattered yellow book. The bag was empty, quite new, and of foreign make. One look inside the book was enough. Ignorant she might be, but there was no need for schooling to tell the Devil's black fist. She pushed it amongst the logs on the hearth and threw on a fir bough to make a blaze. Then she crossed herself for luck and felt better. Regarding the handbag, strange to relate, she had no scruples whatsoever. It served her for years to come.

As for Gisela, she was never seen again.

* * *

Really, it was a pleasure to resume one's old leisurely habits. Bathed and shaved, Ludovic wrapped himself in his father's dressing-gown and enjoyed a cigarette, gazing ruminatively out of the window. This was just the sort of day he liked, grey and gloomy, making his little room seem a cosy paradise in contrast to the world without—and, still more, in contrast to that draughty dingy office, with those pushing young louts; he shuddered. No, he was one of these rather special beings who, lest they curl up and die, must be preserved from the hurly-burly rough-and-tumble—dear me, yes; really, he was very well off where he was—so long as he didn't spoil it all by foolishly allowing worries to intrude. To-day he would coddle himself. Certainly he deserved that. So off you go, you nasty little or big things you, he told them, his worries, and off they went. Both doors shut. Good. So they couldn't come back.

After all, he was busy. He had his hobbies. He lay down on the bed, pulling the quilt up, and arranged the pillows behind his head; then he reached down into his box and found his knitting. Sad to think that these socks might have been finished long since had it not been for that ridiculous venture, the job. His hands occupied, his thoughts flitted on to the next pair. Plain navy silk, moss stitch, and possibly even a tie to match. Lulled by the rhythmic click of the needles

549

a mood of extreme beatitude was just beginning to steal over him when there came a tap on the door.

" Ludo."

Sighing, he laid down his work. Peace, perfect peace. " Yes, Tante Singe," he called out, in his voice patience and reproach evenly mixed. " You may come in."

" Ludo, I——" She stopped short, seeing him in bed. " Oh, I didn't know—are you sick ? "

" Sick ? " he said in surprise. " No." Then, anxiously, as she stood peering at him from the doorway, " Why, do I *look* sick ? "

" N-no . . ." She screwed up her eyes, puzzled. " Not exactly. But what about your—you know ? . . . "

" My job ? " Calmed, he took up his knitting. " My *work*, you mean, Singe? My career? One can't work all the time, my dear auntie. One must keep a sense of proportion in these matters. I'm taking a day off, perhaps ? Is that it ? " He was smiling at her, his head on one side. Teasing her, she knew. " Or," he went on, " maybe I am not very pleased with them, my employers. Or, on the other hand, maybe they are not very pleased with me." He cocked his head the other way, the better to judge her agitation.

" Oh, Ludo, you mean you've been——? "

" Fired ? Tst . . . what a horrid common word—that's the sort of expression one picks up when one makes these regrettable contacts. Well, since you ask, let's say there's been a—a tiff . . . a sort of—lovers' quarrel. That's it. After all, I've been a devoted slave for some time now. The honeymoon's over. Tell me—Singe, come here, tell me now, how d'you like this ? Myself, I can't decide . . ." He shook his head, sighing deeply. " Whether the stripes should be one, or two—what do you think ? Two, an exaggeration, eh? One, perhaps, has more— je ne sais quoi . . . enfin, d'élégance—n'est-ce pas, Singe ? "

" Perhaps," said Singe. " Ludo."

" Mmm . . ." he yawned.

" I'm worried—about Sophie. You don't know where she is ? "

" I ? How should I know ? Eating roast beef with those tedious friends of hers, I dare say."

" She's been out since eight o'clock."

" Really ? I hope she hasn't forgotten our lunch. Yes, she's late. You're right. I've quite an appetite, too. She's getting slack, our Sophie."

Singe was aware that he said this merely to annoy her and so she was careful to make no reply. After all, there were only two people on whom he might vent his annoyance and if one were absent, the other would have to do. Now, looking at him, she judged shrewdly that to-day his malice was not merely the natural expression of his personality but due to some more specific cause—worry, perhaps? She knew him better than he suspected. Now, for instance, she knew that he wanted her to go away and leave him in peace, but instead she stood her ground, there in the doorway, a rather grim expression on her wrinkled face, her eyes fixed upon him so intently that he must have been aware of that steady gaze. He felt it all right, she knew that, even if he made no sign, his fingers moving as nimbly as ever. All his movements were deft, nimble, yet also furtive and rapacious; on the whole, that was how it struck one, watching him: disagreeably. His smooth, pale head shone; flat and sleek, but too small, too compact, dangerous, narrow, slippery, like the head of a stoat. There's never been anyone like him in our family, she reflected. So different from his father—and as for Sophie, why, it was hard to believe they were blood relations. Ludovic had no lovable qualities at all. She herself had found it impossible to love him, even as a child, although she had tried. To love a child—that shouldn't require much effort— and yet with him it had proved impossible. He was a misfit, of course —just as they all were, now; but he had been a misfit even before that.

It had often occurred to her that if circumstances had been otherwise, if their way of life had been allowed to continue—free and easy, reckless, you might say, certainly they had never counted the cost because there had been the land at the back of them all the time . . . but then had they not given, too, as well as taken? They had been able to spend what they liked because of the land, but the land had taught the secret of spending: spend what you like as long as you give what you spend—then Sophie's personality would have expanded, flowered, because she cared not a fig for wealth or position, and had she continued to enjoy these assets, they would merely have been instrumental in spreading happiness, because Sophie had no need of education in that respect, it being her nature to give rather than to take; whereas Ludovic's, by comparison, would have suffered, have become even more stunted, even, perhaps, truly evil. Certainly, had he come into his inheritance, he would have had the power to create more unhappiness, to spread it over a wider field than he had now. Poor Ludo. Perhaps that was what irked him so; that he had been thwarted by circumstance. A sister, an aunt—these were small fry. Not much fun, tormenting them. Yet most of us, she thought, were not bad. On the whole, I think we were respected and admired by our peasants, and some of us—my brother, for instance, and Sophie— were even beloved. But now and again it's as if Nature suddenly turned round and said: " Look here, I'm fed up—there's been too
551

much meddling in what is rightly my business, breeding and so on, so you'd better stop! " And just to show she means it, " You want to see something really bad? " she says, and laughs, because it's her little joke. " All right, if you don't believe me, I'll show you how perfectly disastrous it can be . . ." And she does so, produces her answer, a thoroughbred—and the Rapovski boy's just such another, thought Singe—a creature without a single point, without even the points of common stock; a disaster for all to see. That's it. Nodding to herself, Singe hobbled off into the other room where she began to sort out her work for the day.

" Blast her," muttered Ludovic under his breath. She'd left the door ajar which meant getting up. He couldn't be bothered to, just yet. Blast her, too, for having broken in upon him, bringing with her what he had taken such pains to exclude, his worries.

How very rude they had been, yesterday, at the office. Especially that uncouth old boy, the Chief of Police. So *he* was not sharp enough for this work, wasn't he? *He*, a Bielski—with more brains in his little finger than—ah, but just because he was slow, stupid, and so on, it appeared that that was no reason why he should not work—in a factory, for instance. But, he had reminded them, there was the question of his weak heart, lungs, etc., in short, of his health—aaaah! . . . in *that* case—quite delighted, they had seemed—*then* he must be medically examined. Medically examined? He had almost swooned at the suggestion. A coarse young brute, a semi-qualified quack, the clever-clever son of a kulak, very likely—to handle *him*, with his nerves, his delicate metabolism? Even now the very thought was enough to send his temperature up. Perhaps it had gone up. Cheered by this possibility, Ludovic reached down for his thermometer and slipped it under his tongue. Still, that wasn't the only worry. There was—well, money, and all that other business, too, last night. The fact was he had been doing quite nicely at poker during the slack periods in the office until—well, yesterday, when there had been rather an unpleasant little bother . . . nothing much . . . yesterday had been a bad day all round, really . . . but the little—incident—had served to emphasise the fact—he had always known it, but this *re*-emphasised it, as it were—that if one were to play poker, it was advisable to play only with people one knew. Actually, he had thought he knew them all—even banked on it, in a manner of speaking. And a very promising little bunch of beginners they were, too. Until that assistant to the Chief of Police had taken a hand. Nasty blustering peasant. So then, when he'd got out of there, finally, he'd gone round to Paul Rapovski's, just to cheer himself up, and lost—a bad day, no denying it—quite a tidy sum. He couldn't go *there* again until it was paid. Trouble was, there wasn't a hope of paying it. And he didn't much fancy turning up at the office again—always so tedious, any kind of fuss about cards, although they were only a rabble of filthy peasants—still, all the same, he would prefer *not*. He had half a mind to flit. To Slavnik? But, as per—no cash. He wondered if—what about Sophie? Tell her the whole story—what about that? He grinned, forgetting the thermometer, which dropped out of his mouth. She'd have a fit. It was an idea, though. Might even shock the old girl into coughing up. Normal. Bang on normal. Well, that showed, didn't it, that something was wrong? He was usually sub. Pulse a bit jerky, too. All this worry, of course. Where *was* Sophie, blast her. And what about lunch?

At that moment he heard the outer door slam and the noise as of a whirlwind approach. Ah. That was his sister all right.

" Sophie! " His aunt's scissors dropped with a clatter to the floor. Something in her voice made him prick up his ears. Laying aside his knitting, he sat up and listened.

Sophie had shut the door and was leaning against it, clutching the handle for support. Her beret was askew, her hair in wisps, and her breath came hard and fast as if she had been running.

" Sophie! " Singe gazed at her in terror. " Where have you been? What's happened? Tell me! "

Sophie made a sort of gesture as if she were incapable of speech. She had a small parcel in her hand. She looked at it as if she could not for the minute recollect what it contained. She sat down on her bed and began to unwrap it.

" Oh, yes, " she said. " Here. I got this. It's a hen. For your lunch."

" A *hen*! " Singe dropped her work and came across to look at it. Yes, it was a hen. " But, darling, what possessed you? We could've —but what extravagance! "

" Yes. No, I mean. It's not very large, I'm afraid. I got it because I've no time to cook. It's supposed to be all ready to eat." She wrapped it up again and threw it on the pillow. " You think it'll do? " she said vaguely. " You just cut it up, Singe. I've got to go out again at once. Perhaps I'll be out all day."

" All day? "

" No, " she smiled, seeing the expression on her aunt's face. " All right . . . I'll try to pop back about seven, darling, just for a jiffy." She rubbed her forehead, as if her head hurt her. " They're—they're going away, you see, Singe."

" Away? Oh, *no*, Sophie! Oh, my dear . . ."

" Yes, they are. We've been packing all morning." She frowned

553

as if she had a really bad headache, as if she could scarcely see. " Dreadful things have happened, all at once. I can't tell you now. I have to go. First "—she got up, wandered about—" wait, what did I come for? Oh, yes, a present." In a dream she moved across to the shelf where the crockery was laid out. " Now—let me see . . . what would be—well, these, I suppose." She swept a pile of little plates from the shelf. " They're the best, after all . . . what do you think, Singe? Would they do? "

" I should think they would," said Singe timidly. " They're always nice, you know, to have "—she paused—". . . about." It broke her heart to see Sophie with that look on her face.

" Yes. They are, aren't they? " Suddenly she put the plates down and, leaning with her elbows on the dresser, dug her fists into her eyes. " I can't *think*, Singe," she murmured. " I've so much to think of, but I can't think. Wait. There was something else. Yes." She pushed the plates aside. She was speaking rather hurriedly, her eyes glittering. " You see, these, just these, that's not enough. That's not the *way* it should be done. It's not—you know—*delicate*. Now, what—ah, yes, of course! Dunce that I am. Flowers. That's the *way*, d'you see . . . there are ways and ways and this is the one. Flowers. That's what I came back for. For the flowers." She was muttering, talking to herself, Singe knew. " The money for the flowers. Money. That's it, more money. One mustn't run short of that." She turned, giving her aunt a distracted little smile. " Money, you see, that's important in a case of this kind."

" Sophie, darling——"

" Don't *cry*, Singe. There'll be time for that later." She tossed her beret on to the table and ran her fingers through her hair. " What was I saying? Ah, yes." In a flash she was down on her hands and knees in the corner, tugging at the floorboard.

" Here, Singe. Give me your scissors, quick." She crouched over the hollow, biting her lip; after a little deliberation, she took out a handful of notes and stuffed them into the pocket of her jerkin. Her aunt, who had been watching her, suddenly glanced round.

" Sophie! " she hissed under her breath, and just for a second Sophie seemed to freeze; then, crouching lower, she pressed the floorboard back into place. When that was done, unhurriedly she turned round. Her brother stood in the open doorway, leaning up against the door, apparently engrossed in his knitting, the ball of silk tucked under his arm. Nevertheless, he seemed to be aware of Sophie's eyes upon him, because now he began to whistle very softly to himself. She caught her aunt's eye and Singe gave a slight shake of the head.

"Ah, Ludo," she said pleasantly, getting to her feet.

"Ma soeur?" He paused in his work, his eyebrows raised in inquiry as she came and stood in front of him, the table between them.

"What are you doing here?"

"I live here, you know," he reminded her equably.

"But why aren't you——?"

"At my job?" He pronounced it "chob." His accent was not as good as Sophie's. "Ah . . ." he sighed, "that's a long story. Would you like to hear it?"

I was wrong, thought his aunt, who was sitting on the bed, behind Sophie, and had caught the gleam that had come into his greenish eyes. He is not like a stoat, which is a simple country beast; even does good, killing rats. He is like that animal they had in the Viennese Circus—what was it?—not large, but fierce, and treacherous—the most treacherous in the world. Not a tiger, but like that. Black—it was; I can't remember its name. Perhaps a leopard. No, not a leopard. Ludovic has no spots. He is all one colour—black.

"I could make it snappy," he said, putting his knitting in his pocket and lounging against the door to more studied effect, "if you're pressed."

"Go on, then," said Sophie.

"Once upon a—oh, sorry, you're in a hurry—there was a young man who had good prospects. Unfortunately, he also had a sister . . ."

Sophie said: "Have you any brown paper, Singe, to wrap these plates? Thank you."

"Ah-ha . . . ah-ha . . ." Ludovic craned forward. "So they're going, are they? That's nice. I hope to a good home? I must say I'm relieved in a way. Once or twice lately I've been a bit nervous on their account"—he giggled—"you know what you're like when you're on the rampage—after a drop of . . . where had I got to?"

"The sister," said Sophie. "A piece of that twine, Singe. Thanks."

"Of course, the sister. Well, she was mad. It wasn't generally known at first. But when it became quite clear to everybody that the poor soul had lost her wits, then the employers sent for the young man and said—you have this lunatic sister and we are very keen on respectability and so we are very sorry, but we can't employ you any more. And so his career was—what is it? Ah yes—nipped in the bud. Et voilà—c'est tout! Sad, isn't it? Mais c'est comme ça— la vie."

"You've lost the job."

"Ma chère Sophie! Tu vois, Singe? Folle, si—mais pas tellement bête, quand même."

555

There was a short silence. Sophie finished tying up the parcel, tested the knots, and bit off the length of twine with her teeth. When that was done, she stood up and, looking at him very straight, said, in a voice that neither of her relations had heard before: " I hope you didn't go without collecting your wages. I hope, too, that at least they gave you a little something for the information on Mr. Schulman— what's it called—a bonus . . . a pourboire? You know what I mean . . ."

And Singe thought, they have something in common, after all— how else can she know where to hit? She had caught that look as it flashed across his face.

" Because," Sophie went on in that same voice, " you're going to need it, Ludo. The money, I mean."

" Ah? " He was already quite on the alert. " I'm listening," he said, as she paused.

" Good. Listen, then. I have a great deal to think about just now, but as you are here, I might as well say what I have to say, and get it over. It isn't much. You are related to me. God knows how that came about. I think it was a mistake—a mistake I intend to put right. In this way. As from to-day, you are no longer my brother. As from to-day, I am not going to provide for you any more. You must look out for yourself. I don't wish to see you ever again. I am going out now and you must be gone by the time I come back this evening. Understand? "

" Of course." His eyes were narrowed; he was watching her closely, still smiling. " I understand perfectly." Suddenly dropping his jaunty pose in the doorway, in one quick movement he was facing her at the table; his voice no longer lazy, teasing, he spoke very fast, very low, his eyes fixed on hers: " You're going away, that's it, isn't it, Sophie? And you wish to settle your responsibilities before you go. Your friends have asked you to go with them. You cannot live without them, nor they without you. It's a kind of love affair, eh, Sophie? They have been pleading with you all morning, begging you to go with them—they have made the arrangements even—because it can be arranged, you know—that's the situation, isn't it? And you've taken your decision? Bravo! I didn't think you'd have the courage. That's the way it is, isn't it? " He gave her a strange look, at which she seemed to shrink away, passing her hands across her eyes as if they gave her intolerable pain. Singe, who was watching, thought, yes, he has wounded her, but how or where I don't know; badly, that's all I know.

" That's not the way it is at all," Sophie whispered. " As you know very well I couldn't go, even if——"

"Even if?" He was leaning right over the table; glancing over her shoulder he caught sight of Singe, and seeing the distress on her face, too, was struck by an idea. A case of two birds with one stone —one didn't often have the chance. "Ah, but you *would* go, wouldn't you, Sophie?" Relentless, his voice pursued her. "There's nothing to stop you that I can see—if it were not for our little aunt here— because it's quite plain you're not staying on my account, eh?" He drew back, laughing softly, and judged the effect.

"Certainly," she flashed back at him, "Singe is the one who keeps me—not you. My God, Ludo, not you! You get out of my sight, d'you hear? You've—you've brought shame on us all. You're a liar and a spy and—a *cheat*! Ah, you didn't think I knew about that, did you? Why, it's all round the town. Go—go! And if you can find a place where they won't kick you out, stay there! Stay, because you won't find so many. All I ask is that you go away from here— *out of my sight!*"

"Oh, children, children," moaned Singe.

"Don't upset yourself, Sophie. In fact, that is exactly what I had intended to do—to go."

"All right," she said quietly. "I'm glad it's settled," Frowning, she felt in her pocket and brought out a note. "There. That'll see you off the premises. Make the most of it. It's the last you'll ever get from me." She tucked the parcel of plates under her arm, and picking up her beret, made off towards the door.

"When does their train leave exactly?" said her brother.

She turned round, surprised. "Nine o'clock. Nine or a quarter past."

"Ah well—wish them bon voyage from me." His eyes flickered over her. He had the air of enjoying himself, which struck Singe as strange. "Good-bye, my dear Sophie."

She made no reply. As if she were taking it in for the last time, her eyes wandered over the whole room, and softened as they came to rest on the small figure crouched on the bed.

"The hen, Singe," she said. "You know—it just needs cutting up." She attempted a smile, failed, and blundered out.

"Comme elle souffre, notre pauvre Sophie," murmured her brother as the door shut. Singe made no answer. She got up and went across towards Sophie's bed, passing by him without so much as a glance. She picked up the parcel containing the chicken and unwrapped it. The bird was on the small side, but plump, in colour a nice glossy brown. She sniffed it, nodded with satisfaction, and trotted off towards the door. Ludovic came up behind her and touched her shoulder.

"Singe," he said, winningly, humbly, "please believe me. You
557

know you've always been against me—you always take her side. But I didn't give them any information, you know—about that. Truly I didn't."

She looked up at him with a funny little grimace and for a second he thought he had won her round. Her eyes were very bright.

" Of course I know *that*." Her voice was sharp with irritation and disgust. " You don't have to tell *me*. You didn't give it because you didn't have it. You're stupid, Ludovic. So stupid you miss the point." She shook herself free of his hand.

He was a man who could be perceptive when it suited him and now, what with anger and fear and wounded vanity, he was inspired. " *I* miss the point? " He dodged round in front of her, speaking as he had done to Sophie, very fast and low, putting his face close to hers. Although not in the least nervous, Singe did recoil slightly; when excited he was inclined to spit. " I? Not I, ma tante—I would say rather that the boot is on the other foot—it is *you* who miss the point. You heard what she said just now? You saw what a state she was in? They've been at her all day, those British, to get her to go with them —*and she could still go!* But she'll be firm, I think—strong, you know. But from now till nine o'clock—how she'll suffer! Tst . . . tst . . ." What an excellent weapon this was—both edges sharp, both coming in handy. " She isn't ruining her chances because of *me*, Singe—she said that, didn't she? Ah, I'm thankful I haven't that on my conscience, at least." He rolled his eyes piously. " It's a shame about Sophie. She has really too much heart . . . mais, enfin . . ." he shrugged, shaking his head sadly, moving away, " c'est comme ça, la vie."

Without a word his aunt left the room, closing the door behind her. He waited for a moment, and then in two strides he reached it and opened it cautiously a fraction of an inch. He could see her through the glass top of the kitchen door. She was preparing to cut up the chicken; he watched her reach down the chopping board and get things out of a drawer.

Then, closing the door softly, moving as swiftly and silently as the beast to which Singe had likened him, he went over to the corner where he had seen Sophie on her hands and knees. He trod about, until the loose floorboard squeaked. He had it prised up in no time, using one of the knitting needles in his pocket. Then he too fell on his knees. The noise of his own breathing was something he could hear quite outside himself; I don't care, he thought, if she comes back now, so much the worse for her. Excitement raced through his veins; the blood sang in his ears, a song of triumph. None of them had ever liked him, not his father nor Singe nor the servants nor the grooms, not even the Rapovski boys; Sophie had had everything,

558

always; even the Gobelins, although he was the only son, the rightful heir. This way all the old scores would be settled. He settled them, in full, scooping out all that was in the hollow and stuffing his pockets. He replaced the floorboard, trod it down, went into his own room and immediately started to pack. He worked fast. By the time he heard Singe come back into the next room he was ready. Everything went into one suitcase except for the gramophone. He looked to see that the coast was clear and carried his things through the bathroom and along the passage and out of the front door and left them at the top of the stairs. His coat over his arm, he ran down the three flights to the hall where he rapped smartly on the porter's hatch. Only one sort of gentry rapped in that peremptory manner these days, and they were certainly not the tenants. The hatch opened at once.

"I say," Ludovic leaned on the sill. "I've got some stuff upstairs on the top landing. D'you think your young lad could . . . er . . ."

"I should think he could," said the porter slowly, his eyes bulging. "Stefan!" The boy scampered up the stairs, and the porter's wife crowded up behind her husband to take a look; she was a woman Ludovic had always disliked.

"And," he went on, and now there were two notes fluttering in his fingers, "I'd like a droshky—right away."

"Right away!" The porter jumped down off his stool with greater alacrity than Ludovic had ever seen him display before, and came running out into the hall, and dashed off at the double into the street. His wife, too, had come out into the hall. As she seemed to have nothing better to do than stare at him, Ludovic handed her his coat; she was so stunned that she took it, even held it for him as he got into it.

The droshky was there, the baggage stowed in.

"Thanks, my good man." Ludovic pressed the notes into the porter's hand. "Tell him to drive to the station—the Slavnik train. And to look lively about it." They watched, goggle-eyed, as he settled himself in the droshky.

"Go on," prompted Ludovic, a shade impatiently. "Tell him." Coming out of his daze, the porter bellowed at the figure on the box, "Hey, you!"

The driver, a fat, evil-looking fellow, was shaking like a jelly with mirth. Turning round, he gave the porter a broad wink.

"Save your breath, cock. I 'eard." He swung right round to take a good look at his passenger.

"Bleedin' toff, eh?" he jeered.

Ludovic, far from disconcerted by this accusation, inclined his head

559

in a prim little nod of assent. " Exactly," came his chilling reply, " so hurry up."

The driver's astonishment was such that he nearly fell off the box. None of his fares had dared to address him like that for—well, a good many years. With a dreadful oath he whipped up his nag, and as the droshky moved off Ludovic, on an impulse, airily tossed a third note over the side to flutter down at the porter's feet.

" Ah, that's more like it," he told himself, leaning back and turning up the collar of his coat. " That's the way it should be." Count Bielski had come into his own at last.

All the same, it occurred to him that some detail was missing— something that would make all the difference; the finishing touch. Something his father had always had—what was it? But of course. A cigar.

*   *   *

When she had cut up the chicken and laid the table, Singe tapped on Ludo's door and then sat down on her bed waiting for him to come in. She waited for what seemed like a long time. He liked chicken. In fact, he liked food and was even quite greedy, although one would never think it, he was so thin. Presently she tapped on his door again and as there was no answer she opened it and went in and saw that he had taken all his things and gone. For good, that would be. Well, that made one problem the less for Sophie; really you could say it eliminated almost all her problems; leaving only one—the main one. She folded up his sheets; that was something she could spare Sophie—other people's sheets, horrible—and then she closed his door and cleared away the things on the table, putting a plate over the chicken to prevent it getting dry; Sophie might be hungry when she came in, poor thing; she might even need to take provisions with her, for the train.

There were several little jobs to be done, and Singe knew that she ought to be getting on with them, but instead she found herself just pottering, not hurrying at all. She stood by the window, looking out. How unsightly the window-boxes were in this season—the earth frozen hard as iron, powdered with snow; in one corner a ragged tuft of something, dingy, highly unpromising—a biennial, that would be, and in the spring doubtless the customary miracle would happen. They had planned to plant all sorts of things—to have an arbour of bean-stalks, that was one idea—for the summer. In case there should be another party, Sophie had said. In the summer. What a long time ahead.

Here she was, wasting time, dawdling, yet somehow she couldn't

560

tear herself away from this window. And yet there was this train. At nine o'clock, or a quarter past. How strange. She herself had never even been in a train. Only one thing she knew about them— you could miss them. But even if Sophie missed this one, she would be able to take the next. If she came back at seven, just popped in for a jiffy as she had promised, then there would still be time for her to pack and get to the station. Well, then, *you'd* better hurry, Singe scolded herself, instead of day-dreaming like this.

She began folding her own sheets; talking to herself the while, silently, but now and then a little exclamation would escape her. Never even to have been in a train! That does show—doesn't it? Antoinette was quite right. I am sadly out of touch with the world. I really had no idea that she could have gone with them. And just think—if he hadn't . . . well, *she* would never have told me. She would have gone on for ever—staying here with me, never telling me. It needed him to tell me—and thanks are due to him for that. Still, I do feel ashamed that I should have had to be *told* . . . it makes one look, as Sophie would say, a " dashed fool." . . .

" Now," she began to bustle about, " I have a great deal to do."

She sorted the rags, the felt, into bundles, tied up the bag of sawdust with string; there were some odd arms and legs waiting to be assembled: she had intended finishing a torso that day. " Sorry," she said, and felt like God as she dropped them into the waste-paper basket. Then she went out into the kitchen, and started to prepare a tray for herself, carefully, taking her time. She is getting herself a snack, one would have said, watching her. A very odd sort of snack, then one would have said, seeing the tray. On it she had put a jug of water, a glass, and a teaspoon; also a plate and a knife, a couple of sweet biscuits, and a small pestle and mortar, the kind used for pounding spices for Easter cakes. She looked it over, as if checking the items, then nodded, apparently satisfied, and carried it into the other room and set it on the floor beside her bed.

She opened the brass-bound box, intending to examine all her treasures, and then it occurred to her that time was getting on and she fetched the alarm clock from the shelf and put it on the tray, which was of tin, so that the clock made a terrible clatter, jigging up and down on its three legs; you could hardly overlook it, the time, that way.

There were so many things in the box. Photographs and bits of needlework, dance programmes, holy cards and hair ribbons—her whole past was in that box. The trouble was that in spite of the clock, or because of it, she couldn't concentrate. All sorts of memories came crowding into her mind. Summer evenings in the country, sitting on

561

the steps in front of the house; the smell of hay; the mist rising from the lake and the plish-plash of oars, the squeak of rowlocks; great moths blundering through the dusk, buffeting one's face; mosquitoes, and the sound of horses' hoofs at a gallop up the drive. She always galloped up the drive, Sophie. Sophie whistling to the dog. That awful dog of Sophie's, the way he'd bark at anybody, even family, when he was in his place, on Sophie's bed. He's a king, she would say, her arms round his neck, a real king—and so he was, and knew it. Sophie—thought Singe—it's all been Sophie, for me. My own life—look, it's nothing. A few certificates. A photograph—some wedding. There they all were—Father Joseph, too . . . she had no wish to think of Father Joseph—nor yet meet his eyes, even in a photograph. You ought to get a move on, Singe, she told herself. Trains are trains, you know.

Delving deeper, she found a packet of writing paper, envelopes, pen, ink. "You see," she murmured, rather pleased with herself, "I'm not a perfect fool—I laid in stores, I was not unprepared." Reminded of the essential item amongst these stores, once more she plunged into the box, groped about, found what she sought and put it with the other things on the tray. Then she settled down to write.

She had not written a letter for more years than she could remember; indeed, could have counted on the fingers of one hand all the letters she had ever written in her life. She had a very elegant handwriting, nevertheless—there was even a certificate to prove it, there in the box. Now she hesitated, nibbling the pen. After all, there was not so much to say. "That's good hurry up—that's good hurry up——" Impatient, at her elbow, the clock rattled the tray. "All right," she soothed it, "all in good time"; and took it off the tray, putting it on the floor for the sake of a moment's peace. A *short* letter, then. Very well. She began to write:

"My darling Sophie . . ."

*   *   *

"Milly, darling, would you say the worst was over, or——? "

Milly, darling, cross and dishevelled, looked up from where she was kneeling on the kitchen floor, packing a wicker basket.

"No, Sophie, I would not. There are all the books still, and those brats not even dressed . . . oh, my God—*don't* say you've got to go," she wailed.

"Only for a little while, darling. I promised my old auntie I'd pop back about now, you see . . ."

"Oh, Sophie, *please*, angel Sophie . . . just this once, won't she understand? "

562

"Well," Sophie looked doubtful. "Perhaps. But——"

"Look, dear, sweet Sophie, have some more gin. Go on, pour us both some. Yes, and slosh it in—we might as well finish it now—Sophie, listen, you've been absolutely *wonderful* . . . don't, *please* don't desert me now."

"No, Milly, all right," said Sophie. "Not desert—I'd never do that. Have I "—she went on rather wistfully—" you mean I've really been of some use? "

"Use? " said Milly rather absently; having dealt with that one she was already on to the next. "Of course. You've saved my life. D'you know, that makes the *fourth* open packet of Tide. It's too bad, really. How the hell am I to pack them? And two tins of treacle *without* lids. And I ask you, look at all these—ketchup, chutney, all half empty—ugh! All squishy round the neck—well, I'm just not going to pack them, so that's that. I tell you what." She looked pleased, struck by a sparkling idea. " *You* take them. Take them all home. Why ever not? "

"Darling, but—honest Injun? You *mean* it? I don't like to, though . . . such colossal generosity. . . ."

Actually, Milly reflected, she *was* being rather generous. Still—her eyes swept the heap—it was a pretty gruesome collection. Most of the packets and tins only held dribs and drabs of this and that—you couldn't really say she was *wasting* much—and what with the bother, and a bit sordid, too, at the Customs and so on.

"Not at all," she said modestly, even with a certain enthusiasm, "look, there's a box. You pack the whole lot up in that, Sophie, and we'll have it sent round after Vladek's seen us to the station . . . here, there's even one of your favourite tins of salt."

"So it is. The dear." Sophie caressed it, her eyes shining. " That's a keepsake, Milly. I'll treasure it for ever, you know." She tried the little chute apparatus with her finger, but it didn't work. Damaged a bit. Well, it wasn't as if Milly could spare a *new* tin—and perhaps at home she could even mend it. She would try. What a lot of gin she must have had. It wasn't too reliable, this gin, it seemed. In the past it had always made her giggly and cheerful—but just to-day, when one needed it, not. Not at all.

"Look look look! . . . " shrieked Clarissa, dancing into the room, and round the table. "Look what I've got! "

"Clarissa, *please*! It goes right through my head! What is it? Why, it's a *doll*. But you don't like dolls? "

"Ha-ha, *now* I do . . . I do . . ." She seemed quite beside herself, enraptured, but bent on tantalising her mother, too. "This one I like very very very very——"

" *Stop it*, d'you hear? Who gave it to you? "

" Mr. Wragg," said Clarissa, with affected nonchalance, " gave it to me. Just now."

" That was very kind of him," said Milly slowly, fingering the doll. " I hope you thanked him."

" Of course." She smirked naughtily. " I gave him a kiss."

" But——" Milly began, and stopped. What went for dolls might go for kissing, too. She felt rather—well, *helpless*. So all she said was, and timidly, for her: " What are you going to call it? "

Clarissa's eyes opened wide. " Emma," she replied without a second's hesitation, as if she had been inspired, which was in fact the case.

" Emma? " Milly echoed faintly. Sitting back on her heels she stared in amazement at her offspring. " *Emma?* But why? "

" Oh, I dunno. It just came into my head."

" Clarissa, don't you think," Sophie, skilled at reading danger warnings, began tactfully, " it might be better to give her a Slavonian name? Look, she *is* a Slavonian—you can tell by her clothes."

" Oh, all right," agreed Clarissa affably, feeling in some obscure way that she had scored a point. " I'll call her Sophie, then. After *you* . . ." She flung her arms round Sophie. " Because I love you so."

" Did—er—Mr. Wragg give Dermot anything? "

Clarissa spun round, her face aglow. " *Nothing!* " she sang out in triumph, " nothing at all! Only *me . . . me . . . me . . .*"

" You run along and get dressed. You're over-excited."

" Yes, I am. Oh dear." Instead of doing as she had been told she threw herself on her stomach across the kitchen table, and sprawled there, a curtain of lanky fair hair falling to one side, her chin in her hand, her eyes bright as stars. Sophie had to chuckle, but her mother looked rather grim. " You know what? " said Clarissa—just as if she were one of them, Milly couldn't help thinking and really one did get a disturbing vision of things to come. " You know what? I like *coming* —but I like going away even better. I'd like always to be doing that —coming, or going." She rolled over on to her back, her hands stuck into the pockets of her jeans, and yawned with calculated sophistication: " It's the times in between that *bo—or—e* me . . ."

" CLARISSA! "

Over-calculated, the sophistication—she needed no telling, and scrambled off the table pretty fast.

" Get *on!* " said her mother, giving her a smack on the behind as she skipped past. " Sophie, do you think you could . . .? "

" Yes, Milly, of course." Obediently Sophie followed Clarissa out.

It was nearly finished, the packing—although it didn't look it, because of Sophie's hoard. Milly was on her knees fastening up the basket when Larry came in.

" God, what a mess! " He glanced round. " Nothing like finished, is it? What are you going to do with all this junk? "

" *Junk!* " she exclaimed, incensed. " It's all perfectly good house-hold stuff. As a matter of fact, I thought it would be rather nice to—well, I suddenly had an idea, and I'm—I'm giving it all to Sophie. The whole lot."

" Ah! " He examined the bleary old ketchup bottles with interest. " That's thoughtful," he commented at last. " Very thoughtful. A good-bye present, I take it? "

She looked up, detecting in his voice that faint note of sarcasm she had come to know, and dread, in the last few hours.

" Well, yes, in a way. I don't see why not." She floundered, on the defensive at once. It was nerve-racking, having constantly to be on the look-out for the malicious significance that might be lurking behind even his lightest remark. " I mean, it's all useful—at least, it is to her, and she's been such a help. Anyway," she added defiantly, " she was quite pathetically grateful, I can tell you."

He smiled to greet this dear old-timer as it cropped up again; after an absence, it occurred to him.

" Don't worry," he said dryly, " as tips go, it's handsome. Knowing Sophie, I should say she's well satisfied."

Her head bent over the basket, she began to cry. It was not a performance, but unfortunately there was no way of telling that; the little choky noises, quivering of the shoulders, all accurately reproduced; even the big real tear that fell on the wickerwork was indistinguishable from a million previous fakes. After a minute or two she heard the door close. Then, throwing her arms across the lid of the basket, her head on her arms, for the second time in her life, for the second time in two days, in earnest, she wept.

* * *

" You can't go into your carriage yet," screamed Clarissa from the corridor window. " Sophie's doing a surprise."

" Oh," said Milly, " what fun."

" Promise you'll stay out there on the platform? "

" All right." She lit a cigarette and stood there, huddled into her coat. Ten minutes to go. Larry had gone off somewhere. What a horrible station.

" The English stations," said Sophie, coming up behind her, " aren't like this, I suppose."

" Oh, I don't know. All stations are pretty ghastly, I think. Looks as if we're the only people on this train."

" It's the train to the coast," said Sophie, " that's why."

" Oh, I see."

" Milly, I . . . wanted to say . . . something . . ." Her head bent, she was scuffling her feet, frowning terribly.

" Well ? "

" Well—I thought . . . perhaps, that is—we might——" She looked up, caught sight of the clock at the end of the platform, and blurted out, " Perhaps we might meet again? I mean—I might . . . one day, perhaps, who knows—come to England. What d'you think? " She had blushed scarlet.

Surprised, Milly said, " Well, that would be lovely, Sophie, of course. You've got our address. But can you—I mean, can one— I thought it was impossible? "

" I don't know . . . I'd have to find out . . . it may not be quite— well, *im*possible. Though of course," she added slowly, not looking at Milly, staring along the platform, " it wouldn't be—*easy*. Even dashed difficult, I expect." She gave a nervous little laugh.

" Difficult . . . lord, yes, I should think so." Puzzled, she glanced at Sophie, who was behaving so oddly—as if she were . . . well, dreadfully embarrassed. Obviously she was waiting for her, Milly, to say something, but what? She couldn't imagine what Sophie was getting at, and she did look so wretched—why, she would be only too willing to say anything that might cheer her up. Feeling rather embarrassed herself, all she could think of to say was: " Well, you'll be writing to us, won't you? Oh, look! " she cried out with relief, " there's Larry." There never was anything to say on station platforms; actually, she reflected, it would have been better had she dissuaded Sophie from seeing them off. But what with all the last-minute things to attend to . . . well, there it was. " I'd better get in now, Sophie."

" Yes, darling. Go in." She turned. Milly was thankful to see that she was smiling. " Kiss me." They embraced.

" Can she come in now? " yelled Clarissa from the window. She was on guard at the door of the compartment.

" Not yet," said Sophie, coming up to the window, beaming through her tears. " Wait till the train goes. Milly! Ask her to come to the window, Clarissa—please. Milly! " she called, frantic. She had lost sight of her. Along the corridor the blinds were down.

" Sophie," Larry put his hands on her shoulders. " Look after yourself. And thank you for—everything." For a second their eyes met. How sad he looks, thought Sophie. Poor Larry. And Larry, of course, thought the same of her. He bent and kissed her, and

566

was about to mount the steps into the train, when she clutched his arm. She was sobbing. " Make Milly come to the window— *please*."

" Of course, Sophie," he said, and muttered to himself, " If I have to drag her there by her hair."

" Here I am," said Milly.

In her furs, in her little hat, all dressed up to go, how dainty she looked—Sophie gazed up at her adoringly. This was the picture she would remember.

" Darling." She came up close. " Listen. If I——" The train's whistle blew. It went on and on for half a minute. Sophie, having at last summoned words and courage, went on speaking, but words and courage, too, were swallowed up, lost in that piercing noise. When it stopped, the train was already beginning to move. Milly stretched out her hand, and Sophie, clasping it, began to trot alongside.

" Darling," she panted, in a last desperate attempt, " if I could . . ." She was trotting fast, the train gathering speed.

" What? I can't hear . . . Sophie, don't . . . let go, you must . . . good-bye . . . Sophie, *let go* . . . good-bye . . ."

She let go. It was no use. Anyway, this was the end of the platform. They were waving out of the window, now, all four of them. " Good-bye," she whispered, and raising her hand tried to wave back. There they were, being carried away from her for ever. She had lost them, lost them for ever.

There was a barrow heaped with mailbags and she sat down on it, because her legs were shaking under her. Gone. Gone for ever. Now to make one's life again. But how? That was the point. How.

She sat there for some time until a couple of porters, young lads in high spirits, spying her at the end of the platform, drove their trolley towards her, aiming almost directly at her, as a joke, hoping to see her jump. In this they were disappointed; they passed her with an inch or two to spare.

" Silly old hen! " one of them bellowed. " Wake up! " He was angry—nervous, too; it had really been a close shave.

They began loading the mailbags, now and then glancing at her curiously as they worked, the three of them included in the circle of light shed by the arc-lamp above; beyond that there was gloom all round. Her presence was no hindrance to them, but somehow it upset them to see her sitting there.

" You'll have to move now," said the one who had shouted at her before, his voice gruff but polite.

The other stood in front of her in a cheeky way. " He'll come back," he said, winking at his colleague. " You see if he doesn't."

She put her handkerchief in her pocket and got up. " Good night," she said, looking vaguely from one to the other.

" Good night, miss," said the first, rather taken aback. They watched her move off down the platform.

The great yellow face of the clock seemed to grin as it saw her coming. It was late. Ten o'clock. Walk home, of course. Home. Oh, well, she thought wearily, one must just make the best of it. It might be worse. Some people are left with nothing. I've still got a home, of sorts . . . and Singe. Thank God, I've still got Singe.

*　　*　　*

" Now will you let me in? "

" Yes," said Clarissa, " but shut your eyes."

Milly went in.

" Open! There! Isn't it *gorgeous*? "

The compartment was filled with flowers, the air drenched with their scent; the seats were banked with carnations, the expensive multi-coloured variety, heads as big as lettuces and vulgar as carnival favours; ranged on the table by the window a row of pots, fresh from the florist; decked out with Cellophane and bows, each housed a thriving hydra-headed plant, every plant a cyclamen.

" Oh, Christ," murmured Milly, and quickly shut her eyes again.

" I'm devoted to Sophie," she said when Larry came in. " But she does go a bit far. Just tell me what I'm to do with all these? "

He finished stowing away the baggage. Dusting his hands, he took in the display of horticulture, then he looked at her, and gave a little laugh.

" Chuck 'em out of the window, of course," he said pleasantly. " I'm surprised you ask." Picking up *The Times*, he opened the door. " I'm going along to see about breakfast." He was going to be with the children, she knew. " By the way," he added, " I agree Sophie does go a bit far. There's a parcel over there on that seat. I suggest you don't sit on it till you see what's inside."

*　　*　　*

It was a small ship, a motor vessel. All day they had been loading cargo. She had spent most of the day leaning over the rail, watching. At first it had been exciting to see the hams, the sides of bacon, glued up in sacking, swung over into the hold; the cases stencilled in black lettering, BUTTER (it had given one quite a thrill to see the English word), and crates of glass, GLASS, and poultry—geese, at a guess— destined for SMITHFIELD LONDON E.; yes, that had all been very exciting in the morning; now, in the late afternoon, less so. But it was nearly over.

It made a grim picture, this last one that they would carry with them, of Slavonia. The quay was deserted, except for the gang of men at work, and a little cluster of women, some with children, obviously relatives of the crew; at twenty paces or so from the gangplank, there were soldiers on guard, forming a semi-circle, its diameter being the length of the ship; they were armed with rifles, although here and there were one or two with tommy-guns. The stevedores worked stolidly but for the most part in silence; they all seemed to be equipped with tins of English cigarettes. The women hung about, whispering; they wore shawls round their heads and looked blue with cold; now and then one of the little tots squatted in the snow. They had been there all day, and she wondered why they should perform this miserable penance out of sentiment for their menfolk, then as she watched them it occurred to her that they probably had their totally unsentimental reasons; every so often there was a kind of flutter amongst them as if business were being transacted, but when the captain of the guard walked up or down the gangplank the whispering hushed at once and they scattered like hungry sparrows, not far; as soon as he had gone, they closed in again.

Beyond the fringe of soldiery there was a bare expanse of snow and, at quite a distance, the customs sheds. There were more sentries patrolling outside the customs sheds, on the far side of which, enclosing the whole area of the quay, was a high barbed-wire fence, dotted with pillboxes, equipped with searchlights and, she supposed, everything else. Thus it would have been impossible, and the thought struck her as it must inevitably have struck every onlooker, for any mortal thing, unauthorised, to have approached that ship. This was the grisly foreground; beyond the wire, the town of Dvansk lay in a hollow out of sight, and the view from the deck was of slag-heaps and a gasworks and low snow-covered hills which faded into the leaden sky. Grey, and bleak, and so quiet; not even the sound of trams or of church bells —only the thin shriek of the gulls, the slapping of the sea against the wall, the rattle of the crane and the foreman's voice cursing the men when something went wrong.

They had lunched and had tea on board. There was only one other passenger besides themselves, an elderly girl from their own embassy, who was returning for good and whose main preoccupation, explained in detail at luncheon, and again in rather more detail at tea, was to deliver her chosen partner for life, a correspondingly elderly, wheezing, and, it was to be inferred, neurotic mongrel, safe and sound and with the minimum disturbance to its metabolism, into quarantine.

To this end, it appeared, she had caused to be constructed, at some cost to herself, a magnificent kennel of Slavonian pine, the nostalgic odour of which was designed to be of comfort to the prisoner during captivity —at least, that was what she hoped. Would this be allowed? she had inquired anxiously of Larry, upon discovering that he was to be classed as an Information Officer: " A special kennel?—surely they couldn't be so beastly as to . . .? " " I haven't the faintest idea," said Larry. The kennel was out on deck. Clarissa had sat in it herself between lunch and tea and won favour with Miss Bendix by pronouncing it, as a residence, eminently desirable, roomy, and with a scrumptious ponk. The rightful owner, bloated, flea-bitten, ears cauliflowered, was at this moment being coaxed into the scuppers by his self-appointed guardians, and it seemed on the cards that in their company, Miss Bendix's pet might, after four days at sea, lose quite a bit of weight.

They had not been placed at the captain's table, to Milly's disgust, although this scarcely seemed to matter in view of the size of the dining-room and the fact that no one sat at the captain's table but the captain himself, a grizzled old boy with the eyes of his trade— and one other. This other was a youngish man in a brown tweed jacket with squared-off shoulders, who squeaked his shoes by moving his jaws, that is, whilst he ate; although possibly involuntary, if, on the other hand, not, a parlour-trick that was none the less remarkable because, due to the atmosphere prevailing at that table, it could scarcely go unremarked. The captain seemed depressed by his company. Now and then he would lift his huge head and give Clarissa a wink—not, however, the sort of wink one would ever risk responding to; it might simply have been a nervous tic. The young man, who was once or twice served even before the captain, ate very fast, golloping rather, and as soon as he had cleared his plate, filled in time by cleaning his nails with his fork.

Enthralled, at last Clarissa had whispered, " He's not a *sailor*, is he? "

" No," said her father. " He's something quite different." And the captain had raised his head and signalled her with another of his lugubrious winks.

Sailor or not, Milly noticed that this same young man exercised some authority, remaining stationed in a prominent position at the head of the gangplank all afternoon.

Now they were clamping down the hold. She felt the shudder as the engines started up. There was a crowd of people at the head of the gangplank. She wondered where Larry was; they had hardly exchanged a word all day. She heard the tramp of marching feet. A posse of soldiers was approaching across the snow from the customs sheds. As they came up the gangplank she thought they looked terribly well armed, and then noticed with surprise that the bayonets on their rifles were fixed. The captain saluted and stood aside to let them pass. The young man in the tweed jacket pushed himself in front of the captain, and after that the soldiers seemed to take their orders from him. They dispersed, in pairs, swarming all over the ship. Of course, they were searching it, one could see that, but what a funny way to do it. . . . Surely this wasn't the normal way that ships were searched for contraband, diamonds, documents, drugs—and surely even then only in war-time? These soldiers were turning the ship inside out. Suddenly, as she watched them, it occurred to her—it was a different kind of contraband they sought. They were prodding tarpaulins, sticking their bayonets into lockers, under seats, investigating every nook and cranny wherein a human being might be concealed. At that, all the uneasiness, the doubts, the little nameless dreads which she had sensed or half sensed in the past few months crystallised into one sensation; all the shadows of varying shapes and sizes which she had glimpsed or half glimpsed now merged, became magnified, and recognisable as having been different aspects of a single shadow, the shadow of that which was now in concrete form, with which at last she had come face to face—and fear seized her. There was the gangplank. They were still in Slavonia—not yet free.

Instinctively she looked around for the children. They were just behind her, sitting on a bench on either side of Miss Bendix, to whom Dermot, having taken one of his swift fancies—a sign which Milly could not help regarding as propitious for the voyage—was cuddled up close. Clarissa, apparently equally enamoured of Miss Bendix's other half, had her arms round its fat neck and was crooning into its scarred and frilly ear. And Larry—where was he? She must have them all where she could see them—all under her hand; most of all Larry.

Then suddenly she caught sight of him, at the top of the gangplank, head and shoulders above the crowd. He seemed a long way of, the length of the deck between them and all sorts of people, soldiers, and sailors, too, now, doing things with ropes and swearing at the soldiers who got in their way; she could never have reached him. His back was turned to her, he hadn't seen her, he didn't even know she was there, and seeing him like that made her heart give a terrible lurch. Yes, there he was, in conversation with someone, the captain and somebody else—ah, but I've lived this, she murmured, this has all happened before. The soldiers were marching down the gangplank. The ship's siren sounded; it reminded her of the whistle of the train.

" But I've been *blind*," she whispered, the tears that were streaming down her face in truth blinding her, and clinging to the rail she hid her face in her arms, although the dusk was creeping on and everybody was far too busy to notice her. . . . " Blind," she sobbed, " all these years. Longing for what? For something I had all the time . . . and now I've lost it . . . I never knew I had it . . . until it went . . . and now it's gone . . . oh, help me . . . Sophie, *help me* . . . say it's not too late . . . what am I to do? It hurts . . . it hurts so . . . I've lost him and I can't bear it, I can't bear to lose him, I can't . . . I can't . . . *Sophie!* " she cried out as the gangplank rattled back.

She never knew she called Sophie then, that is to say, she never remembered it, because when, still weeping, she lifted her head from her arms, she saw that the gap was already widening between the ship and the shore. Crouched over the rail, through her tears she watched it widen, watched the quay, the intimate and by now familiar view of it, rather, diminish, the details become blurred; and the more blurred, the more the scene as a whole, oddly enough, seemed to come into focus, until at last it was reduced to its sharpest impression, postcard size; and although the picture presented remained the same, grey and grim as ever, its significance, mercifully, had reduced in proportion to its size. Now manageable, to be discarded or retained, stuck into a scrapbook, or given a few days' grace adorning the chimney-piece, or flipped straight into the fire, as the fancy took one, like the card—so also this had become, that was the picture on the card.

Just like the cards, she thought, still sniffing, we bought that day we went to Auschwitz. Now, at a distance, it was like that, and the farther off . . . and for the first time she glanced over her shoulder at the new and more promising view of what lay ahead; they were approaching the harbour bar. Still—she turned back once more, thinking, I won't see it again, I'd better look—yes, awfully like Auschwitz. The snow; the black figures in the snow, the guard still formed up; the searchlights wheeling this way and that, throwing the flat low business-like roofs of the sheds in shadow on the snow, the high wire glimmering behind; a scene with figures, nevertheless inanimate—as far as she was concerned. Removed from it by the stretch of water, she examined it almost with delight. Nothing there could touch her now. Why—so engrossed she hadn't even noticed— already they had passed beyond the bar and were in the open sea. Heavens, what a wind! And the spray—how salt on one's lips!

Tasting the spray, fresh and salt like the wind, she knew, but with a pang of regret, that her mood had passed. Tears and all that—she didn't feel a bit like crying now. Yes, it had gone, and instinctively she knew, too, that it would never assail her again. It was gone for ever, never to be recaptured even had she wished to recapture it, which she did not. The compensations were too immediate and tremendous. She lifted up her face to let the wind blow over it, drying the tears, wetting it with spray, and then she saw Larry coming up the deck towards her.

Putting her hair out of her eyes, it was blowing all over her face— she thought, that's scotched the dream, too. He had never come towards her in the dream. As he came up, she saw that he had something in his hand, a folded sheet of yellow paper. He held it out to her and she moved towards him and took it; as she did so, she noticed that he stepped back away from her at once. They stood for a second looking at each other: she with her hand to her hair, the wind tugging at her skirts, he in the shelter of the funnel, out of the wind.

" Larry," she said, or shouted, rather, " Larry! " Whatever message the paper contained, it could not be as important as what the wind was urging her to say; there seemed to be nothing in the world as important as that: " Listen . . . It was all like a nightmare, wasn't it? A nightmare—d'you hear? " He was watching her, but he made no reply. She lifted up her face and put her hands to her cheeks: " The wind," she cried at the top of her voice, and her words were blown straight towards him on it—" You can't feel it there—it's wonderful! It blows it all away . . . Larry—come here!—Feel it, too! "

Clarissa appeared from nowhere, planting herself between them.

" What's this sea? " she demanded of her father.

" The Baltic," he replied.

" H'm." She gave it one look, the heaving tumbling thing, a splendid look, sour with reservation, even sheer disbelief. Then she slouched off, dragging her new chum behind her.

Larry grinned. He moved up towards Milly and several paces beyond, where he leaned over the rail. She had unfolded the bit of paper and was staring at it, holding it this way and that. It was a signal; in caps, but in pencil, too; hard to read. She looked at the signature, and looked again and then its meaning dawned. Suddenly she cried out: " Darling . . . Larry! Darling . . ." and stumbled up the deck towards him. " This "—she waved it, bawling against the wind—" it says, doesn't it?—that everything's all right? "

He must have heard her, but he was looking towards the land; clustered here and there with lights, it had become grey and shapeless, and was fading fast. She waited, watching him; now his hair, too, was wild.

" Larry! " She was not—and never would be—good at waiting. She tugged at his arm. " Larry, please! "

He stood up then, and turning his back to the land, leaned against the rail, and lifted his head as she had done to let the wind blow over his face. When he looked down at her, he was—or so it seemed to her—smiling. Encouraged, she pressed up close at his elbow.

" Larry? "

He saw how her eyes sparkled, and he bent down to hear what she had to say.

" Darling," she said, " where d'you suppose we'll go next? "

THE END